The Forging

The Clash

Born in Madrid in 1897, Arturo Barea lived in England from 1939 until his death in 1957. The story of his years in Spain is the subject matter of his remarkable autobiographical trilogy *The Forging of a Rebel*. The first volume, *The Forge*, describes his childhood and youth. *The Track* takes him from the age of twenty to twenty-eight – years spent as a conscript soldier in Spanish Morocco, as a businessman and as a husband and father. *The Clash* describes the Spanish Civil War and his own part in that struggle.

Forced to leave Spain, he and Ilsa, the Austrian socialist and journalist who became his second wife, settled in the village of Eaton Hastings near Faringdon in Berkshire. He worked for the BBC during the war, and contributed articles to journals such as *Horizon*, *London Forum* and *The Times Literary Supplement*. Barea published novels and short stories as well as books of criticism, including *Lorca, the Poet and his People* (1944) and *Unamuno* (1952). *The Forge*, *The Track* and *The Clash* (published simultaneously in Flamingo) were first published in English translation and appeared in eight other languages before the first edition in Spanish came out in Buenos Aires in 1951.

Arturo Barea

The Forging of a Rebel

The Clash

translated by
Ilsa Barea

FLAMINGO

Published by Fontana Paperbacks

The Clash first published in English
by Faber and Faber Limited 1946

Published in an omnibus edition
(with *The Forge* and *The Track*)
under the title *The Forging of a Rebel*
by Davis-Poynter Limited 1972

This Flamingo edition first published
in 1984 by Fontana Paperbacks,
8 Grafton Street, London W1X 3LA

Set in 10 on 12pt Plantin
Reproduced, printed and bound in Great Britain
by Hazell, Watson and Viney Limited,
member of the BPCC Group,
Aylesbury, Bucks.

. . . *honour eternal is due to the* BRAVE AND NOBLE PEOPLE OF SPAIN, *worthy of better rulers and a better fortune! And now that the jobs and intrigues of their juntas, the misconduct and incapacity of their generals, are sinking into the deserved obscurity of oblivion, the* national *resistance rises nobly out of the ridiculous details. . . That resistance was indeed wild, disorganized, undisciplined and Algerine, but it held out to Europe an example which was not shown by the civilized Italian or intellectual German.*

RICHARD FORD, *Handbook for Travellers in Spain and Readers at Home.*
London, 1845

Contents

Part I

1. The Lost Village

The August heat was melting the starch. The inside of my collar had become a damp, sticky rag, the outer tissue kept its stiffness, the edge chafed my sweaty skin. As I pushed my handkerchief between neck and collar to get relief, I suddenly saw before me my Uncle José, sliding a neatly folded silk kerchief between his strong throat and starched collar, while we waited for the coach to Brunete, thirty years ago.

I hated waiting in the heat.

Many people and many things die in thirty years. One feels hemmed in by ghosts, a ghost oneself. The little boy who waited on this spot thirty years ago was myself; but that boy no longer existed.

The old inn of San Andrés was the same: there was the shadowy gateway, the courtyard with the chickens pecking between the cobbles, the little taproom where they still sold wine from a goatskin. I checked the inventory of my memory, and the outlines were identical. But I myself was a little dazed and blunted – or maybe things looked flatter and bleaker in this harsh glare. I used to delight in the shops of this street. The street was unchanged, the same old taverns, the same old shops brimming over with farming tools, coarse cloth, sticky sweets and gaudy colour prints for the customers from the villages of Castile and Toledo.

I knew that by the rules of geography Toledo belongs to Castile. Never mind: Toledo is different. It has always been an island in the old map of Spain. It bears the imprint of Roman legions, of the flower of Arab invaders, of knights-in-armour and of Cardinals, royal bastards, who left their Mass for the sword; of generation after generation of Moorish and Jewish craftsmen who hammered their steel, tempered it in the waters of the Tajo and inlaid it with wire of gold.

I had to go there, soon, if I could make myself free to go.

The bus was here at last. Not so very different from the old diligence. The passengers were taking it by assault as they had done when I was that little boy. It was as easy as then to disentangle the two opposite worlds of the villages of Castile and Toledo. Here were the lean, gaunt men from the meagre wheat lands, from Brunete, and their thin, bony wives with bodies exhausted from childbirths and faces made taut by sun and frost. There were the people of the vale of Toledo, from the wine lands of Méntrida, the men a little pot-bellied and hearty, with fair skin under the tan, their women generously plump and noisily gay. I felt a pleasure, which I knew to be childish, in thinking that I was a crossbreed, my father Castilian, my mother Toledan. Nobody could label me, nobody was able to range me within one of these two groups. I looked different from both.

I was out of place. Just as my stiff collar and town suit were out of place among the country clothes of the others. My fleeting pleasure turned sour. The live people around me made me feel a stranger among my own kindred, and the dead who crowded my memory were ghosts.

I took my seat beside the driver. Antonio wore a labourer's jacket, and when the brakes screeched he cursed like a carter. He was out of place at the steering wheel. He should have been handling the long whip which reaches to the ears of the leading mule.

People sorted themselves out while we coasted downhill. They shouted across the bus – family news, shopping news – and the street outside was full of noises. But when the car changed gear to climb the long slope of El Campamento, the drone of the engine, the sun, the dust, and the acrid smell of petrol enforced silence. When we reached the dun-coloured plain of Alcorcón, with its dry harvested fields and dried clay houses, the passengers were dozing or chewing the cud of their thoughts.

So we passed Navalcarnero and Valmojado, and followed the boundary between Toledo and Castile, until we left the main road at Santa Cruz de Retamar, turning east. Now we were on Toledan soil.

It is an ancient highway. When Madrid was nothing but a famous castle, this was the great artery linking Toledo with Avila. Along this road people fought and traded. Moorish warriors descended from the Toledo mountains into the valley of the Alberche, to scale the Sierra and reach the Castilian uplands. And from the high tablelands of Avila and Burgos, knights streamed down to cross the river plains and to wrest Toledo, City of Stone, from the Moors.

I knew that I was showing colour prints of history to myself. But why not? It was a diverting game.

Now the highway was asleep. Nobody used it but the people from the villages along it, with their carts and their donkeys, and sometimes a lorry with local produce. The road led nowhere in these days. It was merely a link between a few forgotten villages.

On this old warrior route, between Santa Cruz de Retamar and Torrijos, lay Novés. I was on my way to Novés now, and I wondered why.

Of course I knew why. I had rented a house for my family in Novés, and this was the first week-end I was going to spend there, at my 'country house'. What had possessed me to take a house at the back of beyond?

I had long wanted a house in the country near Madrid. Two years before, in 1933, we had spent almost a year in the foothills of the Sierra, in Villalba; but I had disliked the shoddy tourist atmosphere. I had wanted a real village for my week-ends. Novés was a real village.

But this was not the real reason why I chose it.

I had no wish to disentangle once more the complicated reasons which I had so often set out to myself. They were not pleasant, but inescapable. Some time ago I had resumed the joint household with my wife, after a separation of nearly a year. It was because of the children, and it did not work. A house in the country at some distance from Madrid meant regaining my liberty to some extent; it would avoid our having to live together. It was also a decent excuse – or what people call decent – in the eyes of others, while it circumvented a new separation which would have smacked of the ridiculous. And it would be good for the health of the children; and for Aurelia, who had been ailing ever since her last childbed. And the weekly rest and change would do me good. I could afford it after all.

Very good and correct reasons. But I would not deceive myself by repeating them over again, even though they were true as far as they went. The worst of introspection is that one cannot stop it at will.

The country outside was drab and monotonous and I was a stranger to the other passengers. There was no escape into contemplation or conversation.

I wondered whether Novés was not simply another defeat of mine, a flight from myself.

There was Maria. Our affair had lasted six years, which was not bad. But I had hoped to shape her to my measure, as I had hoped with Aurelia, a very long time ago. And Maria had developed in her own way. I had failed. Perhaps I was wrong. One cannot force companionship. It was certainly not her fault. But the worst of it was that she was very much in love with me and that she had become possessive. She wanted to absorb me. And that made it so clear that I was not in love with her. The house in Novés meant that I would be able to avoid the inevitable Saturday afternoons and Sundays with Maria.

It would give me a chance to escape from my wife during the week and from my mistress during the week-ends. A most satisfactory state of affairs!

But it was not the problem of the two women alone. Going to Novés meant that I could get away from my weekday isolation into another isolation. The change would be a relief; my isolation in normal life was making me restless. In theory I had resigned myself to a nice bourgeois existence, keeping up the appearances as far as my wife and my household were concerned, spending agreeable hours with Maria, and indulging in my private taste and whims. The truth was that I was tired of both women and had to force myself to play up to them. Money was not really important to me, it never had been. And my ambitions had long been buried – that to be an engineer as well as that to be a writer. When the Republic was young I had cherished political hopes and illusions while I worked hard to organize the Clerical Workers' Union. But I must have lacked the flexibility one needs to become part and parcel of a political organization and to make a political career. And it was sheer ingenuousness to believe that good will was sufficient to do good work.

Yet I could not seriously give up any of my ideals. I could not settle down to be a contented bourgeois.

I still believed that somewhere there existed a woman with whom I might have a contact beyond the physical, with whom I would have a complete life of mutual give and take. I was still unable to keep my fingers off any piece of mechanism in need of repair. I still plunged for months into difficult technical problems which arose in the course of my work, but in reality had nothing to do with it. I disliked the cheap writing which flooded the Spanish book market and continued to believe that I had more to say than many others. I was still a Socialist.

But I had to carry on the life in which I was caught, or which I had made for myself.

I could feel that I was in an intellectual and even physical deadlock. I knew I broke out in spasmodic explosions, in violent disputes and bursts of rage against all around me. It was because I was impotent before the facts of my own life, and my country's.

Novés was a flight from all this. It was my total defeat, because it meant declaring myself an egoist in cold blood.

I did not like this label.

It meant declaring myself disillusioned, hopeless and in need of a refuge. That was it.

We were still in the plain, but the ribbon of the road before us lost itself in a horizon of hills.

Antonio nudged me:

'There's Novés – over there!'

I only saw the line of the road, topped by a gilded ball and cross.

'That's the church tower.'

The bus dived into a gully and lurched through a village street until it came to a stop in the market square before an inn. The shadows were already lengthening, but the sun was still burning fiercely. Aurelia and my eldest daughter were waiting for me; the family had travelled to Novés with the lorry which moved our furniture.

'Well, how far have you got with the house?' I asked.

'Nowhere, we've been waiting for you. The children leave one no time for anything.'

'Papa, our house is very big, you'll see.'

'I've seen it, silly. Do you like it?'

'Yes, but it frightens me just a little. Because it's empty, you see, and ever so big.'

The men had piled up our furniture along the walls by the entrance, a big heap of bedding, suitcases, trunks, and boxes in the middle. The three children were tumbling about, getting under everybody's feet.

'Children or no children, you'll have to lend me a hand.'

'Well, there's a woman of the village who wants to come and be our maid-of-all-work. You must talk to her. I told her to come along as soon as she heard the bus hooting.'

There she was, flanked by a girl of about sixteen, and a man in the forties. The three stood stock-still in the wide doorway looking at me. The man took off his cap and the woman spoke up for them:

'Good evening. My name's Dominga and this here's my girl and my husband. Now you just tell us what you want done, sir.'

'Don't stand there in the doorway, come in. Now, what do you want?'

'Well, the lady will have explained. As she said to Don Ramón – that's the one that keeps the stores – you'll be wanting a daily woman so I've come, sir. So if it's all right with you, here we are.'

'How much do you want, then?'

Peasant fashion, she avoided a direct answer:

'Well, the girl would come and help, and between the two of us, never you fear, we'll have the house shining like a new medal.'

'But, frankly, I don't need two people here.'

'No, sir, the girl would just come to help me, it wouldn't cost you a thing. Of course, if you wanted her to eat here she could, for as I always say, where three eat, four can eat as well. But for everything else there'd only be me. I was in service in Madrid before I married, and I know what the gentry like. And we're honest, you can ask anyone in the village . . .'

'What wages do you want, then?'

'We can start at once, that's what Mariano's come along for, just to lend a hand, as he's out of work.'

'Yes, but now do tell me what wages you're wanting.'

'Well, if it suits you, twenty-five pesetas[1] a month and my meals. Don't worry about beds, we'll be sleeping at home, just round the corner, and if you ever want me to stay a night, you just say so, sir.'

That seemed to be that. The taciturn husband, Mariano, helped me to put up beds and shove furniture about, while the women took care of the children, the supper, and the clothes. The house was a vast old single-storeyed farm building of no less than seventeen rooms, some of them enormous. In what was to be our dining room, the table seemed a little island in the middle and the sideboard a forlorn ornament against the wall, wherever we put it.

Night was falling. We lit three candles and stuck them in the necks of empty wine bottles. They made three pools of light on the table, while all around them was penumbra, alive with black shadows.

'The best thing would be to light a fire, even if it is August,' said Dominga, and so we did. There was a huge open fireplace, bell-shaped, as large as one of the smaller rooms in our Madrid flat. Mariano heaped dry broom on the hearthstone, and the flames leaped up to man's height, drenching the room in dusky red and drowning the puny flicker of the candles.

Even when we had distributed all our furniture, the house was empty and our footsteps sounded hollow. Those rooms would have needed heavy old oaken chests, sideboards with three tiers, canopied beds with four heaped-up mattresses, such as our grandparents had. We soon went to bed, in weary silence, but my two Alsatians howled outside in the courtyard for many hours.

I got up early the next morning. Outside the door, I found Dominga, her daughter, and her husband, waiting. The women scurried off into the house, but the man kept standing there and twisting his cap round and round.

---

[1] In 1935, 25 pesetas were slightly more than sixty pence, or about three dollars, at an exchange rate of roughly one dollar = 7 pesetas. This exchange rate applies to all sums in pesetas mentioned in this book, previous to the Civil War.

'I believe there's nothing more for you to do, Mariano,' I said to him. I thought he was hoping for a tip such as he had been given the night before.

'Well, it's like this, sir. I haven't got a job, so I said to myself: "Let's go there." So now you just tell me what to do.' He gave me a look and added quickly: 'Of course, I don't ask for anything. But some day, if you feel like giving me anything, well, then you'll give what you like, and if not, well, that's all right too. After all, I can always help the women sawing wood and fetching water.'

There was a cobbled farmyard at the back of the house, with room for half a dozen carts and their mule teams. The mangers were ranged along the walls. I took Mariano there.

'Let's see if we can't do something here. Get rid of the cobbles and we'll try to make a garden with a few flowers.'

So I had acquired a family of retainers. At midday I went to see my village.

Novés lies at the bottom of a ravine scooped out of the plain, and is built on the pattern of a fish's spine. There is a very wide main street, through the middle of which flows a stream blackened by the refuse of the whole village. On both sides, short alleys like ribs lead up the steep, rough slopes. When it rains, the bottom of the ravine becomes the bed of a torrent which sluices away the heaped-up muck. Then people are forced to use the bridges which span the whole width of the street at intervals. One of them is high, humpbacked, made of fitted stones; it is Roman. Another is of concrete and the road passes over it. Most of the houses are built of sun-baked clay with a thick coat of whitewash. They all look alike and they all implacably reflect the glare of the sun. There is a square with a few small trees, the church, the apothecary, the Casino, and the Town Hall. And that is all there is of Novés: some two hundred houses.

I followed the dirty brook downstream, because I had nothing else to do. After the last small houses, the ravine opened into a valley sheltered from the winds of the plain and gently green even in August. On both sides of the stream were market gardens with fruit trees, flowers, and vegetable plots. Each garden had its own well and chain pump. A slight murmur of water and clanking of iron was in the air all the time. A mile further on the valley folded up and the little river ran again through a barren ravine sunk into the arid, dusty plain. This was the whole wealth of Novés. Walking back, I noted that most of the chain pumps were silent, and remembered that it was Sunday. But then I began to see more. Many of the garden plots lay abandoned or badly neglected. There were a few small beds of melons which had been cared for, but the big market gardens looked as though nobody had worked there for months. The earth was baked in hard lumps. I looked down a well-shaft by the wayside. The chain with the buckets was rusty, green weeds floated on the water. Nobody had used the pump for a very long time. Back at my house, I talked to Mariano about it. His answer was to the point.

'It's a sin against God, that's what it is. The men without work, and the land abandoned. You won't believe it, but something's going to happen here, something nasty. It's been like this for the last three years, almost as long as we've had the Republic.'

'But how's that? I know the big landowners are refusing to employ labour nowadays, but here in the village, I didn't think there were any big landowners.'

'We've only got four rich men in the village. Things wouldn't go so badly if it weren't for Heliodoro. The others aren't really bad. But Heliodoro has got them all where he wants them, and there's a war on all the time.'

He was no longer taciturn, and his grey eyes came alive in his heavy face.

'I'll tell you something of what's going on here. Before the Re-public came, some of our young people joined the Socialists and some joined the Anarchists, well, less than a dozen in all. I don't know how they had the guts to do it, because the Civil Guards were after them all the time and beat them up often enough. But of course, when the Republic came, the Corporal of the Civil Guard had to lie low at first, and a lot of us joined. Nearly the whole village is with the Socialists or Anarchists now. But Heliodoro has always been the boss here and managed the elections for the deputy of Torrijos. And so now he's doing what he's always done, because before the Republic he was sometimes a Liberal and sometimes a

Conservative, but never on the wrong side. And when the Republic came, well, then he joined Lerroux's crowd and now, because the Right's been getting strong after what happened in Asturias, he's become one of Gil Robles' crowd. And when our lads asked for decent wages Heliodoro got the four rich men of the village together and said to them: 'Those rascals must be taught a lesson.' So then they started chucking people out and only giving work to the ones who swallowed the old conditions. Because there are some like that, too. And then, you know how things happen in a village, most of us have a bit of land and there's always something the matter with the wife, or the garden gets flooded by the rains, and so lots of people owe Heliodoro money. And because he's the man whose word goes in the village, he got hold of the Municipal Secretary and the Mayor and took out papers against everyone so that he could keep their land. And so things are getting ugly. They were ugly two years ago. People went and messed up the gardens. But now it's worse, because now it's the other side that has the power.'

'And the young people, what about them?'

'What d'you suppose they could do? Keep their mouths shut and tighten their belts. When things happened in Asturias[1] two or three of them were taken away, and now nobody dares to say a word. But something will happen some fine day. Heliodoro won't die in his bed.'

'Have you got trade unions here, then?'

'We've got nothing. The men meet at Eliseo's. He's got a tavern and he's turned it into a Workers' Casino, and there they talk. Eliseo went and joined the Anarchists out there in the Argentine.'

[1] The various references to events in Asturias in this and the following chapters allude to the events of October 1934, when the workers' associations called a general strike, which was followed by revolutionary risings in Asturias, Barcelona, and Madrid, so as to prevent the coming to power of the right-wing leader Gil Robles and his party, the CEDA (Confederación Española de Derechas Autónomas), with a clearly Fascist programme. The armed rising of the Asturian miners, stronger than the other abortive movements, was suppressed by General Ochoa's Legionaries and Moors, then for the first time used on the soil of the Peninsula and against Spaniards. The ensuing violent measures of oppression during the 'Two Black Years' (Bienio Negro) roused public indignation to such a degree that Gil Robles was never called upon to form a Government. – Author's Note.

'I suppose you've got a club secretary, or something of the kind?'

'We haven't got a thing. What the men do is to meet and talk. Because nobody wants trouble with the Corporal.'

'I must go and have a look at your Casino.'

'You can't go there, sir. It's only for the poor. You've got a Casino in the market square, that's for the gentry.'

'I'll go there, too.'

'Well, then, they'll chuck you out of one or the other, sir, to be sure.'

'And what are you a member of, Mariano?'

'I hope you won't get annoyed, but it's like this: When the Republic came, the same thing happened to me as to the others, we were all for it, and I joined the trade union – the UGT. But there, you see, it hasn't helped us much, to tell you the truth.'

'I'm a member of the UGT, too.'

'The devil you are.' Mariano stared at me with great seriousness. 'What a mess! Well, you've got yourself into a tight spot here!'

'We shall see. I don't expect the Corporal will beat me up.'

'You never know.'

In the afternoon, Mariano and I went to the 'Poor Man's Casino', as he called it. The place was a former stable, a huge room with crossbeams, a billiard table in the middle, a small bar at the back, and a score of scratched tables along the bare walls. An ancient radio set built on sham Gothic lines stood in a corner. The billiard table fascinated me; I could not imagine how it ever landed in Novés. It had eight elephantine legs, and eight men could have slept comfortably on its top. The cloth was riddled with tears drawn together with twine. Apparently the table was used for everything, even for an occasional game of billiards; a match was just going on, in which the twine and chance directed the balls. Mariano led me to the bar.

'Give us something to drink, Eliseo.'

The man behind the bar filled two glasses with wine without saying a word. There were about forty people in the room. Suddenly I tumbled to the fact that they had all fallen silent and were watching us. Eliseo stared straight into my eyes. At the first glance, his face gave you a shock. An ulcer had gnawed away one of his nostrils, and a few hairs were sticking out between the livid, greenish seams of the wound. It looked like a biblical, a medieval sore. But the curious thing was that the man was so detached from his blemish that he provoked neither pity nor physical revulsion. Eliseo was in the middle forties, short and squat, dark, suntanned, with quick, shrewd eyes and a sensual mouth. The way in which he looked me up and down while he drank a sip of wine was a provocation. When I set down my empty glass, he said:

'And you, why have you come here? This is the Workers' Casino, and if you hadn't been with Mariano, I wouldn't have served you.'

Mariano intervened:

'Don Arturo is one of us, he belongs to the UGT.'

'Is that true?'

I handed Eliseo the membership card of my trade union. He scanned every page and then called out:

'Boys, Don Arturo is a comrade!' He turned to me: 'When we heard you were coming here we all said:"Another son of a bitch, as if we hadn't enough of them anyhow!" '

He left his corner behind the bar to join me, and in the centre of the clustering men I had to report on events in Madrid: how the Right was organizing and how the Left was coming to life again after the 'Black Year' of repression. The wine was cheap, the drinks were on me and they began to talk. There were great hopes and great plans. The Left would come back into the Government and things would be different this time. The rich would have to choose between paying decent wages and giving up their land so that the others could work it. Novés would have a big communal market garden with a lorry of its own, which would carry greens and fruit to Madrid every morning. And they would finish the school building.

'The scoundrels!' said Eliseo. 'Have you seen our school? The Republic put up the money for it and they sent us a beautiful drawing from Madrid of a house with big windows and a garden. But Heliodoro and his gang convinced the Madrid gentlemen that the school should be built out in the plain, above the valley. And there they started building. Heliodoro got a lot of money for the site, which was his, of course, and up there in the dust you can see the four unfinished walls.'

'Next time we'll build it ourselves, down in the orchards. They're so beautiful, it's a real blessing from God,' said another.

'You can't imagine, Don Arturo,' said Eliseo, 'how glad I am that you're one of us. Now we'll show them that we aren't just a few poor yokels. But you'll have to look out. They'll try to get you.'

That evening I went to the 'Rich Man's Casino'.

There was the obligatory big saloon with marble-topped tables and men drinking coffee or coffee-and-brandy, a billiard table, and a tobacco-laden atmosphere, and behind it a smaller room crowded with card players. A plump little man, womanish in voice, skin, and gestures, made a beeline for me:

'Good evening, Don Arturo, that's right, you've come to join us, haven't you? You already know our Heliodoro, don't you?' I knew the tight-lipped man to whose table I was gently propelled. He was my landlord. The plump little man babbled on: 'Excuse me for a tiny little moment, I've got to get the coffee ready, you know, but I won't be long.' Everything was arranged for me. Heliodoro introduced me to the two black-coated men at his table – 'Our two doctors, Don Julián and Don Anselmo' – and asked me the obvious questions: had I settled down, had the move been difficult, and so forth. I have never been good at small talk, and this was as boring as any. The effeminate little man brought coffee and asked me the same questions all over again, until one of the doctors cut him short:

'José, enter Don Arturo in the list.'

José produced a fat leather-bound notebook and thumbed it, giving me a glimpse of pages filled with columns of figures and headed by names.

'Now, let's see. How many are there in your family?'

'But surely I won't have to enter all my children as members of the Casino!'

'Oh, this hasn't anything to do with the Casino. This is our local Medical Aid Association. I put you on the list and it gives you a right to medical assistance whenever you need it.'

'But I've got a doctor in Madrid.'

Don Julián grunted:

'All right, if you don't want it, we won't put you down. But I warn you, if you've an urgent case in your family and you aren't a subscriber, my colleague here will send you a nice little bill. If you've a splinter in your thumb and he lances it, he'll put it down as "for a surgical operation, two hundred pesetas".'

'And if I call you in?'

'It's he who makes out the bills in any case. It would come to the same thing.'

'All right, then, put me down. My wife, four children, and myself. Six in all.'

'In what category, please, Don Julián?'

'Don't ask obvious questions, José. In our category, of course.'

'Five pesetas per month, Don Arturo. And what about your servant?'

'Isn't she a member of your Association already?'

'Well, yes, she's on our list, but she doesn't pay. So she's been struck off. And if she has an accident at work, you'll have to pay.'

Don Julián sniggered:

'Say she burns her hand on the frying-pan. For a surgical operation and treatment, two hundred pesetas.'

'Put the servant down, then.'

'Two pesetas. D'you want to pay now? I'm the cashier. It won't take me a second to make out the receipts.'

José pocketed the seven pesetas and tripped away, to reappear with a pack of cards.

'One hundred pesetas in the bank, this deal.'

He went straight into the back room and sat down on a high chair behind the biggest table.

'One hundred pesetas, boys, if nobody stakes more.'

Baccarat. The customers flocked to his table, the most important looking monopolizing the chairs. José was still shuffling the cards when a haggard man in mourning called out: 'Banco!' and put a hundred-peseta bill on the table. He seemed to be the local gambler, for people murmured behind his back and nodded sagely when José dealt and raked in the stakes. A large-boned old man muttered behind the loser: 'A bad start, Valentín.'

'Just the usual thing, Uncle Juán. Anything to avoid a change.'

The old man said no more, and the man called Valentín went on staking against the bank and losing. The others rarely played more than two pesetas; they were following the duel between the bank and

Valentín. 'The same as every night,' said someone near me. People began to play against Valentín, who after an hour announced that he had used up all his cash. José asked for a continuation. The gambler protested:

'That's not fair.'

'But, my dear Valentín, it isn't my fault if you've run out of cash.'

'Heliodoro, give me a hundred pesetas.'

They went quickly.

'Heliodoro, I'll sell you my mule.'

'I'll give you five hundred pesetas for her.'

'Let's have them.'

Heliodoro was pushing the five banknotes along the table, when the old man who had spoken to Valentín before interposed his hand:

'Don't sell your mule, Valentín.'

'I've a right to do as I like.'

'All right, then, I'll give you one thousand for her.'

'When? Now, at once?'

'Tomorrow morning.'

'I don't need them tomorrow.' Valentín took the five bills and Heliodoro scribbled a few lines on a piece of paper.

'Here, sign the receipt, Valentín.'

The luck changed. Valentín heaped up bills in front of him and José had to restock the bank with cash again and again. Suddenly somebody opened the door from the street and shouted:

'Good evening!'

José gathered in the cards and his money, the others grabbed theirs, and in an instant all were sitting at the marble-topped tables and chatting boisterously. Horses' hoofs sounded on the cobbles and stopped outside the Casino. A pair of Civil Guards entered, a corporal followed by a constable.

'Good evening, gentlemen!'

José contorted himself, bowing and scraping. The Civil Guards kindly accepted a coffee each. Drinking his cup, the Corporal suddenly lifted his head and stared at me:

'You're the stranger, eh? I know already that you went to Eliseo's this afternoon.' He waxed avuncular: 'I'll give you some good advice

—no one here will interfere with you, you can do as you like. But no meetings, eh? I want no gentlemen Communists here.'

Carefully he wiped his moustache with a handkerchief, rose and walked out, followed by his silent henchman. I was dumbfounded. José sidled up to me.

'Better be careful with the Corporal, Don Arturo, he's got a foul temper.'

'As long as I commit no offence, I'm no business of his.'

'It's not for me to say anything, but it isn't right for you to frequent Eliseo's. Nobody goes there except the rabble from the village, and that's God's own truth. But of course, you don't know the people yet.'

Heliodoro said nothing; he listened.

The man Valentín joined us with a shining face and a fistful of banknotes.

'You've cleaned up today,' said Heliodoro.

'Enough to make up for this evening, and for yesterday, and if the Guards hadn't turned up, blast them, I'd have taken the shirt off little José's back.' He thumped José's plump shoulder.

'You wait till tomorrow,' said José.

'Here are your six hundred pesetas, Heliodoro, and thanks.'

'What's this?'

'Your six hundred pesetas.'

'You don't owe me anything – well, yes, the hundred pesetas I gave you a while ago. The five hundred were for the mule.'

'But d'you think I'd give you my mule for five hundred? She's worth two thousand at least!'

'You won't give her? You *have* given her. Have you sold me your mule, or not? Yes or no? Here are witnesses, and I've got your receipt in my pocket. So there's nothing more to discuss.'

Valentín leaned forward:

'You son of a bitch – '

Heliodoro laid his hand on his hip pocket and smiled. He was a quiet, inconspicuous man, with taut lips.

'Look here,' he said, 'let's keep things straight and quiet. If you don't want to lose, don't gamble. Good night, gentlemen.'

He walked off with dignity, without looking back, but a man I had not noted before stepped up, watching Valentín's every movement. Old Uncle Juán tried to steer the gambler away.

'Now, you keep quiet, and no foolishness! You've sold your mule and you can't alter it. If only it would teach you a lesson.'

'But that son of a bitch – ' Valentín's eyes were watering with rage – 'here's his tame gunman to cover him, too – '

José went round with a tray full of glasses of brandy.

'Now then, now then, let's have peace. After all, I've lost more than anyone.'

But the game did not start again. Soon afterwards we all went out into the moonlit night. Old Juán joined me.

'We're going the same way. What do you think of our village?'

'I don't know what to say. There's food enough for thought in one day!'

'We've been discussing your visit to Eliseo's in the Casino. I think the Corporal only came to have a look at you.'

'But there is no Civil Guard post in this place, is there?'

'No, they've come over from Santa Cruz. But news spreads quickly. I must say, I for one don't think it's wrong to have done what you did, and so I told the others. But if you don't take a firm stand, you'll find life difficult in our village.'

'Now look here, I've no intention of getting mixed up with things in this place. After all, I'm only coming here on two days a week, and then I need a rest. But if I want to drink a glass of wine wherever I like, no one's going to prevent me.'

I knew I was skirting problems, and I felt in my bones that I would not be able to skirt them for long, as I listened to the calm voice of the old man telling me a story I seemed to have heard hundred of times, only to hate it more each time. Heliodoro was the lord and master of the township. His position as political boss was inherited from his father and grandfather who had been the usurers and *caciques*[1] of the place. Half the ground and the houses were his, and the few men who still worked their own land were dependent on him. At the coming of the Republic, people had hoped for a decent

---

[1] *Cacique* is the current term for the local political 'boss' of the Spanish countryside, who often is the local moneylender as well.

way of living. A few of the independent landowners had dared to pay higher wages. Heliodoro had proclaimed that people had to work for him at the old terms or not at all; his own living was not dependent on the land. Two years ago, the men had become desperate and destroyed trees and fields on Heliodoro's property. From that time on, he employed no labour at all, and since his latest political patrons had come to power, he gave no peace to the other proprietors.

'He fixed us with his lorries, mainly. He has got two, and so he used to carry our grain and fruit to Madrid. Most of us sold our produce direct to him. Then he refused to buy any more and our people tried to hire his lorries from him. He said no. They hired lorries in Torrijos, but because the Deputy comes from there and needs Heliodoro, the hire of the lorries was stopped. Then they hired lorries in Madrid, which was much more expensive. They had to pay double, but still, they sold their stuff in town. Then Heliodoro went to Madrid himself.'

Old Juán explained how the fruit and vegetable market in Madrid was worked. A group of agents called *asentadores*, allocators, had a monopoly on the market sites. They received all produce, fixed the price according to quality and the daily market rates, and allotted the goods to the various stalls. They undertook to sell on behalf of the producer and to pay him the proceeds minus their commission.

'Well, and then, after Heliodoro's visit to Madrid, Paco, who's one of our biggest and wealthiest market gardeners, went with a lorry full of big red pimentos to market, and they were a sight for sore eyes too, and worth a lot of money. Pimentos were fetching two pesetas a dozen, and more, at that time. After three days, Paco came back from town in a fine stew and told us in the Casino what had happened to him. One after another of the allocators had told him that there was no stall available for his pimentos, and that he would have to wait. The fruit had to stay in the lorry till the evening, and then Paco had to rent storing space. Next day, the allocators told him the same old story, and said that the market was flooded with pimentos, but they offered to take the lot off his hands at five hundred pesetas. He refused, naturally, and so another day passed. On the third day, the pimentos were squashed and dripping juice. Paco had to accept three hundred pesetas for the lot, and out of that to pay his storage, his stay at the inn, and the lorry. It was touch and go whether he would not have to pay more money out of his own pocket. When he'd finished telling the story – you can imagine in what a rage – Heliodoro laughed and said: 'You people don't understand business. No one in Novés can sell fruit in Madrid except me.' And so it was. Now, of course, people have to bring him their stuff, take what he decides to pay and dance to his tune if they want to sell anything at all. So that's why he lets his land lie fallow while the village is starving, and earns more money than he ever did from the few of us who still work. And that's why the man you saw in the Casino, and who was his father's electoral agent, has to trail round with him as his bodyguard. Because one thing is certain: Heliodoro will get it in the neck one day. Well, here you are – good night, and come and see me in my mill. It's still working.'

I waited, hand on the doorknob, listening to Old Juán's footsteps dying away. They were the steps of a strong and healthy man, beautifully even. While I tried not to lose the sound, my ear was caught by the noises of the night. Frogs were croaking in the pools of the dirty stream, cicadas were shrilling tirelessly in the gully. There were little splashes and jumps, and the thin whirring sound of nocturnal insects, and the sudden creaking of old beams in some house or barn. A moon of white metal cut the street into two bands, one deep black – where I stood – and the other aggressively white, gleaming on the smooth chalk walls and glinting on the sharp flint stones. The sleeping village was beautiful in this light, but I thought I could hear the heart-beat behind the white walls, a hidden force.

My house was asleep, too. The flames in the fireplace threw huge, fugitive shadows on the walls and the two slumbering dogs were black heaps rimmed with red. I sat down between my dogs and let myself be hypnotized by the twisting flames.

The house felt empty, as I did.

2. Spiders' Webs

In the north-west corner of the Puerta del Sol, Madrid's heart and centre, begins the Calle de Alcalá, which is its most important street. The entrance is as narrow as an alley. In the peak hours, the two streams of passers-by are bottled up on strips of pavement hardly more than a yard wide. The middle of the street is a single compact mass of cars, broken up only when a tram cuts through; when two trams coming from opposite directions pass each other there, the whole street is blocked. You cannot escape and must let yourself drift with the slowly moving crowd. You are smothered in the smell of burning petrol from the cars, of hot metal from the trams, and of the human beings round you. You rub elbows with a porter and a demi-mondaine, and you have the smell of acrid sweat and cheap heliotrope in your nostrils.

Every time you pass the open door of one of the cafés, a thick gust of tobacco smoke and crowd hits you in the face, and further on you dive through the fumes of the frying-pan in which the tavern keeper of Number 5 fries his sardines under the doorway of his establishment. It is useless to cross over to the opposite pavement. There, too, are crowded cafés and another tavern with another frying-pan.

But the two frying-pans mark the end of your labours. Once you have come so far, the street and its pavements widen, you breathe more freely and can rest your ears. For while you are caught in the narrow thoroughfare you are deafened by tram bells and klaxons, by the cries of street hawkers, the whistles of traffic policemen, the high-pitched conversations, and by the patter of the crowds, the rattle of tram cars, the screech of brakes.

Then the street becomes aristocratic. On its gently sloping pavement twelve persons can walk abreast, the tram lines are lost somewhere in the middle, and on both sides cars can pass comfortably three at a time. The buildings are ample and solid, stone to the left in the palaces of the old Customs House and the Academy of San Fernando, steel and concrete to the right. This is a street of banks and big offices and fancy shops, sprinkled with smart clubs, bars, and cabarets, flashing with neon lights at night. At its bottom end the stone building of the Bank of Spain rises on one side, and the War Ministry, hidden in gardens, on the other. Between them is the wide expanse of a square, in its centre a fountain where the goddess Cybele rides in a triumphal chariot drawn by lions and spouting jets of water: silver-grey pavement, white buildings, green trees, and a vast sky whose light drenches and obliterates the foolish architectural details. This length of street, no more than a quarter of an hour's walk from the Puerta del Sol, is the Calle de Alcalá.

You may cross the Plaza de la Cibeles and follow for a further hour a street which bears the name Calle de Alcalá, but to the people of Madrid it is no longer the same street. It is an artificial appendix whose construction we watched at the beginning of this century. We call it 'the other side of the Calle de Alcalá', to make it clear that it is not our street.

In the winter, the winds of the Sierra de Guadarrama sweep down the street and people who have to pass through it walk rapidly. But in fine weather its pavements are turned into a promenade, and the owners of the cafés put their marble tables out in the open. At sunset an enormous, milling crowd moves slowly up and down between the Bank of Spain and the Calle de Sevilla on one side, and between the War Ministry and the Calle de Peligros on the other, without entering the bottleneck at the top. Gesticulating, noisy groups of well-known people sit at the café tables, and the strollers cluster round them to see the famous torero, or politician, or writer, and to listen to what they have to say. The newspaper boys cry out the evening papers until the street is full of their shouts, and people go on waiting for the later editions. Then they gradually disperse in search of their supper.

During the day everything is business; people hurry up and down the Calle de Alcalá and the revolving doors of the banks gyrate incessantly, their glass panes flashing. But by day and night the street has a population of its own, which seems to live on those pavements: toreros without engagement, musicians without orchestra, comedians without theatre. They tell each other their difficulties and miseries and wait for a more fortunate colleague to arrive and solve the problem of a meal for them, for one more day. There are streetwalkers who come and go in the nearest bar, looking anxiously round to make sure that no policeman is near to stop them on their journey. There are flower sellers with their bunches of violets or tuberose buttonholes, assailing the customers of expensive bars and restaurants. There is the man without legs in his little wooden contraption which he propels with his hands; coins rain into his cap day after day, he has never missed a bullfight, good or bad, and Ministers and beggars greet him.

Much later, in the small hours of the night, something like a bundle of clothes lies in the porch of Calatrava Church. It is a woman with an infant in arms who sleep there, wrapped in the same huge shawl. You can see them in the same spot winter or summer. I have watched them during twenty-five years, and to me they were the greatest mystery of the Calle de Alcalá. Were they a phantom, that never grew older? Or was the place a fief passed on from generation to generation in the beggars' guild?

It was in this bit of the Calle de Alcalá that I had my office.

My room was on the top of a tower in one of the highest business buildings. It was a cage of glass and iron, with only two walls of masonry, one which separated it from the other rooms of the office, and another which joined it to the next house. The ceiling was of glass, big, transparent glass slabs in a framework of steel girders. The floor was of glass, smaller, dim glass tiles fitted into a net of steel bars. Two walls, one facing the street, the other facing a wide roof terrace, were plate-glass sheets in steel frames. In winter two enormous radiators fought against the icebox atmosphere. In summer, the cage was shaded with canvas covers, the huge windows and the door to the roof terrace were opened, and the draughts battled against the torrid heat of the sun on glass and steel. I could see the endless, luminous sky dwarfing the white city buildings, and the insect-like crowds in the street below.

My office was a cage suspended over the city, but I called it my confessional. Here the inventors shut themselves up together with me. We discussed their affairs, lying back in the deep leather armchairs or leaning over the draftsman's table, and it was often as though I were their confessor.

The humble, visionary inventor would arrive with his drawings in a leather briefcase bought especially for the purpose – he had never used a case of the kind himself and fumbled with the lock – and let himself drop into the armchair.

'Would you mind shutting the door?' he would ask.

I would turn round to Maria at her typewriter and say:

'All right, Señorita, please leave us alone for the moment. I'll call for you later.'

She would shut the door carefully.

'Well now . . . I've come to see you because Don Julián – he's an old client of yours, of course – told me I could trust you and speak freely.'

The man would entangle himself in his words, trying to evade the necessity of showing his drawings, for fear of being robbed of the millions surely awaiting him.

What a labour it was to convince people of the fact that their 'invention' had been known to the world for years, or that their machine could not function because it was against the laws of mechanics. A few, a very few, saw it and left, bowed down under their knowledge, shattered. You had killed their spirit, and you felt compassion for them. But the great majority looked at you out of feverish eyes, pitying you greatly, and demanded that you should register a patent for them. You were unable to understand their genius. They had come to see you, not in order to convince you of their ideas, but simply to register their patent through you; then they would convince the whole world of their invention.

And since a Spanish patent is a document granted to whoever applies for it in the correct legal form and pays the fees to the State, you had to give in. The inventor was perfectly contented and invited you to lunch with him, and you had to listen to the story of how he had conceived the idea, of the calvary he had passed through, and of his extravagant hopes.

'Imagine', he would say, 'that one out of every thousand inhabitants of Spain buys my apparatus. At five pesetas. That makes one hundred thousand pesetas. And then we take it to America, with a market of millions and millions of people – it'll be millions of dollars, you'll see.'

Yet those were the innocents among the many who passed through my confessional. More frequently the deep leather chairs held great figures in industry and commerce who laid bare all their sense of power, all their cynicism: 'Business is business, you know.'

A professor of chemistry at Madrid University discovered a process by which hitherto insoluble alkaline earth salts became soluble. His discovery implied a revolution in various industries, and the inventor knew it. There was a side to it which immediately affected the general public. In the process of extracting sugar from beet or cane molasses, only fourteen to seventeen per cent of the sugar content of the solution was obtainable, because insoluble alkaline earth salts obstructed the separation of the remainder. By the professor's method, eighty-five to ninety-two per cent could be extracted. This meant that from the same quantity of raw material, five times as much sugar could be obtained as before, and that production costs would be reduced to a fifth.

While the patent was pending in several countries, the managing director of an alcohol distillery turned up in my confessional. His firm figured as Spanish, but German capital was behind it, and it possessed a virtual monopoly of industrial alcohol in Spain.

'Barea, I want to see a copy of that patent.'

'It's still pending, and I can't let you have it without an authorization from the inventor.'

He handed me a letter from the inventor, authorizing me to give him a copy of the patent and further detailed information. When he had read through the material, he asked:

'What's your opinion of the patent?'

'I think it's very interesting. England and Germany have granted it.'

'But do you believe the process will work?'

'He's demonstrated it to me in his laboratory. I don't know about its commercial exploitation, but in the laboratory it's child's play.'

'Hm. I want you to take action for an annulment of the patent.'

This man's company was an old client of ours.

'I'm sorry, but we can't undertake it. We are the inventor's agents, after all.'

'I know that. What I want is that you should take charge of the affair, that's to say, that you should handle it without figuring in public. The only one to figure will be the firm's lawyer. But he doesn't know the first thing about patent law, and so I want you to direct him.'

'But do you realize that an action wouldn't have an earthly chance? The patent is solid, it's genuine, and it can't be declared null and void just like that.'

'I know all that, but . . . well, I'll explain how things are. We buy all residues from molasses for our alcohol production from the Sugar Refinery. The inventor has signed a contract with the Sugar Refinery. That means that, in future, their molasses residues will contain about five per cent of sugar instead of eighty-five per cent. You will understand that we have a right to defend our business interests. As soon as we start proceedings against the patent, the Sugar Refinery must suspend the contract.'

'But that won't give you the annulment of the patent.'

'Of course not. But the inventor is a university professor. And we have capital of several millions. The case will go through all the stages of appeal and it will last years and years. The firm's lawyer gets his fees from us anyhow, so that the only extra expenses will be your fees, and the cost of the action. We won't get the patent annulled, but we'll ruin the inventor.'

We did not accept that deal, but we undertook the defence of our client, the inventor. His contract with the Sugar Refinery was cancelled. The lawsuits consumed his private means, a family fortune of some two hundred thousand pesetas. His patent remained valid. But big business had the last laugh. For five years I had to handle that man's affairs and follow his bitter experiences. A Dutch firm which produced sugar in the Dutch East Indies showed interest in the patent. When this firm had tested the process, it offered five thousand guilders for all patent rights. The inventor rejected the proposal with indignation. The answer was that they only wanted to acquire the patent in defence of their interests – for who would want to put it into practice, with a sugar surplus on the world market and the sugar business in a crisis owing to surplus production? A US enterprise was even more brutally direct: 'We don't know what to do with the Cuban sugar, and you want us to pay cash for the right to produce five times more of a product we cannot sell?'

I felt no interest in the inventor as an individual. But I was fascinated by the economic problem the patent case represented. In Spain, sugar was one of the most expensive of all primary commodities. It was the unofficial monopoly of a trust which controlled the sugar-beet prices and had its strong tendrils in politics, so as to maintain prohibitive customs duties on imported sugar. The sugar-beet growers in Aragon were paid starvation prices for the raw material; the consumer, who had no other choice in buying, had to pay an exorbitant price for the finished product. To the Spanish poor, sugar was a luxury article, and had been ever since Spain lost Cuba. I remembered only too well the frugality with which my mother had measured the small spoonful of sugar for her beloved coffee.

And this was not an isolated case by any means. Through my confessional of glass and steel passed dozens of the big sharks, each with his own special, discreet recipe for multiplying his capital, whatever the cost. To my confessional came men who crossed Europe by air and signed fabulous contracts between the coming and going of a plane. Expensive agents of their masters who kept somewhere in the dim background, they arrived in impeccable clothes which did not always suit them, polished, suave, bland, convincing in their deals, often incredibly brutal and primitive in their enjoyments after business. I had to see them dressed to kill, and naked, in business and at play, for it was my job to be the agent of those agents.

I have met many sane businessmen and industrialists, honest within the limits of their human search for more money and greater scope, and I never believed they were evil just because they were businessmen. But there were those others, those who hadn't names like Brown or Mueller or Durand or Pérez, but who were called the 'British', the 'Nederland', the 'Deutsche', the 'Ibérica', with the impunity of the anonymous; who destroyed countries to increase that intangible, irresponsible power of theirs. Their agents and managers, the people someone like myself would meet, had only one standard: dividends. But to the trust or combine it was important that they should appear legally honest. If it was necessary to bribe a Minister, the firm gave the money, but its agent had to know how to do it in such a form that no one would ever be able to prove where the money had come from.

From my vantage point in the economic machinery I came to know those concerns which could afford to give free shares to impoverished or avaricious kings, and to make or unmake a Government, only to have laws passed of which not only the country at large but often even Deputies of the Chamber were ignorant.

But they were too powerful for mere words to reach them.

I knew who had paid two hundred thousand pesetas for the vote of the highest law court in Spain, in order to procure a decision in his favour in a lawsuit which determined whether Spain should have an aircraft industry of her own or not. I knew that the Catalan cloth manufacturers depended on the mercy of the chemical concern, Industrias Químicas y Lluch, which was nominally Spanish but in fact belonged to none less than the I.G. Farbenindustrie. I knew who had given and who had taken thousands of pesetas to procure a verdict which meant that the Spanish public would not be able to buy cheap radio sets. I knew the intricate story of how, thanks to the stupid blindness of Spain's barrack-room dictator, an international firm assumed control of the whole Spanish milk industry, ruined thousands of small businessmen, ruined the dairy farmers of Asturias, and forced the public to pay dear for milk with reduced nutrition value.

But what could I do about it?

Those men and those things passed through my confessional. I was a very small cog in the machinery, but the driving power had to pass through me. And yet, I was given no right to think and see for myself; they considered me as complementary of them, as one man more who was starting on their career. And they confessed themselves to me.

At school I had found myself caught in the wheels of a hypocritical educational system which traded in the intelligence of its charity pupils, so as to attract as boarders the sons of wealthy mine-owners. In the army, I had found myself caught in the wheels of the war-makers, shackled by the Military Code and by a system which made it impossible to furnish proof of corruption, but easy to destroy a little sergeant, had he tried to rebel. Now I found myself caught in yet another system of cogwheels, seemingly less brutal, but infinitely more subtle and effective. I could rebel – but how?

You might go to a judge and tell him that the manager of a certain alcohol distillery was attempting to rob an inventor of the fruits of his work, and a nation of cheap sugar. But the judge did not exist for such matters; he existed so as to prosecute you if you committed the offence of violating professional secrets. Those other things were not an offence, they were legitimate business. The company had the legal right to combat a patent it thought invalid; the inventor had the legal right to defend himself. If he was unable to do so, lacking the millions he would need to fight an anonymous concern during five years of lawsuits, that was not the fault of the judge or the law, but the inventor's bad luck.

If I denounced the deal before a judge, he would laugh me out of his presence, and my boss would put me in the street. I would lose my name as a loyal intelligent worker and find all doors shut to me. I would starve, haunted by my family's reproaches. They would call me an idiot. I might have to go to prison for slander. For slandering those who took the cream from the milk of Madrid's ¢hildren, who stole sugar from them, for slandering honourable and decent people who followed their legitimate business.

I thought of all this while I listened to the lawyer of the German Embassy, young Rodríguez Rodríguez. He was explaining the action by which we were to attack the patents for the manufacture of bearings for railway coaches. What was at stake was an order of the Northern Railway Company for several thousands of special bearings, an order which involved a million pesetas or so. The bearings the patents for which he wanted to attack were the speciality of a French company, and the competitor was the German Reichsbahngesellschaft.

Rodríguez Rodríguez was the prototype of a Madrid playboy. His father had for years been the lawyer of the German Embassy – and of many concerns of German heavy industry. He himself had succeeded his father, although he had nothing but the title and degree of a lawyer. He served the Germans in a double capacity. The lawsuits he undertook did not gain public attention, as those of greater forensic lights would have done; and he loaned himself to all kinds of machinations with an easy unconcern. Immensely vain of his position, he had come back dazzled from his last journey to Berlin. As soon as we had finished discussing the patent action he proposed, he poured forth praise of German doctors and hospitals as he had found them when he was treated for a broken arm. And then they had made him a member, not just of the National Socialist Party, but of the SS. He showed me a photograph of young men in black shirts, he himself in the middle.

'Now, what do you think of that?'

'You look superb in uniform . . . Now, tell me frankly, Rodríguez, what the hell do you want out of this Nazi business? You're Spanish.'

'Of course I am, and they wouldn't have taken me if I hadn't been a member of Falange. It's an honour to become a member of the SS, don't you see? And besides, I'm convinced Hitler's ideas are right. They're what we Falangists want for Spain. We need the sort of thing here that Hitler's done in Germany. Remember what the mob did in Asturias. If they hadn't been made to feel a firm hand, we would now have a Spanish Lenin and be Russia's colony.'

'I won't discuss your ideas about the workers and the Republic, they're your affair. But don't you think you're going to make us into Hitler's colony, which surely means going to the other extreme?'

'So what? I should be delighted. That's exactly what we need in Spain – a whiff of German civilization.'

'Now look here, friend Rodríguez – we've worked together for quite a few years – you know what's happening in Germany better than I do. You know what we may expect from Junkers, and Schering-Kahlbaum, and the I.G. Farben. You can't deny to my face, after all we've seen, that they are the masters of Germany.'

'My dear Barea, in this world there are only two possible attitudes: either you get eaten yourself, or you eat the others. Of course I have to look after my future. And after my country's too.'

'That's why you put on a German uniform?'

'But I'm working for my country that way. It's not a disguise. It simply means that we are working to make Spain into a strong nation.'

'Who's working?'

'Our friends, the Germans, and a handful of good Spaniards like myself, who will have to put things into practice. Believe me, I'm not the only National Socialist in Spain.'

'No, I know there are quite a lot of them, unfortunately. I don't know whether they all have their Party uniform, but they're in it somehow.'

'Of course they won't let just anyone put on their uniform, and they don't make them members like me. But after all, in my position, I'm almost a German subject.'

'With the slight difference that you're a Spaniard. I know they send you to Germany with a diplomatic passport, and a lot of errands and messages. But all the same, I don't think it's good business that you've let yourself in for.'

'Time will show. And you'll change your mind, Barea. You'll have to, you see.'

He left. I had my lunch and took the bus to Novés.

A little bridge rising in a steep hunchback over a damp, green gully lined with aromatic herbs and populated by thousands of frogs. All around, the dun earth of Castile, cut into parallel lines by ploughed furrows. In front of the bridge, the gate of the flour mill, overhung by the grape vine on the wall. The big house a single splash of whitewash, made to look harder and whiter by the sunlight and the background of grey soil, by the gay frame of the vine and the green band of the gully which carries live blood through the dry fields.

I entered the flour mill and found myself in a cool gateway. Light, white dust floated in the air. In the corner gyrated two cone-shaped stones which crushed grain for fodder. The grain steamed under the pressure and a fine vapour arose, greedily inhaled by two patient donkeys at the door.

To the left, behind a wooden partition with a window, was Old Juán's office. So he said with a flourish, but at the same time he laughed at the description, for he found it difficult to write with his knotty fingers. In his grandfather's time accounts were cut on wooden slats with a knife, a notch for each sack of milled grain.

He chuckled and showed me a bundle of tallies, polished by the hands which had handled them for many years.

'I still keep the accounts for many people of my own age this way. But I have to keep those damned books as well!'

He led me through a narrow door into the mill proper, and it was as though we had come out of the land of sun into the land of snow. The roof of the hall was some fifty feet above our heads and had big, plate-glass windows. From the roof down stretched a thicket of beams and tubes, wheels and belts. But none of it was of iron, all was wood. And in the course of the years, the fine dust of milled grain had settled in the minutest cracks and crannies, and had clothed each piece in white velvet. It was like a snow-bound forest. Spiders had scaled the heights and hung their webs from rafter to rafter, from corner to corner. The white dust had lined them, and they were like pine branches laden with snow. The panes of the high, tall windows, powdered with impalpable dust, let through a pale winter sun which laid grey shadows on the machinery. The monotonous noise of the rocking cradle which sifted flour from bran was almost like the sound of a lumberman's saw in the mountains.

'Here you see our whole wealth.'

'This is an old place, Uncle Juán.'

'My grandfather built the mill. He must have been a progressive man for his time, because he installed a steam engine. It's still there.'

When I looked at the steam engine, I realized what people will think of our own notions of mechanics in a thousand years' time. It was an ancient thing with a misshapen flywheel, half buried in the ground, red with the rust of half a century, fretted by wind, sand, and dripping water, chinky, cracked, crumpled. It stuck out of the ground like the skeleton of an antediluvian animal struggling to the surface, its rods the broken arms and its enormous piston the neck of a monster stricken and twisted by a cataclysm.

'I've had an electric engine for many years now.'

'And do you make money?'

'I used to make it. They brought wheat from Torrijos and Santa Cruz to my mill. At times even from Navalcarnero and Valmojado. Then Torrijos built a mill for itself, and so did Navalcarnero. It was Navalcarnero that did me most harm, because it's on a railway line. But you know, what finished us off was politics. Since the time of the dictatorship, one's had to live on the village, and must be grateful to live as it is. Well, I can't complain. I'm nearing seventy-five, my sons have their living, and I'll die here in peace.' He stopped and pondered. 'If they let me. . . .'

'I don't think anyone will quarrel with you. And as you say, when one's seventy-five, one doesn't expect many more changes in one's life.'

'I don't know – really, I don't know. We old people see many things, or we feel them. It may be just our inborn fear of dying. When in 1933 the lads went out to the fields and cut down my trees and killed my few heads of cattle and burned the ricks and destroyed the vegetable garden – believe me, it didn't frighten me very much, because something like that had to come. But then things happened in Asturias and now it looks as if we were all going mad. Things will come to a bad end. To a very bad end. And very soon too, Don Arturo. The people are starving, and hunger is a bad counsellor. . . .

'There's nothing but misery in the village. The half-dozen people who could give work to the others won't do it, some out of anger and some out of fear of Heliodoro. The land lies fallow and the people haven't got enough to eat. Don Ramón, God bless him – '

'Who's Don Ramón?'

'He's the village grocer. You must have seen his shop behind the Casino. He's a good, kind man, only he's crazy about the Church, and it's just as if they'd bewitched him. Don Ramón is one of the best – which doesn't mean that he wouldn't give you a few grammes under weight, though. Well, it used to be like this: every time anybody came to him and said: "Don Ramón, do let me have some beans, or a bit of dried cod, and bread, and I'll pay you as soon as my husband starts working again," he let the woman have something and put it down in his books. If they paid him, it was all right, but they often didn't or couldn't. When people had some misfortune, or when somebody in their family died, he took his pencil and ran it through the account: 'Don't worry, woman, that's settled. And may God forgive me, as He may forgive the one who's dead.' But then, between Heliodoro and Don Lucas – '

'Now, who's your Don Lucas?'

'Our priest, and he's one of the sharp kind. I was going to say, between the two of them, they've won him over, and now he doesn't give a breadcrumb to the poor any more. Because Don Lucas told him it was a mortal sin to help the godless, and Heliodoro said it was necessary to get a tight grip on those rascals, and if Don Ramón wanted to help them, he – Heliodoro – would get a tight grip on Don Ramón.'

He made a long pause.

'The worst of it is that the people take it all in silence. In the morning they sit down in the plaza, on the stone wall along the road, and keep silent. In the evening they go to Eliseo's Casino and keep silent there. In 1933 a few of them came near my mill, but they had some respect for me and knew they could always get a piece of bread in my house when they needed it, and so they went away again. But next time they come – and they will come – I don't know . . . For they'll come soon. You'll see.'

Suddenly, Old Juán's pride as a host swept away his pessimism. He took an old earthenware Talavera jug, ingenuous blue flowers on a milky ground, and led me to a huge wine jar stowed away in a small room.

'Let's have a drink. You won't get another like it in Madrid.'

Slowly we drank the cool, rough wine which frothed in purple bubbles against the glaze. We handed each other the jug and drank from the same side, as in an ancestral peace rite.

Aurelia was in a bad temper that day. After lunch we took the children for a walk in the orchards. She had prepared a snack which we went to eat by a stream at the bottom of the green gully. But her face did not change. In the end, she said:

'This village is so boring.'

'What's the matter now?'

'Nothing. It's just as if we belonged to a different race.'

'Well, what's happened now?'

'Nothing has happened, exactly. But you must see that those people are boycotting us. Because of course the better families in the village know by now that you're a Socialist and don't go to Mass and are seen in Eliseo's Casino. And naturally, all one gets in the street is a 'Good morning', if that. And you must understand that I won't make friends with the country people.'

'Why not? I should like you to.'

'You would. But I think you ought to preserve your standing and —'

'And what? Go to the parties of the Reverend Father and invite Heliodoro's wife to our house? I'm sorry, but I won't. You can do as you like, but I haven't come here to go to parties.'

'Of course, you go away early on Mondays, and I stay here the whole week long.'

We grew sharp and bitter, both of us. The rest of Sunday passed in heavy boredom. When I left to catch my bus on Monday morning, the whole house was sleeping. I went away with a sense of liberation.

3. Unrest

I was about to finish signing my bunch of letters. It was the pleasantest hour in the confessional. The sun had sunk behind the tall buildings on the top of the Calle de Alcalá. A cool breeze blew into my room and made the canvas curtains belly and crackle. In the street down below, people began to cluster for their daily stroll. The noise of the beehive came up as a dull drone puncuated by the cries of the newspaper boys selling the early evening papers, the shrill tinkle of tramway bells and the bark of klaxons. It was a noise we no longer heard, but which was there, day after day.

When a sudden silence fell, it was so strong and unexpected that I stopped writing. Maria interrupted her typing and turned her head. The typewriters in the outer office stopped. It lasted only an instant. Then a shot sounded, and it was followed by a deafening roar from the multitude. Amidst the shouts I caught the sound of people running in all directions and of iron shutters being pulled down with a clatter. Then came a few more shots and the musical note of breaking glass. We ran out on to the roof terrace.

A wide space in the street below was deserted. At the fringe of this sudden void, crowds of people were running madly. Opposite us, at the corner of the Phoenix Building, some half-dozen people were leaning over a bundle on the ground. It looked ludicrous from our height. We could see the street in its full length. At our feet it widened into a sort of square, where the Gran Vía and the Calle de Caballero de Gracia joined it. Some cars were standing, probably abandoned by their occupants, and a tram had stopped and was quite empty. From our altitude the men in the little group were soundless and small, they were gesticulating like puppets in a show. Two of them lifted a still smaller figure, doubled up at the waist. A stain was left on the grey asphalt of the pavement. It looked black. A heap of newspapers beside it flapped in the wind.

Shock Police[1] arrived in an open lorry. The men clambered swiftly out, truncheon in hand, as though they intended to attack the lonely group. A taxi appeared in the still square. The wounded man and those who supported him boarded it, and the taxi sped up the street. The Shock Police hurried to the doors of the cafés. People again flooded into the street and formed groups which the police dispersed.

I finished my mail and we all went downstairs. But police stopped us on the first floor of the building. The Café La Granja had a door which opened on to our staircase, and there the police had been posted. They demanded identity papers and searched all of us. When we reached the front door, we found the wife of the concierge sitting on a chair and recovering from an attack of nerves under her husband's care, while a police officer took notes. There was an intense smell of ether in the air. The woman was saying:

'I was just standing in the doorway and looking at the people walking past until the lads came who sell the *Mundo Obrero*. "Now there'll be a row as usual," I said to myself. Because the young gentlemen of *FE* were already standing in the door of the café with their papers and their sticks. But nothing happened. The boys with the *Mundo Obrero* came running and crying out their paper just as they do every day, and then the young gentlemen started crying out their *FE*, but nobody paid much attention. So it looked as if nothing was going to happen this time, until one of the lads of the *Mundo Obrero* stopped here at the corner with two of his friends. And then a group of four or five of the others came up at once and pulled away his papers, and they came to blows. The people all around ran away, and then one of the young gentlemen drew something out of his

---

[1] The *Guardia de Asalto*, here translated Shock Police, was set up by the Spanish Government in the early days of the Republic, as a corps loyal to the Republican authorities and qualified to replace the old Civil Guard, the rural constabulary which traditionally served the interests of the great landowners and their *caciques*. – Author's Note.

pocket and shot the lad with the papers. Then everyone ran away and the poor boy was left lying because he couldn't get up.'

For weeks, it had been a daily occurrence that the Falangists waited for the Communist paper to appear in the streets, and then began to cry out their own review, *FE*. The people who sold those papers were not professional newspaper vendors but volunteers from each party. After a few moments the two groups would be involved in a row which ended in faces being slapped, in an occasional broken head, and, inevitably, in soiled and trodden newspapers scattered all over the pavement. Timorous people would feel frightened and hurry off, but as a rule the passers-by considered these scenes a stimulating spectacle in which they themselves often felt moved to take a hand.

This time it was serious.

The next afternoon, signs of unrest became visible from half past five onwards. Workers who had finished in their shops at five seemed to have agreed to meet in the Calle de Alcalá. You could see them arrive and walk up and down in little groups with their meal packets under their arm, exhibiting themselves provocatively between the tables on the terrace of the Aquarium, the smart café in which the bigwigs of Falange met. The number of police posts had been increased; people were made to pass on. You could see groups of Falangists passing groups of workers, exchanging looks and mumbling insults. The conflict was still to come.

When the first shouts of *Mundo Obrero* came, they were answered by shouts of *FE*. For a few minutes, the cries filled the street with their challenge, and the supporters of each party flocked round their newspaper sellers to buy a copy. Suddenly one of the groups – from our altitude we could not see which – scattered; there was a scuffle, and at once the whole street became a battlefield. The Shock Police hit out with their truncheons at everyone within their reach.

Very soon the superior strength of the workers became clear, and a group of Falangists took refuge in the Aquarium. All the window panes in the door of the café were smashed. Glass showered on the pavement, and broken chairs and tables rolled on the ground. A carload of Shock Police fell upon the assailants. Once more the Calle de Alcalá was left deserted except for the Shock Police and a few passers-by who hurried through.

After supper I went to the People's House. In the half-empty café I found a group of men I knew, discussing the events of the evening and the day before. When each one had made an excited speech, an elderly man said:

'The worst of it is that all these violent happenings are only cooking the stew for the benefit of the Communists.'

'So what – are you afraid of them?' said another mockingly.

'I'm not afraid, but what I see is that they're getting into our own ranks. To the Falangists everyone is a Communist, and of course we'll defend ourselves when they hit out at us. But at the same time we have to tell people to be patient, and so they go over to the Communists.'

'Well, you're one of Besteiro's reformists, aren't you? You believe that things can be settled with velvet gloves. And that's a mistake. The Right is united – and we pull in all directions, each group on its own, and what's worse, each of us calls the others dirty dogs. The whole thing's mucked up.'

The man who spoke banged a bundle of papers down on the table.

'Just read this, they're all our papers, Left papers. And what's in them? The Communists attacking the Anarchists, and the other way round. Largo Caballero together with Araquistain attacking Prieto, and the other way round. I'll leave out Besteiro, because nobody listens to him any more, and anyhow he never talks about revolution in the streets. But all those others talk about it, each about his own brand of revolution. If we don't get together quickly, the same thing will happen here as happened in Austria: Gil Robles and Calvo Sotelo dictators, and the Vatican dictating.'

'That won't be so easy. The people will rise as they did in Asturias.'

'And the same thing will happen as happened then, or worse, don't you see? Don't think I'm talking of what might happen in the moon. That old ditherer, Chapaprieta, won't be able to save his Government, and as soon as they've got him to resign – as they will – our dear Mr President, old "Boots", will have to do one of two things, either make Gil Robles Premier, or dissolve the Cortes. And he won't dare to dissolve the Cortes, because it would cost him his job, whether the others win the elections or we do.'

I did not take much part in the discussion, but I thought the pessimist was largely right. I was afraid he was right.

The then Premier, Chapaprieta, was clearly the head of a transition government, intended to mark time. He was a man without the backing of a political party, without a majority in the Cortes, in office only to steer the Budgets through. Gil Robles, the leader of the Right, would not fail to exploit the opportunity of bringing things to a head.

It was the most favourable situation for the parties of the Spanish Right. The parties of the Left were utterly disunited. It was not so much a disagreement between Republicans pure and simple and Socialists or Anarchists, but the deep split which followed from the fight for the masses in which each Left party had staked its bid. Azaña, the leader of the Left Republicans, commanded a large section of the middle class and could hope to win over a considerable part of the workers. The socialist trade unions of the UGT controlled a million and a half workers, the anarchist unions of the CNT the same number or more. The number of adherents was difficult to establish exactly, and the boundaries of influence were shifting. And both fought for the decisive influence among the workers. But there was also a struggle within each of the organizations. Officially, the UGT acknowledged the principles of the Socialist Party, the CNT those of the Anarchist. The opinions among their members were not always governed by the official line. The Socialist Party itself, and with it the trade unions under its influence, were divided into a left wing under Largo Caballero, a centre under Indalecio Prieto, and a right wing under Besteiro. The CNT was split, less clearly but no less deeply, into the supporters of 'direct action' and the supporters of 'syndical action,' political anarchists and anarcho-syndicalists. In both great trade union centres there was a group which favoured, and a group which opposed, the fusion of both into a single trade-union association. On the whole, it was the left wing of the Socialists and the UGT which worked for such a rapprochement. But to complicate matters, it was in this left wing that the influence of the Communists began to make itself felt, and there existed an open and ingrained hostility between Communists and Anarchists.

It is very Spanish to 'let oneself be blinded only to rob a neighbour of his eye', as the proverb says. So it could happen that Anarchists were pleased when Communists were attacked by Falange, and that Communists did their best to attack the Anarchists by means of official oppression, coming from a Government equally hostile to the Communists themselves.

I think all of us who did not belong to a party bureaucracy counted those divisions and subdivisions of the Left over and over again in mental despair. And yet it seems to me now that, in stressing the splits of the Spanish Left, we were and are falling into a grave error.

For all those paralysing splits and fights obsessed only the political leaders of each group and their collaborators, or immediate supporters – a minority. The average man who belonged to the Left felt differently. Out of instinct, out of emotion, if you prefer it, and without theoretically marshalled arguments, the vast majority of the Spanish working-class Left wanted a union which would wipe out the resentments and differences that had scarcely ever been real to them. Yet the experience of the result of union was very real: the Republic had been born out of an agreement between the organized Left parties. In the Asturias rising, the miners had fought under the slogan of UHP, 'Union of Brother Workers'. And the longing for such a 'union of brothers', mystical and strong, was alive among the masses in that second half of 1935, when it was clear that without it the Right would assume absolute power and send many thousands more into the prisons, to rot with the political prisoners who had been there since Asturias.

It took a long time before the confused urge of the members and supporters was converted into measures of common self-defence by the leaders of the Left.

The united front of the Right, however, embracing leaders, members and sympathizers, impressed itself on me – and others like me – in daily incidents.

I saw it most clearly on the minute battlefield of Novés.

I like walking in the lonely, vast lands of Castile. There are no trees and no flowers, the earth is dry, hard and grey, you seldom see the outline of a house, and when you meet a labourer on his way, the greeting you exchange is accompanied by a distrustful glance, and a savage growl from the wayfarer's dog who refrains from biting you only thanks to the harsh order of his master.

But under the sun of the dog days, this desolate landscape has majesty.

There are only three things, the sun, the sky, and the earth, and each is pitiless. The sun is a live flame above your head, the sky is a luminous dome of reverberating blue glass, the earth is a cracked plain scorching your feet. There are no walls to give shade, no roofs to rest your eyes, no spring or brook to cool your throat. It is as though you were naked and inert in the hand of God. Either your brain grows drowsy and dulled, in passive resignation, or it gains its full creative power, for there is nothing to distract it and your self is an absolute self which appears to you clearer and more transparent than ever before.

A burning cigarette in the midst of the deserted plain assumes gigantic proportions, like a loud-spoken blasphemy in an empty church. The flame of the match disappears in this light and becomes less flame than ever. The blue smoke of the match mounts in slow spirals, gathers and thickens in the still air to a whitish little cloud and sinks down to your feet, grown cold and invisible. The earth swallows it. The air presses it down to the earth. The light dissolves its blue against the blue of the sky. When you throw away your cigarette stub, the white smoking patch seems more disgraceful than if you had thrown it on the richest carpet. There it stays to tell everyone that you have passed.

Sometimes I have felt so intensely like a criminal leaving a trail that I picked up the stub, crushed it out on the sole of my shoe and put it in my pocket. At other times, when I found a cigarette end lying in the field, I have picked it up out of sheer curiosity. If it was still damp, it meant that somebody was near. A cigarette rolled with coarse paper would indicate a farm worker, a machine-made cigarette a man from the town. Brittle edges and yellowing paper meant that the man had passed days or even months ago. When I saw those signs I would breathe more freely, for in the lonely plains of Castile, an instinctive fear is reborn in you and you love solitude as a defence.

That morning I had gone for a solitary walk in the fields round Novés and come back with an active mind, my brain washed clean, but my body tired and parched. I sat down at one of the tables José had put before the entrance of the Rich Men's Casino.

'Something very cool, José!'

He produced a bottle of beer covered with dew. He leaned over my table and asked, as they all asked:

'How do you like our place?'

'Well, I like it. I prefer villages which are not townified. Perhaps it's because I'm fed up with the town.'

'If you had lived here all your life like me you would want to get away.'

'Of course . . .'

Opposite the Casino the road dipped down and a low stone wall bordered it on the side of the gully. A dozen men were lined up along it. They were watching us in silence.

'What are they doing there, José?'

'They're waiting for something to happen. For a windfall. But if the moon doesn't fall. . . . You see, Don Arturo, it's customary for the men who are out of work to come here in the mornings and wait until somebody hires them for some small job or other.'

'But it's almost noon, and Sunday into the bargain. Who the devil would hire them today?'

'Oh, they just come because they're used to it. And then, on Sundays the gentry come here for their glass of vermouth, and sometimes one of them has an errand to be run, and that means a few coppers. And sometimes one of the men dares to beg a little money. The poor devils must do something after all. They deserve what they've got, though.'

'Do you mean they deserve to starve to death?'

'Goodness me, I don't mean starve to death, as you put it, because one isn't quite hard-hearted, after all. But it's a good thing for them to learn their lesson. That'll teach them not to get mixed up with Republics and things, and to go wanting to put the world in order. Because you've no idea, sir, what this place was like when the Republic came. They even let off rockets. And then they started at once demanding things, for instance, a school. There it is, up there, half finished. If they don't put the money up themselves, their Republic won't.'

On the road there emerged a horseman on a black horse covered with scars and sores. A gaunt figure encased in tight black trousers which moulded his calves like the fashionable trousers of the nineteenth century, a black riding coat with rounded tails and a bowler which must have been black in its time, but now was the colour of a fly's wings. A Quixote in his late seventies, with few teeth left, but bushy brows over lively black eyes, a goatee and a few snow-white tufts of hair sticking out from under his hat. He dismounted, threw the reins over the horse's neck and beckoned one of the men sitting on the stone wall.

'Here, take him to my house.'

The man caught the reins and dragged the horse past the Casino into a doorway beside the pharmacy, some ten yards from where I sat. The rider came towards me, beating a tattoo on his shin with his riding whip.

'How d'you do, I've been waiting to meet the Madrileño. Do you mind if I sit down here?' He did not wait for my assent but simply sat down. 'What's yours? Beer? José, two beers.' He paused and looked at me. 'Possibly you don't know who I am. Well now, I'm their accomplice' – he nodded towards the two village doctors who had just arrived and sat down at another table, hunting in pairs as usual – 'that's to say, I'm the apothecary, Alberto de Fonseca y Ontivares, Licentiate in Pharmaceutics, Bachelor of Science – Chemistry – landowner and starveling to boot. These people here never fall ill, and when they do fall ill, they haven't any money, and farms produce nothing but lawsuits. Now tell me about yourself.'

He was amusing, and I gave him a brief sketch of myself and my work. When I explained my profession, he clutched my arm.

'My dear fellow, we must have a talk. Do you know anything about aluminium?'

'Yes, of course. But I don't know exactly what interests you about aluminium and whether my kind of knowledge is likely to be any good to you.'

'Never mind, never mind, we must have a talk. I've made a most interesting discovery, and we must have a talk. You'll have to give me advice.'

I was by no means pleased at the prospect of having one of those cranky inventors next door to me in the village, but it was impossible not to respond.

The man who had led away the horse came back, took off his cap and stood there, waiting, a couple of yards from us. Don Alberto gave him a stare.

'What are you waiting for? A tip, eh? All right, this is a red letter day – here you are – but don't think it will happen every time. And what's that you've got there in the pocket of your blouse?'

The man reddened and mumbled:

'Doña Emilia gave me a piece of bread for the kids.'

'All right, all right, may you enjoy it.'

I stood up. Don Alberto wanted to discuss his discovery, but I had not had my meal and I did not like looking at the silent men lined up along the wall.

We had our discussion later in the day, in the back room of the pharmacy. Doña Emilia listened, her knitting needles clicking. Her chubby hands moved swiftly. Otherwise, she consisted of tight rolls of fat in calm repose. Sometimes she looked at her husband over her spectacles. A sleepy cat in an old rep armchair opened its eyes, two green eyes with a vertical black slit, whenever its master raised his voice. The room was dark, not because of lack of light, for light entered freely through a wide window opening into the sunlit street, but because everything inside the room was dark: dark purple, almost   black   curtains   and   carpets,   the   four   armchairs raisin-coloured, darkened by age, the wallpaper a blackish blue with tarnished gilt scrolls.

Don Alberto explained:

'As I told you this morning, I'm a landowner. May God give us good earth! I've got a big field rather like a graveyard, all studded with stone slabs, and four miserable cottages in the town. The tenants don't pay rent, and the ground lies waste. But I have to pay the taxes every year, like clockwork. Thank goodness, we've got a bit of our own and this pharmacy to live on. As you saw, every day, no matter what weather God sends us, I saddle my horse and we go off for a ride in the fields. You can't imagine how often I've taken a ride across my fields. Then, one day, I saw a fellow squatting on the ground there and digging little holes. I wondered what he was up to, so I accosted him and asked: "What are you doing, my good man?" and he answered in poor Castilian: "Nothing, just pottering. Do you know who owns this land?" "I do," said I. "It's quite good soil, yes, isn't it?" he answered. "Not bad if you want to sow paving stones." He stared at me and changed the subject and started telling me that he was a German and liked Spain very much, and so on. He told me he thought of building a little house in the country. He found the landscape round here very pleasant, he said. Now, you see, you've got to have a very thick skin to say that without blushing. Because that landscape is as bare as my palm. I said yes to everything and thought: "Now what has this rogue got up his sleeve?" When he was out of sight, I went back to my piece of land, collected a few lumps of the soil and shut myself up here in the back room. My dear friend' – Don Alberto said this very solemnly – 'my soil is bauxite. Pure bauxite.'

He gave me no time to show my amazement, but changed from enthusiasm to rage with lightning speed.

'And that German is a scoundrel. That's why I called you in.'

Doña Emilia dropped her knitting in her lap, raised her head, wagged it and said: 'What's your reason, Albertito?'

'Be quiet, woman, let us talk.'

The knitting needles resumed their monotonous seesaw, and the cat again shut its green eyes. Don Alberto went on:

'A few weeks ago he turned up here. He had decided to build himself a house in this marvellous spot, he said. He had liked my land so much. And as it wasn't arable land, he assumed that I would be willing to sell it cheaply, because he wasn't exactly rich. I couldn't refrain from saying: "So it's a little house in the country you're wanting to build – a little house with big chimneys, eh?" He showed himself most astonished. "Yes, yes, don't play the innocent now. You think I don't know what you're after. Luckily, I haven't quite forgotten my chemistry." My good German chuckled broadly and said: "Good, now we will understand one another better, yes? You must realize that I have to look after my business and if you hadn't got wise to what's in your soil it would have been more economical from my point of view. But never mind. How much do you want for your land?" I said: "Fifty thousand duros – two hundred and fifty thousand pesetas." My German laughed loudly and said: "Now, don't let us waste our time. The site has been registered in accordance with the Law of Mining Sites. So we have the right to expropriate your ground and the adjacent land. I offer you five thousand pesetas in cash and twenty thousand in free shares of the company we will set up. Think it over and you'll see that it's best for you." I told him to go to the devil. But now he's sent me a summons to appear before the judge to settle the question of the expropriation of my land in amity. What would you advise me to do? Those scoundrels think they'll get my land for a chunk of bread.'

What advice could I give to this village apothecary? If Germans were mixed up in the affair, the prospectors were doubtless financed by some important firm in Germany; and no one knew the power and the means at the disposal of those people better than I. Don Alberto had the choice between getting a handful of pesetas and entering on a lawsuit, with the result that the pesetas he might be paid in the end would not cover the costs of the brief. Obviously, they had him in a trap and there was no escape for him.

I explained the legal situation and advised him to try to hold out for the biggest possible sum, but not to involve himself in litigation.

He waxed indignant.

'So those rogues come from abroad and rob us of the fruits of our labour? That's the whole history of Spain. Those people come here where no one wants them and take the best for themselves. There you have Rio Tinto and the Canadiense and the Telephones and the Petrol Monopoly and I don't know what more. And in the meantime, we can starve! What we need is a strong Government. What we need is that the Chief should take the whole thing into his own hands.'

'The Chief? What Chief?'

I knew very well whom he meant. Gil Robles was being built up as the great Leader, the *Jefe*, and his name coupled with the title 'Chief' was being dinned into our ears. But I did not feel like accepting this chieftainship unchallenged.

Don Alberto said: 'There's only one Chief. The man who'll save Spain: José Maria Gil Robles. The man whom the whole nation backs.'

It had always been one of my incurable weaknesses, one which had earned me much enmity, that I tended to revert in the middle of a serious, polite conversation to the mode of expression of a Madrid street urchin and of a soldier in the African Army – to blurt out what I thought with the greatest directness and in the worst language.

I answered Don Alberto with a grin:

'Well, I don't think that our country will be put in order by that church rat.'

Don Alberto turned a flaming red, more intensely red because of the white frame of his hair; he rose and flashed a wrathful glance at me. The knitting needles stopped short and the cat got to its feet, arched its back and clawed the rustling chair cover. Solemnly and melodramatically, Don Alberto pronounced judgement:

'You will realize, Don Arturo, that you and I cannot continue to exchange words.'

I had to leave, somewhat ashamed and annoyed with myself for having lost my sense of fitness, and yet rather amused by the attitude the good man had struck. But there came a sequel to that conversation, one week later.

I was standing before the church tower, figuring out its structure. Its foundations were Roman, and the brick walls built on the square hewn stones very many years later were doubtless Moorish work. It would have been pleasing to know the hardships the ancient tower had gone through at the time it was a fortress, or a watchtower, or whatever it might have been.

A fat voice spoke to me from under the porch:

'Sightseeing, eh? Haven't you the courage to come into the church? We don't devour anybody here.'

Don Lucas, the priest, was standing in the porch of the church and watching me with a slightly mocking glance.

'I was looking at the architectural muddle of this tower. But I would indeed like to have a look at the church, if its Cerberus has nothing against it.'

'Cerberus has nothing against it. This is God's House, open to everyone. Of course, if it's antiquities you're after, there'll be little for you to see. This is just a big barn of a building.'

The church deserved the term. Smooth walls, whitewash on mortar and stone, with half a dozen altars ranged along them, each with its saint in life size, made of papier-mâché and painted in gaudy colours. A wealth of embroidered altar cloths, stiff with starch, bronze candelabra and paper flowers smothered in dust. A confessional on each side of the High Altar. Behind the entrance a Christ on the Cross, the Holy Water stoup on one side and the font on the other. Two rows of benches down the middle, and a score of chairs with straw seats scattered here and there. The only pleasant thing was the coolness of the nave.

'It's true that there isn't much to see.'

'I'll show you our treasure.'

He took me to the sacristy: two huge commodes with plated locks, presumably the most valuable stuff in the whole church, a vaulted niche with an old wooden carving of the Child Jesus, a pulpit, a bench along the wall, a monkish armchair, some church utensils laid out on the commodes. On the front wall the oil painting of a Saint Sebastian with a somewhat feminine body, a painting of the chromolithographic school of the late nineteenth century.

The priest – well filled and fleshy, rather like a pig with his very small eyes and thick, bristling hair and stubble on his chin, bristles on the broad, heavy hands, thick, red lips, altogether a peasant polished by the Seminary – sat down in the armchair and invited me to take a seat on the bench beside the pulpit. He took out a leather cigarette case and we both rolled ourselves a cigarette. He puffed some smoke and then looked straight at me.

'I've noticed, of course, that you don't go to church on Sundays. I know you're one of those Socialists and have dealings with the low people of our village. I must tell you, when you set up house here and I saw your wife and children, I thought: "They seem the right kind of people. Pray God it be so." But – it seems I was mistaken.'

He did not say this in an insulting manner. When he made his little pause after the 'but', he did it with a mild, almost evangelical smile, as though he apologized for his daring. Then he stopped, looking at me, his two heavy hands on the table.

'Well now. It's quite true that I have socialist ideas, and that I don't go to Mass on Sundays, nor my people either. And it's also true that, if all that means being the wrong kind of people, well, then we are the wrong kind of people.'

'Don't get bitter, Don Arturo. I didn't want to molest you. But you see, I can understand it in a way if one of those yokels doesn't believe in God and the Devil. But to find someone who appears to be an intelligent man thinking as they do . . .'

'The fact that I don't go to church doesn't necessarily mean that I don't believe in God.'

'Now don't tell me that you're one of those Protestant heretics – it would pain me greatly – but in that case I would not be able to tolerate your presence in this Sacred House for a single moment.'

'In this Sacred House which is the House of God and therefore open to everyone, isn't it? Don't be afraid. I'm no heretic. It didn't occur to me to change the label. The trouble with me, I think, is that I've suffered from too much so-called religion all my life. You can rest assured, I've been brought up in the lap of Holy Mother Church.'

'But why don't you go to church, then?'

'If I tell the truth, we shall probably quarrel.'

'Just speak out. I prefer to be plain and to know where I am.'

'Well then, I don't go to church because you clergy are in the Church, and we don't get on together. I was taught a faith which by its doctrine was all love, forgiveness, and charity. Frankly, with very few exceptions, the ministers of the faith I have met possess all sorts of human qualities, but just not those three divine qualities.'

Don Lucas did not enter this field. He chose a tangent:

'What should we do then, in your opinion? For instance, what should I do? Or, to put it clearly, what would you do if you were in my place?'

'You're pushing me into the personal sphere. It is possible that you yourself are one of those exceptional priests I've mentioned, and some of whom I have known and still know. But if you want to hear what I would do in your place if I were a priest, it's quite simple; I would drop the post of Chairman of Catholic Action – that's what you are, I think – so as to obey your Master's Law "Render unto

Caesar that which is Caesar's", and that other Word which says that His reign is not of this world. And then I would use the pulpit for teaching the Word of Christ, not for political propaganda, and I would try to convince all people to live together in peace, so that the poor need no longer perish, lined up along the stone wall of the road waiting for a piece of bread as for a miracle, while the rich let the soil lie waste and each night gamble away enough money to wipe out all the hunger in Novés.'

It was now that the priest took offence. His lips went greyish white and quivered.

'I don't think you can claim the right to teach me my duties. In this place there are a good many of the rabble who need one thing, and one only: the stick. I know you think our Chief is a "church rat". But whether or not it pleases your friends, the revolutionaries, who want to push Spain into the greatest misery – he is the man who will create a great Spain. I'm sorry to say that you and I can't be friends. You've come to disturb the tranquillity of this place. We'll each fight for his own side and God will help those who deserve it.'

I left the church in a pensive mood. This was a declaration of war in due form from the masters of the village, although I had not yet interfered in the village life.

It also gave me a practical demonstration of the unity within the Right wing. Don Alberto was an old Monarchist. Don Lucas was a politicizing priest. Heliodoro was nothing but a ruthless usurer, exploiting the political game. The two doctors had not the slightest interest in the Church or in politics, so long as they had their racket. Valentín gambled his farm away. Others believed they had the bounden duty to stand against the workers, simply because they themselves belonged to the landed class. None of them had strong political or religious ideals, and yet they sallied forth as one man to defend a policy and an ideal. Was it precisely their lack of convictions which permitted them to unite? Was it the existence of ideals which made it difficult for us of the Left to be united?

The logical inference was that those men united to defend their property and their position. But why could not the leaders of the Left unite to defend what position and chance of position they had? Why was it that the men in the street, the common people, the workers, the farm labourers, and the miners, were always ready to get together – and not their leaders?

It was not I who asked this. In those days of the Indian summer of 1935 all Spain asked this question, even our enemies.

4. Ballot

Unrest and uncertainty made me seek for something unchanged and secure in human relationship. But my mother was dead.

My mother had died in harness, seventy-two years old, tirelessly working, however tired she may have felt, helping my sister Concha through her many pregnancies, taking over the care of the children and the housework, helping her by taking a post as concierge in a tenement house so that Concha and Agustín, her husband, should have free lodging, helping them with her own scanty earnings through the long periods when Agustín, a skilled cabinet maker, was out of work during the series of strikes in his trade.

There had been a hard time, before I myself had won through to comparative prosperity, when my mother and Concha had to accept the assistance of charitable institutions. There existed a Home for Washerwomen, founded by Queen Maria Christina; my mother applied, not for herself, but for children's clothes on Concha's behalf, and received help from the nuns who ran the Home. There also existed a State institution called 'Drop of Milk', *Gota de Leche*, where mothers of small children could obtain free milk. Concha applied, and was granted a daily milk ration for which she waited in a queue, while our mother looked after the children. But they had to pay for this charity by figuring in the lists of those who regularly attended Mass, and by presenting the parish priest's certificate to show that they had partaken of Holy Communion. This did not make it easier to accept charity.

My mother never grew bitter. She was proud of her usefulness and bore with the 'things of life', as she would say, with a cheerful resignation and sceptical hopefulness. But it made me bitter, and at times, when I felt least able to help, unjust towards my sister.

It was natural that my mother should go to help her daughter. But it hurt and irked me that my mother was so little part of my own home because she was unable to get on with Aurelia. Clearly as I realized the defeat and emptiness of my marriage, I could not bear strictures from others, not even from my mother, still less from my brother, my sister, my brother's wife, and my sister's husband, who all agreed in disliking the woman who was, after all, my wife.

My mother died in 1931. I had little inner contact with the rest of the family. But now, when the open failure of my marriage was an accepted fact and I felt the chill of a great change in my bones, I resumed a closer friendship with my brother and with my brother-in-law. We three had been much together when we were young boys. We knew a lot about each other, without having to explain anything. The women, my wife, my sister, and my sister-in-law, hated one another and met as little as possible. Agustín, short, square, slow to speak and slow but capable in his movements, with a hidden vein of shrewd satire and plenty of horse sense, placid and reliable, gave me a feeling of rest and safety, and when he spoke he was as infallible as Sancho Panza at his best. But it was difficult for him to go out and leave Concha with the nine children, harassed and overworked as she was.

Thus Rafael, my brother, thin, colourless, and acid, more restless and more sceptical than I, became more than ever my silent companion.

When I dissolved my home in Madrid and set up my family in Novés, he let me have a bedroom in his flat. Escaping from the stale, sour atmosphere and the shallow gossip of his wife, we would go out after supper to walk through the streets, to stay for a while in cafés or bars where we had friends, and then to walk on in heated and pointless discussion or in the familiar morose silence. And on some of the evenings I would go out with Maria.

But my relationship with Maria was also in a stage of restlessness.

When I first came to the office, Maria was the least attractive of the four typists. She was seventeen then, with black eyes and hair, angular and bony. Her olive skin looked dirty, her neck was long and thin, her chest flat. And she was highly strung and active, rapid of comprehension. She was not particularly well educated, but quick on the uptake and a good typist. I took her on as my secretary and we worked well together.

Maria's face was pitted with pockmarks. This made her very unhappy and she was continually conscious of it. It gave her comfort when I began to tell her about the difficulties of my married life and my hopes of finding The Woman, because I tried to explain that I did not think so much of physical beauty as of mutual understanding, of harmony, of fusion. I was unaware at the time that I was seducing the young girl. Maria's plain face denied her that homage which is freely given to attractive women in the Spanish streets. She had no other contact with men than myself. And I imagine that I had the kind of fascination for her which mature, experienced men so often have for very young women. In slow stages our intimacy grew. During those years the scrawny girl became a ripe woman with a harmonious body. We slid into a love affair, inevitably, since I wanted to find someone to whom I could give affection and who would understand my language. The community at work and her ardent will to please me were a substitute for love.

We were discreet in our relationship, but did not try to hide it. It was an open secret. In the true tradition of a Spanish marriage, in which the wife does not overmuch mind an affair of her husband's, as long as it does not absorb him forever and as long as there are no illegitimate children, I had no great trouble with Aurelia. She did not feel her fundamental position threatened by Maria, and we had a few acrimonious discussions, but no more. There was no difficulty on the side of Maria's family either. She lived with her mother, a brother, and a younger sister. The mother knew of our relationship, but ignored it in silence, I think because she regarded Maria as a girl who would never marry and therefore had the right to enjoy her life as best she could.

We had agreed that we would both remain completely free, but six years had created a very close intimacy between us. Even though I had never been in love with her, I had been content in those six years.

Now I was no longer content. Nor was she.

One Saturday morning Maria tackled me:

'Are you going to Novés this afternoon?'

'Yes, of course.'

'I'm fed up with this arrangement. Every Sunday I'm left alone, and I'm getting bored. My sister goes out with her girl friends and I can't go with her.'

'I don't see why not.'

'Most Sundays they go to a dance. If I go I must dance too, because they all know I love dancing, and I can't pretend I don't.'

'Well, what more do you want then? If you feel like it, go to a dance and dance yourself, of course. You know I'm not jealous. But I can't stay here on Sundays. We're together all the week. Anyhow, we thrashed all this out in advance, and you agreed with me about it.'

But Maria insisted that I should stay in Madrid. She did not want me to stay every Sunday, only from time to time, and particularly this time. I sensed she had something definite in her mind and let them know in Novés that I would not come for the week-end.

On Saturday night we went to the theatre together. Maria showed more interest in the details of life in Novés and in discussing my wife's behaviour than in the play. On Sunday we made a day of it and went to El Escorial. When we were lying in the grass, before us the overpowering range of mountains which encircles the monastery, Maria suddenly said:

'Now, what do you intend to do?'

'What about?' The question had caught me by surprise and produced no mental association in me, although we had discussed my matrimonial affairs off and on during the day.

'About Aurelia.'

'You mean, what can I do? I can only get a divorce, and I can't see why I should. It would be bad for the children, they would be much worse off without me, and it wouldn't do me any good either. I'd have to stay alone and live in a boarding house, or stay for good in my brother's flat. I'd live less comfortably and spend much more money. It would have been worth while if I'd found my woman.'

I did not mean to be cruel. I had been talking spontaneously, just as I had talked for years, about my own problems. Maria watched me, and her eyes were full of tears.

'I don't mean anything to you, then . . .'

'But – child – our case is something quite different.'

'Of course it's different. For you a pastime and for me a closed door.' She began to weep bitterly.

'But listen, what is it you want me to do? To get a divorce and live with you? Or to marry you?'

She wiped away her tears and smiled.

'Of course, you silly.'

'But don't you see that it wouldn't do? Now, everybody is tolerant about us and shuts both eyes. The moment we do what you want, they would all be against us, and particularly against you. Can't you see? In the office they wouldn't keep you on, probably neither of us, but certainly not you. . . .'

'Once we lived together it wouldn't matter. I would stay at home.'

'All right, granted. But you don't see things as they are. If we lived together, they would treat you as an ordinary tart. If we married, they would treat you as the woman who has seduced a married man and destroyed a home. Even your family wouldn't like it, I presume.'

'Never mind about all those things. I'm of age and can do as I like. If it's only that – it doesn't matter to me what people call me.'

'But it matters to me.'

'Look how little you love me!'

The conversation rang hollow and false, but we went on and on. From that excursion we came back in an antagonistic mood. I understood Maria's attitude and hopes, but I had no intention of realizing them. A divorce followed by a joint household or marriage would have meant no more than an exchange of one woman for another, with the prospect of more children and the boredom of married life without love. Maria was in her own right while she worked with me as my secretary and listened to my personal worries and problems; she was in her own right as my comforter. She would lose all this in a marriage. I would lose the secretary and the comforting listener.

My attitude and line of action were coldly and pointedly selfish. I knew that. It gave me a chill feeling in the pit of my stomach. I did not like myself, and I did not like her. She had broken our pact. I knew she was right in her way, and I thought I was right in mine. It was not as though she just wanted to get her man; she was convinced that her affection for me would make me happy, that even if I was not in love, I was very fond of her, and that I had no hope of ever meeting the woman of whom I used to talk and think. After all, she knew very well that I was thirty-eight years old, an age at which a man begins to be a fatalist in matters of love, or a sceptic.

But I was not altogether a sceptic. And it was not that I wanted to get rid of her or to exploit her coldly. We had had our good times. But I knew that the imposition of a life together would destroy the friendship and fondness born out of loneliness and grown in loneliness.

Our discussion was closed, but it left a tension in the air. Maria did not repeat her demand, but she intensified her attentions to me, down to the smallest matters. She wanted to show me that she was a perfect woman not only as a lover but also as a housewife. Her tactics were wrong. I was not interested in living with a good housewife. She only made me feel irritated and bored. It amused but also annoyed me to see how Maria tended to behave as though we were a good bourgeois couple. We often went to a night club to dance, but now Maria began to tell me that we ought to behave more discreetly.

'If anyone saw us like this, he would think there was something behind it.'

'My dear girl, he would only think what's true.'

'But I don't want people to think I'm one of those women. I love you just as if you were my married husband.'

By the end of 1935, I was in a state of acute irritability and desperation. I avoided contact with both women, and I could not escape either.

At that time began the campaign for the impending elections. For several weeks the mass excitement and the knowledge of what was at stake swept all private problems from my mind.

When Premier Chapaprieta submitted the Budgets to the Cortes, the Right began a systematic obstruction. Chapaprieta had to resign. President Alcalá Zamora – 'Boots' – was an old fox in politics, a *cacique* from Andalusia who during the Monarchy had kept himself in power by managing elections in his district, and who in the last stage of the Monarchy had turned himself into a Republican.

Chapaprieta's resignation involved the position of the President. Gil Robles held the majority in the Cortes, and the President would have to call upon him to form a Cabinet. Alcalá Zamora was not opposed to a Right-wing and Catholic Government; he was a militant Catholic. But he preferred to become the Dollfuss of Spain himself, rather than to leave this role to Gil Robles. And Gil Robles had attempted to put pressure upon Alcalá Zamora, a fact which the old boss could not easily forget.

The President entrusted Portela Valladares, an independent Republican, with the formation of the Government. The idea was that he would use all the resources of governmental power to prepare elections in favour of the moderate Centre, the group which Alcalá Zamora wanted to represent and which would then sway the votes of the Cortes in one or the other direction.

But the game was obsolete. It had been played with success in support of the Monarchy ever since 1860. But now the country was no longer politically indifferent; it was full of effervescence, deeply divided into two opposite camps. Alcalá Zamora's game had no chance of success; it was never even properly started. As soon as Portela Valladares announced his Cabinet, it was attacked by both Right and Left. He resigned. In December 1935, Alcalá Zamora dissolved the Cortes and announced the 16th of February 1936 as the date for the new elections.

The constitutional rights of citizens were restored. The propaganda battle began. The Right hoisted the anti-Communist flag and frightened prospective voters with accounts of the great damage which a Left victory at the elections would do to the country. They predicted chaos, and gave colour to their prediction by multiplying provocative street incidents. The parties of the Left formed an electoral block. Their list of candidates comprised all shades from Republicans to Anarchists; they focused their propaganda on the atrocities which had been committed against the political prisoners after the Asturias rising and on the demand for a general amnesty. Yet at the same time the dissension between the parties of the Left grew. The Left press devoted at least as much space to mutual attacks as to attacks against the Right. Everyone feared a Fascist *coup d'état* and voiced this fear, and proclaimed his particular brand of Revolution as the only way out. Largo Caballero accepted the title of Spain's Lenin and the support of the Communists. His group told the masses that a victory at the elections would not be the victory of a democratic bourgeois State but of a revolutionary State. The Anarchists also announced the coming victory of a revolutionary State, not after the pattern of Soviet Russia, but based on 'libertarian' ideals. After the 'Two Black Years' of oppression, it was like an intoxication. The lid was off. Every single individual was discussing the political situation and taking active part in the propaganda for his ideas.

I entered the fray in Novés.

Eliseo received me with a shout of welcome when I entered the Poor Men's Casino:

'We've been waiting for you. We've decided to prepare for the elections here, and we want to set up an Electoral Committee.'

'A very good idea.'

'But we want you to organize the whole thing. We don't know anything about anything here, and we do want to do things well. Heliodoro and his gang have got it all organized on their side. They're promising the people everything under the sun, and at the same time they threaten them if they don't behave. And hunger is a bad counsellor. Now, you've got friends in Madrid, so if you help us we'll get meetings and make propaganda. Anyhow, you know what I mean.'

I had my roots in Madrid and not in Novés, but I could not refuse to take an active part in what I believed to be a decisive moment for Spain and for our socialist hopes. These people needed someone who could not be intimidated by the Corporal of the Civil Guard or trapped by dubious manoeuvres, someone who could save them from committing foolish or illegal acts and thus giving the other side a handle. It crossed my mind that it would give me satisfaction and diversion to plunge myself into the elections and that it would keep me aloof from the two women as well.

I saw instantly that a victory of the Right, and even perhaps a victory of the Left, would mean that I would have to leave the village at once. But Novés was drawing to an end for me anyhow.

I accepted the task.

The first thing I did was to seek contact with Carlos and Antonio.

Carlos Rubiera was an old member of the Socialist Youth Organization, whom the Party put forward as a candidate at the elections. We had worked closely together in 1931 to found the Clerical Workers' Union in Madrid; our trade union had flourished and gained victories, Carlos was well away on his political career. He had often invited me to join the Socialist Party as a member or to become an official of the trade union; I had refused, because I felt unfit for a political career, but we had remained good friends. He was a very gifted orator and organizer.

Antonio was a Communist, and an old friend of mine. I knew exactly how honest, how poor, and how narrow-minded he was. He had been a little clerk who earned a pittance and had no prospects in life other than to go on earning a pittance and keep himself and his mother just above starvation level. In 1925, while Antonio was in a sanatorium with tuberculosis, his mother died in misery. When he reappeared in Madrid, cured, he earned just enough to live. It would not have been enough for any vice, but smoking and drinking had been cut out by his tuberculosis, and Antonio had become afraid of women since his illness. He became a Communist, one of the earliest Communists in Spain, and he followed his faith with the zeal of a fanatic. In 1936 he was a minor Party official.

Rubiera and Antonio let me have propaganda material for Novés, gave me hints on organizing an electoral committee, and promised to send Left speakers to the village.

The next Saturday afternoon we set up the Electoral Centre of the Popular Front in Novés.

That evening José called me aside and led me to his house, at the back of the Rich Men's Casino. While his wife served coffee to the customers, José hauled out a bottle of cognac.

'You'll excuse my inviting you here, but we must have a talk. I've got to give you some advice.'

'Oh, well, thanks. But I don't remember having asked you.'

'Don't get annoyed, Don Arturo. It's a friend's advice, because friends must show themselves when they're most needed. I've a great respect for you and your family, and I can't keep my mouth shut any longer. It's not as if I had a personal interest in the question. I'm concerned with my business, and that's all. But I know our village, and you're a stranger here. You won't change it.'

'And what exactly is your advice?'

'That you shouldn't get mixed up in these elections. Let the people settle their own affairs, and don't play Don Quixote. Of course – if you've got it into your head to go on working with Eliseo's gang, you'll have to get into the bus as soon as the elections are over, and never come back. If they let you go, that is . . .'

'You mean to say, if the Right wins the elections.'

'Or the Left. You believe things will change here if the Left wins, but that's your mistake. Things will go on here as always. They won't let their land go, one way or the other. And where there's money there's a way. You never know what's going to happen. After all, we're all mortal.'

'Good. That's the message Heliodoro gave you for me?'

'If you want to take it that way. . . . It's true he told me that you ought really to be warned and that he couldn't very well do it himself. But this is my own idea, because of my esteem for you.'

'Many thanks, José. But I don't think I'll change my mind. It may well be that you're right and that I'll have to pay for this by getting out of the village. But I have to stick to my people.'

'Well, think it over. And just in case – but this is really my own idea – don't walk about too much at night when you're alone. Our people here are very rough, and there's been trouble at every election.'

When I reported this conversation in Eliseo's Casino, it caused a great stir; whenever I went out at night afterwards, two hefty young men with cudgels accompanied me everywhere.

I went to Santa Cruz de Retamar to see the Corporal of the Civil Guard about the legal formalities. He received me with a surly face.

'And who ordered you to get mixed up in all this?'

'I've a right to do so, haven't I? I'm a householder in Novés and have the right to take part in the village life.'

'All right. Here are your papers. I should stay quietly in my house, if I were you, because if I'm not very much mistaken, there'll be trouble at the elections. For me the situation is quite simple. It's my duty to maintain order, whomever it may affect. So you have been warned. Look out.'

Carlos Rubiera and Antonio kept their promise. Four speakers of the Popular Front were coming to Novés on Sunday: one of the Republican Left, one Socialist, one Communist, and one Anarchist. With the exception of the Republican, who was a middle-aged man, they were all young lads, completely unknown in politics. The news produced an upheaval at Eliseo's.

'We need the ballroom!'

The ballroom belonged to the inn where the bus stopped and where the post office was installed. I went to see the owner.

'We should like to rent your ballroom for a meeting next Sunday.'

'You'll have to ask Heliodoro, he's booked it for the whole time until Election Day for meetings of the Right. I can do nothing for you.'

Heliodoro received me in his office with the pomp of a great man of affairs, entrenched behind a huge walnut table and surrounded by piles of paper. He answered with a frosty little smile:

'I'm extremely sorry, but I can't help you. I need the room.'

Discouraged, I went back to Eliseo's. We could not arrange an open-air meeting in the middle of January. But Eliseo hit upon the solution.

'They're dirty rogues, those people. Heliodoro can't rent the ballroom, because, you see, it is rented by the municipality. The Municipal Council pays Rufino' – the inn-keeper and postmaster – 'so-and-so much per year, and the only right he's got is to set up a buffet when there's a dance. He just can't sub-let it.'

I returned to Heliodoro. He bridled.

'I've rented the ballroom, and I've got the receipt here. If you want to enter a legal action against Rufino and the Municipal Council, you're welcome, but please leave me out of it. . . .'

I went to the Corporal and explained the case. He shrugged his shoulders. There wasn't anything he could do. I lost patience.

'Now listen. The other day you told me you were here to maintain order, whomever it might affect. The ballroom is here for the free use of the whole population. I won't cancel the meeting, and the meeting will be held in the ballroom. You can settle it however you like, that's to say, if you don't want the thing to go beyond mere words. And I can tell you something: this won't be a matter of a few village lads. Tomorrow I shall inform the parties which organize the meeting, and report the things that are going on here, and the responsibility will fall on you, because it's your obligation to solve such questions without further trouble.'

The Corporal of the Civil Guard beat a retreat. There was unrest in the villages and towns of the province, which had suffered particularly severely from the vindictiveness of the landowners during the 'Two Black Years'. The Corporal foresaw that it would come to an open conflict for which he would be made responsible in the end. That same night he spoke to Heliodoro. And Heliodoro conceded me the ballroom.

'This is a personal favour out of consideration for you and the Corporal. I don't want trouble which would lead to a serious incident, any more than you. What we want is public order.'

During those weeks, I spent almost every evening in Novés and went back to Madrid early each morning. On one of those evenings, Aurelia handed me a letter:

'Here, José brought it for you. And he's been telling me plenty of things. I can't think why you've got to go and interfere in those elections.'

The letter was a communication from the Novés Farmers' Circle – the official name of the Rich Men's Casino – informing me that the General Assembly had decided unanimously to cancel my membership. We celebrated it at Eliseo's that night. The Novés Workers' Circle made me its honorary member. After that, we went out to stick the posters of the meeting on walls and hoardings.

It turned out a radiantly sunny day. The plain in which Novés is ensconced is one of the coldest spots of Spain in winter. The winds from the Sierra de Guadarrama which sweep it freeze the soil deep down. But the village in its gully is sheltered from the winds, and on sunny days people prefer to stay out in the open, so as to get away from their dismal houses. The place comes alive. The women sit on low stools outside their house doors and chat, and their children run round playing; the men stand in groups in the market square and the young people go for walks in the orchards, holding hands.

That Sunday the village looked alien. From the early morning onwards, people from the near-by villages arrived for the meeting of 'those Madrid people'. The main street was filled with peasants and land workers accompanied by their wives and children, all shouting greetings at each other, all noisy and excited. The ballroom was hung with Popular Front posters and its door stood wide open. People went in and out in a continuous stream to show each other the new sight. At midday a number of women turned up with chairs which they planted along the walls, determined not to lose the spectacle or their seats, even if it meant waiting for hours.

The ballroom was an old stable converted into a place for entertainment by the simple expedient of putting up a wooden platform and framing it with draperies of red calico. A little side door led to this dais from the inn stableyard. A sheet hung between the two red draperies served as a screen for films or as a curtain for theatrical performances. When there was a dance, the band occupied the dais. At the other end of the room a sort of balcony had been fixed to the wall; it would be reached by a ladder with a cord for a railing, and was reserved for distinguished guests at theatrical functions, and for the film projector at other times. The floor was beaten earth, and some tiles were missing in the roof so that the sunbeams came through, or the rain, or the snow.

On the dais we had set up the table for the chairman, with a dozen chairs in a semicircle behind it, and a smaller table for the speakers, both covered with the tricolour of the Spanish Republic in calico. The meeting was to start at three in the afternoon and we had arranged that the speakers should first have a meal at my house. Some of the village lads went to the edge of the gully and lined up at the side of the road to warn us of the coming of the car. At noon the pair of Civil Guards arrived and took up their posts outside the ballroom door. They loaded their carbines with ostentatious care.

'Are you going to kill us, then?' an elderly woman asked with a smile.

The Corporal gave no answer, but looked at the woman out of lack-lustre eyes. A few of the men went at once to Eliseo's and told me of the incident.

'You can't imagine what his eyes were like when he looked at the poor woman. Do you think there will be trouble?'

Eliseo brought a pistol out of his house and stuck it under his belt, in the pouch of his blouse.

The car arrived at half past twelve and was received by the cheers of hundreds of people. Heliodoro must have hated it. I had to shut the doors of my house to prevent an invasion.

The only one of the speakers who knew the village was the Socialist, a member of the Land Workers' Union of Toledo. The three others were from Madrid. The Republican was a short little man who looked like a natty clerk. He spoke slowly and with great emphasis, and was unable to say a single sentence without mentioning Azaña. The Anarchist was a young waiter, bright and agile, who seemed to be rehearsing for the meeting by indulging in a stream of words whenever he said anything. He found his match in the Communist, a young metal worker who let loose a torrent of phrases sprinkled with quotations from Marx and Lenin. The four of them were a little nervous.

'Now tell me what the people in this place are like,' said the Communist.

'Just as in all the other villages. They're above all interested in the land and the school.'

'That's one of the things the Party will do first – we're going to organize the Komsomols – I mean, the Kolkhoses – in Spain as they've done in Russia, with model farms and cattle and splendid dairies. In the Ukraine —'

I cut him short: 'Listen, it seems to me that you won't establish any dairies here, not even with goats. There are no more than two cows in the whole village, and I don't think they've ever seen a pasture in their lives!'

'Well, what have they got here?'

'Excellent orchards, corn land, and a *cacique* who owns half the village.'

'All right, we'll liquidate him.' He said it as simply as if he had destined a chicken for the oven.

'Democracy's what we need, democracy and tolerance – a lot of tolerance,' said the Republican. 'Don Manuel' – Azaña – 'is right. Don Manuel said to me one day: "Those Spanish villages, those rotten boroughs, need schools, friend Martínez, schools and bread, and the elimination of their parasites." '

'Don't kid yourselves, we Spaniards are all Anarchists at heart. We can't make do here with Socialism or Communism, and you' – the Anarchist addressed the Republican – 'have nothing to lose here. What we need is a new society with the cornerstones —'

'Hear, hear! But first, I don't want to have to listen to your speeches twice over, secondly, let's leave our dirty linen at home, and thirdly, we're going to eat now,' I said. I was not happy about the meeting, particularly when the conversation at table followed the same channels.

When we entered the platform from the side door, we saw before us a moving carpet of heads and a splash of motley gay colour in the background. They had put the women in the 'boxes' as a precaution, and their garish kerchiefs and blouses shone out. The men were standing; outside the entrance there were over two hundred people who had not found room in the ballroom. The doors stood wide open so that they should hear the speeches, and the men jostled each other and stretched their necks to see.

Teodomiro, the Mayor, a creature of Heliodoro's, was sitting on one of the chairs behind the presidential table.

'Well, well, what are you doing here?' I asked him.

'I represent the authorities.'

There was nothing to be said against this. I opened the meeting. The Communist, as the youngest of the four speakers, took the first turn. He started by explaining the assets of a Popular Front. He spoke rather well, with a certain nervousness and big gestures, but with fluency and conviction. The public, well disposed in advance, lapped up his words and interrupted him from time to time with applause. Then he touched on the subject of the Asturian rising.

'. . . one of the great aims of this alliance of the Left is to free our prisoners. We all have a prisoner to set free, a murder to avenge. In the name of those who were assassinated at Oviedo . . .'

Applause interrputed him. The Mayor rose, waving his hands, then banged his fist on the table.

'Silence, silence!' A surprised silence fell. What was that fellow going to say? Teodomiro turned to the Communist: 'If you mention Asturias once more, I'll suspend the meeting. I represent the authorities here.'

I told the speaker in a whisper to limit himself to propaganda for the elections and to leave out Asturias, since this was better than to lose the meeting. But Teodomiro clearly had his instructions; he interrupted the speaker at every sentence after that. In the end the young man was thrown out of his stride. The Republican leaned over to me.

'Let me deal with this. I'm an old fox.'

I told the boy to come to an end in the best possible manner, and then Azaña's little man faced the public.

'I wanted to speak to you and explain my personal opinions, which in very many points coincide with those of my friend, the previous speaker. But we must respect the authorities as represented by our friend the Mayor, and as I don't wish him to interpret my words in an adverse way, I will speak to you in the words of Don Manuel Azaña, words which he pronounced at the public meeting of Comillas and to repeat which I do not believe his Worship the Mayor will refuse me the right.'

'Quite so, quite so,' said Teodomiro.

'Well then, at Comillas Don Manuel said . . .' and the little man, who must have had a fabulous memory, recited entire passages of the famous speech which had moved the whole of Spain, passages which denounced the policy of the Church, the oppression of Asturias, the tortures inflicted on political prisoners, the scandals of racketeering and corruption, the deeds of violence committed by Falange. The public roared applause and hardly let him finish. Teodomiro was purple in the face and took council with the Corporal. The Corporal shook his head. There was nothing to be done.

The Socialist followed, and he had learned his lesson. Slyly he asked Teodomiro:

'I suppose you've nothing against my quoting words of Largo Caballero?'

The struggle was won. The Socialist and the Anarchist spoke, and the public was delirious, just as much because 'their' speakers had scored a victory over the local powers and had carried through the meeting, as because of what they said. Everyone felt that this was less a defeat of the Mayor's little game than of his boss, Heliodoro, and the Corporal of the Civil Guard.

When at the end of the meeting, some people started singing the Internationale, I rose.

'I'll only say a few words to conclude this meeting. You saw what happened, and I suppose you also saw what might have happened. If you want all this to finish well, go out slowly, don't sing, don't shout in the street, don't stand about in groups – go home, or wherever you want to go, but don't give any occasion for trouble.'

'Do you mean to insinuate that I've come here to put my foot in it and provoke something?' grunted Teodomiro.

'Oh, no, you've come here to represent the authorities and to avoid disturbances. There haven't been any disturbances during the meeting, thanks to you, and now I don't want any to arise in the street. Let him who hath ears . . .'

The meeting of Novés became famous in the region, and meetings were held in all the little villages around. The Popular Front found ample ground between Santa Cruz de Retamar and Torrijos.

But what happened in Novés on a small scale, happened throughout Spain, not always with the same turn of events. During the period known as the 'Two Black Years', the parties of the Right had entrenched themselves in the countryside and now they spared neither coercion nor promises nor gifts. Their efforts were particularly hectic in the cities. A giant poster showing Gil Robles addressing the multitude covered the whole front of a big house in the Puerta del Sol. So as to sow confusion among the members of the Anarchist trade unions, they published posters against the Communists, signed with the initials CNDT, very similar to the Anarchist 'CNT'. Cardinal Gomá, Primate of Spain, issued a declaration in which he claimed that the Pope himself had asked him to appeal to the Spanish Catholics so that they should give their votes to the parties defending the Faith. Inmates of charitable institutions, cloistered nuns and the servants of big houses were taken to the ballot box in groups. In the working-class districts the offers of payment for each vote in favour of the Right rose to fifty pesetas.

The elections of February the 16th were a victory of the Popular Front. The Chamber met with 265 Deputies of the Left, 64 of the Centre, and 144 of the Right.

The highest number of votes had fallen to Julián Besteiro, who was not a professional politican and whose theories were not shared by a great many workers, but who seemed to embody the longing of the Spanish people for culture, decency, and progressive social development.

When the high tide of enthusiasm had passed, the mass of voters went home. The politicians resumed their fight for power. The Popular Front began to disintegrate after the first session of the Cortes. It appeared as though the voice of the people had not been heard.

Novés underwent a change. The public offices were given to the people who had the best contact with the Popular Front Deputy for Torrijos. But the men who met at Eliseo's had played out their role as soon as they had voted, and Heliodoro brought the full weight of his economic power to bear upon the new administrators. There was no more work than before for the men who waited sitting on the stone wall along the road. 'It will come very soon now, you'll see,' said Old Juán. 'You won't change things without trouble.'

A fortnight after the elections I moved my family back to Madrid.

5. Lining Up

I had found a large and inexpensive flat in the Calle del Ave María, a street hardly more than three hundred yards from the Puerta del Sol, yet belonging to the oldest working-class quarter of the city. I liked it because it was near the centre and my place of work. But it had another attraction for me. It was one of the streets which led to El Avapiés, the quarter which had dominated my boyhood. My mother had lived three streets further down. My old school, the Escuela Pía, was so near that I could hear its clock striking the hours at night. Each street and each corner held a memory for me, and there were still old friends of mine living in the shabby tenement houses.

Aurelia, my wife, went there reluctantly. She admitted that the flat had the advantage of size, important enough for the four children, but all the other tenants were merely workers, and she considered ourselves as belonging to a higher social category, too good for such surroundings.

I suppose what I wanted was to get back to my own roots.

It was on the very morning when the lorry with our furniture arrived that Angel and I met.

The men who had come with the lorry began to unload and carry things upstairs. One of them was different from the four others who were big, heavy, sluggish porters. He was in the middle forties, short and very wide across the shoulders, his round face mobile like a monkey's. He worked harder than anyone else, smiling all the time and showing two rows of tobacco-blackened teeth. He drove the others on, pushed each piece of furniture into its exact place, made faces at the children or told a funny story to enliven his work, and bounded indefatigably to and fro.

When everything had been moved in I gave a twenty-five-peseta note to the driver, to be distributed among the five. When the little man bounced up to him, and asked for his duro, the driver stared.

'Why the devil should I give you a duro?'

'What d'you think? I've worked for it like the others.'

'And who asked you to work? If the gentleman called you in he'll pay you himself.'

'I thought he was one of your men,' I said.

'Oh no, sir, we thought he belonged to you.'

'Now look – I'll explain. But can I have a fag?' I gave him a cigarette. He lighted it, very much at his ease, and said: 'I'm Angel, you see. They call me Angelito hereabouts. I've got nothing to smoke and I'm out of work – and it's not because I don't want to work but because there just isn't any. I saw the car with the furniture and said to myself: "Let's lend a hand. We'll get something out of it, even if it's no more than a glass of wine." Now, if you people don't want to shell out a bean, that's just bad luck for me. I won't ask anything of the gentleman, because it's you whom I've saved a lot of work, and so it's you who ought to pay me. But if you won't, never mind. *Salud*!'

He spat on the pavement and stalked away composedly.

I called him back.

'Don't go off like that. It's true that you might have asked beforehand. But we'll find something for you.'

The lorry drove off and I felt like a drink, so I invited Angel to the bar in the ground floor of the house. In the doorway he asked me:

'Do you like wine?'

'Indeed I do.'

'Then let's go to the tavern at Number Eleven, they've got a white wine that's good. I mean, if it's all the same to you. Because in this bar they ask forty centimos for a glass of beer, and for the same money I can drink four glasses of wine, the same size, over there. And I'll tell you something, I've been hungry for a glass of wine for months!'

We went to the tavern, I gave Angel his duro, and he told me his story.

He lived in the next street, the Calle de Jesús y María, as a concierge in a poor tenement house; he was married, but luckily he had no children; he had started as an errand boy in a chemist's shop, become a helper in the laboratory, and ended as an employee in one of the big pharmaceutical stores.

'And then, two years ago, I had words with one of the bosses, because I told him I had no intention of going to Mass. So they chucked me out. And I've been out of work ever since.'

'Because you didn't go to Mass?'

'That's what I'm telling you. After Asturias they went and set up the Sacred Heart, with its little altar and all, in the middle of our store. And they told us we had to be there with a burning candle at the Feast of Consecration. They turned eight of us out into the street. Then, when I was applying for another job, those dirty swine wrote a letter saying quite simply that they had had to dismiss me because of Asturias. What had happened was that at the time when the fight was on in Asturias, our trade union told us not to go to work, and so I stayed at home two days. I'm only sorry because of my wife, she's had a thin time of it. Now I want to send her to her own people, they're quite well off and have got a farm in the province of Burgos. And I'll take the firm's Asturian certificate, and they'll have to take me on again and pay my arrears.'

It was one of the Popular Front projects to enforce the re-engagement of staff dismissed during the reprisals for October 1934.

On the following day Angel turned up at my new flat. 'I've come because, what with the moving-in, you'll be needing a lot of things here in your flat. I can install the light for you, paint the rooms, go shopping, or take the children for a walk. I've taken a fancy to your family.'

For a few weeks Angel spent his time tearing layers of old paper from the walls, filling holes with plaster and painting the rooms. He continued to come when everything was in order; he helped in the house, and took the children for walks in the Retiro in the evenings. I liked him and he gave me the affection of a privileged family valet. He was the classical Madrileño, bred in the streets, cocky, carefree, and alert as a bird, always merry and very shrewd. In a few weeks' time he belonged to the circle that met every night in Emiliano's bar downstairs.

And so did I. For I could not take friends into the chilly emptiness of my so-called home life, and I did not want to stay there in irritation and isolation, or in empty disputes. Nor did I want to go out with Maria every night. But I needed to be with people who would make no demands on me, when I had finished with the complicated, often repellent and often disturbing operations of my day's work.

Every night after supper Rafael came to fetch me and we went down to Emiliano's bar to drink our coffee. There we met Funi-Funi. He had been at school with Rafael, and I had known him since I was a boy. He had been given his nickname at school because he first sniffed – 'Fnn-fnn' – and then sneezed every time he lifted his head and sniffed after every second word he talked. His nose was a tiny, soft blob with two holes stuck on to his round face, and he could not breathe through it properly. He was very shortsighted and wore big round glasses; his optician had to figure out a new kind of bridge for them, because otherwise they would never have stayed on. The moustache above his broad lips rose in rough bristles like a porcupine's quills, and the whole looked rather like the moon-shaped face, fringed with spikes, of some grotesque fish.

Funi-Funi lived close by and used to come to the bar to have a political discussion with Manolo, our concierge's young son. Funi was an Anarchist intellectual, imbued with political theory and abstract philosophy; Manolo was a skilled mechanic with communist sympathies, who swallowed every book on Marxism that fell into his hands. Rafael and I used to sit down with them, and Angel would join us.

For several nights Angel sat listening to the conversation with strained attention, losing the thread between names and quotations which meant nothing to him. From time to time he interrupted Funi.

'Who's the bird you're talking about now?'

Funi-Funi would explain about Kant, or Engels, or Marx, or Bakunin, and Angel would make odd faces while he listened. Then one night he hit the table with his flat hand and said:

'Now it's my turn. All those things you've been talking about day after day, and all those things you've just told us are just stories. I'm a Socialist. All right. And I've never read that Marx or that Bakunin, and they don't interest me a bit. I'm a Socialist for the same reason that you're an Anarchist and Manolo a Communist. Because we're fed up with things. There you go and get born into this world, and when you're beginning to understand what's what, you find that Father's out of work, Mother with child, and the cooking pot empty. Then they send you to school so that the Friars should give you food by way of charity, and as soon as you can, even before you've learned to read, off with you to work like a man. You get four coppers from the master and nothing from your mates, but all the time it's: "Boy, bring me a glass of water." "Boy, take out those pails." "You'll get a kick in the pants." And you get it too. Until you're a grown man, and then you earn a duro. A measly five pesetas. So what happens? You get infatuated, you marry, you have children, and next thing, you're out of work. Then your wife goes a-charring, the kids go to the Friars' school to get free soup, and you can run round in circles in the streets and curse. Well, and that's why I'm a Socialist, because of all the ugly things yours obediently, Angel García, has had to swallow in the forty-odd years of his life. And now I tell you – shut up about Bakunin and Marx. UHP! Do you know what that stands for? Union of Brother Workers. Just like the people of Fuenteovejuna, all as one. That's what counts. Because we don't get anywhere with all that balderdash from one side and the other, we just kick each other instead of getting together. And that's why the others will thrash us!'

Angel's rhetorical fire and gesticulations had attracted the other customers and they pressed round our table. When he ended they cheered him, and from that evening on he was the most popular speaker in all the taverns of the quarter. There he would stand and hold forth:

'What about the priests? Well, the priests can go and say their Mass and let anyone who wants it have his confession or extreme unction. I won't say anything against that, because everyone is free to believe what he believes. But they shouldn't get a centimo from the State, and they should have to pay taxes on their business. So-and-so many Masses per year, so-and-so much income tax . . .

'And the rich? I wouldn't do away with the rich. If someone makes a lot of money because he's smart, well let him do what he damn well likes with it. But when he dies, then his money and his property go to the State. None of your inheritances, and none of your wealthy young gentlemen doing nothing. And there'll be limits to being rich. Beyond that limit not a centimo. Because in this business of the rich, it's the money we've got to settle, not the men. If someone has got money let him spend it, or put it in a drawer, but there won't be any more people living on dividends and interests. The State will have to look after their business and there'll be an end to all that coupon cutting. You understand me, something like what they've got in Russia. Over there, they give one of the Stakhanovites a hundred thousand roubles as a bonus, but he's got to go on stakhanovizing, because they've no Treasury bonds or shares which bear interest there. Here, if they give someone a hundred thousand duros, he puts them in the bank, and starts on the high life, and chucks his hammer on the scrap heap. And that's all wrong.'

Angel treated me as though he were my henchman and wet-nurse at the same time. But he never knew how much moral support he gave me. The foolish and funny things he said when he was trying to brush away intellectual and political complications outside his ken were exhilarating, because behind them stood his sturdy loyalty and common sense, his belief that sooner or later all the working people would get together and settle their world sensibly and firmly. And he seemed irrepressible and indestructible.

Most days, before I went home for supper, and coffee and discussion downstairs in the bar, I left my office together with Navarro, our draftsman, and had a glass of wine with him at the tavern of the 'Portuguese'. There I looked at the melancholic, drowsy drunkard in the corner who was my old friend Plá, an aging and hopeless bank clerk, and listened to Navarro's problems, thinking of my own.

Navarro had dreamed of becoming an artist when he was young, and had become a draftsman in the Topographical Institute. His civil servant's pay was pitiful, and in the afternoons he made commercial publicity drawings, or mechanical sketches to accompany our patents. He knew nothing about topography, publicity, or mechanics, but he had learned how to make impeccably correct drawings, just as a shoemaker's apprentice learns how to put nails into shoe soles. His drawings were perfect in line, but they had to be checked very carefully because it meant nothing to him to have left out a wheel or a screw.

He was married and had two sons, sixteen and twenty years old. His work permitted him to keep his household on a comfortable level and to let his sons study for a professional career. But he himself had become a money-making automaton. His wife ruled the house, and she was entirely under the influence of her Father Confessor, a Jesuit, on the one side, and of her brother, a Captain in the Civil Guard, on the other. Between them, the three of them managed the house and the sons who had realized as young boys that their father was a nobody, while The Family, their family, was the mother's, with an illustrious surname and a Captain Uncle who had fierce moustaches and a post in the Ministry of the Interior. Both went to the Jesuit College in the Paseo de Areneros, and they represented Navarro's gravest problem.

'I can't think what to do with the boys, Barea. Their uncle has put them into that Falange thing, and now they go round with life preservers in their pockets, and provoke rows with students at the university. They egg them on at their school and send them to the university to make trouble. What should I do?'

I could speak frankly and even brutally to Navarro:

'To tell you the truth, Juanito, you're simply not capable of doing the only thing which would solve the problem. And the worst of it is that it's you who will pay the piper.'

'But what can I do, in God's name? Tell me what I can do.'

'Buy a strong stick, get hold of the Captain, the Father Confessor – and your wife – and tickle their ribs a bit. And then take the boys and deal with them.'

'You're a barbarian, and you wouldn't dream of doing it yourself.'

'All right, I'm a barbarian, and that's exactly why I would not have got myself into that particular mess of yours. But you're good, meek, and helpless.'

'But I don't want my boys to get mixed up in politics! Ever since their uncle came back from Villa Cisneros where they sent him for taking part in the August Revolt, he's been filling their whole mind with stories about heroism and heroics. And they'll be badly caught one day. But what can I do, Arturo, what can I do?'

His only consolation was to drink a glass of wine at the Portuguese's and to see all the Walt Disney films shown in Madrid.

As one of his few intimate friends, I saw him quite often in his home and came to know the atmosphere of absolute, freezing intolerance in which this modest and tolerant man had to live. His wife eternally quoted her brother or her Father Confessor: 'Pepe told me . . . Father Luis said we ought . . .' Navarro was haunted by a hopeless longing for a home where he could sit in his armchair in the midst of his family, with gaiety and warmth around him.

He arrived at the office one morning with a deeply worried face and wanted to speak to me.

A few days before, a tumultuous row had broken out between Right- and Left-wing students at the Central University. It had started with cuffs and blows as usual and had ended in shots: there had been one dead. Somebody had fired a pistol and a Republican student had been killed. During one of the following nights, Navarro had been working very late at home and had found himself without matches; he had looked for a box in the pockets of his elder son's jacket and found a short club made of a lump of lead tied with cord to a stick. The lead was stained with dried blood. In the morning, just after the son had left home, saying he was going to the University, the police had come to fetch him. He was hiding in his uncle's house.

Navarro was desperate: 'Of course, the police will find him sooner or later. Or, what's worse, the others will have singled him out and they'll get him as soon as they can. Because each group keeps a list of the ones who stand out on the other side.'

'It's just a youthful affair,' I said unconvincingly.

'Youthful – stuff and nonsense. That's the work of grown-up men. People like his uncle and the black frocks get the boys involved and use them as cannon fodder so that they kill each other. I wonder if they won't employ my Luis, though. If the Right wins, it's on the cards that they will call in my Luis, and give him a living. And they'll promote the Captain to Major and Father Luis to Canon. It's I who have all the worries. His mother is in high spirits because of the boy's feat, his uncle calls him a hero, and his little brother has brought me a letter from the Reverend Fathers saying that they lament what happened – I don't yet know what has happened – but that we must all be patient because it's in the service of God and Spain. And here am I, his father, made a complete fool of!'

I was thinking that Navarro was unable to influence the course of his own life because he was shackled by his own character and his circumstances, and was just feeling an almost supercilious pity, when I caught myself up: was I not in a very similar state? Was anything achieved if one decided to submit to things as they were? Was it not better – perhaps – to rebel once and for all, and to know that it was one's own fault if everything crashed?

All the signs indicated that everything was going to crumble and crash. The country was drifting towards a catastrophe. Though the Right had lost seats in the Parliament, it had gained in the sense that all its supporters were now prepared to wage war on the Republic in every possible field. And they were in good positions to do so. The Right could count upon a great part of the Army officers, the clergy, home-grown and foreign capital, and the barefaced support of Germany.

The Republican parties, in the meantime, were subject to the pressure of the country which demanded that the reforms promised during the election should be put into force without further delay, and each of the parties exploited this demand to attack the others. Alcalá Zamora had been deposed as President of the Republic, and Azaña had been appointed in his place; this robbed the Republic of one of its ablest constructive brains. The Basque Countries and Catalonia increased the difficulties by their particular claims. The workers distrusted a Government in which there were no socialists of any shade whatsoever and which kept on temporizing. The debates in the Cortes were nothing but a mêlée in which the Right made the best use of the situation. Gil Robles, doubly defeated because his claims to Chieftain had been so flamboyant and his electoral strategy so unsuccessful, disappeared as the leader of the Right, and Calvo Sotelo replaced him.

As soon as the Government began negotiations about the Statute of the Basque Countries, then Galicia, Valencia, Old Castile, and León in their turn presented a claim to autonomy. When it came to the point of reinstating the workers and employees who had been dismissed from their posts afer the October Rising in Asturias, some of the firms affected closed down, and others refused to take the men back. Angel had applied for his re-engagement; he was still out of work. Strikes broke out all over Spain and fantastic rumours were rampant. Everybody expected an insurrection of the Right. The workers were ready for a violent counter-move.

In the higher civil service and in the judiciary, the obstruction was barely disguised. The young man who had shot at the Socialist Jiménez de Asua was acquitted, although he had killed the detective who was guarding the Deputy; the acquittal was granted on the ground that he was mentally deficient and infantile – just a boy to whom his father, a high Army officer, used to give pistol ammunition 'to melt down and make lead soldiers, because it kept the boy amused'.

Day after day I stumbled on object lessons in my contacts with the Ministry of Labour and with our clients.

When I was a child, the Puerta de Atocha was the easterly boundary of Madrid. Beyond it was only the terminus of the Saragossa and Alicante railway lines, and a few houses scattered in the hills. Sometimes, when my mother wanted to escape from the unbearable summer heat in our attic, she prepared a cold supper and we went down the Atocha valley, to lie in the grass and eat our supper in the open. It was a poor people's outing. Dozens of workers' families camped near us in the yellow grass.

At that time, the Basilica of Atocha, never to be finished, and the Ministry of Public Works were under construction. The Madrid milkmen sent their goats to browse on the hillocks between the heaps of building material. My childish imagination was deeply impressed by the immense excavations, by the cemented foundations and the stone blocks straggling in the field, which were to become the new Ministry. Sculptures by Querol, destined for the frontispiece, were lying about half unwrapped: gigantic horses' legs, naked female bodies, all sawed into bits as though by a monstrous crime.

The edifice cannot claim great artistic merit. It was planned around 1900, and is a huge bulk of mixed Doric, Roman, and Egyptian elements, striving to be monumental and succeeding merely in being disproportionate. But to my child's eyes it was a cyclopic work which was to outlast centuries.

In the ground floor of this building I passed a long stretch of my life. And I was to see the giant pillars of the entrance, which had loomed in my infancy, crash down in splinters, hit by a bomb.

When the big building became the Ministry of Labour, the Patent Office was housed on its ground floor. For fifteen years I went nearly every day into those vast stone halls and glass-roofed office rooms.

The fields in which I had eaten my supper and played thirty years before had been converted into pretentious modern steets. But farther on, white stone blocks still littered the waste ground at the foot of the unfinished basilica's ugly white-and-red tower, and women, tired from work as my mother had been, sat in the evenings on the benches of the dusty gardens.

The chief of the Patent Office, with the title of Director-General, owed his post to a political appointment and changed with every Government. I had to deal with the three permanent officials, and to crowd all my business into the brief hours when they were available.

Don Alejandro, Departmental Chief, was tall, scrawny, with glittering blue eyes, thin lips and nose. His impeccable dignity hid a clever trickery, ever ready to pull a fast one if it involved no risk.

Don Fernando, Head of the Patents Department, was a merry, fat man with a pendulous belly, always harassed, always in a hurry, and always too late; he had a moon face and a savage appetite embittered by flatulence and hyper-acidity which he tried to drown in bicarbonate. His favour was not for sale, but a case of champagne bottles softened him, a letter from a Deputy calling him 'My dear friend' melted him. He had been young in a period when politicians appointed and dismissed the civil servants, when each change of Government meant a hundred posts suddenly vacant and quickly refilled. He had been bred in awe of politicians, and still felt it.

Don Pedro, Head of the Trade Marks Department, was a tiny, fragile man, with a little shaven head crowned by a toupee, rather like the cowlick of a naughty boy, and a gentle, womanish voice. He came of a wealthy family and was deeply religious, without vices great or small, methodical, meticulous, fastidious, the only man who came to the office in time and who never left before the end of office hours. He was incorruptible, and impervious to political pressure. Only a priest could ever make him change his mind, for a priest was infallible to him.

I had to steer the interests of about a thousand clients past these three men. I had to remember that Don Alejandro admired the Germans and sent his sons to the German College, that Don Fernando kowtowed to Deputies, and Don Pedro obeyed the Church. I could obtain astounding results by fencing cleverly with a few banknotes, an amiable letter from a German personage, an amiable letter from a politician, or an amiable letter from a prominent Father.

And I knew from direct experience that the Patents Office was only a small sample of Spanish Administration.

There had been the case of the representative of a foreign firm who had come specially to Madrid by air, to settle the account for aircraft engines supplied to the Spanish Army. The account amounted to a hundred thousand pesetas and had been endorsed by the Finance Ministry. Our client thought he would only have to call and receive the money. I had to explain about the forms he would have to fill in so that the date for payment would be fixed – and that some of the money owed by the State to veterans of the Cuban war had not been paid because the date of payment had never been settled. I had then to indicate to whom a commission might be acceptable; the client left by the next passenger aircraft, carrying with him the money of his firm minus twenty thousand pesetas – five per cent commission.

I worked out the reasons for, and the inferences from, this state of affairs in the long hours while I waited in the cool stone halls of the Ministry. A great many of the civil servants came from the middle class and remained in the middle class, trying to live up to an ideal of independence and ease which was not within the reach of their meagre salaries. They had felt the power of connections. They had found it easier to cede to pressure than to resist, easier to accept a tip than to wax indignant, because indignation meant the risk of transfer and banishment to an obscure provincial post. Or if they were independent, like Don Pedro, they were still bound to their education and class, doubly submissive to the moral rule of their spiritual advisers in this general hopeless corruption.

How could these administrators have been other than opposed to the Republic which threatened their benefactors and advisers, and their own precarious position in the machinery of the State?

And on the other side there were the clients.

There was Federico Martínez Arias. He was the manager of a rubber manufacturing company in Bilbao. He was an old client and on friendly terms with me. Of humble origin, he had worked himself up to a safe position in the society of Bilbao; he was the Consul of two Latin-American Republics. In Spain he had become wealthy, in America he would have reached the millionaire class. He used to have endless discussions with me on social and economic problems. He was greatly influenced by Taylor and Henry Ford, and mixed their ideas with a dose of Spanish feudalism.

'I belong to the school of thought which says that a worker must be well paid. In our factory we pay the best wages in the whole of Bilbao.'

Beyond the pay, he wanted to organize and supervise the workers, giving them decent houses, decent cities, comfort, schools, culture, leisure, but all under the rule and control of the factory.

'The workers have not the right qualities to do it for themselves. They are like children, you've got to lead them by the hand so that they don't stumble. . . . The worker does not need more than a good house, good food, a bit of diversion, and the certainty that his living is safe.'

'But in your opinion he must accept it and not start thinking and discussing.'

'He doesn't want to. Just look what Ford has done with his thousands and thousands of workers. What trade union has ever given them as much as Ford? Labour must be organized by the State. The worker is part of the State mechanism.'

'Goodness me, have you turned Nazi, Don Federico?'

'No, but I do admire the Germans. It's a marvel what that man Hitler has achieved. We want a man of his kind here in Spain.'

But he was not a political fanatic, nor a religious one. He believed. He believed in the divine mission of the Leader as the head of the national family, a very Catholic and Spanish concept; he also believed in the submission of the serfs. 'Even if the Leader is wrong – what would become of an army if the soldiers were to start discussion?'

'If the soldiers could speak out, we might not get wars, Don Federico.'

'Certainly. And what would it lead to? Life is a struggle, even the grass blades bore through a stone so that they can grow. Read Nietzsche, Barea.'

'But you call yourself a Christian, Don Federico.'

'I know, I know – pacifist blah. "Peace on earth" – yes, but remember what follows: "to men of good will." You aren't going to tell me, I hope, that those Socialists and Communists preaching red revolution are men of good will?'

Don Federico called on me at the office, and after talking over his outstanding affairs, he said suddenly:

'I've come to take you with me to Bilbao.'

'What for?' I was not astonished, for our business often made it necessary to go to the other end of the country at a moment's notice.

'What for? To work for me. Get out of this hole. You'll never get anywhere here. I offer you the post of attorney to the firm, at one thousand pesetas per month and a commission.'

The offer was tempting. The salary was high as salaries go in Spain, the chances it opened were better. It would have meant surmounting the last barrier between me and an upper-class exist-ence. Attorney to the Ibérica in Bilbao would have meant being accepted into the society of Bilbao, one of the most powerful groups in Spain. It would have meant a prosperous future. It would have meant renouncing once and for all everything – everything, that is, of which I still had the Utopian dreams! – and hadn't I told myself I had to be a good bourgeois?

I did not know then as I know now that this incident was a critical juncture in my whole life. It was nothing but the voice of my instinct which prevented me from accepting.

'Don Federico, I'm afraid you can't very well take me on. Do you know that I'm almost a Communist?'

He gaped.

'Of all the absurd things I've heard in my life, this beats the lot. You a kind of Communist! Don't talk nonsense. Pack your suitcase and come to Bilbao. I know you can't do it tomorrow. Tell your chief he's got to find someone in your place, I'll leave you three months for it. And I'll pay you your salary as from today so that you can arrange for the move comfortably. Don't say anything now. I will write you an official letter as soon as I am in Bilbao, and you can answer then.'

The letter came, a very formal business letter, and I answered it in the best business style. I did not accept.

A few days later Don Federico's great friend, Don Rafael Soroza, owner of an important dolomite deposit, came to the office. He patted me on the shoulder.

'So you're coming to join us in Bilbao, eh?'

'No, sir, I'm staying here.'

'But, my dear fellow, you're an idiot – forgive my frankness. Just in a few days . . .'

'What about these days?'

'In these days we need men like you.'

He launched forth into politics and economics. While I listened, I remembered Don Alberto de Fonseca y Ontivares, the apothecary of Novés. The man before me represented a parallel case, with a different final twist. Soroza was in the late fifties, sturdy, expansive, and cheerful; but the later half of his life had been disturbed by business. He came of a patriarchal family from the Asturian mountains. Though his father had made him study law and follow the career of a lawyer, he had lived quietly in his little village after his father's death, farming his land. Then German prospectors arrived.

Few people know with what meticulous thoroughness German agents investigated the soil and subsoil of Spain for some twenty years. And few know that there exist dozens of companies, apparently of genuine Spanish complexion, which serve as cover for the most powerful German concerns, often not so much to do business themselves as to prevent others from doing it.

The Germans found dolomite in one of Don Rafael Soroza's properties, and tried the same game with him which they had played so successfully with the apothecary of Novés. But by pure accident the piece of land was already registered as a mining site, because it included an abandoned coal mine, and the rights were the property of Don Rafael's family. The Germans set up a limited company, installed Don Rafael as its manager, and so Don Rafael began to earn money without knowing how he did. Germany took shiploads of dolomite.

'You just imagine the same amount of magnesia consumed all over the world because of people's digestion. The Germans buy all the magnesia I am able to extract from the dolomite, and now they're asking for greater quantities. It's an excellent insulator, and they're going to use it for refrigerators and for covering all the pipes in the ice factories. It's better than asbestos. We must take out a patent.'

Don Rafael registered innocuous patents which protected the rights to use magnesia as a non-conductor of heat. The Rheinische Stahlwerke, the I. G. Farbenindustrie, and Schering-Kahlbaum sent us patents protecting the extraction of magnesium from dolomite and its exploitation for mechanical purposes. German firms were busy investigating the use of magnesium and its alloys in internal combustion engines. The raw material was to come from Spain, and a ring of patents impeded its industrial exploitation.

When Don Rafael had ended his discourse, I told him:

'In short, you've turned Falangist.'

'No, Barea, no. It's something much bigger. I'm a member of the National Socialist Party. You know that my partners are Germans, and they've let me join, although I'm a foreigner. Now what do you say, Barea?'

'That you've got yourself into a mess, Don Rafael.'

'Nonsense, man. The Cause is making progress with giant strides. In one or two years' time we'll have Fascism here, and then we'll be a nation such as we ought to be. It won't last more than a year as it is. Mark my words. . . . And now, tell me, when are you going to join Don Federico? He belongs to us too.'

'As a matter of fact, I'm staying in Madrid. The climate of Bilbao is bad for me, and I'm in a sound position here.'

'I'm sorry to hear it. Well, you know your own business best.'

I did not dare to tell him that I was a Socialist as I had told Don Federico. He would have fainted. But what the devil had he to do with the Nazi party? I could figure it out in the case of Rodríguez Rodríguez, who had spent his life in the German Embassy. But this Asturian gentleman-farmer?

He supplied me with the answer himself when he called me to his Madrid office to decide on a few pending matters.

'I'm leaving tomorrow, and wanted to settle these points with you before I go.' With childlike gaiety he added: 'I've got guests at home, you know.'

'Are you going on a bear hunt?'

Bears are still to be found in the mountains where Don Rafael had his manor house.

'Nothing of the kind. They've sent a few German lads to me. They're on a research tour – geology, mines, topography – and some engineers are coming as well, I believe, to look round for a good airport site. It's a pity we have the Republic, for, believe me, with the help of the Germans and with what we have ourselves, this could be a great country.'

'You have not done so badly, personally.'

'No. But that is how things are in the whole of Spain: we're treading wealth under our feet and don't know it. Spain is the richest country in the world.'

'Yes. And look how our people live.'

'But why is it so, tell me, why? It's the fault of that handful of demagogues who have become the masters of this country. Remember what they did to Primo de Rivera and how they would not let him run things as he wanted to. But all this won't last much longer. We're going to make an end of all those Freemasons, Communists and Jews, at a single stroke, Don Arturo – at a single stroke.'

'But there aren't enough Jews in Spain for your stroke, Don Rafael, unless someone invents them.'

'We shall find them, Barea.'

6. The Spark

Don Manuel Ayala had wired us to meet him on the airfield at Barajas. We were waiting for him, my chief and I.

A Douglas used on the lines to Barcelona and to Paris stood out glaringly new between the old Fokkers. I went up to it and studied the fuselage. Something at the back of my mind made me uncomfortable and marred my pleasure. I did not know what, and it bothered me, because I had always been in love with aviation. I had to grope for it.

Whatever I knew of the theory of aerodynamics I owed to the Junkers *v*. Ford case, in which I had been acting for our client. It was some time now since the last Junkers and Heinkel patents had passed through my hands. I wondered what they were up to just now.

When Captain Barberan in Morocco had taken me up into the air in his crate and when he spoke of his dream of a Transatlantic flight, it had been beautiful.

I remembered the first flights I had ever seen, and my delight as a small boy. There was that long, exciting walk in the flat grounds of Getafe while I waited for the arrival of Vedrines, the first man to fly from Paris to Madrid. There were the three afternoons when I tramped through the fields to the Velodrome at Ciudad Lineal until the weather was fine enough and Domenjoz could show us what looping-the-loop was.

I would have liked to fly in that Douglas to Barcelona high above the wild coast of Catalonia and the translucent water, and see the shimmering, shifting light of sun and clouds on range beyond range of distant mountains.

I stopped and focused my troubled memory.

It had happened in the twenties, when Junkers had built a four-engined aircraft to tour the world and bring home contracts for the big airlines planned just then by various countries. Junkers was our client. The Germans tried to obtain a commercial air base in Seville, where the tower for the anchorage of the Zeppelin had been constructed. Spain could be a key position in the network of communications with America. There had been many and complicated moves in the game, and one of them was the lawsuit between Junkers and Ford about the patent for aircraft with wings placed below the fuselage.

My old chief and I had had to go to the airport of Getafe when the four-engined Junkers was due to arrive in Madrid on its propaganda tour. A solemn reception was planned and the King of Spain was to be there. When the monster arrived, a little after the scheduled time, the King and his aides-de-camp inspected it thoroughly; the King insisted on being taken up for a trial flight, and diplomatic engine trouble had to be evolved. But while the official formalities were still going on, a German scientist explained the features of the machine to several Spanish officers who had come with the possibility of an army contract with Junkers in mind, and my chief and I went with them.

The man had the title of doctor, but I never caught his name. He was small and thin and sandy-haired, with thick glasses riding on the bridge of a pendulous nose. His hands were enormous. I remembered having thought that they looked like the skinned hands of a big ape. When he moved his bony fingers, the articulations seemed to jump out of their sockets and to assume strange shapes.

First he folded those hands on his back, behind the heavy tails of his coat, and led us through the cabin where the luxurious armchairs for the passengers were lined up. Then he took us through tunnel-like passages which ended in the engine rooms, and finally we came to the pilots' compartment, separated from the passengers' cabin by a sliding door.

The pilots' compartment was shaped like an elongated hemisphere, corresponding to the curved part of the aircraft's nose. Its outer wall consisted of a duraluminium frame and glass panels. The seats of the two pilots were raised in the centre of the half globe, as though suspended in mid-air, and commanded a free field of vision in almost all directions.

Here the little doctor freed his hands and began to explain in Spanish:

'Now that you have seen the machine' – he stopped all praise by weaving those bony fingers in the air – 'I will show you something more interesting.'

With surprising agility he bounded along the curved glass floor and began to unscrew some of the cylindrical rivets placed where the duraluminium bars crossed. Hollowed sockets with a screw thread appeared underneath.

'As you see, it suffices to unscrew the rivets to uncover the threaded socket into which you can screw the legs of a machine gun in a few moments – these – and these – are for the machine gunner's seat. You take away this glass panel here, and the barrel of the machine gun is adjusted so that it protrudes. Here on both sides – here – and here – there is room for two more machine guns, so that the aeroplane is protected and equipped to attack another aeroplane. And now come with me, gentlemen.'

He ran in front of us with small, bouncing steps to the passengers' cabin. There he showed us how the legs of the armchairs were screwed to the floor.

'They can be taken off in two minutes, and this room is empty. Into these sockets you screw equipment for airborne troops and if necessary for bomb storage and releasing gear. Here are the trapdoors. . . . Now I will show you where the bombs are to be installed.'

Underneath the huge wings he unscrewed other mock rivets and demonstrated the sockets which were to receive the bomb racks. He bounded on his toes and his bony fingers danced while he gloatingly repeated the procedure:

'Here – you see – and here! Now what do you think of it? In a single hour we can transform the planes of a commercial airport somewhere in Germany, say in Berlin, and come to bomb Madrid. Ten hours after the declaration of war we can bomb the enemy's capital. And if it is we who declare war, five minutes after the declaration. Ja, ja, this is Versailles!'

The old and famous balloon pilot who was with us and whom I knew well turned to me and muttered:

'That fellow is as loathsome as a spider. One feels like squashing him underfoot.'

I had been very glad at the time that the Spanish Army contracts for bomber aircraft did not go to Junkers, in spite of the enticing demonstration the cadaverous doctor had given the staff officers.

I had managed not to think of the incident too often since then. But it had changed my views on the future of aviation. It had poisoned my pleasure in flying. It was bothering me just now. There had been Abyssinia. There was Hitler. It was so easy to drop bombs on defenceless towns: you took the rivets off the sockets and fixed the machine guns and bombing gear.

I was getting morbid, I told myself. This Douglas with its sober English comfort was nothing but a luxury vehicle to make flying a pleasure.

The plane from Seville circled and made its landing. We went to meet our client. He was not alone, and I did not recognize his companion. A funny pair they made, plodding across the field.

Don Manuel Ayala was short and squat, in the middle seventies, desiccated and burned by the sun, a sharply pointed nose in the wrinkled, furrowed face, bright mouse eyes behind old-fashioned gold-rimmed glasses fastened to his lapel with a black silk cord, a white, tobacco stained moustache drooping over his small and very thin mouth. The man with him was old, heavy, and uncouth. I thought he was big until I realized that only his extremities were big: hands and feet so huge as to be shapeless, and a large head lolling on disproportionately wide shoulders. He had a coarse peasant face, clean shaven, but blue black from the roots of the hair. What made him look comic was his suit. It was as though a giant had been ill in hospital, lost half his weight, and now came out into the street for the first time in his old clothes. They hung loosely on him, as on coat hangers. But he walked with sure, firm steps.

Then I recognized him. I had never seen him out of his clerical garb before. he was our client's brother, the Jesuit – Father Ayala.

Whenever Don Manuel Ayala had come to Madrid, he had asked me to accompany him. He had lived seventy years of his life cloistered in a small village in the province of Huelva and never gone further than on a sporadic visit to Seville. He administered the landed property he had inherited from his father and sold its produce, but otherwise he led the life of a recluse. He grew exquisite wines which were treated with care, and in his old age he suddenly decided to launch them on the market. Somebody gave him an introduction to our firm, and we provided a set of trade marks, labels, and model bottles for his wines and cognacs. He was merry and loquacious, easygoing and a little cynical about himself. He considered his wish to become a famous winegrower as the sudden whim of old age, but was resolved to indulge it, just as he suddenly took to air travel when he came to Madrid.

'At my age one is no longer afraid of anything. Why shouldn't I give myself the pleasure? I'm only sorry to be so old just when all these new things are turning up.'

He felt awe and pride for his brother, the Jesuit, who was so holy and so important that nothing might be said about him. In 1930, the year before the coming of the Republic, he had taken me along for the first time when he went to see his brother at the Jesuit Residence in the Calle de Cedaceros. I had found Father Ayala repulsive. He was dirty and greasy, his habit slovenly, his huge, stiff-soled boots never cleaned, the nails of his splay fingers edged with black. I had no glimpse of his mind, but I knew the strength of the man. At that time, the threads he held in his fingers led to the Royal Palace, to the Cortes, to aristocratic salons, and to officers' rooms in important garrisons. But he never appeared in public. I knew he now lived in civilian clothes in a Seville tenement house together with two other Jesuits. Why did he suddenly accompany his brother on this trip to Madrid, by air, unexpectedly? What new spider's web was he weaving?

Father Ayala left us when we reached our office and Don Manuel apologized for him: 'The poor man is very worried about what is going to happen.'

He went on explaining while the lift took us upstairs.

'You know, when the Republic dissolved the Order, my brother went to Seville and took a tiny little flat with two others. They're still living there, a communal life. There are hundreds like them in Spain. Of course, quite a lot left the country, but gradually they've been coming back. Now things are going to change, and their place is here, don't you see?'

When we finished our business talk, Don Manuel invited me to have lunch with him, 'because my brother has abandoned me and you know the best corners'.

The old man was deeply religious; he lived a bachelor's life and had hardly had any contact with women. But he had a weakness for good food and good wine. When we were installed in one of those 'corners' he liked, Don Manuel asked me:

'Now tell me how things are going in Madrid, politically.'

'As far as I am concerned, I'm very pessimistic. The Left groups are quarrelling with each other, and the Right is out to ruin the Republic. And now some idiot has had the idea of making Azaña President and so immobilizing a man – perhaps the only man – who might have been able to govern the country in its present state.'

'Yes, yes, and that's a great advantage for us. Believe me, Largo Caballero and Prieto and all those people aren't important. The only dangerous man is Azaña. Azaña hates the Church and he's the man who's done us most harm. Now his teeth are drawn. Otherwise it would have been necessary to eliminate him before doing anything.'

'*Caramba*, Don Manuel, that's a side to you I'd never suspected – that you should think of killing anyone!'

'Not I, no, I can't kill a fly myself. But I must admit that certain things may be necessary. That man is the ruin of Spain.'

'The ruin of your Spain, you mean.'

'Man alive, of yours as well. Because you're not going to tell me you're on the side of that Communist rabble!'

'Perhaps not. But certainly not on the side of the Falangists. Now look, Don Manuel, I don't believe in the Monarchy. I'm for the Republic with my whole heart.'

'Psh, I don't care about Monarchies or Republics. There you have Portugal with an ideal Republic. An intelligent man at the top, the Church respected and in the place that's due to Her – that's what I like.'

'You talk as if you were your brother.'

'If you only could hear my brother! And I agree with him. Communism! Do you know that the Society of Jesus solved the social question centuries ago? Read history, my dear fellow, just read it. Then you'll see what the missions in America did, particularly the one in Paraguay. The Society administered the country and no one went hungry. No one, get that straight. The Indians have never been so happy as they were then. When one of them needed a blanket, he got it, as a gift, not for sale. The Fathers even found them wives, if necessary. They needed no money. It was a paradise, and a model administration.'

'And a mine of wealth for the Holy Fathers, I presume.'

'Now don't be a demagogue. You know that the Society is strictly poor.'

'You won't deny that it had influence, and still has it.'

'I won't deny anything. But neither can you deny that the Society had many enemies and that the poor fellows must have means of defence.' He stopped and thought. 'If only they had done as my brother told them in time . . . but they wouldn't listen. When Don Alfonso said he would go, and make way for the Republic, my brother advised against it. With a few regiments everything could have been settled in a couple of days. Well, you saw what happened.'

'I know your brother has excellent contacts.'

'Oh no, no, the poor man never left the Residence except for a little walk. But the Holy Fathers consulted him, because – although it's not for me as his brother to say so – he's a great person. But always his simple self. You have met him after all. Don't you agree?'

It was true. Father Ayala had never changed. There were others of his Order to be men of the world. He had shown his uncouth contempt and guarded his power. I told Don Manuel that I agreed. Mellowed by the meal, he expanded.

'Good times are just around the corner, Barea. Nearer than you think. Now we have the means, and we have the leader. This Calvo Sotelo is a great man. He's the man of the Spain of the future – of the very near future.'

'You don't think we shall get another military rising as in 1932? Or do you?'

'And why not? It's a patriotic duty. Rather than get Communism we have to man the barricades. But it won't be necessary. The whole nation is with us, and all the muck will be swept away at a single stroke. Maybe not even that will be necessary. Calvo Sotelo will become the Salazar of Spain.'

'Yes, most people seem convinced that it will come to an explosion overnight. But if the Right take to the street, I think there'll be few of them left to tell the tale. The country is not with them, Don Manuel.'

'If you call that mob "the country", no. But we have the Army and the middle class, the two live forces of the country. And Azaña will not get rid of that with a laugh, as he did in August 1932.'

'Then, according to you, Don Manuel, we shall have a paternal Government, Paraguayan or Portuguese style, in August 1936?'

'If God grants it, Barea. And He will.'

We finished the lunch pleasantly joking, for neither of us wanted to go further in showing his thoughts to the other. I never saw either of the two brothers again.

On Monday I sent my eldest daughter on a holiday to the mountains with Lucila, Angel's wife, who was going to stay on her family's farm near Burgos, while her husband was still out of work.

It was the 13th of July 1936. When I had seen them off, I went directly to the Ministry with my briefcase.

The rooms of the Patent Office stood empty. A crowd of people clustered round the door to Don Pedro's office. I saw Don Pedro himself gesticulating and vociferating behind his desk, his eyes filled with tears. I asked one of the employees:

'What the devil is going on here?'

'Good Lord, don't you know? They've killed Calvo Sotelo!'

Many of the staff belonged to the Right, particularly four or five typists, daughters of 'good families', and a far larger group of sons of similarly good families, some of whom were members of Falange. Now they were standing round Don Pedro's desk, making a sort of chorus to his outcries at the assassination of the political leader.

'It's a crime against God! Such a man, so clever, so good, such a Christian, such a gentleman, killed like a mad dog —' he moaned.

'We'll settle the account. They'll have little time to rejoice. Now the only thing we can do is to go out into the street.' Thus the response of the chorus.

'No, no, for God's sake, no more bloodshed – it is not Christian. But God will punish the evildoers.

'God will do it? Well then, we'll lend God a helping hand,' replied a very young man.

I went away. There was no work to be done in the Patent Register that day.

The news had caught me by surprise, as it had caught the whole town. Yet it was obvious that the killing of Calvo Sotelo was the answer to the killing of Lieutenant Castillo of the Republican Shock Police. The only question was whether it would prove to be the fuse which would light the powder keg. And my daughter in the train to Burgos! If I had known in time, I would have stopped the journey. Though she might be better off in a small hill village than in Madrid once things started to happen. But – small village? I had seen what could happen in Novés. And the only thing I knew about Lucila's family was that they were well off and considered important people in their village, which was not exactly a guarantee of safety if the countryside was in an uproar. I walked on to the Glorieta de Atocha, not knowing what to do.

The wide expanse of the square was like an ant heap, not because of the assassination of Calvo Sotelo, but because of the preparations for Saint John's Fair, the *Verbena de San Juán*. The foundations for the hundred and one amusements of the Fair were set up on the paving stones. There were the simple wooden frames for the canvas walls of the junk stalls, there was the circle of steel rails for the merry-go-round. A row of men clinging to a cable slowly raised a tall pole from which flapped a circular canvas. Two mechanics streaked with grease adjusted and hammered the pieces of an old steam engine. The men were in vests, with bare arms, and sweated profusely in the July sun. Peeling and flaking pieces of bedaubed wooden horses were piled up in a heap. Smoke rose from the minute chimneys of the caravans of the fair people. And the female tightrope walker was walking around with drooping breasts, her armpits sweaty, looking after the food and helping out the artists who had turned themselves into carpenters. Wagons and lorries unloaded packing cases and indefinable, bulky objects. The children and the onlookers contemplated the assembling of the stalls with ecstatic attention.

Madrid was preparing for its amusement. Who thought of Calvo Sotelo?

I was wrong. Nobody failed to realize the significance of his death. The people of Madrid felt the fear of soldiers about to depart for the front. Nobody knew when and where the attack was to begin, but everybody knew that the hour had come. While the fair people were setting up the merry-go-rounds, the Government had proclaimed a 'state of alert'. The Building Trade Union of the CNT declared itself on strike, and some of the UGT members, who wanted to go on working, were assaulted. The Government shut down all centres of the Right-wing groups, without distinction, and arrested hundreds of their people. It also closed the *Ateneos Libertarios*, the local centres of the Anarchists, and arrested hundreds of their members. It was clear that they intended to avert the conflagration.

In the Calle de Atocha, I met my Communist friend, Antonio, with four others.

'Where are you going?'

'We're on sentry duty.'

'Don't be stupid. They'll only arrest you. Anybody can see a mile off that you're out on business. Your friend there couldn't show more clearly that he's carrying a pistol if he tried.'

'But we've got to be in the streets to see what's going on. We must protect our branch!' The local branch of the Communist Party, of which Antonio was secretary, had its office near by. 'And we don't even know whether the police aren't going to close it down. Of course we've cleared all our people out of the office.'

'What you should do is set up a stall at the Fair.'

Antonio gasped: 'This isn't a joke, you know.'

'No, it certainly isn't a joke. I mean it. It's quite simple. Go and buy a few toys in a store, at once, now, get hold of a few boards for a trestle table, and a blanket, and set up a stall in the Fair. I know a tradesman quite near, in the Paseo del Prado, who's a friend of mine and will let you use his telephone even during the night, because he doesn't close his bar during the *Verbena*. So you can stay there and keep informed without making yourselves conspicuous.'

They did it, and I helped them. That very afternoon Antonio set up a stall with cheap toys at the side of the Botanical Gardens. The members of his local branch who manned the pickets came and went, stopped to finger the toys and pass on their news. The first sensational piece of news came in the middle of the afternoon: the Socialist Party, all the trade unions belonging to the UGT, and the Communist Party had concluded a mutual assistance pact and pledged their support to the Republican Government. Antonio was full of enthusiasm and impatience behind his toys.

'Why don't you join the Party?'

'Because I'm no good for your discipline, as you know.'

'But we need people now.'

'I'll think it over. First let's see what happens.'

None of us doubted that the Right would carry out its rising. My brother Rafael and I went to the *Verbena* that night, fetched Antonio away from his post and sat down in the open outside my friend's bar. The Fair was not yet in full swing and there were few people merry-making, although there was no lack of groups of police, Shock Police, and workers. The public at large, usually so ready to enjoy summer nights in the open, was afraid of gatherings.

'The greatest problem', said Antonio, 'is the Anarchists in the CNT. They're capable of making common cause with the Right.'

'Don't be an idiot.'

'I'm not an idiot. Now look here, who can understand their going on strike just now and starting to shoot up the UGT people? We've already had to give protection to some of our comrades on their way home this evening. It's worst in the University City. Particularly since the Government has been stupid enough to shut the *Ateneos*. Not that I like the Anarchists – I'd like to get rid of all of them – I'd like to get rid of all of them – but all the same we can't afford to let them go over to the Fascists!'

'No fear. Did they go over in Asturias? When the hour comes to fight – if it does come – they'll be with us.'

'You're an optimist. And I'm afraid you've got a soft spot for the Anarchists.'

I was stubborn in my hope.

That week was one of incredible tension. Calvo Sotelo's funeral was turned into a demonstration by the Right and ended in shooting between them and the Shock Police. In the Cortes, Gil Robles made a speech in Calvo Sotelo's memory, which was officially described as a declaration of war. Prieto asked Casares Quiroga to arm the workers, and the Minister refused. Detentions and assaults were on the increase in all districts of Madrid. Building trade workers of the UGT went to work in the University City under police escort, for the CNT continued to attack them. Expensive cars, with their luggage carefully covered so as to escape attention, left the town in considerable numbers on the roads to the north. People began to flee from Madrid and from Spain.

On Thursday rumours ran riot. Fantastic stories circulated, and the evening papers loaned colour to them. Officially, nothing had happened. The Army had not revolted in Morocco, nor had a military rising taken place in southern Spain. The phrase used to calm the public was as equivocal as the rumours: 'The Government has the situation well in hand.' To stress this fact, broadcasts were started on the same subject. They had the opposite effect. If nothing was happening, why all this nervousness?

Outwardly, Madrid looked as though it were celebrating its fiesta. In that broiling heat, the people lived more in the streets at night than in their asphyxiating houses. The café terraces, the doorways of bars and taverns, the gateways of tenement houses were choked with groups of people who talked, disputed, and passed on news or rumours. But in spite of all the tension, an undercurrent of vague optimism survived.

On Friday night – July the 17th – our circle in the bar of my house was very large. At eleven o'clock, the Calle del Ave María seemed to overflow. The balconies of the houses stood wide open and the voices of the radio sets poured through them. Every bar had its loudspeaker on. The people sitting on the terraces carried on their discussions in shouts and screams. Gossiping women were sitting in the doorways and flocks of childen played and made a noise in the middle of the street. Taxis carrying members of the Workers' Militia on their round drove up and down the slope. Their brakes screeched when they stopped outside one of the bars.

The loudspeakers bawled out news, and the street submerged in silence to listen and to hear.

'The Government has the situation well in hand.'

It was strange to hear the phrase proclaimed in a badly synchronized chorus along the street, from different altitudes. No two voices were the same: they reached one's ear clashing and repeating each other. A loudspeaker in a fourth floor room somewhere down the street was left behind and shouted into the silence the word 'hand'.

'They should leave it in our hands,' said Fuñi-Fuñi.

'Yes, so that you can shoot us,' cried young Manolo.

'We Anarchists are as good anti-Fascists as you are. Or better. We have been fighting for the revolution in Spain for nearly a century, and you only started yesterday. And now, as things are – you're sending your masons to work like a lot of sheep, and the Government refuses you arms. What do you expect? Do you think the Fascists are going to give you higher wages in the University City because you're good little boys? You're a nice lot. The builders going to work —'

'We're disciplined. Do you want to give the others a handle so that they can say we have gone into the streets? Let the Fascists do it, and then you'll see.'

'Yes, yes, leave them to it, and you'll see what happens once they're in your house, while you're on your way driving lorries with cement for their public works!'

'And if only you go on shooting at our own people, the Fascists won't get into our houses, I suppose? What logic!'

'The logical thing about it is that you have not yet found out that the hour has come to make the revolution.'

'Of course I haven't found it out. What has come is the hour to defend ourselves when they attack us. After we've crushed them, thanks to the action they've taken, we can make the revolution.'

'I don't agree.'

'All right. Go on killing builders.'

On the following day, Saturday, July the 18th, the Government openly announced that there had been insurrections in many of the provinces, although it continued 'to have the situation well in hand'. Rumours and news, inextricably mixed, chased each other: Morocco was in the hands of Franco; the Moors and the Foreign Legion were disembarking in Seville; in Barcelona the battle was raging; in the provinces a general strike had been declared; the Fleet was in the hands of the rebels – no, it was in the hands of the sailors who had thrown their officers overboard. In Ciudad Lineal a few Falangists had attempted to seize the transmitter of the Navy Ministry, or, according to other reports, they had seized the buildings of film studios in Ciudad Lineal and had installed their headquarters there.

Under the avalanche of contradictory reports, the people reacted in their own way.

'They say that . . . but I don't believe it. What can four generals do? As soon as they start leading the troops out into the street, the soldiers themselves will finish them off.'

'Well, I've been told that . . . but it's just the same with me as with you, I can't believe it. It's all an old wives' tale. Maybe some drunken playboy has marched into the street to proclaim a rising – in Villa Cisneros.'

Villa Cisneros was the place in Northwest Africa where the Republican Government had deported Right-wing promoters of the anti-Republican military rising in August 1932.

As the afternoon neared its end, it was no longer rumour, it was an admitted fact that a military rising had taken place in several of the provincial garrisons and that there was street fighting in Barcelona. But 'the Government had the situation well in hand'.

My brother and I went down into Emiliano's bar to have a quick coffee. Our friends had gathered.

'Sit down here,' cried Manolo.

'No, we're going to the People's House to see what they're saying there.'

We were just about to leave when the radio interrupted its music and the voice we had begun to know so well said brusquely:

'An urgent order has been issued to the members of the following trade unions and political organizations to report immediately to the centre of their respective groups.' The speaker went on to enumerate all the trade unions and groups concerned; he enumerated all the groups of the Left. The bar was in a tumult. A few of the men drew pistols.

'Now it's the real thing. And they won't catch me unprepared!'

Within two minutes the bar had emptied. Rafael and I hurried back to our flats to tell our families that we might not come home

during the night, and then we met again. Together we hastened to
the secretariat of the Clerical Workers' Union. There they were
doing nothing but drawing up a list of the members who reported,
and telling us to wait. We decided to go to the People's House after
entering our names.

I had a funny feeling in my throat when I saw the streets of
Madrid.

Many thousands of workers were on their way to report to their
trade union, and many of their organizations had their seat in the
People's House. From the outlying districts to the centre of the city
the houses were pouring forth men all going in the same direction.
On the roof of the People's House burned a red lamp which was
visible from all the attics of Madrid.

But the People's House lay in a narrow, short street lost in a maze
of equally narrow and short old streets. And so it happened that the
House seemed more and more unapproachable the more the
multitude thickened. At the beginning, sentries of the Socialist
Youth Organization checked the membership cards in the doorway.
Then they had to demand the cards at the two corners of the street.
By ten o'clock sentries were guarding the entrances to all the streets
in a two hundred yards' radius of the House, and within this circle
thronged thousands of persons. All the balconies of all the houses
stood open and countless loudspeakers were shouting the news:

The Right had taken to open insurrection.

The Government was tottering.

Rafael and I dived into the living mass of the crowds. We wanted
to get through to the tiny room where the Executive Committee of
the Socialist Party had its office. The stairways and the narrow
corridors of the People's House were blocked. It seemed impossible
to advance or recede a single step. But those workers in their
boilersuits asked us:

'Where do you want to go, compañero?'

'To the Executive.'

They flattened themselves against the wall and we were pushing
through, when we were deafened by a surging shout, by the roar:

'Arms! Arms!'

The cry was taken up and re-echoed. At times you heard the

whole syllable and at times a cacophony of 'a-a-a'. Suddenly the
multitude was welded into a single rhythm and repeated:

'Arms, Arms! Arms!'

After the third cry there was a pause, and they started afresh. The
clipped rhythm leaped along the corridors and down the stairs, and
won through to the streets. A fine dust silted down from the
vibrating ceiling. Through the open windows, with a bodily impact,
came the shout of a hundred thousand people:

'Arms!'

7. The Clash

I felt sluggish after the meal and tired from my night without sleep. It was good to rest my drowsy head on Maria's thigh and relax like a contented animal. I stared upwards into the tops of the pine trees and the bits of blue, luminous sky between their branches. Maria began to play with my hair and to stroke my neck. A quick wave of desire lapped over my weariness and repose. The scent of resin was clinging to the skin.

Then we lay side by side in the pile of dry pine needles.

'Let me sleep a bit, will you?' I said.

'No, I won't. Tell me what happened last night.'

'Nothing at all happened. Let me sleep now. I'll tell you later.'

'But I don't want to let you sleep. Tell me what happened. What should I do with myself while you're asleep? Get bored?'

'Sleep a bit, too.'

'I won't let you sleep. Look, if you like, we can walk down to the village early this evening and stay at the inn overnight. But I won't let you sleep now.'

We were enmeshed in a senseless, unfriendly discussion. My nerves were raw and taut from last night's excitement, from the weary listlessness which always invaded me after sexual contact, from the blurred, distorted, nagging vision of the happenings of the last twenty-four hours, from sheer hunger for sleep. In the end we shouted at each other. I rose.

'Now we'll go to the station at once. I'm going back to Madrid. If you like come with me, and if not, do as you please.'

We walked down through the pine wood, silent and sullen. To slide on the pine needles which polish one's shoe soles until they shine had always been exhilarating; that afternoon we only cursed when we skidded on the slope. We found it irritatingly ludicrous to slip and to land on our backsides. And we had to walk down a long slope for more than an hour until we reached the little village in the hills.

'No train until five. Let's drink a glass of beer.'

There were few people in the inn: four or five couples of holiday-makers and four Civil Guards playing cards, their belts unstrapped, their coats unbuttoned. Two of them sat there in their shirtsleeves. They gave us a glance and went on with their game. After a few moments one of them turned round and said paternally:

'A little quarrel, eh?'

A young man in the corner stood up and came towards us. I had not seen him; his table was in the gloom and I was still blinded by the sun outside.

'What are you doing here, Barea?'

'Spending Sunday in the country. And you?'

'I'm staying here for a month or so, to have a good rest. I feel almost like going back to Madrid, what with the things that are happening, but my wife says I'd be silly to do it, and I suppose she's right. A few shouts for Calvo Sotelo, and then – a pricked balloon! Last night when I heard the radio I thought it was going to be serious, but this morning people came out here with their snacks and their bottles of wine to spend the day here, just like other Sundays. Just like you yourself. There have been fewer of them, though, to tell the truth.'

'I don't really know what to say to you. Last night I too thought it was serious. Today I can't make up my mind what to think. I was almost inclined to stay here for the night, but I've had a row with the girl and I'm going back at five.'

'Stay here.'

'What for? I would if it were only to stay with you for a while and have a talk. But I prefer going back to staying a night with a bad-tempered face beside me. And anyway, I'm done up, my nerves are all on edge.'

'You can come home with me if you like.'

'No thanks. I'll take the train back.'

One of the Civil Guards was watching us all the time. It did not surprise me, for Hernández was known as a Socialist and in the small mountain village everyone was aware of it. He went there every summer to strengthen his weak lungs; his work – he was a printer – was bad for his health, and he used to rent a woodcutter's shack among the pines for himself, his wife, and his children.

When Maria and I rose at half past four, the Civil Guard Corporal who had watched Hernández and myself put on his uniform coat. While he was buttoning it up, I went to Hernández' table to say goodbye.

'So you're really going?'

'Yes. Come to Madrid with me.'

'I'd like to. But I'll only go when they send for me. They know where I am. As long as they don't call me back, things can't be very serious.'

The Corporal went out of the door in front of me and turned round in the road.

'Your papers.'

He looked twice at my *cedula personal*, the identity paper which also registers the category of the owner's income. I saw that he was impressed and astonished. He stared at me doubtfully.

'How is it you know Hernández?'

'I've known him since we were boys,' I lied.

'Do you carry arms?'

'No.'

'By your leave.' He passed his hands over my body. 'All right. You can go.'

Twenty-four hours later the Civil Guard had taken over the little village in the Sierra. Early in the morning, they shot Hernández by the roadside. But I learned this, and knew that I had escaped the same fate by a narrow margin, only many days later. At the time, Maria and I climbed the torturous road which led up to the tiny station building, in morose silence.

The railway track runs on a ledge of the Sierra between two tunnels, the village lies embedded in a circle of serried, pine-grown hills. Only at the bottom of the valley is there a meadow where cows graze. It was very peaceful to look down from the bench on the station. The cows were gently browsing, the air was drenched with the scent of pines, the blue sun-filled sky was calm, without a breath of wind. When one of the cows raised its head, the air carried up the clear, mellow sound of its bell.

The station canteen-keeper said:

'It's early for you to be going back.'

'Yes, but it will be very crowded later on.'

'And how are things in Madrid?' As though Madrid were thousands of miles away. The canteen-keeper's small children clung to his trousers and watched us with wide-open eyes. Smiling, I answered his question:

'It's a little confused at the moment.'

The train, a short train which came from Segovia, carried few passengers. The people who had gone to the Sierra from Madrid had not yet abandoned the pleasure of the pine needle carpet. An elderly couple in our compartment, well-to-do provincials, looked at us questioningly. After a while, the man offered me a cigarette.

'Did you come from Madrid this morning?'

'Yes, we did.'

'Are things very unruly there?'

'Oh well, much ado about very little. As you see, people went to the Sierra as usual for their Sunday.'

He turned to his wife.

'Now you see I was right. These women are always afraid of something. A new Government, that's all.'

'You're probably right. But I shall have no peace until we're with Pepe. Don't you agree?' She turned to Maria for support, and told her about their son who was at the University in Madrid and – 'God guard us!' – had gone in for Left politics. He belonged to the Students' Association. And she could not stay quiet.

The women went on talking, and I withdrew into my corner and reviewed in my mind the happenings of the past night.

Rafael and I had succeeded in pushing our way through to the cubicle at the end of a long passage where the Socialist Party Secretariat was housed. Carlos Rubiera was there, Margarita Nelken, Puente, a couple more whom I knew by sight, tackling a torrent of people, telephone calls, shouts and written notes which were passed to them from hand to hand along the corridor.

Carlos Rubiera saw me.

'Hullo, what brings you here?'

'I've come to see if I can be of any use.'

'You're just in time. Go and help Valencia.' He showed me an officer in the Engineers' uniform who was sitting at a small table. 'Hey, Valencia, here's someone you may be able to use.'

We shook hands and Valencia asked:

'You've been in the Army?'

'Four years in Morocco – Sergeant in the Engineers. We belong to the same Arm.'

'Good. At present I'm in command of the guard here. We've got Puente and his boys, and an inexhaustible number of volunteers. The bad thing is that we have no arms and no ammunition, and that most of the lads have never handled a rifle in their whole life. They're all in the big room on the terrace. We'll see what Puente says.' Puente was the commander of the Socialist Militia.

It amused me to note the contrast between the two. Valencia was very much the officer, slim, erect, his uniform fitting like a glove. A long, oval face, grey eyes, a fine, straight nose and full mouth. In his early forties. The grey mass of his hair, black and white threads mixed and swept back in faint ripples, gave a sternness to his head which the gay eyes and the mouth belied. It was impossible not to sense his firm energy.

Puente, a baker by profession, must have been about ten years younger, although his round, fresh face made it difficult to assess his age. But the lines of his face were blunted and harsh. He had a town suit which did not fit his solid, strong body. He looked as though it would have suited him better to stand there in a sleeveless vest and exhibit his naked muscles and hairy chest.

It was Puente who steered Rafael and myself through the clogged passages and stairways to the saloon. There one could breathe. It was a large assembly room which opened on to a roof terrace. No one who did not belong to the Militia had been allowed through; there were no more than fifty persons, standing about in groups. In every group one man was holding a rifle and the others were mobbing him, because each one wanted to hold the rifle for an instant, handle the trigger and take aim, before passing it on the next. Puente clapped his hands, waiting for the men to line up before the dais.

'All those who don't know how to handle a rifle – to the left!'

'Shall we get rifles?' shouted a few voices.

'Later, later. Now listen. Our friend Barea here has been a sergeant in Morocco. He'll explain to you all about how a rifle works. And you' – he turned to those who had gone to the right and therefore claimed to be familiar with rifles – 'come along with me. We'll relieve our comrades who are posted in the streets.'

He marched off with his men, and there we were left standing on the platform, Rafael and I, in front of thirty-odd curious faces. I wondered whether I had forgotten the mechanism of a rifle in twelve years, selected a Mauser and began to take it to pieces, without saying a word. It was an old Mauser of 1886. My fingers found their way back instinctively to their old practice. The red cover of the table before me was soon plastered with oily parts.

'If there's any mechanic among you, step forward.' Five men pushed themselves to the front. 'I'll explain to you how the pieces fit together. You will find it easier to understand than the others, and later you can explain it to them in groups of two or three. In the meantime my brother here will explain the theory of firing to the rest.'

Rafael took another rifle and marched his men out on to the terrace. After half an hour each of the mechanics was ready to take on a small group. Rafael was left with two difficult cases, men who seemed incapable of holding a rifle straight. 'You've got the oaf platoon,' I said into his ear. I went and looked down from the terrace.

The house on the other side of the street, some six yards away, had all of its balconies open and all its lights lighted for me to see. There were dining rooms with a lamp in the middle illuminating the table. In one, a woman was collecting what was left over from supper. In another, the empty table was covered with a dark-green cloth with embroidered flowers along its edge. The owner of the flat was leaning in shirtsleeves over his balcony railings. In the flat below the family was having supper. Then there were bedrooms and sitting rooms, all different, each with its own personality, and all alike. From every flat came the voice of a radio set, all the same, each with its own pitch, pouring music over the heads of the mass packed in the street, a dense, black mass of moving heads. A wave of heat rose from below; it smelled of sweat. Sometimes a soft breeze swept this billow of human warmth from the terrace, and then it smelled for a few seconds of trees and flowers. The noise was so intense that the building throbbed with it, as though it were trembling. When the music stopped and the hundred loudspeakers cried: 'Attention! Attention!' you heard the multitude fall silent with a dull rolling sound which died away in the distance in the streets of the quarter. Then only coughs and grunts came, until someone commented on a piece of news with a joke or a blasphemy. A firm voice shouted 'Silence!' and a hundred mouths repeated the command, drowning everything else for seconds. As soon as the announcement was over, the rumbling noise grew worse than ever.

By midnight the Government had resigned. A new Government was being formed. Over my head a voice said: 'Dirty dogs'.

I looked upwards. On the top of the roof swayed a red flag, almost invisible in the darkness of the night; above it, the red lamp. From time to time, when a shiver of the flag dipped a fold into the red glare, it flashed in a sudden blaze. In a corner of the wall, a winding iron staircase led to the roof. Somewhere on the top I saw the faint glow of a burning cigarette. I climbed up. At the highest point, on an open platform above all the roofs, I found a militia lad.

'What are you doing here?'

'I'm on watch.'

'Because they might come over the roofs?'

'Yes, because they might.'

'Whom do you mean?'

'The Fascists, of course.'

'But you can't see anything from here.'

'I know. But we've got to watch out. Imagine what would happen if they caught us by surprise.'

The iron platform rose into the dark. Below was the bulk of the building, crudely lighted. The sky was clear and powdered with flickering stars, but there was no moon. Round us shimmered the flow from the lights of the streets of Madrid and dwindled away into darkness. The street lamps of the suburbs cut through the fields in parallel threads of beads, white flames which seemed to flicker like the stars. The noise of the street came to us muffled through the huge bulk of the house. Twenty steps, and it seemed a different world. I leaned my elbows on the railing and stayed for a long while, quiet.

Then they called us to a belated supper. From somewhere they had produced roast lamb and some bottles of wine for the guard. We ate and talked. The people were still calling for arms. Puente said to me:

'We've got twenty rifles and six cartridges per rifle in the building.'

'Then we're in the soup.'

'Well, it will all be settled now. I suppose they'll give the Government to our Party, to the Socialists. Anyhow, it will have to be settled soon. The Fascists are in Valladolid, and marching for Madrid. But don't tell any of the lads here.'

I went back to the terrace, while Puente had to inspect his men. The long waiting began to wear down the crowd. Some people nodded, sitting on the stairs and in the passages, others leaned against the wall and dozed. I climbed up to the little platform and saw the dawn begin as a faint white sheen in the east.

The loudspeakers started again: 'Attention! Attention! . . . The new Government has been formed!'

The speaker made a pause and then read the list of names. People fished hastily in their pockets for a piece of paper and a pencil. All the sleepers had awakened and were asking: 'What did he say? What did he say?'

The speaker went on with his litany of names. It was a national Government, he had said. Then the name of a Minister without Portfolio rebounded over the heads: Sánchez Román. It was impossible to hear more. The multitude burst into a roar: 'Traitors – treason!' And above the medley of curses and insults surged the cry: 'Arms! Arms!' The roar grew and swelled. In the stairways and corridors the crowds wanted to move, to go up, to go down. The building quivered as though it were worn out and ready to crumble in a cloud of dust.

A new shout rose: 'To the Puerta del Sol!' The short word 'Sol' whipped through the air. The dense mass in the street swayed and moved. The People's House poured forth an unending stream from its doors.

'Sol! Sol!' The cry was still cracking through the air, but from farther away. The crowd below thinned out. Daylight slowly filled the street with a pale, almost blue haze. The People's House was empty. The first rays of the sun caught us with Puente and his Milicianos, left alone on the terrace. Up on the roof, from his iron balcony, the sentry cast a long, misshapen shadow over the tiles.

'What are we going to do?' I asked Puente.

'Wait for orders.'

Down in the street a few groups of people were standing in heated discussion. Isolated words drifted up to us.

'Don't you think we ought to go to the Puerta del Sol?' I asked.

'No. Our orders are to wait. We must keep discipline.'

'But not under this Government.'

The Milicianos echoed my words. One of them began to cry openly. I said to Puente:

'I'm very sorry, but I can't help it. I came here last night of my own will to help in any way I could. I was willing to go everywhere with you, and to be posted anywhere. But I'm not willing to serve under a Sánchez Román. You know as well as I do what his being a Minister means. It means that this Government will try to make a deal with the generals. I'm sorry.'

I shook hands with him. It was not easy. The militiamen turned round, and some of them leaned their rifles against the parapet of the terrace:

'We're going too.'

Puente swore at them, and they took up their rifles again, except two who marched out behind Rafael and myself. We walked through the emptied house. A few people moved on the stairways like ghosts. We gulped down a scalding cup of coffee in the bar and went out into the deserted street.

A street cleaner was spraying the pavement with the jet from his hose and the smell of a moist dawn hung in the air.

But from the centre of Madrid, from the Puerta del Sol, sounded a tremendous clamour, a muffled bellow which made the air throb and which grew louder as we came nearer. At a street corner a tavern stood open, with a table in a doorway. On the table, a coffee urn on a charcoal heater, a basin with water, cups and saucers, a row of liquor bottles. We stopped to take another cup of coffee and a glass of cognac. The tavern's radio interrupted its crooning: 'Attention! Attention!' The tavern keeper increased the volume: 'A new Government has been formed. The new Government has accepted Fascism's declaration of war on the Spanish people!'

One of the two Milicianos who had come with us from the People's House said: 'Then it's all right, Salud.' He walked off and then turned back. 'But one never knows with those Republicans in the Government.'

When we reached the Puerta del Sol, the crowd had dispersed and the shutters of the bars were clanking open. The people who carried on their discussions in groups and clusters along the pavement went in to have their breakfast. A radiant sun rose over the houses. The day was going to be hot. Taxis passed by, cluttered with militiamen; many of them carried flags with the inscription 'UHP'. The Sunday buses lined up to carry the people into the open country. Beside us a conductor shouted: 'Puerta de Hierro! Puerta de Hierro!' Groups of boys and girls and whole families came in driblets to climb into the buses with rucksacks on their backs.

'What a night!' exclaimed a man as he sat down.

I remembered that I had arranged to meet Maria in the Puerta del Sol at seven in the morning on Sunday and go to the Sierra with her for the day. This was Sunday. It was half-past six. I did not want to go home – there was nothing I could do – and it was a spendid morning.

'Listen,' I said to Rafael, 'tell Aurelia that I won't be home till late tonight. Give her some explanation, say I had work to do at the Union. Or anything. I'll wait for Maria here and go with her to the Sierra. I've had enough.'

That was what had happened on the night of the 18th. Last night – though it seemed far away. The conversation of the others droned on and on. I was tired, annoyed with the whole day, annoyed with Maria, annoyed with myself, unwilling to go home and be shut in with my wife on top of it all.

Then we were in Madrid. People stormed the tram. We preferred to walk. The first buses crowded with holiday-makers came back from the banks of the Manzanares. Outside the station was a traffic block. A policeman with a white helmet was trying to unravel it with great shouts and gesticulations. There were lorries full of people singing at the top of their lungs. A luxury car with suitcases heaped on the luggage rack coasted by.

'They're running away, they're running away!' yelled the men in the lorries. The big car swept past them in silence; the road which led away from Madrid was free. Yet the shout had not been threatening; it had been excited, but merry: the crowd made fun of people who fled from Madrid out of fear.

The gaiety died out in the streets as soon as we had passed the hill of San Vicente. Pickets of Milicianos asked for our papers at the street corners. Police had drawn a cordon at the entrance of every street leading to the National Palace. Few people were about, and they all hurried. More cars with Party emblems painted on their doors and the inscription 'UHP' passed us at great speed. People greeted them with the raised fist. A dense smoke column rose at the bottom of the Calle de Bailén. A loudspeaker told us through an open window that General Franco had demanded unconditional surrender from President Azaña. The Republican Government had answered by a formal declaration of war.

A few churches were burning.

I took Maria to her house and hastened home.

The streets round the Plaza de Antón Martín were choked with people. They were filled with an acrid, dense smoke. They smelled of burned timber. The Church of San Nicholás was on fire. The dome had a helmet of flames. I saw the glass panes of its lantern shatter and incandescent streams of molten lead run down. Then the dome was a gigantic, fiery ball with a life of its own, creaking and twisting under the impact of the flames. For an instant the fire seemed to pause, and the enormous cupola cracked open.

The people scattered, shouting:

'It's coming down!'

The dome came down with a crack and a dull thud and was swallowed by the stone walls of the church. A hissing mass of dust, ashes, and smoke rose. Broken glass tinkled shrilly. Suddenly made visible by the fall of the cupola, a fireman's ladder was swaying in the air. A fireman at the top was pouring his jet on to the market stalls in the Calle de Santa Isabel and on the walls of the cinema beside the church. It was as though a harlequin had suddenly been left alone, ridiculous and naked, in the middle of the stage. The people cheered, and I did not know whether they meant the fireman or the collapse of the dome. The fire roared on, muffled, behind the stone walls.

I walked into Serafín's tavern. His whole family was in the back room, the mother and one of his sisters in hysterics, and the bar was full of people. Serafín was running from the customers to his mother and sister and back, trying to do everything, his round face streaked with sweat, half-crazed and stumbling at every step.

'Arturo, Arturo, this is terrible, what's going to happen here? They've burned down San Nicolás and all the other churches in Madrid, San Cayetano, San Lorenzo, San Andrés, the Escuela Pía—'

'Don't worry', a customer who sported a pistol and a red-and-black scarf challenged him. 'There are too many of those black beetles anyhow.'

The name Escuela Pía had shaken me: my old school was burning. I hastened down the Calle del Ave María and found Aurelia and the children outside the house among the neighbours. They greeted me with cries:

'Where have you been?'

'Working all day long. What's going on here?'

Twenty neighbours started giving me information: Fascists had fired at the people from the churches, and so the people had stormed the churches. Everything was burning . . .

The quarter smelled of fire, a light rain of ashes filtered down. I wanted to see for myself.

San Cayetano church was a mass of flames. Hundreds of people living in the tenement houses alongside had dragged out their furniture and stood there, dumbly staring at the fire which threatened their own homes. One of the twin towers began to sway. The crowd screamed: if it fell on their houses, it would be the end. The tower crashed on the pavement.

In front of San Lorenzo a frenzied multitude danced and howled almost within reach of the flames.

The Escuela Pía was burning from inside. It looked as though shattered by an earthquake. The long wall of the school in the Calle del Sombrerete, with its hundred windows of cells and classrooms, was licked by tongues of fire which stabbed through the window grilles. The front was demolished, one of the towers crumbled, the porch of the church in ruins. Through the side door – the entrance for the poor pupils – firemen and Milicianos came and went in ceaseless action. The glow of the central fire in the gigantic building shone through the opening.

A group of Milicianos and a Shock Police officer came out of the door. They carried an improvised stretcher – boards across a ladder – and on it, wrapped in blankets, a small figure of which nothing was visible but the waxen face under a thatch of white hair. A pitiful old man, quavering, his eyes filled with fright: my old teacher, Padre Fulgencio. The multitude opened a path in silence, and then men put him into an ambulance. He must have been more than eighty years old. A stout woman beside me said:

'I'm sorry for poor old Father Fulgencio. I've known him ever since I was a tiny little girl. And to think of him going through all this now! It would have better for him if he had died. The poor man has been stricken with paralysis for many years, you know. Sometimes they carried him up to the choir in a chair so that he could play the organ, because his hands are all right, but from the waist down he's like dead. He wouldn't feel it if you were to stick pins into his legs. And you know, all this has happened because the Jesuits got hold of the school! Because before that – and believe me, we can't stand the black frocks – but all of us here liked the old Fathers.'

'Padre Fulgencio was my chemistry teacher,' I said.

'Then you know what I mean. Because that must have been quite a long time ago. Well, I mean to say, you aren't old. But it must have been a good twenty years ago.'

'Twenty-six.'

'There, you see. I wasn't far out. Well, as I was telling you, some years ago, I don't remember if it was before the Republic or just after, the school changed so that you wouldn't have recognized it.'

The fire was crepitating inside the church. The building was a shattered shell. The woman went on, hearty and verbose:

'The Escolapians – you know, they were nice and, mind you, I don't like the black frocks generally – went and joined one of those Catholic School Associations, or whatever they were called, but it was all managed by the Jesuits. You remember how it was when the Father Prefect used to go to the Plaza del Avapiés and give us coppers, and my own mother went and kissed his hand. But you see, all that was over and done with when the Jesuits came. They started that what-d'you-call-it, the Nocturnal Adoration, and then the fine young gentlemen came and prayed. Nice prayers, I can tell you! Didn't we see them drilling in the schoolyard and getting in arms? And then, would you believe it, this very morning they started firing at us with a machine gun from the windows up there and people could hear it in the whole quarter!'

'And were there any casualties?' I asked.

'They caught four or five over there in the Mesón de Paredes Street and Embajadores Street. One was killed on the pavement there, the others have been taken away, no one knows where.'

I went home in profound distress. I felt a weight in the pit of my stomach as if I wanted to cry, and could not. I saw flashes of my boyhood, I had the sensation of the feel and smell of things I had loved and things I had hated. I sat on the balcony of my flat without seeing the people who walked through the street and stood there in groups, talking loudly, trying to sift the conflict within me. It was impossible to applaud the violence. I was convinced that the Church of Spain was an evil which had to be eradicated. But I revolted against this stupid destruction. What had happened to the great library of the College, with its ancient illuminated books, its unique manuscripts? What had happened to the splendid collections of Physics and Natural Science? All that wealth of educational material! Had those priests and those Falangist boys really been so incredibly stupid as to expect the College to serve as a fortress against an enraged people?

I had seen too much of their preparations not to believe in their use of churches and monasteries for their stores of arms. But I still hated the destruction, as much as I hated those who drove the people to it. For a moment I wondered where Padre Ayala was, and whether he liked the outcome of his silent work.

What would have happened if our old Father Prefect had thrown open the gates of the Church and the College and stood there himself under the lintel, in the face of the crowd, upright, his grey hair stirred by the wind? They would not have attacked him, I was sure of it.

Later I was to learn that my dream had not been vain: the parish priest of the Church of Santa Paloma had put the keys into the hands of the militia and his church with its art treasures was saved, although the papier-mâché saints were smashed and the metal ornaments used for the war. And similarly San Sebastián, San Ginés, and dozens of other churches had been preserved, some of them for the bombs to come.

But that evening I felt laden. The fight was on, it was my own fight, and I was repelled and chilled to the core.

Rafael took me to Antonio's stall at the Fair. There were still people about and the customary amusements functioned. But Antonio was wildly excited and about to leave. The garrison of the big barracks, the Cuartel de la Montaña, had fired from a machine gun at a lorry carrying members of the Socialist Youth returning from the Puerta de Hierro. The police had drawn a cordon round the barracks. It was the headquarters of the insurrection in Madrid, it seemed.

'We must go there,' Antonio said. I refused. There was nothing I could do. I had seen enough, I was dead tired. Rafael went off with Antonio and I returned home. I slept four hours and woke just after four in the morning. It was bright daylight. In the street below people were talking and disputing. I dressed and went down. A taxi with Milicianos stood in the Plaza de Antón Martín. The men were drinking milk at the dairy which belonged to Serafín's brother-in-law. I joined them and drank two glasses of cold milk out of the icebox.

'Where are you going?'

'To the Cuartel de la Montaña. It's getting serious there.'

'I'm coming with you.'

Shock Police stopped our car in the Plaza de España. I walked on to the Calle de Ferraz.

The barracks, in reality three different barracks joined together, is a huge building on the crest of a hill. In front of it lies a wide glacis on which a whole regiment has room for its drill. This terrace slopes down to the Calle de Ferraz on one side and is cut short above the Northern Railway Station on the other. A thick stone parapet runs along its whole length, with a sheer drop of twenty feet to a lower glacis which separates the barracks from the public gardens of the Calle de Ferraz. At the back, the building looms high over the wide avenue of the Paseo de Rosales and the open country to the west and northwest. The Cuartel de la Montaña is a fortress.

Rifle shots were cracking from the direction of the barracks. At the corner of the Plaza de España and the Calle de Ferraz a group of Shock Police were loading their rifles in the shelter of a wall. A multitude of people were crouching and lying between the trees and benches of the gardens. A wave of furious shots and cries was surging from them, and from others I could not see, nearer to the barracks. There must have been many thousands ringing the edifice on its hill. The pavement on the other side was deserted.

A plane came flying towards the barracks at great altitude. People yelled: 'It's one of ours!'

The day before, Sunday – that Sunday on which we had gone to the Sierra in the morning, hoping that the storm had blown over – groups of officers on the two airfields of Madrid had attempted an insurrection, but had been overpowered by the loyal forces.

The machine flew in a wide curve and banked down. I could not see it any longer. A few moments later the ground and the air shook. After dropping its bombs, the plane made off. The crowd went mad with joy, some of the people in the gardens stood up, waving and throwing their caps into the air. A man was making a pirouette when he fell, shot. The barracks was firing. The rattle of machine guns rose above all the other noises.

Shouting and screaming, a tight cluster of people appeared on the other side of the Plaza de España. When the mass arrived at the street corner, I saw that it had in its midst a lorry with a 7.5 centimeter gun. An officer of the Shock Police was trying to give orders on how to unload the cannon. The crowd never listened. Hundreds of people fell upon the lorry as though they wanted to devour it, and it disappeared beneath the human mass like a piece of rotting meat under a cluster of black flies. And then the gun was on the ground, lifted down on arms and shoulders. The officer shook himself, and shouted for silence.

'Now as soon as I've fired it off you're to carry it over there as quickly as you can, do you understand me?' He pointed to the other end of the gardens. 'But don't kill yourselves. . . . We've got to make them believe that we've got plenty of guns. And off with all of you who aren't helping.'

He fired off the field-gun and even before the barrel had come to rest the dense mass of men closed in and carried it one hundred, two hundred yards further on. Again the gun roared, and again it started on its crazy run over the paving stones. It left in its wake people hopping on one foot and screaming with pain: the wheels had rolled over men's feet. Machine-gun bullets were spraying the street very close to us. I took cover in the gardens and threw myself down behind a stout tree trunk, just behind two workers lying on the lawn.

Why the devil was I here – and without any kind of weapon in my pockets? I knew perfectly well that it was sheer useless folly. But how could I be anywhere else?

One of the two men in front of me raised himself on his elbows. He gripped a revolver with both hands and rested it against the tree trunk. It was an enormous, ancient revolver with a nickel-plated barrel and a sight that stuck out like a wart. The cartridge drum was a shapeless bulk above the two hands clutching the butt. The man pressed his face perilously close to the weapon and pulled the trigger, laboriously. A terrific bang shook him and a pall of stinging smoke made a halo round his head.

I almost leaped to my feet. We were at a distance of at least four hundred and fifty yards from the barracks, and the front of the building was completely screened by the trees of the gardens. What did that damned fellow think he was firing at?

His companion took him by the shoulder. 'Now let me have a shot.'

'No, I won't. It's my revolver.'

The other swore. 'Let me have a shot, by your mother!'

'No, I won't, I've told you so. If they bump me off the revolver is yours; if not, you can just lump it.'

The other turned round. He had a clasp-knife in his hand, almost as big as a cleaver, and he brought it down on his friend's behind. 'Give me the revolver, or I'll prick you!' He stabbed at his buttocks with the point of the knife.

The man with the revolver jumped and bellowed. 'It's gone in!'

'Now you see – you let me have a shot or I'll puncture you.'

'Here you are, but hold tight, it kicks.'

'D'you think I'm an idiot?'

As though following a fixed ritual, the other raised himself on his elbows and clutched the butt with both hands, so deliberately and ceremoniously that it looked almost like a supplication. The nickel-plated barrel lifted slowly.

'Go on, get it over!' shouted the owner of the revolver.

The other turned his head.

'Now it's you who's got to wait. It's my turn. Now I'll show those bastards!'

Again we were shaken by the crash, again the acrid smoke clung to the ground around us.

The bangs of mortars and the rattle of machine guns went on at the barracks. From time to time the gun roared at our back, a shell made the air throb, and the explosion resounded somewhere in the distance. I looked at my watch: ten o'clock. Ten! It was impossible.

Just then a silence fell, followed by a pandemonium of cries and shouts. Through the confused noise rose the words: 'Surrender! White flag!' People burgeoned from the ground. For the first time I saw that there were women as well. And all of them started running towards the barracks. They swept me along. I ran with them.

I could see the stone stairways in the centre of the parapet which led from the lower to the upper glacis; they were black with tightly packed people. On the terrace above a dense mass of bodies blocked the exit.

A furious burst from the machine guns cut through the air. With an inhuman shriek, the crowds tried to scatter. The barracks spouted metal from its windows. Mortars sounded again, nearer now, with a dry crack. It lasted some minutes, while the wave of cries was more frightful than ever.

Who gave the order to attack?

A huge, solid mass of bodies moved forwards like a ram against the barracks, against the slope leading upwards from the Calle de Ferraz, against the stone stairs in the wall, against the wall itself. An immense cry rose from the multitude. The machine guns rattled, ceaselessly.

And then we knew in an instant, though no one told us, that the barracks was stormed. The figures in the windows disappeared in a flash, other figures whipped past the windows after them. The tide of screams and the firing now sounded inside the building. A Miliciano emerged in a window, raising a rifle high into the air and throwing it down outside. The multitude answered with a roar. I found myself part of a mass which pushed on towards the barracks. The glacis was strewn with bodies, many of them twitching and slithering in their own blood. And then I was in the barracks yard.

The three tiers of galleries enclosing the square yard were filled with running, yelling, gesticulating people who waved rifles and called senselessly to their friends down below. One group was chasing a soldier who forged ahead, crazed, but swerving aside whenever anyone crossed his path. They had run almost the whole round of the gallery when somebody tripped the soldier up. He fell. The group of people closed round him. When they separated, there was nothing to be seen from the yard where I was.

A giant of a man appeared in the highest gallery, bearing on his huge hands a soldier who threshed the air with his legs. The big man shouted:

'Here he comes!'

And he threw the soldier down into the yard. He fell, revolving through the air like a rag doll, and crashed on the stones with a dull thud. The giant lifted his arms.

'And now the next!'

A crowd had gathered in the corner of the arms depot. The rifles were there. One militiaman after the other came out, brandishing his new rifle, almost dancing with enthusiasm. Then there was a new rush at the door.

'Pistols – Pistols!'

The depot began to pour forth black boxes, passed from hand to hand over the heads. Each box contained a regulation pistol – a long-barrelled Astra calibre 9 – a spare cartridge frame, a ramrod, and a screwdriver. In a few minutes the stones of the yard were spattered with black and white patches – for the inside of the black boxes was white – and with grease-stained paper. The depot door was still spitting forth pistols.

It has been said that there were five thousand Astra pistols in the Cuartel de la Montaña. I do not know. But that day, empty black-and-white cases dotted the streets of Madrid. What was not found, however, was ammunition. It had been seized at once by the Shock Police.

I walked out of the barracks.

When I served my first few months in the Army, a conscript soldier destined for Morocco, it had been in these barracks; that was sixteen years ago.

I had a glimpse of the officers' mess in passing. Dead officers were lying there in wild disorder, some with their arms flung across the table, some on the ground, some over the window-sills. And a few of them were young boys.

Outside on the glacis, under the glare of the sun, lay corpses in hundreds. It was quiet in the gardens.

8. The Street

On Tuesday morning, the day after the storming of the barracks, I went to the office and had a conference with my chief on what course to follow in the circumstances. We decided that our office would continue to function and the staff come to work in the mornings as usual. We even attempted to co-ordinate our work for the day, but gave it up as soon as we realized that postal communications had been uncertain. I took a briefcase full of papers which had to be registered and submitted in the Patent Office and left for the Ministry.

Two floors below us was the head office of Petróleos Porto-Pí S.A., a company set up by Juán March after the organization of the Oil Monopoly, with scarcely any other purpose than that of claiming fantastically high compensation for alleged oil-bearing properties from the Spanish State. The door stood open and I saw two Milicianos with rifles slung over their shoulders and pistols in their belts rummaging through the drawers. One of them turned round and saw me standing at the door.

'Come in!'

I entered. The Miliciano went past me to the door and shut it. Then he addressed me:

'Now, my fine bird, what brings you here?' He had grasped his pistol and held it with the muzzle pointing to the floor. 'Just you drop your nice little case there and put your hands up!'

He did not search me for arms but simply emptied all my pockets on to the desk. My notecase attracted his attention. He drew out the wad of papers and began to scan them. In the meantime the other Miliciano rifled the briefcase.

'I think you're barking up the wrong tree,' I said.

'You shut up and speak when you're spoken to.'

'All right. I suppose one is allowed to smoke. Tell me when you're through.'

I had not yet lighted my cigarette when the man shoved the UGT membership card under my nose.

'Whose is this?'

'Mine, I should say.'

'Do you mean to tell us that you're one of us?'

'I do. But it's a different question whether you're going to believe me or not.'

'I'm not swallowing fairy tales. Whose is this *cedula personal*?'

'Mine too, I imagine.'

He turned to his companion. 'I told you this was a good rat trap! We've caught a bird already. A *cedula* of the hundred-pesetas class, just like the bigwigs, and a UGT card! What do you have to say to that?'

'It's possible, but it's a bit unlikely, it seems to me. Leave him for a moment and look at what I've got here.'

When they had finished thumbing official and legal documents and trying to decipher the complicated designs for a liquid-air installation, they resumed their cross-examination.

'Explain who you are and what all those scrawls mean.'

I gave them circumstantial explanations. They took me down to the concierge, who was pale with fear but confirmed what I had said.

'It seems we've got to take a look at that office.'

We went up to our office in the lift and I led them into the confessional.

'Now, what is it you want to know?'

'Well, we want to know what kind of office this is and what people you've got here.'

'I'll show them to you, that will be the best way.' I said to Maria: 'Tell everybody to come here—'

'Don't you move,' one of them said to her and pushed the button on the desk. Carlitos, our office boy, came in.

'Hullo, kid, you're buttons here, aren't you? Now listen, get everyone of the staff in here, just as if this gentleman here had sent for them. You know who he is?'

'Hell, of course I know. You're on the wrong track, pal.'

But he brought in our employees one by one. They stood in a silent semicircle and waited.

'Now you can introduce them,' the leader of the pair said.

'The best thing will be for you all to show your Union cards. The only person here who hasn't got one is our chief – here he is – and he's one of the partners of the firm.'

The two Milicianos accepted the facts, although they clearly showed their desire to search the office. Before they left, they fired off their parting shot:

'All right – but we'll come back. This outfit will have to be taken over. It's goodbye to employers now, and you' – this was directed to our chief – 'can look round elsewhere for your meal-ticket.'

It was getting late for the Ministry; the patent departments would close within an hour, and there would be no taxis to be had. I walked down the stairs with the two Milicianos. Now they turned friendly.

'You know, my lad, what with you looking like a bourgeois louse and with the figure on your *cedula*, we thought you must be one of those Falangists. Because they carry our Union cards in their pockets, you know. And then you turned up in the door of that robbers' den!'

'I looked in precisely because I was astonished to find anyone in that place just now – and so you've made me late for the Ministry with these papers of mine!'

'We'll take you there in a jiffy, don't you worry.'

Outside was a car and two militiamen with pistols from the Cuartel de la Montaña in their belts. When they saw us coming, they laughed broadly.

'Have you bagged him?'

'No, he's one of ours, we're going to take him to his Ministry.'

That was my first experience in a requisitioned car with a self-appointed driver. We started with a violent jerk and shot down the Calle de Alcalá in defiance of all traffic regulations. Passers-by raised their clenched fists, and we all, including the driver, returned the salute. The car responded with a swerve and the driver tore at the wheel so that we tumbled over one another. There was nothing to be done except to wait for the moment when the madly careering car would crash into another mad car or lorry passing us, brimful with Milicianos who would raise their clenched fists, or when it would dash on to the pavement, crush a couple of pedestrians and end up against a lamp post. But nothing happened. We crossed the Paseo del Prado through a maze of boards and girders, the dismantled skeletons of fair-stalls and merry-go-rounds.

When we came to the Ministry, my companions decided that they wanted to have a look at it; they had never been in a Ministry.

Shock Police posts at the entrance would not let anyone through who did not possess a pass; when the militiamen walked up the broad stairs, trying to follow me, a corporal barked at them:

'Where are you going?'

'We're going in there with him.'

'Are they coming with you, sir?'

'Yes.'

'Have they got passes?'

'No.'

'Then you have to ask for forms over there and wait for your passes.'

'Well, if you come in, you know where to find me,' I said with a childish feeling of triumph.

In the Register everything was topsy-turvy. A dozen employees of patent agencies were waiting in the hall, but the places behind the windows of the counters were deserted. A few of the employees of the Ministry were standing in the middle of the hall and discussing the latest events with the others. One of the Register people saw me and said:

'If you've got anything for us, Señor Barea, let me have it, I'll register it for you. It's not exactly my job, but no one else has turned up. Well, one has – Don Pedro himself.'

'I should have thought he would prefer not to leave his house today.'

'You don't know him then. Go in and see him.'

Don Pedro was buried in mountains of papers and working feverishly.

'How are you, Arturo, do you want anything?'

'Nothing, sir. They told me you were here, and I came in to say good morning. I tell you frankly that I didn't expect to see you today.'

'What should I do in your opinion? Go into hiding? I've never done harm to anyone and I haven't ever meddled in politics. Of course – I have my opinions which you know, Barea.' He changed to the more distant form of address.

'I know them; they seem to me a little dangerous just now.'

'Of course they are. But if one has a clear conscience, one isn't afraid. What I am, though, is shocked and horrified. Those people respect nothing. One of the priests of San Ginés came to my house. He is still there, shivering and trembling, and making my sisters almost die of fright. And those burning churches . . . I can't believe that you approve of all this, although you do belong to the Left.'

'I don't approve of it, but then I don't approve of rifles stored in churches either, nor of conspiratorial meetings held by Christian Knights at two in the morning.'

'They were forced to defend themselves.'

'So have we been, Don Pedro.'

There we were off again, careful not to hurt each other's feelings too much, neither of us hoping to come to any agreement with the other, yet both trying to behave as though discussions were still of value. I was not very attentive. I knew his arguments as much by heart as I did my own. I thought about the man himself.

His religious faith was so strong, his integrity so complete, that he was unable to admit even the possibility that anyone professing the same faith might have a lower moral standard than he himself. He was a simple, childlike man who after the death of his parents had taken refuge in an almost monkish life together with his sisters; he had a private chapel in his house and thus was aloof from the political life of the sacristies; he neither smoked nor drank, and I imagined that he had never known a woman.

There was something else I knew about him. In 1930, a clerk in a patent agent's firm had developed tuberculosis. He was earning 200 pesetas per month, was married, and had two children. His illness had presented him with an insoluble problem. To give up work or to apply for admission to one of the State Sanatoria would have meant starvation for his family. The illness made rapid progress, and the moment came when he was unfit to go to work. His firm paid him three months' salary and dismissed him. The employees of the private patent firms and of the patent departments in the Ministry collected money for him, and I asked the three chiefs of the Patent Office for their contribution. A few days later Don Pedro called me to his room and shut the door. He enquired about the result of the collection, and when I told him that it had netted four hundred pesetas, he exclaimed: that was bread for one day, and hunger for the future. I explained that we were not able to do what would be necessary to provide a place in a sanatorium for the man and financial support for his family in the meantime. Don Pedro said that everything was settled, including the recommendation to the sanatorium which would cut short all the red tape; he was going to pay for the cure; I was to tell the consumptive man's wife that his friends had collected enough money to pay her 200 pesetas per month for the duration of her husband's illness. 'Nobody will know, because we can manage all this between you and me.'

It had been arranged as Don Pedro suggested. The clerk was cured, he lived with his family in the north of Spain. Neither he nor his wife ever learned what had happened. When the young man was dismissed from the sanatorium, Don Pedro had wept with joy.

How could I have quarrelled with this man, whom I respected, much as I disagreed with all his beliefs and political ideas? The discussion dragged on painfully. In the end Don Pedro rose and held out his hand.

'I don't know what is going to happen here, Barea, but if anything does happen . . .'

'If anything happens to you, let me know.'

I went out into the streets.

The workers' militias had occupied all the barracks of Madrid: the conscript soldiers had been discharged. The police had arrested hundreds of persons. News from the provinces was still contradictory. After a fierce battle, Barcelona was finally in the hands of the Republicans. So was Valencia. But the list of provinces which the insurgents had caught by surprise was long.

Crossing the Plaza de Atocha, I wondered what course the War Ministry would follow. A general mobilization? General Castello had the name of being a loyal Republican. But would he dare to arm the people? Would President Azaña bring himself to sign the decree?

Milicianos had drawn a cordon across the Calle de Atocha.

'You can't get through, man, they're firing from the roof up here. Get yourself under cover round the corner.' I heard the crack of a rifle shot. Two Milicianos on the other side of the street fired back, one with a rifle, the other with a pistol. In the doorway of the house where I stood there was a cluster of people and two more militiamen.

'I think I can get through as long as I stick to the front of the houses.'

'All right, if you like. Have you got papers?'

I showed him the UGT card and he let me through. Shots crackled from the roof. I kept very close to the wall of the house and stopped when I had passed it. A group of men came out of the entrance. Two of them were carrying the limp body of a boy of sixteen. His head was oozing blood, but he was alive. He moaned: 'Mother – Mother —'

The whole quarter of Avapiés seemed in an uproar round the Plaza de Antón Martín. Shots sounded from many roofs. Milicianos were chasing snipers over the roofs and through the skylights. Somebody said that two or three Fascists had been killed in the Calle de la Magdalena. But the people showed little alarm. Men, women, and children from the tenements were in the streets, all looking up at the upper storeys of the houses, all shouting and shrieking.

A strong voice shouted the order which I then heard for the first time: 'Shut the balconies!'

The street resounded with the clatter of the wooden laths of window and balcony blinds. Some windows stayed open, and people pointed at them with their fingers.

'Señora Maña!' someone kept on shrieking. After a while a fat woman came out on an open balcony. 'Shut your balcony, quick!' And the fat woman rolled down the blinds without a word.

Then it grew quieter. The houses showed blinded fronts. A little boy squeaked: 'That window's open, over there!'

On a third floor a window stood wide open and its curtain flapped, leisurely. A Miliciano growled: 'Some son of a bitch could fire at us from behind that curtain.' People round him began to scream: 'Shut that window!' The curtain went on flapping, like a challenge. A militiaman took up his stance on the opposite pavement and loaded his rifle. He took aim. The mothers clutched their children and edged away from the man, who stood in the middle of the deserted space and fired. Broken glass clinked. One of the men entered the house and came out with a little woman, shrivelled and humped by old age, who cupped her hand to her ear. The others shouted in chorus:

'Who's the tenant of the flat up there, Señora Encarna?'

When at last the old woman understood, she answered with perfect gravity:

'And that's what you've called me for, children? That's the staircase window. The Fascists live on the first floor. They're bigoted devils, they are.'

Within a few seconds the balconies of the first floor were thrown open. A Miliciano leaned out from the last window in the row: 'There's nobody here – they've flown!'

Furniture and crockery rained down on the paving stones.

The loudspeakers interrupted their music, and the crowd clamoured for silence. The shower of furniture ceased. The Government was speaking:

'The Government, on the point of finishing with the criminal sedition fostered by military who have betrayed their country, requests that the order now about to be re-established should remain entirely in the hands of the public forces of law and order, and of those elements of the workers' associations which, subjected to the discipline of the Popular Front, have shown such abundant and heroic proof of lofty patriotism.

'The Government is well aware that Fascist elements, in despair at their defeat, are trying to sham solidarity and join with other turbid elements in an effort to discredit and dishonour the forces loyal to Government and People by displaying an alleged revolutionary fervour which expresses itself in incendiarism, looting, and robbery. The Government commands all its forces, whether military or civilian, to quell any such disturbances wherever they may encounter them, and to be prepared to apply the utmost severity of the law to those who commit such offences. . . .'

The pieces of furniture stayed there, strewn over the pavement. Milicianos stood guard beside the spoils.

The people clustering in ardent discussions were cheerful; now the insurrection was beaten, the Right would soon realize what Socialist rule would be like. The blindfolded, sombre street became illuminated and almost festive.

At the entrance of the Calle de la Magdalena appeared three lorries packed with standing Milicianos who shouted rhythmically: 'UHP – UHP – UHP.'

The street took up the cry, with raised fists. When one of the lorries stopped and the militiamen came tumbling out, the crowd clotted around them. Many of men had rifles and army leather straps; there were some women in men's clothes, in blue boiler suits.

'Where have you come from?'

'We've had a good day – we've given the Fascists a beating they won't forget so quickly – we've come from the Sierra – the Fascists are in Villalba, but they won't have much guts left to come to Madrid. We met a lot of soldiers going in the other direction when we were coming back.'

'But how is it that they let you come back?' a stout woman asked a man who seemed to be her husband, a mason by the traces on his overall, in the middle forties, somewhat the worse for drink.

'Now listen to her! Who would have the right to stop us? When we saw it would soon be getting dark, we all said it's time to go home to bed, so that the ladies shouldn't get frightened without us. Some of the lads stayed behind, but they had taken their wives along.'

After supper a boisterous crowd thronged the streets, fleeing from the suffocating heat of their houses and still optimistically discussing the Government declaration and the impending end of the insurrection. Rafael and I set out to make a round of the most popular meeting places of the quarter. I wanted to see the people.

First we went to the Café de la Magdalena. It is a very old café and music hall, where, in the last century, generations of gypsy dancers and flamenco singers had paraded, to be followed by 'national and foreign dancers' who came nearer and nearer to strip-tease acts as the era of the cakewalk, machicha and rumba passed. There was always a core of simple-minded customers, workers, and strangers who came to have a drink and stare at crude variety numbers, and round them a fringe of prostitutes with their pimps lying in ambush and the police never far away.

That night some two hundred people blocked the entrance, all trying to get in. Two Milicianos with rifles over their shoulders guarded the door. Rafael and I were determined to get through, and we made it. The rowdy who was porter and ticket collector at the same time never asked for our tickets, but greeted us so unctuously with a 'Salud, comrades' that Rafael muttered: 'He thinks we're plain-clothes cops.'

The huge saloon was crammed with couples of sweating men and women, who swayed and pushed in a futile attempt to follow the strident tune of the dance band, all braying brass and bleating saxaphones. Above their heads hung a streaky pall of bluish smoke turned grey by the dust. They smelled like a truckload of sheep doused with cheap eau-de-Cologne. The men and women were clad in workmen's overalls as though in a uniform, and a pistol was stuck in almost every belt. The big Astra pistols from the Cuartel de la Montaña glinted blue, and their burnished mouths glittered in the garish light.

When the band stopped, the mass howled: 'More – more!' They struck up the *Himno de Riego*, the Republican anthem. The multitude sang the chorus to the words of the popular parody:

> *Simeon had three old cats*
> *And gave them food on a plate* . . .

When it was over, they howled louder than before. The small jazz band intoned a crazy Internationale, with drums, cymbals, and jingling jazz bells. All the people stopped, raised their clenched fists, and sang religiously:

> *Arise, ye starvelings from your slumbers,*
> *Arise, ye criminals of want* . . .

A swarthy, bulky man with frizzed black hair falling over his ears and neck, a black-and-red scarf wound round his throat, towered above the others and roared: 'Long live the FAI!'

At the Anarchists' war cry, it seemed for an instant as though it would come to a brawl. The air was thick with insults. Black-and-red scarves gathered at the back of the saloon. Nervous fingers fumbled at belts and hips. Women squealed like cornered rats and clutched at their men. The Internationale broke off as though choked by a huge fist.

A little man in the ludicrous coat of a waiter had jumped on to the dais and was screaming something, while the big white drum behind him made a frame for his contortions and punctuated them with its thuds. The crowd fell silent, and the little man shrieked with a grating voice:

'Comrades' – he must have thought that he had better not use the Communist style of address alone, and corrected himself ' – or fellow workers! We've come here to have a bit of fun – don't forget we are all brothers in the struggle against Fascism, all brother workers – UHP!'

The saloon shook when the crowd repeated the three magic letters in a staccato rhythm. Then the band struck up a galloping fox trot, the couples started to dance in a furious whirl. They had more room to dance now; many had left.

Rafael and I were edging out, when a mass of flesh bulging out of a tight boiler suit hooked itself on my arm, with opulent breasts almost at the height of my shoulders and a wave of cheap, cloying scent: 'Come on, sweetie, buy me a drink. I'm dying of thirst.'

I had seen her many a night walking on her beat at the corner of the Plaza de Antón Martín. I freed my arm.

'I'm so sorry, but we've got to go. We've been looking for a friend, but he isn't here.'

'I'll come along with you.'

I did not dare to give the woman an aggressive refusal; a mischievous phrase could easily provoke an attack from those temperamental so-called Milicianos, particularly as Rafael and I were too well dressed for the place. The woman clung to us until we came to the Plaza de Antón Martín. There we took her into the Bar Zaragoza, bought her a beer, and disappeared. She was swallowed by a delirious mass of half-drunken men and women, of pistols and black-and-red handkerchiefs, menacing splotches of colour in a swaying sea of heads.

We crossed the street and went into Serafín's tavern. The small bar was cluttered, but we walked through to the back room. There were familiar faces. Old Señor Paco was there, the politicizing carpenter, with a new, shiny leather belt and the straps of a soldier, a rifle between his knees, holding forth to an enthralled audience:

'As I say, we had a fine day in the open, there in the Sierra. Just as if we'd gone shooting rabbits. Near Villalba a post of Shock Police stopped us in the middle of the road, and sent us up to a hill top between rocks and scrubs with a corporal and two constables. The wife had cooked a tortilla to take along, and Serafín had filled my leather bottle with wine in the morning, so everything was fine. The worst of it was that we all got scorched among the stones there, because the sun shone straight down on us. But we didn't see the tip of a Fascist's nose, and we've had a very nice day. There were some shots from the direction of the road, and for a time we heard machine guns, but very far away. The corporal said he had posted us there so that the others shouldn't sneak through the hills, and he also said things were very serious over near Buitrago. Well, so that was that. We've eaten splendidly, my nose is peeling from the sun, and we've had a first-class day. Most of us came back in the evening. The Lieutenant of the Shock Police wanted us to stay, but what the hell, we aren't soldiers, I said. Let them stay there, that's what they're paid for.'

'Are you going back tomorrow, Paco?'

'At six in the morning, if God will it. Well, of course, that's just a manner of speaking, because we've done with that sort of thing now.'

There was a man in the circle whom I had never seen before. He smelled of gasoline and had cold grey eyes and thin lips. He said:

'We've had an even better day. We've made a clean up.'

'Have you been chasing Fascists across the roofs?'

'That's for kids. We've been selling tickets for the Other World in the Casa de Campo. We led them out like sheep. A shot in the neck, and that was that. We haven't got much ammunition to spare.' While he was speaking, his hand made a gruesome shadow play in the air. Cold shivers ran up and down my spine.

'But that's all the Government's affair now, isn't it?'

He stared at me with his frosted eyes.

'Pal – the Government, that's us.'

We talked of him while we walked home, Rafael and I. If that kind of person got power there would be a frightful slaughter. But it was to be hoped that the Government would step in. We looked at each other and shut up.

When we came to the street corner, where two Milicianos stopped us and asked for our papers, we heard from the far end of the Calle del Ave María the noise of shouts, running feet, a shot and a cry. Then the running feet sounded again, further away, and the street lay silent. The pair of Milicianos did not know what to do. One of them turned to us: 'Shall we go?'

The street was deserted, but I sensed the people whispering behind the closed doors of the houses. One of the Milicianos loaded his rifle, the other followed suit. The bolts clanked loudly. Down the street someone cried: 'Halt!'

The militiamen answered the shout. Two shadows moved towards us, keeping close to the walls. Before our groups met, we saw the dead man.

He was lying across the gutter, a tiny black hole in his forehead. He had a cushion of blood under his head. The fingers of his outflung hands were contracting. The body jerked and then lay still. We bent over him, and one of the Milicianos lighted a match close to his mouth. The little flame burned unwaveringly and lighted up the gaping face and glazed eyes. The big black-and-red scarf looked like a wound in the throat. It was the man who had shouted 'Long live the FAI!' in the Café de la Magdalena.

One of the Milicianos said philosophically: 'One less.' Another went to telephone. Three mounted guard over the corpse. The house doors opened and curious faces drew near, grey disks in the darkness.

I could not sleep. The heat choked me, and through the open balcony entered the noise of the street and the music from the loudspeakers. I got up and sat on the balcony in my pyjamas.

I could not continue to drift.

When I had gone to the People's House on Saturday, I had done so because I wanted to serve in the ranks of the anti-Fascist formations in the capacity in which I would be most useful. I knew that what we lacked and needed above all were officers, closely knit groups of trained men who could lead and organize bodies of militia. I was ready then to do such work and to exploit my hated experiences in the Moroccan War. But Azaña had nominated the Government of Martínez Barrio with Sánchez Román as a discreet negotiator, a Government clearly created so as to make a deal with the rebels, and when the Commander of the Socialist Militia had told his men to accept it with discipline, even while the masses were roaring with fury and forcing the President to rectify his step within an hour, I had walked out. I was unable to submit to this sort of blind political discipline.

I had rubbed elbows with the mass of Milicianos, of people calling themselves Milicianos and accepted as such, for three days and nights. This was a pseudo-military machinery of which I did not want to become a part.

But I could not continue on the fringe of events. I felt the duty and I had the need for action. The Government stated that the rising had finished, but it was evident that the contrary was true. The rising had not yet begun in full earnest. This was war, civil war and a revolution. It could not finish until the country had been transformed either into a Fascist or into a Socialist state. I did not have to choose between the two. The choice had been taken for me by my whole life. Either a Socialist revolution would win or I would be among the vanquished.

It was obvious that the vanquished, whoever they would be, would be shot or locked up in a prison cell. That bourgeois life to which I had tried to resign myself and against which I had been struggling had ended on the 18th of July 1936. Whether I would be among the victors or the vanquished, a new life had begun.

I agreed with Prieto's statement in *Informaciones*: This was war, and a long war at that.

A new life meant hope. The revolution which was the hope of Spain was also my own hope for a fuller, cleaner, more lucid life.

I would get away from the two women. Somewhere I would be needed. I would shut myself up in work as though behind the walls of a fortress. For the Government simply had to take things in hand.

And supposing it was unable to do so? If revolution meant the right to kill with impunity – where would we end? We would kill each other for a word, for a shout. The revolution, Spain's hope, would turn into the bloody orgy of a brutal minority. If the Government was too weak, it was up to the political groups to take the lead and to organize the fight.

But I was still under the impression of what I had seen that very night in the quarter of El Avapiés. I had seen the mass of prostitutes, thieves, pimps and gunmen in a bestial frenzy. This was not the mass which had stormed the Cuartel de la Montaña, mere human bodies against machine guns. This was the scum of the city. They would not fight. They would not carry through a revolution. But they would rob, destroy, and kill for pleasure. That carrion had to be swept away before it infected everything.

I had to find my own people. We needed an army. Tomorrow, today, I would go and see Rubiera. We would work together again, as we had done years before and we would achieve something useful.

For a short time I dozed on the balcony. One of the children in the room behind me began to cry. I wondered what would happen to my children. The office was going to stop work. On what were the people out of work going to live? I had the means to hold out for months; but what would happen to those who lived on their weekly wages and had received their last pay envelope on Saturday the 18th?

A motor horn was barking impatiently down in the street. It was daybreak. My boy in there was crying more loudly. The door of our house clanked open and Manolo, the concierge's son, came out, leather straps, rifle and all. I called down: 'Where are you going?'

'To the Sierra, with the boys here. There will be a bit of shooting. Do you want to come along?'

The lorry was full of militiamen in the blue boiler suits which by now seemed to have become a uniform. Most of them wore the five-pointed star of the Communists. There were three girls among them.

The lorry lumbered up the street, its occupants singing at the top of their voices. Downstairs a door was thrown open; the smell of freshly made coffee was wafted up to my balcony. I dressed and went down to Emiliano's bar. The manager, Emiliano's brother, had red-rimmed eyes, puffed with sleeplessness.

'It's a dog's life. Emiliano will have to come here and do his own work. Tomorrow I'm going to the front.'

The first customers drifted in, the night watchman, the Milicianos who had been on guard in the street, the baker's men, a driver.

'Salud!'

'Salud!'

A band of sparrows was pecking among the paving stones and hopping on the balcony rails. From a window high up came the call of a caged quail? 'Pal-pa-la – pal-pa-la!'

The street was deserted and flooded with peace.

9. Man Hunt

The work at our office was practically at a standstill. The firm was faced with the problem of whether to carry on in a void or to shut down altogether and risk being taken over by a workers' committee. For at that time, such committees had begun to take control of private firms, factories, and tenements in each case in which the owners were known to sympathize with the Right or had deserted their offices and buildings, either because they were guilty of conspiracy with the rebels or because they were afraid of staying on. In this emergency, the workers and employees set up committees which carried on the work; other committees were formed by trade unions, and imposed their control on firms the owners of which were suspect.

This movement was an act of self-defence against economic collapse. It developed without order or concerted action, and there were many cases of bad faith or crude theft. Yet with all its blemishes and errors, it prevented Madrid from being starved within one week, and it prevented the black market from flourishing.

Our chief decided that to maintain his unproductive business would be a lesser evil. It looked as though the situation would soon be settled by events outside his control. Already on July the 18th, one of our staff had disappeared and not even his family knew his whereabouts. Two of our men who had been officers reported to the War Ministry and were posted away from Madrid. Our two German employees had vanished. There were three men and four typists left, apart from myself and Carlitos, the office boy. We agreed to keep the office open from ten to twelve. There were no further difficulties, since the patent business had nothing to do with the war, involved nothing but papers, and did not arouse the interest of any of the workers' groups which assumed control of undertakings whose products had more immediate value.

My brother Rafael was the accountant of a perfumery wholesaler's. His chief was an intelligent autocrat hated by the whole staff; within twenty hours of the murder of Calvo Sotelo he had crossed the frontier together with his family. His staff took over the store, with the backing of the Communist Party to which the most active of the employees belonged, and tried to carry on the business on which their living depended. As I had time hanging on my hands, I often went there and observed how it worked; but the same thing happened in some hundreds of warehouses and stores all over Madrid. Simultaneously, each trade union and each party group began to organize its own militia. That was the time of the militia battalions with high-flown names apparently taken from penny dreadfuls, such as the 'Red Lions' or the 'Black Eagles'.

It was also the time of the vouchers.

One morning, two militiamen with rifles over their shoulders and the black-and-red scarf of the Anarchists wound round their throats turned up at my brother's store and presented to him, as the man in charge, the following voucher:

Valid for
        5000 safety razors
        5000 sticks of shaving soap
     100,000 razor blades
        5000 bottles of branded eau-de-Cologne
         10 50-litre flagons of barber's eau-de-Cologne
        1000 kilos of toilet soap

My brother refused to accept the voucher: 'I'm sorry, but I can't give you what you ask for. And by the way, whom do you want all this for?'

'Look at the stamp: the Anarchist Militia in the Círculo de Bellas Artes. . . . What do you mean, you can't let us have it? That's a joke.'

'No joke at all, pals. I wouldn't accept that kind of voucher unless it was endorsed by the War Ministry.'

'All right, then we'll take you with us.'

To be taken to the Círculo de Bellas Artes meant the risk of being found at dawn in the Casa de Campo, with one's neck shattered by a bullet. The two Milicianos were alone, while there were plenty of men with pistols in their pocket about in the store. My brother told the two to wait and rang up the command of the Anarchist Militias in the Círculo. They had not heard of the voucher and asked my brother to bring the two Milicianos and the voucher to them. There it turned out that the men had attempted a bold theft; the Anarchists shot them that night.

Yet vouchers which had to be accepted piled up on my brother's desk, papers which no one would ever redeem. The only money which reached the cashier came in payment for the scanty orders from tradesmen carrying on their business, but as no credit was granted any more, they bought nothing but goods whose sale was absolutely certain. Food began to be frighteningly scarce.

The trade unions which enforced the acceptance of their vouchers could not refuse to issue meal vouchers to their members. They had taken over many cafés and restaurants in the city; when a trade-union member wanted a meal, he was given a stamped voucher from his organization and went to one of its restaurants. Meal vouchers became valid tender when wages began to peter out. At first, people squeezed in at small café tables as best they could. Then the tables were pushed together in the middle of the room and converted into long mess tables. People sat down next to each other as they arrived, though they tried to snatch a seat near the kitchen door. Meals were distributed at one o'clock sharp. There was no bread; many people brought a roll or a chunk of bread along in their pockets. A stream of women and children passed through, all coming to carry their food home in a pot tied into a napkin or large handkerchief. The menu was based on rice and potatoes boiled with meat, the ration was practically unlimited. Albacete was in the hands of the Government, so that communications with Valencia were safe, and Valencia poured the rice and potatoes into Madrid, where all supplies were taken over by the trade unions. Each organization seized as much as possible and shared the food out among the communal restaurants under its control. Empty churches served as storehouses. The smell of a badly kept grocer's shop streamed out into the streets from wide-open church doors.

In my brother's office the staff distributed the money among themselves at the end of the month, and the meal vouchers every day. But their stock of perfumery goods was rapidly dwindling. They were beginning to feel desperate.

The Government was powerless in the face of the chaos. There was no group which would accept orders from it.

The political parties were subdivided into their local branches, the trade unions into trade groups as well as local branches. Each of the groups and branches set up its own communal feeding centre, its own supply service and storehouse, its own militia battalion, its own police, its own prison, its own executioners, and a special place for its executions. They all made propaganda to attract new members, except for the UGT. The walls of Madrid were covered with appeals: 'Join the CNT'. 'Join the Communist Party'. 'Join the POUM'. The Republicans pure and simple did not count. People flocked to the centres of the organizations, let themselves be introduced by one or two old members, and obtained a membership card.

Fascists found this a useful subterfuge. They selected the groups which were least strict in their requirements and joined in large numbers. Some people paid heavily for a membership card antedated by two or three years. With this backing, Fascists would commandeer their own cars and use them to save their friends and to kill off their enemies. Criminals found cover by the same method. They, too, would form their own police and proceed to rob and kill with impunity. No one was safe. Consulates and embassies opened their gates to refugees; some of them set up refuges on a grand scale, ran them as luxury hotels and bought whole houses for the purpose.

Side by side with all that chaos, misery, and cowardice, the other thing which was alive behind the bombastic names of Red Lions and Black Eagles began to assume shape. The excursions to the Sierra were stopped. Positions were established in the hills. Loyal officers set out to mould that embryo of an army. Every group could create a militia battalion, but now the arms, the few arms available, were in the hands of the War Ministry; they were distributed to the volunteer militias, but they in turn had to accept the Ministry's rule in order to exist. At the same time, parties and trade unions competed in showing each other a model of discipline and bravery.

The Rebel Army under General Mola was thrown back behind

Villalba; Toledo was retaken; Saragossa was attacked through the province of Huesca; a force was landed in the Balearics; Ceuta was raided.

But there was still no cohesion, although there was plenty of enthusiasm. Party pride seemed stronger than the feeling of common defence. A victory of an Anarchist battalion was paraded in the face of the Communists; a victory of a Communist unit was secretly lamented by the others. The defeat of a battalion was turned into ridicule for the political group to which it belonged. This strengthened the fighting spirit of the individual units, but also created a hotbed of mutual resentment damaging the military operations as a whole and circumventing a unified command.

I had gone to see Antonio, the Communist, and Carlos Rubiera, the Socialist. I told Antonio that I wanted to work, but refused to join a party militia; the leaders of the Clerical Workers' Union, which I had helped to found together with Rubiera five years earlier, told me that I might be useful in helping to organize the Clerical Workers' Battalion. I tackled the task with something like despair. I doubted the response of the white-collar workers.

They allotted us a commandeered house with a tennis court in the aristocratic Barrio de Salamanca. Fifty volunteers started their military training on that court. We had our theoretical instruction in the enormous marble hall with its pretentious Doric columns; there we ranged benches taken from a near-by school, installed a dais, a huge blackboard and a map of Spain. The War Ministry let us have two dozen rifles and one spare cartridge case per rifle.

I made them form platoons on the tennis court and began to lecture them on the handling of a rifle. Before me I had a double file of anaemic faces perched on starched collars, with a sprinkling of coarser heads topping blouses or braided, tight-fitting livery coats; most of my volunteers were clerks, but a few were office boys and messengers. Some were very young and some old. Many had spectacles which made their eyes glitter and their faces look nervous.

After the first two minutes of my instruction one of the recruits stepped out of the file.

'Now look here, all that's stuff and nonsense. The only thing we need to know is how to shoot. Then give us a rifle and we'll march to wherever we have to. I haven't come here to play at soldiers.'

I ordered them to fall out, took them to the hall and stepped on to the platform.

'Now, you all want a rifle and you all want to go to the front to fire off your rifle and to kill Fascists. But none of you wants to go through the military instruction. Now, suppose I give a rifle to every one of you this moment, pack you into a couple of lorries and place you on the crest of Sierra – in face of Mola's army, with its officers and sergeants who are used to giving commands, and its soldiers who are used to obeying orders and who know what each order means. What would you do? Each of you would run about by himself and fire off bullets, I suppose. Do you think the men you would have to face are just rabbits? And even if you went shooting rabbits in a party of ten or twelve, you'd have to know how to do it if you didn't want to shoot each other.'

We went back to the tennis court and continued the instruction. Many times I was interrupted when someone exclaimed: 'We're wasting our time – anybody knows how to throw himself down when he's got to!' It was the same with each new batch of volunteers. But slowly a unit began to emerge, although it still had nothing but two dozen rifles passed from platoon to platoon. It was the beginning of the Battalion *La Pluma*, The Pen.

In those days, Angel practically lived in my flat. Since his wife had gone away, he helped Aurelia with the house, the children, and the shopping, as he had done in the first weeks of our acquaintanceship. He knew so many people in the quarter in which he had been born and bred that he always found something for our meals. One day he turned up pushing a wheelbarrow with two sacks of potatoes, and followed by a train of women. He stopped before the door of our house and cried:

'Make a queue, please.'

The women obediently stepped into line, and Angel produced a scale and weights out of thin air, by a conjurer's trick.

'Two pounds each, my girls, and mind no one comes twice!'

When the potatoes in the first sack had disappeared, Angel opened the second sack and swept the queue with a glance.

'Friends, I need potatoes myself. These here are for me.' He weighed out twenty pounds and put them in the first sack. 'And now, let's get rid of what's left.'

' Angel went for potatoes to the market of Mataderos where the goods trains were unloaded. His quick tongue always secured him the friendship of the man in charge of the distribution to the tradesmen. He was a street vendor himself, he would say; that was what he did for his living, and the poor people of El Avapiés got something to eat as well. 'Now look, pal. Here you are giving the potatoes to a shopkeeper of the Barrio de Salamanca, so that he can feed the rich and the Fascists. Won't you let me have two sacks?' Then he would invite the man to a cup of coffee and cognac early in the morning and get his two sacks. Once the Anarchists from a branch in the neighbouring street wanted to expropriate the two sacks of potatoes, but the women almost rioted against them, and Angel obtained the protection of the Anarchists' leaders.

Then came days when even Angel found no potatoes, because no potatoes reached Madrid. Aurelia took the children to her parents. I was about to leave the flat, when Angel said: 'If you'll come to my room with me, I'll go along with you. I've nothing to do today.'

I accompanied him to the Calle de Jesús y María. The street begins in the Plaza de Progreso, among the houses of the well-to-do people, and for a stretch of fifty yards the inhabitants of its old houses are small tradesmen and skilled workers. So far the street is paved with big square porphyry blocks. Then it narrows down and changes its face. The paving is made of sharp-edged pebbles, the houses are low, squalid, and rickety, the people who live in them are very poor workers and prostitutes. The tarts lounge in the open doors and fill the street with their quarrels.

Angel lived on the ground floor of a small tenement house stuck between two brothels. His flat was a single big room divided into a bedroom, dining room, and kitchen by thin partition walls. There was nothing in the bedroom but a double bed and a night table. The kitchen was half the size of the bedroom. Light and air entered through the door and through a barred window which opened on to a courtyard three yards square, containing the lavatory for all the tenants of the ground floor and the water tap for the whole house.

The room, now deserted, smelled of mildew and urine. I waited for Angel while he changed in the bedroom.

Suddenly, an explosion shook the house. Angel came out, still struggling into his coat. Piercing cries and the patter of feet sounded outside. Angel and I went out into the street. People were running wildly. A few yards away, several women were lying on the ground and shrieking. One of them was dragging herself along on a belly torn to bleeding tatters. The walls of the houses and the paving stones were spattered with blood. Then we were all running towards the injured.

In the last house of the wide stretch of the street was a clinic for nursing mothers. At that hour there had been a queue of women, most of them carrying a child, waiting for the distribution of milk. A few yards further down, prostitutes had been following their trade. A bomb had fallen in the middle of the street and sprayed the mothers and the street walkers. A woman propped up on her bleeding arm stump gave a scream and let herself drop heavily. Near me was a bundle of petticoats with a leg sticking out, bent at an impossible angle over a swollen belly. My head was swimming. I vomited into the gutter. A militiaman beside me cursed and was sick. Then he began to tremble and broke out into spasmodic laughter. Someone gave me a glass of neat brandy and I poured it down my throat. Angel had disappeared. Some men were busy picking up the wounded and the dead and carrying them into the clinic. A man stuck his head out of the gate, white hair and spectacles over a blood-stained surgeon's overall, stamped his foot, and yelled: 'No more room! Take them to Encomienda!'

Shrieks sounded from the Plaza del Progreso. Angel was beside me, his coat and hands splashed with blood.

'Another bomb in the Plaza del Progreso!'

Groups of people came running down the street in frenzied fear, pairs of men carrying someone between them, women with children in their arms, all screaming and shrieking. I saw nothing but arms and legs and bloodstains in motion, and the street rocked before my eyes.

'Go to Encomienda! There's been one here too.'

The whirling mass of arms and legs disappeared through the Calle de Esgrima.

We went back to Angel's flat and washed. Angel changed again. When we came out of the house, the neighbours told us that a plane had flown low over Madrid from north to south, dropping bombs all along its course. It had left a trail of blood from the Puerta de Toledo to Cuatro Caminos. By accident or because the pilot guided himself by the open spaces, most of the bombs had fallen in public squares and many children had been hit.

That was on the 7th of August 1936. That evening and that night, Fascists were firing from windows and from skylights. Many hundreds were arrested. There were mass executions of suspects during the night.

Antonio sent for me while I was at home in the evening. The local branch of the Communist Party was organizing pickets to paint the street lamps blue and to see to the blackout. Rafael, Angel, and I went. We worked in small groups, each protected by two armed Milicianos; but it was an almost hopeless task to improvise a blackout in August, in Madrid. Shuttered houses were stifling. It was impossible to stay in any public place with the shutters closed. We had to compromise. People were to avoid the rooms facing on to the street and stay in the inner rooms, using only candles. It was easy to paint the street lamps blue, with a mixture of water, aniline dye, and plaster; only a few tenuous, white rays filtered through. We turned off every other lamp.

The streets looked ghostly in our wake, night black, with white dots on the pavements and blue, sickly blobs of light a little higher up in the dark. Sometimes the front of a house was lighted by the fugitive glow of a candle carried through a room in the house opposite, which turned a balcony into a yellow square of light, streaked by the black lines of the railing, and leaped distorted along the walls. The people thronged the streets as they did every night, but they were only half visible in the penumbra, shapeless black bulks from which voices came and, at intervals, the dazzling spark of a lighter or the little red glow from a cigarette outlining a few heads.

Some lorries arrived carrying Milicianos returning from the Sierra and from Toledo. Their headlights were switched on; the crowds caught in their beams looked livid and naked. The cry went up: 'The lights – turn out the lights!'

Brakes screeched, and the lorries rolled slowly on amid the sound of breaking chairs and pitchers. The red light of the rear lamps glowed like a bloodshot eye. In the darkness it was as though nightmare monsters were panting there, about to spring.

By midnight the whole quarter lay in deep shadow. In the Calle de la Primavera we stopped under a street lamp which had been forgotten. One of us climbed up, while another reached him the brush soaked in blue dye. A shot cracked, a bullet ricocheted on the wall above the lamp. Somebody had shot at us from one of the houses opposite. The people lounging in the street took refuge in doorways. We marched out the tenants of the four houses from which the shot might have come. The concierge and neighbours identified them one by one. Then we weeded out those who had been in the street from the others, and started to search each flat in turn. All the tenants surged after us and asked us to go into their flats with them; they wanted to clear themselves, and at the same time they were afraid that a stranger might have hidden in their rooms. We searched through attics and lofts full of cobwebs and old rags, we climbed up and down stairs, we caught dust and dirt on our clothes and banged against rafters and invisible nails. At four in the morning we had finished; we were filthy and sleepy, it was broad daylight, but we had not found the sniper. Somebody had brought a huge pitcher filled with steaming coffee and a bottle of brandy. We drank greedily.

One of the men said: 'That bird's saved his skin.' As though in answer, Angel exclaimed: 'Let's go to Mataderos and see the ones who were polished off this time.'

At first I refused to go, and then I suddenly gave in. It was easier. I dug my fist into Angel's ribs and said to him: 'You're a brute – after what we saw yesterday afternoon, too!'

'God save us – come along, then you'll get rid of the bitter taste of seeing those mangled kids yesterday. Do you remember the woman with child, who had her leg doubled up on her navel? Well, she was still alive and she gave birth in the clinic. Then she died. A boy, it was. Nobody in the whole quarter knows her.'

The executions had attracted far more people than I would have thought possible. Families with their children, excited and still drowsy with sleep, and militiamen with their girls were walking along the Paseo de las Delicias, all in the same direction. Requisitioned cars and lorries were passing by. Crowds and cars had collected at the entrance to the vegetable market and the slaughterhouses at the Glorieta. While carts and trucks with green vegetables came and went, militia pickets on duty meandered round and asked anyone who caught their fancy for his papers.

Behind the slaughterhouses a long brick wall and an avenue with stunted little trees, not yet rooted in the sandy soil under that ruthless sun, run along the river. The landscape is arid and cold with the chill of the cemented canal, of sand, and of dry, yellow tufts of grass.

The corpses lay between the little trees. The sightseers ambled from one to the other and made humorous remarks; a pitying comment might have provoked suspicion.

I had expected the bodies. Their sight did not shake me. There were about twenty of them. They were not mangled. I had seen far worse in Morocco and on the day before. But I was shaken by the collective brutality and cowardice of the spectators.

Vans which belonged to the City of Madrid arrived to collect the corpses. One of the drivers said: 'Now they're going to water the place and make it nice and spruce for tonight.' He chuckled. It rang like fear.

Somebody gave us a lift back to the Plaza de Antón Martín. We entered Emiliano's bar to have our breakfast. Sebastian, the concierge at Number Seven, was there with a rifle leaning behind him. He left his coffee when he saw us and started to explain with extravagant gestures: 'What a night – I'm dead beat! I've accounted for eleven.'

Angel asked: 'What is it you've done? Where have you been?'

'In the Pradera de San Isidro. I went with lads of my union and we took some Fascists with us. Then friends from other groups turned up and we had to lend them a hand. I believe we've got rid of more than a hundred this time.'

I felt hollow in the pit of my stomach. Here was somebody whom I had known almost since I was a child. I knew him as a cheerful, industrious man who was fond of his children and of other people's children; doubtless rather crude, with little brains, but all the same honest and forthright. Here he was turned into an assassin.

'But Sebastian – who dragged you' – I used the formal pronoun *usted* instead of the customary, familiar *tú* – 'who in the world has dragged you into such things.'

He looked at me out of shame-filled eyes.

'Oh well, Don Arturo' – he did not dare to speak to me in the way he had spoken for over twenty years – 'you're not going to start with sentimentalities, I hope. We must make an end of all those Fascist swine.'

'That's not what I was asking you. I want to know who dragged you into these doings.'

'Nobody.'

'Then why are you doing it?'

'Well, someone has to.'

I said nothing and he began to stammer.

'The truth is . . . the truth is, to tell you the truth in confidence . . . it's like this. You know I found work a year or so ago with a recommendation from the CEDA, which my landlord got for me. And after the February elections I didn't need their scrap of paper any more and went back to my own union, of course. The boys all pulled my leg because I had belonged to the CEDA, and because they said I had turned a reactionary, and so on. Naturally I told them I was as good a revolutionary as they. Then one day they took some Fascists for a ride and one of our boys said to me: "Now then, up with you, come on, as you're always talking of killing Fascists." And you can imagine the rest. I was between the devil and the deep sea, because it was either the one or the other, either I had to finish off one of those poor devils, or the lads would have bumped me off. Well, since then I've simply been going there, and they tell me when there's something doing.'

He stopped and pondered, and then shook his head slowly.

'The worst of it is, you know, that I'm beginning to like it.'

He stood there with a drooping head. It was repulsive and pitiful. Emiliano's brother gulped down a glass of brandy and swore. I swore too. Then I said:

'Sebastian, I've known you all my life, and I used to respect you.

But now, I tell you – and you can denounce me on the spot – that I won't ever speak to you again.'

Sebastian lifted the eyes of a whipped dog, full of water. Emiliano's brother blasphemed and smashed his empty glass on the marble slab:

'Get out!'

The man walked out meekly, with bowed shoulders. None of us saw him again, and days later we heard that he had gone to the front. He was killed by a bullet, in an attic in front of the Alcazar of Toledo.

At eleven o'clock that morning, a middle-aged woman in black came to see me in the office. She was tearful and agitated: 'I'm Don Pedro's sister. They arrested him this morning. I've come to you because he told me to get in touch with you if anything happened. . . . I don't know where they've taken him. I only know that the men who came for him were Communists and took him away in a car.'

I went to Antonio and explained the case. 'If I were you, I wouldn't interfere in this mess,' he said. 'From what you tell me he's a Rightist and known as such. So no one can help him.'

'All right, maybe we can't save him, but we must try, and you've got to help me try.'

'I'll help you to find him if it's true that our people have arrested him, but I won't interfere in any other way. I've got enough unpleasantness with these matters as it is.'

We found out to which tribunal Don Pedro had been taken, and went there together. The men in charge let us see the denunciation. Whoever had written it knew the Ministry inside out; it described in great detail how Don Pedro had behaved on the day of Calvo Sotelo's assassination, explained his religious creed and stated that he had a private chapel in his house and kept a priest in hiding there. The denunciation ended with the statement that he was a rich man and possessed a numismatic collection of considerable value.

'You see, there's nothing to be done,' said the man who showed us the papers. 'Tomorrow we're going to take him for a ride.'

I took a deep breath and said: 'You accuse him of belonging to the

Right. He does. It is also true that he is a practising Catholic and a rich man, if that's an offence, and that he has a collection of antique gold coins. But I don't think that's a crime.'

'It isn't. We know that the fellow who denounced him is a son of a bitch who only put in that bit about the collection so as to make us go for the old man. Don't you worry. We may take him for a ride, but we aren't thieves.'

'I know, or I wouldn't be working with the Party. But as you see, the only concrete thing against him is the story about the priest he's hiding. It doesn't surprise me of the man. I believe he would be capable of hiding me too if the Fascists were after me. But tell me, has the priest taken active part in the rising?'

'I don't think so. He's just a priest of San Ginés who's got the jitters and gone into a burrow like a rabbit, but I don't believe he's any good for a man's job any more, he's over seventy.'

'Then you must admit that it wasn't a crime to hide him. And now I'm going to tell you another thing the man you've arrested has done.' I told them the story of Don Pedro and the consumptive clerk. 'It would be a crime to execute a man who had acted like that,' I ended.

'I can't do anything about it, my lad. What you can do, if you like, is to stand surety for his good faith yourself. The other members of our tribunal will see whether they find it a strong enough guarantee. But I would advise you not to do it, because we might just as easily have to lock you up yourself.'

Don Pedro was set free that afternoon. I went again to see Antonio and reported the fact to him.

'I knew it. They asked me plenty of questions about you. And apparently they couldn't find anything concrete against the old man. It's a pity that we can't investigate every single case in the same way, but it's quite impossible, I assure you.'

He stopped and went on after a long pause: 'You know I'm counsel for the defence on one of the tribunals? Come with me this afternoon, you can stay as a witness. We must finish half a dozen cases tonight. I personally believe that the Government ought to take the whole thing into its own hands. On the day of the bombing, the tribunals didn't even sit and pass sentence, everyone who was brought in was shot, and that was that. The people wouldn't listen to reason. The same thing happened when Badajoz was taken by the Fascists and our people were slaughtered in the bull-ring there. Before that you could straighten out some of the cases, but now it's getting more and more difficult every day. The worst thing about this job I've taken on is that, in the long run, one is drawing suspicion on oneself by defending others and trying to see that things are done decently. I think I'll chuck it up and let them do their dirty work alone.'

He took me to one of the most popular churches in Madrid, which had been turned into a prison and a tribunal. The offices had been installed in the priest's house, the prison in the crypt. The church stood in a small, dingy street, but the priest's old, two-storey house was embedded in high, modern buildings in one of the big streets of the town. We entered a narrow doorway and walked through a long corridor with stone walls and stone floor, dark, dank, and oppressive. Then the corridor turned at a right angle, and we stood in the entrance to a wide, flagged courtyard with two carpets of well-tended lawn in the middle and potted flowers along the walls. Before us was the huge coloured glass window in the back wall of the church. The sun shone on the bits of glass in their leaden frames and made them glint. Sparks of blue, red, green, and purple fell on flagstones, grass and walls, and the flagstones were mottled with green and the lawn with deep purple. While we walked past, each piece of glass in turn sent out a flash of its own pure colour. There was an age-old grapevine covering the south wall with its green leaves and golden-green grapes, and a flock of sparrows which did not scatter at our steps.

The militiamen on sentry duty sat on canvas chairs in the shade, smoking and contemplating the birds.

Antonio and I climbed a narrow stairway and found ourselves in a room, which must have been the parish priest's. A missal lay open on a lectern near the balcony. Half of its left page was covered by a huge gilt Q fringed with red arabesques. The book was printed in a clear, old letterpress and the first letter of each chapter and each verse was painted by hand. The initials of the chapters were gilded, the initals of the verses were smaller and painted only in red. A voice at my back said: 'It is prohibited to take away the prayer book.' A Miliciano was sitting in the upholstered leather armchair behind an old, massive desk covered with green cloth. He was a boy of twenty-three or so, strong, with broad shoulders, a broad grin and broad, milk-white teeth.

'You wouldn't believe how many people are after that book. But it looks pretty here, don't you think? One of our comrades can sing Mass and sometimes he does it for us.'

While we were chatting, another man entered, in the forties, with a fierce moustache, black and crooked teeth and lively grey eyes. His *Salud* sounded more like the growl of a dog than like a salute, and he started at once to swear, displaying an inexhaustible vocabulary of blasphemies. When he had vented his bad temper he dropped heavily into a chair and stared at us.

'Well,' he said after a while, 'today we'll liquidate all the Fascists we've got here. A pity it's only half a dozen, I'd prefer six dozen.'

'What's bitten you today, Little Paws?' asked the young Miliciano.

I looked at the older man's hands. They were huge, with knotted fingers, and broad, chipped nails like spades, rimmed with black.

'You can call me Little Paws as much as you like, but if I get hold of one of those dirty dogs today and smack his face, his head will fly off its socket. Do you know whom we found this morning in the meadow when we counted up? Lucio, the milkman, as cold as my grandfather in his grave. They shot him in the neck and the bullet came out through his Adam's apple. You can imagine the row. One of our oldest Party comrades, turned to cold meat under our very noses! They stuck one those little rubber balls for kids into his mouth so that he shouldn't crack a joke. And for all I know, we rubbed him out ourselves, because we helped out some other comrades when they came with their lot, and we didn't know them. Somebody's playing tricks on us. We went to see Lucio's mother and she told us that last evening three comrades had come to fetch him in a Party car. She must have seen something in our faces, because she insisted we should tell her what had happened. And so we told her, and I won't say any more about it. Now we've got to warn all our comrades to be on their guard and not fall into a trap, and we must try and catch out the others. What have you got there?'

'Three new-comers.'

'That's not much. All right, let's settle yesterday's lot.'

The young Miliciano, Little Paws and a third taciturn man constituted themselves a People's Tribunal, with Antonio as counsel for the defence. Two Milicianos brought in the first prisoner, a twenty-year-old boy, his elegant suit dirty with dust and cobwebs and his eyelids reddened.

'Come nearer, my fine bird, we won't eat you,' Little Paws jeered at him.

The militiaman in the armchair took a list from the desk and read out the name and the details. The accused belonged to Falange; several comrades had seen him selling Fascist newspapers, and on two occasions he had taken part in street fights. When he was arrested, a lead bludgeon, a pistol, and a Falange membership card were found on him.

'What have you got to say for yourself?' the judge in the chair asked.

'Nothing. I've had bad luck.' The prisoner fell back into a defiant silence, his head bent, his hands rubbing against each other. Little Paws leaned forward from his chair:

'All right. Take him away and bring the next one.'

When we were alone, the judge asked: 'Are we all agreed?'

The three of them and Antonio all answered in the affirmative; the Fascist would be taken out and shot that night.

The next to be brought in was a grey-haired man near the fifties, his face distorted by fear. Before the judge began to speak, he said:

'You're going to kill me, but I'm an honest man. I've worked all my life and I've earned everything I possess by my own labour. I've never mixed in politics.'

Little Paws rose with a threatening movement, and for an instant I thought he was going to hit the man. 'You shut up, you mangy cur!'

The judge searched among the papers. There was a wallet among them, which Antonio grasped and searched. The judge said:

'Be quiet, Little Paws. . . . We don't kill anyone here if it isn't necessary. But you've got to explain a few things. We have a concrete denunciation; it states that you're a bigoted clerical.'

'I'm a Catholic, but that's no crime. There are priests who are Republicans.'

'That's true, there are some – though I wouldn't trust them an inch. But the denunciation says that you've given money to the CEDA.'

'That's a lie.'

'Thirdly, one of your nephews who often comes to stay in your house is a Falangist, and one of the worst at that.'

'I won't deny it. But what have I got to do with it? Haven't any of you a relative who belongs to the Right?'

Antonio had been checking and comparing papers. Now he called me to him while the accused man went on explaining that he had a shop in the Calle de la Concepción Gerónima, that he never left his shop, that he never mixed in politics. . . .

Antonio silently handed me two papers, one the denunciation, the other an IOU for ten thousand pesetas, lapsed months before. 'The same handwriting,' I whispered. Antonio nodded. 'That's why I wanted you to look at them!' He turned round and interrupted the prisoner in his stream of words:

'Explain this.' He held out the IOU.

'But there's nothing to explain about it, it hasn't anything to do with politics. I loaned the money to an old friend of mine who was in difficulties. I hoped it would help him to get out of them, but it didn't work. He's a rolling stone, and he just spent it. I forgot about the IOU, I simply happened to have it in my pocketbook with the other papers.'

'We must check up on it. What's your friend's address?'

When he had given it, Antonio told the two Milicianos to take the prisoner out of the room. Then he put the two papers on the desk side by side.

'We must clear up this story. We must get that other fellow here at once. You know I'm dead against those anonymous denunciations. If someone has something to denounce, let him come and do it face to face. As it is, we're liquidating people who haven't done anything, or who are just bigoted, and some who are just fools.'

The young judge nodded, Little Paws muttered something. While they waited for the denouncer to arrive, they proceeded with the other prisoners. Three were sentenced to death in the half-hour's interval. Then two militiamen brought in the man whose address the prisoner had given. He was still young, thin, with a tired face, his hands and legs trembling. Antonio showed him the anonymous letter at once.

'You wrote this, didn't you?'

The man stuttered: 'Yes . . . yes . . . I'm a good Republican, I'm one of your people . . .' Then his voice gained a little firmness: 'That man is a dangerous Fascist, brothers.'

'Now, then, we're not your brothers or anything of the sort. They didn't feed me out of the same trough as you,' growled Little Paws.

Antonio spread out the IOU and asked:

'And this paper here – brother – won't you tell us what it means?'

The man could not speak. He trembled and shook. Antonio sent the guard for the prisoner and waited until the two stood facing each other. Then he said: 'Well – here you have the man who denounced you.'

'You, Juán – why? What have you got against me? You aren't political either. And I have been like a father to you. There must be a mistake somewhere, gentlemen. But, let me see – this is your writing —' He suddenly screamed, shaking the other by the arm: 'Answer me!'

The denouncer lifted a pallid face with bluish lips which quivered helplessly. The other let go his arm and stared at us. Nobody spoke. Then Little Paws rose and let his hand fall on the shoulder of the denouncer, who jumped, and said: 'That settles you, friend.'

'What are you going to do to him?' asked the older prisoner.

'Nothing. A bullet through the head, that's all,' said Little Paws. 'This swine's blood must be blacker than the priest's frock.' He jerked his thumb towards the silken cassock hanging behind the door.

The judge got up. 'Well now, this affair is cleared up, you are free. And this other man stays here.'

'But you can't kill him for this. After all, it's me he has denounced, and I forgive him as I hope God will forgive me.'

'That's our affair, don't worry.'

'But no, no, it's my affair. I can't go away from here before you give me your word that nothing is going to happen to him.'

'Now look here, don't be a damn' fool, and get out of here,' said Little Paws. 'You caught us in a soft hour, now don't try to make us turn back, because then we might take you both for a ride. Hey, you there, take that man away and lock him up.'

The two Milicianos led the denouncer away, but the man he had denounced refused to go. He implored and begged the tribunal and in the end knelt down.

'I beg you, gentlemen – for the sake of your own mothers – of your children – of whatever you love in the world! I would never be free from remorse all my life. . . .'

'This fellow must have been to the theatre more often than was good for him,' shouted Little Paws. He took him by the elbow and lifted him from his knees without visible effort. 'Now be off with you, go home and say a paternoster if you like, and leave us alone.'

I stood on the balcony and saw the man stumbling down the street. A cluster of people from the next house stared at him, then stared at the rectory door, and whispered among themselves. An elderly woman cried after him: 'Got out by the skin of your teeth, eh?'

The man glared at her as though he were drunk.

The sixth prisoner was a coal merchant from the same street, a primitive man of tremendous physical strength, with a brutal, bloated face. The judge snapped at him: 'So you've been paying money to Gil Robles – to the CEDA – have you?'

'Me?' The coalman opened his bleary eyes. 'And you've dragged me here to tell me that? I've got nothing to do with that cur. I'm here because somebody's out for my blood. But I've nothing to do with that lousy fellow. I'm an old Republican. By this cross!' He blew a loud kiss on his crossed thumbs, black as cinder. The judge laid a receipt on the desk. 'Then what's this?'

The coalman took it between his huge fingers and began to spell out: 'Confederación Española de Derechas Autónomas – CEDA? – what the hell – ten pesetas.' He gaped at us. 'I don't know what to say. I did pay them. But to tell you the truth, you see, a poor fellow like me isn't much good at books and so on, and so when I saw all those stamps and that bit about Confederation, I thought "It's the insurance." And now it looks as if those dirty swine had stolen two duros out of my pocket and got me into the soup as well.'

'Do you realize that we can shoot you for paying money to the CEDA?'

'Me? Damnation! After they've stolen my money, too? You're crazy, the lot of you.'

Little Paws hit him in the ribs so that he swivelled round and faced him. 'You there – look me in the eyes and answer: Did you or did you not know that the money was for the CEDA?'

'Hell, how often have I got to tell you the same thing over again? If I say so, then it is so, gospel truth. They've diddled me out of those two duros, as sure as my name's Pedro. May God grant that they have to spend it on the doctor's bill.'

'You speak of God quite a lot,' grumbled Little Paws.

'As it comes, lad. It's useful to have Him at hand so that you can swear at Him sometimes, and then He sometimes helps you out.'

When the coalman was told that he was free, he said: 'I knew it anyhow. The wife started weeping like a waterfall when your boys came to fetch me, but I told her you wouldn't take me for a ride. Not me. The whole quarter's known me for the last twenty years, and they can tell you whether anybody's ever seen me mixed up with the priests. I was the first to vote for the Republic. Never mind, boys, anybody can put his foot in it from time to time. Come along and have a drink on me now!'

We heard him lumbering down the creaking stairs.

'That's all for today,' said the judge.

'You've put a fast one over on me – two out of six have got away. But at least we've got that stool pigeon left. I'll settle accounts with him tonight,' said Little Paws.

We walked through the big, cool, stone nave of the church, through pools of deep shadow and swathes of coloured light. Someone was singing a flamenco song high up in the dusk; metal tinkled. A Miliciano perched on the top of the High Altar was wrenching off brass candelabra and throwing them down into the hands of another who stood at the altar's foot and dropped each piece on a mountain of metal scraps. 'That's all for cartridge shells,' said Antonio.

The wood of the altars was bare and ugly. The crippled images lying on the ground had lost their respectability. Old, worm-eaten wooden statues leered with noseless faces. Plaster-covered stuffing stuck out from many-coloured robes. From the gilt screen in front of the High Altar hung a collection box, its lid secured with a big lock and smashed by a hammer blow. The Child Jesus lay on one of the altar steps, a sky-blue ball spangled with silver stars, dangling a pair of minute feet and topped by a two-pronged stick. One of the prongs ended in the papier-mâché head of a fair-haired child with blue eyes, the other in a chubby, pink hand, its thumb doubled on the palm, the four other fingers sticking out rigidly. The tunic was missing, but a shabby coat was wrapped round the stick and turned it into a scarecrow, with the blonde head hanging sideways and smiling archly.

'Put a cigarette in his mouth, then he'll look like a good proletarian,' the Miliciano shouted from the height of the altar. 'Imagine all the money they got out of the silly, bigoted old women with the help of the little angel! But if one of them had lifted the petticoats and seen that broomstick underneath, she would have fainted, don't you think?'

I thought of the stage-setting in the Church of San Martín as I used to see it when I was a boy: the image taken out of its niche on the eve of the Saint's Day; the rural landscape rigged up with lamps hidden behind boards and empty sardine boxes loaned by the fishmonger of the Calle de la Luna; the priest cursing the smell, while the pious women of the parish covered up those boxes with rugs and sheets in the sacristy; scarlet, gold-studded cloth hoisted on to the High Altar, the holes gnawed by mice in the course of the years disappearing in its rich folds; the trappings taken down at the end of the Novena, in a shower of dust and cobwebs, while the Saint's image lolled on the floor like the wax doll in an empty shop window.

Bit by bit, I recognized the pieces of scenery in the despoiled church before me. Here were the ladders of worm-eaten pinewood, which had been blazing with votive candles. Here was the shrine, open and void. It smelled of rancid wax and crumbling wood. The empty space in the golden arch where the Child Jesus had been was festooned with spiders' webs.

Yet above the broken trumpery rose the inaccessible stone pillars and cross-vaults, dark with age and smoke. The organ towered across the nave and aisles. Late sunlight filtered through the windows in the slender lantern of the dome.

10. Menace

The Battalion *La Pluma*, the battalion of the penpushers, was organized; it had its officers and formations which took over the new recruits; it had still no arms and no equipment. Gregorio, one of my office colleagues, was made its captain, mainly because his experience in dealing with Ministry officials seemed to make him particularly fit for negotiations with the War Ministry. He went there day after day, came back with empty hands and exclaimed that only the Anarchists were able to squeeze arms out of the Ministry's depots, because they called the officers Fascists and traitors and threatened them with being taken for a ride if they did not give them arms.

My own work as organizer and instructor was over. I had nothing to do. The couple of hours at the office were nothing. I hated having to go round Madrid as did so many thousand others, raising a clenched fist when a car filled with Milicianos passed, shouting 'Long live' or 'Down with' together with the crowd, saluting the body of fallen militiamen carried past under a red shroud, and being afraid of an error, a denunciation, a sniper's bullet.

In Serafín's tavern we were talking of a man who had fallen in Toledo. Serafín asked me whether I had known him. 'Since he was so high,' I said and raised my flat hand to indicate the height of a young boy. Two minutes later a couple of armed militiamen entered, with a little man at their heels, who pointed me out to them. The Milicianos took me by one arm each and said: 'Come along.' It was lucky that I was surrounded by people who had known me all my life. In the course of the explanations it emerged that the little man had denounced me as having given the Fascist salute.

One morning, Navarro, our draftsman, came to me with a crazed face. His two sons had been arrested and taken to the Círculo de Bellas Artes; the younger one had come back at midnight, set free because he was not yet sixteen. He knew nothing about his brother's fate. Could I do anything? I went to Fuñi-Fuñi and discussed the case with him, but not hiding my opinion that it was hopeless, because the boy had been mixed in university brawls and in all probability wounded one of his adversaries. But we could at least attempt to find out his fate for certain.

Fuñi-Fuñi found it out. The student had been shot in the Casa de Campo during the previous night; the family could try to find and take away his body, but it might already be buried in a cemetery. I told the father. After this I did not see him for many days. Then I happened to go into the Tavern of the Portuguese, and there I found Navarro, drunk. He called me to his table and I sat down. We said nothing for a long while. Then he looked at me and said:

'What can I do, Barea? I don't belong to the Right, as you know. I belong to you. But your people have killed my son. What can I do?' He flung his face down on his crossed arms and sobbed. His shoulders heaved in jerks, as though someone were hitting him on the chin at regular intervals from under the marble table. I got up softly and left him.

Angel established himself as my bodyguard. 'You're much too trustful, and say just what comes into your mind to anybody,' he declared. 'Think of your row with Sebastian. If he takes it into his head to denounce you to his gang they'll bump you off.' He went with me to the office in the mornings and waited patiently in the doorway until I came out. When I was talking to somebody he kept out of sight, but not out of reach of my voice. Whenever I tried to put him off, he would say: 'I won't go. You look too much like a Señorito, someone will have a go at you some day. But not while Angelito is with you.'

In desperation I took Angel along when I visited Antonio another time to see whether he could not give me something useful to do. In one of the rooms of the Party Secretariat I saw thousands of books dumped on the floor. 'The boys in the Sierra have asked for books, and so we've cleared out the libraries of some of the Fascists,' said Antonio. 'Let me handle this for you,' I begged him. 'I don't think all these books are good reading for the Milicianos out there.' Nobody else seemed to bother, so I dived into the surf of books, together with Angel. There were some rare old editions which I salvaged, and text-books which were put aside and turned out to be very useful at a later stage. But after a week, when the books were classified, I was again left without anything to do.

Then I remembered the patent of a very simple hand grenade which had gone through my hands. Its inventor, Fausto, was an old mechanic whom I had come to know well. The ordnance factory at Toledo had just taken up its production when the insurrection broke out. This was the kind of weapon which was needed now. I saw Fausto and asked what had been done about his invention.

'I really don't know. The officers of the factory have all disappeared, and now they've got a workers' committee, and nobody knows anything about anything. I've been there.'

'Would you like to get things going?'

He was delighted, but sceptical. I spoke of the matter to Antonio, who had proved most accessible to me, and he in his turn sent me to see the Comandante Carlos of the 5th Regiment.

The Communist Party had taken the first big step towards the formation of an army by organizing the 5th Regiment, not as a loose militia, but as a closely knit and disciplined body. Volunteers flocked to it. The idea caught on among the masses outside the political groups, because it seemed something beyond party ambition and propaganda. In those late August days the 5th Regiment was already a myth, as well as a very concrete fact.

Its commander, Carlos, came from somewhere in Central Europe, I imagined, but he had lived in America for years and spoke excellent Spanish. I showed him the model of the grenade, explained its possibilities, and when I left he gave me an authorization to collect the several hundreds of grenades in stock in Toledo and to investigate the chances of resuming their production. He accompanied me through the vast building. I saw recruits drilling, who moved and acted like trained soldiers, and I said so, profoundly impressed, but Comandante Carlos shook his head discontentedly. He wanted to show me a workshop for hand grenades set up by Asturian miners; it did not belong to the 5th Regiment, but supplied all the fronts.

In the workshop, men and women were filling pieces of iron tubing with dynamite and fixing short fuses. We stumbled over dynamite cartridges, filled bombs and cigarette stubs in a hellish medley. I felt most uncomfortable.

'But, Carlos, this place is going to blow up any minute.'

'I can't do anything about it. They are free to do as they like. They're under no kind of discipline, and nobody will ever persuade them that they are crazy, because they have been handling dynamite all their lives and think they know everything there is to know about it.'

At eleven in the morning we left the workshop. At half past eleven an enormous explosion shook the district of Salamanca, and the hand-grenade workshop was wiped out.

A few days later, Fausto and I went to the ordnance factory in Toledo in a little car which the Communist Party had put at our disposal.

The city of Toledo was in Government hands, but the Alcazar was held by a strong force of cadets, Falangists, and Civil Guards with their families, under the command of General Moscardó. They had ample ammunition and food stocks, and the old fortress, with casemates scooped out of the living rock, defied the armament of the militia. The struggle had gone on since the beginning of the rebellion. The militia had occupied all the buildings which dominated the Alcazar and set up a battery outside the town on the other bank of the river Tajo. Several assaults had failed. At the time we went there, the Government had offered to pardon the rebels if they surrendered, and they had rejected the offer. There was talk of a new and final assault. There was also talk of the advance of an enemy column towards Toledo and Madrid. Oropesa had been taken by them.

When we arrived at the ordnance factory down in the valley, we knew only that a workers' committee had taken the plant under its control; but it became clear at once that there reigned an atmosphere of mutual distrust. Nobody knew anything, nobody was ready to make a decision. Fausto remembered in what part of the building the grenades were stored. We found them, but the man in charge said:

'You can't take them away without an order from the War Ministry, approved by the Workers' Committee.'

'Never mind, we'll settle that,' Fausto answered. 'But the main thing is that you should go on producing them.'

'Well, you see . . . it's like this: we do produce something.'

They were producing 'something' indeed, something which consumed material and justified the payment of wages. They had been producing thousands of screws needed for the grenade, and two workers at automatic lathes were continuing to produce them. Miles of steel wire had been turned into springs, and percussion pins were still being produced on a large scale, but none of the other parts of the grenade, not even the explosive charge.

'We had to shoot the explosives expert,' said the *Responsable*. 'For sabotage. He absolutely refused to give us explosives for rifle cartridges, so we confiscated his whole stock. But then the cartridges exploded. So we had to shoot him.'

'Of course, if you put mitramite, which is what was in stock here, into a rifle cartridge, it blows up the whole rifle,' said Fausto.

The man shrugged. 'I tell you, the cartridges exploded in the rifle, and that's sabotage.'

Before we went away, depressed and helpless, the man took us with a mysterious mien into a corner and showed us a switchboard. 'What do you think of that? If the Fascists come here we've prepared them a nice surprise. If you pushed down this lever now, not one of the workshops would be left. They're all mined, with a dynamite charge underneath. But that's a secret.

In the car Fausto said: 'I don't know whether to laugh or cry. We shall have to produce the thing in Madrid. Carlos might help. Let's have a look at Toledo.'

We were at the bottom of the sun-drenched valley. The Tajo purred where it flowed into the reservoir of the power plant. Poplars hemmed the path with their green and their shade, people were picnicking, drinking, and laughing in the river meadow. The towering rock of the town showed its tawny flanks flecked with tufted grass and cistus, and its crown of city walls. Far away on the other side of the river a cluster of men dispersed and revealed the outline of a toy cannon, at its muzzle a wad of cotton-wool smoke. Something went screeching through the air. Then came a dull thud followed by a second thud from behind the city walls on the crest of the hill. The echo of the two shots rumbled between the sheer rock walls of the gorge at Alcántara Bridge.

Now we could hear the crackle of rifle shots up in the town, but they sounded like squibs let loose on a fairground.

We went as far as the corner of the Zocodover, the market square of Toledo. Broken chairs, trees with their branches lopped off, twisted iron bars, the bandstand smashed, clothes and old papers scattered here and there, the fronts of the houses scarred, jagged glass splinters fringing the window frames, the balcony of a hotel swinging loose in the air. In the middle of the square was nobody, there seemed to be nothing but a silent void. Taking cover from the fire of the Alcazar in doorways and behind jutting corners, Milicianos and Shock Police in dark blue uniforms crouched in ridiculous positions, vociferating and gesticulating, letting off shots, shouting orders, blowing shrill whistles. Sometimes a puff of smoke, as though from a smoker sitting behind a window, was wafted out of the rosy, enigmatic façade of the Alcazar, but it was impossible to hear the sound of the shot among the hundreds of shots from the crowd at the foot of the fortress. It was like a sound film when the synchronization of sound and picture goes wrong: the actor opens his mouth to speak, but you hear the voice of the woman who listens to him with closed lips.

'Let's get out of it,' Fausto growled. Later on he said: 'We're going to lose the war if this is a symbol.'

We passed commandeered cars and lorries. Militiamen and militia girls were making merry; they were laughing and singing, the men drank from leather bottles and their girls tickled them in the armpits so that the wine spattered. Once more the shots sounded like fairground squibs, and the cannon on the other side of the river decorated its muzzle with a fluff of cotton wool. In tomorrow's papers we would see the photograph of a pretty girl letting off a gun.

Near Getafe a small plane was doing stunts in the air, a sun-gilded fly showing off its glinting back and belly. People stared at it and blocked the pavement; a convoy of militia cars blocked the road. Fausto sounded the motor horn.

'Go to hell,' shouted one of the Milicianos and stayed there in the middle of the road, staring into the air.

When we came to Toledo Bridge we had to give the right of way to a municipal van coming from the Pradera de San Isidro. Fausto glanced at me: 'Do you think it's carrying something? It's a bit late for that.'

The garbage vans collected the bodies of those who had been executed and took them to the cemetery.

Fausto drove faster, and we overtook the van. Its iron doors were shut. Then it bumped over a hole in the road, and loose iron bars clanked in its hollow bowels. It was empty. I wiped some drops of sweat from my forehead.

Antonio had left a message at home; he wanted to see me as soon as possible. I found him in the Party Secretariat, very busy and surrounded by Milicianos who had come from the Sierra. He asked me curtly: 'Do you know English?'

The militiamen turned round and watched me with curiosity.

'Well, I don't speak English, but I read it and I translate from it quite fluently. If that's any good to you.'

'Go into the next room and speak to Nicasio.'

'Antonio told me you want some work to do,' the other secretary said. 'The Foreign Ministry needs people who understand English. So if you like –' He scribbled out a note and rang up somebody.

'Go there and ask for Velilla, he's a Party comrade and will tell you all you want to know.'

Shock Police guarded the Foreign Ministry. I had to wait in the enormous entrance where the sergeant on duty had a desk. All except one of the iron doors were shut. It looked like the reception desk of a prison. Then a young man, masked by big, horn-rimmed glasses and a mop of unruly hair, came straight towards me. 'You're Barea, of course.' He took the note out of my fingers and tore it up without having read it. 'They need people who know languages in the Press Department.'

'I know French well, but I don't speak a word of English. I can translate from it, though.'

'You won't need more. Let's see the Head of the Department.'

A single desk lamp threw a circle of light on heaped-up papers and a pair of white, cushioned hands. Two palely glinting discs stuck on to an egg-shaped blob moved in the dusk beyond the region of the beam from the lamp. Then I took in the head, a pallid, hairless dome, and smoked glasses in tortoiseshell rims. The two soft hands rubbed one against the other. Then a three-cornered tongue pushed out between the lips and curved up towards the nostrils; it looked almost black in that light.

Velilla introduced me to Don Luis Rubio Hidalgo, who invited me to take a seat, tipped up the conical light shade so that the room, he himself, and his heavily lidded eyes without lashes became visible, and began to explain.

He was the Chief of the Press and Propaganda Department at the Foreign Ministry. His office included the censorship of foreign press reports; he would like me to join them as a censor for press telegrams and telephonic press dispatches. The work was done in the Ministry during the day and in the Telefónica during the night, from midnight to eight in the morning. It was for this night work that he needed me. I could start the following evening. The salary was four hundred pesetas per month. I would be taken to work by one of the Ministry's cars. It was sufficient for him that I could translate from English.

I accepted the job. It sounded interesting. But I disliked my new chief, and said so to Velilla. 'Nobody likes him,' he answered, 'but he is in the confidence of the Minister. We distrust him. There are two boys in his department who are comrades, but we must see that we get the whole thing into our hands. Come and see me as often as you can. You will have to join our cell, there are eleven of us.' He ran on, with an engaging mixture of simple faith and involved argument. He believed that the war would be over in a few weeks and Spain become a Soviet Republic. I disagreed, but found him likable; I felt ready to work with him.

When I told the whole story to Angel, who had waited for me outside the Ministry, he grumbled because it would mean being out at night when, as he said, the Milicanos shot off their rifles at anything that moved because they were afraid, and when the phantom cars of Falange went about their murderous business. But he would look after me. When I told him I would be fetched by car and he would have to stay at my flat so that my wife and children

should not be left alone, he grumbled again and was proud. All my
friends in Emiliano's bar were pleased and intrigued by my new job.
It dominated the conversation, until all its aspects had been thrashed
out. Then everyone began to discuss politics. A few days before,
Largo Caballero had taken over the Government, Manolo summed
up the general opinion by saying: 'Now something will get done.
This is a war government, and now the rifles will go to the front. No
more parading up and down the streets – Prieto will show those
people something!' Prieto had been made Minister of War.

'Yes, you watch out,' said Fuñi-Fuñi. 'No more trips to Toledo
for you!'

'But I'm already a member of a battalion, only it hasn't got any
arms yet. As soon as they give us arms, I'll be the first to go.'

'All right, so it's no more Toledo, is it?' the other insisted, and the
customary quibble began. It was cut short by a distant noise which
came nearer: motorcycles, motor horns, sirens. We all rose. A
dispatch rider came racing down the street, the exhaust of his
motorcycle open, his siren sounding ceaselessly. In those days, when
Madrid had no air raid warning system, the alarm was given by the
motorcyclists of the Town Council who had sirens mounted on their
vehicles.

The women and children of the house came down to take shelter
in Emiliano's cellar. The men crowded into the bar. The iron
shutters clanked down, and a few women screamed at the noise.
Then the people grew quieter and spoke softly, for they all listened.
The drone of planes came close and went away, came back, and
seemed to hover overhead. Downstairs in the cellar a child began to
cry, other children followed suit, some of the mothers shrieked in
hysterical rage. Up in the bar the men stared at each other.

Then the hum of the engines no longer sounded in our ears.
Somebody rolled up the shutters. We flocked out into the street. It
was very still, the night was dark and decked with stars. People went
to their flats to see with their own eyes that nothing had happened,
but the men soon came down again. Nobody seemed able to sleep.
The women came after the men: the children were afraid that the
planes might come back. At dawn the street was crowded.
Newcomers brought news from other quarters of the town: bombs

had fallen in the district of Cuatro Caminos, and there had been many casualties. We had not heard the bombs. After sunrise, Manolo's militia friends arrived in their car. They were going to Toledo. He had not slept? Nor had they. 'Come along, we'll have our siesta out there.'

They rolled down the street, singing the Internationale. In the evening they brought Manolo back, dead. While they were taking their siesta in the fields, a plane had dropped a bomb close to the car. Manolo had a tiny orifice in his forehead. He had not wakened. He still slept placidly, pale from the sleepless night.

The Fascists had entered Talavera de la Reina.

At six that evening I went to the Foreign Ministry and Don Luis introduced me to my future colleagues and the work. I read through the journalists' output from the day before and he explained the principles of his censorship. I was given an official pass which authorized me to go anywhere in Madrid at night, and an identity card. At a quarter to midnight a car came to fetch me from my house. All the neighbours saw me off.

I felt elated and light-headed. During the day I had been sorting out the new situation with Aurelia and with Maria. I had explained to myself and to the two women, one after the other, that I would have to work during the night and to sleep during the day. I would no longer be able to meet Maria in the afternoons, as she had demanded. I would no longer have to struggle with the other's clinging and cloying nearness at home, where I had stayed more since the air raids had begun. At daybreak I had discussed my future work with Aurelia; she had been quick to see the disadvantage which it implied for her, and she had opposed my 'getting mixed up in those things'. In the afternoon I went to see Maria; she had resented my absence from the office in the morning and had her doubts about the new arrangement, but accepted it with good grace. It separated me more clearly from my home; it coincided with her belief that a victory of the Government and the social revolution in its wake would bring about my final separation from Aurelia and my agreement to a life together with her. She found it natural that I wanted to take an active part in the war. Her own young brother had just joined a volunteer battalion. Thus my new work held out new hope to her. I saw it, but made no comment. I would be inside the fortress of my work.

The car carried me through deserted streets, their darkness streaked with the feeble rays of light filtering through blinds and tavern doors. It was a new, chilling Madrid. Five times in the course of our short route a pair of Milicianos gave us the 'Halt!', dazzled us with their pocket lamps and scrutinized our papers. The official Ministry Pass did not impress them; when at last I held out my UGT card, one of the sentries said: 'Why didn't you show that one first, comrade?'

The last control was at the door of the Telefónica. It was too dark to see anything but smooth concrete walls towering over the narrow Calle de Valverde. A Shock Police sentry in the door took me to the guard room, where a lieutenant examined the Ministry papers and then passed me on to the Workers' Control.

The control desk was a sort of counter at one side of the big entrance hall, manned by a dark-skinned, unshaven, burly man who had tied a huge black-and-red scarf round his throat in a slovenly knot.

'What d'you want, brother?'

He pushed aside the official papers. 'OK – but what is it you want here?'

'As you see, I'm going to censor the reports of the foreign journalists.'

'What's your organization?'

'The UGT.'

'All right, you'll find one of your people up there. He's daft. But we'll have to settle that business with the foreigners. They're Fascists, all of them. The first one who does anything wrong – you just bring him to me. Or simply ring me up. And keep your eyes skinned when they talk their lingo. I can't think why they're permitted to talk their own language. Hell, if they want to make reports, let them do it in Spanish and pay for a translator. Then they come down the stairs with a lot of noise, talking their English, and nobody knows when they're calling one the son of a bitch. Well, your office is on the fifth floor, and these two will go with you.'

A pretty, flirtatious girl took me and the two Milicianos up in a lift; then we walked through long, dim, twisting passages with many doors and entered the last door of all. The narrow room smelled like a church and the darkness which filled it was suffused with a violet glow. A small circle of light was sharply outlined on the desk. The glow and the smell of wax came from the violet carbon paper wrapped round the bulb in place of a blackout shade. The censor on duty, a tall, bony man, rose and welcomed me. Two shadowy bulks at the other end of the room moved: the orderly and the dispatch rider, the smooth moon face of an elderly valet and the meagre, dusky face with lively eyes of a bootblack.

Then I plunged into the work and did not emerge for many nights. The organization was simple. The journalists had their own room on the fourth floor; there they wrote their reports in duplicate and submitted them to the censor. One copy was returned to the correspondent, stamped, and initialled, the other sent to the telephone room by orderly. When the connection with Paris or London was established, the correspondent read out his dispatch, while a switch censor sitting by his side checked the text and through his earphones controlled the service conversation as well. If the journalist wanted to transmit his report by telegram or radio, the censored copy was sent by dispatch rider to Transradio.

The big American agencies and Havas had teams of reporters who worked in shifts and produced a stream of what they called snaps; the more important British and American newspapers had their special correspondents. The majority spoke English, but there were a number of Frenchmen and a sprinkling of Latin-Americans.

My colleague and I were suppose to deal with all of them. He knew colloquial English, I could read the English of technical reviews and of books. His French was very thin, mine was not bad. But none of us had ever worked with the press. Our orders were strict and over-simple: we had to cut out everything that did not indicate a victory of the Republican Government. The correspondents battled against this rule with all their wit and technique. Perea and I pooled our knowledge and often called in one of the switch censors; we searched the dictionaries for double meanings and cut out a phrase when it remained obscure to us. At the beginning I thought that I would soon have a clearer view of the work and be able to turn it into something positive. But the opposite happened. As the autumn went on, the Republican forces suffered one defeat after another, and the journalists did their level best to get their reports of the facts through; the Frenchmen used *argot*, the Englishmen and Americans their respective slang, and they all tried to catch the switch censor napping by putting some insinuating words into their conversations with their editors, or by inserting into their dispatches little phrases not contained in the original text.

The most important battle in September was that for the Alcazar of Toledo. Colonel Yagüe's column was marching up the Tajo valley and drawing near to Toledo. The Government forces tried to take the fortress before the relief column arrived. Part of the Alcazar was blown up; but the defenders held out in the rock casemates and in the ruins. On September the 20th – I remember the date because it is my birthday – big tank cars were driven to Toledo and the Alcazar's cellars were flooded with petrol and set on fire. The attempt failed. On the same day a well-equipped column of volunteers coming from Barcelona paraded through the streets of Madrid and was cheered by the crowds: the men had come to fight Yagüe's army.

At that time the Government tried to suppress the wild tribunals by creating a new, legalized form of Popular Tribunal in which a member of the judiciary acted as the judge, and milita delegates as his assessors; it authorized militia squads to track down and arrest Fascists, so as to eliminate the terror of the man hunt. But the tide of fear and hatred was still rising, and the remedy was hardly better than the disease.

It was the official policy to pass only reports according to which the Alcazar was about to fall, Yagüe's column halted, and the Popular Tribunals a pattern of justice. I felt convinced that our news and censorship policy was clumsy and futile. But when I dealt with the journalists I disliked the glib assurance with which they took our defeat for granted and tried to squeeze out sensations, and then I carried through the official orders with a savage fury, as though by cutting out a phrase I were cutting out a hated and dreaded fact.

When I went to the Foreign Ministry in the evening to receive my instructions for the night, I usually had a talk with Don Luis, who seemed to single me out. He would tell me stories of how extremists had threatened him because he had let through an unfavourable piece of news, or of how he had been taken to task because some correspondent or other had sent out reports in the diplomatic bag of his embassy; of how he had fallen under suspicion and was afraid of being taken for a ride one fine day. He was on good terms with the Communists – after all, I was there because they had recommended me! – and Don Julio, the Minister, who backed him, was very much favoured by them. But the Anarchists . . .

He would end each of his perorations by opening the drawer of his desk and showing me a pistol. 'Before they get me, I'll get one of them! Well, anyhow, take great care and don't let anything pass, and above all, watch over your colleague who is weak, very weak!'

In the last week of September, Fausto, the inventor of the hand grenade, came and fetched me away from my day sleep. He had a written order of the War Ministry to collect the grenades stored in the ordnance factory, but he had no means of transporting them. The hundreds of cars and vans which were driven aimlessly round Madrid were in the hands of Milicianos, the Ministry had no control over them. Each militia group would willingly fetch the grenades for its own unit, but not for the Army Depot.

'If Prieto hears about it, the bombs will be fetched,' I said.

'Yes – but will Prieto know about it before the Fascists enter Toledo? I'm going there myself and I want you to come along.'

I went with him. The Toledo road was choked with Milicianos and cars, coming and going. Some shouted that the Alcazar had fallen, and some that its fall was a question of hours. Near Toledo the crowds thickened. The rock was wreathed with the bursts of explosions. Ambulances drove slowly over Alcántara Bridge, and the people greeted them, raising their clenched fists. We drove on to the ordnance factory, but gave up all hope as soon as we heard that the factory lorries stood ready to transfer to Madrid the whole stock of brass tubing and the machinery for cartridge production. Fausto was in despair. Neither of us was in a mood to drive up to Toledo. I suggested going back to Madrid via Torrijos so that I could stop at Novés.

In Torrijos the streets were blocked by carts. People were loading them with clothes, mattresses, and furniture, jostling each other and shouting. 'The Fascists are coming,' said an old man in answer to my question. 'The Fascists will get us. Yesterday they dropped bombs from their planes, and killed a lot of people, and this morning we could hear their guns. And the people who've passed through here! They've come from all the villages, even from Escalonilla, which is only half an hour from here.'

Novés was almost deserted. A few women hurried through the street. Both casinos had their doors shut. I asked Fausto to drive on to Old Juán's mill. There I found the old man tying up bundles with his two mill hands. He was amazed at seeing me. 'You'll have to hurry, the Fascists are coming. We're moving to Madrid tonight.'

'They won't be here as quickly as all that,' I said.

'Listen, Don Arturo, those fellows are already on the road. They dropped bombs here two days ago. They killed two cows of the village, and Demetria and her child and husband. People saw pickets of Moors on the Extremadura Road early this morning. I tell you, if you don't hurry, you won't get away. We'll meet in Madrid, Don Arturo, and then I'll tell you what happened here. It was horrible.'

We left Novés in the direction of Puebla de Montalbán so as to reach the Extremadura Road. When we got there Fausto glanced round and stopped the car. 'So that's that. What shall we do? Go back via Toledo?'

'The road to Madrid is still free, I believe. Let's take it – but step on it.'

The road was deserted. It was strewn with heaps of clothing and armament, caps, coats, straps, blankets, rifles, tin plates, and mugs; the ditches were littered with them. Rifle and machine-gun shots sounded in the distance, from the direction of Toledo we heard the dull explosions of five bombs. Fausto drove on at top speed. We began to pass Milicianos sitting by the road, barefooted, their boots or sandals lying beside them. There were more and more of them; then we overtook others who were marching on laboriously, most of them without their rifles, in shirtsleeves or open vests, their faces and bare chests burned red. They shouted at us to give them a lift, and screamed insults when our little car drove past them. We expected a shot in the back. Then the road became crowded. Trudging Milicianos mingled with peasants walking at the head of a mule or donkey which carried their wife and children, or driving a cartload with bundles and crockery, their family perched on top of the bedclothes. So we reached Navalcarnero.

An officer and a few men of the Shock Police had drawn a cordon across the road. They stopped militiamen in their flight, made them deliver their arms and ordered them to line up in the plaza. The little garrison had a solitary machine gun set up in the square: it stemmed the threatening panic. The people of Navalcarnero were packing and shutting up their houses.

They stopped our car, too. Fausto and I scrambled out and explained the aim of our journey to the officer, whose face was a mask of sweat-streaked dust. We simply had to get through to Madrid and report to the War Ministry, Fausto concluded, so that army lorries could be sent out to collect the ordnance material before the Fascists arrived and got it.

At that instant a group of Milicianos with rifles pushed through the crowd and seemed about to break through the cordon by force. The officer left us standing and climbed on to the roof of our car. 'Halt – go back, or we fire! Now, listen . . .'

'Shut up with your lousy commands. Let us through, or we'll get through by our guts,' shouted one of the Milicianos.

The officer shouted back: 'All right, you may pass through, but listen to me first!' The disarmed Milicianos surged round the car. Fausto muttered: 'If we get out of this, today's our real birthday!'

But the officer spoke well. He called the militiamen cowards to their faces, he made them see how shameful it would be to go back to Madrid in their state, he told them that they had been dirty curs to throw their rifles into the ditch. Then he explained that they could reorganize in Navalcarnero and stay there until the forces arrived which were under way from Madrid. In the end he shouted: 'That's all – those of you who've got guts will stay, the others can go on. But they must at least leave us their rifles so that we can fight!' A deafening clamour drowned his last words. He had won.

The officer jumped to the ground and at once sent armed pickets back along the road to collect as many rifles as possible. Then he turned to us, wiping his brow: 'Now you can go on, comrades.'

It was almost dark when we reached Madrid. We had left the

vanguard of the refuge carts in Alcorcón. I went straight to the Foreign Ministry and spoke to Rubio Hidalgo. 'Don't worry,' he said. 'The Fascists have already been halted, and the Alcazar won't last out this night. A few Milicianos have stampeded, that's all. The most important thing is that you shouldn't let through any news of this kind. Tomorrow morning there will be good news, you'll see.'

That night I had to battle against the journalists. One of them, a young, supercilious Frenchman who worked for the *Petit Parisien*, tried so many tricks and blustered so much that I threatened him with arrest. I don't remember more than that I shouted myself and gripped my pistol. In the morning it was no longer possible to conceal the face that the rebels had advanced as far as Maqueda on the Extremadura Road, a village nearer to Madrid than Puebla de Montalbán where we had passed a few hours earlier, and as far as Torrijos on the Toledo Road. Their column on the Extremadura Road threatened Madrid, the other threatened Toledo. The Government capped this piece of news with the announcement that the Alcazar had fallen; this had to be officially denied later on. Some days afterwards, on September the 27th, the rebels entered Toledo. The ordnance factory was not blown up and they occupied it intact.

The censorship work was turned into an unending nightmare. My colleague on the night shift was so panic-stricken that he had to go; I worked alone from nine in the evening to nine in the morning, hardly knowing what I did. The nearer Franco's forces drew to the capital, the more cryptic became the dispatches of the journalists, the more pressing their manner. With the mounting menace and fear, a new wave of killings swept the city. The food situation grew more and more difficult, only the communal restaurants were able to provide meals. There was a strict curfew starting at eleven o'clock; it was dangerous to be out in the streets. On September the 30th the Government decreed the incorporation of all militias into the regular army, which did not exist yet. I ate in the canteen of the Telefónica or in a near-by café and Angel took food home to my family. Snipers' shots cracked through the dark under my windows. I lived on black coffee and brandy during those nights.

When I crossed the street in the early morning to have breakfast I saw the thin stream of refugees from the villages, with their donkeys and carts and gaunt, yellow dogs. They travelled by night for fear of being bombed in daylight. The first batches were billeted in big, requisitioned houses, those who came later had to camp in the avenues of the city. Mattresses were heaped up under the trees in the Castellana and Recoletos, and the women did their cooking at open fires on the pavement. Then the weather changed and torrential rains chased the refugees into the overcrowded houses.

Old Juán of Novés came to see me one morning. I took him to my café and he began to tell me his story, in his slow, equitable manner.

'I was right, Don Arturo. Old people are not often fooled. The things that have happened! When the rebellion broke out, our people went mad. They arrested all the rich men of the village and all those who worked with them – me too. But they let me out after two hours. The lads knew that I never mixed in politics and that there was always a piece of bread in my house for everyone who needed it. And then, you see, my boy is in the Shock Police, and so I became a Republican through him. Well, they set up a tribunal in the Town Hall and shot all of them, including the priest. Heliodoro was shot first. But they buried them all in hallowed ground. The only one who escaped was José, the one from the Casino, because he often gave a peseta or so to the poor people when they hadn't anything to eat. It's always useful to light a candle to the devil! Well, so the families of the men who were shot went away, and our people at first wanted to share out their land, and then they wanted to till it communally. But they couldn't agree and there was no money. They requisitioned my mill, but of course they hadn't any grain to mill, and it was much the same thing in all the other villages. A few joined the militia in Madrid, but most of us stayed on and lived on our garden produce and on what had been stored in the rich men's houses. Then the rebels came nearer, and the people who'd been most active, like Elisro, got away. But we others thought we had nothing to fear and stayed on. A few left when the first bombs fell, but you know how attached one is to one's own home and land, and so most of us stayed. Until the people from other villages passed through on their flight and told us that, when they enter a village, the Fascists shoot all the men and shave the women's hair off. . . .'

'So, what with one thing and another, we all decided to get away.

But it was at the very last minute, the day you passed through. The others were already in Torrijos and Maqueda, and their two groups joined and cut us off from Madrid on the roads. So we had to walk across the fields. They were chasing us. When they caught a man he got a bullet through his head. They drove the women back to the village with their rifle butts. The Moors gleaned the fields afterwards, and when they got hold of a young woman they tumbled her on the ground. You can imagine the rest. They did it to a girl who was a servant at Don Ramón's. They threw her down in a ploughed field and called their comrades, because the girl's very pretty. Eleven of them, Don Arturo. Marcial, one of my mill hands, and I were hidden in a thicket and saw it happening. Marcial was so scared that it upset his innards and he dirtied himself. But afterwards he dared to come with me and we picked her up. She's here in the General Hospital, but they don't know yet whether she will be all right or not. Because, you see, we couldn't manage to carry her on our backs, and so she had to walk along with us across the fields for two days, until we got to Illescas, and from there they took her to Madrid in a cart. . . . I'm all right here, I'm with relatives, and so are some of the others. But there's something I want you to see, Don Arturo, because it's so frightful. It's the place where they've put the poorest of our people, those who haven't got anybody here in the town.'

After a meal in the canteen, Old Juán made me go with him, although I was stupid with tiredness. He took me through a marble portal with wide marble stairs and Doric columns, into a big hall. When he opened the entrance door, the stench of excrement and urine hit me in the face. 'But what is this, Uncle Juán?'

'Don't ask me. It's sheer misery. All the lavatories are broken and blocked. The people were bewildered by this place, you see, and didn't know what to do with it, so they smashed it all up. . . . I told you it was frightful.'

In one of the reception rooms of the palace, a horde of women, children, and old people, filthy, unkempt, evil-smelling, lived in a litter of truckle-beds, crockery and pieces of furniture. A woman was washing napkins in a washbowl; the dirty water slopped over and trickled under one of the camp beds, in which an old man was lying in his drawers, smoking. Three women were quarrelling round a table. The blue-green tapestry hung from the walls in shreds, the marble mantelpiece was chipped, the fireplace choked with refuse and muck. Two small children were squalling; and a third sat in a corner, clutching at a dirty little mongrel which barked ceaselessly and shrilly. In another corner stood an iron bedstead, with a goat tied to one of its legs.

While I stared, Old Juán said: 'Here are the people of Novés – you don't recognize them? Well, I told you they were the poorest of all, and I don't suppose you ever saw them. They were too poor to talk to you. In the other rooms are people from three or four other villages. They all hate each other, and they're always fighting because one's got a better place than the other, and some have a washbasin and some not, and so on. In the end they destroy everything so that the others shouldn't get it, the mirrors, and the lavatory bowls, and the pipes. There's no water left except in the garden pond.'

'But can't someone put it in order? Somebody must have brought them here, after all.'

'Nobody. When they arrived with their donkeys and carts, some militiamen got hold of them in the middle of the street and put them in here. They do send them meal vouchers, but nobody cares about them apart from that.'

It was on that day that Franco proclaimed himself the Caudillo – the Dictator – of Spain, I remember.

During the days that followed, the caravans of donkeys and carts with tired men, women, and children squatting on their bundles, never ceased. Battalions of Milicianos were hastily organized and sent out. Every day news came which showed how the armies of the rebels were fanning out like locust swarms, advancing on Madrid from all sides, from the Sierra de Gredos and the Alberche valley, passing by Aranjuez, through Sigüenza, in the Sierra de Guadarrama. Many people thought the war would end quickly; if the rebel armies closed the ring, if they cut communications with Albacete, Valencia, and Barcelona, Madrid would be lost.

On October the 13th, Madrid heard enemy gunfire for the first time.

I had lost my hopes and plans of arriving at a better understanding of the foreign journalists' way of working, and of thus gaining some influence on their attitude. The journalists, their reports, my life in the Telefónica by night, the life of Madrid by day, were converted into a rapidly moving strip of pictures, some clear, some blurred, but all so fleeting that it was impossible to focus attention on any one of them. I could no longer decipher the hand-written sheets some of the correspondents submitted to the censorship; it looked as though they were made intentionally illegible. In the end I made a ruling that every dispatch had to be typed. It helped a little. One of the Frenchman made it his excuse for leaving, but when he protested against my 'high-handed measure' I saw that he was afraid. He was an exception. While I slashed their reports according to orders, I admired the personal courage of the correspondents, although I resented their detachment. They went out, risking the bullet of a foreigner-hating Miliciano, or the capture by Moors in the fluctuating fighting, so as to produce a few meagre lines of a military report, while we could not pass the sensational articles they would have liked to write – or did write and pass on in some unimpeachable diplomatic bag.

So I saw myself sitting there in the darkness, behind the livid light-cone, working in the dark, when everybody thought I knew what was happening. I knew nothing except that the ring round Madrid was drawing closer, and that we were not equipped to meet the menace. It was difficult to sit still. Sometimes, when I walked past a group of slightly tipsy pressmen who had tried to get the better of me the whole night long, and had perhaps got it, I longed to have a row with them. What to us was life and death, meant nothing but a story to them. Sometimes, when the Anarchist of the Workers' Control in the hall downstairs told me again that all those foreign journalists were Fascists and traitors, I felt a twinge of sympathy. When I saw a certain one of them sprawling on the bed in the telephone room, snoring while he waited for his call to come through, I remembered how he had baited us in the certainty of Franco's prompt entry into the town, and I hated the brute.

I found it impossible to be friendly with Maria when she rang me up and demanded that we should meet. All our lives had come to a dead end.

The air raids became an almost daily occurrence. On October the 30th a single aircraft killed fifty little children in Getafe. The Building Trade Unions sent out men to dig trenches round Madrid and to construct pill-boxes and concrete barricades in the streets. The streets filled with refugees no longer from outlying villages, but from the suburbs of Madrid, and the nights were punctuated with distant gunfire. Elite units went out to man trenches not very many miles away; militiamen came, fleeing from the contact with tanks. La Pasionaria met them on the outskirts of the town and mustered her best strength to put new heart into them. The CNT – the Anarchist Trade Union Centre – sent two Ministers into the War Government. The journalists were writing reports which tried to say that we were lost, and we tried not to let them say it.

In the evening of November the 6th, when I went to the Foreign Ministry to receive my orders for the night, Rubio Hidalgo said:

'Shut the door, Barea, and sit down. You know, the whole thing is lost.'

I was so inured to his dramatic statements, that I was not impressed and only said: 'Really? What's the matter?' Then I saw papers burning in the fireplace and others stacked and packeted on the desk, and asked: 'Are we going to move?'

He wiped his gleaming pate with a silk handkerchief, passed his dark, pointed tongue over his lips, and said slowly:

'Tonight, the Government is transferring to Valencia. Tomorrow, Franco will enter Madrid.'

He made a pause.

'I'm sorry, my friend. There's nothing we can do. Madrid will fall tomorrow.'

But Madrid did not fall on the 7th of November 1936.

Part II

. . . When the senses
Are shaken, and the soul is driven to madness,
Who can stand? When the souls of the oppressed
Fight in the troubled air that rages, who can stand?

WILLIAM BLAKE

1. Madrid

The siege of Madrid began in the night of the 7th November 1936, and ended two years, four months, and three weeks later with the Spanish war itself.

When Luis Rubio Hidalgo told me that the Government was leaving and that Madrid would fall the next day, I found nothing to say. What could I have said? I knew as well as anybody that the Fascists were standing in the suburbs. The streets were thronged with people who, in sheer desperation, went out to meet the enemy at the outskirts of their town. Fighting was going on in the Usera district and on the banks of the Manzanares. Our ears were forever catching the sound of bombs and mortar explosions, and sometimes we heard the cracking of rifle shots and the rattle of machine guns. But now the so-called War Government was about to leave, and the Head of its Foreign Press Department expected Franco's troops to enter. . . . I was stunned, while he spoke on urbanely. The drawer in which he kept his melodramatic pistol was half open.

'We're going tomorrow, too,' he was saying. 'Of course, I'm referring to the permanent staff only. I should very much like to take you with me to Valencia, but you'll understand that I'm unable to do so. I hope – the Government hopes, I should say – that you will remain at your post up to the last moment.

He paused, and moved his smooth face sideways, and his smoked glasses glinted. I had to say something, for he made a pause. 'Of course,' I said.

'That's good. Now I'm going to explain the situation to you. As I mentioned already, the Government will move to Valencia tonight, but no one knows it yet. Written instructions will be left with General Miaja, so that he can negotiate the surrender with the least possible loss of blood. But he doesn't yet know it himself, and he won't know until after the Government has gone. Now you will realize the task that falls upon you. It is absolutely necessary to keep the Government's move a secret, otherwise a frightful panic would break out. So what you have to do is to go to the Telefónica, take over the service as usual – and not let a single reference through. I'm going to leave early in the morning with my staff and with all the foreign journalists who can't risk being found here when Franco enters. I'll spend the night at the Gran Vía Hotel, and if necessary you can report to me there.'

'But if you take the journalists away, they must know what is going to happen.'

'Not that the Government's moving. They may guess something, and of course, we've told them that the situation is extremely grave, so grave that the Government must ask them to leave, and is putting cars at their disposal. Some will stay, but that doesn't matter. I told them that they won't have our censorship facilities any more, because the military are taking over, and that there won't be any service in the Telefónica. So those who are staying behind are the correspondents who are safe in their embassies, risk nothing, and will be glad to be on the spot when the troops enter.'

'Then you feel sure that they will enter?'

'My dear fellow, what do you think half a dozen Milicianos can do? Tell me: what could they do against the Foreign Legion, the Moors, the artillery, the tanks, the aviation, the German experts – what could anyone do? I grant you that they may not enter Madrid tomorrow on the dot, but that would not make any difference, except that there would be more victims – they would enter the day after tomorrow, that's all. Well, I meant to tell you: you can pass the report that as a precautionary measure the Government has organized the evacuation of the press services. Everybody knows that by now. Tomorrow there'll be a proclamation that the Government has decided to move to Valencia, to conduct the war from a focal point, free from the impediments which must hamper any war administration in a front-line town.'

'What shall I do tomorrow, then?'

'As there will be nothing you can do, you will close the censorship when your shift is over, go home, and take care of your own skin, because nobody can tell what may happen. I'll let you have the wages for our commissionaire who acts as your orderly and for the dispatch riders; you can pay them tomorrow, and they can go home, or do whatever they feel like. I'm going to leave you some money for yourself, so that you have something on which to fall back if things go badly for you.'

He gave me two months' salary, eight hundred pesetas, then he rose and took my hand, shaking it solemnly as though at a funeral. I could not tell him anything of what I felt, so I looked down. From his desk, big glistening photographs showing rows of dead children stared at me, and I stared back.

Dully I asked: 'What are you going to do with these photographs?'

'Burn them, and the negatives as well. We wanted to use them for propaganda, but as things are now, anybody on whom they were found would be shot on the spot.'

'So you won't take them with you?'

'I'm cluttered up with papers anyhow,' and he went on explaining something, but I did not listen. I knew the pictures. They had been taken in the mortuary in which the school children of Getafe, killed by bombs from a low-flying Junkers a week before, had been lined up, each with a serial number on its chest. There was a small boy with his mouth wide open. I felt as though Rubio in his fear were sacrificing those dead children over again. 'Let me take them,' I said. He shrugged his shoulders and handed me the photographs and a box with negatives. 'If you care to take the risk. . . .'

On my way home I concentrated on the problem of how to save the photographs from destruction. There would be a fight. I knew, without giving it much thought, that our people would try to get at the men behind the steel curtain, with their bare knives if necessary.

The others would not come in as easily and smoothly as that smooth, frightened man had said. But they might come in, they probably would come in, and then the denunciations, arrests, searches, and executions would start at once. It would be a death warrant to have those photographic documents in one's house. But I could not let them go. The faces of those murdered children had to reach the eyes of the world.

At home I found my sister Concha, her husband, and her nine children waiting for me. Agustín, unperturbed and slow as always, told their story. That morning, their district – the outlying workers' district on the other side of Segovia Bridge – had been attacked by the Fascists. They had fled together with all the neighbours, crossing the bridge under shell-fire. Now the Fascist troops were entrenched on the other bank of the river and advancing into the Casa de Campo. Their house was a heap of rubble. They had saved some bundles of clothes and my sister's sewing machine. For the moment they were staying in Rafael's small flat, because Concha preferred not to live together with Aurelia, my wife.

It seemed absurd to make any permanent arrangements. Within twenty-four hours we might all be in the same situation. I suggested that everyone should get a few things ready for a sudden, last-minute flight. Then I left for the Telefónica.

I found the correspondents in the wildest excitement, waiting for their calls, passing on the latest news from the suburban front, and deputizing for one another if a call came through in the absence of the man who had booked it. The tables in the journalists' room were littered with coffee and spirits, all the telephones seemed to ring at once, all the typewriters were clacking. Nobody referred to the Government's move in my hearing.

From the window in the censorship I heard people marching out towards the enemy, shouting and singing, cars racing past with screeching motor horns, and behind the life of the street I could hear the noise of the attack, rifles, machine guns, mortars, guns, and bombs. Then I sat down to censor the dispatches.

Towards two in the morning somebody brought the news that the Fascists had crossed three of the bridges over the Manzanares, the Segovia, Toledo, and King's Bridges, and that there was hand-to-hand fighting in the courtyards of the Model Jail. This meant that they were within the town. I refused to pass the news so long as I had no official confirmation, and went to the telephone room to see that the embargo was kept. The big American, over six feet, two hundred and twenty pounds or so, who had drunk steadily throughout the evening, turned aggressive; Franco had entered Madrid and he was going to let his paper know about it, in one way or other. The Republican Censor hadn't any say any more. He took me by the coat lapels and shook me. I drew my pistol and put him under the guard of two Milicianos. He dropped heavily on to one of the emergency beds and started snoring wheezily. When the last correspondents had sent off their dispatches, the switch censors and I were left alone with the snoring bulk on the camp bed.

Our nerves were centred in our ears. We listened to the mounting noise of the battle. The American was sleeping off his whisky very noisily. Somebody had thrown a grey blanket over him, and his two enormous feet in black, thick-soled shoes stuck out, laid together as neatly as the feet of a corpse.

There was no need to talk, we were all of the same mind and knew it.

The Gran Vía, the wide street in which the Telefónica lies, led to the front in a straight line. The front came nearer. We heard it. We expected from one moment to the next to hear under our window shots, machine-gun bursts, hand grenades, and caterpillar chains of tanks clanking and screeching on paving stones. They would storm the Telefónica. There was no escape for us. It was a huge trap, and they would chase us like trapped rats. But we had pistols and a few rounds of cartridges each. We would shoot it out through corridors and stairways, to the end. If we lost, it would be our bad luck. We would not wait for them to kill us. We would fight as best we could.

A puny young man, the Madrid reporter of the Barcelona agency *Fabra*, came into the room with a blanched, twitching face, drew me into a corner and whispered: 'Barea – the Government has fled to Valencia!'

'I know. Don't get scared, shut up. I've known about it since six o'clock. We can't do more than we are doing.'

He trembled and was on the point of bursting into tears. I filled him up with brandy like an empty bottle, while he lamented the fate of his children. Then he was sick and fell asleep.

The battle noise had abated. We opened the windows to the Gran Vía. It was a grey dawn. While the cold morning mist drifted in, a dense bluish cloud of tobacco smoke and human warmth streamed slowly out through the upper part of the windows. I made the rounds of the offices. Most of the correspondents had gone, a few slept on camp beds. Their room was fuggy with cold smoke and alcohol fumes, and I opened a window. The four men of the switch control were sleepily waiting for their relief. The girls sitting at the switchboards belonged to the morning shift, their lips were freshly painted and their hair slicked. The orderlies brought thick, black coffee from the canteen, and we poured a small glass of brandy into each cup.

One of the switch censors, a quiet, grey-haired man, untwisted a little roll of paper and brought out two lumps of sugar. 'The last,' he said.

Across the street a convoy of cars was lined up before the Gran Vía Hotel. I went down to take leave of Rubio Hidalgo. The newspaper vendors were selling their morning papers. It was no longer a secret that the Government had gone to Valencia. Madrid came under military law and would be governed by a defence council, the *Junta de Defensa*.

'And now what, Don Luis?' I asked. 'Madrid has not fallen yet.'

'Never mind, stick to what I told you yesterday. Your work is done, now look after yourself. Let the *Junta de Defensa* take over the censorship with a couple of officers, while it lasts. Madrid will fall today or tomorrow – I hope they haven't cut the road to Valencia yet, but I'm not so sure we'll get through. The whole thing is finished.' He was very pale in the sunlight and the nerves under his thick white skin quivered.

I went back to the Telefónica, gave Luis, the orderly, and Pablo, the dispatch rider, their wages, and said what Rubio Hidalgo had told me to say. Luis, an elderly commissionaire of the Ministry, ceremonious and a little unctuous in his manner, a resigned, simple, and shrewd man underneath, turned ashen. 'But they can't chuck me out, I belong to the Ministry staff, I'm a permanent employee of the State and have my rights!'

'Well, you could go to the Ministry and see if you can get anywhere with your claim. I doubt it. They're clearing out, my poor Luis.' I felt savage. 'I'm going home myself, our work here is over.'

While I lingered on, a switch censor came to tell me that Monsieur Delume wanted to book his early morning call to Paris and insisted on transmitting his report. 'We haven't received any orders to stop press calls,' the man said, 'but how can I let the journalists speak with their people abroad before their dispatches are censored? And now you say you have shut down for good! Do you think we should cut their calls off ?'

I tried to state Rubio Hidalgo's case, but even while I was speaking I made up my mind. I had entered the censorship not as a paid civil servant but as a volunteer in the war against the Fascists. The foreign press, our link with the outer world, could not remain without a censoring control, but it could not be silenced either; nor was it right to leave everything to the military censors of whom Don Luis had vaguely spoken. There existed no such thing, the military had other tasks and worries. At the best, army censors would force the foreign correspondents, particularly those eagerly waiting for Franco's entry, to use other channels of communication. Whatever Rubio or his kind might decree, only those who were defending Madrid – whoever they were – had the right to order me to abandon my post.

I interrupted myself in the middle of a sentence and told the man: 'I'll come along with you and talk to the others. We can't let things go on like this.'

I held council with the four switch control censors, who were employees of the American Telephone Company, but had been commandeered to help out the official censorship. We decide that I should go to the Ministry, and if necessary to the new defence authorities, and obtain a ruling. In the meantime, they would censor the journalists' reports to the best of their knowledge. I collected the Press Department stamps and went to the Plaza de Santa Cruz.

The glass-roofed courts of the Foreign Ministry were filled with disputing and gesticulating groups. In the middle of the biggest group Faustino, the majestic Chief Doorkeeper, was holding forth, while the sergeant of the Shock Police detailed to guard the building stood by.

'Those are the orders I've received from the Under-Secretary,' Faustino was declaring, 'and you will leave the building this very moment, gentlemen.' He rattled a big bunch of keys like a sacristan about to lock up his church.

'What's going on here?' I asked.

The torrent of explanations was so unintelligible that I turned to Faustino for an answer. He hesitated. It was plain what was going on in his mind. I was a mere nobody, with no place in the official hierarchy, while he was the Chief Doorkeeper of Spain's chief Ministry, the power behind the throne of each Minister, more lasting than they, and the dictator in the basement of the old palace. But since his whole world had been turned upside down, he decided to answer me.

'Well, you see, sir, this morning the Under-Secretary rang me up and told me the Government had gone to Valencia, he was leaving that very moment, and I was to shut up the Ministry. He said the staff would have to go home as soon as they arrived.'

'Has he sent you a written order to shut up the building?' I asked.

This had not occurred to him. 'No, sir. It was the Under-Secretary's personal instruction.'

'I beg your pardon. You said just now that it was a telephonic instruction.'

'You won't tell me that I can't recognize his voice!'

'You won't tell me that voices can't be imitated.' I addressed the sergeant in a tone of command: 'On my responsibility, you will see to it that this Ministry is not closed unless by written order from a competent higher authority.'

He stood to attention. 'I wouldn't have gone anyhow, even if the building had been shut up, because I haven't received orders. But what you say seems OK to me. Don't worry, this place won't be shut up by anybody while I'm here.'

I turned round to see what the others said.

There were some twenty of us standing in the middle of the frosty, flagged court: ten employees in stiff white collars, incongruous in that Madrid of the Militias, five or six commissionaires in blue braided uniforms, and half a dozen workers of the Ministry printing office. I saw an incredulous hope mixed with fear in all but five faces, and found it not difficult to understand. The Ministry, the part of the State machinery in which some of them had spent their whole life, had vanished overnight. They might have believed in the reality of the war, the revolution, the danger in which Madrid stood, the threatening entry of Franco and his troops, but they were incapable of believing that the edifice of the State could suddenly crumble, and in its fall bury the salaries, the social position, the basis of the existence of its employees. Those modest middle-class people with the lustre of civil servants, most of them without any political conviction, saw the ground drop away from under their feet. They were helpless and homeless now that the Ministry was about to shut down. They did not belong to a trade union. Where could they go, what could they do? They would find themselves out in the street unsupported by a political group or union, unable to apply for protection from the immediate danger of being shot. On the other hand, the rebel army might enter the city that very day, and they would have been employees of the Republican Government almost up to the last hour. It was too late to join either of the camps. My intervention gave them new hope and spared them any responsibility for action. If Franco were to take Madrid, it would have been I, the revolutionary, who had seized the Ministry by brute force and compelled them to go on working. If Madrid were to hold out, they would be among the brave men who stayed on, sticking it out, and nobody would be able to deny them their rights as servants of the Republic.

They all shouted approval. They were backing me, and Faustino withdrew slowly from the scene, muttering and shaking his bundle of keys.

Torres, a young printer, offered to go with me to the *Junta de Defensa*, but neither he nor I knew where to find it. In the end we decided to appeal to Wenceslao Carrillo, an old labour leader whom we both knew and who was an Under-Secretary in the Ministry of the Interior. As we expected, he was still in Madrid and at his office, a cold, dank stone box, smelling of worm-eaten paper and cellar dampness. About two dozen people were crowded into the ridiculously small cubicle and the air was foul with smoke. Carrillo stalked up and down in the middle of the cluster of employees and

Shock Police officers. The old Socialist used to exude a robust, sanguine optimism, but that morning he was in a bad temper, his eyes suffused with red from a sleepless night, and his face congested. He spoke brusquely as always, but without his sly twinkle.

'Well – and you, what d'you want?'

I explained the situation at the Foreign Ministry: it was not right to shut the Ministry and its censorship while there were embassies and foreign journalists in Madrid. For the moment I had prevented it from being shut, but I needed an official order, something to regularize the position.

'And what do you want me to do? I'm in the same boat. They've gone and here's Wenceslao to face the music. The devil take them. Of course they didn't tell me they were going, because if they had told me. . . . Look here, settle it somehow among yourselves. Go to the *Junta de Defensa*.'

'But where is the *Junta de Defensa*?'

'How the hell should I know, my boy, Miaja's the master, and Miaja's running round the town and letting off shots. Well, the best thing you can do is to go to the Party and get instructions there.'

We did not go to the Socialist Party, which was what Wenceslao Carrillo meant. I had lost all confidence in its power of assuming responsibilty and authority in a difficult situation, and my companion Torres, and old member of the Socialist Youth Organization, had recently joined the Communists. We went to the Provincial Committee of the Communist Party. There they told us that the *Junta de Defensa* had not yet constituted itself; but Frades, one of their leading men, would be the secretary to the Junta's Executive Committee. Frades explained that our case could not be settled until the Junta existed in due form; we should come to see him the following day, and in the meantime I had better not leave the Ministry. He did not question my intervention at the Ministry, nor did I ask his opinion; we never discussed this point, because it seemed obvious that no post of any importance in Madrid should remain abandoned.

Torres and I walked back, so immersed in our immediate problem and the danger from pro-Fascist elements within the bureaucracy which we both suspected that we did not think much of the battle going on two miles away. Luis, my orderly from the Telefónica, made an emergency bed for me in the press room at the Ministry on one of the huge, soft, mulberry-coloured sofas. He was in his commissionaire's uniform, coming and going with the perfect tact of a trained flunkey, and wildly excited under the bland surface: Don Luis had wanted to throw him out into the street like a useless old rag, and I had saved his existence, he said. He was convinced that I would obtain official sanction for my act, and that I would stay at the head of the censorship. I thought it possible that I would be shot, but I was too exhausted to care. I telephoned to the switch control in the Telefónica and asked them to censor the dispatches during the night. Then I slept like a log.

The following day Torres and I went to the palace of the banker Juán March where the *Junta de Defensa* had installed some of its offices. Frades handed me a paper with the printed letterhead *Junta de Defensa de Madrid, Ministerio de la Guerra* – Defence Council of Madrid, War Ministry. It said: 'This Defence Council of Madrid decrees that pending a new order from this same Defence Council the whole personnel of the Ministry of Foreign Affairs shall continue at its posts. The Secretariat. Signed: Frades Orondo. Dated: Madrid, 8th November 1936. Stamped with the stamp of the Junta's Executive Committee.' I still have the paper.

When we arrived back at the Ministry, the portly Faustino came up to me and said in a hushed voice:

'The Under-Secretary is in his room.'

'All right, leave him there. Hasn't he gone to Valencia, then?'

'Oh yes, but his car broke down.'

'I'll see him later. Now be so kind as to call the whole staff to the press room.'

I showed the order of the *Junta de Defensa* to the gathered employees and said: 'I think what ought to be done now is to form a Popular Front Committee which will be responsible for the conduct of affairs. Apart from that, you will all have to stay at your posts until there are detailed orders from Valencia.'

Torres, who was young and ingenuous, wanted to do things in the grand style. He asked Faustino to unlock the Ambassadors' room, and added: 'As a lot of you don't belong to any political organization, all of us who do will meet in the Ambassadors' room.'

There were nine of us, the six printers, two office employees, and myself. Torres took the chair. He was small and thin, and his insignificant body sank far too deep into the upholstery of the Minister's chair.

The Ambassadors' room was a long hall almost filled by an enormous central table. The walls were hung with red-and-gold brocade, the chairs had curved gilt backs, and red velvet seats, the claws of their legs bit deep into the flower bunches of the carpet. A leather folder with the coat-of-arms embossed in gold lay on the table in front of each seat. Torres in shirtsleeves addressed the six printers in their blue blouses and us three dishevelled clerks with a solemn: 'Comrades!'

The big room dwarfed and smothered us. We shouted loudly in our discussion. When we left, the carpet was smeared with cigarette ash and the brocade impregnated with smoke. While we filed out, Faustino came in and threw all the windows wide open to cleanse his sanctuary; but we were well content. We had formed a Popular Front Committee, of which Torres was chairman and I secretary. We had also founded the Foreign Ministry Employees' Union. An hour later all the personnel had joined.

The sergeant of the Shock Police called me into his room and shut the door with ostentatious care. 'Now, what are you going to do with that fellow?'

'Which fellow?'

'That Under-Secretary. He ought to be wiped out.'

'Don't be a damned brute.'

'I may be a brute, but that fellow is a Fascist. Do you know what happened to him? He was afraid to go through Tarancón, because of the Anarchists, and so he's come back. Didn't you know the story? All Madrid knows it. The Anarchists of Tarancón were waiting for the Government and the bigwigs when they ran away last night, and wanted to shoot all of them. The only one who had guts enough to deal with them was our own Minister, Don Julio, but there were some who ran away in their pyjamas and dirtied them too, I bet.'

I went to see the Under-Secretary. Señor Ureña's eyes were dilated behind his spectacles, his face faintly green like a church candle. He offered me a seat.

'No, thank you.'

'At your pleasure.'

'I only wanted to tell you that I hold this order of the *Junta de Defensa* according to which the Ministry is not to close down.'

'Well – it's for you to say —' There was no mistaking that the man was racked by fear and his mind haunted by visions of firing squads.

'That's all I wanted to say.'

'But I must leave for Valencia this afternoon.'

'There's nothing on my side to prevent you. You are the Under-Secretary of Foreign Affairs. I'm just a wartime employee of the censorship. You, I suppose, have your instructions direct from the Government. The only thing I had to tell you was that this Ministry of Foreign Affairs would not close down. Nothing else concerns me.'

'Oh, all right then, all right, very many thanks.'

Señor Ureña left that afternoon, and Madrid saw him no more. Torres gave me an order signed by the Popular Front Committee to the effect that I was to take charge of the Press Department. In the day censorship room sat an elderly man with a white thatch of hair, the journalist Llizo, mild-mannered and of a shining honesty, who received me with a cry of relief.

'Thank goodness this is being settled. Do you know that the journalists put through their reports without any censorship yesterday?'

'What the devil – the switch censors were going to look after that!'

'Yes, that may be, and they certainly seem to have done so during the night. But you know, quite a lot of the journalists used to book their calls from here and telephone their dispatches through from the Ministry press room, because it was more comfortable, and we used to do the switch censoring here. The Telefónica people must have put through the calls because they believe the reports were censored and checked here as usual. Or perhaps it was just a muddle. Anyhow, here you can see what was sent out to the world yesterday.'

I looked through the sheaf of papers and my stomach turned over. The suppressed feelings of some of the correspondents had flared up; there were reports breathing a malicious glee at the idea that Franco was, as they put it, inside the town. People abroad who read it must have thought that the rebels had conquered Madrid and that the last, weak, disjointed resistance would soon come to an end. There were just and sober reports as well; but the general picture that arose was one of a hideous muddle – which certainly existed – without the blaze of determination and fight which also existed and which was, in the slang of the journalists, the 'real story'. I had never been as completely convinced of the need for a war censorship as when I read those petty and deeply untrue reports and realized that the damage abroad had been done. It was a defeat inflicted by the man who had deserted.

On the same day, a haggard, shy man in mourning, who looked as though he suffered from stomach trouble, came to see me. 'I'm the State Controller of the Transradio Company. I heard that you got things going here, and so I thought I would consult you. You see, I have to censor all the radio telegrams, and most of them are from foreign embassies. You belong to the Foreign Ministry, so you might be able to help me, since everybody else has gone away. Frankly, I don't know what to do. You see, I'm not a man of action.' He straightened his tie and handed me a packet of telegrams. I explained that I had no authority to intervene in his affairs and tried to send him to the *Junta de Defensa*.

'I've been there. They told me to go on censoring as usual, that's all – but now look, what shall I do with this?' He picked out a telegram directed to 'His Excellency Generalissimo Francisco Franco, War Ministry, Madrid.' It was a flowery message of congratulation to the conqueror of Madrid, signed by the President of one of the smaller Spanish-American Republics.

'That's easy,' I said. 'Send it back with the service note: "Unknown at the above address." ' But if this telegram was not particularly important from a censorship point of view, there were others in code from embassies and legations whose support of Franco was unequivocal. There were radio messages from Spaniards with a foreign embassy address – anti-Republican refugees – to 'relatives' abroad, which showed the time-honoured pattern of simple code messages. The most prolific telegram sender was Felix Schleyer, the German businessman whom I knew to be one of the most active Nazi agents, but who was protected by a spurious extra-territoriality as the Administrator of the Norwegian Legation in the absence of its Minister, then residing in St Jean de Luz.

To help the controller of the radio company, I took it upon myself to decide which telegrams to hold back and which to send. But I was under no illusion. We were fumbling, we were not equipped to deal with the matters abandoned by those in charge. Yet we could not abandon them too. I was hot with resentment and contempt for the bureaucrats who had scrambled to safety, too sure of the fall of Madrid to make any provision for the continuation of the work. The case of the radio telegrams, which did not immediately concern me, brought it home to me that the breakdown had occurred in all the administrative offices of the State, and that those who had stayed on in Madrid had to set up emergency services following the rules of a revolutionary defence, not the rules of precedence.

I reorganized the foreign press censorship with the five members of the staff left behind by Rubio Hidalgo. Some of the journalists showed us a sullen resentment; they chafed under the re-established control. 'Now they'll be sending out their poisonous stuff through their diplomatic bags,' said one of the censors.

What we had set up was a very flimsy structure. We were cut off, without instruction and information, without any superior authority short of the *Junta de Defensa*, and the Junta had other worries than to look after the foreign press censorship. Nobody there was certain to which department we belonged. I could not get through to Valencia by telephone. Yet I felt pride in carrying on.

Around us, Madrid was swept by a fierce exultation: the rebels had not got through. Milicianos cheered each other and themselves in the bars, drunk with tiredness and wine, letting loose their pent-up fear and excitement in their drinking bouts before going back to their street corner and their improvised barricades. On that Sunday, the endless November the 8th, a formation of foreigners in uniform, equipped with modern arms, paraded through the centre of the town: the legendary International Column which had been training in Albacete had come to the help of Madrid. After the nights of the 6th and 7th, when Madrid had been utterly alone in its resistance, the arrival of those anti-Fascists from abroad was an incredible relief. Before the Sunday was over, stories went round of the bravery of the International battalions in the Casa de Campo, of how 'our' Germans had stood up to the iron and steel of the machines of the 'other' Germans at the spearhead of Franco's troops, of how our German comrades had let themselves be crushed by those tanks rather than retreat. Russian tanks, anti-aircraft guns, planes, and munition trucks were arriving. There was a rumour that the United States would sell arms to the Spanish Republic. We wanted to believe it. We all hoped that now, through the defence of Madrid, the world would awaken to the meaning of our fight. Therefore the foreign- press censorship of Madrid was part of its defence, or so I thought.

On one of those mornings, the new siege guns brought up by the rebels began their dawn bombardment. I was sleeping in an armchair at the Ministry, when I was awakened by a series of explosions in the neighbourhood. The shells were falling in the Puerta de Sol, in the Calle Mayor, in the Plaza Mayor – three and two hundred yards from the building. Suddenly the stout walls trembled, but the explosion and destruction for which my nerves were waiting, did not follow. Somewhere in the upper storeys there was shouting and running, half-clad people came pattering down the stairs, Faustino in a dressing-gown, his wife in a petticoat and bed-jacket, her spongy breasts flapping, a group of Shock Police in shirtsleeves. In the west court, a cloud of dust silted down from the ceiling.

A shell had hit the building, but not exploded. It had gone through the thick old walls and come to rest in the door to the dormitory of the Shock Police guard. There it was, monstrously big, lying across the threshold. The wood of the inlaid floor was smouldering, and on the wall opposite was a jagged hole. A row of volumes of the Espasa-Calpe Dictionary had been shattered. It was a twenty-four centimetre shell, as big as a child. After endless tele-phoning hither and thither, a man from the Artillery Depot arrived to dismantle the fuse; the shell would be fetched away later on. The Shock Police cleared the western half of the building, and we waited in the other court. After a short while, the artillerist emerged triumphantly, in one hand the brass fuse cap, in the other a strip of paper. The guards carried the huge, harmless shell into the court and set it up. Somebody translated the words on the paper that had been hidden in the hollow of the shell. It said in German: 'Comrades, don't be afraid, the shells I charge do not explode. – A German worker.' The big wrought-iron gates were thrown open and the shell exhibited under the portal. Thousands of people came to stare at the shell and the strip of paper. Now the workers in Germany were helping us – we were going to win the war! *No pasarán, no pasarán* – They will not pass! A plane, glittering like a silver bird in the sunlight, was flying high overhead. People pointed to it: One of ours – the Russians – Long live Russia! The plane made a loop, banked and dropped a stick of bombs over the centre of the town. The crowd scattered for an instant and then drifted back to restore its faith by looking at the dud shell on its table, flanked by Shock Police sentries.

I went home, fetched the photographs of the murdered children of Getafe, and took them to the Communist Party office, to be used for propaganda posters.

In the morning of November the 11th, Luis came to tell me that two foreigners were waiting for me in Rubio's office.

When I entered the dark, musty room which still carried the traces of sudden flight, I saw a youngish man with strong, high-coloured mobile features, horn-rimmed glasses and a mop of crinkled brown hair, walking up and down, and a pale, slight woman with prim lips and a bun of mousy hair leaning against the desk. I had not the faintest idea who they were. The man slapped a bundle of papers on the desk, and said in bad Spanish, with a guttural accent:

'Who's the man in charge here? You, I suppose?' He put his question in an aggressive tone which I resented. I answered curtly: 'And who are you?'

'Look, comrade, this is Comrade Kolzoff of *Pravda* and *Izvestia*. We come from the War Commissariat – and we want to know a few things from you.' She spoke with a French accent. I looked at the bundle of papers. They were the press dispatches sent out without the censorship stamp on November the 7th.

The Russian snapped at me: 'This is a scandal. Whoever is responsible for this kind of sabotage deserves to be shot. We saw them in the War Commissariat when somebody from the Ministry brought them in an envelope to be sent to Valencia. Was it you who let the journalists get away with it? Do you know what you have done?'

'I know that I have prevented this kind of thing from going on,' I retorted. 'Nobody else has bothered about it, and you too have come somewhat late in the day.' But then I began to explain the whole story, less annoyed by Kolzoff's imperious manner than pleased because at long last someone cared about our work. I ended by telling them that so far I was in charge of the censorship by nobody's authority except my own and that of the improvised Popular Front Committee, consisting of nine men.

'Your authority is the War Commissariat. Come along with us. Suzana will provide you with an order of the Secretariat.'

They took me in their car to the War Ministry where I found out that the woman called Suzana was acting as responsible secretary to the Madrid War Commissariat, apparently because she had stayed on and kept her head. She had been a typist. Groups of militia officers came and went, people burst in to shout that their consignment of arms had not arrived, and the man Kolzoff intervened in most of the discussions on the authority of his vitality and arrogant will. I was glad to come under the War Commissariat. Alvarez del Vayo, who was already my supreme chief in his capacity as Foreign Minister, had been appointed Commissar General. I did not yet know him personally, but I was swayed by the popular feeling for him: he was the first of the Ministers who had come back to Madrid and made contact with the front line of the besieged city. It was common talk that he alone had stood up to the Anarchist group at Tarancón like a man; people remembered that it was he who had told the truth about our war to the diplomats assembled at Geneva. I hoped that under the conditions of a state of siege, the foreign press censorship would remain divorced from the Foreign Ministry's bureaucracy in the Valencia rearguard.

The written order I received from the War Commissariat on November the 12th said:

'Having regard to the transfer to Valencia of the Ministry of Foreign Affairs and to the indispensable need for the Press Department of the aforesaid Ministry to continue functioning in Madrid, the General War Commissariat has decided that the aforementioned office of the Press Department shall henceforward be dependent on the General War Commissariat, and furthermore that Arturo Barea Ogazón shall be in charge of the same, with the obligation to render a daily report of its activities to the General War Commisariat.'

On the evening of that day, Rubio Hidalgo rang up from Valencia; he was coming to Madrid to settle things. I informed the War Commissariat. They told me not to let him touch any papers, but to bring him to the War Ministry; they would speak to him.

'And supposing he doesn't want to come?'

'Then bring him here between two men from the Shock Police.'

I had been avoiding Rubio's room. It belonged to an official head of the department who might sit there in state, undisturbed by the work of others. Moreover, I disliked the very smell of that room. But when Rubio Hidalgo arrived from Valencia, I received him in his own office, behind his desk, and at once passed on the order from the War Commissariat. He grew even more pallid and blinked his hooded eyes, but he said: 'Let us go then.'

At the Commissariat he kept still under the crude, outspoken reprimands, then played his cards. He was the Press Chief of the Foreign Ministry: the War Commissariat must be opposed to any wild and disorganized action, since it recognized the authority of the Government in which the Chief of the War Commisariat was a Minister. Rubio's legal position was unassailable. It was agreed that the Foreign Press and Censorship Office at Madrid would continue to depend on him in his capacity as Press Chief. It would be under the Madrid War Commissariat for current instructions, and through the Commissariat under the *Junta de Defensa*. The Foreign Ministry's Press Department would continue to cover the expenses of the Madrid office, the censored dispatches would continue to be sent to Rubio. He was suave and conciliatory. Back at the Foreign Ministry, he discussed the details of the service with me; the general rules for the censorship continued to be the same, while military security instructions would reach me from the Madrid authorities. We agreed that the censorship offices would have to be moved to the Telefónica altogether. The journalists were clamouring for the transfer; most of them lived in hotels near the Telefónica, and they found the repeated journey to and from the Ministry, through shell-spattered streets, most inconvenient. We also had an interest in relieving the Telefónica employees from their emergency censoring and in covering all the shifts with our own scanty staff. Rubio promised to send another censor from Valencia. He departed with expressions of friendship and appreciation for our arduous work. I knew that he hated me far more deeply than I hated him.

When we had settled down in the Telefónica, I went out for a few hours' walk. It was my first free spell since November the 7th. My brain was drugged, I wanted to have some air. It was unthinkable to go home. I walked towards the district of Argüelles, the residential quarter overhanging the Manzanares valley, which had been shattered by concentrated bombing in the first days of the siege, when the rebel tanks had stood ready to climb up the slope to the Plaza de España. They had begun climbing up the slope, but they had been thrown back, almost in sight of the bronze statue of Don Quixote. But the part of Argüelles around the Paseo de Rosales and the Calle de Ferraz, which was to have been the breach in the defence ring, had since been evacuated and declared part of the front-line zone.

The night fogs had gone and the sky was mercilessly brilliant. I saw every rent and hole in the Cuartel de la Montaña. The gardens at its feet were rank and dirty. Some of the holes framed the sunlit walls of an inner court. The building was a big, hollow shell which caught the sounds from the front and gave them back, amplified. The rattle of a machine gun down by the river echoed in the galleries of the barracks.

So far there were signs of human life, the noises of people in some part of the abandoned barracks, Miliciano units marching through the avenues in the direction of the front, sentries standing in doorways. I wanted to turn into the Paseo de Rosales, but a soldier sent me back: 'You can't go there, brother, it's swept by the machine guns.' So I went down the parallel street, the Calle de Ferraz. It was deserted. As I walked on, the dead street took hold of me. There were absurdly intact houses side by side with heaps of rubble. There were houses cleft through cleanly, which showed their entrails like a doll's house. In the few days that had passed, the fogs had peeled the paper from the walls, and long pale strips fluttered in the brisk wind. A tilted piano showed its black and white teeth. Lamps were swinging from the rafters of vanished ceilings. Behind the glass knife fringe of a window frame a shamelessly smooth mirror reflected a rumpled divan.

I passed bars and taverns, one whose floor had been swallowed by the black gulf of its cellar, another with the walls standing undisturbed, but the zinc bar corrugated, the clock on the wall a twisted mass of wheels and springs, and a little red curtain flapping in front of nothing. I went into a tavern which was not damaged, but only deserted. Stools and chairs were standing round red-painted tables, glasses and bottles were standing as the customers had left them. There was thick, slimy water in the rinsing basin of the bar. Out of the neck of a big square flagon, blackish with the dried dregs of wine, a spider crept slowly, stood straddled over the rim on its hairy legs and stared at me.

I walked away quickly, almost running, pursued by the stare and the cry of the dead things. The tram rails, torn from the paving stones and twisted into convulsive loops, blocked the path like angry snakes.

The street had no end.

2. In the Telefónica

When you are in danger of death you feel fear, beforehand, or while it lasts, or afterwards. But in the moment of danger itself you attain something I might call power of sight: the percipience of your senses and instincts becomes so sharpened and clarified that they see into the depth of your life. If the danger of death persists over a long, unbroken period, not as a personal, isolated sensation, but as a collective and shared experience, you either lose your power of imagination to the point of insentient bravery or numb passivity, or else that power of sight grows more sensitive in you until it is as though it had burst the boundaries of life and death.

In those days of November 1936, the people of Madrid, all of them together, and every single individual by himself, lived in constant danger of death.

The enemy stood at the gates of the city and could break in at any moment. Shells fell in the streets. Bombers flew over the roofs and dropped their deadly loads, unpunished. We were in a war and in a besieged town; but the war was a civil war and the besieged town held enemies in its midst. No one knew for certain who was a loyal friend and who a dangerous hidden enemy. No one was safe from denunciation and error, from the shot of an overexcited Miliciano or of a masked assassin dashing past in a car and spraying the pavement with machine-gun bullets. What food there was might disappear overnight. The air of the town was laden with tension, unrest, distrust, physical fear, and challenge, as it was laden with the unreasoning, embittered will to fight on. We talked side by side, arm in arm, with Death.

November was cold, damp, and hung with fogs. Death was filthy.

The shell which killed the old street seller at the corner of the Telefónica flung one of her legs far away from the body into the middle of the street. November caught it, smeared its slime and mud on what had been a woman's leg, and turned it into the dirty tatters of a beggar.

The fires dripped soot. It dissolved in the dampness and became a black, viscous liquid that stuck to one's soles, clung to one's hands, hair, face, and shirt collar, and stayed there.

Buildings slit open by bombs exhibited shattered, fog-soaked rooms with swelling, shapeless furniture and fabrics, their dyes oozing out in turgid dribbles, as though the catastrophe had happened years before and the ruins stayed abandoned ever since. In the houses of the living, the fog billowed through the broken window panes in chill wads.

Have you ever leaned by night over the kerbstone of an old well where the waters sleep far down? Everything is black and silent and you cannot see the bottom. The silence is dense, it rises from the bowels of the earth and smells of mould. When you speak a word, a hoarse echo answers from the deep. If you go on watching and listening, you will hear the velvet padding of slimy beasts on the walls of the shaft. Suddenly one of the beasts drops into the water. The water catches a spark of light from somewhere and dazzles you with a fugitive, livid, steely flash, as though of a naked knife blade. You turn away from the well with a cold shudder.

That is how it felt to look down into the street from one of the windows high up in the Telefónica.

At times the silence filled with dreaded sounds, that silence of a dead town, was ripped, and the shaft of the well came alive with piercing screams. Bundles of light swept through the street alongside the screeching sirens mounted on motorcycles, and the drone of bombers invaded the sky. The nightly slaughter began. The building quivered in its roots, the windows rattled, the electric lights waxed and waned. And then everything was choked and drowned in a pandemonium of hisses and explosions, of red, green, and blue glares, of twisting, gigantic shadows cast by crashing walls and disembowelled houses, of madly tolling fire bells, of whistles, of shouts, of cries. The broken glass showering down on the pavement tinkled musically, almost merrily.

I was exhausted beyond measure. I had a camp bed in the censorship room at the Telefónica, and slept in snatches by day or night, constantly wakened by enquiries or by air raids. I kept myself going by drinking strong black coffee and brandy. I was drunk with tiredness, coffee, brandy, and worry. The responsibility for censoring the international press had fallen on my shoulders, together with the care of the war correspondents in Madrid. I found myself in perpetual conflict between the contradictory orders from the Ministry in Valencia on the one side, and from the *Junta de Defensa* or the War Commissariat of Madrid on the other, short of staff, incapable of speaking a word of English and forced to face a horde of journalists nervously excited by their own work at a battle front barely a mile away. And we had to work in a building which was the landmark for all the guns shelling Madrid and all the bombers flying over the city, and which every one of us knew to be a mantrap.

I stared at the journalists' reports, trying to make out what they wanted to convey, hunting through pedantic dictionaries to find the meaning of their double-edged words, sensing and resenting their impatience or hostility. I never saw them as human beings, but merely as grimacing puppets, pale blobs in the dusk, popping up, vociferating, and disappearing.

Towards midnight an alert was sounded and we went into the narrow corridor which offered shelter from flying glass in the little lobby behind the door. There we continued to censor reports by the beams of our electric torches.

A group of people was groping through the passage. 'Can't those journalists keep quiet while the raid's on?' one of us grunted.

They were correspondents who had just come from Valencia. A couple of them had been in Madrid before and gone away on November the 7th or so. We exchanged greetings in the semi-darkness. There was a woman among them.

I took them back to the office when the brief alert was over. I could not make out the faces of the newcomers in the dim light of the lamp wrapped in its purple carbon paper. Other journalists arrived with urgent messages about the raid, which I had to dispatch at once. The woman sat down at the desk: a round face with big eyes, blunt nose, wide forehead, a mass of dark hair that looked almost black, too-broad shoulders encased in a green or grey coat, or it may have been some other colour which the purple light made indefinite and ugly. She was over thirty and no beauty. Why in the hell had those people in Valencia sent me a woman, when I had my hands full with the men anyhow? My feelings towards her were strictly unfriendly.

It was irritating having to look up the many new words war and its weapons threw up every day; it made me very slow at my work. The woman was watching me with curious eyes. suddenly she said in French: 'Can I help you with anything, *camarade?*'

Silently, I handed her a page with a number of baffling idioms. I wa displeased and slightly suspicious when I saw how quickly and easily she ran her eyes along the lines, but I consulted her about a few terms, to get rid of the heap of papers. When we were alone I asked her: 'Why did you call me "comrade"?'

She looked up with an expression of great astonishment.

'Because we are all comrades here.'

'I don't think many of the journalists are. Some of them are Fascists.'

'I have come here as a Socialist and not as a newspaper correspondent.'

'All right, then,' I said, 'let it pass at comrades.' I said it harshly and against my inclination. That woman was going to create complications.

I checked and endorsed her papers, billeted her in the Hotel Gran Vía, just opposite the Telefónica, and asked Luis, the orderly, to pilot her through the dark street. She walked down the passage, straight and terribly serious in her severe coat. But she knew how to walk. A voice behind me said. 'She's a member of the Shock Police!'

When Luis came back he exclaimed: 'Now there's a woman for you!'

'What, do you find her attractive?' I asked him, astonished.

'She's a fine woman, Don Arturo. But perhaps too much of a good thing for a man. And what an idea to come to Madrid just now! She doesn't even know five words of Spanish. But I think she'll be all right if she's got to be out in the streets all by herself. She's got plenty of guts, that woman.'

The following day she came to the censorship for her safe-conduct and we had a long talk in conventional French. She spoke frankly about herself, ignoring, or not even noticing, my resentment. She was an Austrian Socialist with eighteen years of political work behind her; she had had her share in the February Rising of the Viennese workers in 1934, and in the underground resistance movement following it; then she had escaped to Czechoslovakia and had lived there with her husband, as a political writer. She had decided to go to Spain as soon as the war broke out. Why? Well, she thought it was the most important thing in the whole world for Socialists, and she wanted to do something for it. She had been following events in our country through the Spanish Socialist papers which she deciphered with the help of her French, Latin, and Italian. By university training she was an economist and sociologist, but for many years she had invested her time in propagandist and educational work within the labour movement.

I groaned internally: so a highbrow woman intellectual had fallen to my lot!

Well, since she was determined to get to Spain, she had got there, goodness knows how, with borrowed money, on the strength of the promise of some Left papers in Czechoslovakia and Norway to take her articles, but without a salary or budget for telephone reports or cables, with nothing but a few powerful letters of introduction. The Spanish Embassy in Paris had sent her on to the Press Department, which had decided to pay for her food. Rubio Hidalgo had taken her back to Valencia in his convoy, but she thought that at least one labour journalist ought to report directly from Madrid, and so she had come back. She would write her own stuff and serve as a kind of secretary to a French and an English journalist, who were willing to pay her quite a lot; so she would be all right. Not that this was very important. She had put herself at the disposal of our propaganda department and considered herself under our discipline.

A neat little speech. I did not know what to do with her; she seemed to know too much and too little. Also, I thought her story a bit fantastic, in spite of the letters she had shown me.

A plump and jovial Danish journalist came into the room, one of the men who had arrived together with the woman. He wanted me to pass a long article for *Politiken*. I was very sorry: I could not censor anything in Danish, he would have to submit it to us in French. He spoke to the woman, she glanced through the handwritten pages and turned to me.

'It is an article on the bombing of Madrid. Let me read it for you. I have censored other Danish articles for the Valencia censorship. It would make it difficult for his paper if he had to re-write and send it in French.'

'I cannot pass reports in a language I don't understand.'

'Ring up Valencia, ask Rubio Hidalgo, and you'll see that he will let me do it. It's in your own interest, after all. I'll come back later to hear what he says.'

I did not much like her insistence, but I reported the case to Rubio when I had my midday telephone conference with him. I found that I could not pronounce the woman's name, but there was no other foreign woman journalist in the town. To my surprise, Rubio agreed at once and asked: 'But what else is Ilsa doing?'

'I don't really know. She'll write a few articles, I suppose, and type for Delmer and Delaprée for a living.'

'Ask her to join the censorship. The usual pay, three hundred pesetas a month, plus her expenses in the hotel. She might be very useful, she knows a lot of languages, and is very intelligent. But she's a bit impulsive and naïve. Ask her today.'

When I invited her to become a censor, she hesitated for a brief moment and then said: 'Yes. It isn't good for your propaganda that none of you can speak with the journalists in their professional language. I'll do it.'

She started that very night. We worked together, one one each side of the wide desk. The shadow from the lampshade fell on our faces, and only when we were leaning over the papers did we see the other's nose and chin in the light cone, foreshortened and flattened by the glare. She was very quick. I could see that the journalists were pleased and talked to her in rapid English, as though to one of themselves. It worried me. Once she put the pencil down and I watched her, while she was absorbed in her report. It must have been amusing, because her mouth curved in a faint half-smile.

'But – this woman has a delightful mouth,' I said to myself. And I suddenly felt curiosity and wanted to see her more closely.

That night we talked for a long time on the propaganda methods of the Spanish Republican Government, such as we saw them mirrored in the censorship rules I explained to her, and such as she had seen them in the results abroad. The terrible difficulties under which we laboured, their causes and effects, had to be suppressed in press reports. Her point of view was that this was catastrophically wrong because it made our defeats and social diseases inexplicable, our successes unimportant, our communiqués ludicrous, and because it gave foreign Fascist propaganda an easy victory. I was fascinated by the subject. From my own experience in written propaganda, although I had worked from a commercial angle, I believed our methods to be ineffective. We tried to preserve a prestige we did not possess, and lost the opportunity for positive propaganda. She and I saw with astonishment that we wanted the same, although in different formulas and coming from widely different starting points. We agreed that we would try to make our superiors change their tactics, and that we were in a key position to do so in the foreign press censorship of besieged Madrid.

Ilsa did not go back to her hotel room. She admitted that the night before, when Junkers and Capronis had showered down incendiary bombs, she had not like being there, cut off and useless. I offered her the third camp bed in the office and was pleased when she agreed. So she slept in snatches and censored in snatches through the night, as I did while Luis gently snored in his corner.

We worked round the clock during the following day, and we talked at every free moment. Rafael asked me how I could find so much to talk about with her; Manolo told her that her conversation must be singularly fascinating; Luis nodded his head sagely. When she went out to type her own articles and stayed away with some of the English-speaking journalists, I was impatient and restless. News from the front was bad. The noise from the trenches knocked at our windowpanes the whole day long.

After midnight I threw myself on my camp bed under the window, while Ilsa took over the censorship of the night dispatches.

I could not sleep. It was not only that people kept coming and going. I was in that stage of nervous exhaustion which makes one go on and on in a weary circle, in mental and physical bondage. During the past nights, I had not slept because of the raids, and I had had my brief share of fire-fighting when incendiary bombs fell in one of the courtyards of the Telefónica. Now I was drugged with black coffee and brandy. A dull irritation was mounting in me.

Then Ilsa, too, lay down on the bed along the opposite wall and soon fell asleep. It was the quietest time, between three and five. At five one of the agency men would come with his endless early morning chronicle. I dozed in a sullen, semi-lucid stupor.

Through my dreams I began to hear a tenuous purr very far away, which quickly came nearer. So I would not sleep this night either, because the bombers were coming! I saw through the purple-grey darkness that Ilsa opened her eyes. We both propped our heads on one of our hands, half sitting, half lying, face to face.

'I thought at first it was the lifts,' she said. The big lifts had been humming all the time in their shafts behind the wall.

The aeroplanes were circling directly overhead and the sound drew nearer. They were coming down, slowly and deliberately, tracing a spiral round the skyscraper. I listened stupidly to the double-toned whirr of their propellers, a low note and a high note: 'To sleep – to sleep – to sleep.'

Ilsa asked: 'What are we going to do?'

What are we going to do? Like that. In a cool, detached voice. Who was this woman that she thought it was a joke? My head kept on hammering the stupid words in time with the engines: 'To sleep – to sleep – to sleep.' And now that idiotic question of hers: 'What are we going to do?'

And was she going to make up her face now? She had opened her handbag, taken out a powder puff and passed it over her nose.

I answered her question brusquely: 'Nothing!'

We stayed on, listening to the drone of the engines circling inexorably overhead. Otherwise there was a deep silence. The orderlies must have gone down to the shelters. Everyone must have gone down to the shelters. What were we doing here, listening and waiting?

The explosion lifted me from the mattress by at least an inch. For an infinitesimal moment I felt suspended in the air. The black curtains billowed into the room and poured a cascade of broken glass from their folds on to my blanket. The building, whose vibration I had not been feeling, now seemed to swing back into place in a slow movement. From the streets rose a medley of cries. Glass was crashing on stone. A wall crumbled softly. I guessed the muffled thud of the wave of dust and rubble pouring into the street.

Ilsa rose and sat down at the foot of my bed, in front of the flapping curtains. We began to talk, I do not remember of what. We needed to talk and to have the feeling of a refuge, like scared animals. The damp fog, carrying a smell of plaster, came in gusts through the windows. I felt a furious desire to possess that woman there and then. We huddled in our coats. Overhead the drone of aircraft had ceased. There were a few explosions very far away. Luis poked his frightened face through the door.

'But did you stay up here, you and the lady? What lunacy, Don Arturo! I went down to the basement and they sent me out with a rescue party while the bombs were still falling, and I had to carry a few who were just a nasty mess. So perhaps it would have been better to stay up here. But I didn't think I was leaving you alone, I thought you would come down too, of course – '

He ran on with his nervous, jerky chatter. One of the agency correspondents came with the first 'snap' on the big raid. He reported that a house in the Calle de Hortaleza, twenty yards from the Telefónica, had been totally destroyed. Ilsa went to the desk to censor his dispatch in haste, and the faint gleam that came through the purple-grey carbon paper round the bulb illuminated her face. The paper was being slowly scorched and smelled of wax, the odour of a church in which the big candles of the Main Altar have just been put out. I went with the journalists up to the twelfth floor, to see the green fires which ringed the Telefónica.

The morning came with a watery sun, and we leaned out of the window. The Calle de Hortaleza was partly closed to traffic by a cordon of Milicianos. The firemen were helping to clear away debris. People were rolling up their blinds and drawing back their curtains. All the window-sills and balconies were littered with glass. Someone started sweeping the glittering heap down into the street. It tinkled on the pavement. Suddenly the figure of a drowsy woman or man wielding a broom appeared in every balcony door and window. The broken glass rained down on both sides of the steet. The spectacle was absurdly funny and hilarious. It reminded me of the famous scene in *Sous les Toits de Paris*, when a human figure appears in every lighted window and joins the chorus of the song. The glass clattered gaily on the stones, and the people who were sweeping it down exchanged jokes with the Milicianos in the street who had to take cover from the downpour.

I saw it as something apart from myself. My own anger was still mounting. Now I would have to find another room for our office, because one could not even dream of new windowpanes.

At ten o'clock Aurelia arrived, determined to persuade me that I should come home for a short while; I had not been there for at least a week. She would arrange it so that the children would stay with her parents, and we would be alone in the flat. For two months or more we had not been alone. I was repelled by the proposal, and our exchange of words became acrid. She jerked her head towards Ilsa and said: 'Of course, since you are in good company . . .!' I told her that she would have to take the children away from Madrid. She said that I only wanted to get rid of her; and, seriously as I felt about the removal of the children from the multiple dangers of the town, I knew that she was not quite wrong. I tried to promise her that I would come to see her the following day.

At midday we were installed on the fourth floor in an enormous conference room. It had a huge table in the middle and four desks lined up under the four windows. We ranged our three camp beds along the opposite wall, a fourth one in the far corner. The windows opened to the Calle de Valverde, facing the battle-front of the Manzanares valley. The big conference table had a shrapnel scar; the house in front of us was slashed by a shell; the roof of another behind it was gnawed away by fire: we were in the wing of the Telefónica most exposed to artillery fire from the blue hills beyond the maze of low roofs. We replaced the missing panes with cardboard and hung mattresses over the windows behind the desks which we selected for censoring. The mattresses would keep out shrapnel, and nothing would keep out a shell anyhow.

We were gay while we made our preparations. The big room was bright and friendly compared with the one we had abandoned. We decided that it should be our permanent office. Ilsa and I went to lunch in one of the restaurants still functioning in the Carrera de San Jeronimo; I was tired of the canteen food, and did not feel like sitting with the journalists in the Hotel Gran Vía, only to listen to a conversation in English I could not understand. While we passed the deep crater of the bomb which had smashed through the gas main and the vaulting of the Underground, Ilsa took my arm. We were crossing the expanse of the Puerta del Sol, when someone plucked at my sleeve.

'Can you spare me a moment?'

Maria was standing behind me with a hag-ridden face. I asked Ilsa to wait for me, and went a few steps with Maria who burst out at once:

'Who's this woman?'

'A foreigner who's working with me in the censorship.'

'Don't tell me stories. She's your lover. If she isn't, why should she be glued to your arm? And in the meantime, you leave me alone, like an old rag one throws away!'

While I tried to tell her that it didn't mean anything to a foreigner to take a man's arm, she poured forth a torrent of insults and then started to weep. Openly crying, she walked away, down the Calle de Carretas. When I joined Ilsa, I had to explain the situation; I told her briefly of the failure of my matrimony, of my state of mind between the two women, and of my flight from them. She made no comment, but I saw the same faint astonishment and disgust in her eyes which I had caught in the morning when I had been quarrelling with my wife. During lunch I felt driven to annoy and provoke her; I wanted to break through her calmness; afterwards I had to make sure that I had not destroyed the frankness of speech between us, and talked, mainly of the torture of being a Spaniard who could not do anything to help his people.

By midnight, after a day when we had had to carry the main load of the censorship, with little help from other staff, our fatigue became overpowering. I decided to close down the office between one o'clock and eight in the morning, except for very urgent and unforeseen cases. It was a liberation to think that I would not have to read through long, futile military surveys at five in the morning. It was impossible to go on working eighteen hours a day.

While one of the other censors dozed at the desk, Ilsa and I tried to sleep on our hard camp beds. The crack of rifle shots and the occasional rattle of machine guns were sweeping in waves through the windows. It was very cold and damp, and it was difficult to shut out the thought that we were in the direct firing line of the guns. We went on talking as though we were holding fast to each other. Then I slept like the dead for a few hours.

I do not remember much of the following day. I was doped by sleeplessness, black coffee, brandy, and despair; I moved in a semi-lucidity of senses and brain. There was no raid, news from the front was bad, Ilsa and I worked together, talked together, and were silent together. That is all I know.

At midnight, Luis made the three beds and pottered round the room. He chose the bed in the far corner for himself; there he hung his braided coat over a chair, took off his boots and wrapped himself in the blankets. Ilsa and I lay down on our camp beds, at a foot's distance from each other, and talked softly. From time to time I stared at the profile of the censor on duty, pallid in the shaft of light. We talked of what we had lived through in our minds, she in the long years of revolutionary fight and defeat, I in the short, endless months of our war.

When the censor packed up at one o'clock, I bolted the door behind him and turned off all the lights except the desk light in its carbon-paper shade. Luis was snoring peacefully. I went back to bed. The room was in darkness outside the purple-grey pool on the desk and the small, ruddy island round the single electric stove. Fog filtered through the windows together with the sounds of the front, and made a mauve halo round the lamp. I got up and pushed my bed close to hers. It was the most natural thing in the world to join our hands and close the circuit.

I woke at dawn. The front was silent and the room quiet. Fog had thickened in it, and the halo of the desk lamp had grown to a globe of purple-grey, translucent and glowing. I could see the outlines of the furniture. Cautiously I withdrew my arm and wrapped Ilsa in her blankets. Then I pushed my bed back into its old place. One of the iron legs screeched on the waxed floor boards, and I stopped in suspense. Luis continued his rhythmical breathing, scarcely a snore any more. Recovering from my fright, I drew my blankets tighter and went to sleep again.

In the morning, the most extraordinary part of my experience was its naturalness. I had not the feeling of having known a woman for the first time, but of having known her always; 'always', not in the course of my life, but in the absolute sense, before and outside this life of mine. It was the same sensation we sometimes feel when we walk through the streets of an old town: we come upon a silent little square, and we know it; we know that we lived there, that we have know it always, that it has only come back into our real life, that we are familiar with those moss-grown stones, and they with us. I had not even the masculine curiosity that watches out in the morning for what the woman with whom we have slept will say and do. I knew what she was going to do and what her face would look like, as we know something which is part of our own life and which we see without watching.

She came down from the washroom of the telephone girls with a fresh face, powder specks still adhering to the damp skin, and when Luis went out to fetch our breakfast we kissed gaily, like a happy married couple.

I had an immense feeling of liberation, and seemed to see people and things with different eyes, in a different light, illuminated from within. My weariness and annoyance had gone. I had an airy sensation, as though I were drinking champagne and laughing, with a mouth full of bubbles which burst and tickled and escaped merrily through my lips.

I saw that she had lost her defensive seriousness and severity. Her grey-green eyes had a gay light in their depths. When Luis spread out the breakfast on one of the tables, he stopped and glanced at her. In the security of knowing that she did not understand Spanish, he said to me:

'She's good to look at today.'

She realized that he was talking of her. 'What is it Luis said about me?'

'That you are better looking this morning.' She blushed and laughed. Luis looked from one to the other. When he and I were alone, he came up to me and said: 'My congratulations, Don Arturo.'

He said it without irony and quite without roguery. In his straightforward mind, Luis had seen clearly what I did not yet know with my brain: that she and I belonged together. With all his profound devotion to me, whom he considered to have saved his existence, he decided simply and clearly to be the guardian angel of our love. But he did not say any further word of comment.

For it was so that at that time I did not know what he knew. While all my instincts had felt and seen that this was 'my woman', all my reason battled against it. As the day went on, I found myself caught in those carefully formulated mental dialogues which arise from a reasoned struggle against one's instincts: 'Now you're in it . . . now you're tied up with yet another woman . . . you've run away from your own wife and you're running away from your mistress of many years' standing, and now you fall for the first woman who comes along, after knowing her five days. She does not even speak your language. Now you are going to be together with her all day long, without any possible escape. What are you doing? What are you going to do? Of course you do not love her. It's just an odd attraction. It's impossible that you should be in love with her. You have never been in love yet.'

I put myself in front of Ilsa, looked into her face and said with the wondering voice of one who states a problem he cannot solve:

'*Mais – je ne t'aime pas!*'

She smiled and said in a soothing voice: 'No, my dear.'

I was angry.

In those days, members of the International Column, who had known Ilsa, or known about her, from her life outside Spain, began to visit the Censorship and to have long conferences with her. One day Gustav Regler came, a German with a pasty, furrowed face, in big boots, a heavy jacket with sheepskin collar, his whole body twitching with nerves. Ilsa had just thrown herself on her camp bed to take half an hour's rest, and I was censoring at the desk. The German sat down on the foot of her bed and talked to her. I watched them. Her face was animated and friendly. While she spoke, he laid one of his hands on her shoulder, and then he laid it on her knee. I felt an overpowering desire to kick him out.

When he had gone, with a casual nod for me, I went over to her and said: 'He wanted to make love to you.'

'Not really. The International Column is in the thick of it, and he's no soldier. He tries to escape from his nerves by pretending that he needs a woman – and I happen to be here.'

'Do as you want,' I said roughly, and sat down on the edge of the bed. For a moment I leaned my forehead on her shoulder, then I straightened up and said furiously: 'But I'm not in love with you.'

'No,' she said serenely. 'Let me get up. I'll take over the shift, I'm quite rested. Now you have a sleep.'

She went to the desk and began to read, while I looked at her from my camp bed and kept on thinking that the wall behind her faced the front. Isolated shrapnel shells burst over the roofs. I was happy.

During the night we listened to the ring of mortar explosions. In the grey, wet dawn we went to the window and heard the horizon of noise quieten down. One of the men from the Workers' Control came and showed me a Mexican rifle: Mexico had sent arms. The fighters circling overhead were ours; they were sent by Soviet Russia. In the Casa de Campo, German and French comrades were fighting and dying for us, and in the Parque de Oeste the Basque unit was digging in. It was very cold, and our windowpanes were starred with small holes. The foreign journalists reported small, infinitely costly, local advances of the Madrid forces, and small, dearly bought, threatening advances of the ring of encirclement. But there was a joyful hope in us, underneath and above the fear, menace, muddle, and petty cowardice which went on, inevitably. We were together in the fear, the menace, and the fight; people were simpler and friendlier to each other for a time. It did not seem worth while to pretend; there were so few things that mattered. Those nights of fire and fighting, those days of stubborn, grinding work were teaching us – for a short time – to walk gaily in step with Death and to believe that we would win through to a new life.

The siege and defence of Madrid had lasted twenty days.

3. The Siege

The assault was over and the siege was set.

A small stair leads from the last storey of the Telefónica up to its square tower. There the city noise recedes, the air grows more transparent, the sounds more clear. A soft breeze blows on days of calm, and on windy days you seem to stand on the gale-swept bridge of a ship. The tower has a gallery facing with its four sides to the four points of the compass and you can look out over a concrete balustrade.

To the north are the pointed crests of the Guadarrama, a barrier changing colour with the course of the sun. From deep blue it turns into opaque black; when its rock reflects the rays of the sun it grows luminous, at sunset it glows in copper tints; and when the darkened city puts on its electric lights, the highest peaks are still incandescent.

Over there the front began, invisibly curving round distant crags and gullies. Then it turned west, following the valleys, and bending towards the city. You saw it first from the angle of the gallery between its north and west sides, a few smoke plumes and shell bursts like puffs from a cigarette. Then the front came closer, along the shining arc of the river Manzanares which took it south and through the city itself. From the height of the tower, the river appeared solid and motionless, while the land round it was shaken by convulsions. You saw and heard it move; that part of the front sent out vibrations. The ground carried them to the skyscraper, and there they mounted its steel girders until they were amplified under your feet to a tremor as of distant railway trains. The sounds reached you through the air, unbroken and undisguised, thuds and explosions, the clatter of machine guns, the dry crack of rifle shots. You saw the flashes from the gun muzzles and you saw the trees in the Casa de Campo swaying as though monsters were scraping against their top branches. You saw ant-like figures dotting the sandy banks of the river. Then there came burst of silence when you stared at the landscape, trying to guess at the secret of the sudden stillness, until ground and air trembled in spasms and the shining smoothness of the river broke up in quivering ripples.

Up on the tower, the front seemed nearer than the street at the foot of the building. When you leaned over to look down into the Gran Vía, the street was a dim, deep canyon, and from its distant bottom vertigo dragged at you. But when you looked straight in front, there was the landscape and the war within it spread on a table before you, as though you could reach out and touch it. It was bewildering to see the front so close, within the city, while the city itself remained intangible and aloof under its shield of roofs and towers, below the red, grey and white divided by a labyrinth of cracks which were its streets. Yet then the hills across the river spat out white points, and the mosaic of roofs opened in sprays of smoke, dust, and tiles, while you still heard the ululating shells pass by. They all seemed to pass by the tower of the Telefónica. Thus the landscape with its dark woods, tawny fields, and glittering river sand was fused with the red tiles, the grey towers, and the street down below, and you were plunged in the heart of the battle.

The storeys above the eighth floor of the building were abandoned. The lift usually arrived empty at the thirteenth floor, where a few artillerymen manned an observation post. The men's boots thumped on the parquet of the wide rooms and made them ring hollow. A shell had crashed through two floors, and the snapped rods, the bent steel girders of the frame, were hanging like tatters into the jagged hole.

The girl who took up the lift, perched on her stool like a bird, was pretty and merry. 'I don't like coming up here,' she would say. 'It's so lonely now, I always think the lift is going to shoot out of the tower into thin air.'

Then you dropped down into Madrid like a stone, while the walls of the shaft closed up above you, the metal doors clanked and a smell of grease, hot iron, and sprayed varnish enveloped you.

The town was alive and tense, palpitating as a deep knife wound in which the blood wells up in gusts and the muscles twitch with pain and vigorous life.

They were shelling the centre of Madrid, and this centre overflowed with people who talked, shouted, pushed, and showed each other that they were alive. Platoons of Milicianos – soldiers, we were beginning to call them – were coming from the front and marching to the front, cheered and cheering. Sometimes people broke into song with raucous gusto. Sometimes steel grated and clanked on stone when a tank passed, its turret open and a small figure peeping out with its hand upon the lid, like a jack-in-the-box escaping from a giant pot. Sometimes a big gun passed and stopped at the street corner so that people could finger its grey-green paint as if they were afraid of its being unreal. Sometimes a huge ambulance, red crosses on milk-white ground, passed and left silence in its wake, and the silence was torn by a stuttering motorcycle weaving its way round people and cars. Then somebody would shout: 'You'll be late!' and the din of the crowd would burst out afresh.

Everything was as fleeting as pictures on a screen, fleeting and spasmodic. People talked in shouts and laughed in shrill outbursts. They drank noisily with a great clatter of glasses. The footsteps in the streets sounded loud, firm, and quick. In daylight, everyone was a friend, by night everyone might be an enemy. The friendliness was shot with a feeling of drunkenness. The city had attempted the impossible, it had emerged triumphant and in a trance.

Oh yes, the enemy was there at the gates, twelve hundred yards from this corner of the Gran Vía. Sometimes a stray rifle bullet made a starred hole in a windowpane. So what? They had not entered that night of November the 7th, how could they enter now? When shells dropped on the Gran Vía and the Calle de Alcalá, starting at the higher end near the front and tracing 'Shell Alley' down to the statue of the goddess Cybele, people clustered under the doors on the side of the street which was considered safer and watched the explosions at thirty yards' distance. Some came from the outlying districts to see what a bombardment was like and went away contented with shell splinters, still faintly warm, for a keepsake.

The misery of it all was not on exhibition. It was hidden away in cellars and basements, in the improvised shelters of the Underground and in the hospitals where they had neither instruments nor medicaments to deal with the never ending stream of wounded people. The flimsy houses in the working-class districts collapsed from blast, but their inhabitants were swallowed by other flimsy, overcrowded houses. Thousands of refugees from the villages and suburbs were stowed away in deserted buildings, thousands of women and children were taken away by evacuation convoys to the east coast. The clutch of the siege was still tightening and more units of the International Column, grown to two brigades, were poured into the gaps of the defence. Yet the elation which carried us beyond our fears and doubts never petered out. We were Madrid.

Life was slowly going back to settled conditions in our new censorship room. We looked round and found each other hollow-eyed, drawn, begrimed, but solid and human. Newcomers among the journalists were inclined to treat those who had settled in as veterans, and Ilsa, the only woman, as a heroine. The guards in the Telefónica changed their tone; some of the foreigners had overnight become comrades. Others were just beyond the pale, such as the big American, who faded out of the picture and was replaced by a man of a very different calibre, commanding trust.

Ilsa was silently given the right of citizenship in the Telefónica by most of our men and followed by the whispering hostility of most of the women. I left it to her to deal with the English-speaking journalists, not only because her energies were fresh and I over-wrought and exhausted, but also because I had to admit that she was doing what we had never been able to do: by handling the censorship with greater imagination and leniency, she improved relations with the foreign correspondents and influenced their way of reporting. Some of the censorship employees resented it and I had to back her with my authority, but through Suzana of the War Commissariat came qualified approval from the General Staff where the censored dispatches were read before going to Valencia. Soon Ilsa's method was put to a hard test.

National Socialist Germany had officially recognized Franco and sent General von Faupel as a special envoy to Burgos. Most of the German citizens had been evacuated by their Embassy, and the Embassy itself had closed down. But there was no declaration of war, only German nonintervention, in the guise of technical and strategical support for the rebels. On a grey November day, our police raided the German Embassy in Madrid and confiscated papers and arms left there. It was technically a breach of extra-territoriality, but the foreign correspondents who had witnessed the raid submitted reports speaking with unexpected accuracy of the links between the Embassy and the headquarters of the Fifth Column. Only – according to our strict official rules – we had to stop their reports: we had to suppress any reference to police measures unless they were released in a communiqué from Valencia. The correspondents were furious and bombarded us with demands and requests. It grew late, and they were afraid of missing the deadline. I rang up the War Commissariat, but only Michael Kolzoff was there to give instructions and he told me to wait for an official statement.

Ilsa was less furious and more worried than the journalists. When an hour of waiting had gone, she took me aside and asked me to let her pass the reports in the order in which they had been handed in. She would sign the dispatches with her initials, so that the responsibility would rest on her, and she was prepared to face the very grave situation which would arise from her breaking a clear order. But she was not prepared to turn the good will of the correspondents into bad will against her better knowledge and to let the German version monopolize the morning press of the world. Somewhat melodramatically, she said: 'I'm responsible not to your Valencia bureaucracy but to the labour movement, and I won't allow this to be messed up if I can help it.' I refused to let her shoulder the responsibility alone. We released the reports about the raid on the Embassy.

Late at night I was rung up by Kolzoff and threatened with courtmartial for myself and Ilsa. On the following morning he rang up again and took everything back: his own superiors, whoever they were, had been delighted with the results of our act of insubordination. Rubio, speaking from Valencia, followed the same line, although he stressed the serious character of the step Ilsa had taken in 'her impulsive manner', as he called it. But for the time being she had carried the day and, aware of her advantage, attempted to follow it up.

After the first week when the bombing and shelling of Madrid was news, the correspondents began to chafe under the restrictions imposed on their reports from the front. Ilsa argued that we should give them access to new material, on the principle that 'you must feed the animals at the zoo'. There was nobody except our own office to deal with them. The military could not be expected to release more than they did. The journalists, on the other hand, were little interested in the social aspects of our fight; or if they were interested, they either turned them into black-and-white left-wing propaganda for readers already convinced, or into bogies to scare comfortable people abroad. We could not suggest subjects for them, but we ought to enable them to write something of the story of Madrid. It was our opportunity, since we were at the switchboards.

One day when Gustav Regler came from the front, heavy-footed in his new dignity as political commissar with the XIIth Brigade – the first of the International Brigades – he launched forth in an impassioned speech in German. Ilsa listened attentively, and then turned to me: 'He's right. The International Brigades are the greatest thing that has happened in the movement for years, and it would be a tremendous inspiration to the workers everywhere, if only they knew enough about it. Think of it, while their governments are organizing NonIntervention . . . Gustav is willing to take journalists to his headquarters and General Kleber would see them. But there's no point in it if we don't pass their stories on principle. I'm going to do it.'

Again it was an audacious step and an immediate success. The correspondents, headed by Delmer of the *Daily Express*, and Louis Delaprée of *Paris-Soir*, came back with glimpses of the best there was in the International Brigades, genuinely impressed and with a news story bound to make headlines. The ball was set rolling. Yet after a week or so it appeared that only the International Brigades figured in the press dispatches, as though they were the sole saviours of Madrid. Ilsa was beginning to feel qualms; she had got more than she had bargained for. I was angry, because I found it unjust that the people of Madrid, the improvised soldiers in Carabanchel and the Parque de Oeste and the Guadarrama, were forgotten because there was no propaganda machine to publicize them. Even before instructions came from the General Staff in Madrid and the Press Department in Valencia, we restricted the space for reports on the International Brigades. It left me with a bitter feeling of cleavage between us, the Spaniards, and the world.

In those days Regler asked me, as the only Spaniard with whom he had any contact, to write something for a front-line paper of his Edgar André Battalion. I wrote a jumble of conventional praise and personal impressions; I voiced my early instinctive fear that the international units would be like the Spanish Foreign Legion I had know in its selfish courage, brutality, and recklessness, and my relief at realizing that there existed in them men driven by a clean political faith and by love for a world without slaughter.

Ilsa worked her way through the article because she was to translate it; she was beginning to read Spanish fairly fluently, though we still had to converse in French. Then she said unexpectedly: 'Do you know that you can write? That is, if you cut out all the pompous ornaments which remind me of the Jesuit Baroque churches and write only your own style. This thing is partly awful and partly very good.' I said: 'But I've always wanted to be a writer,' stuttering like a schoolboy, hot with pleasure at her and her judgement. My article was never used, it was not what the Political Commissar had wanted, but the incident was doubly important for me. She had disinterred my old ambition, and I had admitted my suppressed resentment against the foreigners in so many words, talking myself free of it.

It was thrown back at me in a caricature, on the same day, I think. The Austrian labour leader, Julius Deutsch, made General of the Spanish Republican Army in honour of the Workers' Militia which he had helped to organize and which had fought the first battle against Fascism in Europe, came to visit Ilsa. He was touring our zone together with his interpreter Rolf, and he had been given not only a car but a militia captain as a political commissar and guide. While the two were speaking with Ilsa, trying, as I saw clearly and with annoyance, to persuade her to leave the dangers of Madrid, their Spanish guide told me that they were spies 'because they were always speaking that lingo instead of speaking like Christians'. The man was really upset and excited: 'Now tell me, *Compañero*, what do they seek in Spain? It can't be anything decent. I tell you they are spies. And the woman must be one too.' It made me laugh and gave me a shock even while I was talking sense to him: I was one of those Spaniards, too.

Angel was standing before me in the motley uniform of a Miliciano, blue boiler suit over several layers of torn pullovers, a greasy peaked cap with a five-pointed star, a rifle in his hand and a huge sheathed knife in his belt, everything caked with mud and his grimy face split by an enormous grin.

'Christ alive, I thought I'd never find you in this labyrinth. Well, so here I am. I didn't die, oh no, sir, and they didn't kill me, either. I'm going strong, I am.'

'Angel, where have you sprung from?'

'From somewhere over there.' He pointed with his thumb over his shoulder. 'I was getting bored in my dispensary and things were getting hot somewhere else, so I went there. So now I'm a Miliciano, and a real one, I can tell you.'

In the middle of October, Angel had been taken on as dispensary assistant in one of the first emergency hospitals. He had vanished on the evening of November the 6th and I had not heard of him since.

'Yes, on the evening of the 6th I went down to Segovia Bridge. Well, what should I tell you? You know they gave us a thrashing – the Moors, the Legionaries, and the tanks. As though the world had come to an end. They killed nearly all of us.'

'But you were left.'

'Yes. But . . . well, I don't know about that, because you see, I don't really know if I am left. I'm only beginning to realize it now. Somebody came up to me yesterday and said: "Angelillo, you're going to be a corporal." So I said: "Hell, why?" And the other bird said: "Because you've been made one." I was thinking he'd made a mistake, because as far as I knew, we weren't exactly in barracks, but in a hole in the earth digging hard to make a trench. So then I began to get on to things. The *Tercio* and the Civil Guard were peppering away at us from a couple of houses. And there it was. They hadn't killed me. So I asked a fellow by the name of Juanillo, a neighbour in our street: "Juanillo, lad," I said, "what day is it?" He started counting on his fingers, scratched his head and said to me: "Well – I don't rightly know." '

'Angelillo, I believe you're a bit drunk.'

'Don't you believe it. It's just that I'm afraid. I only took three or four glasses in company with my friends, and then I said to myself, I'll go and see Don Arturo – if they haven't killed him yet, that is. Your missus told me you don't ever get out of this place, so I came here. But I won't say I wouldn't like to take a glass with you, if you've no objection. . . . All right, then, later. And I've nothing to tell you, as I said before. Nothing. It's just been a lot of bangs all the time since the 6th until today, because we've finished our trench now. Of course, they're still shooting, but it's different. Before, they were peppering us in the middle of the street, and round the corners, and even inside the houses. But now we've set up a real hotel, I can tell you.'

'But where are you now?'

'The other side of Segovia Bridge, and we'll be in Navalcarnero in a couple of days, you'll see. And what's happening to you?'

It was as difficult for me as it was for him to give an account of things. Time had lost its meaning. November the 7th seemed to me a date in the remote past and, at the same time, yesterday. I remembered flashes of things seen and done, but they bore no relation to the chronological order of events. We could not narrate what we had lived through, Angel and I, we could only seize upon incidents. Angel had spent those days killing, drowned in a world of explosions and blasphemies, of men killed and left behind, of crumbling houses. He remembered nothing but a blur, and a few lucid moments in which something had printed itself on his memory.

'War's a crazy thing, you don't know what's happening,' he said. 'Well, of course, you do know a few things. For instance, one morning a Civil Guard stuck his head out from behind a wall and I tried to take aim at him. He wasn't looking at me, but somewhere over to my right. He knelt down outside the cover of the wall and drew up his rifle. I fired, and he fell like a sack, with his arms spread out. I said: "So there, you swine." At that moment, somebody beside me said: "I've got a sharp eye, haven't I? I laid him out." So I said: "It seems to me you've got a bit mixed up." So then we ended by punching each other there on the spot, about whether it was him or me that had killed the man. We're always together now, and when we sight a Fascist, we take it in turns to fire first, once him and then me. I've scored three by now. But to talk of something else – Doña Aurelia's told me all sorts of things, that she can't go on like this, and that you've got mixed up with a foreign woman here in the Telefónica, and that she'll have to do something desperate one day. Hell, you know what women are!'

I introduced Angel to Ilsa. He took to her at once, winked at me twice and began to tell her endless stories in his rapid Madrileño slang. She did not understand more than a few stray words, but listened with the right expression of interest until I took him away to the bar of the Gran Vía Hotel across the street. We were drinking their golden Amontillado when shells began to fall outside.

'Does it often get like this, then?' Angel asked.

'Well, only every day and at any time.'

'I'm going back to my trench. We're more polite there. It doesn't suit me at all to be on leave here and get smashed up. . . . What do we think of the war out there? Well, it'll end very soon. With Russia helping us, it'll all be over in a couple of months. They've been doing us fine. Have you seen our fighter planes? As soon as we've got a few more of them, it will be goodbye to Franco's German friends. That's one of the things I just can't understand. Why did those Germans and Italians have to go and get mixed up in our row, when we've done nothing to them?'

'I think they're defending their own side. Haven't you noticed that this is a war against Fascism?'

'Now listen – haven't I noticed? If I started to forget it, they'd remind me every hour with their mortars. Don't think I'm as dumb as all that. Of course, I damn' well know that those generals on the other side are hand in glove with the generals down there in Italy and Germany, because they're all pups from the same litter. But still, I don't understand why the other countries are just keeping quiet and looking on. At least, yes, I can understand it about the people at the top, because they're the same everywhere, German and Italian and French and English. But there are millions of workers in the world, and in France they've got a Popular Front Government. And what are they doing?'

'I don't understand it either, Angel.'

He paid no attention to me and went on: 'I won't say they ought to send us an army of Frenchmen, because we're good enough ourselves to cut those sons of bitches to pieces. But at least they ought to let us buy arms. That's something you don't know about, because you're in the town here, but out there we're fighting with our bare fists, and that's God's own truth. At first we hadn't any rifles to speak of, and we had to agree that whoever was nearest the enemy should have a shot at firing. Then the Mexican sent us a few thousand rifles, blessed be their mothers. But it turned out that our own cartridges were a bit too big for their barrels and stuck. So then they gave us hand grenades, at least, that's what they called them. They're tin cans like water coolers and they're called Lafitte bombs, and you've got to give a tug at a kind of fork and throw them very quickly and then run away, because otherwise they explode in your hand. And then they gave us some pieces of iron tubing filled with dynamite, which you've got to light with your burning cigarette. And the other side are hotting up things for us with their mortars, and the mortar bombs drop on your head without your noticing them. Have you seen one of their mortars? It's like a chimney pipe with a spike at the bottom. They set up the pipe at an angle and drop a bomb the size of an orange in its muzzle, with little wings and all, to make it fly well. When the bomb hits the spike at the bottom of the pipe, the powder in its bottom takes fire, and it shoots sky-high and falls down right on our heads. And there's nothing you can do about it unless you want to spend the whole day gaping at the sky, because it doesn't make any noise. The only thing we can do is to build our trench in angles and stay in the corners. They may kill one of us, but not a whole row as they did to begin with.'

'Stop a bit and have a rest. You're running on like a clock-work toy.'

'It's because your blood boils when you start talking about all those things. I'm not saying the French haven't done anything at all, because they did let us have some machine guns, and people say a few old planes too, but the point is that they don't do things openly as God wants them to. If Hitler sends planes to Franco, why can't the French let us have planes, and with a better right too? After all, we're defending them as well as ourselves.'

I felt too much as he did to say anything, except to remind him that there was Soviet Russia and the International Brigade.

'I'm not forgetting them, but they don't count. Soviet Russia's under an obligation to help us anyway, more than anyone else. A nice thing it would be if Russia shrugged her shoulders and said things just can't be helped!'

'The Russians could have said it. After all, they're a long way away, and there was no need for them to risk war with Germany.'

'You say things you don't really believe, Don Arturo. Russia's a socialist country and has got to come and help us, that's what they've got Socialists – well, Communists – over there for. And as to Germany declaring war: Hitler's just one of those big dogs that bark a lot, but if you hit them with a stone they run away with their tails between their legs. . . And now I must go back to my own place. I'm getting used to mortar shells out there, but I don't like the noise of your shells here. It doesn't sound right in town. *Salud.*'

A convoy of Foreign Ministry cars was leaving Madrid to take stray members of the staff and their families to Valencia. Aurelia and the three children were going with them, and I was seeing them off.

It was good so. The children would be safe. Aurelia had wanted me to come with them and the last days had been burdened with disputes and bickerings that seemed more futile than ever. She had been convinced from her first glance that 'the woman with the green eyes', as she called Ilsa, was the current cause of my attitude; but she was less afraid of the foreigner, who in her view was only having a brief adventure with me, than of Maria, who might establish herself more firmly if I stayed alone in Madrid. She had suggested that I should install her and the children in the basement of the Telefónica, which had been thrown open to nearly a thousand homeless refugees. I had taken her through that pit of misery, noisy and evil-smelling, and explained why it would be wrong to put the children there; but though she had given up her idea, she had insisted that I should go away as the rest of the Ministry had done. In her eyes I only wanted to stay on in Madrid to have more licence to roam. She repeated it even while I was saying goodbye to the children.

I went back to the Telefónica. In the narrow Calle de Valverde there was an endless queue of women and children, drenched by the frosty morning drizzle, stamping their feet, clutching shapeless bundles. Four evacuation lorries, with crude boards for benches, waited a bit further on. Just as I came to the side door of the building, a group of evacuees filed out, women, children, old people, greenish faces, crumpled clothes which carried the stench of the overcrowded shelter in their creases, the same shapeless bundles which the people in the waiting queue carried, the same bewildered, noisy children, shouts, cries, blasphemies, and jokes. They clambered on to the lorries and settled down somehow, a single mass of bodies, while the drivers started their cold, coughing engines.

Now the women in the queue surged past the sentries into the narrow door. The stream caught me and carried me past the Workers' Control Post, down the basement stairs, through the maze of passages. Before and behind me mothers pushed on to seize a free place. Shrill voices were crying: 'Here, Mother, I'm here!' Bundles opened and poured filthy bedclothes into a miraculously free corner, while the occupants of the pallets right and left cursed the newcomers. At once the damp clothes began to steam and the thick sour air became more dense and muggy.

'When are we going to eat, Mother?' cried a dozen children around me. The refugees were starved.

I fought my way upstairs and back to the big, cold, grey room where Ilsa was sitting on her camp bed, listening to the complaints of three people at once, arguing and answering with a patience which seemed wrong to me. I turned to our orderlies: they were cursing as I did.

Rubio rang up from Valencia and told me that I should transfer there. I said I could not go, I was under orders from the Madrid Junta. He gave me instructions about the office. Half an hour later Kolzoff gave me another set of instructions. I shouted through the telephone, in despair; I had to know whose orders I was supposed to follow. There was no decision to be had from either quarter.

I took Delmer, who alone of the English correspondents emerged from the fog of my indifference, to see the clowns Pompoff and Teddy; he made an article out of them. I spoke for hours with Delaprée on French literature and on the utter hatefulness of violence. It did not help much. It irritated me when I saw Ilsa advising and helping some newcomer or other after fifteen hours of work, pumping the last ounce of her energy into an unimportant conversation, only to turn to me with a drawn face and fall silent.

At four in the morning I went down into the second basement which was asleep under the glare of electric bulbs. The silence was full of snores, groans, coughs, and mumbled words. The men of the Shock Police post were playing cards. They gave me a glass of brandy; it was tepid and smelled of sleep. The rooms had the warmth of flesh slowly stewing in its own exudation, of a broody hen, and the brandy had the same warmth and the same smell.

I leaned out of the window for a long while afterwards to rinse my lungs and throat. I could not sleep. I was under a spell. I wanted to take the generals who called themselves saviours of their country, and the diplomats who called themselves saviours of the world to the shelters in the basement of the Telefónica. To put them there on the pallets of esparto grass, damp from November fog, to wrap them in army blankets and make them live and sleep in a space of two square yards, on a cellar floor, between crazed hungry women who had lost their homes, while shells were falling on the roofs outside. To leave them there one day, two days, more days, to drench them in misery, to impregnate them with the sweat and the lice of the multitude and to teach them living history – the history of this miserable, loathsome war, the war of cowardice in top-hats gleaming under the chandeliers of Geneva and of traitor generals coldly murdering their people. To tear them away from their military bands and tail-coats and top-hats and helmets and swords and gold-knobbed canes, to dress them in fustian or blue twill or white twill like the farmhands, the metal-workers, the masons, and then to throw them out into the streets of the world with a three days' stubble and fug-reddened eyes.

I could not think of killing or destroying them. It was monstrous and stupid to kill. It was sickening to see an insect crushed under one's foot. It was marvellous to watch the movements of an insect for hours.

Everything round me was destruction, loathsome as the crushing of a spider underfoot; and it was the barbaric destruction of people herded together and lashed by hunger, ignorance, and the fear of being finally, totally, crushed.

I was choked by the feeling of personal impotence in face of the tragedy. It was bitter to think that I loved peace, and bitter to think of the word pacifism. I had to be a belligerent. I could not shut my eyes and cross my arms while my country was being wantonly assassinated so that a few could seize power and enslave the survivors. I knew that there existed Fascists who had good faith, admirers of the 'better' past, or dreamers of bygone empires and conquerors, who saw themselves as crusaders; but they were the cannon fodder of Fascism. There were the others, the heirs of the corrupt ruling caste of Spain, the same people who had manoeuvred the Moroccan war with its stupendous corruption and humiliating retreats to their own greater glory. We had to fight them. It was not a question of political theories. It was life against death. We had to fight against the death-bringers, the Francos, the Sanjurjos, the Molas, the Millán Astrays, who crowned their blood-drenched record, selling their country so as to be the masters of slaves and in their turn the slaves of other masters.

We had to fight them. This meant we would have to shell or bomb Burgos and its towers. Cordova and its flowered courtyards, Seville and its gardens. We would have to kill so as to purchase the right to live.

I wanted to scream.

A shell had killed the street vendor outside the Telefónica. There was her little daughter, a small, brown, little girl who had been hopping round between the table in the Miami Bar and the Gran Vía café like a sparrow, selling matchboxes and cigarettes. Now she turned up in the bar in a shiny, bright black cotton dress.

'What are you doing?'

'Nothing. I come here since they killed my mother. . . . I'm used to it, I've been doing it since I was so small.'

'Are you alone?'

'No, I'm with Grandmother. They're giving us meals at the Committee, and now they're going to take us to Valencia.' She hopped up to a big, beefy soldier of the International Brigades: 'Long live Russia!' Her voice was high and clear.

No, I could not think in political terms, in terms of party or revolution. I had to think of the crime it was to send shells against human flesh and of the need for me, the pacifist, the lover of Saint Francis, to help in the task of finishing with that breed of Cain. To fight so as to sow, so as to create a Spain in which the command of the Republican Constitution: 'Spain shall renounce war' would be truth and reality. The other thing – to forgive – was Christ's alone. Saint Peter took to the sword.

Over there, the front was alive and sent the echo of its explosions to our windows. Over there were thousands of men who thought vaguely like me and fought, hoping for victory in good faith, ingenuous, barbarous, scratching their lice in the trenches, killing and dying and dreaming of a future without hunger, with schools and cleanliness, without overlords or usurers, in sunshine. I was with them. But it was difficult to sleep.

When all those visions and emotions, thoughts and counter-thoughts crowd into one's brain, when day and night shells and bombs shake the walls and the front line draws nearer, and when sleep is sparse and work long, difficult and full of contradictions, one's mind takes shelter behind the tiredness of the body. I did not work well. Everything was clear and safe while I was together with Ilsa, but as soon as she worked and I looked on, I was uncertain even of her. She did not suffer the civil war in her own flesh as I did; she belonged to the others who went the easy way of political work. In the evenings, when I had drunk wine and brandy to get over my tiredness, I told stories until I found a reason to shout with excitement, or had sudden rows with any journalist who seemed to treat Spaniards more like natives than the others. Every second day I demanded clear and unified instructions for our work from Valencia and from the War Commissariat, and every time I was told by Rubio that I was actually in Madrid against his orders, and by Kolzoff or his friends that everything was in order. When Maria rang up, I was first rude to her and then took her out for a drink because there was so much pain everywhere and I did not want to cause more.

Ilsa looked at me out of quiet eyes which seemed full of reproach, but she did not ask me about anything which had to do with my private life. I wanted her to ask, I would have had an outburst if she had done so. She held the work of the office in firm hands while I tortured myself with doubts. Then came the day when Rubio told me over the telephone that I ought to realize that I was under the authority of the Ministry, not under that of the *Junta de Defensa*, and when the people in the War Commissariat told me the exact opposite, I rang up Rubio again. He gave me strict orders to report to him in Valencia. I knew that he hated me and was waiting for an opportunity to take me away from the work I had usurped, but I was tired of shilly-shallying. I would go to Valencia and have it out, face to face. At the back of my mind was the urge to escape from an ambiguous situation.

The Junta refused to give me a safe-conduct to Valencia, because my job was in Madrid and no orders from Valencia could relieve me from it; Rubio Hidalgo had not the power to give me a safe-conduct. It was an impasse.

Then I met my old friend Fuñi-Fuñi, the Anarchist, now one of the leaders of the Transport Workers' Union. He offered me a safe-conduct and a place in a car to Valencia for the following day. I accepted. Ilsa said very little. She had once more refused Rubio's invitation to go to Valencia.

On December the 6th I left Madrid, feeling like a deserter who is going into a grim battle.

4. The Rearguard

The car that took me to Valencia belonged to the FAI and carried three leaders of the Anarchist militia. One of them, García, was their commander at the Andalusian front. Although they knew that I was not an Anarchist and although I told them that I had collaborated with the Communists, they accepted me as a friend, since their Madrid headquarters had given me the freedom of their car. And I accepted them because their harsh comments on the men who had abandoned Madrid to its fate fitted my mood. I was convinced that the officials who had gone to Valencia on November the 7th were now working hard to regain control of the capital without having to go back there themselves. I was one of the chief witnesses of cowardice and lack of responsibility, and so they would obviously try to get rid of me in an unimpeachable manner. That was why I had been called to Valencia and that was why I obeyed the order.

I began to speak of the problems which choked me. García listened carefully, and his shrewd questions helped me to go on speaking. It was a relief. I described the story as I saw it, the censorship before the night of November the 7th, the functioning of the office in the Telefónica, the role of the Defence Junta, the orders from Valencia, the muddle, the strain, the neglect. The road to Valencia is long, and I talked on to clarify my own mind, while García continued to listen and to put terse questions. When we arrived in the city, we went into a bar to have a drink together before going our separate ways. Only then did García say:

'Well, *compañero*, now give me that fellow's address. We'll pay your boss a visit tonight.'

I was startled: 'What for?'

'Never mind, people sometimes disappear overnight here in Valencia. They're taken to Malvarrosa, or to Grao, or to the

Albufera, get a bullet in the neck, and then the sea carries them away. Sometimes they're washed ashore, though.'

His face was as gravely thoughtful as ever. I tried a different line of approach.

'I don't think he deserves all that. Firstly, I don't believe that Rubio's a traitor to the Republic. He worked with Alvarez del Vayo for a long time, you see. And secondly he's one of the few people we have who knows something about the foreign press. And then, after all, my affair is my own personal affair.'

García shrugged his shoulders: 'All right, if you say so. You'll have to lie on the bed you've made for yourself. But I tell you, one day you'll be sorry for it. I know that type. We're going to lose the war because of them. Or do you believe we don't know about the many things the censors let through? That man is a Fascist, and we've been realizing it for quite a long time. We've warned him too, more than once. You can say what you like, he'll be taken for a ride sooner or later.'

It shook me out of my smouldering resentment against the Ministry. I knew only too well that the foreign censorship committed far more blunders by banning than by passing news or comment; I saw how distant from those Anarchists I was in my judgement, how distant in my feelings, despite the anger and indignation which linked us together.

I went alone to the Press Office.

It was early in the morning. The sun shone from a cloudless sky. After the December fogs and gales of Madrid, the air of Valencia was heady wine. I walked slowly through an outlandish world where the war existed only in the huge anti-Fascist posters and in the uniforms of lounging militiamen. The streets were blocked by cars and thronged with boisterous, well-dressed people who had time and leisure. The café terraces were crowded. A band was playing march music in the middle of the big market square. Flower-sellers carried sheaves of white, red, and rose-pink carnations. The market stalls were heaped with food, with turkeys, and chickens, with big blocks of almond paste, with grapes, oranges, pomegranates, dates, pineapples. A shoe-cleaner assaulted me, and I let him polish my dusty shoes. There was no whistle of shells in the air. When I passed a lorry with evacuated children from Madrid I wanted to speak to them, because I was as bewildered as they were.

The Press Office had been installed in an old palace. I climbed a shabby, sumptuous staircase and found myself in a reception room with faded red brocade on the walls; from there a casual orderly sent me on through a chain of small rooms overflowing with typewriters, roneos, rubber stamps, and packets of paper. People I did not recognize came and went. I stood there like a yokel, until the commissionaire Peñalver discovered and welcomed me as though I had returned from the realm of death. 'You simply must stay with us while you're in Valencia,' he said. 'There is no room anywhere, and your brother's already sleeping with us. I'll tell Don Luis at once that you're here.'

He received me in state, very much the head of the department despite the squalid pomp and disorder of his surroundings, affable, urbane, non-committal, his saurian eyes half hidden by the smoked glasses and the dark arrowhead of his tongue flickering across his lips. I said nothing of what I had meant to say when I left the Telefónica. In Madrid I had cut easily through his bland phrases; but here in Valencia he was in his own fief, and I but a quixotic fool, unable either to submit and conform or to take the way of savage decision which García, the Anarchist, had offered.

Rubio Hidalgo told me he was sorry, but he had not the time to discuss outstanding matters with me that day; I might come back the next morning. I went away. From a street hoarding the blank eyes of the children killed in Getafe, the children of the salvaged photographs, stared at me. A propaganda poster. A very effective appeal. It crossed my mind that I had imagined it differently, and yet I had passed on the negatives of those photos for that very purpose.

I did not know what to do with myself.

In the afternoon I went to see my children and Aurelia in the small village where they had been given a billet. The narrow-gauge railway that took me there was as slow as a mule-drawn cart. The village was under the administration of an Anarchist workers' committee which had commandeered a few big houses for the Madrid evacuees. I found Aurelia in a huge farm building with mighty rafters and decaying mortar-and-stone walls, large reception rooms, a bewildering number of stairs, a damp, sombre garden and an orchard with a few orange trees. It sheltered only mothers with their children, twenty-two families, about a hundred persons in all. The committee had requisitioned beds and bedding and set up dormitories in the biggest rooms. It looked like a hospital or one of the old wayside inns with communal bedrooms.

In Aurelia's room ten beds were ranged in two rows along the main walls. She and the three children shared two beds close to the balcony which let in a blinding flood of sunlight. The place was clean and whitewashed, the four mothers seemed to get on well together. Within the first quarter of an hour of my stay I found that there existed a violent group antagonism between the various dormitories. The women were well cared for and had little to do beyond looking after their broods and being interested in each other. The committee provided milk for the children and issued vouchers for food rations. One of the women in Aurelia's dormitory, whose husband had been killed in the first days of the rising, was being entirely supported by the committee and received a daily shower of small gifts from the village people, clothing for the children, sweets, and flowers.

The children had settled down happily in the strange surroundings and were playing in the orchards. Aurelia paraded the husband who was 'something in the Foreign Ministry' before all the inmates of the big house, including the hostile clans of the other rooms. Towards the evening she asked me:

'What are your plans for tonight?'

'I'm taking the last train back to Valencia. Peñalver's let me have a bed in his house. I'll come and see you again as soon as possible.'

'No. Tonight you are going to stay here. I've arranged the whole thing.'

'But there's no room for me here.'

'Oh yes, there is, I told you I'd arranged everything. The women are going to sleep in other rooms tonight, as soon as the kids are asleep, and so we'll be alone.'

'Do stay, Papa . . .'

I felt an infinite repugnance and at the same time a wave of affection and pity. We had lost our home in Madrid and everything that makes life pleasant; the children hemmed me in and did not let me move; Aurelia's eyes implored. I stayed.

That night I did not sleep at all. It is so difficult to lie.

The room was lighted by two little oil lamps whose sickly glow filled it with shadows. Within reach of my arm, the children slept placidly in the other bed. Aurelia slept beside me. And I was lying by being there. I lied to the children by pretending a harmony with their mother which did not exist. I lied to their mother by feigning a tenderness which was dead and had turned into physical revulsion. I lied to Ilsa there in Madrid. I lied to myself by finding false justification for my presence in a bed in which I did not want to be, should not have been, could never be any more.

In the morning I took the first train to Valencia and slept in the close carriage until fellow-travellers woke me. I went to Peñalver's house and slept on there until midday. In the afternoon Rubio told me that he had no time for our talk and was forced to postpone it. The following day he had gone to Madrid. When he came back I heard from others that he had installed Ilsa formally as head of the Madrid office. He told me nothing, except that he would settle my case as soon as he had time. I waited, and did not force the issue. I waited from one day to the other. Once Rubio went to Madrid on a hurried journey; when he came back he put me off more openly, with a more insolent tone in his voice. I had a violent altercation with him, but I stayed and waited. My fight, so clear-cut in Madrid, appeared helpless and meaningless in Valencia, where I was alone and helplessly floundering.

A week passed, nerve-racking and slow. The sky was uniformly clear, the nights uniformly peaceful, the life of the city unbearably gaudy. Every night my hatchet-faced landlord, Peñalver, produced a packet of cards and a bottle of gin. My brother Rafael, who had gone to Valencia after the evacuation of his family, sat around, silent and morose. At midnight Peñalver would go to bed, befuddled. I could not sleep.

I was collecting stories. With the pressure of Madrid on my mind, I tried to understand the process of the organization of the war. But as I was waiting, idle and supernumerary, I never met any of the people who must have been working feverishly at the time. I only saw the hangers-on, the small fry of the bureaucracy settling down in safety to justify their existence. The minor employees of the Foreign Ministry, who had left Madrid because they had been ordered to do so or because they had been afraid, told malicious tales, and often the point of their malice was turned against the fools who had stayed in Madrid and muddled things up. They all thought that I had come to Valencia to stay, because it was the sensible thing to do. According to their version, the high State functionaries were greatly annoyed because those who organized the defence of Madrid behaved as though they had been heroes and the official evacuees to Valencia cowards. 'You must admit that you people arrogated powers,' someone said to me. 'Yes, because you had written off Madrid,' I retorted. But it was patent that anything I could say would fall into a void, would sound empty and declamatory. I remembered the Anarchist García with an uneasy feeling of comradeship, mixed with loathing; so I fell silent, listening, and watched.

They told me that Rubio Hidalgo had said he would put me into the Postal Censorship at Valencia 'to rot there', and that I would not be allowed to go back to Madrid. They told me that he had spoken with great indignation of the day when I had been quick to usurp his chair and desk in the Ministry. They hinted that Ilsa was to be left in the Madrid office until things were settled – unless she committed a blunder at an earlier stage; Rubio would manage her easily, it was felt, because she was a foreigner without backing and without any knowledge of Spanish to speak of. Others told me that she was politically inconvenient and would shortly be expelled from Spain, especially if she continued to be so friendly with foreign journalists as to make herself suspect. With all that, she had become a legend.

I visited my children regularly, but I did not spend another night in the village. After a bitter quarrel I spoke no more to Aurelia and she knew that I would never come back.

I sat with my brother in cafés and bars, dazed by the noise, and went out to the beach to watch the people swirling round the fashionable beach restaurants or to stare at the frying-pans in the open kitchen of *La Marcelina*, where rice simmered under wreaths of chrome-red crawfish and chunks of golden-skinned fried chicken.

The rice in the Gran Vía Hotel of Madrid, which we had been eating day after day, was a sickly pink paste. On the wooden platforms overlooking the sands and the sea, where tables had to be booked in advance, the women of the town evacuated from Madrid were fighting a grim battle of competition with their colleagues of Valencia. A wealth of loose cash was spent in hectic gaiety. Legions of people had turned rich overnight, against the background of the giant posters which were calling for sacrifices in the name of Madrid.

A new brand of organizers was invading the offices.

My landlord, Peñalver, commissionaire in the Foreign Ministry, awoke one morning with the inspiring idea of setting up a Cyclists' Battalion recruited from the ranks of Ministry orderlies. He had a bicycle and was able to ride it, so were his two sons, both dispatch riders at the Ministry. He started canvassing his idea in the various other departments and after a few days appeared in a brand new captain's uniform, with an order authorizing him to organize a battalion and a voucher for expenses in his pocket. After this, he began to consider leaving the Ministry for good as soon as he had assembled his unit. But in the meantime he had his innings.

I heard that Louis Delaprée had died. During the last days of my work in Madrid he had had a row with his paper, the *Paris-Soir*, because his impassioned reports of the killing of women and children by indiscriminate bombing had not been published, not being topical any more. That was in the days when Mrs Simpson monopolized the front pages. When I had said goodbye to him he had been sitting on my camp bed, his face more pallid than ever, a brick-red scarf round his throat, and had told me that he would have a very serious word with friends in the Quai d'Orsay about the French consulate's brazenly pro-Fascist conduct. 'I hate politics, as you know, but I'm a liberal and a humanist,' he had said.

He had left in a French aircraft; it also carried a Havas correspondent and a delegate of the International Red Cross who had investigated the killing of political prisoners from the Model Jail at the beginning of the assault on Madrid. Not far from the city the French plane was attacked, machine-gunned, and forced down by an unidentified aircraft. The Havas man lost his leg, the Red Cross delegate was unharmed, the pilot bruised, and Delaprée died a painful, lingering death in a Madrid hospital. Rumours claimed that the atacking aircraft had been Republican, but Delaprée denied it in the endless lucid hours of his agony. I could not believe it.

It was to attend the funeral service that Rubio Hidalgo had hurried to Madrid with a sheaf of glowing flowers in his car, and it was after his return that I had heard the spate of stories about Ilsa's strong but precarious position and my own impending exile in the postal censorship.

Journalists came to Valencia from a spell in Madrid, and their effusive praise of Ilsa's régime worried me more than the vague rumours. I saw her exposing herself to envy, entangling herself in a net of bureaucratic rules which she ignored or did not know, and I saw her going away from me, on her own road.

I began to write a diary-like letter to her, in French. It was stiff, uneasy, and self-conscious, and I knew it. As I had entered the Madrid censorship on the recommendation of the Communist Party and grasped the reins after November the 7th with their consent, I went to see one of the Party secretaries. He had told me that the censorship muddle would have to be cleared up by the Government, that we all had to support the reorganization of the State machinery in every way, that I was in the right but would have to wait for an official decision. I waited. It was all very reasonable and it drove home to me that I did not belong.

There came a letter from Ilsa in answer to a note in which I had urged her to join me in Valencia. She would come for a few days' leave, after Christmas, and she hoped that I would return with her to Madrid. Luis, our orderly, would give me more details, she was about to send him off to Valencia for a brief holiday and he ought to arrive shortly after her letter. I went to the Ministry; no car had come from Madrid. When I returned a few hours later, somebody mentioned vaguely that he had heard of a car accident in which two journalists and an orderly had been wounded. No, they did not know exactly who they were.

The hospital of Valencia was an enormous building looking like a convent, with vaulted rooms, cold stone walls, dark corners, where the dying were hidden away, and a slab with the name of a saint on the door of each room. The stone flags and huge tiles of the floor rang with footsteps, glasses and crockery clicked, the air was dense with the odour of carbolic. The old order was broken up by the war. A crowd of visitors had installed themselves on chairs and bedsteads, closing in on the sick and wounded. The vaults hummed like a giant beehive.

Nurses and medical orderlies had become gruff and exasperated. They pushed their way through the clustering people without answering questions. I tracked down the English journalist; he had nothing but scratches, he would sleep in the hotel that night. But he passed me on to Suzana of the War Commissariat who had taken him along in her car: she had a deep gash on her forehead which had to be stitched up, and she knew that Luis was gravely injured. I could not find him. Nobody knew where he was. A bed to which I was directed stood empty. He might have died, or it might all have been a mistake. I walked through a maze of cold corridors and found him, in the end, on a stretcher outside the door of the X-ray department.

The tenderness on his face when he saw me was so intense that it hit me like a blow. I knew he was doomed. A thin thread of saliva mixed with blood ran out of the corner of his mouth, his gums were greenish and had receded from his teeth, his skin had turned ashen and his limbs were totally paralysed. Only his eyes, lips, and fingers were alive. The doctor let me accompany him and showed me, in silence, the shadow picture on the other side of the fluorescent screen: the spinal column broken in the middle of the back, two of the vertebrae an inch apart.

Afterwards I sat down by the side of his bed. Luis laboured to speak, and said:

'The letter, in my jacket.' I found a fat envelope in the coat hanging at the foot of the bed. 'Now it's all right. You know I'm going to die?' He smiled, and it was a grimace. 'It's funny, I was so afraid of the bombs. Do you remember that night in the Telefónica? If you want to run away from Death you run straight into Her arms. Life's like that. I'm sorry because of my daughter. Not because of my wife.' He put a bitter stress on his 'not'. 'She'll be glad, and I too. Give me a cigarette.'

I lighted the cigarette for him and pushed it between his lips.

From time to time his fingers closed round the stub and lifted it away, and he spoke.

'Don Arturo, don't let that woman get lost. I was right. She's a great woman. Do you remember that night she came to Madrid? And she loves you. We've talked a lot. Do you know that she speaks Spanish already? At least, we understood each other, and we spoke a lot about you. She's in love with you and you're in love with her. There are many things I see clearly now. You know, it's always said that one doesn't see things clearly until one's about to die. Don't let her go, it would be a crime, for you and for her. She's coming here on the 26th. You'll be happy, both of you, and you'll remember poor Luis. You've got her letter safe, have you? I was worrying about it all the time.'

The agony of peritonitis is shattering. The belly lifts the sheets, steadily, inexorably swelling. The bowels are crushed by the tremendous pressure and in the end pushed out of the mouth in a loathsome paste of mixed excrement, blood, and bubbles of gaseous stench. Luis' wife could not stand it and deserted her place at the head of his bed, and I stayed on alone for long hours, ceaselessly wiping his mouth. His eyes were to the last moment alive, resigned and affectionate, and he said goodbye to me very softly, choked by froth.

Ilsa came to Valencia on December the 26th. They put flowers into her hotel room on behalf of the department because she was a 'heroine'. She was tired and her round face looked haggard, but she was strong and buoyant. When I met her, everything in the world fell into place again.

The following midday, her friend Rolf came to look for me in the smoking room of the hotel: an agent of the Political Police had waited for her at the reception desk and taken her away. She had met Rolf on the stairs and told him to notify me and Rubio Hidalgo.

I saw the avenue near the abbattoir of Madrid, its rickety, dusty little trees, tumbled bodies in the grey light of dawn, the nervous titter of passers-by, the ugly blasphemies of evil people, I remembered the old woman I had seen dragging a small boy by the hand and pushing a piece of pastry into the half-open mouth of a dead man. I saw the tribunal where Little Paws had asked for more people to be taken for a ride. I saw Ilsa before a tribunal of men who believed anything of a foreigner, and I saw her stretched out on the sand of the beach, the water lapping at her feet. The clock in the room ticked slowly. I had a pistol. We all had pistols.

I rang through to the Press Department and asked for Rubio Hidalgo. He cut me short. He had heard, he would do everything in his power and would soon find out what had happened. Yes, I said, he would have to find out soon. He told me that he would come to the hotel at once. There were other strangers around me; Rolf had brought Julius Deutsch, the Austrian, who knew her well. I think he rang up Largo Caballero's secretary. Rubio came and monopolized the telephone. I had laid my pistol on the table before me. They all looked askance at me as though I were a madman, and told me to be calm.

I said it did not matter whether she appeared that night or not, other people would die in Valencia, that was all. I put two filled cartridge frames on the table. Rubio rang up the Foreign Minister.

Then they told me that the whole thing was cleared up; it had been a stupid denunciation, nothing more; she would be back soon. I did not altogether believe them. The clock went very slowly. She came back two hours later, smiling and self-possessed. I could not speak to her. The other people crowded round and she told them her story with a wicked relish. The agent who had detained her had asked her questions on the way to the police, which indicated that she had been denounced as a 'Trotskyist spy'. There had been no concrete accusation, but her friendship with the Austrian Socialist leader Otto Bauer had loomed large. While two people cross-examined her – in a very clumsy and uncertain way, she said, which gave her the feeling of being mistress of a ludicrous rather than a dangerous situation – the telephone had started ringing. After the first call they had asked her whether she was hungry; after the third or fourth they had brought her a sumptuous lunch; after the sixth or seventh they had asked her opinion about the man Leipen who had apparently denounced her, a little Central European journalist who for a time had worked in the Press Department and whom I did not even know. She had told them that she thought him a twister, but nothing worse, and left it at that. In the end they had treated her with the greatest affection, as a friend of the family.

It did not matter that she had never realized the whole extent of her danger. She was back again, alive. I stayed with her.

That night the moon of Valencia shone like molten silver. Valencia has gardens and fountains, it has a wide promenade flanked by palm trees, it has old palaces and churches. Everything was dark, from fear of enemy aircraft, and that polished moon lorded it over the city. The small, bright disc rode on a blue-black sky studded with tiny, white, flickering flames, and the earth was a field of black and silver.

After supper we went out and walked through the light and darkness. There was a scent of cool, moist soil, of thirsty roots drinking the sap of the ground, of breathing trees, of flowers opening to the moon and the shadows. We walked along the pillars of palm trees whose broad fans rustled like parchment, and the sand crunching under our feet caught sparks from the moon as though the world were of crystal. We spoke softly, so that the moon should not shut her eyes and leave the world blinded.

I do not know what we said. It ran deep as talk runs in a nuptial night. I do not know how long it lasted. Time had no measure and stood still to watch us walking beyond its orbit. I do not know where we went. There was garden and moon, sand, and leaping fountains, rustle of dry leaves in pools of shadow, and we went on, hand in hand, disembodied, following the murmur of the cradle-song.

In the morning we went to the sea, speaking soberly of the struggle in front of us, until we would go back to our posts in Madrid and work together. We walked past the village of El Cabanel, white, frail-looking huts of fishermen and workers. Where the beach curved away from people and houses, we sat down in the sand. It was yellow, fine, and warm like human skin. Sea and sky were two shades of the same soft blue, fusing without a borderline in the dim haze. Shallow waves ran up the beach and their glassy crests carried flicks of sand. The sand grains rode on gaily like mischievous gnomes until the wave toppled over with a gentle splash and left them ranged in long motionless ripples, the trace of the sea's lips.

My neck was lying on her bare arm, skin on skin, and I felt the currents running below our skins, as strong and imperious as the forces beneath the blue surface of the sea.

'I don't know any more where I end and where you begin. There is no borderline.'

It was peaceful. We had no need to talk much about ourselves. We had each said a few sentences: she would have to write to her husband and tell him that their marriage had come to an end. I would try to straighten out my own private mess with the least possible hurt to those whom I had involved.

'You know that it will be a lot of pain for the others, and pain for ourselves as well as happiness. One's got to pay, always.'

'I know.'

But everything seemed apart from our life together, the only life we could feel. The muddled, complicated, entangled matters of which I knew in my brain referred to somebody else. I told her of my boyhood, of my delight when I could bury my head in my mother's lap and feel her light fingers in my hair. That was my self still. It belonged together with Ilsa's slow smile and the small shells she dug out of the sand, shells white as milk, golden as bread from a peasant's oven, deep rose as a woman's nipples, smooth and polished as a shield, curled and grooved as a perfect fan.

Then we were hungry and plodded through the yellow sand to a small beach tavern. There we sat on the wooden platform, looking at the sea and talking of Madrid. The waiter brought an earthenware pan with the saffron-yellow Valencian rice and pointed to two slender red crawfish on its top: 'From the comrades over there.' A fisherman at the corner table rose, bowed, and said: 'We thought that the foreign comrade ought to have a chance of eating the real thing. We've only just caught those *langostinos*, they're quite fresh.'

The rice smelled tangy and we drank tart red wine with it.

'Hasn't the new year begun today?'

'Still three days to go.'

'You know, it's odd, but it's only today that I found out that we can share a life in daylight and gaiety, a normal life.'

'Will you always tell me things I've been thinking of?'

It was beautiful to be childish. I felt as strong as never before. We walked out on the beach, lay in the sand and collected more of the golden and pink shells. When we went home in the crowded, clattering tram, the shells in Ilsa's pocket clicked like castanets.

5. Front Line

'The story has moved from Madrid to Valencia because of the non-intervention racket,' I heard a foreign correspondent say. 'Of course, everything still depends on whether Madrid holds out or not – I've heard that the Nationalists are going to resume their offensive against the Great North Road – but we've got to stay in contact with the Valencia Government.'

It was true. Madrid was in the war, but Valencia was in the world. The laborious work of administrative organization and diplomatic traffic had come into its own; it was necessary although it bred a parasitic life. Yet I knew that I could not become part of it without losing my last shred of faith. I had to go back to Madrid. I wanted to have a share in the handling of foreign propaganda from there. This meant that I would have to learn how to exert an indirect influence on the outside world, converting that which to us was naked life and death into raw material for the press. It also meant that I would have to return to Madrid, not in opposition to the 'proper channels' of the Press Department, but in agreement with them.

This was difficult to work out within myself. I revolted against it even while I believed in Ilsa's diagnosis. She was profoundly uneasy at the thought of once again having to face the Spanish authorities by herself, at the head of a key office, yet without the slightest knowledge of official rules and regulations. She wanted me there to help her in collecting the factual material which she would hand out to journalists in search of copy. It now seemed worth while to me. I read foreign papers in Valencia and forced myself to observe their methods of reporting. Ilsa hoped that Julio Alvarez del Vayo, with his journalistic experience, would see her point, but she was very doubtful whether the Minister's friendliness towards her would outweigh his press chief's venomous dislike of me. I was sceptical, yet willing to let her try her best.

Suddenly all obstacles dissolved into thin air. I was waiting in an ante-room of the Ministry when Ilsa came out from an interview with Don Julio with a blank expression that sat oddly upon her, and told me that Rubio Hidalgo was waiting to see us both. He received us with great warmth and informed me that he was sending me back to Madrid as Head of the Foreign Press Censorship with Ilsa as my deputy. Ignoring my bewilderment, he went on smoothly: his secretary would settle the administrative details; our salaries would be slightly raised; the Ministry would foot our living expenses; otherwise, there was not much he could tell me; I knew the ropes, none better; and Ilsa seemed to have bewitched the foreign journalists into a constructive attitude – although I would have to guard her from an excess of kindness and indulgence, to which she was inclined.

It was just as well that I had donned my official face; I was at a complete loss. Ilsa seemed to know something about the background of the sudden change, for she chatted with a studied impulsiveness, mentioned by the way that she was glad Rubio had realized the impracticability of his plan to send his Valencia censors to Madrid in turn, and expressed her concern at the appointment of Major Hartung. Was he to be our chief, or just liaison officer with the General Staff?

Who the hell was Major Hartung?

'That man has nothing whatsoever to do with you,' said Rubio. 'You, Barea, are responsible for the department in Madrid together with Ilsa, and you both work directly under me. I am sure you will do it better than ever before. We'll send you food parcels and whatever you need. Take care of yourselves. I'm sorry, but you will have to leave for Madrid tomorrow.'

Everything was arranged, the car, the petrol quota, the safe-conducts, the Ministry papers, even rooms in the Gran Vía Hotel, since it would be too strenuous to go on sleeping on camp beds in the office. This time our work would run in regular grooves. I gave the answers that seemed expected of me. Rubio Hidalgo slapped me on the shoulder and wished us good luck.

Not even Ilsa knew exactly what had happened, but at least she had grasped one thread of the tangle. An Austrian, calling himself

Major Hartung, had turned up in the Telefónica on Christmas Eve, sent to Madrid by official car on some undefined mission. He had talked a lot about the need for a military Press Office, casting himself for the role of Chief Publicity Officer with the General Staff in Madrid, stressed his allegedly enormous journalistic experience, and boasted of his acquaintance with the Minister. Ilsa had regarded him as a jovial braggart and failed to take him seriously. He was now in Valencia, apparently about to go back to Madrid with some kind of press appointment in his pocket. Rubio Hidalgo saw in him a menace to his own office, and turned to us in his quandary. So, through no merit or act of our own, the road back to our joint work was cleared.

The road from Valencia to Madrid had changed in the bare four weeks since I had travelled in the opposite direction. There were fewer control posts at the roadside, many of the pickets and barricades in the villages had disappeared, the remaining sentries had a businesslike air and scanned our papers carefully. The most important crossroads were in the hands of the Shock Police. We overtook military vehicles and a chain of light tanks moving towards Madrid. The air of the hills was crisp and exhilarating, but at dusk, when we climbed the uplands, the wind bit into our skin. From the height of Vallecas, the white skyscrapers of the city rose out of a pool of dark mist and the front rumbled in the near distance. Our car plunged down the slope, past the concrete pillars of street barricades, and then we were suddenly back at home; in the Telefónica.

Two days later, the rebels launched two attacks, one at Las Rozas against the North Road, the Corunna Road, which was the link with El Escorial, and the other in the Vallecas sector, against the road to Valencia. They captured Las Rozas and penetrated deeper into the northwestern fringe of the city. A new stream of people in flight swept through the streets and choked the tunnels of the Underground stations. The International Brigades stopped the gap at Las Rozas. The Government attempted to organize a large-scale evacuation of noncombatants to the Mediterranean coast. We heard the swelling roar of the battle through the windows of the Telefónica during our working hours and through the windows of our hotel room during the few hours of sleep. Those were days of hunger and cold. The lorries which entered the city carried war material, not food. There was hardly any coal left, and the cardboard in place of the broken windowpanes did not keep out the bitter frosts. Then a thick blanket of chilly fog spread over the town and smothered the noise. The shelling stopped. The offensive was broken off. Only then did I look round and take stock.

While I had been away, the foreign journalists had come to take it for granted that the Censorship Office should help them personally, as well as censor their dispatches. Men of the International Brigades came and went, bringing us their letters and snatching a few words with people who spoke their language. Correspondents who had no assistant to pick up material for them came and exchanged impressions and information with us. Our office provided newcomers with hotel rooms, and helped them to get petrol vouchers. Ilsa had established official relations with *Servicios Especiales*, a branch of the Military Security Police, which at our request granted safe-conducts for certain sectors of the front to foreign journalists. The Political Commissars of the International Brigades visited us as a matter of course and gave us information which we could pass on to the journalists.

The Russian General Goliev, or Goriev, who was attached to Miaja's staff as an adviser and at the same time as chief of the detachments of Russian technicians and tank-men detailed to the Madrid front, sent regularly for Ilsa in the small hours of the morning and discussed current press problems with her. So far as I could make out, his appreciation of her work had gone far to strengthen her difficult position and to neutralize the enmity of those foreign Communists who considered her undesirable because she was critical and independent of them. Sometimes, when Goliev's Spanish Adjutant, childishly proud of his post, came to fetch Ilsa at three in the morning, I went with her.

The Russian general perturbed and impressed me. He was fair, tall, and strong, with high cheek-bones, frigid blue eyes, a surface of calm and constant high tension underneath. He was not interested in people unless they forced him to consider them as individuals; and then he was curt. His Spanish was good, his English excellent; his capacity for work was apparently unlimited. He was watchful and correct in his treatment of Spanish officers, but ruthlessly detached and cold in his discussion of Spanish problems, in so far as he touched upon them at all, that is to say, whenever they impinged on his military considerations. He lived, ate, and slept in a gloomy, dank cellar room. There he saw the bald, bullet-headed Mongolian commander of the tankists, a man with a cellophane-covered map forever under his arm, or the employees of the Soviet Embassy, and dealt with them rapidly and, to judge by the sound, brusquely. Then he would turn to us, giving his concentrated attention to the problems of press and propaganda. He never attempted to give us orders, but clearly expected us to follow his advice; at the same time, he accepted a surprising amount of argument and contradiction from Ilsa, because – as he said – she knew her job but was no Party member.

Every morning he scrutinized the censored press dispatches of the previous day, before they were sent on to the Ministry in Valencia by a War Commissariat courier. Sometimes he disagreed with our censoring, and said so, sometimes he explained points of military intelligence value of which we ought to be aware, but as a rule he focused his attention on the trends of foreign opinion revealed by the correspondents, and more particularly by reports to conservative and moderate newspapers. The noticeable change in their tone, from open animosity against Republican Spain to straight reporting had impressed him. He had conceived a predilection for the sober articles of the *New York Times* correspondent, Herbert Matthews, and for the *Daily Express* reports of Sefton Delmer's, whose carefully dosed shrewdness disguised by a whimsical style amused him as much as his erratic typing; but he showed a cavalier disregard for the reports of Communist newspapermen.

From time to time, Goliev probed into Ilsa's political ideas which he found inexplicably near to and far from his own, so that he would stare at her in puzzled interest. Once he ended by saying to her 'I cannot understand you. I could not live without my Party Membership card.' He tended to leave me alone because he had classified me as an emotional, romantic revolutionary, useful enough in a way, but unreasonable and intractable. No doubt he was right from his point of view. He was so honest and blatant about it, that I accepted his manner and repaid it in kind, by my silent scrutiny of this new breed, the Red Army officer, single-minded, strong, ruthless, and beyond my touch. He seemed a man from Mars. But he was more or less of my own age, and I could not help imagining what his experiences had been in 1917.

A few doors further on in the cellar passage, and in a different world altogether, was General Miaja. Operations were directed by the General Staff, and he, the nominal C.-in-C., had little say in them. And yet he was more than a figurehead. In that period, when the role of the Defence Junta had shrunk and the new administration did not yet function, he acted as Governor of Madrid and held a considerable part of the administrative power in his hands, without making much use of it. He had the sly shrewdness of a peasant who does not want to be entangled in things beyond his understanding, and he knew to a nicety his own value as a symbol of Madrid's resistance. He knew that he was at his best whenever he could sum up the feelings of the men in the trenches and the streets in rude, blunt words, such as he liked and shared with them, and that he was at his worst when it came to the game of politics or the science of strategy.

Miaja was short, paunchy, red in the face, with a long thick nose and incongruous spectacles which made his eyes frog-like. He liked drinking beer even more than he liked drinking wine. When the foreign press censorship, which he neither understood nor cared about, came under his authority by the rules of martial law and the state of siege, he found it mainly awkward. With Ilsa, who was saved from his dislike of intellectuals only by her plumpness and her fine eyes, he never quite knew how to deal, but he thought me a good fellow: I enjoyed drinking with him, cursing highbrows and politicians together with him, and matching the barrack-room language in which he found relief from his official dignity. As long as I did not embroil him with 'those fellows in Valencia' he was willing to back me within his own kingdom of Madrid.

The courtyard of the Ministry of Finance, into which you emerged from the underground headquarters, had been cleared of the litter of sodden papers that filled it in the days of November.

Then you had trodden on reports on economic planning and taxation reform of the eighteenth century, on bleached State Loan certificates and sheaves of agrarian statistics, all thrown out from the vast archive vaults when they were being converted into bomb-proof offices. Now, the courtyard was packed with lorries, cars, motorcycles, and occasionally a bevy of light Russian tanks just arrived from a Mediterranean port. The smell of damp mould and of rats' nests still stuck to the stone slabs which the sun never touched, but it was mixed with the stench of petrol and hot metal.

On the first floor of the drab building were the offices of the Military Government of Madrid, the Army Judiciary, and of *Servicios Especiales*. This Intelligence Department was headed by a group of Anarchists who had taken over the abandoned office when the Government machine had been rushed to Valencia in the early days of November. I have never dealt with any police authority which tried to be so meticulously just, so sparing in the use of its power; and yet some of the agents attached to the department were shady and obnoxious, very much the *agent provocateur* type, mixing old spy methods with a new, truculent brutality which was alien to the ideas of their temporary chiefs.

The man who dealt with matters connected with foreigners was Pedro Orobón, whose brother had been famous among the collaborators of the great Anarchist Durruti. Pedro was small, dark, thin, with shrewd, sad, kind eyes in an ugly monkey face, a childlike smile and nervous hands. He was utterly unselfish, an ascetic believer with a burning, incorruptible sense of justice, of the breed which gave Spain a Cardinal Cisneros and an Ignatius Loyola. Frank, helpful and ready to be your friend as soon as he trusted you, he would have shot his best friend had he found him guilty, and you knew this about him all the time. But you also knew that he would have fought with all the strength of his being against any punishment he believed unjust, that he would never have accused anyone without being convinced of his guilt, and before having exhausted every means of clearing or justifying him. To him, an aristocrat had the moral right to be a Fascist, because his environment had moulded him in a certain way; Pedro would have liked to give him pick and shovel and make him earn his bread with his hands – and he would have thought it possible that this way of living might open the aristocrat's mind to the ideals of Anarchism. But a worker gone Fascist or a traitor pretending to be a revolutionary were to him past redemption; they had sentenced themselves. He had respect for other people's convictions and was willing to work with all militant anti-Fascists; he and Ilsa trusted each other, and he treated me as a friend. Yet even while he himself worked as part of the war machine without dimming his ideas, he was worried about the Anarchist Ministers' participation in the Government, because he feared the trappings of power and the dilution of ideals for them.

I had soon every reason to be grateful for Orobón's scrupulous fairness.

Hartung, the Austrian whose vague promotion had made Rubio Hidalgo send me to Madrid, had turned up armed with papers which made him Chief Press Officer with the Army at the Central Front. He was extremely loquacious, expounded his plans – he would of course manage everything with the General Staff, provide our office with a fleet of cars and whatever else its importance warranted, and so forth – and went off. Soon we heard that he had presented himself everywhere in his brand-new uniform of a Spanish Artillery major, thrown out grandiloquent and nebulous hints, and left distrust behind him wherever he had entered. When I broached the matter in one of my telephone conversations with the head office in Valencia, Rubio Hidalgo told me to disregard that madman and swindler as well as his papers which seemed to make him my superior. The journalists began asking embarrassing questions about the new man.

Some days later, two agents of the Military Police came and asked Ilsa whether she had had anything to do with a countryman of hers, a so-called Major Hartung; when I intervened and explained the connection, they told us both to come with them. In *Servicios Especiales* we found our Anarchist friends puzzled, somewhat worried, yet ridiculing any idea that we had been arrested. Nevertheless we were not allowed to leave the building and spent hours in the dingy ante-room, together with a motley collection of people who had been seen speaking or having a drink with Hartung: there was an attaché of the Soviet Embassy, the correspondent of a Swiss newspaper, a Norwegian woman journalist, and Professor J. B. S. Haldane. The

Russian walked silently up and down, the Norwegian was frightened, Professor Haldane sat down at a deal table and filled in a number of old blanks bearing the signature of His Gracious Majesty King Alfonso XIII, giving himself beautiful titles and interesting things to do. Ilsa spoke to the German girl Hilda who worked with the Anarchists in *Servicios Especiales*, and explained that the huge man in the leather jerkin which rode up his belly was a famous scientist, Nobel Prize winner and a great friend of the Republic's, upon which Hilda shyly invited him into their room. Haldane came out soon, rather disgruntled, and all I could understand of his English harangue was that he was disappointed because they had not threatened to shoot him at dawn, but had offered him, of all things, a cup of tea!

From the guarded remarks of our friends, I realized that Orobón and his colleagues were resisting pressure from the Special Military Judge in charge of the Hartung affair to put us all into jail on suspicion of conspiracy with a foreign spy. The Judge, an army officer and a Freemason with a strong bias against Socialists and foreigners, found it most suggestive that all the people rounded up by the agents as having had contact with Hartung were foreigners, with the exception of myself. The chiefs of *Servicios Especiales* objected to the summary injustice against people who, in their opinion, had proved their loyalty more clearly than the Judge himself, and against journalists who had happened to stray into Hartung's hotel. In the end, Orobón rang up General Goliev and let Ilsa speak to him; then I spoke briefly with General Miaja, who said that the Judge was his friend and that he could not interfere with the judiciary, but anyhow, he would speed up matters and see to it that we should not be kept away any longer from our work.

Once again I felt caught in a trap, when I entered the faded reception room where a natty Colonel sat enthroned behind a paper-laden desk, a perfectly groomed young girl in riding breeches beside him as his secretary. In clipped tones the Colonel asked me a number of questions, of which the young girl took notes, with an occasional giggle. The brocade chairs gave out a stale odour of dust and damp.

What were my relations with Hartung? I answered that I had seen him only once, in my official capacity. The Colonel had an outburst of barrack-yard rage: 'None of your tales! You're in with a pack of foreign Fascists, and I know how to deal with the likes of you . . .!' I was just calling him a sabotaging Fascist, when the 'phone rang and I heard the Colonel say, 'Yes, *mi general* . . . of course, *mi general* . . . at your orders, *mi general*.' He was scared, of the telephone and of me. After putting down the receiver, he started tendering me carefully worded apologies: maybe the whole thing was a mistake; Hartung might well be nothing but a dangerous kind of lunatic, the man had not slept during the night and devoured any food he got hold of. 'Even that sort of rice the Milicianos eat,' said the Colonel with contemptuous disgust.

Ilsa's interrogation lasted a few minutes, during which the Colonel tried to make her say that the shady man Hartung had been promoted to a position of power by Alvarez del Vayo and Rubio Hidalgo because they had dark reasons of their own; but she had found it easy to parry his clumsy insinuations. Haldane ambled off with a chuckle, tugging at his leather jerkin. I believe he put on the fantastic tin hat from the last war which he sported in Madrid, as though it were Mambrino's helmet. The Norwegian was almost in tears, the Russian disappeared quietly. We went back to the Telefónica. Hartung was kept imprisoned and it was never cleared up whether he was more than an adventurer with a touch of megalomania. The incident was closed. Rubio Hidalgo was affectionate during our telephone conversations the following days: there had been no scandal and everything was nicely settled. Yet I knew well that, but for the refusal of *Servicos Especiales* to send us all to prison without further ado, and but for the intervention from higher quarters, we might have been caught in a purposeless, dangerous tangle, caught in the cog-wheels of machinery hostile to everything we stood for.

They rang me up from the Military Emergency Hospital in the Palace Hotel. A wounded Miliciano wanted them to get in touch with me. His name was Angel García.

I felt convinced that Angel was in grave danger. In my confused mind I saw him doomed, as all the simple men of good faith seemed doomed in the unequal struggle. The day was foggy and dirty. The battle noise to the south of the city was carried through the streets by gusts of wind. I took Ilsa with me, afraid of being alone with a dying Angel.

We found him stretched out on his belly, splashed with mud, streaks of drying blood on his torn, dirty shirt. There it is, I thought. He turned his face and grinned. His eyes crinkled in impish merriment. A huge, grimy bandage covered him from the waist downwards and another spanned his shoulder blades.

'Now, that's nice! Well, here I am: I've been born again! Those Moors, the dirty bastards, have been trying to violate me.'

I had seen cases of that sort in Morocco, and felt sickened. But Angel burst into a guffaw. His teeth, which ought to have glistened white in his berry-red face, were stained a dark brown by tobacco juice.

'Now you're on the wrong track, Don Arturo. What d'you think of your Angelillo? Oh no, it's not that. It's only that those gentlemen have shot me through the ass, I beg your pardon, ma'am. And a nice shot it was, too. You see, we made a night attack on a machine-gun nest that annoyed us, and they sprayed us with bullets, so the only thing we could do was to stick to the ground like limpets and bury our heads in the mud. I've still got some on my face – see? Well then, a bullet struck me in the shoulder, grazed my spine and went right through one of my buttocks, and all the way along it touched nothing but flesh. No bones broken. If I hadn't stuck so flat to the ground it would have made a tunnel through me from my shoulder blade to my footsole. But they don't get me, no, sir.'

I was gulping down hysterical laughter. Of course, what other wound would have been right for Angel? It was just like him. Wasn't he indestructible? Doomed – nonsense, he was more alive than I was. He stank of mud, sweat, blood and carbolic acid, but he winked at me and wriggled on his belly, babbling on about the nice shelter he had rigged up for himself at the front in Carabanchel and how we would get drunk together the first day he was out of bed, because you didn't need your buttocks for drinking, did you? Nor for other things.

A young boy lying in the bed opposite was getting irritated by Angel's flow of jokes. He launched forth in a bitter tirade. He had been wounded near the Jarama, and his wound was no joke. His unit, the 70th Brigade, had been sent into action without sufficient armour and automatic weapons, just because they were Anarchists of the FAI and the CNT, and the neighbouring brigade, which was Communist, was excellently equipped but kept in the rear.

'We made three attacks, *compañero*, and the Fascists gave us hell. The third time we got the position we wanted, and we mightn't have stuck it if we hadn't wanted to show those other rogues who we were. But it was a lousy trick of theirs. We'll have to shoot it out with the Communists sooner or later.'

Angel grew angry and screwed round his neck to glare at the young boy. 'Listen, you fool, I'm a Communist myself and I won't let you insult my people. We can shoot too, if that's your game.'

'I didn't mean you. I meant your bosses. It's always the poor devils who pay, people like you and me and the many others who don't live to tell the tale.'

'What bosses?' said Angel. 'No boss puts a fast one over on me. There's our Captain, he's been my neighbour for ten years and he's younger than me, and now he starts talking of Party discipline and Army discipline and what not, because you see, it's true, we're an Army now and he's right, only I don't tell him so. They've started peppering us with mortars and we got orders to clear out of the huts we were using as shelters and get down into proper dugouts. But you won't catch me sleeping in a dugout, I don't want to be buried alive and it's too damp for my rheumatics. So when the Captain told me to get myself a dugout, I said to him, you can't tell me anything, I was a Socialist and a Communist and what you will when you were still afraid of your Father Confessor, and I won't be ordered about. So he called me Corporal García and ordered me to get myself a mortar-proof shelter, and he didn't mind if I got it in hell. So I did. I got a lot of doors from ruined houses, and a lot of spring mattresses, and I propped up the doors inside my hut, plenty of them, until if looked like a builder's store, and then I tore off the roof of my hut and put another lot of doors across. The upright doors were like beams, see? Then I shovelled earth on the top of my hut, two feet of it, and then I planted a heap of spring mattresses on top of the earth, and that was my roof. I fixed the springs with wire so they couldn't slip, and the Captain said I'd gone mad.'

'And hadn't you, Angelito?'

'Don't you see? It's all a question of ballistics. Now, when a mortar bomb hits my roof while I'm asleep, it falls on something springy and bounces off. Then one of two things happens: either the bomb explodes in its bounce in mid-air, and that's OK by me, or it goes on bouncing up and down on my mattresses like a rubber ball until it comes to rest on the bed, and then all I've got to do is to collect the mortar bomb next morning and send it back to the other side. So I've obeyed my Captain's orders, you see, discipline and all, and I shan't get buried in a filthy damp dugout either. The others've started collecting spring mattresses too. What price your bosses, you young idiot? We're a revolutionary army, we are.' And he wriggled on his paunch and grinned at the Anarchist who growled: 'You make jokes about your being cannon fodder.'

We were hilarious, Ilsa and I, when we walked back to our office. 'You could turn Angel into a symbol like the Good Soldier Schwejk,' she said, and told me about the book of the Czech rebel. Yet then we had to go on censoring bleak reports of skirmishes and shellings written by people who did not know Angel and his kind.

An extremely competent English journalist who had recently arrived to write human interest stories for the London branch of the Republican Agence Espagne had written up the pluck of Gloria, one of our lift operators, in taking her cage down from the top floor to the basement while shell splinters were clattering on its roof. It was one of the classic tales of the Telefónica, but he had to describe her as a dark Spanish beauty, with a red rose behind her ear, because 'readers in London want their spot of local colour and wouldn't like to miss the Carmen touch'. He was shivering in his greatcoat. Herbert Matthews handed me an account he wanted to send on to his editor, including various items for the treatment of chilblains; to demonstrate that it was no secret code, he pointed a long, sausage red finger, swollen and split open, at a purple chilblain on the tip of his melancholy nose.

Doctor Norman Bethune, the dictatorial chief of the Canadian Blood Transfusion Unit, came stalking into the room with his escort of lumbering, embarrassed young helpers. Ilsa must come with them at once, they had found hidden papers in the flat where they were billeted. And as some were in German, Ilsa would have to translate them. She went and returned hours later with a bundle of letters and filing cards. The card index was that of the members of the German Labour Front in Madrid: employees of Siemens-Halske, Siemens-Schuckert, the AEG, and other big German firms. The letters were the correspondence between my old acquaintance, the lawyer Rodríguez Rodríguez, and his friends in Germany; among them was the photograph he had showed me, centuries ago, to boast his place of honour among the Nazis. Ilsa translated the letter of a high Nazi official, which defended Rodríguez Rodríguez against criticism by saying that his membership in the Catholic Falange was only natural, as Falange corresponded to the National Socialist Movement under Spanish conditions. A number of small incidents which belonged to my former office life fell into place: here was part of the material about the Nazi network in Madrid. But Bethune claimed the letter. In immaculate battledress, his frizzy grey hair slicked back on his long, narrow head, he stood there swaying slightly on his feet and proclaiming that he would take these important papers – his own treasure trove – to Alvarez del Vayo, in the Blood Transfusion van. He knew nothing about the former owner of the flat where his unit was installed. It had been empty.

I came back to the office harassed by an hour's talk with Maria, who had asked me with a dreadful tenderness to give her at least those moments of contact every day, since she was threatened by the loss of the only worthwhile thing in her life. She refused to accept my union with Ilsa; she would get me back; I would see who was stronger in the end; it could not be true that I loved that foreigner. I knew that she was desperately alone; she was a stranger for whom I was sorry. How to end it?

In the Telefónica I found Ilsa tense and excited. Her husband had rung up from Paris. Through an unfortunate coincidence he had never received her letter from Valencia in which she explained to him that she had broken away from their marriage. Over the crackling wire and in precise French, Ilsa had told him what had happened to her, because she did not want to speak to him for a moment under false pretences, but the cruelty of the thing she had done to him left her shaken. She hardly spoke to me. The young censor on duty kept staring at her through his glasses and wagging his horselike head. 'I couldn't help listening,' he said. 'The way she did it – it was one of those things one reads about in novels – I never thought it could happen in real life – it must be a great experience, but I couldn't do it.'

That night she telephoned to Paris again and arranged to go there by air from Alicante; the Spanish Embassy booked a seat for her: she was going to discuss propaganda matters in Paris and to meet her husband so as to define the situation once and for all.

I was in a panic, but I had not the right to ask anything of her. It appeared to me that outside Spain she would be caught by her other life. Her many friends and her political work would drag her back. She had still a profound affection for Kulcsar, who was working at the time as adviser to the Spanish Legation in Prague. Suddenly I could not imagine in my Spanish brain that a woman was capable of going to meet her husband, only to tell him to his face that she had left him for good and meant to link herself to another. Was it that my own muddled life, my dark temper, had exhausted her? Was it that the experience of love had been mine only? It was so difficult to love, even while it was so easy. It seemed to have no place in life as we knew it. Was she leaving me? I had no right to ask anything from her.

She left the next day, alone in a small car. I was afraid for her and afraid of Paris. The Telefónica was an empty shell and the work senseless. I did not sleep unless I drugged myself with brandy. My brain was revolving round the hundred and one chances that she would never come back, against the one chance that she would. The enemy thrusts southeast of Madrid foreshadowed a new drive to cut off the roads. She might come back and her driver, not knowing the new front lines, might blunder on the side roads near the Jarama and land her in a Fascist position. She might come back and be hit by one of the shells which raked the town. Or she might decide to stay abroad and leave me alone.

She came back after six endless days. I was so weak with relief that I gave her a meagre welcome. Her driver told a long tale of how she had bullied the Military Governor of Alicante into giving her one of the official cars, and of how he had obtained petrol by telling the guards at the filling stations that she was the daughter of the Soviet Ambassador – wasn't it crazy anyhow that she had made him drive by night through the snowdrifts of the Mancha? They had got the last petrol at Toboso.

Ilsa had obtained a promise from her husband that he would agree to a divorce as soon as she gave the word after the end of the Spanish War. He had seen that she was utterly certain of herself, but he still hoped that she would snap out of her infatuation with me. The reactions of the outer world to Madrid had depressed her deeply: too many people had wanted to know whether it was true that the Communists held all the safe posts, instead of trying to understand that spirit of Madrid out of which the Left press was making stirring headlines. Still, an increasing number of foreign writers and publicists were coming to Madrid and we would have to look after them; I myself would have to do some journalistic work for the Agence Espagne until the arrival of another correspondent.

I had not much time to spend on arranging my private affairs then, because the wave of work and danger was mounting once more. But I decided to get my divorce from Aurelia and to make the position clear beyond any misconception to Maria; the torture and relief of Ilsa's journey had made it impossible for me to go on in a mesh of relations which had become untrue and wrong. It was not enough that Aurelia was my wife in nothing but in name, and that my contact with Maria was reduced to an hour in a café or a walk in the streets. For the time being, people accepted and respected my life with Ilsa, because we raised it beyond the level of an affair by complete frankness and naturalness; but I knew that this somewhat romantic indulgence would not last and that we could not carry it off indefinitely without giving and taking offence. I did not talk this over with Ilsa; it was my own difficulty, while it was unreal to her, and she only felt that she hated the tangle. But just when I tried to summon my courage for an unequivocal break, Maria told me of the death of her younger brother at the front, and I did not dare to wound her even more. I had to go on meeting her every second day for a drink and a brief walk, feeling nauseated with myself and resentful of her, yet trying to be as gentle as possible within the cruelty of it all.

In desperation I took Maria with me while I traced the damage done by a single three-engined Junkers which had circled low and slowly over the jerry-built cottages of Vallecas, on the evening of January the 20th, and dropped a stick of bombs on the little square where women were sewing and children playing. I had met the father of three of the murdered children, and I thought that I would do what the professional journalists did not do because minor raids were no longer a story for them. The little house of the man, who was a fish-hawker, had been smashed by seven light bombs. His wife had been killed on the doorstep, with a baby in her arms. The two older girls had been killed. A six-year-old boy had lost one of his legs. The smallest girl, aged four, had over a hundred scratches and wounds from shrapnel dust in her little body. The eldest boy, bleeding from his torn eardrums, had carried her to the First Aid Post in his arms. I visited the one-legged boy in the Provincial Hospital and heard the father, Raimundo Malanda Ruiz, tell the story, while the boy looked at me out of staring, opaque eyes.

I imagined that this was a good case history to illustrate nonintervention, but presumably I did not understand the market of foreign public opinion well enough.

Maria did not see what I saw, because she was only interested in keeping something of me; and this indifference made me give up the attempt to find a basis of friendship with her in the common experience of us all. I persuaded her to take up work outside Madrid, aware that I was only putting off the final injury to her.

February was a dark and bitter month. While the battle on the Jarama, the battle for the southeastern approaches to Madrid, was being fought and while sceptical journalists discussed the possibilities of the fall of Madrid after the cutting of its lifeline, the rebels and their Italian auxiliaries took Malaga. Madrid was being starved of food and wine and the tunnels of the Underground, like the basements of the Telefónica, were still clogged by thousands of refugees. And we knew that on the road from Malaga to the east a stream of refugees were trudging on or hiding in the ditches from the machine guns of low-flying German and Italian planes. There were no large-scale air raids on Madrid, only a few bombs were scattered on its outskirts from time to time as an evil reminder. The shelling went on and on. Most of us scurried across the Gran Vía when we went to the hotel for lunch, and I never lost my resentment at Ilsa's slow pace while I was waiting for her in the doorway of the bar, counting the seconds before the next, close-by shell burst.

The horizon of Madrid was suffused with flashes and flares to the south, east, and west. In the southeastern sector, the International Brigades had halted the enemy advance on the Jarama at a terrible price. One of the Englishmen, a longshoreman with simian arms and a low brow, came to see Ilsa and tell her of the death of his friends who used to take him to the Telefónica, of the Cambridge archeologist, and of the young writer, and gave her a pitifully funny photograph of himself in an impressive pose, hand on a plush chair.

But then the first smell of spring was in the air, with a dry, scented wind and fast white clouds sailing the bright sky.

The battle noise coming from the west, heavy mortar thuds and sharp rattle of machine guns, was grateful to our ears. We knew that there, on the slope below the Model Jail where four months earlier Miaja had rallied a handful of crazed volunteers against the invading Moors, Antonio Ortega's Basque regiment had reconquered the Parque de Oeste, inch by inch, and was pressing back the enemy.

Ortega, a bony man with a face carved in wood yet mobile as rubber, had organized his sector so well and was so proud of it that we liked to send him journalists and foreign visitors in search of a whiff of the front. But we ourselves had to know what we wanted others to see. After an interminable, sumptuous, and very gay meal in Ortega's headquarters, and after half an hour of singing songs with his young officers, among them a young painter and an international footballer, he took us through a narrow tunnel. We emerged in the park, in the intricate network of well-kept trenches which crossed the unkempt sand paths. The trees were slashed and torn, but the young leaves were just bursting out of their buds. In the zigzagging trenches the soldiers were peacefully occupied oiling and burnishing metal parts. A few were sitting in dugouts and dozing or reading. From time to time there was a swishing sound and a soft plop, and another star-shaped flower with white splinter petals blossomed on one of the tree trunks.

And then we were in the first line. The trench was surprisingly dry and clean, as Ortega pointed out with professional pride. In the places where a trickle of water came down the hillside, the ground was covered with doors taken from the bombed houses of the Paseo de Rosales. Through slits in the parapet I snatched a glimpse of an earthen ridge where little dust clouds spurted from time to time.

There was the enemy, a hundred-odd yards from us: Moors – Falangists – Legionaries – Italians – a sprinkling of Germans – conscript soldiers from Old Castile. The vast buildings of the University City loomed heavy and shell-pitted in the background. A doll-like figure passed behind a window hole and high up, under the roof of the brick building of the Faculty of Medicine, a machine gun cackled, but I could not think where the bullets went. The sun glittered on a loop of the river.

With the city at our back and the big Basques and Asturians cracking their jokes around us, the enemy was nothing. You had to laugh. We were safe here, the city was safe, victory was safe.

Then Ortega showed off a primitive mortar; the bomb was released by a big spring, as from a catapult. The Basque in charge of the mortar made ready to fire: 'As you're here, comrades, you must see the fireworks. Let's tickle them a bit.'

At the second attempt, the missile went off without a sound, and a second later a sharp explosion shook us. Then the front broke loose. The cracks of rifle shots ran along the parapets and a machine gun to our right began to rattle. The buildings of the University City joined in. A thin 'eeee' sounded in my skull. The hidden power of the explosives was unleashed. We were no longer playing at safety.

Ten days later, armoured Italian divisions launched a big offensive in the stony plain of Alcarria, to the northeast of Madrid. Their tanks overran our forces; they took Brihuega and Trihueque, they were before Torrija and nearing Guadalajara. It was a bid to cut off our northern salient and to seal the road through Alcalá de Henares, which had become essential to Madrid since the Valencia road had to be reached by side roads.

General Goliev took the retreat coolly; he spoke as though we had got the wide spaces of Russia in which to manoeuvre. I do not think that many people in Madrid realized the gravity of the situation. The foreign journalists knew that this was the first open action of the Italian Army in Spain. Here was a great story. But when they reported that Italian armour and Italian infantry formed the spearhead of the advancing rebel forces, they came up against the censorship of their own editors. The fiction of nonintervention had to be conserved. Suddenly, our censorship and the foreign correspondents were thrown together in the wish to get the news of what was happening across to the people and the papers in England, France, and the United States.

Herbert Matthews had a service conversation after reading out one of his telephone reports, in which the man at the other end of the wire, somebody at a desk in Paris, told him: 'Don't always speak of Italians, you and the Bolshevik papers are the only ones who use that propaganda tag.' Matthews, tied down by our censorship rules, came to my desk with tight lips and submitted a service cable he wanted to send: If they had no confidence in his objective reporting, he was going to resign.

The answer from the *New York Times* office said nobody thought he wanted to make propaganda, only that he might have fallen for the official handout of the Republicans.

Herbert Matthews won this fight. Yet when I read, months later, in what form various British, American, and French newspapers had published the reports we had passed in Madrid, I found that most of them had changed the terms 'Italian tanks', 'Italian infantry', etc., to 'Nationalist' forces, tanks, infantry, or whatever fitted, so as to eliminate the awkward evidence of an international war.

Then the tide turned. The Republican fighter planes, provided by Soviet Russia, those 'Ratas' and 'Moscas' which seemed so marvellous to us, battered the advance forces. An Anarchist unit led a big Italian formation into a trap. The International Brigades moved up. The loudspeakers of the Garibaldi Battalion called to the Italians on the other side. Then they advanced, anti-Fascist Italians and Germans together with Spanish units. They took back Trihueque and Brihuega, they took more than a thousand prisoners – all Italians – and they captured the mail bag and documents of a Brigade staff.

Gallo, the Communist Commisar of the International Brigades, and Pietro Nenni, the Italian Socialist leader who was everywhere with his unobtrusive friendliness, brought us postal orders sent home to their families by Italian soldiers in Spain, blood-stained diaries, still uncensored field-post letters, which we gave to correspondents who wanted irrefutable proof of their correctness in reporting on nonintervention. War Commissariat cars took journalists out to recaptured towns. I think that their reports after the victory of Guadalajara made good reading, so that they could no longer be bowdlerized; they turned it into a propaganda victory of ours.

The front line was stabilized much farther to the northeast than it had been before the Italian rout, although hopes of a decisive advance towards Aragon petered out. Yet after Guadalajara, Madrid was no longer isolated; the semicircle of the siege was no longer threatening to become a ring. There was a steady trickle of visitors. No one spoke of the fall of Madrid any more. The reorganization of the civil authorities was speeded up. Rubio was more curt on the telephone. Foreign delegations arrived, were led through Argüelles and Cuatro Caminos, through the Duke of Alba's Palace and, if they felt like it, through Ortega's trenches; they paid their respects to Miaja, looked at one or the other model factory under the workers' control, and at one or the other school for adults and home for orphaned children, and left.

One of the delegations we had to show round was headed by the Austrian Social-Democrat Friedrich Adler, then Secretary of the Labour Socialist International. He hated the existence of a Popular Front and the collaboration with the Communists so much that he never asked any of us a question; he disapproved of Madrid in offensive silence, and the young Right-wing Socialists who had been tactfully detailed by the Junta to accompany him asked me who the unfriendly old man was and why he was so much like a walking corpse. He left a feeling of hostility behind, which was the only result of his visit.

Then more journalists and writers came. Ernest Hemingway arrived, was taken over the battleground of Guadalajara by Hans Kahle of the International Brigades, and worked with Joris Ivens at the film 'Spanish Earth', while his bullfighter-secretary, Sidney

Franklin, went round the offices to get petrol, permits, and gossip. Martha Gellhorn arrived and was brought to the Telefónica by Hemingway, who said: 'That's Marty – be nice to her – she writes for *Collier's* – you know, a million circulation.' Or was it half a million – or two million? I did not catch it and did not care, but we all stared at the sleek woman with the halo of fair hair, who walked through the dark, fusty office with a swaying movement we knew from the films.

Drinks at the Gran Vía bar and drinks at the Miami bar. Apart from some hard-working 'veterans' of Madrid, such as George Seldes and Josephine Herbst, the foreign writers and journalists revolved in a circle of their own and an atmosphere of their own, with a fringe of men from the International Brigades, Spaniards who touted for news, and tarts. March had turned into April. It was hot in the streets but for the hours when the sharp wind blew from the Sierra. In the evenings, the streets were thronged and the cafés full, people were singing and laughing, while far away machine guns burst out in short spasms as though the front were spluttering with rage. There was no menace in the air for the time being.

I started my divorce proceedings after obtaining Aurelia's unwilling consent. I was restless. The work had no longer much hold over me. We had had our share in the fight, but now everything seemed flat. Propaganda had seized upon the cliché of Heroic Madrid and had become easy and shallow, as if our war were not growing in scope and evil ramification.

Whenever Angel came on an evening's leave and, half tipsy, told me of a new trick they had invented in the trenches, of his abortive adventures with women, and his hopeless longing for his wife, he helped me. Agustín, my brother-in-law, helped me when he explained how life among his neighbours and in the workshops went on. I took Ilsa to Serafín's tavern, where I had been at home as a young man, and was glad when she liked the baker and the butcher and the pawnbroker who were my friends, or when an unknown worker sitting on the bench of the back room gave her a few edible acorns out of his pockets, just because he liked her face. All this was real. Other things were wrong. But my own life cleared.

On an April afternoon, when Ilsa for the first time wore her new grey coat and skirt instead of her soldier-like jacket, I walked with her through the oldest, narrowest and most crooked lanes of Madrid and showed her the *Cava Baja* where I had waited for the diligence to Brunete as a boy and for the bus to Novés as a man. I showed her corners and fountains in deserted, ancient streets, where I knew every stone. While we walked across the sun-filled squares and through shadowy alleys, women in the house doors looked after us and gossiped. I knew exactly the words in which they were discussing us.

From the escarpment of Las Vistillas, near a gun emplacement, I looked down at the Viaduct across the Calle de Segovia and beyond the river to the Casa de Campo, where the enemy was, and saw myself trotting up the slope with my mother, tired from her washing by the river.

I told her tales of my childhood.

6. The Shock

They had sent us a delegation of British women politicians from Valencia; our office was to look after them during their brief stay in Madrid. They had a guide of their own, the putty-faced Simon of Agence Espagne, and the Valencia departments were very much concerned about them. There were three MPs, the Duchess of Atholl, Eleanor Rathbone, and Ellen Wilkinson, and a society welfare worker, Dame Rachel Crowdy. It took Ilsa some time to din their names, political attributes, and range of interests into my head; I was not feeling too kindly towards the stream of well-meaning but usually self-centred visitors who had been touring Madrid ever since the victory of Guadalajara had eased the grip of the siege. In exchange, the grip of bureaucracy was tightening; I was acutely aware of a change in the air, and the fashion of sightseeing seemed to me part and parcel of it.

I left the personal contacts with the party to Ilsa and arranged a tour of Madrid on the obvious lines: introduction to Miaja in his musty cellar vault; visits to the flattened-out workers' houses in Cuatro Caminos and to the empty ruins of Argüelles; Sunday morning in the Protestant Church of Calatrava, with its ingenuous, honest parson and a few earnest young men in uniform singing hymns; a glimpse of the front from some comparatively safe place; a reception by Miaja in due form; a visit by the Duchess of Atholl – without any of us to guide her – to the gutted palace of the Duke of Alba, where she would be able to check and disprove on the spot the Grandee's hostile statements to the press. The shelling, which had become singularly intense during the last few days, would provide the background noise.

First came the introductory visit to Miaja. The four women waited in the ante-room, looking excited, while we cajoled Miaja into seeing them. He liked having an opportunity to grumble at the demands of the many people who came to pay him their respects. Twice he asked Ilsa who the hell those women were, and twice he asked me why the hell I did not produce young and pretty women, or at least sensible people who supplied arms for our troops. 'If they're making me into a vaudeville turn they ought at least to give me presents, a machine gun or a plane, and then I'll sign a photograph for them if they like.' But he came out meekly enough and listened to their little speeches 'to the Defender of Madrid', looking down his long nose and answering with a few gruff words. Ilsa did her translating with a hidden flourish which made me suspect that she had edited what both sides had said. Miaja grunted: 'Tell them to come to a tea party tomorrow afternoon, since you think they're so important. As they're English we must give them tea. The devil take it. They shouldn't expect too much of us, tell them, because there's a war on here. *Salud.*'

I felt almost as surly as he did. I was unable to take part in the English conversation, but I wanted very much to ask them rudely whether they couldn't do anything about nonintervention without a sightseeing trip. Moreoever, I resented Simon's slick showmanship. When we walked through a side street in Cuatro Caminos where the only thing left of a row of houses were the outlines of their flimsy foundations, an old woman came up to show us, with a dramatic instinct and sparse words, the place where her hearth had been. Simon looked as pleased as though he had stage-managed the encounter, or so I thought. I was in no mood to be just; it was a good thing that I had to do nothing but to provide the silent Spanish background.

The shelling was still growing in intensity, and it was spraying the centre of the town along 'Shell Alley'. When we drove back from the suburbs, wisps of grey smoke floated in the air the whole length of the Calle de Alcalá, and people walked very near to the house doors on the so-called safe side of the street. We hustled our guests into the Gran Vía Hotel.

I wanted the women to have lunch with us upstairs in our room, partly because I did not want them to get their image of Madrid from the tawdry cosmopolitan atmosphere of the public dining room. But they preferred to see life in the basement, and so I arranged for lunch there. The foreign correspondents rose from the long table, where they were sitting with their friends from the International Brigades, and chose their victims among the visitors, while a crowd of soldiers, tarts, and anxious mothers taking shelter with their children were milling about, shouting, eating, drinking, and waiting for a lull in the bombardment. Through the skylights came the sound of shell bursts and the wafts of acrid fumes, but the noise and the smell inside drowned them. It was a successful lunch.

After the black coffee I took the party up to the entrance hall; we were scheduled to visit Ortega's artillery observation post and our two cars were waiting outside.

In the hall there was a thin haze of smoke and an unusually dense crowd. The manager made a beeline for me:

'Don Arturo, would you please come along at once? There's been a fire in your room upstairs and the firemen are just dealing with it. It must have been a shell.'

I had heard the firebell tinkling while we were finishing our meal.

We pushed our way through the curious people blocking the stairs and the corridor. Our room was grey and smudged with smoke. There were burns on one wall and on the wardrobe, the chairs were tumbled on the ground, two firemen were just withdrawing a hose and another was tearing a smouldering curtain from its rod.

No shell had hit the room, so much was clear at a glance. But a big, triangular piece of a shell was lying on the table. It was still warm. Before it dropped, its force spent, it must have been hot enough to set the curtain on fire. That was all. Two eggs in a bowl on the side table were intact. My cigarettes had disappeared. The tablecloth was torn, a few plates were smashed; the table had been set for Ilsa and me as it was every day. Her shoes which had been lined up on a rack under the window, covered by the long curtain, were a pitiful heap of scorched, twisted, tortured-looking leather. There were stains of soot and water on pillows, and clothes. It had been nothing.

Ilsa stared ruefully at the small leather corpses of her shoes and complained that a new blue pair, much beloved by her, was shrivelled and shapeless. The Englishwomen kissed her, because they had saved her life through their presence. Hadn't she said that except for them she and I would have ben lunching at that table even while the shell fragment struck it?

I heard Ilsa saying that it didn't look as if it would have been as serious as all that, even if we had been in the room; the women were making much of her, while I said nothing. Nothing had happened. I took them down to the entrance once more. Our drivers were waiting, and it was not right to let them stay much longer in the Gran Vía during the afternoon shelling.

The street was filled with glaring sunlight and curls of slowly thinning smoke. Dull thuds sounded from further up Shell Alley. The porter informed me that our drivers were waiting round the corner in the Calle de la Montera, which was safer. I walked ahead of the women to find the cars. At the corner itself a gust of the familiar acrid smell hit me. Out of the corner of my eye I saw something odd and filmy sticking to the huge show window of the Gramophone Company. I went close to see what it was. It was moving.

A lump of grey mass, the size of a child's fist, was flattened out against the glass pane and kept on twitching. Small, quivering drops of grey matter were spattered round it. A fine thread of watery blood was trickling down the pane, away from the grey-white lump with the tiny red veins, in which the torn nerves were still lashing out.

I felt nothing but stupor. I looked at the scrap of a man stuck on to the shop window and watched it moving like an automaton. Still alive. A scrap of human brain.

Like an automaton, too, I took the elbow of the elderly woman beside me, whose honest red face was paling, and made a few steps forward to help her on. There was a fresh grey-white scar in the paving stones at the corner. The post of the old newspaper woman. I stopped. What was it I meant to do? I was hollow inside, emptied and without feelings. There seemed no street noise in the void around me.

I strained myself to hear. Somebody was calling me.

Ilsa was clutching at my arm and saying in a rough, urgent voice: 'Arturo, come away from here – Arturo!'

There were those foreign women. We had to take them somewhere. Ilsa was supporting the heavy, grey-haired one. The car was just in front of me. But my feet were sticking to the ground and when I tried to lift them I slithered. I looked down at those feet of mine. They were standing in a small sticky puddle of coagulating blood.

I let Ilsa push me into the car, but I never knew who else was inside. I believe that I rubbed my shoes on the car mat once, and I know I said nothing. My brain was blocked. Stupidly, I looked through the window and saw buildings and people move past. Then we were outside the tall house in which Ortega had set up his observation post with the telemeter of which he was so proud. He was there himself to do the honours. His young officers were ragging me because I had turned myself into the guide of a duchess. Everything was normal and it was easy to answer their jokes.

They took us up to the top floor. The wide windows overlooked a large sector of the front and of the city. One after the other our guests looked through the telemeter and let Ortega show them enemy gun emplacements, camouflaged trenches, the white and red buildings of the University City, the flash and smoke of a firing battery and the place where its shells hit their target. While he led them out on to the balcony to explain the lines of the front, I looked through the telemeter myself.

It was focused on a low building wreathed in white smoke-puffs. They were shelling it, and I wondered what their target was. I adjusted the telemeter. What I recognized in the field of vision was the chapel of the Cemetery of San Martín. The place where I had played on countless days of my boyhood while my Uncle José was there on his official visits. I made out the old brick building, the courtyards, the gallery with its white niches. One of the smoke wads dissolved and I saw the hole the shell had torn into the thick wall.

As though I had been looking into a magic crystal globe, I saw the images of my childhood in the frame of the telemeter lens.

The old cemetery with its sunlit courtyards. The row of rose-trees laden with flowers. The old chaplain, and the cemetery keeper with his flock of boys more or less my own age. The transfer of long-buried people when the cemetery was closed down. My Uncle José inspecting the decorations in the chapel before the funeral ceremonies. Bones of an ashy grey colour spread out tenderly on a sheet so white that it looked bluish. Hollow bones thrown into the bonfire of the keepers, together with the mouldy planks from burst coffins. Myself chasing butterflies and tiny lizards between the trellises and cypresses.

'We must go,' Ilsa murmured into my ear.

Through the balcony I saw streets filled with sun and people, and in the open grounds of Amaniel, green with spring grass, a dark patch, spires of cypresses wreathed in another white cloud, very far away and daintily small.

We had to go to Miaja's tea party for the British ladies.

The General had invited a few people from the Propaganda Ministry to help him with the foreigners. They had prepared a sumptuous spread in one of the big rooms of the underground department. The walls were stained and flaking, but orderlies brought bunches of flowers and served the unfamiliar tea with a smirk on their faces. While I kept up a running banter with the staff officers, Ilsa acted as interpreter in the conversation between the General and the Duchess, toning down questions and answers.

'Why the devil is she asking about Russian instructors to our air force? Tell her that we've got splendid lads of our own—why the hell isn't she interested in them?'

'Oh, I know the way generals talk from my own husband,' the Duchess said briskly.

When the drinks came, Miaja lifted his glass and said in his best French: 'To peace!'

The Duchess gave back: 'And to liberty, for peace can be bought at too dear a price.'

'*Salud!*' Ellen Wilkinson cried from the other end of the table.

When our guests had gone back to the Hotel Florida, we worked for a few hours in the Telefónica and then walked across the street to the Gran Vía Hotel. They had given us a couple of airy new rooms, on the same side of the house as the one that had been hit. We were very tired, but while Ilsa shrank away from more noise, I had to be among people. Simon was giving a party to a few Americans and some Germans from the International Brigades on another floor of the Gran Vía, and I went with him. There was nobody I liked. Major Hans was everything I imagined a raw-boned Prussian officer to be;

Simon petted a white-blonde girl with a baby-skin and a hard mouth; they were all drinking and showing off their toughness, and none of them thought of the war as our war, as Spain's torture and pain. I drank with them and burst out into a tirade to which only one person, an American film critic whose name I never knew, listened with sympathy. I shouted at them that they had come to Spain to seek their own ends, not out of a simple faith, and that they were not helping us; that they were smug and glib and we barbarians, but that at least we felt and knew what we were doing. Then my excited mood died down. I was a complete stranger among people who had every right to dislike me as I disliked them. I went down and found stillness with her.

When I woke up at eight in the morning, I did not want to wake Ilsa. The blackout curtains were split by a thin, bright gap. I wanted to take a bath, but found that we had forgotten to move soap, shaving tackle, and toothbrushes over from our old bathroom. I went out to fetch them.

Our old room was flooded with sun. It still smelled of smoke and scorched leather, and there were half-dried pools of water on the floor. It was a radiant morning. The smooth front of the Telefónica across the street was dazzlingly white. I stood by the window and looked down into the street to see whether they were not just sprinkling the pavement and producing the scent of moist earth I loved. An explosion sounded from the upper end of the street. The morning shelling had begun, punctual like the milkman. There were few people about in Shell Alley. Idly I watched a woman crossing the street a little higher up, and suddenly I wondered: wasn't that Ilsa? She was sleeping in the near-by room, I knew it, but this woman was so like her, the same size, the same body, seen from the back, the same dark-green costume. I was staring at the woman's back when the high whistle of a shell tore through the air. It hit the Fontalba Theatre just above the booking office. The woman swayed and fell, and a dark stain began to spread. One of the Shock Police sentries ran up to her, two men sprinted across the street beneath my window, and the three picked up the body. It sagged and slipped through their hands. Her limbs hung as though all her joints had been smashed by hammer blows.

I went back to our room and found Ilsa standing by the window in her dressing-gown. I looked at her and my face must have been odd, because she came over to me and said: 'What's the matter with you?'

'Nothing.'

There was another whistle, and my eyes instinctively followed the direction of the sound. A window opposite up in the fifth floor of the Telefónica was boarded up. The boards buckled in and spat splinters into the air, a dark phantom shape entered the hole and then the torn boards bulged outwards again. I ducked and dragged Ilsa down to the floor with me; we were in the line of flying shrapnel and masonry.

Squatting on the floor I had an attack of nausea, a sudden violent contraction of the stomach as when I had vomited in the shambles of the Moroccan War fifteen years earlier. But at the time I did not remember that. I cowered in a corner, trembling, unable to control my muscles which had acquired a life of their own. Ilsa led me down to the vestibule of the hotel, into a dark corner behind the telephone boxes. I drank a couple of brandies and my trembling ceased. The dark corner where I was sitting faced across the shadowy hall to the entrance. The sun was glittering and licking through the revolving doors. It was like being in a cave opening out into the fields, like awakening from a vivid dream within strangely distorted bedroom walls. At that moment my whole life suffered a distortion.

The others did not notice it. Even Ilsa only thought I was feeling a transitory after-effect of yesterday's shock. The British party had gone, and we resumed the strenuous daily routine. Yet I refused to lunch upstairs, as Ilsa wanted, and insisted on our taking our meals in the basement at the noisy table of the journalists, where I never spoke much and people were used to my morose face.

When we went up to our room before going on duty again, I saw a tiny orfice in the cardboard which replaced one of the windowpanes, and found a steel splinter embedded in the opposite wall.

We were arranging our books on a shelf beside the window. It was quiet, people were strolling and chatting in the street, everything had the light, colour, and smell of spring. The sky was clear blue and the stones of the houses looked warm with sun. A Shock Police sentry at the corner of the Telefónica paid compliments to every girl that passed him, and from my window it was easy to see that some of the girls crossed the street only to stroll past him and hear what the handsome lad had to tell them. The revolving door of the Telefónica behind him kept turning, and the glitter of its panes threw bundles of light across the shadow at the foot of the building.

Three people were crossing the Grand Vía, a soldier and two girls. One of the girls wore a black dress and carried a parcel wrapped in pink paper, bright and gay against the black. Ilsa remarked that the girl walked like a young animal, and I told her:

'If a woman walks like that we say she is *una buena jaca*, a fine filly, because she moves with the grace of a young and skittish horse.'

Then the shell whistled, and it felt as if it had passed a few yards from our faces. The soldier threw himself flat on the ground, his arms flung over his head. The shell burst in front of him with a flash and a cloud of thick black smoke. The Shock Police sentry disappeared as though swallowed by the wall of the building. The two young girls dropped like two empty sacks.

I was clinging to the window-sill, my mouth filled with vomit, and saw through a haze how people hurried away with the two bodies. Then the street was deserted and the pink parcel lay there in the middle of dark stains. Nobody collected it. The deserted street was gay and spring-like, with an inhuman indifference.

It was the hour when our afternoon shift began. We crossed the street to the other corner of the Telefónica.

I sat at my desk and stared at the meagre dispatches of journalists who had nothing to report except that the shelling of Madrid continued with unabated and monotonous intensity. Ilsa was pacing up and down, her poise shattered. Suddenly she sat down at a typewriter and wrote something at great speed. When she had finished she rang up Ilsa Wolff, the German journalist who ran the UGT Radio which broadcast to foreign workers in various languages, and in distinction to whom our Ilsa used at that time to be called *Ilsa de la Telefónica*.

They spoke in German and I was not interested. But then Ilsa rose, took her coat and said to me: 'I must do something, otherwise I can't forget that pink parcel. I must speak to my own workers at home – they'll still know my voice in some place – and I've told Ilsa Wolff that I simply must broadcast today instead of her.'

I knew at once what she meant. There had been many duds among the shells, and we were all firmly convinced that there was some sabotage in the German factories which supplied Franco with armaments. Ilsa was going to cry out to her Austrian workers. But few of them would hear her. When she went out into the street I sat there listening for the sound of bursting shells.

There was too little work to do. I was obsessed with tracing the course the shells might have taken. The piece of metal which had set the curtain of our window on fire had followed a curve which meant that it would have hit her head, if we had lunched in our room as usual. The minute steel splinter which a few hours ago had pierced the cardboard in the window-frame of our new room had bored deep into the opposite wall. Had we eaten there as Ilsa had wanted, her head would have been midway between the hole in the pane and the hole in the wall. I was haunted by images of her, in the shape of the woman whom I had seen hit in the street that morning, or sitting at our table with a hole in her head.

Journalists came and went, and I spoke as much or as little to them as usual; in the end I handed over the censoring to old Llizo and started to write.

I do not remember that story well; it would be of interest to a psychiatrist. Like a dream it mixed sights and visions: the shop window of the Gramophone Company, a display of black discs showing the white, cock-eared dog on their gaudy labels; the smooth pane reflecting the passing multitude, a phantom multitude of living beings without life; the black records enclosing in their furrows a multitude of ghost voices; everything unreal, and the only real thing above them – on the surface of that solid glass pane – a scrap of palpitating brain, still living, the antennae of its severed nerves lashing out in a desperate voiceless cry to a deaf multitude. And then I put the woman behind the glass panel, lying still, a hole in her head, the corners of her lips like a question mark in a faint smile, very serene. It was no story.

When Ilsa came back, quietened and tired, I was still sitting at the typewriter. I handed her the pages I had written. When she came to the description of the woman, she gave me a scared glance and said without thinking:

'But it's me you've killed here.'

I took the pages from her and tore them up.

The routine work went on, but we had a guest whom I liked and respected, John Dos Passos, who spoke about our land workers and peasants with a gentle understanding, looking from one to the other out of wondering brown eyes. He helped us that evening; I saw that Ilsa's eyes were following my gestures with a suppressed anxiety and that she kept the conversation going so as to lead me back into normal contacts.

I find that John Dos Passos mentions this encounter in one of his sketches in *Journeys between Wars*. This is what he says:

> In the big quiet office you find the press censors, a cadaverous Spaniard and a plump little pleasant-voiced Austrian woman. . . . Only yesterday the Austrian woman came back to find that a shell-fragment had set her room on fire and burned up all her shoes, and the censor had seen a woman made mincemeat of beside him. . . . It's not surprising that the censor is a nervous man; he looks underslept and underfed. He talks as if he understood, without taking too much personal pleasure in it, the importance of his position as guardian of those telephones that are the link with countries technically at peace, where the war is still carried on with gold credits on bank ledgers and munitions contracts and conversations on red plush sofas in diplomatic ante-rooms instead of with six-inch shells and firing squads. He doesn't give the impression of being complacent about it. But it's hard for one who is more or less of a free agent from a country at peace to talk about many things with men who are chained to the galley benches of war.
>
> It's a relief to get away from the switchboards of power and walk out into the sunny streets again.

But I was chained to myself and split in myself.

When I was seven I went to school one morning and saw a man running round a street corner towards me. Behind him sounded shouts and the patter of an invisible crowd. The stretch of street where we were was empty except for the man and me. He stopped close to me and pushed something into his mouth. There was a bang, I saw the man's cap hurled into the air, and black scraps flying, there was a flash, and then I found myself at a first-aid post, where people were pouring water with a penetrating odour down my throat.

When I was nine years old, I was sitting on the balcony of my uncle's flat one morning reading a book. Suddenly I heard a dull thud in the street down below. On the opposite pavement lay the body of a woman, smashed on the stones. She had her eyes tied with a white handkerchief which was turning first red and then almost black. Her skirts were gathered above her ankles with a green curtain cord. One of the tassels of the cord dangled over the kerbstone. The balcony began to sway and the street to reel before my eyes.

When I was twenty-four years old, and I saw the room in the barracks of the Civil Guard at Melilla, which looked as though the dead men leaning over the window-sills and in the corners had splashed each other with their blood as during a battle in a swimming pool in the summer, I had vomited. With the stench of slashed bodies eternally in my nostrils, I had been unable to stand even the sight of raw meat for over three years.

It all came back.

I was listening with my whole body for the whistle of a shell or the drone of an aircraft among the thousand noises of the street; my brain was trying feverishly to eliminate all the noises which were not hostile and to analyse those which held a threat. I had to fight ceaselessly against this obsession, because it threatened to tear the weave of whatever I was doing, hearing, or saying. People and things near me grew blurred and twisted into phantom shapes as soon as they were out of direct contact with me. I was afraid of being shut up and alone, and afraid of being in the open among people. When I was alone I felt like an abandoned child. I was incapable of going alone to my hotel room, because it meant crossing the Gran Vía, and

I was incapable of staying alone in my room. When I was there, I stared at the white front of the Telefónica, with its bricked-up window-holes and black window-holes and the pock-marks of dozens of shells. I hated it and I stared at it. But I could no longer bear to look down into the street.

That night I ran a high temperature and although I had not eaten, I vomited bitter stomach juice in spasmodic convulsions. The following day my mouth filled with the sour liquid at the sound of a motorcycle, a tram, the screech of a brake, at the sound of air-raid sirens, the drone of planes, and the thud of shells. The city was full of those sounds.

I knew what was happening to me and fought against it: I had to work and I had no right to show nervousness or fear. There were the others before whom I had to be calm if I wanted them to be calm. I clung to the thought that I had the obligation not to show fear, and so I became obsessed with a second kind of fear: the fear of being afraid.

The people, apart from Ilsa and my brother-in-law, Agustín, who had become senior orderly at our office, only knew that I was not feeling well and seemed in a particularly black mood. The journalists themselves were urging a transfer of the censorship office to safer quarters; at their request, the telephonic room was installed downstairs in the basement of the Telefónica, yet even so they had to cross Shell Alley too often. It had become an unreasonable risk. Ilsa had been almost the only person to defend our continued stay in the Telefónica; she had an affection for the very walls of the building and felt part of it. But by then the situation had become untenable even for her.

We changed our rooms in the hotel to the back where our windows opened into a chimney-like yard that caught and held every sound. I was shaken by bouts of fever and bouts of sickness. I neither slept nor ate. For a day, I stayed in the dark corner of the hotel hall, doing office work other than actual censoring, while Ilsa carried on in the Telefónica. It was she who obtained Rubio Hidalgo's consent to move our office to the Foreign Ministry. Some of the journalists urged the transfer to one of the quiet and almost shell-proof suburbs, but it would have taken a long time and a lot of wiring; in the Ministry the press-room and censorship were still wired and had thick stone walls, even though the building was within the habitual range of the siege guns.

The Telefónica had been hit by over one hundred and twenty shells, and although not a single life had been lost within its walls during that time, the journalists and censors alike had a feeling of impending disaster.

On May the 1st the Foreign Press and Censorship Department of Madrid moved back to the Foreign Ministry in the Plaza de Santa Cruz. I waited for the move in my corner at the back of the hotel vestibule, fighting myself and lost within myself. I did not know at that time that Ilsa was crossing the shelled street and working on the fourth floor of the Telefónica for eight days with the absolute conviction that she was doomed to be killed. I even left it to her to collect all papers and bring them to the Ministry with the help of Agustín.

The day after they left the Telefónica, a shell entered through one of the windows of our deserted office and exploded by the main desk a few minutes after five. At five sharp every afternoon Ilsa had taken over and sat down at that very desk.

The Foreign Ministry is built round two big, flagged, glass-covered inner courts and divided by a monumental staircase which leads up from the triple entrance. Arched galleries circle the two courts in two tiers; the upper gallery has a parqueted floor and gilt railing, the gallery on the ground floor has large flagstones and it echoes under the heavy vaulting. The office rooms open on to the galleries. The building is of stone and brick, with enormously stout walls. Two towers with pointed slate roofs flank it. It is an island amid silent old streets, near the old Plaza Mayor of the Auto-da-fés and bullfights, and near the noisy Puerta del Sol. Below the building are vaulted cellars and mighty passages dating from an older age.

The Ministry is dignified, chilly, and unfriendly, with its stones, which seem to sweat dampness on rainy days, and the heavy iron bars before its windows. The cellar vaults once belonged to the jail of the Royal Court. Second-rate sculptures made by artists whom the Spanish State subsidized stand stupidly and incongruously around the courts.

Ilsa and I installed ourselves in one of the small rooms. The censorship moved back to its old quarters, and Rubio Hidalgo's office was opened for formal occasions, but hardly ever used. It smelled stale. To save the journalists unnecessary trips through the spatter of shells, a kind of canteen was set up; orderlies brought food – poor food – from the Gran Vía Hotel in a service car. Whenever the shelling moved near and thuds came from the Plaza Mayor there was the vault of the cellar staircase with fifteen feet of stone and mortar thickness above it, a perfect shelter.

The noise and bustle of the transfer had torn me out of my daze. Away from the glaring façade of the Telefónica I lost one of the elements of my obsession, but the others did not disappear with the move as I had secretly hoped. I went down to the Ministry library in the basement vaults and listened from there for the sound of Ilsa's heels on the flags of the court. I forced her to stay within the building, but I could not force her to stay in my sight, because she had to do two men's work to cover up the fact that I was not working. She was amused with the Ministry, content because the journalists seemed to like it, and busy making our small room livable; she, and Agustín's steady, good-humoured common sense kept me from lapsing into a broody melancholy dangerously near to something worse.

After a few days, when I saw I was not sleeping in the new place either, I asked the Ministry's physician to examine me and give me some drug. He gave me a medicine based on morphine. Ilsa thought I should rather fight it out mentally, but she did not understand: I simply could not sleep. That night I went to bed early, reeling with exhaustion and sleeplessness, and took the prescribed dose.

I sank down into a gulf. The outlines of the room dissolved. Agustín was nothing but a shadow moving against endless yellow walls which lost themselves in dark depths. The light was a faint glow which grew steadily more faint. My body lost the feeling of weight and I was floating. I slumbered.

An infinite terror invaded me. Now, at that very moment, the shelling was going to start afresh. I would be tied to my bed, unable to move or to protect myself. The others would go down to the basement and leave me alone. I battled desperately. The drug had worked upon the motorial nerve centre and I could not move. My will did not want to submit, it did not want to sleep or to let me go to sleep. Sleep meant the danger of death. My brain sent out urgent orders: move – jump out of bed – speak – scream! The drug held it own. I was shaken by waves of deep-seated nausea, as if my entrails had torn loose from me and were moving furiously, with hands, claws and teeth of their own.

Someone was speaking close above my head, trying to tell me something, but it was too far away, although I saw the shadows of enormous heads looming. I was being hurled into bottomless pits, falling into voids, with a horrible pressure in my stomach, and at the same time trying to push upwards and to resist the fall and the crash at the invisible bottom of the abyss. I was being dismembered; my limbs were converted into a shapeless, woolly mass and then became invisible, although they were still there, and I was trying to recapture those arms and legs, those lungs and bowels of mine which were dissolving into nothingness. Phantasmagoric faces and monster hands and floating shapes caught me, lifted me, dropped me, carried me hither and thither. And I knew that at that very moment the explosions would start again. I felt myself dying of disintegration of the body, with only an incommensurable brain left to pit all its energies against death, against the dissolution of the body to which it was attached.

I have never been certain whether it was the threshold of death or madness at which I stood that night. Nor did Ilsa ever know whether she saw me drifting towards death or madness.

Slowly my will was stronger than the drug. At dawn I was awake, covered with cold sweat, mortally exhausted, but able to think and move. There came a second wave of frenzy in the afternoon, when I rolled on my bed and fought to retain my senses while Ilsa, who dared not leave me alone, had to answer the questions of unfriendly Polish visitors – Alter and Ehrlich – by the table in our room. I saw their faces in distorted, leering shapes and tried not to cry out. It seems that I did moan, however.

The worst part of my experience, and of all the stages of experience through which the war shock took me, was that I was the whole time aware of the process and its mechanism. I knew that I was ill and what I had to call abnormal; my self was fighting against my second self, refusing to submit to it, yet doubting whether I had the strength to win my fight – and thus prolonging the struggle. I doubted whether that other self which produced the abject fear of destruction was not really right, and I had to suppress those doubts so as to live on among the others.

When I got up and returned to work, I felt set apart from the others, who themselves appeared abnormal to me because they did not share my own anguish. I could not emerge from introspection, because I was forced to keep a conscious check on myself, and this constant self-observation made me observe the others in a new way.

I lost my interest in the office work which the others carried on in set tracks and against a growing passive resistance from the head office in Valencia. What occupied me was how to understand the springs that moved other people in our war, and to understand the course of the war itself.

It seemed to me that small, unreasoned and unreasonable things were driving each individual to fight, things which stood for shapeless and deep emotions. A particle of palpitating grey matter had set off a hidden train of thoughts and emotions in me. What was it that set off others? Not what they said in well-ordered words.

A few days after I had recovered from my nightmare ride, I wrote my first short story, about a Miliciano in a trench who stayed there because the Fascists had destroyed his wife's sewing-machine, because he had to be there, and finally because a blindly hitting bullet had crushed a fly which he loved to observe on a sunlit spot of the parapet. I brought it to Ilsa, and I saw that it struck her. If she had said that it was no good, I think I would never have tried to write again, because it would have meant that I was unable to touch hidden springs.

But this was only a slight relief. I could not get away from the vision of the war with which I had risen from my stupor. Our war had been provoked by a group of generals who were in their turn manoeuvred by the sectors of the Spanish Right most grimly determined to fight any development within the country which might threaten the privileges of their caste. But the rebels had committed the mistake of resorting to outside help and of converting the civil war into an international skirmish. Spain, her people, and her Government no longer existed in a definite form; they were the objects of an experiment in which the States standing for international Fascism and the State standing for Communism or Socialism took part, while the other countries looked on as vitally interested spectators. What was happening to us was a signpost for the future road of Europe and possibly the world.

The spectator countries favoured one or the other of our two fronts; their ruling classes leaned towards the camp of international Fascism, a part of their working people and intellectuals leaned more or less clearly towards international Socialism. An ideological guerrilla warfare was going on in Europe and America. Recruits for the International Brigades came from all countries, and all countries refused to supply the Spanish Republic with the arms it needed. The avowed reason was to avoid an international war; yet some groups may have hoped that Spain would provoke war between Soviet Russia and Germany and many were curious to see the strength of the two opposing political ideologies tested, not in the field of theory but of arms.

It seemed to me beyond doubt that the ruling groups of Europe expected to retain mastery of the situation after a defeat of Communism and a weakening of militant Fascism, which could then be usefully exploited and handled by them. Thus it was part of their game to protect Fascism from the danger of finally losing its war in Spain, for Fascism was the lesser evil, or rather a potential boon. This meant nonintervention, and the surrender of the Republican Government into the hands of Soviet Russia, of the rebels into the hands of Germany and Italy.

We could not win the war.

The statesmen of Soviet Russia would not be so foolish as to carry their intervention to a point when it would mean war with Germany, in a situation in which Russia would be left alone and Germany enjoy the support of the ruling classes and of the heavy industries of all the other countries. Soon the Russians would have to tell us: 'We can't do more for you, carry on as well as you can.'

We were condemned in advance. And yet we were carrying on a ferocious fight. Why?

We had no other choice. Spain had only two roads before her: the terrible hope, worse than despair, that a European War would break out and force some of the other countries to intervene against Hitler's Germany, and the desperate resolution to sacrifice ourselves so that others should gain time for their preparations and so that one day, after the end of Fascism, we would have the right to demand our compensation. In any case we would have to pay in blood, in the currency of a savage destruction of our own soil. It was for this that the many thousands who faced death at the front were fighting with a Credo and a political conviction, with faith, and with the hope of victory.

When I had reached this conclusion, it was sheer intellectual torture. I had nothing with which to soften it. I saw in my mind the corpses piling up, the destruction spreading without cease, and I had to accept it as necessary, as inevitable, as something in which I had to take part, although I lacked the consolation of a blind faith or hope. At that stage, it became more intolerable than ever to see that there was so little unity on our side. Among the leaders of the struggle, the ideal to save the Republic as the basis for democratic growth had evaporated; each group had turned monopolist and intolerant. For a short time I had forgotten the atmosphere there was away from the front of Madrid. Now came the news of street fighting among anti-Fascists in Barcelona. The civil servants sent back to Madrid from Valencia were very meticulous about their political label. We who had tried to carry on in the days of the November crisis were out of place, and it had become dangerous for us to vent our feelings.

But there were still many men like Angel and the shy, gawky Milicianos he brought to the Ministry to see Ilsa and me, boys who clutched a pitiful bunch of rosebuds in their fingers, who had come from olive fields and brick kilns to fight for the Republic and wanted to hear me read Federico García Lorca to them. There were the men I met when I took Ilsa to Serafín's tavern on quiet evenings, tired workers, fatalistic, grumpy, and unshaken. There was the girl who ushered people into her porter's lodge during shellings because her grandfather had done so until shrapnel had killed him.

I wanted to cry out to them and to the world. If I was to stay on fighting against my nerves and my mind, relentlessly aware of myself and the others, I had to do something more in this war than merely supervise the censorship of increasingly indifferent newspaper dispatches.

So I continued to write, and I began to speak on the radio.

7. Crying Out

At the outbreak of the Civil War, Spanish radio stations, the semi-official ones as well as the numerous amateur transmitters, had been commandeered by political groups and used for their propaganda, not so much of a general as of a partisan and sectional character. The outcome was confusion and muddle, less noted since few of the stations were at all audible abroad, and none in all parts of Spain. When the Government regained its hold on public life, it began by accepting this state of affairs as a lesser evil, but then, step by step, imposed its authority and ended by decreeing the cessation of all party stations and the functioning only of transmissions under official control.

One morning, the State Controller of Transradio, the same shy, haggard civil servant who had made me shoulder his worries about radio-telegrams in the first days of the siege, turned up at the Ministry to confront me with a new puzzle.

The Spanish State had a contractual right to use the short-wave station EAQ, the transmitter of the Transradio Company, during certain hours every day. This service came under the authority of a Government Delegate, but the Controller did not know which was the competent Ministry. A small team of speakers had been broadcasting official communiqués in Spanish, French, Portuguese, English, and German, and culled items from the Spanish press to compose their news bulletins. Since the beginning of the reorganization of broadcasting matters, however, the Government Delegate had failed to pay the speakers' salaries, and by now only the Spanish and the Portuguese broadcasters were left to carry on.

The Controller had officially nothing to do with the broadcasting side; but he was worried at this neglect of one of the best weapons at the disposal of the Republic, and he had discussed matters with the

Workers' Committee whose members felt as he did. Something had to be done, otherwise the only short-wave station of Madrid would close down so far as propaganda was concerned. The speakers could not weather it out any longer. The Portuguese was half starved anyhow, and went about in shoes without proper soles. He, the Controller, had attempted to argue the case with one of the Junta's secretaries in the Ministry of the Interior and with his own superiors, the postal authorities, but when they found that the EAQ broadcasts were destined for foreign consumption they had lost all interest. At bottom, they thought foreign propaganda a useless luxury; they knew nothing about it; and anyhow, the only official body concerned with foreign matters was the Foreign Ministry. The Foreign Ministry was in Valencia, and I knew, said the Controller, how impossible it was to get Valencia to do anything for and in Madrid. But now I was back in the Foreign Ministry. Would I do something?

I was no less ignorant of the whole affair than the Controller. Miaja, as the Governor-General of Madrid, could have intervened, but I felt that it was futile to approach the General with this intricate problem. Yet I shared the Controller's conviction that we had to act. The only thing which occurred to me on the spur of the moment was that the Portuguese speaker might eat in our canteen and, if he had nowhere to go, sleep on a divan in one of the Ministry's empty, dust-sheeted rooms. I asked the Controller to send me the Portuguese and promised to think over the entire problem.

I was glad to be given something concrete with which to grapple. The censorship was running in settled grooves. Ilsa had the help of a new censor, the white-blonde Canadian girl Pat whom I distrusted. The head office in Valencia, where Rubio had left the reins in the hand of his new assistant, Constancia de la Mora, was balking our requests on behalf of the journalists with tiresome consistency. There were more visitors and more special correspondents on lightning trips to the Madrid front; General Goliev had been transferred to the Basque front. The shelling went on and on; and my nightmares lasted.

The Portuguese Armando came to see me, slovenly, unshaven, a skeleton frame covered with twitching nerves, his clothes miserably frayed. His bony, hooked nose and the gapped teeth in his wide mouth did not matter; his eyes were alive and intelligent under a domed forehead and his hands long and slim, with terse, neat gestures. He spoke without pause of the political crimes being committed out of indifference and corruption of the mind, and he caught my imagination with his picture of what could be done if the radio station were used for intensive propaganda directed to the Americas. When I broached his own situation, he countered all proposals with a savage pride: he wanted no alms, the salary for over three months' work was due to him, and he had no cause to accept charity from anyone. If he starved to death, it would be a good, clear case of official sabotage. In the end Ilsa talked him round, and he joined me at the long table of our improvised canteen, where journalists and passing visitors ate together with the censors, dispatch-riders, and orderlies.

It may have been because his burning, relentless, high-pitched indignation at things as they were coincided with my own frame of mind: we became friends.

I learned from Armando not only about the unexploited possibilities of the EAQ station, but also about the need for a directing control and censorship of the broadcasts. It had happened before – and now I realized how – that journalists, whom we stopped sending off a piece of news because it was banned by Military Intelligence, protested sharply and proved that the same report had gone out on the air for all the world to hear.

Among the regular visitors to my office was a man I will call Ramón, a Spanish journalist attached to Miaja's headquarters and used by the General as a private secretary and publicity agent. I spoke to Ramón of the radio muddle, and he quickly understood that I thought Miaja ought to intervene, but did not know how to make him. Two days later Miaja sent for me.

'Now what's this damned story about the radio? You boys are always trying to drag me into one of your messes. One day I'll chuck the whole damned bunch of you out.'

Ramón gave me an accomplice's grin. After my simple explanation, the General wiped his eyeglasses and called his secretary.

'Make out a paper thinggammyjig for Barea. He's in charge of the radio censorship now. And you know, my boy – you're a sucker!'

I started to tell him about foreign propaganda, the EAQ station and its potential importance, but Miaja cut me short and Ramón produced a few bottles of beer out of the bedroom. A few days later, however, I was summoned again: the General gave me a 'paper' with his signature, which made me his Commissioner at the EAQ station, with full powers.

My most urgent task was to find out which official department had to pay the speakers. I called in the Government Delegate – whom I had superseded – and asked him to render an account of his administration on the following day; he never turned up. The Workers' Committee brought me a bundle of letters from sympathizers overseas who had sent small donations of which there was no trace. This made it a matter for the police, and I handed it on; not however to my friends the Anarchists, for Pedro Orobón had been killed by a shrapnel splinter and the tolerant, human, selfless leadership of his friend Manuel replaced by a new system, more impersonal and more political, under a young Communist.

I still did not know which Ministry would pay the speakers and put up the money for the special valves bitterly needed by the station. Rubio Hidalgo, when I raised the point in one of our sporadic telephone conversations, made it perfectly clear that he was annoyed at my having meddled with something outside my office. Broadcasting was a matter for the Propaganda Ministry which had a Delegate in Madrid, Don José Carreño España. I sent a memorandum to Don José and received no answer.

At this, I called a council of war consisting of the Controller, the Workers' Committee, and the two speakers. I told them that I had not yet solved the financial question. I believed in the importance of their work. If they wanted to cease broadcasting in view of the difficulties and the official neglect, I could do nothing. If they were willing to go on until I found a way out – which I thought I could find – I would do my best. The speakers could eat in our canteen, since the food problem would otherwise be insoluble for them, and I would help with the programmes. Ilsa would find friends in the International Brigades to broadcast in foreign languages.

They agreed to carry on, sceptically, yet too much in love with their station to let it close down.

I solved the matter of the speakers' pay by sheer chance. Carreño España and I met in Miaja's room, and the General presented us to each other. I said: 'I'm glad to know you exist after all.' 'How's that?' Miaja grunted, and Don José asked the same in more elaborate words. 'Because memos addressed to you seem to get nowhere.' Then, of course, the whole story came out; we all agreed that it had been an office blunder; the Madrid Delegate of the Propaganda Ministry declared that the commitment would be honoured, and I had made yet another friend in official circles. . . .

In those weeks, the Madrid front held little military interest. Hemingway had to find material for his articles by investigating the reactions of his friends in the bullfighting world and by keeping in contact with the Russian colony in the Hotel Gaylord; when we stood in the ring of inane, marble statues in the Ministry court, his jokes told me how near he was to understanding Castilian double meanings – and how far, in spite of his obvious wish to speak to us man to man. Delmer (who was deeply annoyed because we failed to procure from either Valencia or from Careño España a permit to use his big camera) and Herbert Matthews visited the Aragon front and came back disgusted with the sector held by POUM units. Most of the correspondents only stayed on in Madrid because something was bound to break, in their opinion. But what came was the collapse of the northern front.

We were self-centred in Madrid; we thought that the rearguard – the 'rotten rearguard' – of Valencia and Barcelona belonged to another world which we did not even try to understand. But Bilbao was fighting, Asturias was fighting, and they seemed to belong to us. And Bilbao fell.

I heard it first from foreign correspondents whose editors in London and Paris wanted them to report on Madrid's reaction to the news which had been broadcast from the other side. We knew nothing, officially. Rumours had been going round, but there were strict orders to press and radio not to publish anything except official communiqués; so far no communiqué had told the story of the fall of Bilbao, but many had spoken of its victorious defence. This news policy was humiliating in its stupidity. I went to Miaja and stated my conviction that this night's broadcast to America would have to deal with the fact of Bilbao's fall; if we were going to be silent about it, it would hurt our moral standing more than the fall itself. Miaja refused to make a decision: any order had to come from Valencia, he could not assume the responsibility and he did not know how to give the news. I suggested that I would write a talk on the subject and show it him before broadcasting.

'I can't imagine how the devil you can put it so that it doesn't hurt us,' Miaja said. 'But you can write it by all means; there's still time for me to tear it up and leave the Valencia people to cope.'

I wrote a talk. As a device, it was directed to the blockade-running ship's captain nicknamed Potato Jones, and it was merely a profession of faith. It said that Bilbao had fallen, it explained what it had meant to our Spain and what it would come to mean again; that we were fighting on and that there was no time to weep for Bilbao. Miaja read it, thumped on his desk, and ordered me to broadcast the talk. He also rang up the only newspaper which was scheduled to appear the following day and told the editor to print my piece. In this form, Madrid read about Bilbao.

That was the first time I spoke into a microphone. The engineers and guards of the building thronged the narrow room and I saw that I moved them. I had a lump in my throat and the feeling that here was a force entrusted to me. So I told the Workers' Committee that I would broadcast a talk every day after the news bulletins for Latin America, at a quarter past two in the morning. The speaker had announced me as 'An Unknown Voice from Madrid', and I wanted this to remain my radio name. This was what I wanted to be.

The day was burdened with double office work since I had to censor all talks broadcast from Madrid. I went through it mechanically, forever listening to the thuds of shells. When the shelling came too near, I went down to the vaults of the library and wrote there. The new foreign journalists who came and went hardly ever became real persons to me. I remember the young Dane Vinding. He arrived with great plans, amusedly recalling that his father had fled from Madrid during the November raids, and then came to ask me for shelter, a trembling wreck, after seeing a little boy torn by a shell in the Gran Vía. I spoke to him about myself, so as to give him a fellow feeling; but at his first sally into the streets he was caught in a shooting brawl in one of the cafés and, escaping, faced a phantom car of the Fifth Column, swishing past with a rattle of tommy-guns: I had to send him back to Valencia. I also remember the German Communist George Gordon, crippled and twisted by the Nazis in body and mind. He worked for Agence Espagne and quickly began to agitate for people of a sterner political discipline to be put in mine and Ilsa's places, when he found that we did not let him monopolize all scoops and influence our treatment of the journalists. I found him slimy, with a crooked mouth, a sliding glance, sidling movements, and no spontaneous warmth or interest; I underrated him. From him and the circle of young foreign Party workers he collected I turned more than ever to people I knew to be genuine.

Torres, the printing worker who had founded the Popular Front Committee of the Ministry together with me, came to us with his difficulties. He had become secretary of the Communist cell, but he knew that he was ignorant and helpless and therefore submitted his political worries to Ilsa who, after conscientiously reminding him that she did not belong to the Party and was indeed disapproved of by it, would explain to him what, in her opinion, he ought to do, and what the Party line would be. He never found it odd that he let himself be guided by her, as long as it helped his work; he never admitted that he was acting against the discipline of his Party. But to me he came with other problems. He was married; he had not the courage to break away from it altogether as I had done, although he was unhappy and in love with another woman; he envied me; he wanted to speak of the relationship between men and women. Then again he told me of the Fifth Columnists he feared were among the bureaucrats of the Ministry. I contradicted him. There was nothing left in the building which could have been of interest to the enemy, and the people he suspected were scared elderly employees, faithful servants of the old ruling caste, such as the doorkeeper Faustino who greeted me with an obsequious bow and a bilious glance, but by no means dangerous. Then one day Torres arrived in great excitement and burst out:

'Now there you are, you and your talk of harmless scared old men. . . . In San Franciso el Grande, the Shock Police have caught one of them sending heliograph messages to the rebels in the Casa de

Campo by tugging at the cord of a blind, and there was a pocket mirror tied to one of the slats, and that's how he signalled news of troop movements on our side. If you'd seen the man! He was just like a wrinkled old bat. And you see, the worst of it is, the art treasure left in San Francisco el Grande is our responsibility – I'm one of the Controlling Committee – and we thought we could trust some of those bigoted old fools because they've looked after it so long. But you can't trust anybody except our own people.'

He pestered me to go with him and see the works of art still left in the old monastery which for half a century had been one of the National Monuments. It was his responsibility before the people and weighed upon him; but he wondered what I would think of it: was it really great art?

I began to go out again and to teach myself to behave as everybody else did. In the night I would speak to the outer world as the voice of Madrid, so I had to be one of the people of Madrid. With Ilsa, I spent quiet hours in the back room of Serafín's tavern while he told me stories of his street. He took me down into the pawnbroker's cellar where he and his friends slept on empty wooden shelves, the shelves where pawned mattresses used to be piled, so as to be safe from shells. The women slept in the neighbouring cellar on camp beds. But Serafín had a purple bruise on his forehead which never waned and was the butt of countless jokes: every time he jumped because of an explosion, he bumped his head against the upper shelf and every time he wanted to get out of his bunk to help clear up the mess left by a shell in the street, he bumped it too. His fear and his courage both gave him bruises.

I told this story over the wireless, as I told the stories of street-cleaners watering Shell Alley and washing off dark trickles of blood, of tramway bells tinkling and giving me courage during raids, of a telephone girl crying until her eyes and nose were swollen, but sticking to her post while the windowpanes were shattered by blast, of old women sitting and knitting under the porches of a front-line village where Pietro Nenni took me in his car, of children picking up shell-fuses, still warm, in the street behind the Ministry and making a game of it. I believe that all the stories I wrote and broadcast at the end of a day in the bleak, echoing Ministry, were stories of ordinary people living in that mixture of fear and courage which filled the streets of Madrid, and its trenches. All their fears were mine, and their courage warmed me. I had to pass it on.

Miaja had put a driver and a small car, one of the Italian Balillas captured after Guadalajara, at mine and Ilsa's disposal for our broadcasting. After one o'clock, when the press censorship was closed, it took us through empty streets where sentries stopped us and asked for sign and counter-sign. The station was in the Calle de Alcalá, in a tall building whose top floor had housed big, well-equipped studios. The shelling had made the upper floors uninhabitable, and an emergency studio and office had been installed in the basement. You walked down a small concrete staircase and found yourself in a dirty, narrow passage, dank and pervaded by the smell of the doorless lavatory which opened into it, exhibiting white tiles and dripping water pipes. The small cubicles ranged along the corridor had originally served to store coal; each had a grating set high in the wall and opening out into the street just above pavement level. One of those coal cellars had been cleared out and converted into a studio by the simple means of army blankets strung up on the walls for sound-proofing. It held a gramophone turntable, a small switchboard and a suspended microphone.

The coal cellar next door had been turned into the office. It had half a dozen chairs and two huge, old, ink-stained desks. A big iron stove in the middle was kept burning even on the hottest summer nights, because the cellars sweated dampness. Thus the room was filled with steam, thickened and coloured by tobacco smoke. The passage and the empty cubicles were littered with pallets stuffed with esparto grass. There slept the family of the concierge, the engineers, a few employees of the company, the messenger boys, the militiamen posted there, two Assault Guards, and an assortment of children who had nowhere else to go. Everybody talked and shouted, the children squeaked, and the concrete walls resounded. Sometimes it was necessary to cut the transmission for a moment and to shout for silence, with a couple of curses to lend force to the command.

At the far end of the passage a round hole opened, like a well shaft; a winding iron stair led into a cellar hole, ten feet square and of solid concrete, where my friend the Controller had his office. Under the green glow of the lampshade he looked like a ghost, with his thin frame and loose clothes, and the sudden silence behind the thick walls made you feel as though you had descended into a tomb. There we would sit with the Secretary of the Workers' Committee, a spare man from the Mancha with jutting cheekbones and small, glinting eyes, and plan our programmes. There we would read the first letters addressed to the 'Voice of Madrid'. One was from an old Spanish miner in the United States. He said – and I think I remember the exact words of his utterly simple letter: 'When I was thirteen I went underground to dig coal in Peñarroya. Now I am sixty-three, and I am still digging coal in Pennsylvannia. I am sorry I cannot write better, but the Marquess and the priest of our village did not grant us any schooling. I bless you who are fighting for a better life, and I curse those who do not want our people to rise.'

While I read my nightly talk, the entire population of the basement used to assemble in the blanketed studio. The men seemed to feel that they had a share in my broadcasts, because I spoke their language, and they were possessively critical of them. The control-room engineer in Vallecas made a point of ringing me up and telling me whether I had once again been too soft for his taste or not. The simplest among the men had a predilection for biblical denunciations of the powers of evil on the other side; some of the workers were shocked and fascinated by the harshest pieces of realism I wrote; the employees found my style too uncouth and devoid of rotund, polished passages, not literary enough; most of them were astonished that they could follow every sentence easily, without intellectual stumbling. I had no theory; I was fumbling to express what they dimly felt, in the clearest possible language, and to make people overseas see below the surface of our struggle.

The man whose reactions were most illuminating to me was the sergeant in command of the Shock Police post at the Ministry. He held himself at my disposal with the unquestioning loyalty of a henchman, following the orders of his predecessor who had stood by me on November the 7th. Convinced that I was a worthwhile target for the Fifth Column, he refused to let me out of his sight after dark and accompanied me to the radio station with a silent, childlike pride. There he would stand in a corner, towering above the others, and blink when he was touched. His face was flat and rugged, as though carved out of a weather-beaten stone slab, and his eyes were pale.After a few weeks of listening to my broadcasts he entered my room, gulped, blinked, and handed me a few sheets; he had written down the bad things he had done and seen being done in his years of service in the Army and the Civil Guard. Now he wanted me to turn his story into a broadcast, as an atonement to the people. His handwriting was much like the old miner's who had written from Pennsylvania.

The new Republican Government under Dr Negrin had been in office for some time. Negrin himself had made his first, grimly sober broadcasts; Indalecio Prieto was rumoured to have cleaned up the General Staff; Army discipline was being tightened up, the Party character of the units reduced, the role of the Political Commissars restricted. There were troop movements on the sectors west of Madrid, the roads from the coast saw a constant flow of war material, many more new fighter planes were flying overhead, war correspondents arrived from Valencia. I was given a series of stringent orders by HQ: Prieto was in the town, but his stay was to be kept secret; as soon as the operation started, no reports other than the war communiqués were to be passed by the censorship; private as well as diplomatic telegrams and radio messages were to be held up for several days; correspondents were not allowed to go to the front.

Offensive operations began in a broiling July heat. The Lister, Campesino, and International Brigades were in action. The battle for Brunete was joined. The Republican thrust, supported – for the first time – by successful air operations, gained ground due west of Madrid in a bid to cut the enemy's lines, turn his flank and force an evacuation of his positions in the University City. But then the offensive was halted; in spite of their remarkable technical improvement, our forces were too weak to increase their pressure before the enemy had time to bring up reinforcements. After the advance came a reverse; Brunete and Quijorna, taken at great cost, were lost again and wiped out in the process.

Torres and I climbed the crooked, cobwebbed stair to the western turret of the Ministry. Through the skylight we looked down on the chess-board of slated roofs and on the vast battlefield. Far away in the plain, too far for our eyes to make out any detail, was a mass of smoke and dust, split by flashes, and from its dark base an immense smoke column rose into the bright sky. The war cloud heaved and quivered, and my lungs trembled with the vibration of sky and earth. Fine dust floated from the old beams of the turret, clearly visible against the light that came through the panes. Down on the Plaza de Santa Cruz people were going about their affairs, and on the roof opposite a black-and-white cat sat down by a chimney, stared at us, and began to slick its ears.

The dreaded nausea crept from my stomach into my mouth. There, below the apocalyptic cloud, was Brunete. In my mind, I saw the dun-coloured village, its mud walls whitened with chalk, its miry pond, the desolate fields with their dry, bleached, stone-hard clods, the merciless sun of the threshing floors, the powdered wheat chaff stinging one's throat. I saw myself as a boy walking down the village street, the Madrid Road, between my Uncle José and his brothers, he in his town suit and they in their corduroys, but all of them carrying their smell of dry earth and swat dried by sun and dust; for even after many years in town, my Uncle José still had the skin and smell of a peasant from Dry Castile.

There, behind that dark, flashing cloud, Brunete was being killed by clanking tanks and screaming bombs: its mud houses crumbled in dust, the mire of its pond spattered, its dry earth ploughed up by shells and sown with blood. It seemed to me a symbol of our war: the forlorn village making history by being destroyed in a clash between those who kept all the Brunetes of my country arid, dry, dusty, and poor as they were, and the others who dreamed of transforming the dust-grey villages of Castile, of all Spain, into homesteads of free, clean, gay men. It was also a personal thing to me. The soil of Brunete held some of the roots of my blood and of my rebellion. Its harsh, dry heritage had always battled within me against the joyful warmth I had received, as a legacy, in the other stream of blood from that other village of my youth: Méntrida with its wine lands, its green meadows, its slow running river between reeds – Méntrida, a speck out there in the plain, far from the sinister cloud, yet in the bondage of the men who were turning the fields of Spain into barren waste.

In the night after that day, I cried into the microphone what I had felt in the tower facing the front.

The journalists, so close to the focus of the war and yet unable to report on it, were persistent and angry. They all sent out air force and army communiqués, but they quarrelled with me, and I quarrelled with them, because I stuck to orders and did not let them say more. At the start of the offensive, the precautions were clearly necessary. The radio-telegrams which the Controller put on my desk, and which we delayed four days, included a good many messages that sounded highly suspicious; the German agent Felix Schleyer, still administrator of the Norwegian Legation, produced an outburst of private telegrams; an astonishing number of people with an impeccable diplomatic address had developed family trouble. Yet once operations were in full swing, I thought it in our own interest to let the journalists send out reports of their own. I went to Prieto in the General Staff, and after a heated discussion obtained a relaxation of the rules.

Yet my relations with the journalists had suffered under our mutual irritation; they noted that requests for permits, which had been so quickly dispatched before, were being delayed, and had little idea of the struggle between our office and the reborn bureaucracy which lay behind it. To them I was the source of the trouble, and I did not even try to undeceive them or to soothe them down, although I knew that they raised complaints with Prieto and the Valencia office, and that the Valencia staff, at least, was not displeased with this fact. George Gordon came back from a trip to Valencia, shrouded in political importance, and I went out of my way to be more than usually rude to him. Rubio Hidalgo appeared for half a day, insisted that the temporary contract with the girl Pat should not be prolonged because she had passed a dispatch calling Prieto the 'roly-poly' Minister (which in his opinion was against the national dignity), expounded a plan to install a Spanish journalist, mainly known for his feud with the *Times* correspondent, as Madrid propaganda director for both press and radio, found me more refractory than ever, and worse than that when he hinted at the bad impression caused by my divorce and my relationship with Ilsa.

It was evident that more than one campaign of a personal and half-political kind was under way. I was too exhausted to care, or it may have been that I secretly welcomed them.

When the offensive was over; my divorce in its final stage; the International Anti-Fascist Writers' Congress, with its exhibition of intellectuals posturing on the background of fighting Madrid and discussing the political behaviour of André Gide, over and done with, I fell into a stupor.

Maria came once a week to threaten and implore me; I worked myself up into a state of rage, disgust, and dislike until I was able to be brutally frank to her. She never came again, but wrote anonymous letters. Aurelia's mother, who recognized her daughter's share of responsibility in the wreck of our marriage, formed the habit of visiting Ilsa and me regularly; when she first came, the employees of the Ministry watched through half-open doors so as not to miss a thrilling row, and when they found that the old lady was on affectionate terms with her ex-son-in-law's future wife, it gave them an even more sensational, because more revolutionary spectacle. 'It's still like in a foreign novel,' said the horse-faced censor to me. 'I wouldn't have thought that Spanish people could behave like this.' I listened to everything and did little except write my broadcasts.

At that time people who were no more than casual acquaintances began to speak to me about my mistake in wanting to marry the foreigner instead of merely carrying on with her; so long as they believed that a Spaniard had 'conquered' a foreign woman, their male fellow-feelings had been tickled, but now they saw me breaking their whole code of behaviour and thought it morally wrong. It chimed in with Rubio's hints and filled me with a weary loathing, an additional excuse to despise the whispers I caught about my growing slackness, my outbursts of anger, my insecure health. Those whispers almost pleased me and I courted them. Only when I saw how Ilsa was worried and harassed, and when Torres, or my old sergeant, or Agustín, or Angel, or the old friends in Serafín's tavern showed their belief in me, did I shake myself into spasmodic action.

While I was in the throes of this crisis, Constancia de la Mora came on her first visit to Madrid. I knew that she had virtually assumed the control of the Censorship Department in Valencia and that she did not like Rubio; that she was an efficient organizer, very much a woman of the world who had joined the Left of her free choice, and that she had greatly improved the relationship between the Valencia office and the press; I was also aware that she must have found it irksome that we in Madrid invariably acted as if we were independent of their – of her – authority. Tall, buxom, with full, dark eyes, the imperious bearing of a matriarch, a schoolgirl's simplicity of thought, and the self-confidence of a grand-daughter of Antonio Maura, she grated on me, as I must have grated on her. Yet when she advised Ilsa and me to take our long overdue and obviously much-needed holiday, I was prepared to trust her intention. I had to relax and sleep; and I wanted to find out what the Valencia people meant to do with us.

Ilsa was pessimistic. She had evolved a theory that we had become mere survivors of the revolutionary pioneer days, since we had failed to adapt ourselves to the changes in the administrative system. She was no more prepared than I to surrender her independence of judgement and her unbureaucratic ways, but she had begun to think that there was no room for them any more, and I had outgrown my position – she knew that I had deliberately brought my insubordination, impatience and anger to the notice of the powers that be – as she had outstayed her welcome and usefulness as a foreigner without party backing. I brushed her apprehensions aside, not because I thought them wrong, but because I did not care if they were right.

General Miaja asked me to arrange for an acting radio censor, gave permission to use the driver and car during our holiday as 'the only pay you'll ever get for courting trouble', and supplied us with safe-conducts from and to Madrid.

The road to Valencia was not the straight road across the Arganda bridge which we had travelled in January. We had to go a round about route through Alcalá de Henares, scaling bare red hills and returning to the hot, white road after weary hours. I slept most of the time on Ilsa's shoulder. Once our car stopped to give room to a long file of miserable, mangy, spavined mules, donkeys, and horses. Dust and flies were clogging the sores of the exhausted beasts which seemed to carry all the ills and evils of the world on their sagging backs. I asked the gypsy who squeezed past our mudguard: 'Where are you taking this collection?'

'Meat for Madrid. Give us a fag, comrade.'

On the hills lavender was in bloom, a blue haze, and when we came down into the valley, the stream was edged with clumps of rose-red oleander. Then the hollow of Valencia wrapped us in moist and sticky heat, in noise and the smell of crowds.

We reported to Rubio's office. He was devastatingly polite: 'If you had let us know you were arriving this evening, we should have received you with flowers, Ilsa . . . No, we won't discuss shop any more. You go and have your rest – what's your address? Altea? Very nice indeed – and don't worry about the Madrid office. We'll see to everything, you've done your bit.'

After a fitful sleep in the steaming, mosquito-infested hotel room we escaped into the bright, hot morning. The town was gaudy and crowded. I left Ilsa to herself while I went to visit my children and speed up the final divorce formalities with the local magistrate. It meant some greasing of palms; and it meant that I had to harden myself against the sense of the injustice I was inflicting on the children. I was astonished at being so callous. Aurelia was at the hairdresser's, and I had long hours alone with them. It would have pleased me to take my younger daughter with me, but I knew that no compromise was possible.

On my return to town I found Ilsa at our meeting place in the café, talking gravely to the same police agent who had arrested her in January. He was a hulking man with a deeply furrowed, humorous face, who addressed me before I could say anything: 'I'm sorry you were first with Ilsa, I'd have liked to try out my chances with her. Never mind, it's because of her that I'm about to tell you something as a friend.'

What he told us with a wealth of detail was that, according to his authoritative information, Rubio and Constancia had no intention of letting us go back to our posts in Madrid. Constancia had fixed my successor, a secretary to the League of Anti-Fascist Intellectuals recommended by Maria Teresa León. 'You see, those Spanish women don't like a foreign woman having so much influence. And then, they're all new and eager Party members.' There had been more than one complaint against us. Ilsa, for instance, had passed an article for the Stockholm Labour paper, which criticized the elimination of the Socialist and Anarchist Trade Unions from the Government, and this was taken to be a pointer to her own political sympathies. Some of the German Communists working in Madrid (I at once thought of George Gordon) maintained that she was a Trotskyite, but so far their campaign had been discredited by the Russians. Ilsa's old enemy Leipen was bombarding the authorities with denunciations of her, in which he advised against letting her leave Spain, because she knew too many people in the international labour movement. Aurelia was filling the Ministry with abuse of Ilsa and myself whenever she came to fetch my salary, which I had transferred to her and the children. We would do better, in sum, to set our own friends in motion and to cut our stay in Valencia short – it was not healthy for us.

There was very little we could do on the strength of his confidential information. It all fitted, but how could we prove anything? How could we fight this combination of personal dislikes, political intrigues and the ineluctable laws of a state machine during a civil war? Del Vayo was no longer Foreign Minister; his successor, a politician of the *Izquierda Republicana*, would not have known about us; it would have been childish to demand an explanation from Rubio Hidalgo, and I could not have trusted my self-control. We spoke to a few people who were in a position to act, should we disappear without any trace. Our only way was to go back to our place in Madrid as soon as we had recovered some strength for the coming test.

We went to Altea.

The road along the rocky coast of Levante, the *Costa Brava*, took us across terraced hills at the foot of the blue, barren mountains, through crumbling towns with resounding names – Gandía and Oliva and Denia and Calpe – through stony, herb-grown gorges and past whitewashed farms with an arched portico and curled tiles on their roofs. At the first vineyard I stopped the car. The old field guard came, looked at the number plate, grumbled: 'From Madrid, eh? How are things there?' and gave Ilsa a heap of golden-green grapes, a few tomatoes, and a cucumber. We passed through villages, bumping on the cobbles, and saw old women in black sitting on low stools outside the swinging bead curtains of their house doors, by their side a box heaped with long bars of the greenish soap which country people of the region made of the residues of their oil-press and caustic soda. In Madrid there was no soap.

By dusk we reached the little roadside inn at Altea, a whitewashed, clean-smelling hall, dark polished dressers, rush-plaited chairs and a breeze from the sea. Our tiny bedroom was filled with the smell of the sea mixed with a scent of garden and freshly watered earth, but outside our window was nothing but a dark haze, water and air fused, a star-powdered blue-black sky above it, and a chain of gently swaying specks of light drawing away into the blue darkness. The men of Altea were out fishing. That night I slept.

Altea is almost as old as its hill; it has been Phoenician, Greek, Roman, Arabic, and Spanish. Its flat-roofed white houses, plain walls pierced by window-holes, climb the hill in a spiral which follows the mule-track with its age-polished, worn stone steps. The church has a slender tower, the minaret of a mosque, and a blue-tiled dome. The women walking from their silent, dark houses down to the shore where the men are mending their fishing nets carry on their heads water pitchers of a light yellow clay, with a swelling curve, a narrow base, a graceful neck, an amphora-shape of their own which the local pottery reproduces only for Altea after the ageless pattern. The ancient port is deserted, but the lateen sails of the Altea fishermen still reach the African coast on fishing and contraband trips. Around the hill are olive and pomegranate groves, and terraces of cultivated land scooped out from the rock. The coastal road is new, and round it a new village has sprung up, wealthier and less soil-bound than the town on the hill, with a police-station, a few taverns and inns, and the villas of rich people from the outside world. It has left the hill-town more secluded in itself than ever. After all the changes it absorbed it has become immutable.

I felt the shock of this peace and immutability in my marrow. It made me sleep in the nights and think during the days. This place ignored the war. The war only served to increase the market value of its fishing hauls. Politics? Only a few young men with a bee in their bonnet had volunteered for the fight, and if age classes were being called up now, it was a cruel injustice. Politics and wars were always the same, a matter for a few politicians and a few generals quarrelling for power, each out for himself. There had been supporters of the Left and Right in Altea, there had been a few rows, but now everything was at peace. If the others, the Fascists, came, the people of Altea would go on just as they were now. Sometimes the sound of naval guns or of bombs was carried to the village by the wind. Then it was better not to leave the waters of the port, to leave fishing for another night. Prices were rising.

A few miles from Altea the war was knocking at the coast. On the Rock of Ifach, 'Little Gibraltar', as it was called, there was a naval observation post in the ruins of the ancient watchtower. Men of the International Brigades, sent to the hospital of Benisa to recover from wounds and exhaustion, came every day in lorries to bathe in one of the three shallow, scalloped little bays at the foot of the rock. When we did not go to the African beach of Benidorm, with blue mountains and palm trees and dung-beetles making their tracks in the hot sand, we went to the Rock of Ifach and stayed with Miguel, the tavern keeper whom I called the Pirate, because he looked like the free, bold pirate of the tales.

He sold wine in an open, reed-covered shack with long benches and plain trestle tables, protected from the glaring sun by plaited rush curtains. He had seen shacks like that in Cuba, he said. His eyes were grey-blue and distant, and his skin golden. He was no longer very young, but he was strong and moved noiselessly like a cat. When we first came into the cool shade he looked us up and down. Then, as though conferring a favour, he brought us wine in a glazed jar and drank with us. He looked at Ilsa and suddenly offered her a packet of Norwegian cigarettes. Cigarettes were very scarce then. 'You're a foreigner. Good. You're with us.' He stated it simply. Then he took us into the smoky kitchen to meet his young dark-eyed wife and his little son in the cot. A sturdy five-year-old girl silently followed each of his steps. His wife stood by the hooded fireplace and said nothing, while he explained:

'Look, this comrade here has come from far away to fight with us. She knows a lot of things. More than I. I told you that women can know about things too, and that we need some of them.'

But she did not like it, she looked at Ilsa with quiet hostility mixed with awe, as though she were a strange monster.

He left the kitchen with us, brought another jar of wine and sat down. 'Look,' he said to Ilsa. 'I know why you've come here. I can't explain. Perhaps you can. But there are many like us in the world. We understand each other when we meet for the first time. Comrades or brothers. We believe in the same things. I would know what you believed even if you didn't speak a word of Spanish.'

He drank his wine ceremoniously. '*Salud!*'

'Miguel, what are you?'

'A Socialist. Does it matter?'

'Do you believe we shall win the war?'

'Yes. Not now, perhaps. What's this war? There'll be others, and in the end we shall win. There will be a time when all people are Socialists, but many will have to die before then.'

I went to see him whenever I was cloyed with the drowsy peace of Altea. He never told me much about himself. He had gone night fishing along these coasts with his father, in a boat with a lantern in the stern. Then he had gone to New York. He had been twenty years at sea. Now he had married because a man must sink his roots into the soil at some stage. He had what he wanted, and he knew what was wrong with the world. I was too tense, I ought to sit in the sun, fishing. He loaned me a rod. That day – I caught a single blue-scaled fish – he himself cooked us a meal: a bucket of fish, fresh from the sea, glinting in the colours of the rainbow, were cooked until the water had sucked out their goodness; then he boiled plain rice in this juice of the sea. That was all. We ate it with gaiety and drank rough red wine.

'You learned it when you were a pirate, Miguel.'

'There aren't any pirates.'

The lorry load of men from the International Brigades arrived. Some had their arms and legs in plaster, some had half-healed scars which they exposed to the wind and sun, lying in the wet sand by the pale, over-scented sand-lilies. At noon, when the sky shimmered with heat, they stormed the shack and shouted for drinks and food. Miguel served them silently. If he had to keep them in order, he always had a strong curse in the right language ready. Later in the afternoon, the men were half drunk and started rows. A Frenchman was the noisiest. Miguel ordered him and his cronies out of the shack. The others left submissively, but the Frenchman came back and reached for his hip pocket. Miguel lunged, caught him and threw him through an opening in the rush curtain as though he were a doll. An hour later he slouched in again. Miguel looked straight through him and said in a very low voice: 'Get out.'

The man never came back. But a few tourists sitting at a small table had witnessed the scene. One of them, a woman with the face of a parrot, said as soon as the lorry had left: 'Now tell me, why are those foreigners here? They ought to have stayed at home. They're having a racket at our expense.'

Another woman who was sitting with her said: 'But they helped us to save Madrid. I know it, I was there at the time.'

'So what?' said the unfriendly woman.

Miguel turned round: 'Those men have fought. They're with us. You're not.'

The husband of the parrot-woman asked hastily: 'What do we owe you?'

'Nothing.'

'But we've had – '

'Nothing.'

They went away, cowed. A few old men from the small white houses by the beach had climbed up the road, as they did every evening. They sat down on low stools outside the rush curtain. Their glowing cigarette ends drew cabalistic signs in the dusk. 'That war – they'll come here too,' one of them mumbled.

Miguel, his face lit by the flare of his match and turned to stern bronze, asked: 'What would you do then?'

'What can an old man do? Nothing. I'd make myself so small they wouldn't notice me.'

'You can do nothing, if they really come,' said another. 'They come and go, but we've got to stick it out here. . . . You know,

Miguel, there are some people in Calpe who are waiting for the Fascists to come, and you're on their black list.'

'I know.'

'What would you do, Miguel?' I asked.

He took me with him to a shed behind the shack. There were two big drums of petrol. 'When they come here,' Miguel said, 'nothing will be free. I'll put my wife and the children in my boat and burn all this. And I shall light a fire on the rock where they used to have a beacon in old times, to tell the people along the coast to flee. But I shall come back one day.'

In front of the dark, rustling curtain, the burning cigarette ends of the old men were a chain of red points. Far out to sea, the lanterns of the fishing boats were a swaying chain of sparks. It was very still and down by the beach a fish jumped.

The next time I was about to visit Miguel, I received a registered letter; Rubio Hidalgo informed me that his department was granting Ilsa and me indefinite leave 'for the benefit of your physical and moral recovery', after which we would be used for work in Valencia. I had, however, taken away an official car of the department without a permit, which I ought to send to Valencia at once. I answered by sending in Ilsa's and my own resignation from any war work in the Foreign Ministry; we were going back to the posts in Madrid from which General Miaja had given us sick leave; the car had been put at our disposal by the General and had nothing to do with the Press Department; we would not accept indefinite leave, because we did not intend to draw pay for work not rendered.

I felt a bitter pain in the pit of my stomach.

8. In the Pit

Back to Madrid. The dull ache which possessed me never lifted.

As though to mock the war and those who were fighting it, the whole breadth of the Spanish landscape unfolded: salt plains by the shimmering Mediterranean; the palm forest of Elche in the noon haze; eyeless, blindingly white Moorish houses on the slope of bare yellow dunes, petrified in the shape of waves; gnarled oak and pine on rocky ridges, unbearably lonely under the infinite dome of the sky; a neat carpet of well-watered, green fields and garden plots spread out before the tall, squalid old houses and many squat church towers of Orihuela; a slow river, women beating linen on flat stones by the water; more desolate bleached hills with blue shadows in their sharp folds; the fiery depth of the sky turning into a soft blue glow; the emerald-green garden of the Murcian plain, with the basalt rock of Monteagudo soaring, fantastically, into an amber evening sky and holding up a many-towered, battlemented fairy-tale castle; then the city of Murcia itself, dingy baroque palaces and bazaar life wrapped in the warm, intimate dusk.

The only beds we could obtain in the overcrowded hotel were camp beds rigged up in an airless lobby. The three open galleries running round the huge stair-well were filled with the strident voices of women and drunken men. The restaurant was overflowing with soldiers, rich farmers, and food-racketeers; food and wine were excellent and preposterously expensive. It was easy to place the Murcians who looked askance at the birds of passage: there were small groups of the old rural owner caste, uneasy, sullen, and silent; there was a self-confident majority of the tenants of old, men who had been cruelly exploited, but had themselves been wont cruelly to exploit their primitive farm labourers, and who now earned un-dreamed of riches from the food ramp; and there were the workers, clumsy, noisy, boisterously showing off the freedom they had won and sporting the black-and-red scarves of the Anarchists so as to scare their hated former masters. There was an atmosphere of forced good cheer and underlying distrust, of electric tension and desperate enjoyment in the place. But the war was there only in the uniforms, and the revolution was there only in the deliberate exhibition of newly acquired affluence and power by those who had been the proletariat of wealthy Murcia.

I hated the place; I think Ilsa was scared by it. We stayed no more than a couple of hours in the stench of our improvised bedroom, and left in the early morning. Hilario, our young driver, shook his head. 'This is a worse rearguard than Valencia. And the food they waste! But what can you expect of those treacherous Murcians anyway?' For in the rest of Spain the people of Murcia have the reputation of being crafty and treacherous.

And on through the hills, long slopes covered with withered grass where sheep were cropping, on to the uplands of Castile.

Great billowing clouds, sailing slowly to the east, laid splashes of shadow on the bleak conical hills which rose out of the plain. There were no trees, few birds – black-and-white magpies and lonely cruising hawks – and no human beings. The plain was tinted yellow, dun, tawny, russet, umber, and elephant-grey, but rarely green. In that great field of loneliness I no longer wanted to shout or scream: we were too little.

Past the ugly garrison town of Albacete, centre of war supplies and the International Brigades; barracks, stucco houses, dusty stunted avenue trees, military traffic, repair shops, refuse heaps. And then we were in Don Quixote's Mancha. The white road fringed by telegraph poles cut an almost straight line through endless, undulating vineyards; their black grapes were covered with thick white dust. A lime pit showed the shallow top layer of fertile, ashy-brown earth, no more than a foot deep, and the lifeless white chalk underneath. The sun burned fiercely and my mouth was filled as though with dust and ashes. But there was no village and no wayside tavern for long hot hours. Then we reached La Ronda. It was market day. Straight-backed women in dusty, black cloth dresses were sitting, motionless, behind boxes of cheap thread and buttons, or behind baskets of grapes. They all looked old before their time, yet ageless, burned into likeness by the same pitiless sun, frost, and winds, made haggard and fierce by the same hopeless fight with the dry soil. On the background of their discoloured mud-brick houses they were a frieze in black, brown, and parchment-yellow. None of them seemed eager to sell. They did not deign to speak. Their dark, shuttered eyes followed Ilsa with a bitter interest. When we acquired a pound of the purple-black grapes from one of them, it seemed a victory over their hostile silence.

I decided to take a secondary road from La Ronda to the Valencia trunk road where we would find a place to give us lunch. The Mancha was inhospitable. But after a mile our car floundered in deep, powdery white dust where the wheels did not grip; we had to slow down to five miles an hour. Now there was something simple and straightforward which could be blamed for our misfortune: my stubbornness in insisting on the side road against the advice of the driver. The three of us broke out into childish jokes which showed how strong our feeling of depression had been. It seemed very funny to be slower than a cyclist wobbling in the deep dust. And then there were trees, pine copses which hid a field airdrome with 'Moscas', the small, fly-like fighter planes supplied by the Russians; and there was a little river, and a mill, and fields. There was life. It did not matter that Hilario had to repair one of the springs in the village forge, after we had limped into Motilla del Palancar. I took Ilsa to the threshing floor where we saw the chaff eddying in the wind, and I took her to an old inn where they gave us eggs and bacon in a cool, flagged room with a hooded fireplace. The light fell through the inverted funnel of the chimney on to the clean brick hearth, and there were old red clay pitchers and jars on the wide mantelpiece. In the wagon yard chickens were pecking grains. We stared at them: starved Madrid was so very near.

A chain of tanks caught us and carried us on towards the city front. The Valencia road was blocked by two streams of military traffic, one coming and one going. It slowed us up. We spent a night in Saelices where we slept on feather mounds in high, old-fashioned beds whose linen had not been changed for months. The mutton stew they gave us was rank with grease. To make up for it, the innkeeper presented Ilsa with an enormous tomato weighing well over two pounds, the pride of his heart and, so he maintained, with a flavour better than cooked ham. Carrying the red, glistening ball, we entered the Ministry on the following morning.

The pale, inhibited girl Rosario who had been appointed chief of the Foreign Press and Censorship Department in my place was plainly embarrassed to see us, but she was courteous and tried to be helpful. Once again, people stared at us from behind half-open office doors. Old Llizo came bravely to tell me how sorry he was that our common work, begun on that unforgettable November the 7th, had ended; he would never change towards me or Ilsa 'who had made the censorship an office of diplomatic importance'. My old sergeant wrung my hand and muttered something about what he would like to do to those bastards, and so forth; he remained at my orders. Yet I could not delude myself into underrating our quandary. Agustín turned the key in the lock of our room. 'I've had to keep it locked the last few days – Rubio wanted to throw out your things just like that. There was a story they gave out that the police had arrested you because you had absconded with the car. None of them thought you would come back to Madrid. Now the girl's ringing up Valencia to tell them you're back, and you'll see: they won't let the journalists speak to you, much less to Ilsa.'

I reported to General Miaja: we would resume our job with the radio, but we were no longer employees of the Foreign Ministry. I told him the story of the car which had been meant as a trap for me. Miaja grunted. He disliked the whole muddle. I had better take care of what those fellows in Valencia would do next: 'We in Madrid are only muck to them, my boy.' It was all right about the car, we would have to go on using it as long as we did night work at the radio. And there wouldn't be any trouble about the radio – yet. He would tell Carreño España. But it might be wise if I got the new Civil Governor of Madrid – 'Yes, my boy, I'm no longer Governor-General, and glad I am to get rid of all that trouble' – to endorse me as chief radio censor. People were getting damned formal these days; that girl Rosario – not much to look at, is she? – had been accredited to him and the Civil Governor and Carreño España, and the devil knew whom with all sorts of pomp and circumstance, and she would have every facility for which I had shouted in vain, just because her official papers were beautifully in order. Journalists would find that she could get things done for them. I should have a look at things and get wise – if I could ever get wise. But I wouldn't.

I had a drink with Miaja after his sermon and left him with that cold, nauseating lump in the pit of my stomach. Yes, our position was extremely precarious. I was still Radio Censor of Madrid and Commissioner of the EAQ station by Miaja's order, but obviously Miaja himself did not think that his orders would stand very much longer. The fact that I received neither salary nor fee would probably give me some more time in which to go on working. But nobody would back me. Ilsa was nothing but my voluntary helper in languages I did not understand, with Miaja's knowledge, but without any appointment. She, too, would be left to carry on the work she had begun, the organization of foreign language broadcasts to the Americas, until the moment when one of the Ministries decided to turn it into a paid job. I might go to the new Civil Governor of Madrid. But I had no stomach to beg for a favour where I had created something in which I believed and which was already bearing fruit. Hundreds of letters from overseas were waiting for the 'Unknown Voice of Madrid', some of them abusive, many naïve, and many touching; all of them showed that those people were listening avidly to something personal and human, off the beaten track. I was convinced that I had chosen the right way of speaking to them. But I was determined not to move a finger for myself. If 'they' – all those people who were going in for a new formal bureaucracy – had so little interest in the essence of the work, they would do better to push me away, as they had pushed away Ilsa and me from the censorship.

I did not speak to anybody more than I could help, and I did not make it easy for anybody to help me. On the day after our arrival, we moved into the Hotel Victoria on the Plaza de Santa Ana, where the Propaganda Ministry had reserved a number of rooms; while we did a full-time job for them (and immediately after our return the work piled up for both of us) they would have to pay our expenses in place of any other compensation. As there was no radio censorship office, I stayed in a small unused room of the Foreign Ministry, waiting for an official instruction to clear out, which was never given; very unwillingly, Rosario told me that Ilsa and I would have to continue the radio censoring there for the time being. She did it reluctantly, because our mere presence in the building created a difficulty for her. The veteran correspondents, most of whom had been absent at the time of our leave and dismissal, were too experienced in their trade not to keep on the best terms with the new authorities, but they still sought out Ilsa, as a colleague, to discuss news with her; the censors still asked our advice when nobody observed them; we still took over foreign guests from Rosario, whenever a short-wave broadcast had to be arranged. It was a division between official and intellectual authority which was hard to bear for both sides.

Rosario did her best to fit me into a secure place; she took me to a banquet given by the Civil Governor, expecting me to settle the matter of the radio censorship with him so that he should find a proper office for me, away from the foreign press. I had been to the front of Carabanchel the day before, I believe, and I had been fighting the old sick feeling that rose in me every time the explosion of a shell had shaken the Ministry; my brain was on fire and I bitterly hated the well-behaved crowd moving decorously from the bar to the side tables. They were all so anxious to shed the last odour of the rude, lousy, desperate rabble which had committed so many atrocities and, incidentally, had defended Madrid when the others left it. The Civil Governor was a well-meaning, well-fed Socialist, evidently prepared to meet me half way when Rosario introduced me. But I did not want to be met half way. I gulped down a few glasses of wine, but they neither warmed nor cooled my overheated mind. Instead of explaining about the radio censorship, I burst into a loud, incoherent, desperate harangue, in which I mixed the rats I had seen in a trench of Carabanchel, and the stupid, simple people who believed that the war was fought for their future peace and happiness, with accusations against sated, reactionary bureaucrats. I wanted to be 'impossible'. I was impossible. I belonged to the impossible, intractable people, and I did not belong to the hedged-in administrators. Whenever I met Ilsa's anguished eyes I shouted more loudly. I felt that I might cry like a hurt child if I stopped shouting. It was soothing to know that I had broken my own neck, and not left it to others.

Then, at a quarter past two in the morning, I went to the microphone in the blanketed cellar room and described the trench in Carabanchel which our men had wrested from the Civil Guards, the stinking shelters through which Angel had guided me, the rotting carcass of the donkey wedged in between burst sandbags, the rats and lice and the people who fought on down there. The secretary of the Workers' Committee, that acidulous man from the Mancha (I thought of the gaunt, black-dressed women in the market square of La Ronda), smiled thinly and said: 'Today you've almost made new literature.' My old sergeant blinked and snuffled, and the engineer of the Vallecas control room rang to say that for once I had spoken as if I had guts.

I felt hilarious and triumphant. When we emerged into the starlighted night, its stillness punctuated by shell thuds, our car would not start; and the four of us, the sergeant, Hilario, Ilsa, and I, pushed it down the deserted slope of the Calle de Alcalá, singing the refrain of *La Cucaracha*:

> *La cucaracha, la cucaracha*
> *Ya no puedo caminar,*
> *Porque la faltan, porque la faltan*
> *Las dos patas de atrás . . .*

The poor old cockroach, the poor old cockroach
Can no longer walk or run,
For her two hindlegs, for her two hindlegs
Are forever lost and gone!

There were nights when the success of an ambitious feature broadcast or of a new series of talks in English or Italian made me believe for a short while that we would be allowed to carry on with work which was so clearly useful. Carreño España agreed to cover our basic living expenses and to let the Portuguese Armando eat in the Hotel Victoria as well, since he had no home and found it impossible to cater for himself. Bread was very scarce in Madrid at that time. Thin slices of bully-beef were the best fare the hotel could provide; on the rare occasions there was meat it made me think of the diseased mules and donkeys on the Valencia road: 'Meat for Madrid.'

But in the Ministry, during the brief hours when we worked there to censor radio talks, the air was laden with tension.

Torres, faithful and worried, reproached us with having missed the right moment to convert ourselves into regular civil servants and employees of the Ministry, with full trade union rights; he began to throw out dark hints of threatening dangers. The sergeant, like a big, clumsy dog, did not know how to express his allegiance; one day, he arrived with a solemn invitation from the Shock Police barracks, took us religiously through every room and workshop there and filled Ilsa's arms with a sheaf of tall snapdragons, yellow, salmon, and scarlet. He, too, warned us of vague and sinister plots. Llizo, the white-haired censor, tried to teach Ilsa the Andalusian way of playing the guitar and apologized for not being able to be with us more often, as this displeased his chief.

George Gordon came, swaggering, and told me – his Spanish was very good – that I might be permitted to keep the radio if I approached the Party in the right way, but he rather thought it was too late; we had played a lone hand too long and this was a thing liable to be misconstrued – or perhaps to be correctly interpreted. Young Pat, the Canadian for whom Ilsa had fought tooth and nail, much against my feeling and advice, at a time when the girl had been jobless and in difficult straits, manoeuvred not to see us when we passed her. The Australian wife of our English radio announcer, a young Communist whom Constancia had sent from Valencia at our request, was at least honest; she made it clear that, to her, we were dangerous heretics or lepers. The more experienced among the correspondents were perturbed but not particularly surprised at seeing us in disgrace; things of the sort were happening all the time. Some of them asked Ilsa to do journalistic work for them, which helped us financially, and most of them were more personally friendly than they had ever been. Ernest Hemingway, back in Madrid, said with a worried frown: 'I don't understand the whole thing, but I'm very sorry. It seems a lousy mess.' He never changed his behaviour towards us, which was more than could be said of many lesser people, Spaniards and non-Spaniards. A tight net was closing in on us; we knew it, and had to keep still.

In the end, after weeks of a muffled, intangible warfare, an English correspondent who felt under an obligation to Ilsa – for in the early days she had risked her position to defend him against political accusations which might have had serious consequences for him – told her in so many words what was going on: George Gordon was asking the other journalists not to have any dealings with us because we were suspect and under police supervision. The story he had told uninformed foreign visitors so as to keep them effectively apart from us (it was my impression that Tom Driberg had been one of those warned off) had lurid features: according to it, Ilsa was either a Trotskyist and therefore a spy, or had committed imprudent acts, but anyhow she would shortly be arrested and at the very least expelled from Spain, while I was so deeply entangled with her that during my broadcasts the transmission was cut and I was speaking into a disconnected microphone without knowing it.

Not even the ludicrous character of those details could diminish the reality of our danger. I knew only too well that, if some people belonging to foreign Communist groups wanted to get rid of Ilsa for personal or political reasons, they would join forces with those Spaniards who rightly or wrongly hated me, and through them would find means to make use of the Political Police.

In those days, the shelling of Madrid grew in intensity after a slack period. There was a night when eight hundred shells were reported by the Fire and Rescue Services to have fallen in ten minutes. The bitter juice of nausea never left my mouth; but I did not know whether it was produced by the recurrent nervous shock which I had only partly under control, or by my despairing, helpless anger at the thing that was happening to us. Again I felt ill, afraid of being alone and afraid of being in a crowd, forcing Ilsa to go down to the shelter and hating the shelter because down there you could not hear the sound of explosions, only feel their tremor.

And I did not know how to protect her. She was very quiet, with a fine-drawn face and big, calm eyes which wounded me. Matter-of-fact and in possession of all her cool power of analysis as she was, I saw her stretched on the rack. But she did not say so. That was the worst.

All her friends tried to show her that she was not alone. Torres brought a young couple to keep her company in the evenings, a captain in a Madrid regiment and Luisa, his wife, organizer of the district branch of the Anti-Fascist Women's League. The girl, lively and eager to learn, was happy to speak to another woman without the undercurrent of envy and jealousy which poisoned her friendship with Spanish girls of her age, and Ilsa was glad to help her by answering and listening. Luisa had organized a sewing and mending workshop at the regimental headquarters and suffered tortures when she saw her husband flirting with a pretty girl there. She was caught between the new rules of conduct and the old, half thinking that, as a male, her man had to play the game with other females and half hoping that he and she might be complete friends and lovers. The old women of her tenement house told her that her husband did not love her, since she was allowed to go out alone to her meetings in the evenings; and Luisa never knew whether they were not somehow right. 'But I can tell you – a Spanish woman would try to take him from me – I'm sure he loves me. And he wants me to work with him. It does happen. Arturo loves you, doesn't he?' And she looked hopefully at Ilsa.

In the empty afternoons, Ilsa played songs for the hotel waiters and for me. She had an untrained, husky voice, deep and soft when she did not strain it, and I liked her singing Schubert. But the Anarchists among the waiters were happy when she played their fighting song, after the Republican anthem and the Internationale. When we sat in the dining room, the waiters brought us their stories about the newcomers. I remember an American delegation which caused a stir because one of the women – the humorist Dorothy Parker – sat at table in a cyclamen-coloured hat shaped like a sugar loaf, surely the only hat worn in Madrid that day. The waiter came and whispered: 'What d'you think's the matter with her so that she can't take the thing off? Perhaps her head is shaped like a cucumber. . . .'

But the days were long. The radio work Ilsa still had to do could not fill them, nor did it exhaust her energy. She began to translate some of the talks I had written; she collected propaganda material; she still furnished the many journalists who came to see her with sidelights on events or with a vision of political developments. It seemed impossible for her not to exert this intellectual influence in some form or other, but it recoiled on her. Cut off from the censorship, shunned by those who were afraid of catching the infectious disease of disfavour, she still had a hold on foreign propaganda from Madrid which remained no secret.

Torres brought me a message from a friend who was a Shock Police captain in the political branch of the police: he offered me a bodyguard, one of his own young men, to watch over Ilsa because otherwise she might be arrested on some pretext and taken for a ride. The captain, whom I then met for the first time, was a Communist; the young policeman, who from that day accompanied Ilsa when she went out alone, and stood on guard outside the hotel when she was indoors, had also joined the Communist Party. Both appeared deeply incensed at the thought that by means of complicated intrigues, 'a few foreigners and a few Fascist-minded bureaucrats', as they put it, were trying to harm somebody who had passed the great test of November 1936 in Madrid, whether as a member of the Party of not. It was curious to see how the growing dislike those men felt for 'interfering foreigners' melted away in her case, because they were bound to her by the overpowering common experience of the early defence of Madrid.

It was so bitter having to accept the bodyguard that it did not bear discussion. It was worse to think of the possibility which we were trying to forestall. I fought not to think of it; I could no longer talk openly to Ilsa, because I could not let her see my whole fear. And she kept quiet, quieter even than before. Anger and hot despair choked me. When she walked off with young Pablo, the guard, talking about John Strachey's book on Fascism which she had loaned him in the new Spanish translation, I felt easy in some part of my mind. He was willing to fight for her. But then it all came back, the whole cruel senselessness of it.

What could I do? I tried to do something. I went to Miaja; but he only explained that nobody had anything against me personally, while there were people who had their knife into Ilsa, and I would doubtless be promoted and protected if I were no longer mixed up with her. Further he did not dare to go openly. I went to see

Antonio, my old friend, who was by then a great man in the Provincial Secretariat of the Communist Party. He was profoundly embarrassed and muttered something about the time I had kept him hidden in my flat to save him from prosecution. He was still my friend, so – frankly, why had I obtained a divorce? Was it necessary? I had always arranged my private life before. It wasn't a good thing for somebody recommended by the Party for an important post such as the censorship. And as to that foreign woman – he didn't know anything officially, but he had heard that some of the German comrades, or Austrian – anyhow, people who ought to know – considered her a kind of a Trotskyist, although it could not be proved because she had been too clever to commit any false move inside Spain. That was it, she was too clever for safety. I had been taken in by her. I ought to leave her; after all, she was only my mistress.

I asked him whether this was the official opinion of the Communist Party; he denied it anxiously, it was only his friendly advice to me. I sent him to hell, and was glad that I was able not to hit him. Later I realized that he had been bewildered, unhappy, and trying to be helpful in his stupid way, but at the time I did not think so.

Up till then I had still found my refuge in the talks I broadcast night after night. In them I forgot the personal side of the matters which burned in my brain, and spoke for the people I met at Serafín's, in the streets, in the shops, in the little park of the Plaza de Santa Ana where not even the shells drove away the lovers, the old women, and the sparrows. But when the nights turned cool, on one of the first days of October, a man with a written instruction from the Valencia Propaganda Ministry was waiting for me in the office: he was the new radio commissioner and censor. And he was a German called Albin, very Prussian to my eyes, something like a Puritan inquisitor to judge by the expression of his bony face. To Ilsa he was barely civil; he just listened to her report on the foreign broadcasts which were scheduled, and turned away. His Spanish was halting and bare, but correct. Would I submit my next talk to him, please? I did, and he passed it. I broadcast two more before I asked him whether he expected me to go on. If he had said yes, I might have done it because my heart was in the work. But he told me coldly that it had been agreed to drop the talks by the 'Unknown Voice of Madrid'.

Some days later, two police agents came to search our room while Ilsa was still in bed. Pablo, her guard, came up at once and smartly told them that his department would see to it that we received fair treatment; they were guaranteeing us. The agents had brought along a sallow, gangling German boy who had to translate every scrap of paper written in French or German; while he was doing so he cast agonized looks at us, twisting his thin arms and legs in pitiful embarrassment. The documents which illustrated mine and Ilsa's range of work during the first year of the siege seemed to impress and disconcert the agents. They took some of my manuscripts, most of our letters, all photographs, and my copy of a Mexican fable – *Rin-Rin-Renacuajo*, the young tadpole, a poem which had pleased me when I heard it during the visit of a delegation of Mexican intellectuals – because President Azaña had mentioned 'toads croaking in their pond' in a recent speech and the fable might contain a hidden political meaning. They also took a copy of Dos Passos's *Forty-Second Parallel*, signed for us by the author, because he had declared himself in favour of the Catalan POUM and Anarchists, and this was a suspect possession. They confiscated my pistol and small arms permit. But then they were at a loss what to do next. The denunciation they were following up had hinted at dark conspiracies plotted by Ilsa, but they had found her record impeccable, our papers all to her credit, and me an almost exemplary Republican. Above all, they did not want trouble with another police group. They looked at Pablo, looked at us, and said they would have lunch with us downstairs. Then they shook hands and left.

The deadly cloud had lifted. The anti-climax made us laugh. It was no longer likely that the police would be used to get rid of Ilsa. I had lodged a sharp complaint against the denouncers, not sparing the man whom I suspected behind the move. At lunch, while we were sitting in amity with the police agents, I had seen George Gordon's face flushed and twitching. A couple of days later he made a movement as though to greet us, but we overlooked it.

I wanted to be merry. I took Ilsa round the corner to the Andalusian bar, Villa Rosa, where the old waiter Manolo greeted me as a lost son, examined her thoughtfully, and then told her that I was a rake, but not a genuine rake, and that she was the right woman to cope with me; he drank a little glass of Manzanilla with us, tremulously, because the war had made him very old. He did not get enough food. When I let him have some tins given us by a friend in the International Brigades, he was so humbly grateful that I could have cried. In the evening we went to Serafín's and plunged into the warm welcome of the cronies. Torres, Luisa, and her husband came with us, gabbling with pleasure. They thought that now our troubles were over and that soon we would do work in Madrid again.

But Agustín, who had staunchly visited us every day, though it could do him no good with his boss Rosario, told me bluntly that we ought to leave Madrid. As long as we stayed on, certain people would resent our very existence. Intrigues might not always go through official channels, and we could not walk about for good with a bodyguard. Moreover, I was going crazy, in his opinion.

I felt in my bones that he was right. But I was not yet ready to leave Madrid. I was tied to it with hurting, quivering nerve-strings. I was writing a story about Angel. If they did not let me broadcast any more, I had to talk through print. I believed I could do it. My very first story (the story of the militiaman who made a fly his pet) had been printed, incongruously enough, in the *Daily Express*, and the fee had overwhelmed me, accustomed as I was to the rates of pay of Spanish journalism. I realized that the story had been published mainly because Delmer had liked it and provided a witty headline and caption, such as: 'This story was written under shellfire by the Madrid Censor – who lost his inhibitions about writing by censoring our dispatches.' All the same, my first piece of simple story-telling had gone out to people who, perhaps, would through it get a glimpse of the mind of that poor brute, the Miliciano. I wanted to go on; but what I had to say had its roots in Madrid. I would not let them drive me away, and I could not go before I had cleared the red fog of anger out of my brain. It swept me, together with the relief that she was alive and with me, every time I watched Ilsa. All my submerged violence rose when I saw her still bound to her rack, still lashed by the ugliness of the thing which people of her own creed were inflicting on her, and still quiet.

The man who helped me then, as he had helped me through the evil weeks that went before, was a Catholic priest, and of all those I met in our war he commands my deepest respect and love: Don Leocadio Lobo.

I do not remember how we first came to talk to each other. Father Lobo, too, lived in the Hotel Victoria, and soon after we had moved in he became a regular guest at our table, together with Armando. The mutual confidence between him and Ilsa was instantaneous and strong; I felt at once the great attraction of a man who had suffered and still believed in human beings with a great and simple faith. He knew, because I said so, that I did not consider myself a Catholic any more, and he knew that I was divorced, living in what his Church called 'sin' with Ilsa and intending to marry her as soon as she had her divorce. I did not spare him violent outbursts against the political clergy in league with the 'powers of darkness', and against the stultifying orthodoxy I had come to hate in my schooldays. Nothing of all this seemed to impress him or to affect his attitude to us, which was that of a candid, detached friend.

He wore no cassock, but a somewhat shiny dark suit. His strong, regular features would have made him an attractive man, had they not been deeply furrowed by his thought and struggle; his face had a stamp of inwardness which set him apart even in his frequent moments of expansion. He was one of those people who make you feel that they only say what is their own truth and do not make themselves accomplices of what they believe to be a lie. He seemed to me a reincarnation of Father Joaquín, the Basque priest who had been the best friend of my boyhood. Curiously enough the origins of both were alike. Father Lobo, like Father Joaquín, was the son of simple country folk, of a mother who had borne many children and worked tirelessly all her life. He, too, had been sent to the seminary with the help of the local gentry because he had been a bright boy at school, and because his parents were glad to see him escape from grinding poverty. He, too, had left the seminary not with the ambition of becoming a prelate, but with that of being a Christian priest at the side of those who were hungry and thirsty for bread and justice.

His history was well known in Madrid. Instead of staying in a smart, influential parish, he chose a parish of poor workers, rich in blasphemies and rebellion. They did not blaspheme less for his sake, but they loved him because he belonged to the people. At the outbreak of the rebellion he had taken the side of the people, the side of the Republican Government, and he had continued in his ministry. During the wildest days of August and September he went out at night to hear the confession of whoever demanded it, and to give Communion. The only concession he made to circumstances was that he doffed his cassock so as not to provoke rows. There was a famous story that one night two Anarchist Milicianos called at the house where he was staying, with their rifles cocked and a car waiting at the door. They asked for the priest who was living there. His hosts denied that there was one. They insisted, and Father Lobo came out of his room. 'Yes, there is a priest, and it's me. What's up?'

'All right, come along with us, but put one of those Hosts of yours in your pocket.'

His friends implored him not to go; they told the Anarchists that Lobo's loyalty was vouched for by the Republican Government, that they simply would not allow him to leave, that they would rather call in the police. In the end, one of the Anarchists stamped on the floor and shouted:

'Oh hell, nothing will happen to him! If you must know, the old woman, my mother, is dying and doesn't want to go to the other world without confessing to one of these buzzards. It's a disgrace for me, but what else could I do but fetch him?'

And Father Lobo went out in the Anarchists' car, into one of those grey dawns when people were being shot against the wall.

Later on he went for a month to live with the militiamen in the front line. He came back exhausted and deeply shaken. In my hearing he rarely spoke of his experiences in the trenches. But one night he exclaimed: 'What brutes – God help us – what brutes, but what men!'

He had to fight his own bitter mental struggle. The deepest hurt to him was not the fury vented against churches and priests by maddened, hate-filled, brutalized people, but his knowledge of the guilt of his own caste, the clergy, in the existence of that brutality, and in the abject ignorance and misery at the root of it. It must have been infinitely hard for him to know that princes of his Church were doing their level best to keep his people subjected, that they were blessing the arms of the generals and overlords, and the guns that shelled Madrid.

The Government had given him a task in the Ministry of Justice which was anything but simple: he had come to Madrid to investigate cases of hardship among the clergy, and he had to face the fact that some of the priests whose killing by the 'Reds' had been heralded and duly exploited came out of their hiding, safe and sound, and demanded help.

I needed a man to whom I could speak out of the depth of my mind. Don Leocadio was most human and understanding. I knew that he would not answer my outcry with admonitions or canting consolation. So I poured out all the turgid thoughts which clogged my brain. I spoke to him of the terrible law which made us hurt others without wanting to hurt them. There was my marriage and its end; I had hurt the woman with whom I did not share my real life and I had hurt our children because I hated living together with their mother. I inflicted the final pain when I had found my wife, Ilsa. I told him that Ilsa and I belonged together, complementing each other, without superiority of one over the other, without knowing why, without wanting to know, because it was the simple truth of our lives. But this new life which we could neither reject nor escape meant pain, because we could not be happy together without causing pain to others.

I spoke to him of the war, loathsome because it set men of the same people against each other, a war of two Cains. A war in which priests had been shot on the outskirts of Madrid and other priests were setting the seal of their blessing on the shooting of poor labourers, brothers of Don Leocadio's own father. Millions like myself who loved their people and its earth were destroying, or helping to destroy, that earth and their own people. And yet, none of us had the right to remain indifferent or neutral.

I had believed, I still believed, in a new free Spain of free people. I had wanted it to come without bloodshed, by work and good will. What could we do if this hope, this future was being destroyed? We had to fight for it. Had we to kill others? I knew that the majority of those who were fighting with arms in hand, killing or dying, did not think about it, but were driven by the forces unleashed or by their blind faith. But I was forced to think, for me this killing was a sharp and bitter pain which I could not forget. When I heard the battle noise I saw only dead Spaniards on both sides. Whom should I hate? Oh yes, Franco and Juán March and their generals and puppets and wirepullers, the privileged people over there. But then I would rather hate that God who gave them the callousness which made them kill, and who punished me with the torture of hating any killing and who let women and children first suffer from rickets and starvation wages, and then from bombs and shells. We were caught in a monstrous mechanism, crushed under the wheels. And if we rebelled, all the vioence and all the ugliness was turned against us, driving us to violence.

It sounded in my ears as though I had thought and said the same things as a boy. I excited myself to a fever, talking on and on in rage, protest, and pain. Father Lobo listened patiently, only saying sometimes: 'Now slowly, wait.' Then he talked to me for days. It may be that the answers I gave myself in the quiet hours on the balcony, while I stared at the Church of San Sebastian cut in two by a bomb, were fused in my memory with the words Father Lobo said to me. It may be that insensibly I made him into the other 'I' of that endless inner dialogue. But this is how I remember what he said:

'Who are you? What gives you the right to set yourself up as a universal judge? You only want to justify your own fear and cowardice. You are good, but you want everybody else to be good too, so that being good doesn't cost you any trouble and is a pleasure. You haven't the courage to preach what you believe in the middle of the street, because then you would be shot. And as a justification for your fear you put all the fault on to the others. You think you're decent and clean-minded, and you try to tell me and yourself that you are, and that whatever happens to the others is their fault, and whatever pain happens to you as well. That's a lie. It is your fault.

'You've united yourself with this woman, with Ilsa, against everything and everybody. You go with her through the streets and call her your wife. And everybody can see that it's true, that you are in love with each other and that together you are complete. None of us would dare to call Ilsa your mistress because we all see that she is your wife. It is true that you and she have done harm to others, to the people who belong to you, and it is right that you should feel pain for it. But do you realize that you have scattered a good seed as well? Do you realize that hundreds of people who had despaired of finding what is called Love now look at you and learn to believe that it exists and is true, and that they may hope?

'And this war, you say it's loathsome and useless. I don't. It is a terrible, barbarous war with countless innocent victims. But you haven't lived in the trenches like me. This war is a lesson. It has torn Spain out of her paralysis, it has torn the people out of their houses where they were being turned into mummies. In our trenches illiterates are learning to read and even to speak, and they learn what brotherhood among men means. They see that there exists a better world and life, which they must conquer, and they learn too, that they must conquer it not with the rifle but with their will. They kill Fascists, but they learn the lesson that you win wars not by killing, but by convincing people. We may lose this war – but we shall have won it. They, too, will learn that they may rule us, but not convince us. Even if we are defeated, we will be stronger at the end of this than ever we were because the will has come alive.

'We all have our work to do, so do yours instead of talking about the world which doesn't follow you. Suffer pain and sorrow and stick it out, but don't shut yourself up and run round in circles within yourself. Talk and write down what you think you know, what you have seen and thought, tell it honestly and speak the truth. Don't produce programmes which you don't believe in, and don't lie. Say what you have thought and seen, and let the others hear and read you, so that they are driven to tell their truth, too. And then you'll lose that pain of yours.'

In the clear, chill nights of October it seemed to me sometimes as though I were conquering my fear and cowardice, but I found it very hard to write down what I thought. It is still difficult. I found out, however, that I could write honestly and with truth of what I had seen, and that I had seen much. Father Lobo exclaimed when he saw one of my stories: 'What a barbarian you are! But go on, it's good for you and us.'

One evening he knocked at our door and invited us to go with him to see a surprise. In his small room was one of his brothers, a quiet workman, and a farm labourer from his village. I knew that his people brought him wine for Mass and wine for his table whenever they could, and I thought he wanted to invite us to a glass of red wine. But he took me into his bathroom. An enormous turkey was standing awkwardly on the tiles, hypnotized by the electric light. When the countryman had gone, we spoke of those simple people who brought him the best thing they had, not caring whether it was absurd or not to dump a live turkey in the bathroom of a city hotel.

'It isn't easy for us to understand them,' Father Lobo said. 'If you do, it's a basis for art like Breughel's or like Lorca's. Yes, Lorca's. Listen.' He took the slim war edition of the *Romancero Gitano* and started reading:

> *And I took her down to the river,*
> *Thinking she was a maiden,*
> *But she had a husband. . . .*

He read on with his strong, manly voice, not slurring over the words of naked physical love, only saying: 'This is barbarian, but it's tremendous.' And he seemed to me more of a man, and more of a priest of men and God, than ever.

In the worst weeks, when it took some courage to be seen with us, he spent long hours at our table, aware that he gave us moral support. He knew more about the background of our tangled story than we ourselves, but he never gave away what he had heard from others. Yet I did not dream of doubting his word when, after the campaign had passed its peak, he suddenly said: 'Now listen to the truth, Ilsa. They don't want you here. You know too many people and you put others in the shade. You know too much and you are too intelligent. We aren't used to intelligent women yet. You can't help being what you are, so you must go, and you must go away with Arturo because he needs you and you belong together. In Madrid you cannot do any good any more, except by keeping quiet as you do. But that won't be enough for you, you will want to work. So go away.'

'Yes, I know,' she said. 'The only thing I can do for Spain now is not to let people outside turn my case into a weapon against the Communists – not because I love the Communist Party, for I don't, even when I work with Communists, but because it would at the same time be a weapon against our Spain and against Madrid. That's why I can't move a finger for myself, and even have to ask my friends not to make a fuss. It's funny. The only thing I can do is to do nothing.'

She said it very dryly. Father Lobo looked at her and answered: 'You must forgive us. We are in your debt.'

Thus Father Lobo convinced us that we had to leave Madrid. When I accepted it, I wanted it to be done quickly so as not to feel it too much. It was again a grey, foggy November day. Agustín and Torres saw us off. The Shock Police lorry, with hard loose boards for benches, rattled through the suburbs. There were few shells that morning.

Father Lobo had sent us to his mother in a village near Alicante. In his letter he had asked her to help me, his friend, and my wife Ilsa; he did not want to bewilder his mother, he said, and he had put down the essential truth. When I stood before the stout old woman with grey hair who could not read – her husband deciphered her son's letter for her – and looked into her plain, lined face, I realized gratefully Don Leocadio's faith in us, His mother was a very good woman.

9. Face to Face

There was no war, nothing but blue hills, the moon-sickle of a wide, shallow beach, and blue water. The cart track alongside the coast was carpeted with deep, loose sand. Where the ground became firm and the sea shells rare, small wooden shacks, half boarding houses and half taverns, had sprung up; for in peacetime San Juán de la Playa had been a holiday resort. A mile further on was the village where Father Lobo's parents and his ailing sister lived a quiet life which drew its warmth from the sons and brothers somewhere at work in the war. For the mother, all life centred in her son the priest.

They had sent us to their friend Juán, the owner of one of the shacks and the most famous cook of rice dishes between Alicante and Valencia. He let me have a small room open to the sea wind and gave me the run of his house and kitchen. I learned how to make *paella* from him. Ilsa arranged with Juán to give lessons to his two girls, which permitted us to live very cheaply. We had little money left. Secretly I always suspected Juán of hoping that I was a hunted aristocrat in disguise, for despite his lukewarm Republicanism he hankered after the splendour of 'quality' to grace his table and give his masterly *paellas* their due.

The November days were hot, still, and sunny on the coast of Alicante. In the afternoons, when the water began to chill, we let ourselves dry in the warm sand and watched the tide recede in gentle ripples. Sometimes I laid lines, but I never caught any fish. When the slow dusk crept up from the sea, we – and the village children – walked along the line of froth left by the lapping water, to hunt the minute crabs which betray their presence only by the tiniest of eddies in the wet, sleeked sand.

I began to sleep at night. By day, Juán let me work in his dining room or in his vine bower facing the sea. Few people came past, and the only other boarder was out, working in an aircraft factory in Alicante. I began to think out a book I wanted to write, my first book, primitive stories of primitive people at war, such as I had woven into my radio talks. But first I had to repair the small, battered little typewriter which Sefton Delmer had thrown away as scrap metal after he had learned how to type on it. I had asked him whether he could let me have it, and he had roared with laughter at the idea that it could still be used. Now it was our only wealth, but it did not yet work. I hated having to write by hand; it was too slow to catch up with my thoughts.

On the scrubbed deal table, I dismantled the typewriter, spread out its thousand-and-one pieces, cleaned them one by one, and put them together without hurry. It was good work. I seemed to hear my Uncle José saying:

'When I was twenty I started writing. At that time only rich people had the steel nibs you use. The rest of us had quills, and before learning how to write I had to learn how to cut and trim quills with a penknife. But they were too fine for my fingers, so I made myself a thick pen out of a cane.'

I, too, had to make myself a pen before writing my first book, and though mine was a far more complicated pen than Uncle José's, I, too, was only about to learn how to write.

In those first days I was happy sitting in the sun, wrapped in the light, scent, and sound of the sea, reconstructing and healing a complicated mechanism (how I love machinery!), my brain confined within the maze of fragile bolts and screws, and the vision of a book, my first book, gaining shape at the back of my mind.

In a silvery night filled with the song of crickets and frogs I heard the heavy drone of planes coming near and waning, and coming near again. There were no more than three dull thuds, the last of which shook our flimsy house. The next day we heard that one of the bombs dropped by the Capronis – I had seen one of them glinting in the light of the moon like a silver moth – had fallen in Alicante, in the middle of a cross-road, laying flat half a dozen mud-built houses and killing a dozen poor workers who lived there. The second bomb had fallen in a barren field. The third has fallen in the garden of an old man. It had destroyed his tomato crop and killed nothing but a frog. It made me angry to hear the hefty aircraft mechanic laugh at the idea of the dead frog. The wounded garden caught hold of me. I could not conceive that a wound to any living thing was a matter of indifference. The whole war was there in the trees and plants torn by a bomb, in the frog killed by blast. This was the first story I wrote on the cured typewriter.

In the fourth week of our stay in San Juán de la Playa, I was awakened by a loud knock at our door; I opened, had a glimpse of Juán's scared face, and then two men brushed past him and filled the door frame: 'Police. Here are our papers. Is this lady an Austrian called Ilsa Kulcsar? Yes? Will you please dress and come outside.' It was before sunrise and the sea was leaden. We looked at each other, said nothing, and dressed in haste. Outside, the two police agents asked Ilsa: 'Have you a husband in Barcelona?'

'No,' she said, astonished.

'No? Here we have an order to take you to Barcelona to your husband Leopold Kulcsar.'

'If the name is Leopold Kulcsar, then he is indeed my legal husband from whom I have separated. You have no right to force me to go to him – if he really is in Barcelona!'

'Well, we know nothing except that we have the order to take you with us, and if you don't want to go we have no other choice but to declare you arrested. Will you come with us voluntarily?'

Before Ilsa had time to answer, I said: 'If you take her with you, you will have to take me as well.'

'And who are you?'

I explained and showed them my papers. They went away to discuss the new problem. When they came back into the room, one of them started: 'We have no order . . .'

Ilsa interrupted: 'I will come with you, but only if he accompanies me.'

The second agent grunted: 'Let's take him, too; maybe we ought to arrest him in any case.'

They gave us just enough time to settle our account with Juán, to ask him to take care of the things we left behind, and to pack a small suitcase. Then they hustled us into the car which was waiting outside.

'Don't worry so much,' said Ilsa. 'As it's Poldi who's started the hue and cry after me, it must be some kind of stupid misunderstanding.'

But it was she who did not understand. I had read the stamp on the agents' papers: SIM – *Servicio de Inteligencia Militar*, Military Intelligence Service. That story about Ilsa's husband was a blind; the trick which had miscarried in Madrid was being tried through another, more powerful agency, in a place where we had no outside help whatsoever. The only thing which astonished me was that they had not searched us. In my pocket I still carried the small pistol Agustín had given me on our departure from Madrid.

They took us along the coastal road to Valencia. After the first half-hour, the two agents began to ask questions, probing into our affairs with a certain guarded sympathy. One of them said he was a Socialist. We discussed the war. They asked me where we might get a decent lunch and I suggested Miguel's place by the Rock of Ifach. To my astonishment, they took us there. Miguel gave them a sour look, watched Ilsa's face and saw it serene, frowned, and asked me what he could cook for us. Then he prepared fried chicken and rice, and sat down with us. It was an unbelievably normal meal. As we slowly drank the last glass of wine, one of the agents said: 'Don't you ever listen to the radio? For days there's been a message for this foreign comrade to get in touch with her husband in Barcelona.' I wondered what we should have done, had we heard it. But whoever listens to police messages at the end of news bulletins?

Mellowed by the sun and the meal, they took us to the car again. Miguel shook hands with us and said: '*Salud y suerte!*' Good luck!

I dozed, exhausted by my own thoughts and by the impossibility of talking with Ilsa. She enjoyed the journey, and when we came to an orange grove she made the agents stop the car so that she could pluck a branch with fruits graded green, yellow, and golden. She took it with her to Barcelona. I could not understand her gaiety. Did she really fail to see her danger? Or, if that legal husband of hers was behind the whole thing, did she fail to see that he might want to take her away from Spain by force and – perhaps – get rid of me for good?

Suddenly, when it was near sunset, the more burly of the agents said: 'If we come to Valencia before dark they'll saddle us with some other assignment. Let's go round the longer way by the Albufera, the foreign comrade will like it, too.'

I sat stiffly and said nothing. The Albufera is the lagoon in which the corpses of killed people had been dumped in the chaotic and violent days of 1936. Its name made me shiver. Recklessly, I put my hand in my pocket and cocked my pistol. The moment they ordered us out of the car I would fire through my coat, and we would not be the only ones to die. I watched the tiniest movement of our guardians. But one of them half dozed and the other chatted with Ilsa, pointing out water-fowl, rice fields, fishermen's nets, explaining about the small villages and the size of the wide, shallow, reed-grown lake. And the car went on at an even pace. We had already passed several spots which would have been excellently suitable for a swift execution without witness. If they wanted to get it done, they would have to hurry up. This was the far end of the Albufera.

I set the safety-catch and let the pistol drop to the bottom of my pocket. When I pulled out my hand, it was cramped and I trembled. 'Are you tired?' asked Ilsa.

It was dark when we arrived in Valencia and were taken up to the SIM office. We were left waiting in a fusty ante-room, with people whispering behind our backs. Officers telephoned to Barcelona, where their head office had recently moved together with the Government; then they came to fire abrupt questions at us, and disappeared again. In the end one of them said, wonderingly: 'They say you're to go to Barcelona with her. But I can't understand what the whole thing's about. Now, you explain to me.' I tried to do so, briefly and noncommittally. They stared at me in distrust. I sensed that they would have liked to keep us in Valencia for investigation; but when I asked whether we were detained or free, I received the answer: 'Free – only we've to keep you under observation since they want you so urgently.'

In the small hours of the morning we left Valencia in another car. The agent who had taken us past the Albufera said goodbye and regretted that he was not sent on with us: he had considered it almost a holiday. But when I was seated, I noticed that our small attaché case was nowhere to be seen, although I had asked for it and been told that it was waiting for us in the car. I went back to the office, I asked the drivers, but everybody disclaimed any knowledge. The case contained my manuscripts and most of the papers which documented our work in Madrid, as far as they were left to us. This meant that we had lost our most important weapon, which we might need bitterly in Barcelona, now the seat of the Government offices, of new bureaucrats who knew nothing of us, and of our old adversaries.

When the car stopped at the Barcelona headquarters of the SIM, it was so early that the chiefs had not yet arrived. Nobody knew what to do with us. For safety's sake, we were taken to still another ante-room with an apathetic guard at the door. Ilsa was certain that things would clear up quickly. I did not know what to think. Were we, or were we not arrested? We spent our time discussing the building, too small to be a palace, too big to be the house of a wealthy bourgeois, with showy tiles in the courtyard and deep-piled carpets in the corridors, old braziers and modern coloured-glass windows showing a coat-of-arms.

A man entered brusquely. Ilsa rose and cried: 'Poldi!' He whipped off his hat, threw me a sombre glance and kissed Ilsa's hand in an exaggeratedly ceremonious and courtly gesture. She said a few sharp words in German and he drew back, almost reeling in astonishment. Later she told me that she had asked him: 'Why did you have me arrested?' and that this accusation had stunned him.

Only then did she introduce us to each other, in French, saying no more than the names. I nodded. He bowed from the hips, a theatrical bow. We did not shake hands or speak.

Her legal husband: deep-set, brown-ringed eyes stared at me, feverish and intense. He had a wide, broad, powerfully domed forehead, made still higher by his incipient baldness; his head sat well on strong shoulders, he was slim, slightly younger and slightly shorter than I. Goodlooking in his way. His jaws rigidly clamped on an embittered mouth whose upper lip had a smeared outline. His thinning hair looked dead. He took stock of me as I took stock of him.

Then he turned to her and sat down by her side on the velvet-covered bench. The guard had saluted him and disappeared. The three of us were alone. While the other two started to talk in German, I went to the window and looked down into the courtyard, first through a yellow, then through a blue, and finally through a red pane. The sunlit walls and the shadows under the arches assumed with each colour new, unexpected depths and perspectives. For a few minutes I thought of nothing at all.

It was difficult for my Spanish mind to assimilate and to gauge the situation. This man had never been real to me before. Ilsa was my wife. But now he, her legal husband, was in the room, talking to her, and I had to keep my nerves quiet. How was he going to act, why had he come to Spain, why had he tracked us down through the SIM, why did the guard salute him so respectfully?

Both were talking in anger, though their voices were still low. Sharp question, sharp answer: they were disagreeing.

The wall opposite threw the warmth of the sun back into my face. The chill which had weighed me down melted away and left nothing behind but a great weariness, the fatigue of a sleepless night and of a twenty-four-hours' journey – God, what a journey! The room was heavy and drowsy with curtains, rugs, and tapestries. I had no share in their unintelligible talk. What I needed was coffee, brandy, and a bed.

Had that man come to claim his wife and take her away? I had the stubble of two days on my chin and felt my skin sticking to my bones in tiredness and tautness. I must have had a villainous face.

What will you do if he tries to take her away? – The question is whether she wants to go, and she doesn't. – Yes, but he is her legal husband, he is a foreigner who can claim the help of the Spanish authorities in taking his wife away; they might refuse her a further stay in Spain – and what then? – We would protest. – To whom, and on what legal grounds? I had not been able to protect her from persecution even in Madrid.

I tried to argue it out in an articulate dialogue with myself. But then their voices were no longer sharp. She was dominating him, convincing him with that warm voice which was so soothing after the icy edge it had before. At this hour the sun would already have warmed the sea on the beach of San Juán. To dip into the shallow water and then sleep in the sand!

Ilsa rose and came towards me: 'We'll go now.'

'Where?'

'To Poldi's hotel. I'll explain later.'

The guards saluted when we left the building. Ilsa walked between him and me. Again, he started to speak in German, but she cut him short: 'We'll speak French now, won't we?' We made the rest of the way in silence. The hotel hall was full of chattering people, among them half a dozen journalists we knew. I was very conscious of my state of squalor. Poldi took us up to his room and told Ilsa where to find his washing and shaving things; he did not speak directly to me. A huge blue trunk stood in the middle of the room, and he showed it off to Ilsa, opening drawers and compartments and pulling out the rod with the clothes hangers. It was all very complicated and did not work well. When he left us alone, Ilsa said in a motherly tone, which angered me:

'The poor boy, it's always the same with him. Any silly new luxury gadget makes him as happy as a child with a new toy.'

I told her gruffly that I was not interested in imitation trunks, and showered questions on her. While we were washing and brushing, she explained. He was in Barcelona on some official mission or other, not yet understood by her; but he had also come to take her away from Spain, forcibly, if she was not willing to go. The reason was that he had heard not only rumours of the political campaign against her, but also stories about me which made him anxious for her fate: that I was a confirmed drunkard, with a litter of illegitimate children, and that I was dragging her down into the gutter with me. He had indeed intended to use his legal standing as her husband to take her away against her will – just as I had imagined – not under the illusion that she would resume her married life with him, but so as to save her and give her the chance of recuperating in sane, peaceful surroundings. The mode of our detention in San Juán de la Playa was due to the fact that he had been unable to get our address in Madrid (an odd thing, as several people had it, both officially and privately) and thus been driven to enlist the help of radio and police; and the SIM policemen seemed only to have acted according to their lights. Apparently he had dropped his orginal plans after seeing her calm, self-possessed, clear-eyed, and happier than he had ever known her, in spite of the obvious difficulties. Now he wanted to discuss things with me and to help us. She ended triumphantly: 'Here you are, with all your nightmares! I told you he would never play me a dirty trick.'

I was not yet convinced; I knew the force of possessive instincts too well. But when the three of us sat together at lunch and I saw more of the man, I began to change my mind. Ilsa was so perfectly natural in her behaviour to him, so friendly and unselfconscious, that he lost the demonstrative arrogance towards me, against which I would have had no defence since he had every right to protect his own pride as best he could. I saw him twisted and straightforward at the same time. A small incident broke the ice between us. We had no cigarettes and tobacco was almost unobtainable in Barcelona. Poldi demanded a packet of cigarettes from the waiter, in an imperious tone which drew nothing but a smile and shrug from the man. It was the overbearing accent of a young boy who does not know how to give orders and tips, and is afraid that the waiter might see through his varnish of worldliness. I intervened, chatted with the man, and in the end we had cigarettes, good food, and good wine. This impressed Poldi beyond measure, so much that I could guess at his adolescent dreams and his difficult youth; he said wistfully: 'You seem to have a knack which I never possessed.' I realized how much his lordly manner was a flimsy armour to cover an inner insecurity and lack of poise.

Yet now that he had accepted me as a man, he was simple and dignified in talking to me about Ilsa. She was the most important human being in the world to him, but he knew, finally, that he had lost her, at least for this period of his life. He did not want to lose her altogether. She would have her cake and eat it, he said: she would have her life with me, as I seemed to be able to make her happy, and she would keep his devotion and friendship. And if I were to hurt her, I would still have to reckon with him.

Poldi said he would try to arrange a divorce, but it would be extremely difficult for the time being. They were married according to Austrian law, and both fugitives from Fascist Austria. In the meantime, he understood that neither of us was doing any practical work in the war, mainly because we had mismanaged all our official relations. We had been crazy to have done important propaganda work in Madrid, without making sure of the appropriate trappings and emoluments. He had know Ilsa to be a romantic, but he was sorry to find me, too, a romantic. She would have to leave Spain until the campaign against her had died down; though only a few persons were behind it, our bureaucratic quarrels had isolated us and brought us into bad odour. He would help us to get all the necessary papers, both of us, since she would not leave me, and we would find useful work to do outside Spain. In fact, Ilsa was much needed there and he was willing to accept her valuation of me. He realized that he had done us harm by unwittingly entangling us with the SIM which considered everything grist that came to its mill; but he would remove any trace of ambiguity in our situation and recover the papers taken from us.

He tried to do all this the same afternoon. Back at the SIM headquarters Poldi again donned the ostentatious behaviour which I had noted and disliked. He was nervous and excited, as though he would soon slide into the depths of depression. He asked one of the SIM chiefs to give us papers to show that the department had nothing against us, even though it had brought us forcibly to Barcelona; but the pallid young man gave him no more than a promise. However, he telephoned an urgent order to Valencia to send on our suitcase with its contents intact, without attempting to gloss over the fact that it had been silently confiscated. Without a paper to show why we were in Barcelona, we would have found no billet; therefore the SIM man said he would send an agent along with us to the Ritz and we would be given a room. He would prefer us to stay there so they would know where to find us. The offer was an order; it demonstrated that, despite Poldi's explanations, the man intended his department to have a thorough look at us, since we had accidentally been brought to their notice. So we went to the Ritz, only recently thrown open to the public, with the red, thick carpets and meticulous ceremony of peacetime but scant food and scanty lighting, and were given a room opening out into the garden. We had not even toothbrushes with us.

The rest of my day was a jumble of conversations and silences, of waiting and walking alongside the others like a puppet on a string. When we closed the door of our room behind us that night, we were too exhausted to talk or think, although we knew that we had been pushed on to the threshold of a new stage in our life. This man had said that I was to leave Spain, to desert from our war, so as to be able to work again. It sounded crazy and wrong. But I would have to think it out, later, when things would have resumed their firm shape.

I was too tired to sleep. The balcony door was wide open and a pale bluish light filled the alien room. My ears laboured to identify a faint, distant purr, and decided that it was the sea. A cock crowed somewhere in the night and was answered by others, near and strident, distant and ghostly. Their chain of challenge and counterchallenge seemed unending.

There followed ten unreal days while Poldi was in Barcelona and his presence dominated our timetable. He spoke to me, he took Ilsa for walks while I wondered at my absence of any conventional resentment or jealousy, he arranged meetings with this or that official, diplomat, or politician, he dragged us along to the SIM headquarters to demand our safe-conducts. The suitcase had arrived, but we were still without a paper justifying our arrival in Barcelona. I tried to find my way through his mind, and my own; I tried to find firm ground under my feet so that I would be able to stay on and work with my own people; and I had again to fight my body and nerves whenever the sirens went or a motorcycle engine spluttered in the street.

While Poldi discussed international affairs he fascinated me by his knowledge and vision. He was convinced that closely knit, revolutionary, Socialist organizations were the only forces able to fight international Fascism wherever they met it, and that the most important battlefield of that war was still the German working class, even while the most important battle was being fought on the Spanish front. He was throwing all his energies into his work as secretary to Jiménez de Asúa, the Spanish Minister in Prague, and his friends risked their lives crossing the frontier to give warning of new bombs and shells being produced in German factories for intervention in Spain. Yet serving the Spanish Republic was only part of the greater war and preparation for the bigger battle to come, the battle in which England and France would be ranged by the side of Soviet Russia, in spite of their murderous and suicidal game of nonintervention. He told Ilsa bluntly that in his opinion she had deserted from the main fighting line by submerging herself altogether in the Spanish War and dropping all her work for Austrian and German socialism. He agreed that she was right in making no effort to mobilize one of her Socialist friends, such as Julius Deutsch of Pietro Nenni, when the political campaign against her became dangerous, because the shabby intrigue might have been magnified into an issue between Socialists and Communists by people inveterately opposed to the collaboration between the two groups, in the necessity of which both Ilsa and he believed.

I listened and marvelled; I remembered that he had shown me the revolver he had been prepared to use against me, had he found it necessary to save Ilsa in this way. And then he agreed that she should throw away her life rather than do an imagined harm to a political principle? The two talked so easily, they used the same language, the same abbreviations of thought, the same associations and quotations; I saw them attuned in everything which touched their social and political ideas, while I was left outside, almost hostile to their analytical logic.

Yet there was an evening when Ilsa and Poldi argued on the aim of their Socialism. When she professed her belief in the human individual as the final value, he exclaimed: 'I've always felt that our philosophy clashes – you know, this means that we are spiritually divorced.' It sounded so high-falutin' to me that I made a silly joke; but then I saw that it had hit him very deeply, and I felt it within myself. In spite of our different logic and language of the mind, I met her where a gulf was between her and Poldi. It was the same as when he said to me: 'She is difficult to understand, isn't she?' and I denied it, astonished. It had hit him and made him jealous as no physical fact could have made him jealous. For he had wanted to dominate and possess her, and his hunger for power and possession had destroyed their marriage.

I thought about myself and I found that my life had made me hate power and possession too much to want anything but freedom and spontaneous union. It was here that we clashed, he and she, he and I. He had had much the same proletarian childhood as I, he had hated the world as it was and become and rebel as I. But his hatred of power and possession made him obsessed with it; he had never outgrown the hurts to his self-confidence.

I saw it with pity and aversion on the day when we finally received our safe-conducts from the SIM. I had passed an ugly hour. Ordoñez, the young Socialist intellectual who had become chief of the department, had played at interrogation, with an equivocal smile and the cruelty of a weakling; but in the end he had ordered his secretary to prepare the papers at once, and we had them in our hands, eager to go. Poldi was scanning a heap of paper connected with his official mission, material on the foreign leaders of the Catalan POUM who had been arrested under the suspicion of an international conspiracy. He spoke to Ordoñez, magniloquently as he was wont to speak within that building, gave an order to one of the agents who stood around, and buried himself in the papers again. The agent brought in a big, lumbering woman, and Poldi interrogated her in a tone which made Ilsa move restlessly in her chair. I too recognized the tone: he heard himself speaking as the great, cold judge – a dangerous ambition. I was pleased that I could answer in the negative when Poldi asked me whether I had ever seen the woman in Madrid.

Then the electric light was cut off. Somebody lighted a candle which threw yellow patches and immense shadows on the walls. The house quivered in its roots; a stick of bombs had fallen. I felt my fingers tremble and fought back the vomit which filled my mouth. Another agent brought in another female prisoner, a small woman with taut, bitter features and the wide, dark eyes of a hunted animal. She went up to Ilsa: 'You're Ilsa – don't you remember me – twelve years ago in Vienna?' They shook hands, and I felt Ilsa go rigid in her chair; but Poldi began to interrogate, the perfect prosecutor in a revolutionary tribunal, and it seemed shameless for us to stay on. I thought I heard how he made his voice ring in his own ears. He must have dreamed that scene; perhaps he had imagined it when he was imprisoned for his share in the great Austrian strike against the last war, an imaginative, uncertain, and ambitious boy. Now he did what he conceived to be his duty, and the terrible thing was that the power over others gave him pleasure. In the yellow light his eyes were hollow like a skull's.

After we had left the building (and I thought that I never wanted to see it again) he spent a long time explaining to Ilsa why he could no longer consider that woman a Socialist. The details escaped me; I had sympathy neither for the POUM nor for their persecution. Poldi might have been right. But however careful and convincing his argument, there was a streak of madness in him. There was in me. But mine was born from the fear and hatred of violence, while his seemed to push him towards a fantastic dream of power. This impression grew in me so much that I did not pay great attention to his plans for Ilsa's and my work abroad. He had no sympathy with my manner of looking at the problems of our war; it seemed only sentimental to him. If he wanted to find work for me, it was as much because it gave him pleasure to have the power of helping me as because he imagined me to be a good propagandist. But I had to find my own way.

Whenever Poldi took us along to his many conversations with young officials of the various Ministries, I tried to assess them. It struck me that most of them were ambitious young men of the upper middle classes who now declared themselves Communists, not, as we had done in Madrid, because to us it meant the party of revolutionary workers, but because it meant joining the strongest group and having a share in its disciplined power. They had leaped over the step of humanist socialism; they were efficient and ruthless. They admired Soviet Russia for its power, not for its promise of a new society, and they chilled me to the bone. I tried to see where I might fit in, because it was torturing to know that nothing of what I had to give was exploited in the war. But the only thing I found to do for myself was to write the book of Madrid which I had planned. I was a has-been.

It was bitterly cold when Poldi left. He looked very ill and was suffering pain; he confessed to a serious stomach complaint rendered worse by his way of living, the late nights, the irregular food, the black coffee and the cognac which he used in the way I knew so well, to whip up his energies. Before going, he spoke again of Ilsa to me: she now looked as she had looked before he had twisted her gaiety and simplicity, and he was glad of it. We would be together often, the three of us, for 'if it were not for Ilsa, blast her, you and I would have been friends'. I did not believe it, but it was good that he felt so. There was no poisoning bitterness between us.

I was left face to face with myself.

In those dark December days, the air raids on Barcelona multiplied, and in January 1938 they grew worse. The Government troops were attacking on the Aragon Front, and Barcelona was the great supply centre. Italian planes had a short way to go from the Balearic Islands. They stopped their engines far out over the sea and glided down over the city, released their bombs, and fled. The first warning was the tremor of the distant bomb, then the electricity was cut off, and much later the sirens sounded. I was back in the clutches of my obsession. I could not stand the bedroom once I woke up. In the street, every confused noise shook me and brought the humiliations of the vomit on me. First I stayed in the hotel hall, listening to the street, looking at the people. Then I discovered the bar in the basement, where I could chat with the waiters and sit under thick walls, and finally I found a small room which was wedged in behind the bar. It was in disuse, and the manager agreed to let me use it for working. There I put my typewriter, and there I worked days and nights, in a feverish excitement bordering on hysteria. When an air raid came I was down in the shelter anyhow and could hide from people; a small grating opening just above the pavement let me listen to the noises outside. I would have liked to sleep down there. I slept in snatches on the plush divan, twisting in nightmares from which I only recovered after drinking a glass of wine. I drank much and smoked much. I was afraid of going mad.

When I could work no longer because the words became blurred, I went out of my cubicle into the bar. There was a motley collection of Spanish officers and officials, of journalists, foreign and Spanish, of the Government's foreign guests and of international racketeers, with a sprinkling of wives and elegant tarts. The noise, the drinks, the discussions and the sight of people saved me from the deadly lethargy which fell on me as soon as I stopped working.

Sometimes, but rarely, I made myself go out and speak to people I knew in some department of the war machine. I still hoped that I might be useful and cure myself within Spain. Yet men such as Frades who had worked with me in the November days of Madrid – how far away they were in this town of business and bureaucracy, where the heart of the fight had grown cold! – told me that it was all very sad, but the best thing for me was to publish a book and then see what happened. Rubio Hidalgo had gone to Paris as head of Agence Espagne, but it was Constancia de la Mora who had succeeded him in Barcelona, and I did not dream of speaking to her of my affairs. The great man in the Foreign Ministry was Señor Ureña, who had certainly not forgotten my share on November the 7th; Alvarez del Vayo – whose wife showed great kindness to Ilsa – was not yet back at the Foreign Ministry, and anyhow he was bound to support others rather than me. I found no one to whom I could speak honestly, as I did to Father Lobo.

The Government and the war machine were working as they had never worked before. There existed an Army now, and an efficient Administration: you need both to fight even a small-scale modern war. I believed the reorganization to have been necessary; and yet it had ruined the urge for freedom, the blundering efforts to build social life anew. My brain assented, and all my instincts rose against it.

I went into the shop to buy a beret. The owner told me, smiling, that his business was improving; the wives of Government officials were again being encouraged to wear hats as a sign that the turbulent, proletarian times were over.

It was all true. Perhaps the men who did not want to give me work in their teams were right. The only hope for Spain, the new Spain, was to hold out until the non-Fascist powers were driven to sell us arms because we were their vanguard – or until they were themselves forced to fight the looming greater war. In all that there was no room for dreams. There was no time or place for the premature fraternity of Madrid. Here, in the Barcelona of 1938, I could not talk to any man in the street as to a friend and brother. They organized a

Madrid exhibition with huge empty bomb cases, with splinters and fuses of shells, with photographs of ruins, children's homes, and trenches. The faces of the murdered children of Getafe again looked down at me.

But Madrid was far away.

Teruel had been stormed by our troops. Correspondents came back with stories of death in fire and ice. Our Norwegian friend, Nini Haslund, organizer of international relief work, told of small girls cowering in a shelled convent and of old women weeping when they were given bread.

A feeling of inferiority was weighing me down. Our soldiers were dying in the snows of Teruel. We were destroying our own cities and men, because there was no other defence against the horror of life in Fascist bondage. And I ought to be there at the front – when I was not even capable of working in Barcelona where the bombs fell. I was a physical and mental casualty, crouching in a cellar room instead of helping the children or the men.

I knew that I could not alter my physical defects, neither my game finger nor my heart trouble nor the scar in my lung tissue. I knew that I was not willing to kill. But I was an organizer and a propagandist, and I did no work as either. I might have been less self-righteous, more elastic in my dealings with the bureaucracy; after all, I had worked with it successfully in the service of patents whose benefits went to the heavy industry I hated. Now, in the great clash, I had put my qualms and aversions above the work. I had driven myself out of my chosen post in the war, out of Madrid. But for my intransigeance and cherished individualism, Ilsa and I might still be doing work which, to the best of my belief, we did better and more unselfishly than most of the others. Or would my shattered nerves have betrayed me in any case? Would the sour, bitter juice of my body – the cud of my warring thoughts – have filled my mouth so that I could not have spoken any longer as the voice of Madrid? Did I escape into an illness of the mind because I could not bear to be face to face with the things my eyes saw, and the others seemed able to overlook?

Slowly, in fits, I was finishing the book which included something of the Madrid I had seen. In the nights I listened to the cocks challenging each other from the roof tops. While Ilsa left me alone in our bedroom I felt exposed to all terrors, an outcast, and when she came I took shelter in her warmth. But I slept little. My brain made its weary round, a blind mule chained to the wheel of a well.

After a period of grappling with the war and coming war, my thoughts always went back to myself. They no longer controlled the emotions which drove me; their net had become threadbare. I was afraid of the torture which precedes death, of pain, mutilation, living putrefaction and of the terror they would strike into my heart. I was afraid of the destruction and mutilation of others because it was a prolongation of my own terror and pain. An air raid would be all this, magnified by the crumbling walls, the rush of the blast, the image of one's own limbs being torn from one's living body. I cursed my faithful, graphic memory and my technically trained imagination, which showed me explosives, masonry, and human bodies in action and reaction, as in a slow-motion picture. To succumb to this terror of the mind would be stark madness. I was terrified of going mad.

It was a profound relief when the sirens went and the danger became real. I would make Ilsa get up and come with me to the basement. There we would sit with all the other guests in dressing-gowns and pyjamas, while anti-aircraft guns barked and the ex-plosions rocked the house. A few times my mouth filled with vomit, but even so it was a relief, because all this was real. After a bombing I always fell asleep.

Then, in the morning, I would go down to the stale-smelling cubicle behind the bar and sit before my typewriter. For a short time, my brain would clear and I would think. Was it true that I had to leave Spain so as not to go mad, so as to be able to work again? I did not believe in Poldi's plans and negotiations. Things would develop by themselves. As each concrete situation faced us we would have to come to a decision. In the meantime the foundations of the future edifice were here, firm and real and indestructible: my union with Ilsa. Poldi had seen it as Maria and Aurelia had seen it, as Father Lobo had accepted it. There at least was no problem. I held on to this one plain thing.

On the evening of January the 29th – a Saturday – the manager came down to the bar to find Ilsa: somebody wanted to speak to her in the hall. When she did not come back for a while, the waiter said: 'The

Police, I think,' and I went after her. She was sitting with one of the SIM agents, her face was grey, and she held out a telegram: 'Poldi died suddenly Friday. Letter follows.' Somebody's signature. The agent had come to make sure that it was no code. She explained the situation carefully to the man and answered his chatty remarks on the hotel and its international racketeers with grave friendliness. Then, holding herself very straight, she walked down the stair to the bar in front of me. Father Lobo was with us then; he had met Poldi, declared him a great and fundamentally good man, and yet seen why Ilsa did not belong to him. Now he was gentle with her.

For a whole night she sat in her bed and fought it out with herself. There was little I could do but stay with her. She held herself responsible for his death, because she thought that his way of living since she left him had destroyed his health. She thought that he had not taken care of himself just because she had left him, and because he had to strengthen his hold on life in some other way than through his feeling for her. So much she told me, but she did not speak much. It did not make it easier for her that she felt no remorse, only sorrow at having hurt him mortally and at the loss of a deep, lasting friendship. They had been marrried fourteen years and there had been many good things in their life together. But she knew that she had failed him because she had not loved him, and it anguished her. She paid her price.

At three o'clock in the morning there was a raid. The bombs fell very near. A few hours later she dropped off into an uneasy slumber; I dressed and went down into the basement. There the charwomen were still at their work, and I had to wait in the hall. A young Englishman – the Second Officer of an English vessel which had been sunk by Italian bombs, as the manager told me – was wandering up and down, up and down like an animal in a cage. He had the eyes of a scared animal, too, and his jaw hung loosely. He paced the hall in the opposite direction to mine and we stared at each other when our tracks crossed.

That Sunday morning was brilliantly blue. Ilsa had promised to act as interpreter for one of her English friends, Henry Brinton, during an interview with President Aguirre of the Basques. Now she came down, still very rigid and pale, drank the morning beverage –

lime-blossom tea with no bread, for the food situation of Barcelona was growing worse from one day to the other – and left me alone. I had enough of staring at the nervous young Englishman and went down to my refuge. My collection of tales was finished, but I wanted to read it through and make corrections. I was going to call the book *Valor y Miedo*, Courage and Fear.

Half an hour later the sirens sounded, together with the first explosions. I went quickly to the bar table; my stomach was rising, and the waiter gave me a glass of brandy. The young Englishman came down the stairs with trembling legs; at the last triangular landing he stopped and leaned against the wall. I went to him. His teeth were chattering. I helped him to sit down on a step and brought him some brandy. Then he began to explain in a laborious mixture of French and English: bombs had fallen on the deck of his ship and he had seen his mates torn to shreds, a couple of days before. It had given him a shock – and he hiccoughed convulsively.

A tremendous crash and roar shook the building, followed by the rumble of masonry knocking against the wall. Shrill screams from the kitchen. A second crash, rocking us and the house. The English officer and I drank the rest of the brandy. I saw my own hand tremble and his shake. The waiter who had run upstairs came back and said: 'The house next door and the one behind us have been smashed. We'll make a hole through our kitchen wall, because there are people calling on the other side.'

And Ilsa was out in the streets.

A herd of cooks in white overalls appeared in the corridor. The white was stained with the red of brick dust. The tall white cap of the *chef de cuisine* was dented. He guided a few women and children in torn, tattered clothes covered with dust. They were weeping and shrieking: they had just been rescued through a hole in the basement wall. Their house had fallen down on them. Two others were still stuck in the rubble. A fat, elderly woman held her belly with her two hands, gave a scream and began to laugh in great guffaws. The officer of the English ship stared at her out of wide-open blue eyes. I felt that my control, too, was slipping, pushed the officer aside with my elbow and slapped the woman in the face. Her laughter stopped and she glared at me.

Slowly the rescued women and children disappeared into the passages. The Englishman had drunk a bottle of wine and was lying across a table, snoring with a painfully contracted face. The waiter asked me: 'And where is your wife?'

I did not know. My ears were full of explosions. Out there, in the street, or dead. I was in a stupor. Through the small windows in the ceiling came the sound of firebells and a fine rain of plaster. It smelled of an old house being torn down.

Where is she? The question hammered on my brain, but I did not try to answer it. It was a murmur like the beating of the blood in my temples. Where is she?

She came down the stairs together with Brinton, and she looked years older than the day before. Upstairs in our room we found only one of our panes cracked, but the house on the far side of the hotel garden had disappeared. The garden was invaded by Venetian blinds twisting like snakes, by broken furniture and strips of wallpaper, and by a big tongue of spilt rubble. Ilsa stared at it and then she broke down. She had been in the street during the bombing and it had not scared her; she had piloted Brinton through the interview with Aguirre, and there had been a flowering mimosa in the President's garden, and an anti-aircraft shell stuck in the pavement of the street. But then the chauffeur had told her that the Ritz was hit or almost hit and in coming back she had been steeling herself against the thing that waited for her. She had helped to kill Poldi. Now she thought that she had left me alone to be killed or to go mad. And I realized that I had thought her dead because of Poldi's death, without admitting it to myself.

That night the sound of pick and shovel, the shouts of rescue workers came into our room together with the crow of the cocks. I remember that an English delegation – John Strachey and Lord Listowel among them – arrived that evening and was taken to the heap of debris beside the hotel, where men still worked by the flare of hurricane lamps to rescue the buried. I seem to remember that the journalists spoke much about a public Mass Father Lobo had said that Sunday morning, and that Nordahl Grieg – the Norwegian writer who was shot down in a British aircraft during a raid on Germany six years later – told me how rescue squads had hauled able-bodied revellers out of a night club where he had been drinking. But I do not remember anything about myself. The following days passed as in a fog. My book was finished. Ilsa was alive. I was alive. It was clear that I had to leave my country if I was not to go mad altogether. Perhaps I was already mad; I wondered about it with a feeling of indifference.

Whatever was done in those weeks of February was done by Ilsa and her friends. She finished the German translations of my stories and sold them to a Dutch tobacco racketeer and general agent, so as to pay our hotel bill. The Spanish manuscript of *Valor y Miedo* was, to my astonishment, accepted by *Publicaciones Antifascistas de Cataluña*. A German refugee – a girl who had been secretary to left-wing writers, had fled from the Nazi régime, starved in Spain, and was suffering from a nervous shock which made her a public menace in shelters – had obtained a visa to England only because Ilsa had persuaded Henry Brinton to help her, and the British Envoy in Barcelona to see the matter through; in her gratitude, the girl took my manuscript to publishers she knew, and I had to do nothing but sign a contract. It was good to know that something of me would survive.

As I was not fit for active service, I was granted a permit to leave the country; but it had to pass through complicated official channels. Julius Deutsch helped, del Vayo helped, I do not know how many others helped to settle the countless formalities which had to be gone through before we obtained our passports and the exit visa. On the few occasions when I myself had no choice but to go out into the street, I thought of little except how not to vomit. When I came back to the hotel I went off into a doze or ennmeshed myself in an endless, pointless discussion with somebody down in the bar. But I do not think people in general noticed that I was fighting mental destruction. Dozens of times I told Ilsa that it was hopeless to pit ourselves against the blind force of circumstance, and every time she told me that if only we wanted to we would survive, because we had many things to do. When I felt beaten and went into a doze, she was desperately furious with me, and made the impossible possible. My weakness forced her out of her own private hell; it gave her so much to do that she almost forgot her fears for me. For she, too, was afraid that I was going mad, and she was not able to hide this fear from my sharpened eyes.

She had learned by letters that Poldi had died from an incurable kidney disease which had already affected his brain and would have destroyed it, dreadfully, if he had lived on instead of dying quickly and mercifully; she had learned from her mother that he had come back from Barcelona quietened, almost happy, proud of her and friendly towards me, determined to rebuild his own life. This released her from her sense of responsibility for his death and left her with the abiding knowledge of the wound she had dealt him. She said that his death had ended her last lap of youth, because it had taught her that she was not stronger than everything else, as she had secretly believed. But now my illness drove her to tap her deepest reserves of strength. As she put it, she was working the miracle of Baron Münchhausen: pulling oneself out of the mire by one's own pigtail. But I saw most of it only through a haze of apathy.

There was one thing, however, a single thing, which I did alone. I procured the papers and took the steps necessary for our marriage. A week before we left Barcelona and Spain, we were married in due form by a caustic Catalan Judge who, instead of a sermon, said: 'One of you is a widow, the other divorced. What could I say to you that you don't know? You are aware of what you are doing. Good luck.'

When we went down the rickety stairs, I wondered that a mere formality could make my heart feel relieved, for nothing was altered. But it was right that we had no longer to fight for an acknowledgement of our life together. Out in the bright, empty street, the wind of early spring whipped my face.

10. No Truce

The clock of the Spanish church tower struck twelve – midnight –
just as the customs official lifted his rubber stamp off its sticky
inkpad. He pressed it on the open page of my passport, and the clock
of the French church on the other side of the frontier tolled in
answer. If we had reached La Junquera five minutes later, they
might have turned us back, for my permit to leave Spain expired
with February the 22nd. I would have had to return to Barcelona
and apply for a prolongation of the permit. But I would not have had
the strength to do it. Rather go to hell and perdition in Barcelona.
Our soldiers had lost Teruel again, they were being driven back
through the icy fields. Why should I flee from an imagined madness?

Now the man was stamping Ilsa's passport.

It was she who had found the car to take us out of the town: one of
the cars of the British Embassy. No other vehicle had been available
for days ahead. The last week had been racked by air raids and
hunger. There was no bread in Barcelona, and no tobacco to assuage
that nagging suction in one's stomach. The morning before we left
we had passed the fish stalls of the Rambla de las Flores in our
desperate search for cigarettes for me; there had been a single heap
of little quayside fish spread out on one of the boards, with a slip of
paper stuck on a wire saying: 'Half-pound – 30 pesetas.' The
monthly pay of a Miliciano had been 300 pesetas. While I watched
the British pennant fluttering on the bonnet of the big car, I had
thought of that pitiful white paper flag.

The customs official was buckling up the straps of our three
suitcases.

He had handled my manuscripts with care and respect; evidently
he believed that I was going to France on some mysterious mission,
since we had arrived at the customs house in a police car. For the

beautiful British car had broken down thirty miles from the frontier and the men in the roadside garage had been unable to repair it. Again I had felt defeated by fate, again I had seen myself as one of the soldiers reeling back from Teruel, doomed by fire and snow; but the garage owner had rung up the local police, and their rickety car had taken us to our destination. It must have been the magic of the British flag and Ilsa's foreign accent. Blind chance had rescued us from blind chance.

And so we had made La Junquera five minutes before twelve, after driving through serried ranks of trees which sprang out of the darkness into the light cone of the car lamps, and through sleeping villages where the rubble of bombed houses littered the road. So it was true that I was leaving my country.

Then we were standing on the road, in front of the barrier. A Spanish carabinero on one side, a French gendarme on the other. The French road was blocked by heavy lorries, with their rear bumpers turned our way: no arms for Spain, I thought. We crossed the barrier, the frontier. The gendarme looked at our passports, casually. I would have to lug our suitcases up the slope to the French customs house, for Ilsa could not carry them; I told her to wait for me by the third suitcase and the typewriter. From one of the lorries a score of oranges came trickling down on to the frozen road, and two of them rolled past me, back to Spain.

When I came into the bare, narrow office, I was engulfed by the fumes of tobacco and a red-hot iron stove. Two men were dozing behind the counter, wrapped in capes. One of them stirred, stretched, yawned, suddenly gave me a sharp look. 'You've just come out of Spain, eh?' and held out his cigarette case. I smoked one with greed before plunging back into the icy clarity of the night. There were no street lamps burning, no more than in Spain; La Junquera had been bombed a couple of nights before, and Le Perthus was next door to it, near enough for a share of bombs.

Ilsa was talking to the Spanish sentry, but I did not feel like it. I grasped the heavy suitcase, she took the typewriter, and we turned our backs on Spain. '*Salud*,' the sentry called out.

'*Salud*.'

We climbed the long, bleak slope without a word.

There was no bed to be had in Le Perthus that night, because the drivers of the lorries which carried oranges from Spain to France had occupied the last free corner. I wished I had picked up one of those oranges. We were hungry and thirsty. The customs official, an elderly Frenchman with long, flowing, black-and-white and tobacco-yellow moustaches, suggested that his neighbour might be willing to take us to Perpignan in his car. He would like to let us stay overnight in the warm customs office, but they had to lock it up at one o'clock. I thought of our scanty money and of the ice-cold night, and decided to interview the man's neighbour. After long minutes of knocking and waiting on the doorstep, a sleepy fat man in a sleeveless vest and half-buttoned trousers opened. Yes, he would take us to Perpignan, but first we would have a drink. He put a bottle of wine and three glasses on the table: 'To the Spanish Republic!'

Even while he was dressing, he and the other man plied me with questions about our war. Then the customs official said:

'I've been in the other war – muck and misery and lice! And now they're pushing us into still another. My boy's just the right age.' From a paunchy, greasy wallet, he took the photograph of a hefty lad ensconced in an ill-fitting uniform. 'That's him. That man Hitler's going to muck things up for us, and the second war will be worse than the first. I'm sorry for you people over there. We don't want wars, what we want is to live in peace, all of us, even if it's not much of a life. But those politicians – to hell with all politicians! And you, what are you?'

'A Socialist.'

'Well, so am I, of course, if you know what I mean. But politics in general are muck. If they kill my boy . . . We didn't fight to have another war on our hands, but if they ask for it they'll get it in the neck again. Only, what I say is, why can't people live in peace?'

It was getting on for three when we reached Perpignan. The streets were deserted, but they were lighted. We gaped at the street lamps which exhibited their light so shamelessly. One of the light cones fell into our hotel room. I made a movement as if to draw the curtains and leave the light outside in the cold of the night.

Ilsa slept the sleep of exhaustion; she had warned me that once in France, she would let herself drop. But I listened to the street noises through the thin crust of my slumber. At seven I was wide awake and could no longer bear being shut up in the room. The walls were closing in on me. I dressed noiselessly and went out into a street full of bustling people and pale, frosty sunshine. A young girl in a white apron, a short black skirt and silk stockings, pretty as a servant girl in a comedy, was arranging the shelves in a baker's shop window. Rolls, buns, *croissants*, pastry, long staves of white bread, on trays whose golden-brown wood looked as though it had been toasted in the oven. The cold air carried a whiff of fresh bread to me; it smelled of sun-drenched women. The sight and smell of the bread made me voraciously hungry, voluptuously hungry.

'Can you give me some *croissants*?' I asked the girl.

'How many, monsieur?'

'As many as you like, half a dozen . . .'

She looked at me out of clear, friendly, compassionate eyes and said: 'You've come from Spain? I'll give you a dozen, you'll eat all of them.'

I ate some in the street and took the rest up to our room. Ilsa was still fast asleep. I put one of the *croissants* on the pillow close to her face, and its smell woke her.

We were walking lazily through the streets, because it was pleasant to stroll and to look at people and shops, although our errand was rather urgent. We had to go to the bank where Poldi had deposited money in Ilsa's name, in exchange for some of our own money which he had needed on his departure from Barcelona. The sum would be just enough to get us to Paris and to allow us two – perhaps three – weeks of rest without immediate financial worries. The future seemed simple and clear. I would soon get well, away from the air raids. In the meantime we would work for our people in Paris. So many articles waiting to be written by her, so many human stories waiting to be written by me. Then we would return to Spain, to Madrid. Everything would come right. We had to be in Madrid in the hour of victory, and we would. The only thing which still had power to hurt Ilsa was the fact that we had not stayed on in Madrid, as was our right and our duty.

But then there was no deposit in Ilsa's name at any of the banks in Perpignan. He must have forgotten about it; his brain had had blackouts.

We counted and recounted our money. At the official rate of exchange, we had brought four hundred francs out of Spain. Not enough for two third-class tickets to Paris or for a week's board at the hotel in Perpignan. We felt stunned. What was there we could sell? We had nothing but shabby clothes, papers, and an old Paisley shawl. Pawn the typewriter? But that would rob us of our tool.

I left Ilsa resting on the bed, escaping into sleep, and went down for a drink in the hotel courtyard. When I saw Sefton Delmer sitting there in the centre of a boisterous group it bothered me. I did not want him to know about our quandary. But he took our presence in Perpignan for granted and spoke only of the new car he had come to fetch, in place of the old, war-worn Ford two-seater which he had taken across the frontier for the last time and would pension off now. I looked at the new car and listened to reminiscences about the exploits of the old little car, and wondered whether the Ford would be chucked on the scrap-heap just like the typewriter which I had mended. I felt a secret bitterness and envy, and asked Delmer what was going to happen to the Ford. Oh, his colleague Chadwick who had brought the new car from Paris would take it over – the fellow there with the sloping forehead. He was going to drive it back to Paris in a couple of hours.

Quaking with excitement, I asked as casually as I could whether Mr Chadwick by any chance had room to take us along in the car. We had little luggage and wanted to go to Paris ourselves. Well – there might just be room if we didn't mind being uncomfortable. I said we did not mind, and went to wake Ilsa, proud as though I had handled Fate well. At five in the afternoon we were on our way to Paris where our driver-host had to be by noon the next day.

The journey was our salvation and my nightmare. In the fading light, every twist of the road on the flats threatened destruction. I was sickeningly afraid of a malicious, senseless accident, of a sudden twist of the cog-wheels to remind us that there was no escape from the crushing mechanism of life. When we began to climb the Central Plateau (on the map this looked like the shortest route to Paris) the roads were frosted and the car slithered on the hairpin bends. Chadwick was a bold and good driver, and I had enough road discipline not to say anything to him, but I had to press myself into Ilsa to still my trembling. With the same blue-print clarity with which I imagined the course and effect of a bomb, I now imagined the skid, the clash, and the cruel mutilation. Once we went into a lonely tavern to warm ourselves and have a quick supper. We lost our road, and found it again. The sleet turned into prickling snow. We went on and on, while I was digging my fingers into Ilsa's arm.

Then, shortly before dawn, when we were planing down somewhere near Clermont-Ferrand, Chadwick stopped the car. He was at the end of his resistance, he had to sleep for an hour or so. Ilsa stowed herself away in the hollow space between the toolbox at the back of the seat, and the low roof. Chadwick fell asleep over the steering wheel. I tried to do the same in my corner, now that I had slightly more room. The cold numbed me and I had to move, as I could not sleep. Cautiously I opened the door, and walked up and down the stretch of road. It was a grey misty dawn, chill and moist. The soil was frozen hard. A few trees along the road were gaunt skeletons. On the top of a near-by hill, a tall chimney overtowering the blurred, dark bulk of a factory was belching forth dark smoke. Workers were passing me on their bicycles, first single, then in droves; their red rear lamps dotted a side-path leading to the factory. Suddenly the screech of a siren split the air; dense white steam spurted from the side of the tall chimney-stack and curled away in the thinning grey mist.

Nausea gripped me when I was not prepared for it. I vomited in the middle of the road, and then I stood there, frozen, trembling, clammy with sweat, my teeth chattering.

Was there no cure for me? Here I had been watching the chimney and the very steam which produced the shrill whistle; I might have known that it was coming; I knew that it meant the beginning of a morning shift of work, and not an air raid. I knew that I was in France, in peace. And yet I was the puppet of my body and nerves.

Not until nearly half an hour passed did I wake the others. Chadwick grumbled because I had let him oversleep past six o'clock; I said that I would have hated to wake him, exhausted as he was. I could not have told him that it would have shamed me too much, had he seen me pallid and trembling.

It was cold and sunny when we entered Paris. Chadwick, in a hurry, gave us the address of a cheap hotel in Montparnasse, and we went there in a taxi. The noise of the city bewildered me. Thinly joking, I said to Ilsa:

'Hôtel Delambre, Rue Delambre – if you pronounce it the Spanish way it become Hôtel del Hambre and Rue del Hambre.'

Hunger Hotel and Hunger Street.

The small bedroom on the third floor smelled of cooking and a dirty street. It had wallpaper with pink and mauve roses like cabbages on a grey-blue ground, a big shameless bed which filled half the space, a yellow wardrobe which creaked but did not quite shut, a deal table, and a white enamel basin with nickelled taps and no hot water. Madame, the wife of the hotelkeeper, had been handsome and was by now formidable, with jet-black eyes and a thin-lipped mouth. Her husband had a big flabby walrus moustache, and a big flabby body; whenever he could, he slipped out of the parlour into the street and left his wife to keep guard behind the glass door. It was cheaper to rent the room for a month, but when we had paid for it in advance we had just enough money left to eat our fill during three days. The small restaurants of the quarter offered set meals at seven francs, with bread *à discrétion* included in the menu; coming out of Spain, one full meal a day seemed enough to us, once our first hunger was stilled. We imagined that we would manage to live on twenty francs a day. To tide us over, there were a few things – our watches, my fountain pen, the Paisley shawl – which we could pawn at the *Mont-de-Piété*, for sums small enough to make us certain of being able to redeem them. And I would begin to earn money without delay.

I went to the Spanish Embassy. The Counsellor, Jaime Carner, received me with sympathy and scepticism, gave me introductions to a couple of Left papers, but warned me that I would find it extre-

mely difficult to break into the charmed circle of French literary sets
without strong backing either by a Party or else by one of the
acknowledged writers. I knew that I would have neither.

Vincens, at the beginning Press Attaché, later head of the Spanish
Bureau de Tourisme - one of the main propaganda agencies – invited
us to lunch, which was very welcome, and gave me another introduction to yet another Left periodical.

Professor Dominois, who had been Poldi's friend, a French
Socialist, staunch supporter of Republican Spain and expert on
Central European politics, summoned us to the Café de Flore,
tumbled out of a taxi, his bulging, stained waistcoat half unbuttoned, his gold pince-nez dancing on a black cord, and his
briefcase spilling papers, and with immense good will expounded
large-scale plans for our future propaganda work – for the Spanish
Embassy.

With a bundle of amateurish translations of my Madrid stories I
made the round of the editors. Some of the sketches were accepted
and set up in print, only to perish 'on the marble', on the slab which
was the graveyard of unimportant contributions; some were
published; and two were even paid. The proofs of a short sketch
which the *Nouvelle Revue Française* took, but never actually
published, helped us to impress Madame and the hotelkeeper for a
whole fortnight. Ilsa was luckier; she placed articles of hers and a
few translations of my tales in Swiss Socialist papers which paid
punctually although meagrely. Later on we met a Swedish girl who
out of enthusiasm (because she recognized Ilsa as the heroine of a
broadcast by a Swedish journalist back from Madrid) translated two
stories from *Valor y Miedo*; the stories were published and paid,
miraculously. Collected in a folder, the sum total of our free-lance
efforts during the first few months looked encouraging. We told
ourselves and one another that, single-handed, we had made people
abroad read about the Spanish war just when they were getting tired
of it and when the press treated it as stale news. But though it had
taken all our combined energy to achieve even so much, it was
shockingly little compared with the task, and it did not satisfy our
need for work. Also, it brought us no more than a sporadic trickle of
cash. Soon we were in arrears with the rent, chained by this debt to a

hotel which we had learned to hate for its very air and for the tiny, greedy ants nesting in its walls; and we often went hungry.

Ilsa was no more fit for systematic work than I was. In the evenings she was feverish and almost immobilized by rheumatic pains; half an hour's walk would exhaust her to the verge of tears. When we had come to France, she had begged me to give her time to recover her strength. Now, it made me furiously angry and depressed when she had to go out in search of work or of a friend from whom to borrow a small sum to keep us going. She found a few lessons, but none of her pupils could afford to pay more than a pittance, and one of them was just able to buy her a white coffee and roll in the café where they met. I found an agency for commercial translations which paid at the rate of one franc per hundred words, with a guaranteed minimum of three francs. They had hundreds of people on their waiting lists, mainly for translations from and into German, but occasionally they sent Ilsa a few lines to translate into French from one of the Scandinavian languages, and they gave me Spanish work to do. Mostly it was a question of short advertisements netting five francs apiece, enough for bread and cheese. But once they sent me a patent to translate into Spanish. When I started to type, one of the letter-levers broke. It was nothing short of disaster, for the patent was long enough to promise warm meals for at least five days. I sat and thought for a long time, while Ilsa was trying to sleep. It was exhilarating and exciting to grapple with a purely mechanical adversity. When I hit upon my great invention and repaired the lever with piano wire, it made me happy for days. I am still proud of it, and the lever is still working.

Yet there were far too many days in endless weeks when we lived on bread and black coffee. This was before we were able to buy a little spirit-lamp, a stewing pot and a frying-pan; we had not even yet asked Madame's permission to cook in our room. The sluttish chambermaid had told us that Madame did not like dishwashing in the basin, and we were too conscious of our standing debt to ask for favours. But even a few consecutive days of bread and coffee at the counter – where the coffee is cheaper and thinner than in the café proper – made us very weak. Neither of us had quite got over the effects of the lean times in Spain. When I was empty of food, my brain grew feverish and sluggish at the same time. Often it seemed more reasonable to stay in bed and doze than to go out and pawn my watch once again, or to borrow five francs from people who had little more than ourselves – for it was still preferable to ask them rather than people who lived a normal, comfortable life. It had been very much easier to go hungry in Spain, together with everybody else and for a reason which made it worth while, than to go hungry in Paris because we found no work and had no money, while the shops were brimming over with food.

Sometimes Ilsa had a spurt of desperate courage and forced herself to ask help from one of her well-to-do friends, afraid that he might resent it as sponging. But she was so scared of meeting Madame's hostile eyes and of being asked when we would pay the rent, that it was usually I who sneaked past the glass door and went out in quest of money for bread and cigarettes. If I waited long enough at the corner of our street, outside the Café de Dôme, I would see somebody whom I knew from Spain, or one of Ilsa's refugee friends, people who would give away whatever they could spare, as easily and naturally as the waiters and I had pooled our cigarettes in Madrid, in the days of scarcity, aware that the other's turn to give or take would come any time.

If the only person I met had just enough money to buy me a coffee in the newly opened, glistening bar of the Dôme, I would gratefully stay there, accept a cigarette from the waiter, and listen to his stories, bandy jokes with the pretty German girl who claimed to be the only painter's model with a Renoir behind, stare back at English and American tourists who had come to get a glimpse of bohemian life, and then return to the hotel, defeated, only to make the journey a second time late at night. When I was lucky, I fetched Ilsa down, walking between her and the glass door in the hotel lobby; then we would eat sausages at the bar, in an elated and mischievous mood because Madame had not accosted us and because we were alive, no longer buried in our stale-smelling room.

Ilsa did not like to stay in the bar. The noise made her restless. She would have a chat with the flower-seller outside, a stout, florid, imperious woman who used to discuss her flowers and the articles in the *Humanité* with Ilsa. Or she would walk round the other corner to the secondhand bookshop behind a narrow blue-painted door, where the wife of the languid, handsome owner – a small, cuddly provocative girl with rolling black eyes and dyed yellow hair – let her browse among the books, borrow a battered volume for a franc, and, in days of affluence, buy a book with the certainty that the shop would take it back at half the price. The bookshop flaunted surrealism, in the primitive guise of absurd, incongruously matched toys hung up in a bird cage or dangling from the wall in front of family portraits of the plush era. But they had very good books. There were two cats, a beautiful dwarf Siamese she-cat and a huge black Persian who was castrated and sat motionless while the Siamese, in heat, dragged herself in frenzy along the floor in front of him.

I felt smothered in the backroom of the bookshop, and it did not give me any pleasure to read pages out of books by André Gide, which seemed beautifully, austerely unreal, remote and chill. I preferred to move among the people in the street and the bar.

Every day, just after dark, a little man arrived at the bar of the Café de Dôme and took up his post at one end of the horseshoe table. He always wore the same shiny dark suit on his round little body and the same rusty bowler hat on his round little head, topping a featureless, round face with a very French moustache. He looked like any old clerk of any old-fashioned notary, one of those notaries who live in ancient, leaning houses and have a gloomy office, where stacks of dossiers tied with red tape pile up in every corner, and an indigenous population of rats grow fat and respectable on a diet of yellowed paper and crumbs of bread and cheese scattered among the files.

The little man would lift his forefinger, slowly and deliberately, crook it, and wave it at the waiter inside the horseshoe of the bar. The waiter would put a glass of colourless liquid in front of the little man, pour into it a few drops from a bottle, and a poisonous yellow-green cloud would mount in the transparent fluid until the whole glass was aglow with it; it was *Pernod*. The little man would plant his elbow on the bar table, bend his hand outward at a right angle, rest his chin on his hand, and stare at the greenish drink. Suddenly he would shake off his meditation; his head would jerk free, his arm extend stiffly from the elbow, his forefinger point accusingly into the void, his eyes pop and swivel in their sockets, in a swift survey of the circle of customers leaning at the bar. Then his finger and eyes would stop, and aim straight at someone's face. The victim would grin and wriggle. The stabbing forefinger would trace signs, affirmative and negative, questioning and persuasive, while the empty features of the little man would contract in a series of rapid gestures, illustrating the rhetoric of the finger. But his body would remain motionless and the words and chuckles which his lips formed never became sound. The grimacing head looked like one of those toy heads of painted rubber which move and gesticulate as you squeeze and release their necks in your hand. Then the play would suddenly stop, the little man would drink a sip of his Pernod and fall back into meditation for a few minutes, only to resume his mute soliloquy in an altered key, with the same mute vigour.

He would go on like this for hours, never moving from his place, from time to time crooking his finger to order another Pernod. People tried to make him speak, but I never heard a word come from his lips. When his eyes looked straight into yours you knew that they never saw you. They were the windows of an empty house; there was nobody left inside the skin of the body. The man had gone quietly mad.

But I was no longer afraid of going mad. My illness had been fear of destruction and fear of the rift within myself; it was an illness which equally threatened all the others, unless they were emptied of thought and will, gesticulating puppets like the little man at the bar. True, the others had built up more defences, or possessed greater powers of resistance, or had fought their way to a greater spiritual clarity than I. But I might fight my own way to clarity, and I might be able to help others in the end, if I traced my mental disease – this disease which was not only mine – back to its roots.

In those noisy summer evenings when I was alone among strangers, I realized that I did not want to write articles and propaganda stories, but to shape and express my vision of the life of my own people, and that, in order to clarify this vision, I had first to understand my own life and mind.

There was no discharge, no release, no truce in the war I carried in myself. So much I knew. How could there have been, when the war riding its course in my country was being dwarfed by the forces lining up for the other war and by the deadly menace to all freedom of spirit?

The drone of passenger planes always carried a threat; it reminded me of the giant Junkers whose cushioned seats could so easily be replaced by bombing gear. I was waiting for German bombs to fall on Paris.

Every Thursday, the air-raid sirens of Paris blew their whistles for a quarter of an hour, beginning at noon; long before the test alert started, I was preparing myself for its impact, without ever preventing the bitter juice of nausea from filling my mouth.

Once I was waiting on a Métro platform and quietly talking to Ilsa, when I vomited; and only in the grip of the convulsion did I become consciously aware of the train rumbling overhead.

In the white-tiled, glistening underground passage of the Châtelet station I was obsessed with the vision of crowds trapped during an air raid combined with a gas attack. I looked at big buildings to assess their potential resistance to bombs.

I was sentenced to a perpetual awareness of the oncoming clash in its physical form, as I was sentenced to feel the helplessness and muddled violence of its victims and fighters in my own mind. But I could not speak to others than Ilsa about it.

The Frenchmen I knew were scarcely hiding their frightened impatience with the Spanish fight; they resented the writing on the wall, because they still clutched at their hope of peace for themselves. The political refugees from Austria whom I met through Ilsa were harassed by their knowledge of developments in their country, recently occupied by Hitler, and by the doom hanging over Czechoslovakia; yet even so they found cover behind their group doctrines, ambitions, and feuds. A single one of them, young Karl Czernetz, realized that international Socialism had lessons to learn from the case history offered by Spain's bleeding body and overwhelmed us with questions about the mass movements, political parties, social and psychological factors in the Spanish war; the others seemed to have their explanations pat. As to Spaniards, those whom I met in official and semi-official departments may have been seared by our war as I was, but they were profoundly afraid of anything outside the sheltering official or party line. I was as much a stranger to them as to the others, although I was far from glorying in an isolation which reduced my radius of action. The alternative, however, was worse, because it would have meant bartering away my independence of thought and expression in exchange for conditional support and help, and for a party label which would have been a lie.

Even in my own ears my purpose sounded crazily audacious: to make people abroad see and understand enough of the human and social substance of our war to realize how it linked up with their own latent, but relentlessly approaching fight. Yet as I strove to control and define my mental reactions, the conviction grew in me that the inner conflicts behind those reactions tortured not only me, the individual, but the minds of countless other Spaniards as well; that indeed they would rend the minds of countless men throughout the world once the great clash engulfed them.

If others, then, felt no urge to search for the causes and the chain of causes, I felt it. If they were content to speak of the guilt of Fascism and Capital and the final victory of the people, I was not. It was not enough; we were all bound up in the chain and had to fight ourselves free from it. It seemed to me that I might better understand what was happening to my people and to our world, if I uncovered the forces which made me, the single man, feel, act, blunder, and fight as I did.

I began to write a book about the world of my childhood and youth. At first I wanted to call it *The Roots*, and describe in it the social conditions among the Castilian workers at the beginning of the century, in the villages and slums I had known. But I caught myself putting down too many general statements and reflections which I believed but could not check, because they did not grow out of my own experience and mind.

I tried to wipe the slate of my mind clean of all reasoning and to go back to my beginnings, to things which I had smelled, seen, touched, and felt and which had hammered me into shape by their impact.

At the beginning of my conscious life I found my mother. Her work-worn hands dipping into the icy water of the river. Her soft fingers stroking my tousled hair. The black-coated earthenware pot in which she brewed her coffee out of a week's dregs. At the bottom of my memory I found the picture of the tall arch of the King's Bridge with the Royal coach guarded by red-and-white horsemen rolling past, high above our heads, washerwomen beating linen down by the river bank, boys fishing rubber balls out of the big black sewer canal, and an Asturian woman singing:

> *Por debajo del puente*
> *no pasa nadie,*
> *tan solo el polvo*
> *que lleva el aire* . . .

> Under the bridge
> nobody goes,
> only the dust
> that the wind blows

There I started. I called the book *La Forja*, The Forge, and wrote it in the language, words, and images of my boyhood. But it took long to write, because I had to dig deep into myself.

About that time we had a windfall; Ilsa earned an English pound, worth 180 francs at the exchange rate of the week. We bought the spirit-lamp and the frying-pan of which we had spoken so much, and two plates, two forks, two spoons, and a knife. I remembered the smell and splutter of the frying-pan in my mother's old attic, and cooked Spanish dishes for us. They were poor people's dishes, but to me they tasted of my country: fresh sardines, potatoes, meat-balls, fried in sizzling oil, even if it was not olive oil. I had never cooked before, but I recalled the movements of my mother's hands: 'Now what was it she did then . . .'

It was something of alchemy and white magic. While I was frying fat sardines in front of the black, useless fireplace, I told Ilsa about the attic, the passage, the staircase, the street, the sounds and the smells of El Avapiés. They overlaid the noises and vapours of the Rue Delambre. Then, before going back to the typewriter, I would stretch out on the floor, my head on Ilsa's lap and her fingers in my hair, and listen to her warm voice.

At the upper end of our short street was the market of the quarter. We went out together to select vegetables for a salad and to find the cheapest fish on the slab. Many times we were saved from another hungry day by cuttlefish, which few people bought and the fishmonger was glad to give away for a mere nothing. They looked ugly, slimy, and unclean. But I stripped off their many layers of transparent skin, until the only thing left was the firm flesh with its mother-of-pearl glints; I prepared a glorious sauce out of their own inky fluid, oil, bay leaves, fried garlic, and a drop of vinegar, in which I simmered the white strips of flesh. And then the whole room smelled like Miguel's kitchen at the foot of the Rock of Ifach. On other days, Ilsa would have an attack of nostalgic cooking and insist on preparing a Viennese dish for once, under my critical eyes. Late in the evening, when I no longer dared to go on typing, afraid of provoking a complaint by other lodgers, we would stroll down to St Germain des Prés, watch the blue glow of the sky, and guard the frail bubble of our gaiety.

When we had a small sum of money beyond the needs of a single day, we were not reasonable. Instead of doling it out carefully, we would celebrate each small victory in a skirmish with existence by eating a full meal in a real restaurant, with the bottle of cheap red wine that went with it. Usually we sat under the striped awning of the Restaurant Boudet in the Boulevard Raspail, because I liked its blend of noisy American students, desiccated Parisian clerks, and stodgy provincial families on an outing, and because I liked gazing at the spacious boulevard with its air of shabby gentility and the fringe of paintings – sunsets, lilac in a blue vase, coy, pink-hued maidens – which was spread out along the kerb on the other side. Also, Boudet's gave a good meal for eight francs or substantial dishes *à la carte*; and they were generous with their white bread, which circulated freely in big baskets filled and refilled by the waitresses.

On hot evenings, when I was smothered by the walls of our close room and wanted to see people and lights, to hear anonymous voices, and feel the slight breeze after dusk, we went to Boudet's even if we had no more than five francs between us. Then we ordered a single dish, sadly refused the wine which the waitress would automatically put on the table, and secure one of the baskets with much bread in it. But it happened early in the summer, when we ordered a dish of macaroni and a second plate, that the elderly, broad-faced waitress leaned over our table and said: 'You must eat more, this isn't good for you.' Ilsa looked up into the friendly face and said lightly: 'It doesn't matter, we can't afford more today. Next time, perhaps.'

Next time we asked for a single dish again, the waitress stood there, solid and firm, and said: 'I'm going to bring you the set meal, it's very nice today. Madame says you've got credit with us and can order what you like.'

I went to see Madame, like a stammering schoolboy. She was sitting behind her cash register, in a black dress, a black-and-white cat by her side, but unlike most of the proprietresses of French restaurants entrenched behind their cash-box, she was not florid and high-bosomed, nor did she wear her black satin like impenetrable armour. She was small, thin, and lively, short in her speech like a mother of many children. Oh yes, it was all right. I did not know when we would get money to pay accounts? That did not matter. We would pay in the end. She cut short my halting explanations of our financial situation: we would order what we needed, on account, and pay when we had the money. It was her risk.

We rationed our visits to Boudet's; but even so we went there often enough when we had no cash for food to cook in our room or when we wanted to breathe freely. By the end of September, we had accumulated a debt of almost six hundred francs. The kindly warmth of the two women never changed; they never assumed a proprietary air. Sometimes I went to eat there merely to bask in their human welcome. How much it helped us to overcome our physical depression, how much it helped me to work without the dread of the next hour when I would have to sneak out and hunt for a few pieces of silver, I cannot tell. But it was certainly my secret ambition then to pay my moral debt – I paid the cash debt, ludicrously, out of two thousand francs I gained on a single lottery ticket bought in cynical despair, with my last ten francs, on a grey rainy day – and to pay it in the face of the world, in print, as I am now doing.

That blue-and-golden September was the September of Munich.

For weeks the Frenchmen round us had been discussing the chances of a peace at any price paid by others than themselves. They began to look askance at foreigners who embodied an uncomfortable warning and the threat of political complications. The ugly word *sale metèque* was spreading. Whatever its origin, its meaning was clear enough: it hit aliens other than Englishmen and Americans in the back. I heard a drunkard spit 'Dirty nigger!' into the yellow-grey face of a half-caste who wore two rows of ribbons from the last war on his lapel. The workers to whose conversations I listened in the *bistro* were confused and uncertain; why should they fight for a bureaucracy going Fascist, for a Government of Big Business? Look at Spain. It showed what happened to the people who risked their lives to defend freedom – isn't it so, Spaniard? It was hard for me to answer them; they did not hate war more than I did; I distrusted their Government as much as they did. Whatever I said about the need to fight for one's chance of a better social order rang hollow, because it had been said so often; the word liberty sounded ironical.

An increasing number of refugees applying at the Préfecture for the monthly or bi-monthly prolongation of their Aliens' Registration Card (the *Récépisse*) were told that they would have to leave the country within eight days. At the corner of the Café de Dôme I heard about many who had left Paris to tramp the roads to the south rather than be arrested and taken across the Belgian frontier – or dumped on the German frontier and left to their fate.

Republican Spaniards, too, met with increasing official disapproval. Franco's armies had cut Loyal Spain into two shrinking areas and were threatening Catalonia. When, in our turn, we went to the Préfecture (on foot, because we had just the amount to pay the fee for the prolongation of our *Récépisse*), we discussed soberly what we would do if they refused us the permit to stay in the country any longer. Go back to Spain – my book half written – my sanity half restored – in the certainty that we would not be given work to do? We had a standing invitation to England, and Ilsa talked of going there almost as if it were her home; but how could we muster the money for the fare within eight days? It was a blind alley. Then, when the morose official prolonged our permits without the slightest hitch, we walked down the stairs hand in hand, like children coming out of school; but my legs felt hollow.

In the evenings people stood about on the boulevards in tight clusters, reading and commenting on the multiple late editions of *Paris-Soir*. Hitler spoke. Chamberlain spoke. What about Czechoslovakia? It was war or no war. In our streets, one of the grocery shops was shut: the owner had gone home to his family in the country. On the following day two more of the shops in the Rue Delambre were shut because their owners had taken their families to the country. It was a nightmare to think what would happen in this Paris if the war were to break out; the very first thing would be chaos in the food supply because those people had no thought but to escape from the bombs. It was bitter and strengthening to think of our people in Madrid who were still carrying on, with the second year of the siege approaching its end.

On July the 14th, when the dull detonations of holiday fireworks had shaken the town and coloured flashes ringed the horizon, I had gone underground, into the shelter of the nearest Métro station, because I could not bear the sounds and the tremor of the earth; in the streets, people had been singing and dancing in a strained, hectic effort to recapture the joyous relief of a half-forgotten victory of freedom. Now, when I knew the threat to be real and not a figment of my brain, I could stand it, for war was inevitable, and war against the aggressor at this moment would save Spain, the world's battered vanguard. And if there was war, it would be better to be in its heart and have a share in it. The French might begin by putting all foreigners into concentration camps, but they would admit us to co-operation in the end, because we were the veterans of their own fight.

It dawned on me then that I was regaining control of myself. I had learned many lessons.

On the day when huge posters mobilizing several French age-classes invaded walls and hoardings, the owner of the Hôtel Delambre called me into the parlour.

'This means war. If the rest of your debt to us is not paid by Sunday, I'll go to the police about it. We can't have foreigners without any income – I've spoken about you to the police anyhow. On Monday we'll shut up the hotel and go away to the country. Paris will be bombed at once, it will be the first town they bomb.'

Ilsa was in bed with flu. I walked through the streets of Paris without wanting to go anywhere. At the Porte d'Orléans, private cars loaded with suitcases and bundles crept forward on a broad front, blocking each other's way out of the city. The railway stations were beleaguered by crowds, sullen, silent, and uneasy. Rows of shops had shuttered doors and windows. This was panic about to break loose.

I went back to our room to look after Ilsa and to eat something. But all we had in store were a few potatoes and half a loaf of bread, infested in all its pores by the tiny red ants which clutched at their pasture and would not be shaken off. I went back into the street and asked the waiter in the Dôme to give me a glass of red wine, which I poured down my throat. He filled it afresh, absent-minded, staring past my shoulder at the stream of cars on the boulevard, cars with big trunks on their luggage-grids.

'Those swine – it's the barracks for us, and they . . . Well, we'll have to cut the throats of quite a lot of people, just as you did in Spain.'

Somebody shook me by the shoulder. 'Well, well, what are you doing here, Barea? And how's Ilsa? Come and have a look at my car. But where *is* Ilsa? How's life?'

It was Miguel, the Cuban, who had drifted into besieged Madrid out of curiosity, out of sympathy, and out of the urge to escape from his own empty life. In Spain he used to say that he loved Ilsa like a sister; now he insisted on seeing her at once. He was appalled at the squalor of our room, appalled at our drawn faces, and he over-whelmed me with reproaches because I had never sought him out in Paris during the past months when he had been flinging away his money. Now, as though to punish me for my constant fear of a blind, cruel, senseless chance, this chance meeting saved us from an encounter with a hostile police. Miguel gave me the money to buy ourselves free from the hotel then and there. We knew where to go;

friends who looked after the empty flat of a Norwegian journalist, with the right to sub-let, had offered us a room which seemed unbelievably bright, clean, and airy, but which we had been unable to take as long as our debt tied us to the hotel. We moved in on the following morning, although the hotelkeeper suddenly asked me to stay: the Pact of Munich had been signed and he no longer thought it necessary to leave Paris and shut his hotel.

Munich destroyed Spain's last hope. It was clear beyond any doubt that no country in Europe would lift a finger to help us against Hitler and his Spanish friends. Russia would have to withdraw her asistance, already painfully reduced; her open intervention in Spain would have meant that the whole of Europe would fall on Russia herself and destroy her. For the immolation of Czechoslovakia and the weak submission of the Great Powers to Hitler's ultimatum had not provoked a wave of anger and contempt for the dictator; they had provoked a tidal wave of fear, naked fear of war and destruction, which bred the urge to deflect that war and destruction on to others.

The Frenchmen with whom I spoke were brutally open. They were ordinary men with small incomes and small ambitions, trying to build up their savings account against old age, disliking the very memory of the last war. They would have welcomed it if, after Czechoslovakia, they could have directed the dictator's greed and fury against another country which he might crush, while his feelings towards France would soften. For France was innocent. France wanted to live at peace with the whole world. The true France repudiated the guilty men, the warmongers, the militant Socialists, the Communists, the Spanish Reds who tried to drag Europe into their war; the true France had signed the Munich Pact.

For a few weeks I, too, felt guiltily glad at the respite from war and made myself forget the smell of putrefaction in the country which still – for how long? – gave us hospitality. It was so great a relief to be in the new room, to learn the trick of how to make three francs provide a meal from Trudy, our generous and hard-worked hostess, and to write at leisure, to be able to think without petty fears hammering at one's brain! It was the first time since our coming to Paris that I could let Ilsa rest at her ease; soon she went to work with her old freshness, forcing me to haul the brightest colours and the sharpest pains of my childhood out of my secret mind and to give them shape in my book.

The autumn sun was dipping Paris in a golden glow. After our meal we used to walk to the Jardin du Luxembourg, slowly, like two convalescents, and sit down on a bench in the sunshine. We had to go early, for the seats filled quickly with children, nurses, and old people. We did not talk much, for to talk of the matters which occupied our thoughts was to conjure up nightmares. It was better to sit still and look at the dance of the fallow chestnut leaves in the sun-flecked avenue.

An old couple was stopping at the bench opposite ours, she small and vivacious, kicking up the sand with the ferrule of her stick, he erect and bony, with a white goatee and white, pointed, carefully waxed moustache. Before he permitted her to sit down he dusted the seat with his silk handkerchief. She wore a dress of black, figured silk, and he carried a silver-handled cane under his arm, like an officer's baton. They spoke to each other in a soft murmur, with courteously inclined heads. When she moved her tapering fingers in their black lace mittens, they looked like the wings of a bird shaking off raindrops.

Ilsa said: 'When we're as old as they, we might be rather like them. At least, it would be nice. You will be a dried-up, lean old man anyhow, and I'll do my best to become a small, wrinkled old lady. We'll take our afternoon walks in a garden, and warm ourselves in the sun, and tell each other about old times, and smile at the dreadful things that happened to us when we were younger.'

'But how will you turn yourself into a little old woman?'

'Just as many others do it. My mother, for example, used to be quite as round as I am now –'

'Come, come, was she?'

'For her size I mean. Really, she was quite plump, and now she's getting fragile and shrinking very pleasantly, though I know it mostly from her photos . . .'

The old man opposite rose, lifted his hat, and stretched out his right hand.

'Look, now they'll dance a minuet!'

But the old gentleman bowed, kissed his lady's finger-tips, and walked sedately down the avenue, his silver-handled cane under his arms. Her fingers escaping from the black mittens moved like the wings of a bird that cannot fly.

'Oh – but you won't do that to me!' Ilsa exclaimed, and her eyes filled with water.

'Of course I will, I'll go to the café and sit with my cronies, and you can stay in the garden all by yourself.' But then I saw that a drop had splashed on to her skirt and was spreading there, and I blinked as though grit had got under my eyelids, for no good reason whatsoever. I had to tell her childish stories, until the corners of her mouth crinkled in laughter and deepened into the question marks which made me feel happy.

I received a parcel of books from Spain: *Valor y Miedo* had been published. But I thought the publishers would not send many copies to Madrid where they belonged; Madrid was cut off from Barcelona.

I read what I had spasmodically written, with the sound of bombs in my ear, and some of it I still liked, though much now seemed of light weight. Yet it made me glad and proud to think that I had torn something straight and simple out of the whirl.

One of the first copies I gave away – the first of all was Ilsa's – went to Vicente, the shop assistant of our Spanish greengrocer. The owner himself, like most of the Spanish fruiterers in Paris, had no liking for the Republicans who wanted to control the export trade, to favour co-operatives, to raise the Spanish workers' wages, and so to curtail private profits. His assistants were Republicans for the very same reasons. Vicente had invited me to the attic where he lived with his thrifty French wife, taken me to the big storehouses in the *Halles* where Spanish packers and porters handled fruit and vegetables coming from Valencia and the Canaries, and told me of his secret fear that France was going the way of Spain, the way to Fascism or civil war. When I gave him my book, he was proud, as though it gave him a share in our fight. He dragged me to the little café near the *Halles* where the Spaniards met. There they used to collect money for the organizations, most of them under Communist leadership, which tried to bring relief to Republican Spain.

The men were shouting and swearing, smoking, drinking, and discussing the way of the world with as much swashbuckling gusto as the people in Serafín's tavern during the months before the clash. They would not admit that things could go wrong in Spain; France, yes – France was going to the dogs because those French had no fight in them, but the people of Spain would show them all. . . . They fingered the pages of my book, looked in it for words to confirm what they said, and slapped me on the back. I still spoke their language. But while I was at ease among them, I kept thinking of the other book which I was writing so as to understand why we were swayed from outburst to passivity, from faith to violence; and it chafed me.

Another of the copies was a bribe to our concierge. The manager of the block of flats in which we lived, a huge modern building with central heating and exorbitant rents, disliked our household because it consisted of foreigners. Once he came and tried to be offensive; at that time a Norwegian couple was living there as well, and the manager declared that he did not like it. The authorities would do well to keep foreigners under even stricter supervision in these turbulent times when they only caused mischief. It was lucky for us that the concierge took our part and gave good reports about us. Thus we religiously paid him his tip at the beginning of the month, because it was more important than food to us to keep him well disposed, and I took pains to do what was just as essential as the tip: I always listened to him. He would intercept me in the courtyard and begin his hardluck story. He had lost a leg in the last war, his chest had caved in, his wife had no understanding for his lost ambitions, and he had to drink so as to keep going.

'Times are bad. . . . Politics, Monsieur! If I had wanted to – now look at this.' He would push me into his lodge and point at a diploma hanging on the wall. 'You see, I was destined for the Bar. Yes, though I'm a humble doorkeeper now, I'm an educated man with a degree. But that cursed war!' This was his cue to turn back his trouser leg and show me his artificial leg, pink like a doll's. 'Here I am, left to rot. This cursed leg ate up my last thousand francs. It hurts me to think of what I might have been.' This was the moment to invite him to a glass of wine in the *bistro*. If I failed to respond, he guessed the state of my finances and invited me, because he longed to display his submerged self and to beg for the listener's admiration. Towards the end of the month, when he had consumed all the tips from all the tenants in the huge beehive, he would pounce on me when I passed and begin to talk with the supplicating eyes of a dog suffering from thirst. He would spread out cuttings describing the many battles in which he had fought as a conscript soldier, and he would open the case with his Croix de Guerre. The cross had worn out the pile of the blue velvet lining. Then he would ask invariably: 'And what do you think of it all?'

When I gave him my book, he weighed it ceremoniously in his hands and said: 'Ah – the Liberty of the People! But let me tell you, we, the Frenchmen, brought Liberty into this world. It was our blood that was shed for the liberation of –' He stopped, twisted his moustache which at once dropped limply back into place, and added: 'You know what I mean.' His wife was gazing at him with the wondering, dark-brown eyes of a cow.

As time went on, my concierge began to speak of certain unspecified difficulties caused by the manager. The point was, there were really too many foreigners in Paris. It was not meant against us as individuals, but he did not think that the lease of the flat would be prolonged on March the 1st. The tenant was never there in person, and some people considered that it was not right to have a centre of aliens in the building. We had many friends, after all, who visited us, hadn't we? Would we not rather go back to our own country?

The collapse of the Spanish front began on the eve of Christmas, at the Ebro. The way to Barcelona lay open. But Madrid still stood. The enemy launched no attack on the besieged city; he left it in the clutch of hunger and isolation. Nini Haslund had come back from her relief work in Spain and told of the despair of the mothers, of their dull, nagging, hopeless despair. But there was no surrender.

Paris had grown dark, foggy, and cold. We were alone in the flat, for our hosts had gone away to the country, fighting their own battle with misery. I had finished my new book, working in spurts when the typewriter was not blocked by the translations which helped us to live, or by Ilsa's laborious and unskilled copying of other people's manuscripts. But when the first rough version of *The Forge* was completed, I sagged. It seemed insolent to hope that it would reach and touch people who wanted to hide from their fears and from their awareness of the social rift within their own world. It might never be printed. I heard it said so often that nobody wanted to hear about anything Spanish. If so, my contribution to the battle would be futile; for writing was to me part of action, part of our war against death and for life, and not just self-expression.

I had struggled to fuse form and vision, but my words were crude because I had had to break away from the conventional rhythms of our literature, if I was to evoke the sounds and images of the world which had made me and so many of my generation. Had I evoked them? I was not sure. I was a learner again, I had to learn how to tell my own truth. The conceptions of art of the professional writers did not help me; they hardly interested me. Twice a French writer had taken me along to a literary gathering, but the self-conscious statements of people gyrating round one 'master' here and another 'master' there had only filled me with astonished boredom and an embarrassing disgust. Now it depressed me to think that I belonged nowhere and so might once again condemn myself to uselessness; and yet it was impossible to act on the beliefs of others and not on my own unless I wanted to lose whatever virtue there might be in me.

When I was very low in spirit, an unknown Spaniard rang me up. He had seen the manuscript *The Forge*, as the reader of the French publisher to whom I had sent it, and he wanted to discuss it with me. The man came, a weak man, split in himself, with his roots in the old Spain and his mind groping towards the new, afraid of the pain which the final clash inflicted on him and the others. He had not greatly liked my way of writing because, as he said, it scared him by its brutality; but he had recommended the book for publication because it had the force to release things which he and others like him kept painfully buried in themselves. I saw his excitement, his relief at the freedom my outspokenness had given him, and I saw with amazement that he envied me. The publisher kept the book, but never answered. It no longer mattered so much, because that other man's words had told me that the book was alive.

In the last days of the year 1938, a bitter frost fell on Paris. Pipes froze in many houses. We were lucky, because the central heating in our flat still worked, and when a young Pole with whom I was friends – he was on the way to becoming a grimly realistic writer of French prose restrained by Gide's influence – rang me up to ask whether we could not rescue him and his wife from their ice-cold, waterless flat, I gladly invited them to stay with us. On the next morning, two police agents called and asked for our guests; they had not informed the Commissariat of their district that they were going to spend a night away from their registered address, and it was only thanks to their satisfactory conduct so far, and to the French Army papers of the young man, that the agents refrained from arresting them. All this in pompous official language and without any civility. Then we were severely warned not to let foreigners stay with us overnight, being foreigners ourselves. Our guests would have to report to the Préfecture, and it would count greatly against them. No, they could not stay until their pipes unfroze, except with the permit of their Commissariat.

When I left the house that day, the concierge called me into his lodge: 'I'm sorry, but I had to tell the police that you had people staying with you overnight who hadn't given me their papers. You see, if I hadn't told them, somebody else would have done it. The manager doesn't like me as it is. I told you things were getting difficult. Well, everyone's got to look out for himself, I say.'

A few days later, I met a young Basque whom I knew slightly in the bar of the Dôme. He told me that the police had asked for his papers three times in a single night, the last time when he was with a girlfriend in her hôtel meublé. He possessed a safe-conduct of Franco's Government, which his father, a manufacturer of San Sebastian, had procured for him at the time when he wanted to cross the frontier into France; the paper had no validity except for the Spanish frontier officials in Irun, but on seeing it, one of the French police agents had said: 'Our apologies, we've nothing against you, but you see, it's high time we cleared France of all those Reds.'

When we went to the Préfecture to get the prolongation of our *Récépisses*, the official subjected us to a lengthy cross-examination. Were we refugees? No, we had our passports of the Spanish Re-

public and could return there. Would we not register as refugees –
we would not return to Spain now, would we? We would not register
as refugees; we insisted on our rights as Spanish citizens. In the end
he told us that we soon would be refugees anyhow, whether we liked
it or not, and then our case would be reconsidered. But he granted us
the prolongation of our papers – this time.

In the drab corridor I met Spaniards waiting for their turn; they
told me of many who had been expelled from Paris and ordered to
provinces in the north of France. Then I saw a familiar face: 'He
looks worried!'

'Didn't you know they'd arrested him and kept him locked up a
few days, just because they knew he'd been a Minister of the
Generalitat?'

It was Ventura i Gassols, the Catalan poet whom intellectual Paris
had fêted a few years before. He scuttled down the stairs, a hunted
animal.

The grey house smelled of rot.

How could I have been fool enough to think that they, those
officials and their bosses, would admit us to co-operation in the war
once it reached France? They were preparing the Maginot Line of
their caste, and we were the enemy to them. They would try to use
the war as their tool. In the end it would devour them and their
country. And we would have to pay the price first. But I did not
want to become the cannon-fodder of a French Fascism. I would not
let ourselves be caught in the trap, doubly defeated.

If we wanted to live and fight, and not to rot and be hunted, we
had to leave France. Get out of the trap. Go to England – a desperate
effort would get us the money, even if we had to ask friends again –
and stay there, free. Not to Latin-America, for our war was fought in
Europe. But away from this stench of decay.

There, within the flaky, stale-smelling walls of the Préfecture, I
was possessed by the urge to escape into freedom. The noises of the
city, dulled by the thick walls, hammered at the back of my skull,
and the horrors of senseless destruction were closing in on me again.

*

The plain-clothes man bowed and said: 'Passports, please.'

As I fumbled in my pocket, I felt my forehead and the palms of my hands go damp. The dread of the last few weeks, when the pack was hunting in full cry, sat in my marrow. And this was our last meeting with the French police.

The man looked perfunctorily at the papers and put his rubber stamps on one after the other of our passports. Then he handed them back, thanked us politely, and shut the door of our compartment with considerate care. The wheels of the fast train were humming, and we kept silence, Ilsa and I, looking at each other. This time, we belonged to the lucky ones; international laws and treaties were still valid for us. Yet the vision of thousands and thousands of others filled the compartment, until I saw nothing else.

Since the end of January the Spanish frontier had been a broken dam, through which the flood of refugees and routed soldiers poured into France. On January the 26th Barcelona had fallen to Franco. The exodus from all the towns and villages along the coast had begun. Women, children, men, beasts, struggling along the roads, through frozen fields, in the deadly snows of the mountains. Pitiless planes overhead, a blood-drunk army pressing from the back, and a small band of soldiers checking its advance, pushed back inexorably and still fighting on, face to the enemy. Poor people with pitiful bundles, fortunate people in overloaded cars cleaving their way through the packed highways, and at the gates of France an endless queue of exhausted fugitives waiting for admission into safety. Admission into the concentration camps which this France had prepared for free men: barbed wire, black sentries, abuse, and robbery, and disease, and the first bunches of refugees herded together without roof or shelter, shivering in the cruel February winds.

Was all France blind? Did Frenchmen not see that one day – soon – they would call upon those Spaniards to fight for French liberty? Or was it that France had given up her own liberty?

The deck of the small steamer was almost deserted. The sea was choppy, most of the passengers had disappeared, Ilsa had gone to lie down in the cabin. A spare, wiry Englishman was sitting on one of the hatches, his feet dangling, and seemed to enjoy the spray which the wind drove into his face. I was sheltering from the gale behind a bulkhead, together with two of the sailors. We exchanged cigarettes, and I began to talk, I had to talk. I spoke about the fight of Spain, and they asked many questions. In the end I was carried away by my scorching anger and poured out all my grievances against France. I asked the two, face to face, the questions I had asked myself:

'Are the French blind, or have they given up their own liberty?'

The two men looked gravely at me. One of them had clear blue eyes and a fresh boyish face, the other had deep-set, black eyes, rough-hewn features and a bare, hairy chest. Then they spoke together, in one breath and with almost identical words:

'Oh no, we shall fight. The others are the ones who won't fight.' And their stress on the words 'the others' sank a deep gulf between the two Frances. The older one added:

'Look, comrade, don't go away from France in bitterness. We'll fight together yet.'

The coast of Dieppe was fading behind us.

Autumn, 1944

Rose Farm House
Mapledurham
Oxfordshire

Arturo Barea

The Forging of a Rebel

The Forge	£2.95
The Track	£2.95
The Clash	£3.50

'One of the key statements of that "desperate hope" by which modern political decency has kept going. It helped educate a generation to the necessity of radical illusions.'

George Steiner

'There is no book in any language which more vividly recreates the years of poverty, political corruption and social violence which finally erupted into the Spanish Civil War.'

Paul Preston, University of London

'Anyone who reads all three novels will end up *understanding* the Spain of Barea's day far better than by reading a dozen works of academic history.'

Martin Blinkhorn, University of Lancaster

FLAMINGO

André Brink

One of South Africa's leading Afrikaner Writers

Looking on Darkness   £2.95

'A novel of stature that explores our cancerous condition more persistently than any other novel has done before, and without benefit of anaesthetic.'   *Alan Paton*

'Brutal, harrowing, desperately sincere.'   *Sunday Times*

An Instant in the Wind   £2.50

'It is difficult to see how any South African novelist will be able to surpass the honesty of this novel.'

World Literature Today

Rumours of Rain   £2.95

'A brilliant achievment.'   *The Times*

'It both enriches our understanding and increases our knowledge of the world we live in.'   *Spectator*

A Dry White Season   £2.50

'Winner of the Martin Luther King Memorial Prize, 1980.

'The revolt of the reasonable . . . far more deadly than any amount of shouting from the housetops.'   *Guardian*

A Chain of Voices   £2.95

This novel transforms a political statement into a compelling and moving artistic achievement.

'A triumph.'   *The Times*

FLAMINGO

Sybille Bedford

A Legacy

More than twenty-five years after its first publication *A Legacy* remains one of the masterpieces of twentieth-century literature.

'A beautiful and brilliant book.' *Bernard Levin*

Against the background of the Kaiser's Germany and the Europe of which it forms part, two families – the Merzes, Jewish upper-bourgeoisie, and the Feldens, landed Catholic aristocracy – are joined in marriage. Out of this union emerges a political and social legacy at once magnificently funny and profound.

'One of the very best novels I have ever read.' *Nancy Mitford*

£2.50

FLAMINGO

FLAMINGO

Flamingo is a quality imprint publishing both fiction and non-fiction. Below are some recent titles.

Fiction

- [ ] Troubles *J. G. Farrell* £2.95
- [ ] Rumours of Rain *André Brink* £2.95
- [ ] The Murderer *Roy Heath* £1.95
- [ ] A Legacy *Sybille Bedford* £2.50
- [ ] The Old Jest *Jennifer Johnston* £1.95
- [ ] Dr Zhivago *Boris Pasternak* £3.50
- [ ] The Leopard *Giuseppe di Lampedusa* £2.50
- [ ] The Mandarins *Simone de Beauvoir* £3.95

Non-fiction

- [ ] On the Perimeter *Caroline Blackwood* £1.95
- [ ] A Journey in Ladakh *Andrew Harvey* £2.50
- [ ] The French *Theodore Zeldin* £3.95
- [ ] The Practice of History *Geoffrey Elton* £2.50
- [ ] Camera Lucida *Roland Barthes* £2.50
- [ ] Image Music Text *Roland Barthes* £2.95
- [ ] A Ragged Schooling *Robert Roberts* £2.50

You can buy Flaming paperbacks at your local bookshop or newsagent. Or you can order them from Fontana Paperbacks, Cash Sales Department, Box 29, Douglas, Isle of Man. Please send a cheque, postal or money order (not currency) worth the purchase price plus 15p per book (maximum postal charge is £3.00 for orders within the UK).

NAME (Block letters) _____

ADDRESS_____

_____

_____

A MESSAGE
TO THE CHARNWOOD READER
FROM THE PUBLISHER

Since the introduction of Ulverscroft Large Print Books, countless readers around the world have confirmed that the larger and clearer print has brought back the pleasure of reading to an ever-widening audience, thus enabling readers to once again enjoy the companionship of books which had previously been denied to them due to their inability to read normal small print.

It is obvious that to cater for this ever-widening audience of readers a new series was necessary. The Charnwood Series embraces the widest possible variety of literature from the traditional classics to the most recently published bestsellers, and includes many authors considered too contemporary both in subject and style to be suitable for the many elderly readers for whom the original Ulverscroft Large Print Books were designed.

The newly developed typeface of the Charnwood Series has been subjected to extensive and exhaustive tests amongst the international family of large print readers, and unanimously acclaimed and preferred as a smoother and easier read. Another benefit of this new typeface is that it allows the publication in one volume of longer novels which previously could only be published in two large print volumes: a constant source of frustration for readers when one volume is not available for one reason or another.

The Charnwood Series is designed to increase the titles available to those readers in this ever-widening audience who are unable to read and enjoy the range of popular titles at present only available in normal small print.

LOST HORIZON

A small plane carrying four passengers takes off from revolution-torn Baskul. But instead of heading for Peshawur and safety, its mysterious pilot flies ever deeper into the Himalayas, finally crash-landing in the unexplored Tibetan wilderness. Met by an elderly Chinese the travellers are conducted to the lamasery of Shangri-La and the hidden valley of Blue Moon. Their strange adventure has only begun . . . First published in 1933 the book, which added the word "Shangri-La" to the English language, is widely regarded as a modern classic and has been enjoyed by countless readers and film, TV and radio audiences.

JAMES HILTON

LOST HORIZON

Complete and Unabridged

CHARNWOOD
Leicester

First published 1933

First Charnwood Edition
published February 1984
by arrangement with
Macmillan London Ltd.
and
William Morrow & Co. Inc.
New York

British Library CIP Data

Hilton, James
    Lost horizon.—Large print ed.
    (Charnwood library series: fiction)
    I. Title
    823'.912[F]   PR6015.I53

    ISBN 0-7089-8170-4

Published by
F. A. Thorpe (Publishing) Ltd.
Anstey, Leicestershire
Printed and Bound in Great Britain by
T. J. Press (Padstow) Ltd., Padstow, Cornwall

Prologue

CIGARS had burned low, and we were beginning to sample the dissillusionment that usually afflicts old school friends who meet again as men and find themselves with less in common than they used to think. Rutherford wrote novels; Wyland was one of the Embassy secretaries; he had just given us dinner at Tempelhof—not very cheerfully, I fancied, but with the equanimity which a diplomat must always keep on tap for such occasions. It seemed likely that nothing but the fact of being three celibate Englishmen in a foreign capital could have brought us together, and I had already reached the conclusion that the slight touch of priggishness which I remembered in Wyland Tertius had not diminished with years and an M.V.O. Rutherford I liked better; he had ripened well out of the skinny, precocious infant whom I had once alternately bullied and patronised. The probability that he was making much more money and having a more interesting life than either of us, gave Wyland and me our only shared emotion—a touch of envy.

The evening, however, was far from dull. We had a good view of the big Luft-Hansa machines as they arrived at the aerodrome from all parts of Central Europe, and towards dusk, when arcflares were

1

lighted, the scene took on a rich, theatrical brilliance. One of the planes was English, and its pilot, in full flying-kit, strolled past our table and saluted Wyland, who did not at first recognise him. When he did so there were introductions all round, and the stranger was invited to join us. He was a pleasant, jolly youth named Sanders. Wyland made some apologetic remark about the difficulty of identifying people when they were all dressed up in Sibleys and flying-helmets; at which Sanders laughed and answered: "Oh, rather, I know that well enough. Don't forget I was at Baskul." Wyland laughed also, but less spontaneously, and the conversation then took other directions.

Sanders made an attractive addition to our small company, and we all drank a great deal of beer together. About ten o'clock Wyland left us for a moment to speak to someone at a table nearby, and Rutherford, into the sudden hiatus of talk, remarked: "Oh, by the way, you mentioned Baskul just now. I know the place slightly. What was it you were referring to that happened there?"

Sanders smiled rather shyly. "Oh, just a bit of excitement we had once when I was in the Service." But he was a youth who could not long refrain from being confidential. "Fact is, an Afghan or an Afridi or somebody ran off with one of our buses, and there was the very devil to pay afterwards, as you can imagine. Most impudent thing I ever heard of. The blighter waylaid the pilot, knocked him out, pinched his kit, and climbed into the cockpit

2

without a soul spotting him. Gave the mechanics the proper signals, too, and was up and away in fine style. The trouble was, he never came back."

Rutherford looked interested. "When did this happen?"

"Oh—must have been about a year ago. May 'thirty-one. We were evacuating civilians from Baskul to Peshawur owing to the revolution—perhaps you remember the business. The place was in a bit of an upset, or I don't suppose the thing could have happened. Still, it *did* happen—and it goes some way to show that clothes make the man, doesn't it?"

Rutherford was still interested. "I should have thought you'd have had more than one fellow in charge of a plane on an occasion like that?"

"We did, on all the ordinary troop-carriers, but this machine was a special one, built for some maharajah originally—quite a stunt kind of outfit. The Indian Survey people had been using it for high-altitude flights in Kashmir."

"And you say it never reached Peshawur?"

"Never reached there, and never came down anywhere else, so far as we could discover. That was the queer part about it. Of course, if the fellow was a tribesman he might have made for the hills, thinking to hold the passengers to ransom. I suppose they all got killed, somehow. There are heaps of places on the frontier where you might crash and not be heard of afterwards."

3

"Yes, I know the sort of country. How many passengers were there?"

"Four, I think. Three men and some woman missionary."

"Was one of the men, by any chance, named Conway?"

Sanders looked surprised. "Why, yes, as a matter of fact. 'Glory' Conway—did you know him?"

"He and I were at the same school," said Rutherford a little self-consciously, for it was true enough, yet a remark which he was aware did not suit him.

"He was a jolly fine chap, by all accounts of what he did at Baskul," went on Sanders.

Rutherford nodded. "Yes, undoubtedly . . . but how extraordinary . . . extraordinary . . ." He appeared to collect himself after a spell of mind-wandering. Then he said: "It was never in the papers, or I think I should have read about it. How was that?"

Sanders looked suddenly rather uncomfortable, and even, I imagined, was on the point of blushing. "To tell you the truth," he replied, "I seem to have let out more than I should have. Or perhaps it doesn't matter now—it must be stale news in every mess, let alone in the bazaars. It was hushed up, you see—I mean, about the way the thing happened. Wouldn't have sounded well. The Government people merely gave out that one of their machines was missing, and mentioned the names. Sort of thing that didn't attract an awful lot of attention among outsiders."

4

At this point Wyland rejoined us, and Sanders turned to him half-apologetically. "I say, Wyland, these chaps have been talking about 'Glory' Conway. I'm afraid I spilled the Baskul yarn—I hope you don't think it matters?"

Wyland was severely silent for a moment. It was plain that he was reconciling the claims of compatriot courtesy and official rectitude. "I can't help feeling," he said at length, "that it's a pity to make a mere anecdote of it. I always thought you air fellows were put on your honour not to tell tales out of school." Having thus snubbed the youth, he turned, rather more graciously, to Rutherford. "Of course, it's all right in your case, but I'm sure you realise that it's sometimes necessary for events up on the Frontier to be shrouded in a little mystery."

"On the other hand," replied Rutherford dryly, "one has a curious itch to know the truth."

"It was never concealed from anyone who had any real reason for wanting to know it. I was at Peshawur at the time, and I can assure you of that. Did you know Conway well—since schooldays, I mean?"

"Just a little at Oxford, and a few chance meetings since. Did *you* come across him much?"

"At Angora, when I was stationed there, we met once or twice."

"Did you like him?"

"I thought he was clever, but rather slack."

Rutherford smiled. "He was certainly clever. He had a most exciting university career—until war broke out. Rowing Blue and a leading light at the Union, and prizeman for this, that and the other—also I reckon him the best amateur pianist I ever heard. Amazingly many-sided fellow—the kind, one feels, that Jowett would have tipped for a future Premier. Yet in point of fact, one never heard much about him after those Oxford days. Of course the War cut into his career. He was full young and I gather he went through most of it."

"He was blown up or something," responded Wyland, "but nothing very serious. Didn't do at all badly—got a D.S.O. in France. Then I believe he went back to Oxford for a spell—as a sort of don. I know he went East in 'twenty-one. His Oriental languages got him the job without any of the usual preliminaries. He had several posts."

Rutherford smiled more broadly. "Then, of course, that accounts for everything. History will never disclose the amount of sheer brilliance wasted in the routine of decoding F.O. chits and handing round tea at Legation bun-fights."

"He was in the Consular Service, not the Diplomatic," said Wyland loftily. It was evident that he did not care for chaff, and he made no protest when, after a little more badinage of a similar kind, Rutherford rose to go. In any case it was getting late, and I said I would go too. Wyland's attitude as we made our farewells was still one of official propriety suffering in silence, but Sanders was very cordial and said he hoped to meet us again sometime.

6

I was catching a trans-continental train at a very dismal hour of the early morning, and as we waited for a taxi Rutherford asked me if I would care to spend the interval at his hotel. He had a sitting-room, he said, and we could talk. I said it would suit me excellently, and he answered: "Good. We can talk about Conway, if you like—unless you're completely bored with his affairs."

I said that I wasn't at all, though I had scarcely known him. "He left at the end of my first term, and I never met him afterwards. But he was extra-ordinarily kind to me on one occasion—I was a new boy and there was no earthly reason why he should have done what he did. It was only a trivial thing, but I've always remembered it."

Rutherford assented. "Yes, I liked him a good deal too, though I also saw surprisingly little of him, if you measure it in time."

And then there was a somewhat odd silence, during which it was evident that we were both thinking of someone who had mattered to us far more than might have been judged from such casual contacts. I have often found since then that others who met Conway, even quite formally and for a moment, remembered him afterwards with great vividness. He was certainly remarkable as a youth, and to me, at the hero-worshipping age when I saw him, his memory is still quite romantically distinct. He was tall and extremely good-looking, and not only excelled at games but walked off with every conceivable kind of school prize. A rather senti-

7

mental headmaster once referred to his exploits as "glorious," and from that arose his nickname. Perhaps only he could have survived it. He gave a Speech Day oration in Greek, I recollect, and was outstandingly first-rate in school theatricals. There was something rather Elizabethan about him—his casual versatility, his good looks, that effervescent combination of mental with physical activities. Sometimes a bit Philip-Sidneyish. Our civilisation doesn't so often breed people like that nowadays. I made a remark of this kind to Rutherford, and he replied: "Yes, that's true, and we have a special word of disparagement for them—we call them dilettanti. I suppose some people must have called Conway that—people like Wyland, for instance. I don't much care for Wyland. I can't stand his type—all that primness and mountainous self-importance. And the complete head-prefectorial mind—did you notice it? Little phrases about 'putting people on their honour' and 'telling tales out of school'—as if the bally Empire was the Fifth Form at St. Dominic's! But then I always fall foul of these sahib diplomats."

We drove on a few streets in silence, and then he continued: "Still, I wouldn't have missed this evening. It was a peculiar experience for me, hearing Sanders tell that story about the affair at Baskul. You see, I'd heard it before, and hadn't properly believed it. It was part of a much more fantastic story, which I saw no reason to believe at all, or well, only one very slight reason, anyway.

Now there are *two* very slight reasons. I dare say you can guess that I'm not a particularly gullible person. I've spent a good deal of my life travelling about, and I know there are queer things in the world—if you see them yourself, that is, but not so often if you hear of them second-hand. And yet . . ."

He seemed suddenly to realise that what he was saying could not mean very much to me, and broke off with a laugh. "Well, there's one thing certain—I'm not likely to take Wyland into my confidence. It would be like trying to sell an epic poem to *Tit-Bits*. I'd rather try my luck with you."

"Perhaps you flatter me," I suggested.

"Your book doesn't lead me to think so."

I had not mentioned my authorship of that rather technical work (after all, a neurologist's is not everybody's "shop"), and I was agreeably surprised that Rutherford had even heard about it. I said as much, and he answered: "Well, you see, I was interested, because amnesia was Conway's trouble—at one time."

We had reached the hotel and he had to get his key at the bureau. As we went up to the fifth floor he said: "All this is mere beating about the bush. The fact is, Conway isn't dead. At least he wasn't a few months ago."

This seemed beyond comment in the narrow space and time of a lift-ascent. In the corridor a few seconds later I answered: "Are you sure of that? How do you know?"

And he responded, unlocking his door: "Because

9

I travelled with him from Shanghai to Honolulu in a Jap liner last November." He did not speak again till we were settled in armchairs and had fixed ourselves with drinks and cigars. "You see, I was in China in the autumn—on a holiday. I'm always wandering about. I hadn't seen Conway for years—we never corresponded and I can't say he was often in my thoughts, though his was one of the few faces that have always come to me quite effortlessly if I tried to picture them. I had been visiting a friend in Hankow and was returning by the Pekin express. On the train I chanced to get into conversation with a very charming Mother Superior of some French sisters of charity. She was travelling to Chung-Kiang, where her convent was, and because I had a little French she seemed to enjoy chattering to me about her work and affairs in general. As a matter of fact, I haven't much sympathy with ordinary missionary enterprises, but I'm prepared to admit, as many people are nowadays, that the Romans stand in a class by themselves, since at least they work hard and don't pose as commissioned officers in a world full of other ranks. Still, that's by the by. The point is that this lady, talking to me about the mission hospital at Chung-Kiang, mentioned a fever case that had been brought in some weeks back—a man who they thought must be a European, though he could give no account of himself and had no papers. His clothes were native, and of the poorest kind, and when taken in by the nuns he had been very ill

10

indeed. He spoke fluent Chinese, as well as pretty good French, and my train companion assured me that before he realised the nationality of the nuns, he had also addressed them in English with a refined accent. I said I ~ouldn't imagine such a phenomenon, and chaffed her gently about being able to detect a refined accent in a language she didn't know. We joked about these and other matters, and it ended by her inviting me to visit the mission if ever I happened to be thereabouts. This, of course, seemed then as unlikely as that I should climb Everest, and when the train reached Chung-Kiang I shook hands with genuine regret that our chance contact had come to an end. As it happened, though, I was back in Chung-Kiang within a few hours. The train broke down a mile or two farther on, and with much difficulty pushed us back to the station, where we learned that a relief engine could not possibly arrive for twelve hours. That's the sort of thing that often happens on Chinese railways. So there was half a day to be lived through in Chung-Kiang—which made me decide to take the good lady at her word and call at the mission.

"I did so, and received a cordial though naturally a somewhat astonished welcome. I suppose one of the hardest things for a non-Catholic to realise is how easily a Catholic can combine official rigidity with non-official broad-mindedness. Is that too complicated? Anyhow, never mind—those mission people made quite delightful company. Before I'd been there an hour I found that a meal had been prepared, and a young Chinese Christian doctor sat down with me to it and kept up a conversation in a jolly mixture of French and English. Afterwards, he and the Mother Superior took me to see the hospital, of which they were very proud. I had told them I was a writer, and they were simple-minded enough to be a-flutter at the thought that I might put them all into a book. We walked past the beds while the doctor explained the cases. The place was spotlessly clean and looked to be very competently run. I had forgotten all about the mysterious patient with the refined English accent till the Mother Superior reminded me that we were just coming to him. All I could see was the back of the man's head; he was apparently asleep. It was suggested that I should address him in English, so I said 'Good afternoon,' which was the first and not very original thing I could think of. The man looked up suddenly and said 'Good afternoon' in answer. It was true; his accent was educated. But I hadn't time to be surprised at that, for I had already recognised him—despite his beard and altogether changed appearance and the fact that we hadn't met for so long. He was Conway. I was certain he was, and yet, if I'd paused to think about it, I might well have come to the conclusion that he couldn't possibly be. Fortunately I acted on the impulse of the moment. I called out his name and my own, and though he looked at me without any definite sign of recognition, I was positive I hadn't made any mistake. There was an odd little twitching of the facial muscles that I had noticed in him before, and he had the same eyes that at Balliol we used to say were so much more of a Cambridge blue than an Oxford. But besides all that, he was a man one simply didn't make mistakes about—to see him once was to know him always. Of course the doctor and the Mother Superior were greatly excited. I told them that I knew the man, that he was English, and a friend of mine, and that if he didn't recognise me, it could only be because he had completely lost his memory. They said yes, in a rather amazed way, and we had a long consultation about the case. They weren't able to make any suggestions as to how Conway could possibly have arrived at Chung-Kiang in the state he was.

"To make the story brief, I stayed there over a fortnight, hoping that somehow or other I might induce him to remember things. I didn't succeed, but he regained his physical health, and we talked a good deal. When I told him quite frankly who I was and who he was, he was docile enough not to argue about it. He was quite cheerful, even, in a vague sort of way, and seemed glad enough to have my company. To my suggestion that I should take him home, he simply said that he didn't mind. It was a little unnerving, that apparent lack of any personal desire. As soon as I could I fixed up our departure. I made a confidant of an acquaintance in the consular office at Hankow, and thus the necessary passport and so on were made out without the fuss there

13

might otherwise have been. Indeed, it seemed to me that for Conway's sake the whole business had better be kept free from publicity and newspaper headlines—and I'm glad to say I succeeded in that. It would have been jam, of course, for the Press.

"Well, we made our exit from China in quite a normal way. We sailed down the Yang-tse to Nanking, and then took train for Shanghai. There was a Jap liner leaving for 'Frisco that same night, so we made a great rush and got on board."

"You did a tremendous lot for him," I said.

Rutherford did not deny it. "I don't think I should have done quite as much for anyone else," he answered. "But there was something about the fellow, and always had been—it's hard to explain, but it made one enjoy doing what one could."

"Yes," I agreed. "He had a peculiar charm, a sort of winsomeness that's pleasant to remember even now when I picture it—though of course I think of him still as a schoolboy in cricket flannels."

"A pity you didn't know him at Oxford. He was just brilliant—there's no other word. After the War people said he was different—I think myself he was. But I can't help feeling that with all his gifts he ought to have been doing bigger work—all that Britannic Majesty stuff isn't my idea of a great man's career. And Conway was—or should have been—*great*. You and I have both known him, and I don't think I'm exaggerating when I say it's an experience we shan't ever forget. And even when he and I met in the middle of China, with his mind a

14

blank and his past a mystery, there was still that queer core of attractiveness in him."

Rutherford paused reminiscently and then continued: "As you can imagine, we remade our old friendship on the ship. I told him as much as I knew about himself, and he listened with an attention that might almost have seemed a little absurd. He remembered everything quite clearly since his arrival at Chung-Kiang, and another point that may interest you is that he hadn't forgotten languages. He told me, for instance, that he knew he must have had something to do with India, because he could speak Hindostani.

"At Yokohama the ship filled up, and among the new passengers was Sieveking, the pianist, *en route* for a concert tour in the States. He was at our dining-table and sometimes talked with Conway in German. That will show you how outwardly normal Conway was. Apart from his loss of memory, which didn't show in ordinary inter-course, there couldn't have seemed much wrong with him.

"A few nights after leaving Japan Sieveking was prevailed upon to give a piano recital on board, and Conway and I went to hear him. He played well, of course—some Brahms and Scarlatti, and a lot of Chopin. Once or twice I glanced at Conway and judged that he was enjoying it all, which appeared very natural, in view of his own musical past. At the end of the programme the show lengthened out into an informal series of encores which Sieveking

15

bestowed—very amiably, I thought—upon a few enthusiasts grouped round the piano. Again he played Chopin chiefly—he rather specialises in it, you know. At last he left the piano and moved towards the door, still followed by admirers, but evidently feeling that he had done enough for them. In the meantime a rather odd thing was beginning to happen. Conway had sat down at the keyboard and was playing some rapid lively piece that I didn't recognise, but which drew Sieveking back in great excitement to ask what it was. Conway, after a long and rather strange silence, could only reply that he didn't know. Sieveking exclaimed that that was incredible, and grew more excited still. Conway then made what appeared to be a tremendous physical and mental effort to remember, and said at last that the thing was a Chopin study. I didn't think myself it could be, and I wasn't surprised when Sieveking denied it absolutely. Conway, however, grew suddenly quite indignant about the matter—which startled me, because up to then he had shown so little emotion about anything. 'My dear fellow,' Sieveking remonstrated, 'I know everything of Chopin's that exists, and I can assure you that he never wrote what you have just played. He might well have done so, because it's utterly in his style, but he just didn't. I challenge you to show me the score in any of the editions.' To which Conway replied at length: 'Oh yes, I remember now—it was never printed. I only know it myself from meeting a man who used to be one of Chopin's

16

pupils. . . . Here's another unpublished thing I learned from him.'"

Rutherford steadied me with his eyes as he went on: "I don't know if you're a musician, but even if you're not, I dare say you'll be able to imagine something of Sieveking's excitement, and mine too, as Conway continued to play. To me, of course, it was a sudden and quite mystifying glimpse into the past—the first clue of any kind that had escaped. Sieveking was naturally engrossed in the musical problem—which was perplexing enough, as you'll realise when I remind you that Chopin died in 1849.

"The whole incident was so unfathomable, in a sense, that perhaps I should add that there were at least a dozen witnesses of it—including a Californian university professor of some repute. Of course it was easy to say that Conway's explanation was chronologically impossible, or almost so; but there was still music itself to be explained. If it wasn't what Conway said it was, then what *was* it? Sieveking assured me that if those two pieces were published, they would be in every virtuoso's repertoire within six months. Even if this is an exaggeration, it shows Sieveking's opinion of them. After much argument at the time, we weren't able to settle anything, for Conway stuck to his story, and as he was beginning to look fatigued, I was anxious to get him away from the crowd and off to bed. The last episode was about making some gramophone records. Sieveking said he would fix

17

up all arrangements as soon as he reached America, and Conway gave his promise to play before the microphone. I often feel it was a great pity, from every point of view, that he wasn't able to keep his word."

Rutherford glanced at his watch and impressed on me that I should have plenty of time to catch my train, since his story was practically finished. "Because that night—the night after the recital—he got back his memory. We had both gone to bed and I was lying awake, when he came into my cabin and told me. His face had stiffened into what I can only describe as an expression of overwhelming sadness—a sort of universal sadness, if you know what I mean—something remote or impersonal, a *Wehmut* or *Weltschmerz*, or whatever the Germans call it. He said he could call to mind everything, that it had begun to come back to him during Sieveking's playing, though only in patches at first. He sat for a long while on the edge of my bed, and I let him take his own time and make his own method of telling me. I said that I was glad his memory had returned, but sorry if he already wished that it hadn't. He looked up them and paid me what I shall always regard as a marvellously high compliment. 'Thank God, Rutherford,' he said, 'you are capable of imagining things.' After a while I dressed and persuaded him to do the same, and we walked up and down the boat-deck. It was a calm night, starry and very warm, and the sea had a pale, sticky look, like condensed milk. Except for the vibration of the

18

engines, we might have been pacing an esplanade. I let Conway go on his own way, without questions at first. Somewhere about dawn he began to talk consecutively and it was mid-morning and hot sunshine when he had finished. When I say 'finished' I don't mean that there was nothing more to tell me after that first confession. He filled in a good many important gaps during the next twenty-four hours. He was very unhappy, and couldn't have slept, so we talked almost constantly. About the middle of the following night the ship was due to reach Honolulu. We had drinks in my cabin the evening before; he left me about ten o'clock, and I never saw him again."

"You don't mean——" I had a picture in mind of a very calm, deliberate suicide I once saw on the mail-boat from Holyhead to Kingstown.

Rutherford laughed. "Oh Lord, no—he wasn't that sort. He just gave me the slip. It was easy enough to get ashore, but he must have found it hard to avoid being traced when I set people searching for him, as of course I did. Afterwards I learned that he'd managed to join the crew of a banana-boat going south to Fiji."

"How did you get to know that?"

"Quite straightforwardly. He wrote to me, three months later, from Bangkok, enclosing a draft to pay the expenses I'd been put to on his account. He thanked me and said he was very fit. He also said he was about to set out on a long journey—to the north-west. That was all."

19

"Where did he mean?"

"Yes, it's pretty vague, isn't it? A good many places must lie to the north-west of Bangkok. Even Berlin does, for that matter."

Rutherford paused and filled up my glass and his own. It had been a queer story—or else he had made it seem so; I hardly knew which. The music part of it, though puzzling, did not interest me so much as the mystery of Conway's arrival at that Chinese mission hospital; and I made this comment. Rutherford answered that in point of fact they were both parts of the same problem. "Well, how *did* he get to Chung-Kiang?" I asked. "I suppose he told you all about it that night on the ship?"

"He told me something about it, and it would be absurd of me, after letting you know so much, to be secretive about the rest. Only, to begin with, it's a longish sort of tale, and there wouldn't be time even to outline it before you'd have to be off for your train. And besides, as it happens, there's a more convenient way. I'm a little diffident about revealing the tricks of my dishonourable calling, but the truth is, Conway's story, as I pondered over it afterwards, appealed to me enormously. I had begun by making simple notes after our various conversations on the ship, so that I shouldn't forget details; later, as certain aspects of the thing began to grip me, I had the urge to do more—to fashion the written and recollected fragments into a single narrative. By that I don't mean that I invented or altered anything. There was quite enough material

20

in what he told me—he was a fluent talker and had a natural gift for communicating an atmosphere. Also, I suppose, I felt I was beginning to understand the man himself." He went to an attaché-case and took out a bundle of typed manuscript. "Well, here it is, anyhow, and you can make what you like of it."

"By which I suppose you mean that I'm not expected to believe it?"

"Oh, hardly so definite a warning as that. But mind, if you *do* believe it, it will be for Tertullian's famous reason—you remember?—*quia impossibile est*. Not a bad argument, maybe. Let me know what you think, at all events."

I took the manuscript away with me and read most of it on the Ostend express. I intended returning it with a long letter when I reached England, but there were delays, and before I could post it I got a short note from Rutherford to say that he was off on his wanderings again and would have no settled address for some months. He was going to Kashmir, he wrote, and thence "east." I was not surprised.

1

DURING that third week of May the situation in Baskul had become much worse and, on the 20th, Air Force machines arrived by arrangement from Peshawur to evacuate the white residents. These numbered about eighty, and most were safely transported across the mountains in troop-carriers. A few miscellaneous aircraft were also employed, among them being a cabin machine lent by the Maharajah of Chandapore. In this, about 10 A.M., four passengers embarked: Miss Roberta Brinklow, of the Eastern Mission; Henry D. Barnard, a U.S. citizen; Hugh Conway, H.M. Consul; and Captain Charles Mallinson, H.M. Vice-Consul.

These names are as they appeared later in Indian and British newspapers.

Conway was thirty-seven. He had been at Baskul for two years, in a job which now, in the light of events, could be regarded as a persistent backing of the wrong horse. A stage of his life was finished with; in a few weeks' time, or perhaps after a few months' leave in England, he would be sent somewhere else. Tokio or Tehran, Manila or Muscat, people in his profession never knew what was coming. He had been ten years in the Consular

23

Service, long enough to assess his own chances as shrewdly as he was apt to do those of others. He knew that the plums were not for him; but it was genuinely consoling, and not merely sour grapes, to reflect that he had no taste for plums. He preferred the less formal and more picturesque jobs that were on offer, and as these were often not good ones, it had doubtless seemed to others that he was playing his cards rather badly. Actually, to suit his own tastes, he felt he had played them rather well; he had had a varied and moderately enjoyable decade.

He was tall, deeply bronzed, with brown, short-cropped hair and slate-blue eyes. He was inclined to look severe and brooding until he laughed, and then (but it happened not so very often) he looked boyish. There was a slight nervous twitch near the left eye which was usually noticeable when he worked too hard or drank too much, and as he had been packing and destroying documents throughout the whole of the day and night preceding the evacuation, the twitch was very conspicuous when he climbed into the aeroplane. He was tired out, and overwhelmingly glad that he had contrived to be sent in the maharajah's luxurious air liner instead of in one of the crowded troop-carriers. He spread himself indulgently in the basket seat as the plane soared aloft. He was the sort of man who, being used to major hardships, expects minor comforts by way of compensation. Cheerfully he might endure the rigours of the road to Samarkand, but from London to Paris he would spend his last tenner on the Golden Arrow.

It was after the flight had lasted more than an hour that Mallinson said he thought the pilot wasn't keeping a straight course. Mallinson sat immediately in front. He was a youngster in his middle twenties, pink-cheeked, intelligent without being intellectual, beset with public-school limitations, but also with their excellences. Failure to pass an examination was the chief cause of his being sent to Baskul, where Conway had had six months of his company and had grown to like him.

But Conway did not want to make the effort that an aeroplane conversation demands. He opened his eyes drowsily and replied that whatever the course taken, the pilot presumably knew best.

Half an hour later, when weariness and the drone of the engine had lulled him nearly to sleep, Mallinson disturbed him again. "I say, Conway, I thought Fenner was piloting us?"

"Well, isn't he?"

"The chap turned his head just now and I'll swear it wasn't him."

"It's hard to tell, through that glass panel."

"I'd know Fenner's face anywhere."

"Well, then, it must be someone else. I don't see that it matters."

"But Fenner told me definitely that he was taking this machine."

"They must have changed their minds and given him one of the others."

"Well, who is this man, then?"

"My dear boy, how should I know? You don't suppose I've memorised the face of every flight-lieutenant in the Air Force, do you?"

"I know a good many of them, anyway, but I don't recognise this fellow."

"Then he must belong to the minority whom you don't know." Conway smiled and added: "When we arrive in Peshawur very soon you can make his acquaintance and ask him all about himself."

"At this rate we shan't get to Peshawur at all. The man's right off his course. And I'm not surprised either—flying so damned high he can't see where he is."

Conway was not bothering. He was used to air travel, and took things for granted. Besides, there was nothing particular he was eager to do when he got to Peshawur, and no one particular he was eager to see; so it was a matter of complete indifference to him whether the journey took four hours or six. He was unmarried; there would be no tender greetings on arrival. He had friends, and a few of them would probably take him to the club and stand him drinks; it was a pleasant prospect, but not one to sigh for in anticipation.

Nor did he sigh retrospectively when he viewed the equally pleasant but not wholly satisfying vista of the past decade. Changeable, fair intervals, becoming rather unsettled; it had been his own

26

meteorological summary during that time, as well as the world's. He thought of Baskul, Pekin, Macao, and the other places—he had moved about pretty often. Remotest of all was Oxford, where he had had a couple of years of donhood after the War, lecturing on Oriental History, breathing dust in sunny libraries, cruising down the High on a push-bicycle. The vision attracted, but did not stir him; there was a sense in which he felt that he was still a part of all that he might have been.

A familiar gastric lurch informed him that the plane was beginning to descend. He felt tempted to rag Mallinson about his fidgets, and would perhaps have done so had not the youth risen abruptly, bumping his head against the roof, and waking Barnard, the American, who had been dozing in his seat at the other side of the narrow gangway. "My God!" Mallinson cried, peering through the window. "Look down there!"

Conway looked. The view was certainly not what he had expected—if, indeed, he had expected anything. Instead of the trim, geometrically laid-out cantonments and the larger oblongs of the hangers, nothing was visible but an opaque mist veiling an immense, sun-brown desolation. The plane, though descending rapidly, was still at a height unusual for ordinary flying. Long, corrugated mountain-ridges could be picked out, perhaps a mile or so closer than the cloudier smudge of the valleys. It was typical Frontier scenery, though Conway had never viewed it before from such an altitude. It was also—which struck him as odd—nowhere that he could imagine near Peshawur. "I don't recognise this part of the world," he commented. Then, more privately, for he did not wish to alarm the others, he added into Mallinson's ear: "Looks as if you're right—the man's lost his way."

The plane was swooping down at a tremendous speed, and as it did so, the air grew hotter; the scorched earth below was like an oven with the door suddenly opened. One mountain-top after another lifted itself above the horizon in craggy silhouette; now the flight was along a curving valley, the base of which was strewn with rocks and the debris of dried-up watercourses. It looked like a floor littered with nut-shells. The plane bumped and tossed in air-pockets as uncomfortably as a row-boat in a swell. All four passengers had to hold on to their seats.

"Looks like he wants to land!" shouted the American hoarsely.

"He can't!" Mallinson retorted. "He'd be simply mad if he tried to! He'll crash and then——"

But the pilot did land. A small cleared space opened by the side of a gully, and with considerable skill the machine was jolted and heaved to a standstill. What happened after that, however, was more puzzling and less reassuring. A swarm of bearded and turbaned tribesmen came forward from all directions, surrounding the machine and effectively preventing anyone from getting out of it except the pilot. The latter clambered to earth and

28

held excited colloquy with them, during which proceeding it became clear that, so far from being Fenner, he was not an Englishman at all, and possibly not even a European. Meanwhile cans of petrol were fetched from a dump close by and emptied into the exceptionally capacious tanks. Grins and disregarding silence met the shouts of the four imprisoned passengers, while the slightest attempt to alight provoked a menacing movement from a score of rifles. Conway, who knew a little Pushtu, harangued the tribesmen as well as he could in that language, but without effect; while the pilot's sole retort to remarks addressed to him in any language was a significant flourish of his revolver. Midday sunlight, blazing on the roof of the cabin, grilled the air inside till the occupants were almost fainting with the heat and with the exertion of their protests. They were quite powerless; it had been a condition of the evacuation that they should carry no arms.

When the tanks were at last screwed up, a petrol-can filled with tepid water was handed through one of the cabin windows. No questions were answered, though it did not appear that the men were personally hostile. After a further parley the pilot climbed back into the cockpit, a Pathan clumsily swung the propeller, and the flight was resumed. The take-off, in that confined space and with the extra petrol load, was even more skilful than the landing. The plane rose high into the hazy vapours; then turned east, as if setting a course. It was mid-afternoon.

A most extraordinary and bewildering business! As the cooler air refreshed them, the passengers could hardly believe that it had really happened; it was an outrage to which none could recall any parallel, or suggest any precedent, in all the turbulent records of the Frontier. It would have been incredible, indeed, had they not been victims of it themselves. It was quite natural that high indignation should follow incredulity, and anxious speculation only when indignation had worn itself out. Mallinson then developed the theory which, in the absence of any other, they found easiest to accept. They were being kidnapped for ransom. The trick was by no means new in itself, though this particular technique must be regarded as original. It was a little more comforting to feel that they were not making entirely virgin history; after all, there had been kidnappings before, and a good many of them had ended up all right. The tribesmen kept you in some lair in the mountains till the Government paid up and you were released. You were treated quite decently, and as the money that had to be paid wasn't your own, the whole business was only unpleasant while it lasted. Afterwards, of course, the Air people sent a bombing squadron, and you were left with one good story to tell for the rest of your life. Mallinson enunciated the proposition a shade nervously; but Barnard, the American, chose to be heavily facetious. "Well, gentlemen, I dare say this is a cute idea on somebody's part, but I can't exactly figger it out that your Air Force has covered itself with glory. You Britishers make jokes about the hold-ups in Chicago and all that, but I don't recollect any instance of a gunman running off with one of Uncle Sam's aeroplanes. And I should like to know, by the way, what this fellow did with the real pilot. Sandbagged him, I should reckon." He yawned. He was a large, fleshy man, with a hard-bitten face in which good-humoured wrinkles were not quite offset by pessimistic pouches. Nobody in Baskul had known much about him except that he had arrived from Persia, where it was presumed he had something to do with oil.

Conway meanwhile was busying himself with a very practical task. He had collected every scrap of paper that they all had, and was composing messages in various native languages to be dropped to earth at intervals. It was a slender chance, in such sparsely populated country, but worth taking.

The fourth occupant, Miss Brinklow, sat tight-lipped and straight-backed, with few comments and no complaints. She was a small, rather leathery woman, with an air of having been compelled to attend a party at which there were goings-on that she could not wholly approve.

Conway had talked less than the two other men, for translating S.O.S. messages into dialects was a mental exercise requiring concentration. He had however, answered questions, when asked, and had agreed, tentatively, with Mallinson's kidnapping theory. He had also agreed, to some extent, with Barnard's strictures on the Air Force. "Though one

31

can see, of course, how it may have happened. With the place in commotion as it was, one man in flying-kit would look very much like another. No one would think of doubting the *bona fides* of any man in the proper clothes who looked as if he knew his job. And this fellow *must* have known it—the signals, and so forth. Pretty obvious, too, that he knows how to fly . . . still, I agree with you that it's the sort of thing that someone ought to get into hot water about. And somebody will, you may be sure, though I suspect he won't deserve it."

"Well, sir," responded Barnard, "I certainly do admire the way you manage to see both sides of the question. It's the right spirit to have, no doubt, even when you're being taken for a ride."

Americans, Conway reflected, had the knack of being able to say patronising things without being offensive. He smiled tolerantly, but did not continue the conversation. His tiredness was of a kind that no amount of possible peril could stave off. Towards late afternoon, when Barnard and Mallinson, who had been arguing, appealed to him on some point, it appeared that he had fallen asleep.

"Dead beat," Mallinson commented. "And I don't wonder at it, after these last few weeks."

"You're his friend?" queried Barnard.

"I've worked with him at the Consulate. I happen to know that he hasn't been in bed for the last four nights. As a matter of fact, we're damned lucky in having him with us in a tight corner like this. Apart from knowing the languages, he's got a sort of way with him in dealing with people. If anyone can get us out of the mess, he'll do it. He's pretty cool about most things."

"Well, let him have his sleep, then," agreed Barnard.

Miss Brinklow made one of her rare remarks. "I think he *looks* a very brave man," she said.

Conway was far less certain that he *was* a very brave man. He had closed his eyes in sheer physical fatigue, but without actually sleeping. He could hear and feel every movement of the plane, and he heard also, with mixed feelings, Mallinson's eulogy of himself. It was then that he had his doubts, recognising a tight sensation in his stomach which was his own bodily reaction to a disquieting mental survey. He was not, as he knew well from experience, one of those persons who love danger for its own sake. There was an aspect of it which he sometimes enjoyed—an excitement, a purgative effect upon sluggish emotions—but he was far from fond of risking his life. Twelve years earlier he had grown to hate the perils of trench warfare in France, and had several times avoided death by declining to attempt valorous impossibilities. Even his D.S.O. had been won, not so much by physical courage, as by a certain hardly developed technique of endurance. And since the War, whenever there had been danger again, he had faced it with in-creasing disrelish unless it promised extravagant dividends in thrills.

33

He still kept his eyes closed. He was touched, and a little dismayed, by what he had heard Mallinson say. It was his fate in life to have his equanimity always mistaken for pluck—whereas it was actually something much more dispassionate and much less virile. They were all in a damnably awkward situation, it seemed to him, and so far from being full of bravery about it, he felt chiefly an enormous distaste for whatever trouble might be in store. There was Miss Brinklow, for instance. He foresaw that in certain circumstances he would have to act on the supposition that because she was a woman she mattered far more than the rest of them put together, and he shrank from a situation in which such disproportionate behaviour might be unavoidable.

Nevertheless, when he showed signs of wakefulness, it was to Miss Brinklow that he spoke first. He realised that she was neither young nor pretty—negative virtues, but immensely helpful in such difficulties as those in which they might soon find themselves. He was also rather sorry for her, because he suspected that neither Mallinson nor the American liked missionaries, especially female ones. He himself was unprejudiced, but he was afraid she would find his open mind a less familiar and therefore an even more disconcerting phenomenon. "We seem to be in a queer fix," he said, leaning forward to her ear, "but I'm glad you're taking it calmly. I don't really think anything dreadful is going to happen to us."

"I'm certain it won't, if you can prevent it," she answered; which did not console him.

"You must let me know if there is anything we can do to make you more comfortable."

Barnard caught the word. "Comfortable?" he echoed raucously. "Why, of course we're comfortable. We're just enjoying the trip. Pity we haven't a pack of cards—we could make up a bridge four."

Conway welcomed the spirit of the remark, though he disliked bridge. "I don't suppose Miss Brinklow plays," he said, smiling.

But the missionary turned round briskly to retort: "Indeed I do, and I could never see any harm in cards at all. There's nothing against them in the Bible."

They all laughed, and seemed grateful to her for providing an excuse. At any rate, Conway thought, she wasn't hysterical.

All afternoon the plane had soared through the thin mists of the upper atmosphere, far too high to give clear sight of what lay beneath. Sometimes, at longish intervals, the veil was torn for a moment, to display the jagged outline of a peak, or the glint of some unknown stream. The direction could be determined roughly from the sun; it was still east, with occasional twists to the north; but whither it had led depended on the speed of travel, which Conway could not judge with any accuracy. It seemed likely, though, that the flight must already

35

have exhausted a good deal of the petrol; though that again depended on uncertain factors. Conway had no technical knowledge of aircraft, but he was sure that the pilot, whoever he might be, was altogether an expert. That halt in the rock-strewn valley had demonstrated it, and also other incidents since. And Conway could not repress a feeling that was always his in the presence of any superb and indisputable competence. He was so used to being appealed to for help that mere awareness of someone who would neither ask nor need it was slightly tranquillising, even amidst the greater perplexities of the future. But he did not expect his companions to share such a tenuous emotion. He recognised that they were likely to have far more personal reasons for anxiety than he had himself. Mallinson, for instance, was engaged to a girl in England; Barnard might be married; Miss Brinklow had her work, vocation, or however she might regard it. Mallinson, incidentally, was by far the least composed; as the hours passed he showed himself increasingly excitable—apt, also, to resent to Conway's face the very coolness which he had praised behind his back. Once, above the roar of the engine, a sharp storm of argument arose. "Look here," Mallinson shouted angrily, "are we bound to sit here twiddling our thumbs while this maniac does everything he damn well wants? What's to stop us smashing that panel and having it out with him?"

"Nothing at all," replied Conway, "except that

36

he's armed and we're not, and that in any case, none of us would know how to bring the machine to earth afterwards."

"It can't be very hard, surely. I dare say you could do it."

"My dear Mallinson, why is it always *me* you expect to perform these miracles?"

"Well, anyway, this business is getting hellishly on my nerves. Can't we *make* the fellow come down?"

"How do you suggest it should be done?"

Mallinson was becoming more and more agitated. "Well, he's *there*, isn't he? About six feet away from us, and we're three men to one! Have we got to stare at his damned back all the time? At least we might force him to tell us what the game is."

"Very well, we'll see." Conway took a few paces forward to the partition between the cabin and the pilot's cockpit, which was situated in front and somewhat above. There was a pane of glass, about six inches square and made to slide open, through which the pilot, by turning his head and stooping slightly could communicate with his passengers. Conway tapped on this with his knuckles. The response was almost comically as he had expected. The glass panel slid sideways and the barrel of a revolver obtruded. Not a word; just that. Conway retreated without arguing the point, and the panel slid back again.

Mallinson, who had watched the incident, was only partly satisfied. "I don't suppose he'd have dared to shoot," he commented. "It's probably bluff."

"Quite," agreed Conway, "but I'd rather leave you to make sure."

"Well, I do feel we ought to put up some sort of a fight before giving in tamely like this."

Conway was sympathetic. He recognised the convention, with all its associations of red-coated soldiers and school history-books, that Englishmen fear nothing, never surrender, and are never defeated. He said: "Putting up a fight without a decent chance of winning is a poor game, and I'm not that sort of hero."

"Good for you, sir," interposed Barnard heartily. "When somebody's got you by the short hairs you may as well give in pleasantly and admit it. For my part I'm going to enjoy life while it lasts and have a cigar. I hope you don't think a little bit of extra danger matters to us?"

"Not so far as I'm concerned, but it might bother Miss Brinklow."

Barnard was quick to make amends. "Pardon me, madam, but do you very much object if I smoke?"

"Not at all," she answered graciously. "I don't do so myself, but I just love the smell of a cigar."

Conway felt that of all the women who could possibly have made such a remark, she was easily the most typical. Anyhow, Mallinson's excitement had called a little, and to show friendliness he offered him a cigarette, though he did not light one himself. "I know how you feel," he said gently.

"It's a bad look-out, and it's all the worse, in some ways, because there isn't much we can do about it."

"And all the better, too, in other ways," he could not help adding to himself. For he was still immensely fatigued. There was also in his nature a trait which some people might have called laziness, though it was not quite that. No one was capable of harder work, when it had to be done, and few could better shoulder responsibility; but the facts remained that he was not passionately fond of activity, and did not enjoy responsibility at all. Both were included in his job, and he made the best of them, but he was always ready to give way to anyone else who could function as well or better. It was partly this, no doubt, that had made his success in the Service less striking than it might have been. He was not ambitious enough to shove his way past others, or to make an important parade of doing nothing when there was really nothing doing. His despatches were sometimes laconic to the point of curtness, and his calm in emergencies, though admired, was often suspected of being too sincere. Authority likes to feel that a man is imposing some effort on himself, and that his apparent nonchalance is only a cloak to disguise an outfit of well-bred emotions. With Conway the dark suspicion had sometimes been current that he really was as unruffled as he looked, and that whatever happened, he did not give a damn. But this, too, like the laziness, was an imperfect interpretation. What most observers failed to perceive in him was

39

something quite bafflingly simple—a love of quietness, contemplation, and being alone.

Now, since he was so inclined and there was nothing else to do, he leaned back in the basket chair and went definitely to sleep. When he woke he noticed that the others, despite their various anxieties, had likewise succumbed. Miss Brinklow was sitting bolt upright with her eyes closed, like some rather dingy and outmoded idol; Mallinson had lolled forward in his place with his chin in the palm of a hand. The American was even snoring. Very sensible of them all, Conway thought; there was no point in wearying themselves with shouting. But immediately he was aware of certain physical sensations in himself—slight dizziness and heart-thumping and a tendency to inhale sharply and with effort. He remembered similar symptoms once before—in Switzerland.

Then he turned to the window and gazed out. The surrounding sky had cleared completely, and in the light of late afternoon there came to him a vision which, for the instant, snatched the remaining breath out of his lungs. Far away, at the very limit of distance, lay range upon range of snow-peaks, festooned with glaciers, and floating, in appearance, upon vast levels of cloud. They compassed the whole arc of the circle, merging towards the west in a horizon that was fierce, almost garish in colouring, like an impressionist back-cloth done by some half-mad genius. And meanwhile the plane, on that stupendous stage, was droning over

40

an abyss in face of a sheer white wall that seemed part of the sky itself until the sun caught it. Then, like a dozen piled-up Jungfraus seen from Mürren, it flamed into superb and dazzling incandescence.

Conway was not apt to be easily impressed, and as a rule he did not care for "views"—especially the more famous ones for which thoughtful municipalities provide garden-seats. Once, on being taken to Tiger Hill, near Darjeeling, to watch the sunrise upon Everest, he had found the highest mountain in the world a definite disappointment. But this fearsome spectacle beyond the window-pane was of different calibre; it had no air of posing to be admired. There was something raw and monstrous about those uncompromising ice-cliffs, and a certain sublime impertinence in approaching them thus. He pondered, envisaging maps, calculating distances, estimating times and speeds. Then he became aware that Mallinson had wakened also. He touched the youth on the arm.

2

IT was typical of Conway that he let the others waken for themselves, and made small response to their exclamations of astonishment; yet later, when Barnard sought his opinion, gave it with something of the detached fluency of a university professor elucidating a problem. He thought it likely, he said, that they were still in India; they had been flying east for several hours, too high to see much, but probably the course had been along some river valley—one stretching roughly east and west. "I wish I hadn't to rely on memory, but my impression is that the valley of the upper Indus fits in well enough. That would have brought us by now to a very spectacular part of the world—and, as you see, so it has."

"You recognise where we are, then?" Barnard interrupted.

"Well, no—I've never been anywhere near here before, but I wouldn't be surprised if that mountain is Nanga Parbat—the one Mummery lost his life on. In structure and general lay-out it seems in accord with all I've heard about it."

"You are a mountaineer yourself?"

"In my younger days I was keen. Only the usual Swiss climbs, of course."

Mallinson intervened peevishly: "There'd be

more point in discussing where we're going to. I wish to God somebody could tell us."

"Well, it looks to me as if we're heading for that range yonder," said Barnard. "Don't you think so, Conway? You'll excuse me calling you that, but if we're all going to have a little adventure together, it's a pity to stand on ceremony."

Conway thought it very natural that anyone should call him by his own name, and found Barnard's apologies for so doing a trifle needless. "Oh, certainly," he agreed, and added: "I think that range must be the Karakorams. There are several passes if our man intends to cross them."

"Our man?" exclaimed Mallinson. "You mean our maniac! I reckon it's time we dropped the kidnapping theory. We're far past the Frontier country by now—there aren't any tribes living around here. The only explanation I can think of is that the fellow's a raving lunatic. Would anybody except a lunatic fly into this sort of country?"

"I know that nobody except a damn fine airman *could*," retorted Barnard. "I never was great at geography, but I understand that these are reputed to be the highest mountains in the world, and if that's so, it'll be a pretty first-class performance to cross them."

"And also the will of God," put in Miss Brinklow unexpectedly.

Conway did not offer his opinion. The will of God or the lunacy of man—it seemed to him that you could take your choice, if you wanted a good enough reason for most things. Or, alternatively (and he thought of it as he contemplated the small orderliness of the cabin against the window-background of such frantic natural scenery), the will of man and the lunacy of God. It must be satisfying to be quite certain which way to look at it. Then, while he watched and pondered, a strange transformation took place. The light turned to bluish over the whole mountain, with the lower slopes darkening to violet. Something deeper than his usual aloofness rose in him—not quite excitement, still less fear, but a sharp intensity of expectation. He said: "You're quite right, Barnard, this affair grows more and more remarkable."

"Remarkable or not, I don't feel inclined to propose a vote of thanks about it," Mallinson persisted. "We didn't ask to be brought here, and Heaven knows what we shall do when we get *there*—wherever *there* is. And I don't see that it's any less of an outrage because this fellow happens to be a stunt flyer. Even if he is, he can be just as much a lunatic. I once heard of a pilot going mad in mid-air. This fellow must have been mad from the beginning. That's my theory, Conway."

Conway was silent. He found it irksome to be continually shouting above the roar of the machine, and after all, there was little point in arguing possibilities. But when Mallinson pressed for an opinion, he said: "Very well-organised lunacy, you know. Don't forget the landing for petrol, and also that this was the only machine that could climb to such a height."

"That doesn't prove he isn't mad. He may have been mad enough to arrange everything."

"Yes, of course, that's possible."

"Well, then, we've got to decide on a plan of action. What are we going to do when he comes to earth? If he doesn't crash and kill us all, that is. What are we going to *do*? Rush forward and congratulate him on his marvellous flight, I suppose."

"Not on your life," answered Barnard. "I'll leave you to do all the rushing forward."

Again Conway was loth to prolong the argument, especially since the American, with his level-headed banter, seemed quite capable of handling it himself. Already Conway found himself reflecting that the party might have been far less fortunately constituted. Only Mallinson was inclined to be cantankerous, and that might partly be due to the altitude. Rarefied air had different effects on people; Conway, for instance, derived from it a combination of mental clarity and physical apathy that was not unpleasant. Indeed, he breathed the clear cold air in little spasms of content. The whole situation, no doubt, was appalling, but he had no power at the moment to resent anything that proceeded so purposefully and with such captivating interest.

And there came over him, too, as he stared at that superb mountain-piece, a glow of satisfaction that there were such places still left on earth—distant, inaccessible, as yet unhumanised. The icy rampart of the Karakorams was now more striking than ever against the northern sky, which had become mouse-coloured and sinister; the peaks had a chill gleam; utterly majestic and remote, their very nameless-ness had dignity. Those few thousand feet by which they fell short of the known giants might save them eternally from the climbing expedition; they offered a less tempting lure to the record-breaker. Conway was the antithesis of such a type; he was inclined to see vulgarity in the Western ideal of superlatives, and "the utmost for the highest" seemed to him a less reasonable and perhaps more commonplace proposition than "the much for the high." He did not, in fact, care for excessive striving, and he was bored by mere exploits.

While he was still contemplating the scene, twilight fell, steeping the depths in a rich velvet-gloom that spread upwards like a dye. Then the whole range, much nearer now, paled into fresh splendour; a full moon rose, touching each peak in succession like some celestial lamp-lighter, until the long horizon glittered against a blue-black sky. The air grew cold and a wind sprang up, tossing the machine uncomfortably. These new distresses lowered the spirits of the passengers; it had not been reckoned that the flight could go on after dusk, and now the last hope lay in the exhaustion of petrol. That, however, was bound to come soon. Mallinson began to argue about it, and Conway,

46

with some reluctance, for he really did not know, gave as his estimate that the utmost distance might be anything up to a thousand miles, of which they must already have covered most. "Well, where would that bring us to?" queried the youth miserably.

"It's not easy to judge, but probably some part of Tibet. If these are the Karakorams, Tibet lies beyond. One of the crests, by the way, must be K2, which is generally counted the second highest mountain in the world."

"Next on the list after Everest," commented Barnard. "Gee, this is some scenery."

"And from a climber's point of view much stiffer than Everest. The Duke of Abruzzi gave it up as an absolutely impossible peak."

"*Oh, God!*" muttered Mallinson testily, but Barnard laughed. "I guess you must be the official guide on this trip, Conway, and I'll allow that if only I'd got a flask of café cognac I wouldn't care if it's Tibet or Tennessee."

"But what are we going to do about it?" urged Mallinson again. "Why are we here? What can be the point of it all? I don't see how you can make jokes about it."

"Well, it's as good as making a scene about it, young feller. Besides, if the man *is* a loonie, as you've suggested, there probably *isn't* any point."

"He *must* be mad. I can't think of any other explanation. Can you, Conway?"

Conway shook his head.

Miss Brinklow turned round, as she might have done during the interval of a play. "As you haven't asked my opinion, perhaps I oughtn't to give it," she began, with shrill modesty, "but I should like to say that I agree with Mr. Mallinson. I'm sure the poor man can't be quite right in his head. The pilot, I mean, of course. There would be no excuse for him, anyhow, if he were *not* mad." She added, shouting confidentially above the din: "And do you know, this is my first trip in the air! My very first! Nothing would ever induce me to do it before, though a friend of mine tried her very best to persuade me to fly from London to Paris."

"And now you're flying from India to Tibet instead," said Barnard. "That's the way things happen."

She went on: "I once knew a missionary who had been in Tibet. He said the Tibetans were very odd people. They believe we are descended from monkeys."

"Remarkably cute of 'em."

"Oh dear no, I don't mean in the modern way. They've had the belief for hundreds of years—it's only one of their superstitions. Of course I'm against it all myself, and I think Darwin was far worse than any Tibetan. I take my stand on the Bible."

"Fundamentalist, I suppose?"

But Miss Brinklow did not appear to understand the term. "I used to belong to the L.M.S.," she shrieked, "but I disagreed with them about infant baptism."

Conway continued to feel this was a rather comic remark long after it had occurred to him that the initials were those of the London Missionary Society. Still picturing the inconveniences of holding a theological argument at Euston Station, he began to think that there was something slightly fascinating about Miss Brinklow. He even wondered if he could offer her any article of his clothing for the night, but decided at length that her constitution was probably wirier than his. So he huddled up, closed his eyes, and went quite easily and peacefully to sleep.

And the flight proceeded.

Suddenly they were all wakened by a lurch of the machine. Conway's head struck the window, dazing him for the moment; a returning lurch sent him floundering between the two tiers of seats. It was much colder. The first thing he did, automatically, was to glance at his watch; it showed half-past one—he must have been asleep for some time. His ears were full of a loud flapping sound, which he took to be imaginary until he realised that the engine had been shut off and that the plane was rushing against a gale. Then he stared through the window and could see the earth quite close—vague and snail-grey, scampering underneath. "He's going to land!" Mallinson shouted; and Barnard, who had also been flung out of his seat, responded with a saturnine: "If he's lucky." Miss Brinklow, whom the entire commotion seemed to have disturbed least of all, was adjusting her hat as calmly as if Dover Harbour were just in sight.

Presently the plane touched ground. But it was a bad landing this time—"Oh, my God, damned bad, *damned* bad!" Mallinson groaned as he clutched at his seat during ten seconds of crashing and swaying. Something was heard to strain and snap, and one of the tyres exploded. "That's done it," he added in tones of anguished pessimism. "A broken tail-skid—we'll have to stay where we are now, that's certain."

Conway, never talkative at times of crisis, stretched his stiffened legs and felt his head where it had banged against the window. A bruise—nothing much. He must do something to help these people. But he was the last of the four to stand up when the plane came to rest. "Steady," he called out as Mallinson wrenched open the door of the cabin and prepared to make the jump to earth; and eerily, in the comparative silence, the youth's answer came: "No need to be steady—this looks like the end of the world—there's not a soul about, anyhow."

A moment later, chilled and shivering, they were all aware that this was so. With no sound in their ears save the fierce gusts of wind and their own crunching footsteps, they felt themselves at the mercy of something dour and savagely melancholy—a mood in which both earth and air were saturated. The moon looked to have disappeared behind clouds, and starlight illumined a tremendous emptiness heaving with wind. Without thought or knowledge, one could have guessed that this bleak world was mountain-high, and that the mountains rising from it were mountains on top of mountains. A range of them gleamed on a far horizon like a row of dog-teeth.

Mallinson, feverishly active, was already making for the cockpit. "I'm not scared of the fellow on land, whoever he is," he cried. "I'm going to tackle him right away . . . ."

The others watched, hypnotised by the spectacle of such energy, though apprehensive also. Conway sprang after him, but too late to prevent the investigation. After a few seconds, however, the youth dropped down again, gripping his arm and muttering in a hoarse, sobered staccato: "I say, Conway, it's queer. . . . I think the fellow's ill or dead or something. . . . I can't get a word out of him. Come up and look. . . . I took his revolver, at any rate."

"Better give it to me," said Conway, and though still rather dazed by the recent blow on his head, he nerved himself for action. Of all times and places and situations on earth, this seemed to him to combine the most hideous discomforts. He hoisted himself stiffly into a position from which he could see, not very well, into the enclosed cockpit. There was a strong smell of petrol, so he did not risk striking a match. He could just discern the pilot, huddled forward, his head sprawling over the

51

controls. He shook him, unfastened his helmet, and loosened the clothes round his neck. A moment later he turned round to report: "Yes, there's something happened to him. We must get him out." But an observer might have added that something had happened to Conway as well. His voice was sharper, more incisive; no longer did he sound to be hovering on the brink of some profound doubtfulness. The time, the place, the cold, his fatigue, were now of less account; there was a job that simply had to be done, and the more conventional part of him was uppermost and preparing to do it.

With Barnard and Mallinson assisting, the pilot was extracted from his seat and lifted to the ground. He was unconscious, not dead. Conway had no particular medical knowledge, but, as to most men who have lived in outlandish places, the phenomena of illness were mostly familiar. "Possibly a heart attack brought on by the high altitude," he diagnosed, stooping over the unknown man. "We can do very little for him out here—there's no shelter from this infernal wind. Better get him inside the cabin, and ourselves too. We haven't an idea where we are, and it's hopeless to make a move until daylight."

The verdict and the suggestion were both accepted without dispute. Even Mallinson concurred. They carried the man into the cabin and laid him full-length along the gangway between the seats. The interior was no warmer than outside, but offered a screen to the flurries of wind. It was the wind, before much time had passed, that became the central preoccupation of them all—the *leit-motif*, as it were, of the whole mournful night-piece. It was not an ordinary wind. It was not merely a strong wind or a cold wind. It was somehow a frenzy that lived all around them, a master stamping and ranting over his own domain. It tilted the loaded machine and shook it viciously, and when Conway glanced through the windows it seemed as if the same wind were whirling splinters of light out of the stars.

The stranger lay inert, while Conway, with difficulty in the dimness and confined space, made what examination he could. But it did not reveal much. "His heart's faint," he said at last, and then Miss Brinklow, after groping in her handbag, created a small sensation. "I wonder if this would be any use to the poor man," she proffered condescendingly. "I never touch a drop myself, but I always carry it with me in case of accidents. And this *is* a sort of accident, isn't it?"

"I should say it was," replied Conway with grimness. He unscrewed the bottle, smelt it, and poured some of the brandy into the man's mouth. "Just the stuff for him. Thanks." After an interval the slightest movement of eyelids was visible under the match-flame. Mallinson suddenly became hysterical. "I can't help it," he cried, laughing wildly. "We all look such a lot of damn fools striking matches over a corpse. . . . And he isn't much of a beauty, is he? Chink, I should say, if he's anything at all."

"Possibly." Conway's voice was level and rather severe. "But he's not a corpse yet. With a bit of luck we may bring him round."

"Luck? It'll be his luck, not ours."

"Don't be too sure. And shut up for the time being, anyhow."

There was enough of the schoolboy still in Mallinson to make him respond to the curt command of a senior, though he was obviously in poor control of himself. Conway, though sorry for him, was more concerned with the immediate problem of the pilot, since he, alone of them all, might be able to give some explanation of their plight. Conway had no desire to discuss the matter further in a merely speculative way; there had been enough of that during the journey. He was uneasy now beyond his continuing mental curiosity, for he was aware that the whole situation had ceased to be excitingly perilous and was threatening to become a trial of endurance ending in catastrophe. Keeping vigil throughout the gale-tormented night, he faced facts none the less frankly because he did not trouble to enunciate them to the others. He guessed that the flight had progressed far beyond the western range of the Himalaya towards the less-known heights of the Kuen-Lun. In that event they would by now have reached the loftiest and least hospitable part of the earth's surface—the Tibetan plateau, two miles high even in its lowest valleys—a

54

vast, uninhabited, and largely unexplored region of wind-swept upland. Somewhere they were, in that forlorn country, marooned in far less comfort than on most desert islands. Then abruptly, as if to answer his curiosity by increasing it, a rather awe-inspiring change took place. The moon, which he had thought to be hidden by clouds, swung over the lip of some shadowy eminence and, whilst still not showing itself directly, unveiled the darkness ahead. Conway could see the outline of a long valley, with rounded sad-looking hills on either side, not very high from where they rose, and jet-black against the deep electric blue of the night-sky. But it was to the head of the valley that his eyes were led irresistibly, for there, soaring into the gap, and magnificent in the full shimmer of moonlight, appeared what he took to be the loveliest mountain on earth. It was an almost perfect cone of snow, simple in outline as if a child had drawn it, and impossible to classify as to size, height, or nearness. It was so radiant, so serenely poised, that he wondered for a moment if it were real at all. Then, while he gazed, a tiny puff clouded the edge of the pyramid, giving life to the vision before the faint rumble of the avalanche confirmed it.

He had an impulse to rouse the others to share the spectacle, but decided after consideration that its effect might not be tranquillising. Nor was it so, from a common sense view-point; such virgin splendours merely emphasised the facts of isolation and danger. There was quite a probability that the nearest human settlement was hundreds of miles away. And they had no food; they were unarmed except for one revolver; the aeroplane was damaged and almost fuel-less, even if anyone had known how to fly. They had no clothes suited to the terrific chills and winds; Mallinson's motoring-coat and his own ulster were quite inadequate, and even Miss Brinklow, woollied and mufflered as for a polar expedition (ridiculous, he had thought, on first beholding her), could not be feeling happy. They were all, too, except himself, affected by the altitude. Even Barnard had sunk into melancholy under the strain. Mallinson was muttering to himself; it was clear what would happen to him if these hardships went on for long. In face of such distressful prospects Conway found himself quite unable to restrain an admiring glance at Miss Brinklow. She was not, he reflected, a normal person; no woman who taught Afghans to sing hymns could be considered so. But she was, after every calamity, still normally abnormal, and he was deeply obliged to her for it. "I hope you're not feeling too bad?" he said sympathetically, when he caught her eye.

"The soldiers during the War had to suffer worse things than this," she replied.

The comparison did not seem to Conway a very valuable one. In point of fact, he had never spent a night in the trenches quite so thoroughly unpleasant, though doubtless many others had. He concentrated his attention on the pilot, now breathing fitfully and sometimes slightly stirring. Probably Mallinson was right in guessing the man Chinese. He had the typical Mongol nose and cheekbones, despite his successful impersonation of a British flight-lieutenant. Mallinson had called him ugly, but Conway, who had lived in China, thought him a fairly passable specimen, though now, in the burnished circle of matchflame, his pallid skin and gaping mouth were not pretty.

The night dragged on, as if each minute were something heavy and tangible that had to be pushed to make way for the next. Moonlight faded after a time, and with it that distant spectre of the mountain; then the triple mischiefs of darkness, cold, and wind increased until dawn. As at its signal the wind dropped, leaving the world in compassionate quietude. Framed in the pale triangle ahead, the mountain showed again, grey at first, then silver, then pink as the earliest sunrays caught the summit. In the lessening gloom the valley itself took shape, revealing a floor of rock and shingle sloping upwards. It was not a friendly picture, but to Conway, as he surveyed, there came a queer perception of fineness in it, of something that had no romantic appeal at all, but a steely, almost an intellectual quality. The white pyramid in the distance compelled the mind's assent as passionlessly as a Euclidean theorem, and when at last the sun rose into a sky of deep delphinium-blue, he felt only a little less than comfortable again.

As the air grew warmer the others wakened, and

he suggested carrying the pilot into the open, where the sharp dry air and the sunlight might help to revive him. This was done, and they began a second and pleasanter vigil. Eventually the man opened his eyes and began to speak convulsively. His four passengers stooped over him, listening intently to sounds that were meaningless except to Conway, who occasionally made answers. After some time the man became weaker, talked with increasing difficulty, and finally died. That was about mid-morning.

Conway then turned to his companions. "I'm sorry to say he told me very little—little, I mean, compared with what we should like to know. Merely that we were in Tibet, which is obvious. He didn't give any coherent account of why he had brought us here, but he seemed to know the locality. He spoke a kind of Chinese that I don't understand very well, but I think he said something about a lamasery near here—along the valley, I gathered—where we could get food and shelter. Shangri-La, he called it. *La* is Tibetan for mountain-pass. He was most emphatic that we should go there."

"Which doesn't seem to me any reason at all why we should," said Mallinson. "After all, he was probably off his head. Wasn't he?"

"You know as much about that as I do. But if we don't go to this place, where else are we to go?"

"Anywhere you like, I don't care. All I'm certain

of is that this Shangri-La, if it's in that direction, must be a few extra miles from civilisation. I should feel happier if we were lessening the distance, not increasing it. Damnation, man, aren't you going to get us back?"

Conway replied patiently: "I don't think you properly understand the position, Mallinson. We're in a part of the world that no one knows very much about, except that it's difficult and dangerous, even for a fully equipped expedition. Considering that hundreds of miles of this sort of country probably surround us on all sides, the notion of walking back to Peshawur doesn't strike me as very hopeful."

"I don't think I could possibly manage it," said Miss Brinklow seriously.

Barnard nodded. "It looks as if we're damned lucky, then, if this lamasery *is* round the corner."

"Comparatively lucky, maybe," agreed Conway. "After all, we've no food, and, as you can see for yourselves, the country isn't the kind it would be easy to live on. In a few hours we shall all be famished. And then to-night, if we were to stay here, we should have to face the wind and the cold again. It's not a pleasant prospect. Our only chance, it seems to me, is to find some other human beings, and where else should we begin looking for them except where we've been told they exist?"

"And what if it's a trap?" asked Mallinson, but Barnard supplied an answer. "A nice warm trap," he said, "with a piece of cheese in it, would suit me down to the ground."

They laughed, except Mallinson, who looked distraught and nerve-racked. Finally Conway went on: "I take it, then, that we're all more or less agreed? There's an obvious way along the valley—it doesn't look too steep, though we shall have to take it slowly. In any case, we could do nothing here—we couldn't even bury this man without dynamite. Besides, the lamasery people may be able to supply us with porters for the journey back. We shall need them. I suggest we start at once, so that if we don't locate the place by late afternoon we shall have time to return for another night in the cabin."

"And supposing we *do* locate it?" queried Mallinson, still intransigent. "Have we any guarantee that we shan't be murdered?"

"None at all. But I think it is a less, and perhaps also a preferable risk to being starved or frozen to death." He added, feeling that such chilly logic might not be entirely suited for the occasion: "As a matter of fact, murder is the very last thing one would expect in a Buddhist monastery. It would be rather less likely than being killed in an English cathedral."

"Like St. Thomas of Canterbury," said Miss Brinklow, nodding an emphatic agreement, but completely spoiling his point. Mallinson shrugged his shoulders and responded with melancholy irritation: "Very well, then, we'll be off to Shangri-La. Wherever and whatever it is, we'll try it. But let's hope it's not half-way up that mountain."

The remark served to fix their glances on the

glittering cone towards which the valley pointed. Sheerly magnificent it looked in the full light of day; and then their gaze turned to a stare, for they could see, far away and approaching them down the slope, the figures of men. "Providence!" whispered Miss Brinklow.

3

PART of Conway was always an onlooker, however active might be the rest. Just now, while waiting for the strangers to come nearer, he refused to be fussed into deciding what he might or mightn't do in any number of possible contingencies. And this was not bravery, or coolness, or any especially sublime confidence in his own power to make decisions on the spur of the moment. It was, if the worst view be taken, a form of indolence—an unwillingness to interrupt his mere spectator's interest in what was happening.

As the figures moved down the valley they revealed themselves to be a party of a dozen or more, carrying with them a hooded chair. In this, a little later, could be discerned a person robed in blue. Conway could not imagine where they were all going, but it certainly seemed providential, as Miss Brinklow had said, that such a detachment should chance to be passing just there and then. As soon as he was within hailing distance he left his own party and walked ahead, though not hurriedly, for he knew that Orientals enjoy the ritual of meeting and like to take their time over it. Halting when a few yards off, he bowed with due courtesy. Much to his surprise the robed figure stepped from the chair, came forward with dignified deliberation, and held out his hand. Conway responded, and observed an old or elderly Chinese, grey-haired, clean-shaven, and rather pallidly decorative in a silk embroidered gown. He in his turn appeared to be submitting Conway to the same kind of ready reckoning. Then, in precise and perhaps too accurate English, he said: "I am from the lamasery of Shangri-La."

Conway bowed again, and after a suitable pause began to explain briefly the circumstances that had brought him and his three companions to such an unfrequented part of the world. At the end of the recital the Chinese made a gesture of understanding. "It is indeed remarkable," he said, and gazed reflectively at the damaged aeroplane. Then he added: "My name is Chang, if you would be so good as to present me to your friends."

Conway managed to smile urbanely. He was rather taken with this latest phenomenon—a Chinese who spoke perfect English and observed the social formalities of Bond Street amidst the wilds of Tibet. He turned to the others, who had by this time caught up and were regarding the encounter with varying degrees of astonishment. "Miss Brinklow . . . Mr. Barnard, who is an American . . . Mr. Mallinson . . . and my own name is Conway. We are all glad to see you, though the meeting is almost as puzzling as the fact of our being here at all. Indeed, we were just about to make our way to your lamasery, so it is doubly fortunate. If you could give us directions for the journey——"

"There is no need for that. I shall be delighted to act as your guide."

"But I could not think of putting you to such trouble. It is exceedingly kind of you, but if the distance is not far——"

"It is not far, but it is not easy either. I shall esteem it an honour to accompany you and your friends."

"But really——"

"I must insist."

Conway thought that the argument, in its context of place and circumstance, was in some danger of becoming ludicrous. "Very well," he responded. "I'm sure we are all most obliged."

Mallinson, who had been sombrely enduring these pleasantries, now interposed with something of the shrill acerbity of the barrack-square. "Our stay won't be long," he announced curtly. "We shall pay for anything we have, and we should like to hire some of your men to help us on our journey back. We want to return to civilisation as soon as possible."

"And are you so very certain that you are away from it?"

The query, delivered with much suavity, only stung the youth to further sharpness. "I'm quite sure I'm far away from where I want to be, and so are we all. We shall be grateful for temporary shelter, but we shall be more grateful still if you'll provide means for us to return. How long do you suppose the journey to India will take?"

"I really could not say at all."

"Well, I hope we're not going to have any trouble about it. I've had some experience of hiring native porters, and we shall expect you to use your influence to get us a square deal."

Conway felt that most of all this was rather needlessly truculent, and he was just about to intervene when the reply came, still with immense dignity: "I can only assure you, Mr. Mallinson, that you will be honourably treated and that ultimately you will have no regrets."

"*Ultimately?*" Mallinson exclaimed, pouncing on the word, but there was greater ease in avoiding a scene since wine and fruit were now on offer, having been unpacked by the marching party, stocky Tibetans in sheepskins, fur hats, and yak-skin boots. The wine had a pleasant flavour, not unlike a good hock, while the fruit included mangoes, perfectly ripened and almost painfully delicious after so many hours of fasting. Mallinson ate and drank with incurious relish; but Conway, relieved of immediate worries and reluctant to cherish distant ones, was wondering how mangoes could be cultivated at such an altitude. He was also interested in the mountain beyond the valley; it was a sensational peak, by any standards, and he was surprised that some travellers had not made much of it in the kind of book that a journey in Tibet invariably elicits. He climbed it in mind as he gazed, choosing a route by col and couloir until an exclamation from Mallinson drew his attention back to earth; he looked round then and saw that the Chinese had been earnestly regarding him. "You were contemplating the mountain, Mr. Conway?" came the enquiry.

"Yes. It's a fine sight. It has a name, I suppose?"

"It is called Karakal."

"I don't think I ever heard of it. Is it very high?"

"Over twenty-eight thousand feet."

"Indeed? I didn't realise there would be anything on that scale outside the Himalaya. Has it been properly surveyed? Whose are the measurements?"

"Whose would you expect, my dear sir? Is there anything incompatible between monasticism and trigonometry?"

Conway savoured the phrase and replied: "Oh, not at all—not at all." Then he laughed politely. He thought it a poorish joke, but one perhaps worth making the most of. Soon after that the journey to Shangri-La was begun.

All the morning the climb proceeded, slowly and by easy gradients; but at such height the physical effort was considerable, and none had energy to spare for talk. The Chinese travelled luxuriously in his chair, which might have seemed unchivalrous had it not been absurd to picture Miss Brinklow in such a regal setting. Conway, whom the rarefied air troubled less than the rest, was at pains to catch the occasional chatter of the chairbearers. He knew a very little Tibetan, just enough to gather that the men were glad to be returning to the lamasery. He

66

could not, even had he wished, have continued converse with their leader, since the latter, with eyes closed and face half hidden behind curtains, appeared to have the knack of instant and well-timed sleep.

Meanwhile the sun was warm; hunger and thirst had been appeased, if not satisfied; and the air, clean as from another planet, was more precious with every intake. One had to breathe consciously and deliberately, which, though disconcerting at first, induced after a time an almost ecstatic tranquillity of mind. The whole body moved in a single rhythm of breathing, walking, and thinking; the lungs, no longer discrete and automatic, were disciplined to harmony with mind and limb. Conway, in whom a mystical strain ran in curious consort with scepticism, found himself not unhappily puzzled over the sensation. Once or twice he spoke a cheerful word to Mallinson, but the youth was labouring under the strain of the ascent. Barnard also gasped asthmatically, while Brinklow was engaged in some grim pulmonary warfare which for some reason she made efforts to conceal. "We're nearly at the top," Conway said encouragingly.

"I once ran for a train and felt just like this," she answered.

So also, Conway reflected, there were people who considered cider was just like champagne. It was a matter of palate.

He was surprised to find that beyond his puzzlement he had few misgivings, and none at all on his own behalf. There were moments in life when one opened wide one's soul just as one might open wide one's purse if an evening's entertainment were proving unexpectedly costly but also unexpectedly novel. Conway, on that breathless morning in sight of Karakal, made just such a willing, relieved, yet not excited response to the offer of new experience. After ten years in various parts of Asia he had attained to a somewhat fastidious valuation of places and happenings; and this, he was bound to admit, promised unusually.

About a couple of miles along the valley the ascent grew steeper, but by this time the sun was overclouded and a silvery mist obscured the view. Thunder and avalanches resounded from the snow-fields above; the air took chill, and then, with the sudden changefulness of mountain regions, became bitterly cold. A flurry of wind and sleet drove up, drenching the party and adding immeasurably to their discomfort; even Conway felt at one moment that it would be impossible to go much further. But shortly afterwards it seemed that the summit of the ridge had been reached, for the chair-bearers halted to readjust their burden. The conditions of Barnard and Mallinson, who were both suffering severely, led to renewed delay; but the Tibetans were clearly anxious to press on, and made signs that the rest of the journey would be less fatiguing.

After these assurances it was disappointing to see them uncoiling ropes. "Do they mean to hang us

68

already?" Barnard managed to exclaim, with desperate facetiousness; but the guides soon showed that their less sinister intention was merely to link the party together in ordinary mountaineering fashion. When they observed that Conway was familiar with rope-craft, they became much more respectful and allowed him to dispose the party in his own way. He put himself next to Mallinson with Tibetans ahead and to the rear, and with Barnard and Miss Brinklow and more Tibetans farther back still. He was prompt to notice that the men, during their leader's continuing sleep, were inclined to let him deputise. He felt a familiar quickening of authority; if there were to be any difficult business he would give what he knew was his to give—confidence and command. He had been a first-class mountaineer in his time, and was still, no doubt, pretty good. "You've got to look after Barnard," he told Miss Brinklow, half jocularly, half meaning it; and she answered, with the coyness of an eagle: "I'll do my best, but you know, I've never been roped before."

But the next stage, though occasionally exciting, was less arduous than he had been prepared for, and a relief from the lung-bursting strain of the ascent. The track consisted of a traverse cut along the flank of a rock-wall whose height above them the mist obscured. Perhaps mercifully it also obscured the abyss on the other side, though Conway, who had a good eye for heights, would have liked to see where he was. The path was scarcely more than two feet wide in places, and the manner in which the bearers manœuvred the chair at such points drew his admiration almost as strongly as did the nerves of the occupant who could manage to sleep through it all. The Tibetans were reliable enough, but they seemed happier when the path widened and became slightly downhill. Then they began to sing amongst themselves—lilting barbaric tunes that Conway could imagine orchestrated by Massenet for some Tibetan ballet. The rain ceased and the air grew warmer. "Well, it's quite certain we could never have found our way here by ourselves," said Conway, intending to be cheerful, but Mallinson did not find the remark very comforting. He was, in fact, acutely terrified, and in more danger of showing it now that the worst was over. "Should we be missing much?" he retorted bitterly. The track went on, more sharply downhill, and at one spot Conway found some edelweiss, the first welcome sign of more hospitable levels. But this, when he announced it, consoled Mallinson even less. "Good God, Conway, d'you fancy you're pottering about the Alps? What sort of hell's kitchen are we making for, that's what I'd like to know? And what's our plan of action when we get to it? *What are we going to do?*"

Conway said quietly: "If you'd had all the experiences I've had, you'd know that there are times in life when the most comfortable thing is to do nothing at all. Things happen to you and you just let them happen. The War was rather like that.

70

One is fortunate if, as on this occasion, a touch of novelty seasons the unpleasantness."

"You're too confoundedly philosophic for me. That wasn't your mood during the trouble at Baskul."

"Of course not, because then there was a chance that I could alter events by my own actions. But now, for the moment at least, there's no such chance. We're here because we're here, if you want a reason. I've usually found it a soothing one."

"I suppose you realise the appalling job we shall have to get back by the way we've come. We've been slithering along the face of a perpendicular mountain for the last hour—I've been taking notice."

"So have I."

"Have you?" Mallinson coughed excitedly. "I dare say I'm being a nuisance, but I can't help it. I'm suspicious about all this. I feel we're doing far too much what these fellows want us to. They're getting us into a corner."

"Even if they are, the only alternative was to stay out of it and perish."

"I know that's logical, but it doesn't seem to help. I'm afraid I don't find it as easy as you do to accept the situation. I can't forget that two days ago we were in the Consulate at Baskul. To think of all that has happened since is a bit overwhelming to me. I'm sorry. I'm overwrought. It makes me realise how lucky I was to miss the War—I suppose I should have got hysterical about things. The whole world seems to have gone completely mad all around me. I must be pretty wild myself to be talking to you like this."

Conway shook his head. "My dear boy, not at all. You're twenty-four years old, and you're somewhere about two and a half miles up in the air—those are reasons enough for anything you may happen to feel at the moment. I think you've come through a trying ordeal extraordinarily well—better than I should at your age."

"But don't *you* feel the madness of it all? The way we flew over those mountains, and that awful waiting in the wind, and the pilot dying, and then meeting these fellows—doesn't it all seem nightmarish and incredible when you look back on it?"

"It does, of course."

"Then I wish I knew how you manage to keep so cool about everything."

"Do you really wish that? I'll tell you if you like, though you'll perhaps think me cynical. It's because so much else that I can look back on seems nightmarish too. This isn't the only mad part of the world, Mallinson. After all, if you *must* think of Baskul, do you remember just before we left how the revolutionaries were torturing their captives to get information? An ordinary washing-mangle—quite effective, of course, but I don't think I ever saw anything more comically dreadful. And do you recollect the last message that came through before we were cut off? It was a circular from a Manchester textile firm asking if we knew of any trade

72

openings in Baskul for the sale of corsets! Isn't that mad enough for you? Believe me, in arriving here the worst that can have happened is that we've exchanged one form of lunacy for another. And as for the War, if you'd been in it you'd have done the same as I did—learned how to funk with a stiff lip."

They were still conversing when a sharp but brief ascent robbed them of breath, inducing in a few paces all their earlier strain. Presently the ground levelled, and they stepped out of the mist into clear, sunny air. Ahead, and only a short distance away, lay the lamasery of Shangri-La.

To Conway, seeing it first, it might have been a vision fluttering out of that solitary rhythm in which lack of oxygen had encompassed all his faculties. It was, indeed, a strange and almost incredible sight. A group of coloured pavilions clung to the mountainside with none of the grim deliberation of a Rhineland castle, but rather with the chance delicacy of flower-petals impaled upon a crag. It was superb and exquisite. An austere emotion carried the eye upward from milk-blue roofs to the grey rock bastion above, tremendous as the Wetterhorn above Grindelwald. Beyond that, in a dazzling pyramid, soared the snow-slopes of Karakal. It might well be, Conway thought, the most terrifying mountain-scape in the world, and he imagined the immense stress of snow and glacier against which the rock functioned as a gigantic retaining wall. Some day, perhaps, the whole mountain would split, and a half of Karakal's icy splendour come toppling into the valley. He wondered if the slightness of the risk combined with its fearfulness might even be found agreeably stimulating.

Hardly less an enticement was the downward prospect, for the mountain wall continued to drop, nearly perpendicularly, into a cleft that could only have been the result of some cataclysm in the far past. The floor of the valley, hazily distant, welcomed the eye with greenness; sheltered from winds, and surveyed rather than dominated by the lamasery, it looked to Conway a delightfully favoured place, though if it were inhabited its community must be completely isolated by the lofty and sheerly unscalable ranges on the farther side. Only to the lamasery did there appear to be any climbable egress at all. Conway experienced, as he gazed, a slight tightening of apprehension; Mallinson's misgivings were not, perhaps, to be wholly disregarded. But the feeling was only momentary, and soon merged in the deeper sensation, half mystical, half visual, of having reached at last some place that was an end, a finality.

He never exactly remembered how he and the others arrived at the lamasery, or with what formalities they were received, unroped, and ushered into the precincts. That thin air had a dream-like texture, matching the porcelain-blue of the sky; with every breath and every glance he took in a deep anaesthetising tranquillity that made him impervious alike to Mallinson's uneasiness,

Barnard's witticisms, and Miss Brinklow's coy portrayal of a lady well prepared for the worst. He vaguely recollected surprise at finding the interior spacious, well warmed, and quite clean; but there was no time to do more than notice these qualities, for the Chinese had left his hooded chair and was already leading the way through various ante-chambers. He was quite affable now. "I must apologise," he said, "for leaving you to yourselves on the way, but the truth is, journeys of that kind don't suit me, and I have to take care of myself. I trust you were not too fatigued?"

"We managed," replied Conway with a wry smile.

"Excellent. And now, if you will come with me, I will show you to your apartments. No doubt you would like baths. Our accommodation is simple, but I hope adequate."

At this point Barnard, who was still affected by shortness of breath, gave vent to an asthmatic chuckle. "Well," he gasped, "I can't say I like your climate yet—the air seems to stick on my chest a bit—but you've certainly got a darned fine view out of your front windows. Do we all have to line up for the bathroom, or is this an American hotel?"

"I think you'll find everything quite satisfactory, Mr. Barnard."

Miss Brinklow nodded primly. "I should hope so, indeed."

"And afterwards," continued the Chinese. "I

should be greatly honoured if you will all join me at dinner."

Conway replied courteously. Only Mallinson had given no sign of his attitude in the face of these unlooked-for amenities. Like Barnard, he had been suffering from the altitude, but now, with an effort, he found breath to exclaim: "And afterwards also, if you don't mind, we'll make our plans for getting away. The sooner the better so far as I'm concerned."

4

"SO you see," Chang was saying, "we are less barbarian than you expected. . . ."

Conway, later that evening, was not disposed to deny it. He was enjoying the pleasant mingling of physical ease and mental alertness which seemed to him, of all sensations, the most truly civilised. So far, the appointments of Shangri-La had been all that he could have wished—certainly more than he could ever have expected. That a Tibetan monastery should possess a system of central heating was not, perhaps, so very remarkable in an age that supplied even Lhasa with telephones; but that it should combine the mechanics of Western hygiene with so much else that was Eastern and traditional, struck him as exceedingly singular. The bath, for instance, in which he had recently luxuriated, had been of a delicate green porcelain, a product, according to inscription, of Akron, Ohio. Yet the native attendant had valeted him in Chinese fashion, cleansing his ears and nostrils, and passing a thin silk swab under his low eyelids. He had wondered at the time if and how his three companions were receiving similar attentions.

Conway had lived nearly a decade in China, not wholly in the bigger cities; and he counted it, all things considered, the happiest part of his life. He liked the Chinese, and felt at home with Chinese ways. In particular he liked Chinese cooking, with its subtle undertones of taste; and his first meal at Shangri-La had therefore conveyed a welcome familiarity. He suspected, too, that it might have contained some herb or drug to relieve respiration, for he not only felt a difference himself, but could observe a greater ease among his fellow-guests. Chang, he noticed, ate nothing but a small portion of green salad, and took no wine. "You will excuse me," he had explained at the outset, "but my diet is very restricted—I am obliged to take care of myself."

It was the reason he had been given before, and Conway wondered by what form of invalidism he was afflicted. Regarding him now more closely, he found it difficult to guess his age; his smallish and somehow undetailed features, together with the moist-clay texture of his skin, gave him a look that might either have been that of a young man prematurely old or of an old man remarkably well preserved. He was by no means without attractiveness of a kind; a certain formalised courtesy hung about him in a fragrance too delicate to be detected till one had ceased to think about it. In his embroidered gown of blue silk, with the usual side-slashed skirt and tight-ankled trousers, all the hue of water-colour skies, he had a cool metallic charm which Conway found pleasing, though he knew it was not everybody's taste.

The atmosphere, in fact, was Chinese rather than specifically Tibetan: and this in itself gave Conway an agreeable sensation of being at home, though again it was one that he could not expect the others to share. The room, too, pleased him; it was admirably proportioned, and sparingly adorned with tapestries and one or two fine pieces of lacquer. Light was from paper lanterns, motionless in the still air. He felt a soothing comfort of mind and body, and his renewed speculations as to some possible drug were hardly apprehensive. Whatever it was, if it existed at all, it had relieved Barnard's breathlessness and Mallinson's truculence; both had dined well, finding satisfaction in eating rather than talk. Conway also had been hungry enough, and was not sorry that etiquette demanded gradualness in approaching matters of importance. He had never cared for hurrying a situation that was itself enjoyable, so that the technique well suited him. Not, indeed, until he had begun a cigarette did he give a gentle lead to his curiosity; he remarked then, addressing Chang: "You seem a very fortunate community, and most hospitable to strangers. I don't imagine, though, that you receive them often."

"Seldom indeed," replied the Chinese, with measured stateliness. "It is not a travelled part of the world."

Conway smiled at that. "You put the matter mildly. It looked to me, as I came, the most isolated spot I ever set eyes on. A separate culture might

79

flourish here without contamination from the outside world."

"Contamination, would you say?"

"I use the word in reference to dance-bands, cinemas, sky-signs, and so on. Your plumbing is quite rightly as modern as you can get it—the only certain boon, to my mind, that the East can take from the West. I often think that the Romans were fortunate—their civilisation reached as far as hot baths without touching the fatal knowledge of machinery."

Conway paused. He had been talking with an impromptu fluency which, though not insincere, was chiefly designed to create and control an atmosphere. He was rather good at that sort of thing. Only a willingness to respond to the superfine courtesy of the occasion prevented him from being more openly curious.

Miss Brinklow, however, had no such scruples. "Please," she said, though the word was by no means submissive, "will you tell us about the monastery?"

Chang raised his eyebrows in very gentle deprecation of such immediacy. "It will give me the greatest of pleasure, madam, so far as I am able. What exactly do you wish to know?"

"First of all, how many are there of you here, and what nationality do you belong to?" It was clear that her orderly mind was functioning no less professionally than at the Baskul mission-house.

Chang replied: "Those of us in full lamahood

number about fifty, and there are a few others, like myself, who have not yet attained to complete initiation. We shall do so in due course, it is to be hoped. Till then we are half-lamas—postulants, you might say. As for our racial origins, there are representatives of a great many nations among us, though it is perhaps natural that Tibetans and Chinese make up the majority."

Miss Brinklow would never shirk a conclusion—even a wrong one. "I see. It's really a native monastery, then. Is your head lama a Tibetan or a Chinese?"

"No."

"Are there any English?"

"Several."

"Dear me—that seems very remarkable." Miss Brinklow paused only for breath before continuing: "And now, tell me what you all believe in."

Conway leaned back with somewhat amused expectancy. He had always found pleasure in observing the impact of opposite mentalities; and Miss Brinklow's girl-guide forthrightness applied to lamaistic philosophy promised to be entertaining. On the other hand, he did not wish his host to take fright. "That's rather a big question," he said temporisingly.

But Miss Brinklow was in no mood to temporise. The wine, which had made the others more reposeful, seemed to have given her an extra liveliness. "Of course," she said with a gesture of magnanimity, "I believe in the true religion, but I'm broadminded enough to admit that other people—foreigners, I mean—are quite often sincere in their views. And naturally in a monastery I wouldn't expect to be agreed with."

Her concession evoked a formal bow from Chang. "But why not, madam?" he replied in his precise and flavoured English. "Must we hold that because one religion is true, all others are bound to be false?"

"Well, of course, that's rather obvious, isn't it?"

Conway again interposed. "Really, I think we had better not argue. But Miss Brinklow shares my own curiosity about the motive of this unique establishment."

Chang answered, rather slowly, and in scarcely more than a whisper: "If I were to put it into a very few words, my dear sir, I should say that our prevalent belief is in moderation. We inculcate the virtue of avoiding excess of all kinds—even including, if you will pardon the paradox, excess of virtue itself. In the valleys which you have seen, and in which there are several thousand inhabitants living under the control of our order, we have found that the principle makes for a considerable degree of happiness. We rule with moderate strictness, and in return we are satisfied with moderate obedience. And I think I can claim that our people are moderately sober, moderately chaste, and moderately honest."

Conway smiled. He though it well expressed, besides which it made some appeal to his own temperament. "I think I understand. And I suppose the fellows who met us this morning belonged to your valley people?"

"Yes. I hope you had no fault to find with them during the journey?"

"Oh no, none at all. I'm glad they were more than moderately sure-footed, anyhow. You were careful, by the way, to say that the rule of moderation applied to *them*—am I to take it that it does not apply to your priesthood also?"

But at that Chang could only shake his head. "I regret, sir, that you have touched upon a matter which I may not discuss. I can only add that our community has various faiths and usages, but we are most of us moderately heretical about them. I am deeply grieved that at the moment I cannot say more."

"Please don't apologise. I am left with the pleasantest of speculations." Something in his own voice, as well as in his bodily sensations, gave Conway a renewed impression that he had been very slightly doped. Mallinson appeared to have been similarly affected, though he seized the present chance to remark: "All this has been very interesting, but I really think it's time we began to discuss our plans for getting away. We want to return to India as soon as possible. How many porters can we be supplied with?"

The question, so practical and uncompromising, broke through the crust of suavity to find no sure foothold beneath. Only after a longish interval came

Chang's reply: "Unfortunately, Mr. Mallinson, I am not the proper person to approach. But in any case, I hardly think the matter could be arranged immediately."

"But something has *got* to be arranged! We've all got our work to return to, and our friends and relatives will be worrying about us—we simply *must* return. We're obliged to you for receiving us like this, but we really can't slack about here doing nothing. If it's at all feasible, we should like to set out not later than to-morrow. I expect there are a good many of your people who would volunteer to escort us—we would make it well worth their while, of course."

Mallinson ended nervously, as if he had hoped to be answered before saying so much; but he could extract from Chang no more than a quiet and almost reproachful: "But all this, you know, is scarcely in my province."

"Isn't it? Well, perhaps you can do *something*, at any rate. If you could get us a large-scale map of the country, it would help. It looks as if we shall have a long journey, and that's all the more reason for making an early start. You have maps, I suppose?"

"Yes, we have a great many."

"We'll borrow some of them, then, if you don't mind. We can return them to you afterwards—I suppose you must have communications with the outer world from time to time. And it would be a good idea to send messages ahead, also, to reassure our friends. How far away is the nearest telegraph line?"

Chang's wrinkled face seemed to have acquired a look of infinite patience, but he did not reply.

Mallinson waited a moment and then continued: "Well, where do you send to when you want anything? Anything civilised, I mean." A touch of scaredness began to appear in his eyes and voice. Suddenly he thrust back his chair and stood up. He was pale, and passed his hand wearily across his forehead. "I'm so tired," he stammered, glancing round the room. "I don't feel that any of you are really trying to help me. I'm only asking a simple question. It's obvious you must know the answer to it. When you had all these modern baths installed, how did they get here?"

There followed another silence.

"You won't tell me, then? It's part of the mystery of everything else, I suppose. Conway, I must say I think you're damned slack—why don't *you* get at the truth? I'm all in, for the time being—but—to-morrow, mind—we *must* get away to-morrow—it's essential——"

He would have slid to the floor had not Conway caught him and helped him to a chair. Then he recovered a little, but did not speak.

"To-morrow he will be much better," said Chang gently. "The air here is difficult for the stranger at first, but one soon becomes acclimatised."

Conway felt himself waking from a trance. "Things have been a little trying for him," he commented with rather rueful mildness. He added, more briskly: "I expect we're all feeling it somewhat—I think we'd better adjourn this discussion and go to bed. Barnard, will you look after Mallinson? And I'm sure *you're* in need of sleep too, Miss Brinklow." There had been some signal given, for at that moment a servant appeared. "Yes, we'll get along—good-night—good-night—I shall soon follow." He almost pushed them out of the room, and then, with a scantness of ceremony that was in marked contrast with his earlier manner, turned to his host. Mallinson's reproach had spurred him.

"Now, sir, I don't want to detain you long, so I'd better come to the point. My friend is impetuous, but I don't blame him—he's quite right to make things clear. Our return journey has to be arranged, and we can't do it without help from you or from others in this place. Of course I realise that leaving to-morrow is impossible, and for my own part I hope to find a minimum stay quite interesting. But that, perhaps, is not the attitude of my companions. So if it's true, as you say, that you can do nothing for us yourself, please put us in touch with someone else who can."

The Chinese answered: "You are wiser than your friends, my dear sir, and therefore you are less impatient. I am glad."

"That's not an answer."

Chang began to laugh—a jerky, high-pitched chuckle so obviously forced that Conway recognised in it the polite pretence of seeing an imaginary joke with which the Chinese "saves face" at awkward moments. "I feel sure you have no cause to worry about the matter," came the reply, after an interval. "No doubt in due course we shall be able to give you all the help you need. There are difficulties, as you can imagine, but if we all approach the problem sensibly, and without undue haste——"

"I'm not suggesting haste. I'm merely seeking information about porters."

"Well, my dear sir, that raises another point. I very much doubt whether you will easily find men willing to undertake such a journey. They have their homes in the valley, and they don't care for leaving them to make long and arduous trips outside."

"They can be prevailed upon to do so, though, or else why and where were they escorting you this morning?"

"This morning? Oh, that was quite a different matter."

"In what way? Weren't you setting out on a journey when I and my friends chanced to come across you?"

There was no response to this, and presently Conway continued in a quieter voice: "I understand. Then it was *not* a chance meeting. I had wondered all along, in fact. So you came there deliberately to intercept us. That suggests you must have known of our arrival beforehand. And the interesting question is, *How?*"

His words laid a note of stress amidst the exquisite quietude of the scene. The lantern-light showed up the face of the Chinese; it was calm and statuesque. Suddenly, with a small gesture of the hand, Chang broke the strain; pulling aside a silken tapestry he undraped a window leading to a balcony. Then, with a touch upon Conway's arm, he led him into the cold crystal air. "You are clever," he said dreamily, "but not entirely correct. For that reason I should counsel you not to worry your friends by these abstract discussions. Believe me, neither you nor they are in any danger at Shangri-La."

"But it isn't danger we're bothering about. It's delay."

"I realise that. And of course there *may* be a certain delay—quite unavoidably."

"If it's only for a short time, and genuinely unavoidable, then naturally we shall have to put up with it as best we can."

"How very sensible, for we desire nothing more than that you and your companions should enjoy every moment of your stay here."

"That's all very well, and as I told you, in a personal sense I can't say I shall mind a great deal—it's a new and interesting experience, and in any case, we need some rest."

He was gazing upward to the gleaming pyramid of Karakal. At that moment, in bright moonlight, it seemed as if a hand reached high might just touch it; it was so brittle-clear against the blue immensity beyond.

"To-morrow," said Chang, "you may find it even more interesting. And as for rest, if you are fatigued, there are not many better places in the world."

Indeed, as Conway continued to gaze, a deeper repose overspread him, as if the spectacle were as much for the mind as for the eye. There was hardly any stir of wind, in contrast to the upland gales that had raged the night before; the whole valley, he perceived, was a land-locked harbour, with Karakal brooding over it lighthouse-fashion. The simile grew as he considered it, for there was actually light on the summit, an ice-blue gleam that matched the splendour it reflected. Something prompted him then to enquire the literal interpretation of the name, and Chang's answer came as a whispered echo of his own musing. "Karakal, in the valley patois, means Blue Moon," said the Chinese.

Conway did not pass on his conclusion that the arrival of himself and party at Shangri-La had been in some way expected by its inhabitants. He had had it in mind that he must do so, and he was aware that the matter was important; but when morning came his awareness troubled him so little, in any but a theoretical sense, that he shrank from being the cause of greater concern in others. One part of him insisted that there was something distinctly queer about the place, that the attitude of Chang on the previous evening had been far from reassuring, and that the party were virtually prisoners unless and until the authorities chose to do more for them. And it was clearly his duty to compel them to action. After all, he was a representative of the British Government, if nothing else; it was iniquitous that the inmates of a Tibetan monastery should refuse him any proper request. . . . That, no doubt, was the normal official view that would be taken; and part of Conway was both normal and official. No one could better play the strong man on occasions; during those final difficult days before the evacuation he had behaved in a manner which (he reflected wryly) should earn him nothing less than a knighthood and a Henty school-prize novel entitled *With Conway at Baskul*. To have taken on himself the leadership of some scores of mixed civilians, including women and children, to have sheltered them all in a small consulate during a hot-blooded revolution led by anti-foreign agitators, and to have bullied and cajoled the revolutionaries into permitting a wholesale evacuation by air—it was not, he felt, a bad achievement. Perhaps by pulling wires, and writing interminable reports, he could wangle something out of it in the next New Year Honours. At any rate it had won him Mallinson's fervent admiration. Unfortunately the youth must now be finding him so much more of a disappointment. It was a pity of course, but Conway had grown used to people liking him only because they misunderstood him. He was not genuinely one of those resolute, strong-jawed, hammer-and-tongs empire-builders; the semblance he had given was merely a little one-act play, repeated from time to time by arrangement with fate and the Foreign Office, and for a salary which anyone could turn up in the pages of Whitaker.

The truth was, the puzzle of Shangri-La and of his own arrival there was beginning to exercise over him a rather charming fascination. In any case he found it hard to feel any personal misgivings. His official job was always liable to take him into odd parts of the world, and the odder they were, the less, as a rule, he suffered from boredom; why, then, grumble because accident, instead of a chit from Whitehall, had sent him to this oddest place of all?

He was, in fact, very far from grumbling. When he rose in the morning and saw the soft lapis blue of the sky through the window, he would not have chosen to be elsewhere on earth—either in Peshawur or Piccadilly. He was glad to find that on the others also a night's repose had had a heartening effect. Barnard was able to joke quite cheerfully about beds, baths, breakfasts, and other hospitable amenities. Miss Brinklow admitted that the most strenuous search of her apartment had failed to reveal any of the drawbacks she had been well prepared for. Even Mallinson had acquired a touch of half-sulky complacency. "I suppose we shan't get away to-day after all," he muttered, "unless somebody looks pretty sharp about it. These fellows are typically Oriental—you can't get them to do anything quickly and efficiently."

Conway accepted the remark. Mallinson had been out of England just under a year—long enough, no doubt, to justify a generalisation which he would probably still repeat when he had been out for twenty. And it was true, of course, in some degree. Yet to Conway it did not appear that the Eastern races were abnormally dilatory, but rather that Englishmen and Americans charged about the world in a state of continual and rather preposterous fever-heat. It was a point of view that he hardly expected any fellow-Westerner to share, but he was more faithful to it as he grew older in years and experience. On the other hand, it was true enough that Chang was a subtle quibbler and that there was much justification for Mallinson's impatience. Conway had a slight wish that he could feel impatient too; it would have been so much easier for the boy.

He said: "I think we'd better wait and see what to-day brings. It was perhaps too optimistic to expect them to do anything last night."

Mallinson looked up sharply. "I suppose you think I made a fool of myself, being so urgent? I couldn't help it—I thought that Chinese fellow was damned fishy, and I do still. Did you succeed in getting any sense out of him after I'd gone to bed?"

"We didn't stay talking long. He was rather vague and non-committal about most things."

"We shall jolly well have to keep him up to scratch to-day."

"No doubt," agreed Conway, without marked enthusiasm for the prospect. "Meanwhile this is an excellent breakfast." It consisted of pomelo, tea, and chupatties, perfectly prepared and served. Towards the finish of the meal Chang entered and with a little bow began the exchange of politely conventional greetings which, in the English language, sounded just a trifle unwieldy. Conway would have preferred to talk in Chinese, but so far he had not let it be known that he spoke any Eastern tongue; he felt it might be a useful card up his sleeve. He listened gravely to Chang's courtesies, and gave assurances that he had slept well and felt much better. Chang expressed his pleasure at that, and added: "Truly, as your national poet says, sleep knits up the ravelled sleeve of care."

This display of erudition was not too well received. Mallinson answered with that touch of scorn which any healthy-minded young English-man must feel at the mention of poetry. "I suppose you mean Shakespeare, though I don't recognise the quotation. But I know another one that says 'Stand not upon the order of your going, but go at once.' Without being impolite, that's rather what we should all like to do. And I want to hunt around for those porters right away—this morning, if you've no objection."

The Chinese received the ultimatum impassively, replying at length: "I am sorry to tell you that it would be of little use. I fear we have no men available who would be willing to accompany you so far from their homes."

"But good God, man, you don't suppose we're going to take that for an answer, do you?"

"I am sincerely regretful, but I can suggest no other."

"You seem to have figgered it all out since last night," put in Barnard. "You weren't nearly so dead sure of things then."

"I did not wish to disappoint you when you were so tired from your journey. Now, after a refreshing night, I am in hope that you will see matters in a more reasonable light."

"Look here," intervened Conway briskly, "this sort of vagueness and prevarication won't do. You know we can't stay here indefinitely. It's equally obvious that we can't get away by ourselves. What, then, do you propose?"

Chang smiled with a radiance that was clearly for Conway alone. "My dear sir, it is a pleasure to make the suggestion that is in my mind. To your friend's attitude there was no answer, but to the demand of a wise man there is always a response. You may recollect that it was remarked yesterday—again by your friend, I believe—that we are bound to have occasional communication with the outside world. That is quite true. From time to time we require certain things from distant entrepôts, and it is our habit to obtain them in due course—by what methods and with what formalities I need not trouble you. The point of importance is that such a consignment is expected to arrive shortly, and as the men who make delivery will afterwards return, it seems to me that you might manage to come to some arrangement with them. Indeed I cannot think of a better plan, and I hope, when they arrive——"

"When *do* they arrive?" interrupted Mallinson bluntly.

"The exact date is, of course, impossible to forecast. You have yourself had experience of the difficulty of movement in this part of the world. A hundred things may happen to cause uncertainty—hazards of weather——"

Conway again intervened. "Let's get this clear. You're suggesting that we should employ as porters the men who are shortly due here with some goods. That's not a bad idea as far as it goes, but we must know a little more about it. First, as you've already been asked, when are these people expected? And second, where will they take us?"

"That is a question you would have to put to them."

"Would they take us to India?"

"It is hardly possible for me to say."

"Well, let's have an answer to the other question. When will they be here? I don't ask for a date—I just want some idea whether it's likely to be next week or next year."

"It might be about a month from now. Probably not more than two months."

"Or three, four, or five months," broke in Mallinson hotly. "And you think we're going to wait here for this convoy or caravan or whatever it is to take us God knows where at some completely vague time in the distant future?"

"I think, sir, the phrase 'distant future' is hardly appropriate. Unless something unforeseen occurs, the period of waiting should not be longer than I have said."

"But *two months*! Two months in this place! It's preposterous! Conway, you surely can't contemplate it! Why, two weeks would be the limit."

Chang gathered his gown about him in a little gesture of finality. "I am sorry. I did not wish to offend. The lamasery continues to offer all of you its utmost hospitality for as long as you have the misfortune to remain. I can say no more."

"You don't need to," retorted Mallinson furiously. "And if you think you've got the whip hand over us, you'll soon find you're damn well mistaken! We'll get all the porters we want, don't worry. You can bow and scrape and say what you like——"

Conway laid a restraining hand on his arm. Mallinson in a temper presented a child-like spectacle; he was apt to say anything that came into his head, regardless alike of point and decorum. Conway thought it readily forgivable in one so constituted and circumstanced, but he feared it might affront the more delicate susceptibilities of a

96

Chinese. Fortunately Chang had ushered himself out, with admirable tact, in good time to escape the worst.

5

THEY spent the rest of the morning discussing the matter. It was certainly a shock for four persons who in the ordinary course should have been luxuriating in the clubs and mission-houses of Peshawur, to find themselves faced instead with the prospect of two months in a Tibetan monastery. But it was in the nature of things that the initial shock of their arrival should have left them with slender reserves either of indignation or astonishment; even Mallinson, after his first outburst, subsided into a mood of half-bewildered fatalism. "I'm past arguing about it, Conway," he said, puffing at a cigarette with nervous irritability. "You know how I feel. I've said all along that there's something queer about this business. It's crooked. I'd like to be out of it this minute."

"I don't blame you for that," replied Conway. "Unfortunately, it's not a question of what any of us would like, but of what we've all got to put up with. Frankly, if these people say they won't or can't supply us with the necessary porters, there's nothing for it but to wait till the other fellows come. I'm sorry to admit that we're so helpless in the matter, but I'm afraid it's the truth."

"You mean we've got to stay here for two months?"

"I don't see what else we can do."

Mallinson flicked his cigarette-ash with a gesture of forced nonchalance. "All right, then. Two months it is. And now let's all shout hooray about it."

Conway went on: "I don't see why it should be much worse than two months in any other isolated part of the world. People in our jobs are used to being sent to odd places—I think I can say that of us all. Of course it's bad for those of us who have friends and relatives. Personally, I'm fortunate in that respect—I can't think of anyone who'll worry over me acutely, and my work, whatever it might have been, can easily be done by somebody else."

He turned to the others as if inviting them to state their own cases. Mallinson proffered no information, but Conway knew roughtly how he was situated. He had parents and a girl in England; it made things hard.

Barnard, on the other hand, accepted the position with what Conway had learned to regard as an habitual good-humour. "Well, I reckon I'm pretty lucky myself, for that matter—two months in the penitentiary won't kill me. As for the folks in my own home town, they'll not wink an eyelid—I've always been a bad letter-writer."

"You forget that our names will be in the papers," Conway reminded him. "We shall all be posted missing, and people will naturally assume the worst."

Barnard looked startled for the moment; then he replied, with a slight grin: "Oh yes, that's true, but it don't affect me, I assure you."

Conway was glad it didn't, though the matter remained a little puzzling. He turned to Miss Brinklow, who till then had been remarkably silent; she had not offered any opinion during the interview with Chang. He imagined that she too might have comparatively few personal worries. She said brightly: "As Mr. Barnard says, two months here is nothing to make a fuss about. It's all the same, wherever one is, when one's in the Lord's service. Providence has sent me here. I regard it as a call."

Conway thought the attitude a very convenient one in the circumstances. "I'm sure," he said encouragingly, "you'll find your mission society pleased with you when you *do* return. You'll be able to give much useful information. We'll all of us have had an experience, for that matter. That should be a small consolation."

The talk then became general. Conway was rather surprised at the ease with which Barnard and Miss Brinklow had accommodated themselves to the new prospect. He was relieved, however, as well; it left him with only one disgruntled person to deal with. Yet even Mallinson, after the strain of all the arguing, was experiencing a reaction; he was still perturbed, but more willing to look at the brighter side of things. "Heaven knows what we

100

shall find to do with ourselves," he exclaimed, but the mere fact of making such a remark showed that he was trying to reconcile himself.

"The first rule must be to avoid getting on each other's nerves," replied Conway. "Happily, the place seems big enough, and by no means over-populated. Except for servants, we've only seen one of its inhabitants so far."

Barnard could find another reason for optimism. "We shan't starve, at any rate, if our meals up to now are a fair sample. You know, Conway, this joint isn't run without plenty of hard cash. Those baths, for instance—they cost real money. And I can't see that anybody earns anything here, unless those chaps in the valley have jobs, and even then, they wouldn't produce enough for export. I'd like to know if they work any minerals."

"The whole pace is a confounded mystery," responded Mallinson. "I dare say they've got pots of money hidden away, like the Jesuits. As for the baths, probably some millionaire supporter presented them. Anyhow, it won't worry me, once I get away. I must say, though, the view *is* rather good, in its way. Fine winter-sport centre if it was in the right spot. I wonder if one could get any skiing on some of those slopes up yonder?"

Conway gave him a searching and slightly amused glance. "Yesterday, when I found some edelweiss, you reminded me that I wasn't in the Alps. I think it's my turn to say the same thing now. I wouldn't advise you to try any of your Wengen-

Scheidegg tricks in this part of the world."

"I don't suppose anybody here has ever seen a ski-jump."

"Or even an ice-hockey match," responded Conway banteringly. "You might try to raise some teams. What about 'Gentlemen *v*. Lamas'?"

"It would certainly teach them to play the game," Miss Brinklow put in with sparkling seriousness.

Adequate comment upon this might have been difficult, but there was no necessity, since lunch was about to be served, and its character and promptness combined to make an agreeable impression. Afterwards, when Chang entered, there was small disposition to continue the squabble. With great tactfulness the Chinese assumed that he was still on good terms with everybody, and the four exiles allowed the assumption to stand. Indeed, when he suggested that they might care to be shown a little more of the lamasery buildings, and that if so, he would be pleased to act as guide, the offer was readily accepted. "Why, surely," said Barnard. "We may as well give the place the once-over while we're here. I reckon it'll be a long time before any of us pay a second visit."

Miss Brinklow struck a more thought-giving note. "When we left Baskul in that aeroplane I'm sure I never dreamed we should ever get to a place like this," she murmured as they all moved off under Chang's escort.

"And we don't know yet why we have," answered Mallinson unforgetfully.

102

Conway had no race or colour prejudice, and it was an affectation for him to pretend, as he sometimes did in clubs and first-class railway carriages, that he set any particular store on the "whiteness" of a lobster-red face under a topee. It saved trouble to let it be so assumed, especially in India, and Conway was a conscientious trouble-saver. But in China it had been less necessary; he had had many Chinese friends, and it had never occurred to him to treat them as inferiors. Hence, in his intercourse with Chang, he was sufficiently unpreoccupied to see in him a mannered old gentleman who might not be entirely trustworthy, but who was certainly of high intelligence. Mallinson, on the other hand, tended to regard him through the bars of an imaginary cage; Miss Brinklow was sharp and sprightly, as with the heathen in his blindness; while Barnard's wise-cracking *bonhomie* was of the kind he would have cultivated with a butler.

Meanwhile the grand tour of Shangri-La was interesting enough to transcend these attitudes. It was not the first monastic institution Conway had inspected, but it was easily the largest and, apart from its situation, the most remarkable. The mere procession through rooms and courtyards was an afternoon's exercise, though he was aware of many apartments passed by—indeed, of whole buildings into which Chang did not offer admission. The party were shown enough, however, to confirm the impressions each one of them had formed already. Barnard was more certain than ever that the lamas

103

were rich; Miss Brinklow discovered abundant evidence that they were immoral. Mallinson, after the first novelty had worn off, found himself no less fatigued than on many sight-seeing excursions at lower altitudes; the lamas, he feared, were not likely to be his heroes.

Conway alone submitted to a rich and growing enchantment. It was not so much any individual thing that attracted him as the gradual revelation of elegance, of modest and impeccable taste, of harmony so fragrant that it seemed to gratify the eye without arresting it. Only indeed by a conscious effort did he recall himself from the artist's mood to the connoisseur's, and then he recognised treasures that museums and millionaires alike would have bargained for—exquisite pearl-blue Sung ceramics, paintings in tinted inks preserved for more than a thousand years, lacquers in which the cold and lovely detail of fairyland was not so much depicted as orchestrated. A world of incomparable refinements still lingered tremulously in porcelain and varnish, yielding an instant of emotion before its dissolution into purest thought. There was no boastfulness, no striving after effect, no concentrated attack upon the feelings of the beholder. These delicate perfections had an air of having fluttered into existence like petals from a flower. They would have maddened a collector, but Conway did not collect; he lacked both money and the acquisitive instinct. His liking for Chinese art was an affair of the mind; in a world of increasing

104

noise and hugeness, he turned in private to gentle, precise, and miniature things. And as he passed through room after room, a certain pathos touched him remotely at the thought of Karakal's piled immensity over against such fragile charms.

The lamasery, however, had more to offer than a display of Chinoiserie. One of its features, for instance, was a very delightful library, lofty and spacious, and containing a multitude of books so retiringly housed in bays and alcoves that the whole atmosphere was more of wisdom than of learning, of good manners rather than seriousness. Conway, during a rapid glance at some of the shelves, found much to astonish him; the world's best literature was there, it seemed, as well as a great deal of abstruse and curious stuff that he could not appraise. Volumes in English, French, German, and Russian abounded, and there were vast quantities of Chinese and other Eastern scripts. A section which interested him particularly was devoted to Tibetiana, if it might be so called; he noticed several rarities, among them the *Novo Descubrimento de grao catayo ou dos Regos de Tibet*, by Antonio de Andrada (Lisbon, 1626); Athanasius Kircher's *China* (Antwerp, 1667); Thevenot's *Voyage à la Chine des Pères Grueber et d'Orville*; and Beligatti's *Relazione Inedita di un Viaggio al Tibet*. He was examining the last-named when he noticed Chang's eyes fixed on him in suave curiosity. "You are a scholar, perhaps?" came the enquiry.

Conway found it hard to reply. His period of

105

donhood at Oxford gave him some right to assent, but he knew that the word, though the highest of compliments from a Chinese, had yet a faintly priggish sound for English ears, and chiefly out of consideration for his companions he demurred to it. He said: "I enjoy reading, of course, but my work during recent years hasn't supplied many opportunities for the studious life."

"Yet you wish for it?"

"Oh, I wouldn't say all that, but I'm certainly aware of its attractions."

Mallinson, who had picked up a book, interrupted: "Here's something for your studious life, Conway. It's a map of the country."

"We have a collection of several hundreds," said Chang. "They are all open to your inspection, but perhaps I can save you trouble in one respect. You will not find Shangri-La marked on any."

"Curious," Conway made comment. "I wonder why?"

"There is a very good reason, but I'm afraid that is all I can say."

Conway smiled, but Mallinson looked peevish again. "Still piling up the mystery," he said. "So far we haven't seen much that anyone need bother to conceal."

Suddenly Miss Brinklow came to life out of a mute, processional stupor. "Aren't you going to show us the lamas at work?" she fluted, in the tone which one felt had intimidated many a Cook's man. One felt, too, that her mind was probably full of

106

hazy visions of native handicrafts—prayer-mat weaving, or something picturesquely primitive that she could talk about when she got home. She had an extraordinary knack of never seeming very much surprised, yet of always seeming very slightly indignant—a combination of fixities which was not in the least disturbed by Chang's response: "I am sorry to say it is impossible. The lamas are never—or perhaps I should say only very rarely—seen by those outside the lamahood."

"I guess we'll have to miss 'em then," agreed Barnard. "But I do think it's a real pity. You've no notion how much I'd like to have shaken the hand of your head-man."

Chang acknowledged the remark with benign seriousness. Miss Brinklow, however, was not yet to be side-tracked. "What do the lamas do?" she continued.

"They devote themselves, madam, to contemplation and to the pursuit of wisdom."

"But that isn't *doing* anything."

"Then, madam, they do nothing."

"I thought as much." She found occasion to sum up. "Well, Mr. Chang, it's a pleasure being shown all these things, I'm sure, but you won't convince me that a place like this does any real good. I prefer something more practical."

"Perhaps you would like to take tea?"

Conway wondered at first if this were intended ironically, but it soon appeared not; the afternoon had passed swiftly, and Chang, though frugal in eating, had the typical Chinese fondness for tea-drinking at frequent intervals. Miss Brinklow, too, confessed that visiting art galleries and museums always gave her a touch of headache. The party therefore fell in with the suggestion, and followed Chang through several courtyards to a scene of quite sudden and unmatched loveliness. From a colonnade steps descended to a garden, in which by some tender curiosity of irrigation a lotus-pool lay entrapped, the leaves so closely set that they gave an impression of a floor of moist green tiles. Fringing the pool were posed a brazen menagerie of lions, dragons, and unicorns—each offering a stylised ferocity that emphasised rather than offended the surrounding peace. The whole picture was so perfectly proportioned that the eye was entirely unhastened from one part to another; there was no vying or vanity, and even the summit of Karakal, peerless above the blue-tiled roofs, seemed to have surrendered within the framework of an exquisite artistry. "Pretty little place," commented Barnard, as Chang led the way into an open pavilion which, to Conway's further delight, contained a harpsichord and a modern grand pianoforte. He found this in some ways the crowning astonishment of a rather astonishing afternoon. Chang answered all his questions with complete candour up to a point; the lamas, he explained, held Western music in high esteem, particularly that of Mozart; they had a collection of all the great European compositions, and some were skilled executants on various instruments.

Barnard was chiefly impressed by the transport problem. "D'you mean to tell me that this pi-anno was brought here by the route we came along yesterday?"

"There is no other."

"Well, that certainly beats everything! Why, with a gramophone and a radio you'd be all fixed complete! Perhaps, though, you aren't yet acquainted with up-to-date music?"

"Oh yes, we have had reports, but we are advised that the mountains would make wireless reception impossible, and as for a gramophone, the suggestion has already come before the authorities, but they have felt no need to hurry in the matter."

"I'd believe that even if you hadn't told me," Barnard retorted. "I guess that must be the slogan of your society—'No hurry.'" He laughed loudly and then went on: "Well, to come down to details, suppose in due course your bosses decide that they *do* want a gramophone, what's the procedure? The makers wouldn't deliver here, that's a sure thing. I figger you have an agent in Pekin or Shanghai or somewhere, and I'll bet everything costs a mighty lot of dollars by the time you handle it."

But Chang was no more to be drawn than on a previous occasion. "Your surmises are intelligent, Mr. Barnard, but I fear I cannot discuss them."

So there they were again, Conway reflected,

edging the invisible border-line between what might and might not be revealed. He thought he could soon begin to map out that line in imagination, though the impact of a new surprise deferred the matter. For servants were already bringing in the shallow bowls of scented tea, and along with the agile, lithe-limbed Tibetans there had also entered, quite inconspicuously, a girl in Chinese dress. She went straightway to the harpsichord and began to play a gavotte by Rameau. The first bewitching twang stirred in Conway a pleasure that was beyond amazement; those silvery airs of eighteenth-century France seemed to match in elegance the Sung vases and exquisite lacquers and the lotus-pool beyond; the same death-defying fragrance hung about them, lending immortality through an age to which their spirit was alien. Then he noticed the player. She had the long, slender nose, high cheekbones, and egg-shell pallor of the Manchu; her black hair was drawn tightly back and braided; she looked very finished and miniature. Her mouth was like a little pink convolvulus, and she was quite still, except for her long-fingered hands. As soon as the gavotte was ended, she made a little obeisance and went out.

Chang smiled after her and then, with a touch of personal triumph, upon Conway. "You are pleased?" he queried.

"Who is she?" asked Mallinson, before Conway could reply.

"Her name is Lo-Tsen. She has much skill with

Western keyboard music. Like myself, she has not yet attained the full initiation."

"I should think not, indeed!" exclaimed Miss Brinklow. "She looks hardly more than a child. So you have women lamas, then?"

"There are no sex distinctions among us."

"Extraordinary business, this lamahood of yours," Mallinson commented loftily, after a pause. The rest of the tea-drinking proceeded without conversation; echoes of the harpsichord seemed still in the air, imposing a strange spell. Presently, leading the departure from the pavilion, Chang ventured to hope that the tour had been enjoyable. Conway, replying for the others, see-sawed with the customary courtesies. Chang then assured them of his own equal enjoyment, and hoped they would consider the resources of the music-room and library wholly at their disposal throughout their stay. Conway, with some sincerity, thanked him again. "But what about the lamas?" he added. "Don't they ever want to use them?"

"They yield place with much gladness to their honoured guests."

"Well, that's what I call real handsome," said Barnard. "And what's more, it shows that the lamas do really know we exist. That's a step forward, any-how—makes me feel much more at home. You've certainly got a swell outfit here, Chang, and that little girl of yours plays the pi-anno very nicely. How old would she be, I wonder?"

"I am afraid I cannot tell you."

Barnard laughed. "You don't give away secrets about a lady's age, is that it?"

"Precisely," answered Chang with a faintly shadowing smile.

That evening, after dinner, Conway made occasion to leave the others and stroll out into the calm, moon-washed courtyards. Shangri-La was lovely then, touched with the mystery that lies at the core of all loveliness. The air was cold and still; the mighty spire of Karakal looked nearer, much nearer than by daylight. Conway was physically happy, emotionally satisfied, and mentally at ease; but in his intellect, which was not quite the same thing as mind, there was a little stir. He was puzzled. The line of secrecy that he had begun to map out grew sharper, but only to reveal an inscrutable background. The whole amazing series of events that had happened to him and his three chance companions swung now in a sort of focus; he could not yet understand them, but he believed they were somehow to be understood.

Passing along a cloister, he reached the terrace leaning over the valley. The scent of tuberose assailed him, full of delicate associations; in China it was called "the smell of moonlight." He thought whimsically that if moonlight had a sound also, it might well be the Rameau gavotte he had heard so recently; and that set him thinking of the little Manchu. It had not occurred to him to picture women at Shangri-La; one did not associate their presence with the general practice of monasticism. Still, he reflected, it might not be a disagreeable innovation; indeed, a female harpsichordist might be an asset to any community that permitted itself to be (in Chang's words) "moderately heretical."

He gazed over the edge into the blue-black emptiness. The drop was phantasmal; perhaps as much as a mile. He wondered if he would be allowed to descend it and inspect the valley civilisation that had been talked of. The notion of this strange culture-pocket, hidden amongst unknown ranges, and ruled over by some vague kind of theocracy, interested him as a student of history, apart from the curious though perhaps cognate secrets of the lamasery.

Suddenly, on a flutter of air, came sounds from far below. Listening intently, he could hear gongs and trumpets and also (though perhaps only in imagination) the massed wail of voices. The sounds faded on a veer of the wind, then returned to fade again. But the hint of life and liveliness in those veiled depths served only to emphasise the austere serenity of Shangri-La. Its forsaken courts and pale pavilions simmered in repose from which all the fret of existence had ebbed away, leaving a hush as if movements hardly dared to pass. Then, from a window high above the terrace, he caught the rose-gold of lantern-light; was it there that the lamas devoted themselves to contemplation and the pursuit of wisdom, and were those devotions now in progress? The problem seemed one that he could solve merely by entering at the nearest door and exploring through gallery and corridor until the truth were his; but he knew that such freedom was illusory, and that in fact his movements were watched. Two Tibetans had padded across the terrace and were idling near the parapet. Good-humoured fellows they looked, shrugging their coloured cloaks negligently over a naked shoulder. The whisper of gongs and trumpets uprose again, and Conway heard one of the men question his companion. The answer came: "They have buried Talu." Conway, whose knowledge of Tibetan was very slight, hoped they would continue talking; he could not gather much from a single remark. After a pause the questioner, who was inaudible, resumed the conversation, and obtained answers which Conway overheard and loosely understood as follows:

"He died outside."

"He obeyed the high ones of Shangri-La."

"He came through the air over the great mountains with a bird to hold him."

"Strangers he brought also."

"Talu was not afraid of the outside wind, nor of the outside cold."

"Though he went outside long ago, the valley of Blue Moon remembers him still."

Nothing more was said that Conway could interpret, and after waiting for some time he went back to his own quarters. He had heard enough to turn another key in the locked mystery, and it fitted

114

so well that he wondered he had failed to supply it by his own deductions. It had, of course, crossed his mind, but a certain initial and fantastic unreasonableness about it had been too much for him. Now he perceived that the unreasonableness, however fantastic, was to be swallowed. That flight from Baskul had *not* been the meaningless exploit of a mad-man. It had been something planned, prepared, and carried out at the instigation of Shangri-La. The dead pilot was known by name to those who lived there; he had been one of them, in some sense; his death was mourned. Everything pointed to a high directing intelligence bent upon its own purposes; there had been, as it were, a single arch of intention spanning the inexplicable hours and miles. But what *was* that intention? For what possible reason could four chance passengers in a British Government aeroplane be whisked away to these trans-Himalayan solitudes?

Conway was somewhat aghast at the problem, but by no means wholly displeased with it. It challenged him in the only way in which he was readily amenable to challenge—by touching a certain clarity of brain that only demanded a sufficient task. One thing he decided instantly; the cold thrill of discovery must not yet be communicated—neither to his companions, who could not help him, nor to his hosts, who doubtless would not.

6

"I RECKON some folks have to get used to worse places," Barnard remarked towards the close of his first week at Shangri-La, and it was doubtless one of the many lessons to be drawn. By that time the party had settled themselves into something like a daily routine, and with Chang's assistance the boredom was no more acute than on many a planned holiday. They had all become acclimatised to the atmosphere, finding it quite invigorating so long as heavy exertion was avoided. They had learned that the days were warm and the nights cold, that the lamasery was almost completely sheltered from winds, that avalanches on Karakal were most frequent about midday, that the valley grew a good brand of tobacco, that some foods and drinks were more pleasant than others, and that each one of themselves had personal tastes and peculiarities. They had, in fact, discovered as much about each other as four new pupils of a school from which everyone else was mysteriously absent. Chang was tireless in his efforts to make smooth the rough places. He conducted excursions, suggested occupations, recommended books, talked with his slow, careful fluency whenever there was an awkward pause at meals, and was on every occasion benign, courteous, and resourceful. The line of demarcation was so marked between information willingly supplied and politely declined that the latter ceased to stir resentment, except fitfully from Mallinson. Conway was content to take notice of it, adding another fragment to his constantly accumulating data. Barnard even "jollied" the Chinese after the manner and traditions of a Middle-West rotary convention. "You know, Chang, this is a damned bad hotel. Don't you have any newspapers sent here ever? I'd give all the books in your library for this morning's *Herald-Tribune*." Chang's replies were always serious, though it did not necessarily follow that he took every question seriously. "We have the files of *The Times*, Mr. Barnard, up to a few years ago. But only, I regret to say, the London *Times*."

Conway was glad to find that the valley was not to be "out of bounds," though the difficulties of the descent made unescorted visits impossible. In company with Chang they all spent a whole day inspecting the green floor that was so pleasantly visible from the cliff-edge, and to Conway, at any rate, the trip was of absorbing interest. They travelled in bamboo sedan-chairs, swinging perilously over precipices while their bearers in front and to the rear picked a way nonchalantly down the steep track. It was not a route for the squeamish, but when at last they reached the lower levels of forest and foot-hill the supreme good fortune of the lamasery was everywhere to be realised. For the valley was nothing less than an

117

enclosed paradise of amazing fertility, in which the vertical difference of a few thousand feet spanned the whole gulf between temperate and tropical. Crops of unusual diversity grew in profusion and contiguity, with not an inch of ground untended. The whole cultivated area stretched for perhaps a dozen miles, varying in width from one to five, and, though narrow, it had the luck to take sunlight at the hottest part of the day. The atmosphere, indeed, was pleasantly warm even out of the sun, though the little rivulets that watered the soil were ice-cold from the snows. Conway felt again, as he gazed up at the stupendous mountain wall, that there was a superb and exquisite peril in the scene; but for some chance-placed barrier, the whole valley would clearly have been a lake, nourished continually from the glacial heights around it. Instead of which, a few streams dribbled through to fill reservoirs and irrigate fields and plantations with a disciplined conscientiousness worthy of a sanitary engineer. The whole design was almost uncannily fortunate, so long as the structure of the frame remained unmoved by earthquake or landslide.

But even such vaguely future fears could only enhance the total loveliness of the present. Once again Conway was captivated, and by the same qualities of charm and ingenuity that had made his years in China happier than others. The vast encircling *massif* made a contrast with the tiny lawns and weedless gardens, the painted tea-houses by the stream, and the frivolously toy-like houses.

The inhabitants seemed to him a very successful blend of Chinese and Tibetan; they were cleaner and handsomer than the average of either race, and looked to have suffered little from the inevitable inbreeding of such a small society. They smiled and laughed as they passed the chaired strangers, and had a friendly word for Chang; they were good-humoured and mildly inquisitive, courteous and care-free, busy at innumerable jobs but not in any apparent hurry over them. Altogether Conway thought them one of the pleasantest communities he had ever seen, and even Miss Brinklow, who had been watching for symptoms of pagan degradation, had to admit that everything looked very well "on the surface." She was relieved to find the natives "completely" clothed, even though the women did wear ankle-tight Chinese trousers; and her most imaginative scrutiny of a Buddhist temple revealed only a few items that could be regarded as some-what doubtfully phallic. Chang explained that the temple had its own lamas, who were under loose control from Shangri-La, though not of the same order. There were also, it appeared, a Taoist and a Confucian temple farther along the valley. "The jewel has facets," said the Chinese, "and it is possible that many religions are moderately true."

"I agree with that," said Barnard heartily. "I never did believe in sectarian jealousies. Chang, you're a philosopher—I must remember that re-mark of yours. 'Many religions are moderately true'—I reckon you fellows up on the mountain are a lot of wise guys to have thought that out. You're right, too—I'm dead certain of it."

"But we," responded Chang dreamily, "are only *moderately* certain."

Miss Brinklow could not be bothered with all that, which seemed to her a sign of mere laziness. In any case she was preoccupied with an idea of her own. "When I get back," she said with tightening lips, "I shall ask my society to send a missionary here. And if they grumble at the expense, I shall just bully them until they agree."

That clearly was a much healthier spirit, and even Mallinson, little as he sympathised with foreign missions, could not forbear his admiration. "They ought to send *you*," he said. "That is, of course, if you'd like a place like this."

"It's hardly a question of *liking* it," Miss Brinklow retorted. "One wouldn't like it, naturally—how could one? It's a matter of what one feels one ought to do."

"I think," said Conway, "if I were a missionary, I'd choose this rather than quite a lot of other places."

"In that case," snapped Miss Brinklow, "there would be no merit in it, obviously."

"But I wasn't thinking of merit."

"More's the pity, then. There's no good in doing a thing because you like doing it. Look at these people here!"

"They all seem very happy."

"*Exactly*," she answered with a touch of

120

fierceness. She added: "Anyhow, I don't see why I shouldn't make a beginning by studying the language. Can you lend me a book about it, Mr. Chang?"

Chang was at his most mellifluous. "Most certainly, madam—with the greatest of pleasure. And, if I may say so, I think the idea an excellent one."

When they ascended to Shangri-La that evening he treated the matter as one of immediate importance. Miss Brinklow was at first a little daunted by the massive volume compiled by an industrious nineteenth-century German (she had more probably imagined some slighter work of a "Brush up your Tibetan" type), but with help from the Chinese and encouragement from Conway she made a good beginning and was soon observed to be extracting grim satisfaction from her task.

Conway, too, found much to interest him, apart from the engrossing problem he had set himself. During the warm, sunlit days he made full use of the library and music-room, and was confirmed in his impression that the lamas were of quite exceptional culture. Their taste in books was catholic, at any rate; Plato in Greek touched Omar in English; Nietzsche partnered Newton; Thomas More was there, and also Hannah More, Thomas Moore, George Moore, and even Old Moore. Altogether Conway estimated the number of volumes at between twenty and thirty thousand;

and it was tempting to speculate upon the method of selection and acquisition. He sought also to discover how recently there had been additions, but he did not come across anything later than a cheap reprint of *Im Westen Nichts Neues*. During a subsequent visit, however, Chang told him that there were other books published up to about the middle of 1930 which would doubtless be added to the shelves eventually; they had already arrived at the lamasery. "We keep ourselves fairly up-to-date, you see," he commented.

"There are people who would hardly agree with you," replied Conway with a smile. "Quite a lot of things have happened in the world since last year, you know."

"Nothing of importance, my dear sir, that could not have been foreseen in 1920, or that will not be better understood in 1940."

"You're not interested, then, in the latest developments of the world crisis?"

"I shall be very deeply interested—in due course."

"You know, Chang, I believe I'm beginning to understand you. You're geared differently, that's what it is—time means less to you than it does to most people. If I were in London I wouldn't always be eager to see the latest hour-old newspaper, and you at Shangri-La are no more eager to see a year-old one. Both attitudes seem to me quite sensible. By the way, how long is it since you last had visitors here?"

"That, Mr. Conway, I am unfortunately unable to say."

It was the usual ending to a conversation, and one that Conway found less irritating than the opposite phenomenon from which he had suffered much in his time—the conversation which, try as he would, seemed never to end. He began to like Chang rather more as their meetings multiplied, though it still puzzled him that he met so few of the lamasery personnel; even assuming that the lamas themselves were unapproachable, were there not other postulants besides Chang?

There was, of course, the little Manchu. He saw her sometimes when he visited the music-room; but she knew no English, and he was still unwilling to disclose his own Chinese. He could not quite determine whether she musicked merely for pleasure, or was in some way a student. Her playing, as indeed her whole behaviour, was exquisitely formal, and her choice lay always among the more patterned compositions—those of Bach, Corelli, Scarlatti, and occasionally Mozart. She preferred the harpsichord to the pianoforte, but when Conway went to the latter she would listen with grave and almost dutiful appreciation. It was impossible to know what was in her mind; it was difficult even to guess her age. He would have doubted her being over thirty or under thirteen; and yet, in a curious way, such manifest unlikelihoods could neither of them be ruled out as wholly impossible.

123

Mallinson, who sometimes came to listen to the music for want of anything better to do, found her a very baffling proposition. "I can't think what she's doing here," he said to Conway more than once. "This lama business may be all right for an old fellow like Chang, but what's the attraction in it for a girl? How long has she been here, I wonder?"

"I wonder too, but it's one of those things we're not likely to be told."

"Do you suppose she *likes* being here?"

"I'm bound to say she doesn't appear to *dis*like it."

"She doesn't appear to have feelings at all, for that matter. She's like a little ivory doll more than a human being."

"A charming thing to be like, anyhow."

"As far as it goes."

Conway smiled. "And it goes pretty far, Mallinson, when you come to think about it. After all, the ivory doll has manners, good taste in dress, attractive looks, a pretty touch on the harpsichord, and she doesn't move about a room as if she were playing hockey. Western Europe, so far as I recollect it, contains an exceptionally large number of females who lack these virtues."

"You're an awful cynic about women, Conway."

Conway was used to the charge. He had not actually had a great deal to do with the other sex, and during occasional leaves in Indian hill-stations the reputation of cynic had been as easy to sustain as any other. In truth he had had several delightful friendships with women who would have been pleased to marry him if he had asked them—but he had not asked them. He had once got nearly as far as an announcement in the *Morning Post*, but the girl did not want to live in Pekin and he did not want to live in Tunbridge Wells, mutual reluctances which proved impossible to dislodge. So far as he had experience of women at all, it had been tentative, intermittent, and somewhat inconclusive. But he was not, for all that, a cynic about them.

He said with a laugh: "I'm thirty-seven—you're twenty-four. That's all it amounts to."

After a pause Mallinson asked suddenly: "Oh, by the way, how old should you say Chang is?"

"Anything," replied Conway lightly, "between forty-nine and a hundred and forty-nine."

Such information, however, was less trustworthy than much else that was available to the new arrivals. The fact that their curiosities were sometimes unsatisfied tended to obscure the really vast quantity of data which Chang was always willing to outpour. There were no secrecies, for instance, about the customs and habits of the valley population, and Conway, who was interested, had talks which might have been worked up into a quite serviceable degree thesis. He was particularly interested, as a student of affairs, in the way the valley population was governed; it appeared, on examination, to be a rather loose and elastic autocracy, operated from the lamasery with a benevolence that was almost casual. It was certainly an established success, as every descent into that fertile paradise made more evident. Conway was puzzled as to the ultimate basis of law and order; there appeared to be neither soldiers nor police, yet surely some provision must be made for the incorrigible? Chang replied that crime was very rare, partly because only serious things were considered crimes, and partly because everyone enjoyed a sufficiency of everything he could reasonably desire. In the last resort the personal servants of the lamasery had power to expel an offender from the valley—though this, which was considered an extreme and dreadful punishment, had only very occasionally to be imposed. But the chief factor in the government of Blue Moon, Chang went on to say, was the inculcation of good manners, which made men feel that certain things were "not done," and that they lost caste by doing them. "You English inculcate the same feeling," said Chang, "in your public schools—but not, I fear, in regard to the same things. The inhabitants of our valley, for instance, feel that it is 'not done' to be inhospitable to strangers, to dispute acrimoniously, or to strive for priority amongst one another. The idea of enjoying what your English headmasters call the mimic warfare of the playing-field would seem to them entirely barbarous—indeed, a sheerly wanton stimulation of all the lower instincts."

126

Conway asked if there were never disputes about women.

"Only very rarely, because it would not be considered good manners to take a woman that another man wanted."

"Supposing somebody wanted her so badly that he didn't care a damn whether it was good manners or not?"

"Then, my dear sir, it would be good manners on the part of the other man to let him have her, and also on the part of the woman to be equally agreeable. You would really be surprised how the application of a little courtesy all round helps to smooth out these problems."

Certainly during visits to the valley Conway found a spirit of goodwill and contentment that pleased him all the more because he knew that of all the arts that of government has been brought least to perfection. When he made some complimentary remark, however, Chang responded: "Ah, but you see, we believe that to govern perfectly it is necessary to avoid governing too much."

"Yet you don't have any democratic machinery—voting, and so on?"

"Oh no. Our people would be quite shocked by having to declare that one policy was completely right and another completely wrong."

Conway smiled. He found the attitude a sufficiently congenial one.

Meanwhile Miss Brinklow derived her own kind of

satisfaction from a study of Tibetan; meanwhile also Mallinson fretted and groused, and Barnard persisted in an equanimity which seemed almost equally remarkable, whether it were real or simulated.

"To tell you the truth," said Mallinson, "the fellow's cheerfulness is just about getting on my nerves. I can understand him trying to keep a stiff lip, but that continual joke-over of his begins to upset me. He'll be the life and soul of the party if we don't watch him."

Conway, too, had once or twice wondered at the ease with which the American had managed to settle down. He replied: "Isn't it rather lucky for us he *does* take things so well?"

"Personally, I think it's damned peculiar. What do you *know* about him, Conway? I mean who he is, and so on."

"Not much more than you do. I understand he came from Persia and was supposed to have been oil-prospecting. It's his way to take things easily—when the air evacuation was arranged I had quite a job to persuade him to join us at all. He only agreed when I told him that an American passport wouldn't stop a bullet."

"By the way, did you ever see his passport?"

"Probably I did, but I don't remember. Why?"

Mallinson laughed. "I'm afraid you'll think I haven't exactly been minding my own business. Why should I, anyhow? Two months in this place ought to reveal all our secrets, if we have any. Mind

128

you, it was a sheer accident, in the way it happened, and I haven't let slip a word to anyone else, of course. I didn't think I'd tell even you, but now we've got on to the subject I may as well."

"Yes, of course, but I wish you'd let me know what you're talking about."

"Just this. Barnard was travelling on a forged passport and he isn't Barnard at all."

Conway raised his eyebrows with an interest that was very much less than concern. He liked Barnard, so far as the man stirred him to any emotion at all; but it was quite impossible for him to care intensely who he really was or wasn't. He said: "Well, who do you think he is, then?"

"He's Chalmers Bryant."

"The deuce he is! What makes you think so?"

"He dropped a pocket-book this morning and Chang picked it up and gave it to me, thinking it was mine. I couldn't help seeing it was stuffed with newspaper clippings—some of them fell out as I was handling the thing, and I don't mind admitting that I looked at them. After all, newspaper clippings aren't private, or shouldn't be. They were all about Bryant and the search for him, and one of them had a photograph which was absolutely like Barnard except for a moustache."

"Did you mention your discovery to Barnard himself?"

"No, I just handed him his property without any comment."

"So the whole thing rests on your identification of a newspaper photograph?"

"Well, so far, yes."

"I don't think I'd care to convict anyone on that. Of course you might be right—I don't say he couldn't *possibly* be Bryant. If he were, it would account for a good deal of his contentment at being here—he could hardly have found a better place to hide."

Mallinson seemed a trifle disappointed by this casual reception of news which he evidently thought highly sensational. "Well, what are you going to do about it?" he asked. Conway pondered a moment and then answered: "I haven't much of an idea. Probably nothing at all. What *can* one do, in any case?"

"But dash it all, if the man *is* Bryant——"

"My dear Mallinson, if the man were Nero it wouldn't have to matter to us for the time being! Saint or crook, we've got to make what we can of each other's company as long as we're here, and I can't see that we shall help matters by striking any attitudes. If I'd suspected who he was at Baskul, of course, I'd have tried to get in touch with Delhi about him—it would have been merely a public duty. But now I think I can claim to be *off* duty."

"Don't you think that's rather a slack way of looking at it?"

"I don't care if it's slack so long as it's sensible."

"I suppose that means your advice to me is to forget what I've found out?"

130

"You probably can't do that, but I certainly think we might both of us keep our own counsel about it. Not in consideration for Barnard or Bryant or whoever he is, but to save ourselves the deuce of an awkward situation when we get away."

"You mean we ought to let him go?"

"Well, I'll put it a bit differently and say we ought to give somebody else the pleasure of catching him. When you've lived quite sociably with a man for a few months, it seems a little out of place to call for the handcuffs."

"I don't think I agree. The man's nothing but a large-scale thief—I know plenty of people who've lost their money through him."

Conway shrugged his shoulders. He admired the simple black-and-white of Mallinson's code; the public-school ethic might be crude, but at least it was downright. If a man broke the law, it was everyone's duty to hand him over to justice—always provided that it was the kind of law one was not allowed to break. And the law pertaining to cheques and shares and balance-sheets was decidedly that kind. Bryant had transgressed it, and though Conway had not taken much interest in the case, he had an impression that it was a fairly bad one of its kind. All he knew was that the failure of the giant Bryant group in New York had resulted in losses of about a hundred million dollars—a record crash, even in a world that exuded records. In some way or other (Conway was not a financial expert) Bryant had been monkeying on Wall Street, and the result

131

had been a warrant for his arrest, his escape to Europe, and extradition orders against him in half-a-dozen countries.

Conway said finally: "Well, if you take my tip you'll say nothing about it—not for his sake but for ours. Please yourself, of course, so long as you don't forget the possibility that he mayn't be the fellow at all."

But he was, and the revelation came that evening after dinner. Chang had left them; Miss Brinklow had turned to her Tibetan grammar; the three male exiles faced each other over coffee and cigars. Conversation during the meal would have languished more than once but for the tact and affability of the Chinese; now, in his absence, a rather unhappy silence supervened. Barnard was for once without jokes. It was clear to Conway that it lay beyond Mallinson's power to treat the American as if nothing had happened, and it was equally clear that Barnard was shrewdly aware that something *had* happened.

Suddenly the American threw away his cigar. "I guess you all know who I am," he said.

Mallinson coloured like a girl, but Conway replied in the same quiet key: "Yes, Mallinson and I think we do."

"Darned careless of me to leave those clippings lying about."

"We're all apt to be careless at times."

132

"Well, you're mighty calm about it, that's something."

There was another silence, broken at length by Miss Brinklow's shrill voice: "I'm sure *I* don't know who you are, Mr. Barnard, though I must say I guessed all along you were travelling *incognito*." They all looked at her enquiringly and she went on: "I remember when Mr. Conway said we should all have our names in the papers, you said it didn't affect you. I thought then that Barnard probably wasn't your real name."

The culprit gave a slow smile as he lit himself another cigar. "Madam," he said eventually, "you're not only a cute detective, but you've hit on a really polite name for my present position. I'm travelling *incognito*. You've said it, and you're dead right. As for you boys, I'm not sorry in a way that you've found me out. So long as none of you had an inkling, we could all have managed, but considering how we're fixed it wouldn't seem very neighbourly to play the high hat with you now. You folks have been so darned nice to me that I don't want to make a lot of trouble. It looks as if we were all going to be joined together for better or worse for some little time ahead, and it's up to us to help one another out as far as we can. As for what happens afterwards, I reckon we can leave that to settle itself."

All this appeared to Conway so eminently reasonable that he gazed at Barnard with considerably greater interest, and even—though it was perhaps odd at such a moment—a touch of genuine appreciation. It was curious to think of that heavy, fleshy, good-humoured, rather paternal-looking man as the world's hugest swindler. He looked far more the type that, with a little extra education, would have made a popular headmaster of a prep-school. Behind his joviality there were signs of recent strains and worries, but that did not mean that the joviality was forced. He obviously was what he looked—a "good fellow" in the world's sense, by nature a lamb and only by profession a shark.

Conway said: "Yes, that's very much the best thing, I'm certain."

Then Barnard laughed. It was as if he possessed even deeper reserves of good-humour which he could only now draw upon. "Gosh, but it's mighty queer," he exclaimed, spreading himself in his chair. "The whole darned business, I mean. Right across Europe, and on through Turkey and Persia to that little one-horse burg! Police after me all the time, mind you—they nearly got me in Vienna! It's pretty exciting at first, being chased, but it gets on your nerves after a bit. I got a good rest at Baskul, though—I thought I'd be safe in the midst of a revolution."

"And so you were," said Conway with a slight smile, "except from bullets."

"Yeah, and that's what bothered me at the finish. I can tell you it was a mighty hard choice—whether to stay in Baskul and get plugged, or accept a trip in your Government's aeroplane and find the bracelets

134

waiting at the other end. I wasn't exactly keen to do either."

"I remember you weren't."

Barnard laughed again. "Well, that's how it was, and you can figger it out that the change of plan that brought me here don't worry me an awful lot. It's a first-class mystery, I'll allow, but for me, speaking personally, there couldn't have been a better one. It ain't my way to grumble so long as I'm satisfied."

Conway's smile became more definitely cordial. "A very sensible attitude, though I think you rather overdid it. We were all beginning to wonder how you managed to be so contented."

"Well, I *was* contented. This ain't a bad place, when you get used to it. The air's a bit nippy at first, but you can't have everything. And it's nice and quiet for a change. Every fall I go down to Palm Beach for a rest-cure, but they don't give it you, those places—you're on the racket just the same. But here I guess I'm having just what the doctor ordered, and it certainly feels grand to me. I'm on a different diet, I can't look at the tape, and my broker can't get me on the telephone."

"I dare say he wishes he could."

"Sure. That'll be a tidy-sized mess to clear up, I've no doubt."

He said this with such simplicity that Conway couldn't help responding: "I'm not much of an authority on what people call high finance."

It was a lead, and the American accepted it

without the slightest reluctance. "High finance," he said, "is mostly a lot of bunk."

"So I've often suspected."

"Look here, Conway, I'll put it like this. A feller does what he's been doing for years, and what lots of other fellows have been doing, and suddenly the market goes against him. He can't help it, but he braces up and waits for the turn. But somehow the turn don't come as it always used to, and when he's lost ten million dollars or so he reads in some paper that a Swede professor thinks it's the end of the world. Now I ask you, does that sort of thing help markets? Of course, it gives him a bit of a shock, but he still can't help it. And there he is till the cops come—if he waits for 'em. I didn't."

"You claim it was all just a run of bad luck, then?"

"Well, I certainly had a large packet."

"You also had other people's money," put in Mallinson sharply.

"Yeah, I did. And why? Because they all wanted something for nothing and hadn't the brains to get it for themselves."

"I don't agree. It was because they trusted you and thought their money was safe."

"Well, it wasn't safe. It couldn't be. There isn't safety anywhere, and those who thought there was were like a lot of saps trying to hide under an umbrella in a typhoon."

Conway said pacifyingly: "Well, we'll all admit you couldn't help the typhoon."

136

"I couldn't even pretend to help it—any more than you could help what happened after we left Baskul. The same thing struck me then as I watched you in the aeroplane keeping dead calm while Mallinson here had the fidgets. You knew you couldn't do anything about it, and you weren't caring two hoots. Just like I felt myself when the crash came."

"That's nonsense!" cried Mallinson. "Anyone can help swindling. It's a matter of playing the game according to the rules."

"Which is a darned difficult thing to do when the whole game's going to pieces. Besides, there isn't a soul in the world who knows what the rules are. All the professors of Harvard and Yale couldn't tell you 'em."

Mallinson replied rather scornfully: "I'm referring to a few quite simple rules of everyday conduct."

"Then I reckon your everyday conduct don't include managing trust companies."

Conway made haste to intervene. "We'd better not argue. I don't object in the least to the comparison between your affairs and mine. No doubt we've all been flying blind lately—both literally and in other ways. But we're here now, that's the important thing, and I agree with you that we could easily have had more to grumble about. It's curious, when you come to think about it, that out of four people picked up by chance and kidnapped a thousand miles, three should be able to

137

find some consolation in the business. *You* want a rescue-cure and a hiding-place; Miss Brinklow feels a call to evangelise the heathen Tibetan."

"Who's the third person you're counting?" Mallinson interrupted. "Not me, I hope?"

"I was including myself," answered Conway. "And my own reason is perhaps the simplest of all—I just rather like being here."

Indeed, a short time later, when he took what had come to be his usual solitary evening stroll along the terrace or beside the lotus-pool, he felt an extraordinary sense of physical and mental settlement. It was perfectly true; he just rather liked being at Shangri-La. Its atmosphere soothed while its mystery stimulated, and the total sensation was agreeable. For some days now he had been reaching, gradually and tentatively, a curious conclusion about the lamasery and its inhabitants; his brain was still busy with it, though in a deeper sense he was unperturbed. He was like a mathematician with an abstruse problem—worrying over it, but worrying very calmly and impersonally.

As for Bryant, whom he decided he would still think of and address as Barnard, the question of his exploits and identity faded instantly into the background, save for a single phrase of his—"the whole game's going to pieces." Conway found himself remembering and echoing it with a wider significance than the American had probably intended; he felt it to be true of more than American banking and trust-company management.

138

It fitted Baskul and Delhi and London, war-making and empire-building, consulates and trade concessions and dinner-parties at Government House; there was a reek of dissolution over all that recollected world, and Barnard's cropper had only, perhaps, been better dramatised than his own. The whole game *was* doubtless going to pieces, but fortunately the players were not as a rule put on trial for the pieces they failed to save. In that respect financiers were unlucky.

But here, at Shangri-La, all was in deep calm. In a moonless sky the stars were lit to the full, and a pale blue sheen lay upon the dome of Karakal. Conway realised then that if by some change of plan the porters from the outside world were to arrive immediately, he would not be completely overjoyed at being spared the interval of waiting. And nor would Barnard either, he reflected with an inward smile. It was amusing, really; and then suddenly he knew that he still liked Barnard, or he wouldn't have found it amusing. Somehow the loss of a hundred million dollars was too much to bar a man for; it would have been easier if he had only stolen one's watch. And after all, how *could* anyone lose a hundred millions? Perhaps only in the sense in which a cabinet minister might airily announce that he had been "given India."

And then again he thought of the time when he would leave Shangri-La with the returning porters. He pictured the long, arduous journey, and that eventual moment of arrival at some planter's bungalow in Sikkim or Baltistan—a moment which ought, he felt, to be deliriously cheerful, but which would probably be slightly disappointing. Then the first hand-shakings and self-introductions; the first drinks on clubhouse verandahs; sun-bronzed faces staring at him in barely concealed incredulity. At Delhi, no doubt, interviews with the Viceroy and the C.I.C.; salaams of turbaned menials; endless reports to be prepared and sent off. Perhaps even a return to England and Whitehall; deck-games on the P. & O.; the flaccid palm of an under-secretary; newspaper interviews; hard, mocking, sex-thirsty voices of women—"And is it really true, Mr. Conway, that when you were in Tibet . . . ?" There was no doubt of one thing; he would be able to dine out on his yarn for at least a season. But would he enjoy it? He recalled a sentence penned by Gordon during the last days at Khartoum—"I would sooner live like a Dervish with the Mahdi than go out to dinner every night in London." Conway's aversion was less definite—a mere anticipation that to tell his story in the past tense would bore him a great deal as well as sadden him a little.

Abruptly, in the midst of his reflections, he was aware of Chang's approach. "Sir," began the Chinese, his slow whisper slightly quickening as he spoke, "I am proud to be the bearer of important news. . . ."

So the porters *had* come before their time, was Conway's first thought; it was odd that he should

140

have been thinking of it so recently. And he felt the pang that he was half prepared for. "Well?" he queried.

Chang's condition was as nearly that of excitement as seemed physically possible for him. "My dear sir, I congratulate you," he continued. "And I am happy to think that I am in some measure responsible—it was after my own strong and repeated recommendations that the High Lama made his decision. He wishes to see you immediately."

Conway's glance was quizzical. "You're being less coherent than usual, Chang. What has happened?"

"The High Lama has sent for you."

"So I gather. But why all the fuss?"

"Because its extraordinary and unprecedented—even I who urged it did not expect it to happen yet. A fortnight ago you had not arrived, and now you are about to be received by *him*! Never before has it occurred so soon!"

"I'm still rather fogged, you know. I'm to see your High Lama—I realise that all right. But is there anything else?"

"Is it not enough?"

Conway laughed. "Absolutely, I assure you—don't imagine I'm being discourteous. As a matter of fact, something quite different was in my head at first—however, never mind about that now. Of course I shall be both honoured and delighted to meet the gentleman. When is the appointment?"

"Now. I have been sent to bring you to him."

"Isn't it rather late?"

"That is of no consequence. My dear sir, you will understand many things very soon. And may I add my own personal pleasure that this interval—always an awkward one—is now at an end. Believe me, it has been irksome to me to have to refuse you information on so many occasions—extremely irksome. I am joyful in the knowledge that such unpleasantness will never again be necessary."

"You're a queer fellow, Chang," Conway responded. "But let's be going—don't bother to explain any more. I'm perfectly ready and I appreciate your nice remarks. Lead the way."

7

CONWAY was quite unruffled, but his demeanour covered an eagerness that grew in intensity as he accompanied Chang across the empty courtyards. If the words of the Chinese meant anything, he was on the threshold of discovery; soon he would know whether his theory, still half formed, were less impossible than it appeared.

Apart from this, it would doubtless be an interesting interview. He had met many peculiar potentates in his time; he took a detached interest in them, and was shrewd as a rule in his assessments. Without self-consciousness he had also the valuable knack of being able to say polite things in languages of which he knew very little indeed. Perhaps, however, he would be chiefly a listener on this occasion. He noticed that Chang was taking him through rooms he had not seen before, all of them rather dim and lovely in lantern-light. Then a spiral staircase climbed to a door at which the Chinese knocked, and which was opened by a Tibetan servant with such promptness that Conway suspected he had been stationed behind it. This part of the lamasery, on a higher storey, was no less tastefully embellished than the rest, but its most immediately striking feature was a dry tingling

143

warmth, as if all the windows were tightly closed and some kind of steam heating plant were working at full pressure. The airlessness increased as he passed on, until at last Chang paused before a door which, if bodily sensation could have been trusted, might well have admitted to a Turkish bath.

"The High Lama," whispered Chang, "will receive you alone." Having opened the door for Conway's entrance, he closed it afterwards so silently that his own departure was almost imperceptible. Conway stood hesitant, breathing an atmosphere that was not only sultry, but full of dusk, so that it was several seconds before he could accustom his eyes to the gloom. Then he slowly built up an impression of a dark-curtained low-roofed apartment, simply furnished with table and chairs. On one of these sat a small, pale, and wrinkled person, motionlessly shadowed, and yielding an effect as of some fading, antique portrait in chiaroscuro. If there were such a thing as presence divorced from actuality, here it was, adorned with a classic dignity that was more an emanation than an attribute. Conway was curious about his own intense perception of all this, and wondered if it were dependable or merely his reaction to the rich crepuscular warmth; he felt dizzy under the gaze of those ancient eyes, took a few forward paces, and then halted. The occupant of the chair grew now less vague in outline, but scarcely more corporeal; he was a little old man in Chinese dress, its folds and flounces loose against a flat, emaciated frame. "You are Mr. Conway?" he whispered in excellent English.

The voice was pleasantly soothing and touched with a very gentle melancholy that fell upon Conway with strange beatitude; though once again the sceptic in him was inclined to hold the temperature responsible.

"I am," he answered.

The voice went on. "It's a pleasure to see you, Mr. Conway. I sent for you because I thought we should do well to have a talk together. Please sit down beside me and have no fear. I am an old man and can do no one any harm."

Conway answered: "I feel it a signal honour to be received by you."

"I thank you, my dear Conway—I shall call you that, according to your English fashion. It is, as I said, a moment of great pleasure for me. My sight is poor, but believe me, I am able to see you in my mind as well as with my eyes. I trust you have been comfortable at Shangri-La since your arrival?"

"Extremely so."

"I am glad. Chang has done his best for you, no doubt. It has been a great pleasure to him also. He tells me you have been asking many questions about our community and its affairs?"

"I am certainly interested in them."

"Then if you can spare me a little time, I shall be pleased to give you a brief account of our foundation."

"There is nothing I should appreciate more."

"That is what I had thought—and hoped. . . . But first of all, before our discourse . . ."

He made the slightest stir of a hand, and immediately, by what technique of summons Conway could not detect, a servant entered to prepare the elegant ritual of tea-drinking. The little egg-shell bowls of almost colourless fluid were placed on a lacquered tray; Conway, who knew the ceremony, was by no means contemptuous of it. The voice resumed: "Our ways are familiar to you, then?"

Obeying an impulse which he could neither analyse nor find desire to control, Conway answered: "I lived in China for some years."

"You did not tell Chang."

"No."

"Then why am I so honoured?"

Conway was rarely at a loss to explain his own motives, but on this occasion he could not think of any reason at all. At length he replied: "To be quite candid, I haven't the slightest idea, except that I must have wanted to tell you."

"The best of all reasons, I am sure, between those who are to become friends. . . . Now tell me, is this not a delicate aroma? The teas of China are many and fragrant, but this, which is a special product of our own valley, is in my opinion their equal."

Conway lifted the bowl to his lips and tasted. The savour was slender, elusive, and recondite, a ghostly bouquet that haunted rather than lived on the

146

tongue. He said: "It is very delightful, and also quite new to me."

"Yes, like a great many of our valley herbs, it is both unique and precious. It should be tasted, of course, very slowly—not only in reverence and affection, but to extract the fullest degree of pleasure. This is a famous lesson that we may learn from Kou Kai Tchou, who lived some fifteen centuries ago. He would always hesitate to reach the succulent marrow when he was eating a piece of sugar-cane, for, as he explained—'I introduce myself gradually into the region of delights.' Have you studied any of the great Chinese classics?"

Conway replied that he was slightly acquainted with a few of them. He knew that the allusive conversation would, according to etiquette, continue until the tea-bowls were taken away; but he found it far from irritating, despite his keenness to hear the history of Shangri-La. Doubtless there was a certain amount of Kou Kai Tchou's reluctant sensibility in himself.

At length the signal was given, again mysteriously, the servant padded in and out, and with no more preamble the High Lama of Shangri-La began:

"Probably you are familiar, my dear Conway, with the general outline of Tibetan history. I am informed by Chang that you have made ample use of the library here, and I doubt not that you have studied the scanty but exceedingly interesting annals of these regions. You will be aware, anyhow,

147

that Nestorian Christianity was wide-spread throughout Asia during the Middle Ages, and that its memory lingered long after its actual decay. In the seventeenth century a Christian revival was impelled directly from Rome through the agency of those heroic Jesuit missionaries whose journeys, if I may permit myself the remark, are so much more interesting to read of than those of St. Paul. Gradually the Church established itself over an immense area, and it is a remarkable fact, not realised by many Europeans to-day, that for thirty-eight years there existed a Christian mission in Lhasa itself. It was not, however, from Lhasa but from Pekin, in the year 1719, that four Capuchin friars set out in search of any remnants of the Nestorian faith that might still be surviving in the hinterland.

"They travelled south-west for many months, by Lanchow and the Koko-Nor, facing hardships which you will well imagine. Three died on the way, and the fourth was not far from death when by accident he stumbled into the rocky defile that remains to-day the only practical approach to the valley of Blue Moon. There, to his joy and surprise, he found a friendly and prosperous population who made haste to display what I have always regarded as our oldest tradition—that of hospitality to strangers. Quickly he recovered health and began to preach his mission. The people were Buddhists, but willing to hear him, and he had considerable success. There was an ancient lamasery existing then on this same mountain-shelf, but it was in a state of decay both physical and spiritual, and as the Capuchin's harvest increased, he conceived the idea of setting up on the same magnificent site a Christian monastery. Under his surveillance the old buildings were repaired and largely reconstructed, and he himself began to live here in the year 1734, when he was fifty-three years of age.

"Now let me tell you more about this man. His name was Perrault, and he was by birth a Luxembourger. Before devoting himself to Far Eastern missions he had studied at Paris, Bologna, and other universities; he was something of a scholar. There are few existing records of his early life, but it was not in any way unusual for one of his age and profession. He was fond of music and the arts, had a special aptitude for languages, and before he was sure of his vocation he had tasted all the familiar pleasures of the world. Malplaquet was fought when he was a youth, and he knew from personal contact the horrors of war and invasion. He was physically sturdy; during his first years here he laboured with his hands like any other man, tilling his own garden, and learning from the inhabitants as well as teaching them. He found gold deposits along the valley, but they did not tempt him; he was more deeply interested in local plants and herbs. He was humble and by no means bigoted. He deprecated polygamy, but he saw no reason to inveigh against the prevalent fondness for the *tangatse* berry, to which were ascribed medicinal properties, but which was chiefly popular because its effects were those of a mild narcotic. Perrault, in fact, became somewhat of an addict himself; it was his way to accept from native life all that it offered which he found harmless and pleasant, and to give in return the spiritual treasure of the West. He was not an ascetic; he enjoyed the good things of the world, and was careful to teach his converts cooking as well as catechism. I want you to have an impression of a rather earnest, busy, learned, simple, and enthusiastic person who, along with his priestly functions, did not disdain to put on a mason's overall and help in the actual building of these very rooms. That was, of course, a work of immense difficulty, and one which nothing but his pride and steadfastness could have overcome. Pride, I say, because it was undoubtedly a dominant motive at the beginning—the pride in his own Faith that made him decide that if Gautama could inspire men to build a temple on the ledge of Shangri-La, Rome was capable of no less.

"But time passed, and it was not unnatural that this motive should yield place gradually to more tranquil ones. Emulation is, after all, a young man's spirit, and Perrault, by the time his monastery was well established, was already full of years. You must bear in mind that he had not, from a strict point of view, been acting very regularly; though some latitude must surely be extended to one whose ecclesiastical superiors are located at a distance measurable in years rather than miles. But the folk

150

of the valley and the monks themselves had no misgivings; they loved and obeyed him, and as years went on, came to venerate him also. At intervals it was his custom to send reports to the Bishop of Pekin, but often they never reached him, and as it was to be presumed that the bearers had succumbed to the perils of the journey, Perrault grew more and more unwilling to hazard their lives, and after about the middle of the century he gave up the practice. Some of his earlier messages, however, must have got through, and a doubt of his activities have been aroused, for in the year 1769 a stranger brought a letter written twelve years before, summoning Perrault to Rome.

"He would have been over seventy had the command been received without delay; as it was, he had turned eighty-nine. The long trek over mountain and plateau was unthinkable; he could never have endured the scouring gales and fierce chills of the wilderness outside. He sent, therefore, a courteous reply explaining the situation, but there is no record that his message ever passed the barrier of the great ranges.

"So Perrault remained at Shangri-La, not exactly in defiance of superior orders, but because it was physically impossible for him to fulfil them. In any case he was an old man, and death would probably soon put an end both to him and his irregularity. By this time the institution he had founded had begun to undergo a subtle change. It might be deplorable, but it was not really very astonishing; for it could

151

hardly be expected that one man unaided should uproot permanently the habits and traditions of an epoch. He had no Western colleagues to hold firm when his own grip relaxed; and it had perhaps been a mistake to build on a site that held such older and differing memories. It was asking too much; but was it not asking even more to expect a grey-haired veteran, just entering the nineties, to realise the mistake that he had made? Perrault, at any rate, did not then realise it. He was far too old and happy. His followers were devoted even when they forgot his teaching, while the people of the valley held him in such reverent affection that he forgave with ever-increasing ease their lapse into former customs. He was still active, and his faculties had remained exceptionally keen. At the age of ninety-eight he began to study the Buddhist writings that had been left at Shangri-La by its previous occupants, and his intention was then to devote the rest of his life to the composition of a book attacking Buddhism from the standpoint of orthodoxy. He actually finished this task (we have his manuscript complete), but the attack was very gentle, for he had by that time reached the round figure of a century—an age at which even the keenest acrimonies are apt to fade.

"Meanwhile, as you may suppose, many of his early disciples had died, and as there were few replacements, the number resident under the rule of the old Capuchin steadily diminished. From over eighty at one time, it dwindled to a score, and then to a mere dozen, most of them very aged themselves. Perrault's life at this time grew to be a very calm and placid waiting for the end. He was far too old for disease and discontent; only the everlasting sleep could claim him now, and he was not afraid. The valley people, out of kindness, supplied food and clothing; his library gave him work. He had become rather frail, but still kept energy to fulfil the major ceremonial of his office; the rest of the tranquil days he spent with his books, his memories, and the mild ecstasies of the narcotic. His mind remained so extraordinarily clear that he even embarked upon a study of certain mystic practices that the Indians call *yoga*, and which are based upon various special methods of breathing. For a man of such an age the enterprise might well have seemed hazardous, and it was certainly true that soon afterwards, in that memorable year 1789, news descended to the valley that Perrault was dying at last.

"He lay in this room, my dear Conway, where he could see from the window the white blur that was all his failing eyesight gave him of Karakal; but he could see with his mind also; he could picture the clear and matchless outline that he had first glimpsed half a century before. And there came to him, too, the strange parade of all his many experiences, the years of travel across desert and upland, the great crowds in Western cities, the clang and glitter of Marlborough's troops. His mind had straitened to a snow-white calm; he was ready, willing, and glad to die. He gathered his friends and servants round him and bade them all farewell; then he asked to be left alone awhile. It was during such a solitude, with his body sinking and his mind lifted to beatitude, that he had hoped to give up his soul . . . but it did not happen so. He lay for many weeks without speech or movement, and then he began to recover. He was a hundred and eight."

The whispering ceased for a moment, and to Conway, stirring slightly, it appeared that the High Lama had been translating, with fluency, out of a remote and private dream. At length he went on:

"Like others who have waited long on the threshold of death, Perrault had been granted a vision of some significance to take back with him into the world; and of this vision more must be said later. Here I will confine myself to his actions and behaviour, which were indeed remarkable. For instead of convalescing idly, as might have been expected, he plunged forthwith into rigorous self-discipline somewhat curiously combined with narcotic indulgence. Drug-taking and deep breathing exercises—it could not have seemed a very death-defying regimen; yet the fact remains that when the last of the old monks died, in 1794, Perrault himself was still living.

"It would almost have brought a smile had there been anyone at Shangri-La with a sufficiently distorted sense of humour. The wrinkled Capuchin, no more decrepit than he had been for a dozen years, persevered in a secret ritual he had evolved,

154

while to the folk of the valley he soon became veiled in mystery, a hermit of uncanny powers who lived alone on that formidable cliff. But there was still a tradition of affection for him, and it came to be regarded as meritorious and luck-bringing to climb to Shangri-La and leave a simple gift, or perform some manual task that was needed there. On all such pilgrims Perrault bestowed his blessing—forgetful, it might be, that they were lost and straying sheep. For 'Te Deum Laudamus' and 'Om Mane Padme Hum' were now heard equally in the temples of the valley.

"As the new century approached, the legend grew into a rich and fantastic folk-lore—it was said that Perrault had become a god, that he worked miracles, and that on certain nights he flew to the summit of Karakal to hold a candle to the sky. There is a paleness always on the mountain at full moon; but I need not assure you that neither Perrault nor any other man has ever climbed there. I mention it, even though it may seem unnecessary, because there is a mass of unreliable testimony that Perrault did and could do all kinds of impossible things. It was supposed, for instance, that he practised the art of self-levitation, of which so much appears in accounts of Buddhist mysticism; but the more sober truth is that he made many exeriments to that end, but entirely without success. He did, however, discover that the impairment of ordinary senses could be somewhat offset by a development of others; he acquired skill in telepathy which was perhaps remarkable, and though he made no claim to any specific powers of healing, there was a quality in his mere presence that was helpful in certain cases.

"You will wish to know how he spent his time during these unprecedented years. His attitude may be summed up by saying that, as he had not died at a normal age, he began to feel that there was no discoverable reason why he either should or should not do so at any definite time in the future. Having already proved himself abnormal, it was as easy to believe that the abnormality might continue as to expect it to end at any moment. And that being so, he began to behave without care for the imminence with which he had been so long preoccupied; he began to live the kind of life that he had always desired, but had so rarely found possible; for he had kept at heart and throughout all vicissitudes the tranquil tastes of a scholar. His memory was astonishing; it appeared to have escaped the trammels of physique into some upper region of immense clarity; it almost seemed that he could now learn *everything* with far greater ease than during his student days he had been able to learn *anything*. He was soon, of course, brought up against a need for books, but there were a few he had had with him from the first, and they included, you may be interested to hear, an English grammar and dictionary and Florio's translation of Montaigne. With these to work on he contrived to master the intricacies of your language, and we still possess in our library the manuscript of one of his first linguistic exercises—a translation of Montaigne's essay on Vanity into Tibetan—surely a unique production."

Conway smiled. "I should be interested to see it sometime, if I might."

"With the greatest of pleasure. It was, you may think, a singularly unpractical accomplishment, but recollect that Perrault had reached a singularly unpractical age. He would have been lonely without some such occupation—at any rate until the fourth year of the nineteenth century, which marks an important event in the history of our foundation. For it was then that a second stranger from Europe arrived in the valley of Blue Moon. He was a young Austrian named Henschell who had soldiered against Napoleon in Italy—a youth of noble birth, high culture, and much charm of manner. The wars had ruined his fortunes, and he had wandered across Russia into Asia with some vague intention of retrieving them. It would be interesting to know how exactly he reached the plateau, but he had no very clear idea himself; indeed, he was as near death when he arrived here as Perrault himself had once been. Again the hospitality of Shangri-La was extended, and the stranger recovered—but there the parallel breaks down. For Perrault had come to preach and proselytise, whereas Henschell took a more immediate interest in the gold deposits. His first ambition was to enrich himself and return to Europe as soon as possible.

"But he did not return. An odd thing happened—though one that has happened so often since that perhaps we must now agree that it cannot be very odd after all. The valley, with its peacefulness and its utter freedom from worldly cares, tempted him again and again to delay his departure, and one day, having heard the local legend, he climbed to Shangri-La and had his first meeting with Perrault.

"That meeting was, in the truest sense, historic. Perrault, if a little beyond such human passions as friendship or affection, was yet endowed with a rich benignity of mind which touched the youth as water upon a parched soil. I will not try to describe the association that sprang up between the two; the one gave utmost adoration, while the other shared his knowledge, his ecstasies, and the wild dream that had now become the only reality left for him in the world."

There was a pause, and Conway said very quietly: "Pardon the interruption, but that is not quite clear to me."

"I know." The whispered reply was completely sympathetic. "It would be remarkable indeed if it were. It is a matter which I shall be pleased to explain before our talk is over, but for the present, if you will forgive me, I will confine myself to simpler things. A fact that will interest you is that Henschell began our collections of Chinese art, as well as our library and musical acquisitions. He made a remarkable journey to Pekin and brought back the first consignment in the year 1809. He did not leave the valley again, but it was his ingenuity which devised the complicated system by which the lamasery has ever since been able to obtain anything needful from the outer world."

"I suppose you found it easy to make payment in gold?"

"Yes, we have been fortunate in possessing supplies of a metal which is held in such high esteem in other parts of the world."

"Such high esteem that you must have been very lucky to escape a gold rush."

The High Lama inclined his head in the merest indication of agreement. "That, my dear Conway, was always Henschell's fear. He was careful that none of the porters bringing books and art treasures should ever approach too closely; he made them leave their burdens a day's journey outside, to be fetched afterwards by our valley folk themselves. He even arranged for sentries to keep constant watch on the entrance of the defile. But it soon occurred to him that there was an easier and more final safeguard."

"Yes?" Conway's voice was guardedly tense.

"You see, there was no need to fear invasion by an army. That will never be possible, owing to the nature and distances of the country. The most ever to be expected was the arrival of a few half-lost wanderers who, even if they were armed, would probably be so weakened as to constitute no danger. It was decided, therefore, that henceforward strangers might come as freely as they chose—with but one important proviso.

"And, over a period of years, such strangers did come. Chinese merchants, tempted into the crossing of the plateau, chanced occasionally on this one traverse out of so many others possible to them. Nomad Tibetans, wandering from their tribes, strayed here sometimes like weary animals. All were made welcome, though some reached the shelter of the valley only to die. In the year of Waterloo two English missionaries, travelling overland to Pekin, crossed the ranges by an unnamed pass and had the extraordinary luck to arrive as calmly as if they were paying a call. In 1820 a Greek trader, accompanied by sick and famished servants, was found dying at the topmost ridge of the pass. In 1822 three Spaniards, having heard some vague story of gold, reached here after many wanderings and disappointments. Again, in 1830, there was a larger influx. Two Germans, a Russian, an Englishman, and a Swede made the dreaded crossing of the Tian-Shans, impelled by a motive that was to become increasingly common—scientific exploration. By the time of their approach a slight modification had taken place in the attitude of Shangri-La towards its visitors—not only were they now welcomed if they chanced to find their way into the valley, but it had become customary to meet them if they ever ventured within a certain radius. All this was for a reason I shall later discuss, but the point is of importance as showing that the lamasery was no longer hospitably indifferent; it had already both a need and a desire for new arrivals. And indeed in the years to follow it happened that more than one party of explorers, glorying in their first distant glimpse of Karakal, encountered messengers bearing a cordial invitation—and one that was rarely declined.

"Meanwhile the lamasery had begun to acquire many of its present characteristics. I must stress the fact that Henschell was exceedingly able and talented, and that the Shangri-La of to-day owes as much to him as to its founder. Yes, quite as much, I often think. For his was the firm yet kindly hand that every institution needs at a certain stage of its development, and his loss would have been altogether irreparable had he not completed more than a life-work before he died."

Conway looked up to echo rather than question those final words. *"He died!"*

"Yes. It was very sudden. He was killed. It was in the year of your Indian Mutiny. Just before his death a Chinese artist had sketched him, and I can show you that sketch now—it is in this room."

The slight gesture of the hand was repeated, and once again a servant entered. Conway, as a spectator in a trance, watched the man withdraw a small curtain at the far end of the room, and leave a lantern swinging amongst the shadows. Then he heard the whisper inviting him to move, the whisper that had already become a familiar music.

He stumbled to his feet and strode across to the

trembling circle of light. The sketch was small, hardly more than a miniature in coloured inks, but the artist had contrived to give the flesh-tones a waxwork delicacy of texture. The features were of great beauty, almost girlish in modelling, and Conway found in their winsomeness an instantly personal appeal, even across the barriers of time, death, and artifice. But the strangest thing of all was one that he realised only after his first gasp of admiration: the face was that of a young man.

He stammered as he moved away: "But—you said—this was done just before his death?"

"Yes. It is a very good likeness."

"Then if he died in the year you said——"

"He did."

"And he came here, you told me, in 1803, when he was a youth?"

"Yes."

Conway did not answer for a moment; presently with an effort, he collected himself to say: "And he was killed, you were telling me?"

"Yes. An Englishman shot him. It was a few weeks after the Englishman had arrived at Shangri-La. He was another of those explorers."

"What was the cause of it?"

"There had been a quarrel—about some porters. Henschell had just told him of the important proviso that governs our reception of guests. It was a task of some difficulty, and ever since, despite my own enfeeblement, I have felt constrained to perform it myself."

162

The High Lama made another and longer pause, with just a hint of enquiry in his silence; when he continued, it was to add: "Perhaps you are wondering, my dear Conway, what that proviso may be?"

Conway answered slowly and in a low voice: "I think I can already guess."

"Can you, indeed? And can you guess anything else after this long and curious story of mine?"

Conway dizzied in brain as he sought to answer the question; the room was now a whorl of shadows with that ancient benignity at its centre. Throughout the narrative he had listened with an intentness that had perhaps shielded him from realising the fullest implications of it all; now, with the mere attempt at conscious expression, he was flooded over with amazement, and the gathering certainty in his mind was almost stifled as it sprang to words. "It seems impossible," he stammered. "And yet I can't help thinking of it—it's astonishing—and extraordinary—and quite incredible—and yet not *absolutely* beyond my powers of belief——"

"What is, my son?"

And Conway answered, shaken with an emotion for which he knew no reason and which he did not seek to conceal: "*That you are still alive, Father Perrault.*"

8

THERE had been a pause, imposed by the High Lama's call for further refreshment; Conway did not wonder at it, for the strain of such a long recital must have been considerable. Nor was he himself ungrateful for the respite. He felt that the interval was as desirable from an artistic as from any other point of view, and that the bowls of tea, with their accompaniment of conventionally improvised courtesies, fulfilled the same function as a *cadenza* in music. This reflection brought out (unless it were mere coincidence) an odd example of the High Lama's telepathic powers, for he immediately began to talk about music and to express pleasure that Conway's taste in that direction had not been entirely unsatisfied at Shangri-La. Conway answered with suitable politeness and added that he had been surprised to find the lamasery in possession of such a complete library of European composers. The compliment was acknowledged between slow sips of tea. "Ah, my dear Conway, we are fortunate in that one of our number is a gifted musician—he was, indeed, a pupil of Chopin's—and we have been happy to place in his hands the entire management of our salon. You must certainly meet him."

"I should like to. Chang, by the way, was telling

me that your favourite Western composer is Mozart."

"That is so," came the reply. "Mozart has an austere elegance which we find very satisfying. He builds a house which is neither too big nor too little, and he furnishes it in perfect taste."

The exchange of comments continued until the tea-bowls were taken away; by that time Conway was able to remark quite calmly: "So, to resume our earlier discussion, you intend to keep us? That, I take it, is the important and invariable proviso?"

"You have guessed correctly, my son."

"And we are really to stay here for ever?"

"I should greatly prefer to employ your excellent English idiom and say that we are all of us here 'for good.'"

"What puzzles me is why we four, out of all the rest of the world's inhabitants, should have been chosen."

Relapsing into his earlier and more consequential manner, the High Lama responded: "It is an intricate story, if you would care to hear it. You must know that we have always aimed, as far as possible, to keep our numbers in fairly constant recruitment—since, apart from any other reasons, it is pleasant to have with us people of various ages and representative of different periods. Unfortunately, since the recent European War and the Russian Revolution, travel and exploration in Tibet have been almost completely held up; in fact, our last visitor, a Japanese, arrived in 1912, and was not, to be candid, a very valuable acquisition. You see, my dear Conway, we are not quacks or charlatans; we do not and cannot guarantee success; some of our visitors derive no benefit at all from their stay here; others merely live to what might be called a normally advanced age and then die from some trifling ailment. In general we have found that Tibetans, owing to their being inured to both the altitude and other conditions, are much less sensitive than outside races; they are charming people, and we have admitted many of them, but I doubt if more than a few will pass their hundredth year. The Chinese are a little better, but even among them we have a high percentage of failures. Our best subjects, undoubtedly, are the Nordic and Latin races of Europe; perhaps the Americans would be equally adaptable, and I count it our great good fortune that we have at last, in the person of one of your companions, secured a citizen of that nation. But I must continue with the answer to your question. The position was, as I have been explaining, that for nearly two decades we had welcomed no new-comers, and as there had been several deaths during that period, a problem was beginning to arise. A few years ago, however, one of our number came to the rescue with a novel idea; he was a young fellow, a native of our valley, abso-lutely trustworthy and in fullest sympathy with our aims; but, like all the valley people, he was denied by nature the chance that comes more fortunately to those from a distance. It was he who suggested that

166

he should leave us, make his way to some surrounding country, and bring us additional colleagues by a method which would have been impossible in an earlier age. It was in many respects a revolutionary proposal, but we gave our consent, after due consideration. For we must move with the times, you know, even at Shangri-La."

"You mean that he was sent out deliberately to bring someone back by air?"

"Well, you see, he was an exceedingly gifted and resourceful youth, and we had great confidence in him. It was his own idea, and we allowed him a free hand in carrying it out. All we knew definitely was that the first stage of his plan included a period of tuition at an American flying-school."

"But how could he manage the rest of it? It was only by chance that there happened to be that aeroplane at Baskul——"

"True, my dear Conway—many things are by chance. But it happened, after all, to be just the chance that Talu was looking for. Had he not found it, there might have been another chance in a year or two—or perhaps, of course, none at all. I confess I was surprised when our sentinels gave news of his descent on the plateau. The progress of aviation is rapid, but it had seemed likely to me that much more time would elapse before an average machine could make such a crossing of the mountains."

"It wasn't an average machine. It was a rather special one, made for mountain-flying."

"Again by chance? Our young friend was indeed

fortunate. It is a pity that we cannot discuss the matter with him—we were all grieved at his death. You would have liked him, Conway."

Conway nodded slightly; he felt it very possible. He said, after a silence: "But what's the idea behind it all?"

"My son, your way of asking that question gives me infinite pleasure. In the course of a somewhat long experience it has never before been put to me in tones of such calmness. My revelation has been greeted in almost every conceivable manner— with indignation, distress, fury, disbelief, and hysteria—but never until this night with mere interest. It is, however, an attitude that I most cordially welcome. To-day you are interested; to-morrow you will feel concern; eventually, it may be, we shall claim your devotion."

"That is more than I should care to promise."

"Your very doubt pleases me—it is the basis of profound and significant faith. . . . But let us not argue. You are interested, and that, from you, is much. All I ask in addition is that what I tell you now shall remain, for the present, unknown to your three companions."

Conway was silent.

"The time will come when they will learn, like you, but that moment, for their own sakes, had better not be hastened. I am so certain of your wisdom in this matter that I do not ask for a promise; you will act, I know, as we both think best. . . . Now let me begin by sketching for you a

168

very agreeable picture. You are still, I should say, a youngish man by the world's standards; your life, as people say, lies ahead of you; in the normal course you might expect twenty or thirty years of only slightly and gradually diminishing activity. By no means a cheerless prospect, and I can hardly expect you to see it as I do—as a slender, breathless, and far too frantic interlude. The first quarter-century of your life was doubtless lived under the cloud of being too young for things, while the last quarter-century would normally be shadowed by the still darker cloud of being too old for them; and between those two clouds, what small and narrow sunlight illumines a human lifetime! But you, it may be, are destined to be more fortunate, since by the standards of Shangri-La your sunlit years have scarcely yet begun. It will happen, perhaps, that decades hence you will feel no older than you are to-day—you may preserve, as Henschell did, a long and wondrous youth. But that, believe me, is only an early and superficial phase. There will come a time when you will age like others, though far more slowly, and into a condition infinitely nobler; at eighty you may still climb to the pass with a young man's gait, but at twice that age you must not expect the whole marvel to have persisted. We are not workers of miracles; we have made no conquest of death, or even of decay. All we have done and can sometimes do is to slacken the *tempo* of this brief interval that is called life. We do this by methods which are as simple here as they are impossible elsewhere; but make no mistake; the end awaits us all.

"Yet it is, nevertheless, a prospect of much charm that I unfold for you—long tranquillities during which you will observe a sunset as men in the outer world hear the striking clock, and with far less care. The years will come and go, and you will pass from fleshly enjoyments into austerer but no less satisfying realms; you may lose the keenness of muscle and appetite, but there will be gain to match your loss; you will achieve calmness and profundity, ripeness and wisdom and the clear enchantment of memory. And, most precious of all, you will have Time—that rare and lovely gift that your Western countries have lost the more they have pursued it. Think for a moment. You will have time to read—never again will you skim pages to save minutes, or avoid some study lest it prove too engrossing. You have also a taste for music—here then, are your scores and instruments, with Time, unruffled and unmeasured, to give you their richest savour. And you are also, we will say, a man of good fellowship—does it not charm you to think of wise and serene friendships, a long and kindly traffic of the mind from which death may not call you away with his customary hurry? Or, if it is solitude that you prefer, could you not employ our pavilions to enrich the gentleness of lonely thoughts?"

The voice made a pause which Conway did not seek to fill.

"You make no comment, my dear Conway. Forgive my eloquence—I belong to an age and a nation that never considered it bad form to be articulate. . . . But perhaps you are thinking of wife, parents, children, left behind in the world? Or maybe ambitions to do this or that? Believe me, though the pang may be keen at first, in a decade from now even its ghost will not haunt you. Though in point of fact, if I read your mind correctly, you have no such griefs."

Conway was startled by the accuracy of the judgement. "That's so," he replied. "I'm unmarried; I have few close friends, and no ambitions."

"No ambitions? And how have you contrived to escape those widespread maladies?"

For the first time Conway felt that he was actually taking part in a conversation. He said: "It always seemed to me in my profession that a good deal of what passed for success would be rather disagreeable, apart from needing more effort than I felt called upon to make. I was in the Consular Service—quite a subordinate post, but it suited me well enough."

"Yet your soul was not in it?"

"Neither my soul nor my heart nor more than half my energies. I'm naturally rather lazy."

The wrinkles deepened and twisted till Conway realised that the High Lama was very probably smiling. "Laziness in doing certain things can be a great virtue," resumed the whisper. "In any case, you will scarcely find us exacting in such a matter. Chang, I believe, explained to you our principle of moderation, and one of the things in which we are always moderate is activity. I myself, for instance, have been able to learn ten languages; the ten might have been twenty had I worked immoderately. But I did not. And it is the same in other directions; you will find us neither profligate nor ascetic. Until we reach an age when care is advisable, we gladly accept the pleasures of the table, while—for the benefit of our younger colleagues—the women of the valley have happily applied the principle of moderation to their own chastity. All things considered, I feel sure you will get used to our ways without much effort. Chang, indeed, was very optimistic—and so, after this meeting, am I. But there is, I admit, an odd quality in you that I have never met in any of our visitors hitherto. It is not quite cynicism, still less bitterness; perhaps it is partly disillusionment, but it is also a clarity of mind that I should not have expected in anyone younger than—say, a century or so. It is, if I had to put a single word to it, passionlessness."

Conway answered: "As good a word as most, no doubt. I don't know whether you classify the people who come here, but if so, you can label me '1914-18.' That makes me, I should think, a unique specimen in your museum of antiquities—the other three who arrived along with me don't enter the category. I used up most of my passions and energies during the years I've mentioned, and though I don't talk much about it, the chief thing I've asked from the world since then is to leave me alone. I find in this place a certain charm and quietness that appeals to me, and no doubt, as you remark, I shall get used to things."

"Is that all, my son?"

"I hope I am keeping well to your own rule of moderation."

"You are clever—as Chang told me, you are very clever. But is there nothing in the prospect I have outlined that tempts you to any stronger feeling?"

Conway was silent for an interval and then replied: "I was deeply impressed by your story of the past, but to be candid, your sketch of the future interests me only in an abstract sense. I can't look so far ahead. I should certainly be sorry if I had to leave Shangri-La to-morrow, or next week, or perhaps even next year; but how I shall feel about it if I live to be a hundred isn't a matter to prophesy. I can face it, like any other future, but in order to make me keen it must have a point. I've sometimes doubted whether life itself has any; and if not, long life must be even more pointless."

"My friend, the traditions of this building, both Buddhist and Christian, are very reassuring."

"Maybe. But I'm afraid I still hanker after some more definite reason for envying the centenarian."

"There *is* a reason, and a very definite one indeed. It is the whole reason for this colony of chance-sought strangers living beyond their years. We do not follow an idle experiment, a mere whimsy. We have a dream and a vision. It is a vision that first appeared to old Perrault when he lay

173

dying in this room in the year 1789. He looked back then on his long life, as I have already told you, and it seemed to him that all the loveliest things were transient and perishable, and that war, lust, and brutality might some day crush them until there were no more left in the world. He remembered sights he had seen with his own eyes, and with his mind he pictured others; he saw the nations strengthening, not in wisdom, but in vulgar passions and the will to destroy; he saw their machine power multiplying until a single weaponed man might have matched a whole army of the Grand Monarque. And he perceived that when they had filled the land and sea with ruin, they would take to the air. . . . Can you say that his vision was untrue?"

"True indeed."

"But that was not all. He foresaw a time when men, exultant in the technique of homicide, would rage so hotly over the world that every precious thing would be in danger, every book and picture and harmony, every treasure garnered through two millenniums, the small, the delicate, the defence-less—all would be lost like the lost books of Livy, or wrecked as the English wrecked the Summer Palace in Pekin."

"I share your opinion of that."

"Of course. But what are the opinions of reasonable men against iron and steel? Believe me, that vision of old Perrault will come true. And that, my son, is why *I* am here, and why *you* are here, and why we may pray to outlive the doom that gathers around on every side."

"To outlive it?"

"There is a chance. It will all come to pass before you are as old as I am."

"And you think that Shangri-La will escape?"

"Perhaps. We may expect no mercy, but we may faintly hope for neglect. Here we shall stay with our books and our music and our meditations, conserving the frail elegancies of a dying age, and seeking such wisdom as men will need when their passions are all spent. We have a heritage to cherish and bequeath. Let us take what pleasure we may until that time comes."

"And then?"

"Then, my son, when the strong have devoured each other, the Christian ethic may at last be fulfilled, and the meek shall inherit the earth."

A shadow of emphasis had touched the whisper, and Conway surrendered to the beauty of it; again he felt the surge of darkness around, but now symbolically, as if the world outside were already brewing for the storm. And then he saw that the High Lama of Shangri-La was actually astir, rising from his chair, standing upright like the half-embodiment of a ghost. In mere politeness Conway made to assist; but suddenly a deeper impulse seized him, and he did what he had never done to any man before; he knelt, and hardly knew why he did.

"I understand you, Father," he said.

175

He was not perfectly aware of how at last he took his leave; he was in a dream from which he did not emerge till long afterwards. He remembered the night air icy after the heat of those upper rooms, and Chang's presence, a silent serenity, as they crossed the starlit courtyards together. Never had Shangri-La offered more concentrated loveliness to his eyes; the valley lay imagined over the edge of the cliff, and the image was of a deep unrippled pool that matched the peace of his own thoughts. For Conway had passed beyond astonishments. The long talk, with its varying phases, had left him empty of all save a satisfaction that was as much of the mind as of the emotions, and as much of the spirit as of either; even his doubts were now no longer harassing, but part of a subtle harmony. Chang did not speak, and neither did he. It was very late, and he was glad that all the others had gone to bed.

9

IN the morning he wondered if all that he could call to mind were part of a waking or a sleeping vision.

He was soon reminded. A chorus of questions greeted him when he appeared at breakfast. "You certainly had a long talk with the boss last night," began the American. "We meant to wait up for you, but we got tired. What sort of guy is he?"

"Did he say anything about the porters?" asked Mallinson eagerly.

"I hope you mentioned to him about having a missionary stationed here," said Miss Brinklow.

The bombardment served to raise in Conway his usual defensive armament. "I'm afraid I'm probably going to disappoint you all," he replied, slipping casily into the mood. "I didn't discuss with him the question of missions; he didn't mention the porters to me at all; and as for his appearance, I can only say that he's a very old man who speaks excellent English and is quite intelligent."

Mallinson cut in with irritation: "The main thing to us is whether he's to be trusted or not. Do you think he means to let us down?"

"He didn't strike me as a dishonourable person."

"Why on earth didn't you worry him about the porters?"

"It didn't occur to me."

Mallinson stared at him incredulously. "I can't understand you, Conway. You were so damned good in that Baskul affair that I can hardly believe you're the same man. You seem to have gone all to pieces."

"I'm sorry."

"No good being sorry. You ought to buck up and look as if you cared what happens."

"You misunderstand me. I meant that I was sorry to have disappointed you."

Conway's voice was curt, an intended mask to his feelings, which were, indeed, so mixed that they could hardly have been guessed by others. He had slightly surprised himself by the ease with which he had prevaricated; it was clear that he intended to observe the High Lama's suggestion and keep the secret. He was also puzzled by the naturalness with which he was accepting a position which his companions would certainly and with some justification think traitorous; as Mallinson had said, it was hardly the sort of thing to be expected of a hero. Conway felt a sudden half-pitying fondness for the youth; then he steeled himself by reflecting that people who hero-worship must be prepared for disillusionments. Mallinson at Baskul had been far too much the new boy adoring the handsome games-captain, and now the games-captain was tottering if not already fallen from the pedestal. There was always something a little pathetic in the smashing of an ideal, however false; and

178

Mallinson's admiration might have been at least a partial solace for the strain of pretending to be what he was not. But pretence was impossible anyway. There was a quality in the air of Shangri-La—perhaps due to its altitude—that forbade one the effort of counterfeit emotion.

He said: "Look here, Mallinson, it's no use harping continually on Baskul. Of course I was different then—it was a completely different situation."

"And a much healthier one, in my opinion. At least we knew what we were up against."

"Murder and rape—to be precise. You can call that healthier if you like."

The youth's voice rose in pitch as he retorted: "Well, I *do* call it healthier—in one sense. It's something I'd rather face than all this mystery business." Suddenly he added: "That Chinese girl, for instance—how did *she* get here? Did the fellow tell you?"

"No. Why should he?"

"Well, why shouldn't he? And why shouldn't you ask, if you had any interest in the matter at all? Is it usual to find a young girl living with a lot of monks?"

That way of looking at it was one that had scarcely occurred to Conway before. "This isn't an ordinary monastery," was the best reply he could give, after some thought.

"My God, it isn't!"

There was a silence, for the argument had evidently reached a dead-end. To Conway the history of Lo-Tsen seemed rather far from the point; the little Manchu lay so quietly in his mind that he hardly knew she was there. But at the mere mention of her Miss Brinklow had looked up suddenly from the Tibetan grammar which she was studying even over the breakfast-table (just as if, thought Conway, with secret meaning, she hadn't all her life for it). Chatter of girls and monks reminded her of those stories of Indian temples that men missionaries told their wives, and that the wives passed on to their unmarried female colleagues. "Of course," she said between tightened lips, "the morals of this place are quite hideous—we might have expected that." She turned to Barnard as if inviting support, but the American only grinned. "I don't reckon you folks'd value my opinion on a matter of morals," he remarked dryly. "But I should say myself that quarrels are just as bad. Since we've gotter be here for some time yet, let's keep our tempers and make ourselves comfortable."

Conway thought this good advice, but Mallinson was still unplaced. "I can quite believe you find it more comfortable than Dartmoor," he said meaningly.

"Dartmoor? Oh, that's your big penitentiary?—I get you. Well, yes, I certainly never did envy the folks in them places. And there's another thing, too—it don't hurt when you chip me about it.

Thick-skinned and tender-hearted, that's my mixure."

Conway glanced at him in appreciation, and at Mallinson with some hint of reproof; but then abruptly he had the feeling that they were all acting on a vast stage, of whose background only he himself was conscious; and such knowledge, so incommunicable, made him suddenly want to be alone. He nodded to them and went out into the courtyard. In sight of Karakal misgivings faded, and qualms about his three companions were lost in an uncanny acceptance of the new world that lay so far beyond their guesses. There came a time, he realised, when the strangeness of everything made it increasingly difficult to realise the strangeness of anything; when one took things for granted merely because astonishment would have been as tedious for oneself as for others. Thus far had he progressed at Shangri-La, and he remembered that he had attained a similar though far less pleasant equanimity during his years at the War.

He needed equanimity, if only to accommodate himself to the double life he was compelled to lead. Thenceforward, with his fellow-exiles, he lived in a world conditioned by the arrival of porters and a return to India; at all other times the horizon lifted like a curtain; time expanded and space contracted, and the name Blue Moon took on a symbolic meaning, as if the future, so delicately plausible, were of a kind that might happen once in a blue moon only. Sometimes he wondered which of his two lives were the more real, but the problem was not pressing; and again he was reminded of the War, for during heavy bombardments he had had the same comforting sensation that he had many lives, only one of which could be claimed by death.

Chang, of course, now talked to him completely without reserve, and they had many conversations about the rule and routine of the lamasery. Conway learned that during his first five years he would live a normal life, without any special regimen; this was always done, as Chang said, "to enable the body to accustom itself to the altitude, and also to give time for the dispersal of mental and emotional regrets."

Conway remarked with a smile: "I suppose you're certain, then, that no human affection can outlast a five-year absence?"

"It can, undoubtedly," replied the Chinese, "but only as a fragrance whose melancholy we may enjoy."

After the probationary five years, Chang went on to explain, the process of retarding age would begin, and if successful, might give Conway half a century or so at the apparent age of forty—which was not a bad time of life at which to remain stationary.

"What about yourself?" Conway asked. "How did it work out in your case?"

"Ah, my dear sir, I was lucky enough to arrive when I was quite young—only twenty-two. I was a soldier, though you might not have thought it; I had command of troops operating against brigand tribes in the year 1885. I was making what I should have called a reconnaissance if I had ever returned to my superior officers to tell the tale, but in plain truth I had lost my way in the mountains, and of my men only seven out of over a hundred survived the rigours of the climate. When at last I was rescued and brought to Shangri-La I was so ill that only extreme youth and virility saved me."

"Twenty-two," echoed Conway, performing the calculation. "So you're now ninety-seven?"

"Yes. Very soon, if the lamas give their consent, I shall receive full initiation."

"I see. You have to wait for the round figure?"

"No, we are not restricted by any definite age limit, but a century is generally considered to be an age beyond which the passions and moods of ordinary life are likely to have disappeared."

"I should certainly think so. And what happens afterwards? How long do you expect to carry on?"

"There is reason to hope that I shall enter lamahood with such prospects as Shangri-La has made possible. In years, perhaps another century or more."

Conway nodded. "I don't know whether I ought to congratulate you—you seem to have been granted the best of both worlds, a long and pleasant youth behind you, and an equally long and pleasant old age ahead. When did you begin to grow old in appearance?"

"When I was over seventy. That is often the case,

though I think I may still claim to look younger than my years."

"Decidedly. And suppose you were to leave the valley now, what would happen?"

"Death, if I remained away for more than a very few days."

"The atmosphere, then, is essential?"

"There is only one valley of Blue Moon, and those who expect to find another are asking too much of Nature."

"Well, what would have happened if you had left the valley, say, thirty years ago, during your prolonged youth?"

Chang answered: "Probably I should have died even then. In any case, I should have acquired very quickly the full appearance of my actual age. We had a curious example of that some years ago, though there had been several others before. One of our number had left the valley to look out for a party of travellers who we had heard might be approaching. This man, a Russian, had arrived here originally in the prime of life, and had taken to our ways so well that at nearly eighty he did not look more than half as old. He should have been absent no longer than a week (which would not have mattered), but unfortunately he was taken prisoner by nomad tribes and carried away some distance. We suspected an accident and gave him up for lost. Three months later, however, he returned to us, having made his escape. But he was a very different man. Every year of his age was in his face and behaviour, and he died shortly afterwards, as an old man dies."

Conway made no remark for some time. They were talking in the library, and during most of the narrative he had been gazing through a window towards the pass that led to the outer world; a little wisp of cloud had drifted across the ridge. "A rather grim story, Chang," he commented at length. "It gives one the feeling that Time is like some baulked monster, waiting outside the valley to pounce on the slackers who have managed to evade him longer than they should."

"*Slackers?*" queried Chang. His knowledge of English was extremely good, but sometimes a collo-quialism proved unfamiliar.

"'Slacker,'" explained Conway, "is a slang word meaning a lazy fellow, a good-for-nothing. I wasn't, of course, using it seriously."

Chang bowed his thanks for the information. He took a keen interest in languages, and liked to weigh a new word philosophically. "It is significant," he said after a pause, "that the English regard slackness as a vice. We, on the other hand, should vastly prefer it to tension. Is there not too much tension in the world at present, and might it not be better if people were slackers?"

"I'm inclined to agree with you," Conway answered with solemn amusement.

During the course of a week or so after the interview with the High Lama, Conway met several others of his future colleagues. Chang was neither eager nor reluctant to make the introductions, and Conway sensed a new and to him rather attractive atmosphere in which urgency did not clamour nor postponement disappoint. "Indeed," as Chang explained, "some of the lamas may not meet you for a considerable time—perhaps years—but you must not be surprised at that. They are prepared to make your acquaintance when it may so happen, and their avoidance of hurry does not imply any degree of unwillingness." Conway, who had often had similar feelings when calling on new arrivals at foreign consulates, thought it a very intelligible attitude.

The meetings he did have, however, were quite successful, and conversation with men thrice his age held none of the social embarrassments that might have obtruded in London or Delhi. His first encounter was with a genial German named Meister, who had entered the lamasery during the 'eighties, as the survivor of an exploring party. He spoke English well, though with an accent. A day or two later a second introduction took place, and Conway enjoyed his first talk with the man whom the High Lama had particularly mentioned— Alphonse Briac, a wiry, small-statured Frenchman who did not look especially old, though he announced himself as a pupil of Chopin. Conway thought that both he and the German would prove agreeable company. Already he was subconsciously analysing, and after a few further meetings he

186

reached one or two general conclusions; he perceived that though the lamas he met had individual differences, they all possessed that quality for which agelessness was not an outstandingly good name, but the only one he could think of. Moreover, they were all endowed with a calm intelligence which pleasantly overflowed into measured and well-balanced opinions. Conway could give an exact response to that kind of approach, and he was aware that they realized it, and were gratified. He found them quite as easy to get on with as any other group of cultured people he might have met, though there was often a sense of oddity in hearing reminiscences so distant and apparently so casual. One white-haired and benevolent-looking person, for instance, asked Conway, after a little conversation, if he were interested in the Brontës. Conway said he was, to some extent, and the other replied: "You see, when I was a curate in the West Riding during the 'forties, I once visited Haworth and stayed at the Parsonage. Since coming here I've made a study of the whole Brontë problem—indeed, I'm writing a book on the subject. Perhaps you might care to go over it with me some time?"

Conway responded cordially, and afterwards, when he and Chang were left together, commented on the vividness with which the lamas appeared to recollect their pre-Tibetan lives. Chang answered that it was all part of the training. "You see, my dear sir, one of the first steps towards the clarifying of the mind is to obtain a panorama of one's own past, and that, like any other view, is more accurate in perspective. When you have been among us long enough you will find your old life slipping gradually into focus as through a telescope when the lens is adjusted. Everything will stand out still and clear, duly proportioned and with its correct significance. Your new acquaintance, for instance, discerns that the really big moment of his entire life occurred when he was a young man visiting a house in which there lived an old parson and his three daughters."

"So I suppose I shall have to set to work to remember my own big moments?"

"It will not be an effort. They will come to you."

"I don't know that I shall give them much of a welcome," answered Conway moodily.

But whatever the past might yield, he was discovering happiness in the present. When he sat reading in the library, or playing Mozart in the music-room, he often felt the invasion of a deep spiritual emotion, as if Shangri-La were indeed a living essence, distilled from the magic of the ages and miraculously preserved against time and death. His talk with the High Lama recurred memorably at such moments; he sensed a calm intelligence brooding gently over every diversion, giving a thousand whispered reassurances to ear and eye. Thus he would listen while Lo-Tsen marshalled some intricate fugue rhythm, and wonder what lay behind the faint impersonal smile that stirred her lips into the likeness of an opening flower. She talked very little, even though she now knew that Conway could speak her language; to Mallinson, who liked to visit the music-room sometimes, she was almost dumb. But Conway discerned a charm that was perfectly expressed by her silences.

Once he asked Chang her history, and learned that she came of royal Manchu stock. "She was betrothed to a prince of Turkestan, and was travelling to Kashgar to meet him when her carriers lost their way in the mountains. The whole party would doubtless have perished but for the customary meeting with our emissaries."

"When did this happen?"

"In 1884. She was eighteen."

"Eighteen *then*?"

Chang bowed. "Yes, we are succeeding very well with her, as you may judge for yourself. Her progress has been consistently excellent."

"How did she take things when she first came?"

"She was, perhaps, a little more than averagely reluctant to accept the situation—she made no protest, but we were aware that she was troubled for a time. It was, of course, an unusual occurrence—to intercept a young girl on the way to her wedding. . . . We were all particularly anxious that she should be happy here." Chang smiled blandly. "I am afraid the excitement of love does not make for an easy surrender, though the first five years proved ample for their purpose."

"She was deeply attached, I suppose, to the man she was to have married?"

"Hardly that, my dear sir, since she had never seen him. It was the old custom, you know. The excitement of her affections was entirely impersonal."

Conway nodded, and thought a little tenderly of Lo-Tsen. He pictured her as she might have been half a century before, statuesque in her decorated chair as the carriers toiled over the plateau, her eyes searching the wind-swept horizons that must have seemed so harsh after the gardens and lotus-pools of the east. "Poor child!" he said, thinking of such elegance held captive over the years. Knowledge of her past increased rather than lessened his content with her stillness and silence; she was like a lovely cold vase, unadorned save by an escaping ray.

He was also content, though less ecstatically, when Briac talked to him of Chopin, and played the familiar melodies with much brilliance. It appeared that the Frenchman knew several Chopin compositions that had never been published, and as he had written them down, Conway devoted pleasant hours to memorising them himself. He found a certain piquancy in the reflection that neither Cortot nor Pachmann had been so fortunate. Nor were Briac's recollections at an end; his memory continually refreshed him with some little scrap of tune that the composer had thrown off or improvised on some occasion; he took them all down on paper as they came into his head, and

190

some were very delightful fragments. "Briac," Chang explained, "has not been initiated, so you must make allowances if he talks a great deal about Chopin. The younger lamas are naturally preoccupied with the past; it is a necessary step to envisaging the future."

"Which is, I take it, the job of the older ones?"

"Yes. The High Lama, for instance, spends almost his entire life in clairvoyant meditation."

Conway pondered a moment and then said: "By the way, when do you suppose I shall see him again?"

"Doubtless at the end of the first five years, my dear sir."

But in that confident prophecy Chang was wrong, for less than a month after his arrival at Shangri-La Conway received a second summons to that torrid upper room. Chang had told him that the High Lama never left his apartments, and that their heated atmosphere was necessary for his bodily existence; and Conway, being thus prepared, found the change less disconcerting than before. Indeed, he breathed easily as soon as he had made his bow and been granted the faintest answering liveliness of the sunken eyes. He felt kinship with the mind beyond them, and though he knew that this second interview following so soon upon the first was an unprecedented honour, he was not in the least nervous or weighed down with solemnity. Age was to him no more an obsessing factor than rank or colour; he had never felt debarred from

191

liking people because they were too young or too old. He held the High Lama in most cordial respect, but he did not see why their social relations should be anything less than urbane.

They exchanged the usual courtesies, and Conway answered many polite questions. He said he was finding the life very agreeable and had already made friendships.

"And you have have kept our secrets from your three companions?"

"Yes, up to now. It has proved awkward for me at times, but probably less so than if I had told them."

"Just as I surmised; you have acted as you thought best. And the awkwardness, after all, is only temporary. Chang tells me he thinks that two of them will give little trouble."

"I dare say that is so."

"And the third?"

Conway replied: "Mallinson is an excitable youth—he's pretty keen to get back."

"You like him?"

"Yes, I like him very much."

At this point the tea-bowls were brought in, and talk became less serious between sips of the scented liquid. It was an apt convention, enabling the verbal flow to acquire a touch of that almost frivolous fragrance, and Conway was responsive. When the High Lama asked him whether Shangri-La was not unique in his experience, and if the Western world could offer anything in the least like it, he answered with a smile: "Well, yes. To be quite frank, it reminds me very slightly of Oxford, where I used to lecture. The scenery there is not so good, but the subjects of study are often just as impractical, and though even the oldest of the dons is not quite so old, they appear to age in a somewhat similar way."

"You have a sense of humour, my dear Conway," replied the High Lama, "for which we shall all be grateful during the years to come."

10

"EXTRAORDINARY," Chang said, when he heard that Conway had seen the High Lama again. And from one so reluctant to employ superlatives the word was significant. It had never happened before, he emphasised, since the routine of the lamasery became established; never had the High Lama desired a second meeting until the five years' probation had affected a purge of all the exile's likely emotions. "Because, you see, it is a great strain on him to talk to the average new-comer. The mere presence of human passions is an unwelcome and, at his age, an almost unendurable unpleasantness. Not that I doubt his entire wisdom in the matter. It teaches us, I believe, a lesson of great value—that even the fixed rules of our community are only moderately fixed. But it is extraordinary, all the same."

To Conway, of course, it was no more extra-ordinary than anything else, and after he had visited the High Lama on a third and fourth occasion, he began to feel that it was not very extraordinary at all. There seemed, indeed, something almost preordained in the ease with which their two minds approached each other; it was as if in Conway all secret tensions were relaxed, giving him, when he came away, a sumptuous tranquillity. At times he had the sensation of being completely bewitched by the mastery of that central intelligence, and then, over the little pale-blue tea-bowls, the cerebration would contract into a liveliness so gentle and miniature that he had an impression of a theorem dissolving limpidly into a sonnet.

Their talks ranged far and fearlessly; entire philosophies were unfolded; the long avenues of history surrendered themselves for inspection and were given new plausibility. To Conway it was an entrancing experience, but he did not suspend the critical attitude, and once, when he had argued a point, the High Lama replied: "My son, you are young in years, but I perceive that your wisdom has the ripeness of age. Surely some unusual thing has happened to you?"

Conway smiled. "No more unusual than has happened to many others of my generation."

"I have never met your like before."

Conway answered after an interval: "There's not a great deal of mystery about it. That part of me which seems old to you was worn out by intense and premature experience. My years from nineteen to twenty-two were a supreme education, no doubt, but rather exhausting."

"You were unhappy at the War?"

"Not particularly so. I was excited and suicidal and scared and reckless and sometimes in a tearing rage. Like a few million others, in fact. I got mad-drunk and killed and lechered in great style. It was the self-abuse of all one's emotions, and one came

195

through it, if one did at all, with a sense of almighty boredom and fretfulness. That's what made the years afterwards so difficult. Don't think I'm posing myself too tragically—I've had pretty fair luck since, on the whole. But it's been rather like being in a school where there's a bad headmaster—plenty of fun to be got if you feel like it, but nerve-racking off and on, and not really very satisfactory. I think I found that out rather more than most people."

"And your education thus continued?"

Conway gave a shrug. "Perhaps the exhaustion of the passions is the beginning of wisdom, if you care to alter the proverb."

"That also, my son, is the doctrine of Shangri-La."

"I know. It makes me feel quite at home."

He had spoken no less than the truth. As the days and weeks passed he began to feel an ache of contentment uniting his mind and body; like Perrault and Henschell and the others, he was falling under the spell. Blue Moon had taken him, and there was no escape. The mountains gleamed around in a hedge of inaccessible purity, from which his eyes fell dazzled to the green depths of the valley; the whole picture was incomparable, and when he heard the harpsichord's silver monotony across the lotus-pool, he felt that it threaded the perfect pattern of sight and sound.

He was, and he knew it, very quietly in love with

the little Manchu. His love demanded nothing, not even reply; it was a tribute of the mind, to which his senses added only a flavour. She stood for him as a symbol of all that was delicate and fragile; her stylised courtesies and the touch of her fingers on the keyboard yielded a completely satisfying intimacy. Sometimes he would address her in a way that might, if she had cared, have led to less formal conversation; but her replies never broke through the exquisite privacy of her thoughts, and in a sense he did not wish them to. He had suddenly come to realise a single facet of the promised jewel; he had Time, Time for everything that he wished to happen, such time that desire itself was quenched in the certainty of fulfilment. A year, a decade hence, there would still be Time. The vision grew on him, and he was happy with it.

Then, at intervals, he stepped into the other life to encounter Mallinson's impatience, Barnard's heartiness, and Miss Brinklow's robust intention. He felt he would be glad when they all knew as much as he; and, like Chang, he could imagine that neither the American nor the missionary would prove difficult cases. he was even amused when Barnard once said: "You know, Conway, I'm not sure that this wouldn't be a nice little place to settle down in. I thought at first I'd miss the newspapers and the movies, but I guess one can get used to anything."

"I guess one can," agreed Conway.

He learned afterwards that Chang had taken

Barnard down to the valley, at his own request, to enjoy everything in the way of a "night out" that the resources of the locality could provide. Mallinson, when he heard of this, was rather scornful. "Getting tight, I suppose," he remarked to Conway, and to Barnard himself he commented: "Of course it's none of my business, but you'll want to keep yourself pretty fit for the journey, you know. The porters are due in a fortnight's time, and from what I gather, the return trip won't be exactly a joy ride."

Barnard nodded equably. "I never figgered it would," he answered. "And as for keeping fit, I reckon I'm fitter than I've been for years. I get my daily exercise, I don't have any worries, and the speakeasies down in the valley don't let a feller go too far. Moderation, y'know—the motto of the firm."

"Yes, I've no doubt you've been managing to have a moderately good time," said Mallinson acidly.

"Certainly I have. This establishment caters for all tastes—some people like little Chink gels who play the pi-anno, isn't that so? You can't blame anybody for what they fancy."

Conway was not at all put out, but Mallinson flushed like a schoolboy. "You can send them to jail, though, when they fancy other people's property," he snapped, stung to fury that set a raw edge to his wits.

"Sure, if you can catch 'em." The American

198

grinned affably. "And that leads me to something I may as well tell you folks right now, now we're on the subject. I've decided to give those porters a miss. I guess they come here pretty regular, and I'll wait for the next trip, or maybe the next but one. That is, if the monks'll take my word that I'm still good for my hotel expenses."

"You mean you're not coming with us?"

"That's it. I've decided to stop over for a while. It's all very fine for you—you'll have the band playing when *you* get home, but all the welcome I'll get is from a row of cops. And the more I think about it, the more it don't seem good enough."

"In other words, you're just afraid to face the music?"

"Well, I never did like music, anyhow."

Mallinson said with cold scorn: "I suppose it's your own affair. Nobody can prevent you from stopping here all your life if you feel inclined." Nevertheless he looked round with a flash of appeal. "It's not what everybody would choose to do, but ideas differ. What do you say, Conway?"

"I agree. Ideas *do* differ."

Mallinson turned to Miss Brinklow, who suddenly put down her book and remarked: "As a matter of fact, I think I shall stay too."

"*What?*" they all cried together.

She continued, with a bright smile that seemed more an attachment to her face than an illumination of it: "You see, I've been thinking over the way things happened to bring us all here, and there's

199

only one conclusion I can come to. There's a mysterious power working behind the scenes. Don't you think so, Mr. Conway?"

Conway might have found it hard to reply, but Miss Brinklow went on in a gathering hurry: "Who am I to question the dictates of Providence? I was sent here for a purpose, and I shall stay."

"Do you mean you're hoping to start a mission here?" Mallinson asked.

"Not only hoping, but fully intending. I know just how to deal with these people—I shall get my own way, never fear. There's no real grit in any of them."

"And you intend to introduce some?"

"Yes, I do, Mr. Mallinson. I'm strongly opposed to that idea of moderation that we hear so much about. You can call it broadmindedness if you like, but in my opinion it leads to the worst kind of laxity. The whole trouble with the people here is their so-called broadmindedness, and I intend to fight it with all my powers."

"And they're so broadminded that they're going to let you?" said Conway, smiling.

"Or else she's so strong-minded that they can't stop her," put in Barnard. He added with a chuckle: "It's just what I said—this establishment caters for all tastes."

"Possibly, if you happen to *like* prison," Mallinson snapped.

"Well, there's two ways of looking even at that. My goodness, if you think of all the folks in the world who'd give all they've got to be out of the racket and in a place like this, only they can't *get* out! Are *we* in the prison or are *they*?"

"A comforting speculation for a monkey in a cage," retorted Mallinson; he was still furious.

Afterwards he spoke to Conway alone. "That man still gets on my nerves," he said, pacing the courtyard. "I'm not sorry we shan't have him with us when we go back. You may think me touchy, but being chipped about that Chinese girl didn't appeal to my sense of humour."

Conway took Mallinson's arm. It was becoming increasingly clear to him that he was very fond of the youth, and that their recent weeks in company had deepened the feeling, despite jarring moods. He answered: "I rather took it that *I* was being ragged about her, not you."

"No, I think he intended it for me. He knows I'm interested in her. I am, Conway. I can't make out why she's here, and whether she really likes being here. My God, if I spoke her language as you do, I'd soon have it out with her."

"I wonder if you would. She doesn't say a great deal to anyone, you know."

"It puzzles me that you don't badger her with all sorts of questions."

"I don't know that I care for badgering people."

He wished he could have said more, and then suddenly the sense of pity and irony floated over him in a filmy haze; this youth, so eager and ardent,

201

would take things very hardly. "I shouldn't worry about Lo-Tsen if I were you," he added. "She's happy enough."

The decision of Barnard and Miss Brinklow to remain seemed to Conway all to the good, though it threw Mallinson and himself into an apparently opposite camp for the time being. It was an extraordinary situation, and he had no definite plans for tackling it.

Fortunately there was no apparent need to tackle it at all. Until the two months were past, nothing much could happen; and afterwards there would be a crisis no less acute for his having tried to prepare himself for it. For this and other reasons he was disinclined to worry over the inevitable, though he did once say: "You know, Chang, I'm bothered about young Mallinson. I'm afraid he'll take things very badly when he finds out."

Chang nodded with some sympathy. "Yes, it will not be easy to persuade him of his good fortune. But the difficulty is, after all, only a temporary one. In twenty years from now our friend will be quite reconciled."

Conway felt that this was looking at the matter almost too philosophically. "I'm wondering," he said, "just how the truth's going to be broached to him. He's counting the days to the arrival of the porters, and if they don't come——"

"But they *will* come."

"Oh? I rather imagined that all your talk about

them was just a pleasant fable to let us down lightly."

"By no means. Although we have no bigotry on the point, it is our custom at Shangri-La to be moderately truthful, and I can assure you that my statements about the porters were almost correct. At any rate, we are expecting the men at or about the time I said."

"Then you'll find it hard to stop Mallinson from joining them."

"But we should never attempt to do so. He will merely discover—no doubt by personal experiment—that the porters are reluctantly unable to take anyone back with them."

"I see. So that's the method? And what do you expect to happen afterwards?"

"Then, my dear sir, after a period of disappointment, he will—since he is young and optimistic—begin to hope that the next convoy of porters, due in nine or ten months' time, will prove more amenable to his suggestions. And this is a hope which, if we are wise, we shall not at first discourage."

Conway said sharply: "I'm not so sure that he'll do that at all. I should think he's far more likely to try an escape on his own."

"*Escape?* Is that *really* the word that should be used? After all, the pass is open to anyone at any time. We have no jailers, save those that Nature herself has provided."

Conway smiled. "Well, you must admit that she's

done her job pretty well. But I don't suppose you rely on her in every case, all the same. What about the various exploring parties that have arrived here? Was the pass always equally open to *them* when they wanted to get away?"

It was Chang's turn now to smile. "Special circumstances, my dear sir, have sometimes required special consideration."

"Excellent. So you only allow people the chance of escape when you know they'd be fools to take it? Even so, I expect some of them do."

"Well, it has happened very occasionally, but as a rule the absentees are glad to return after the experience of a single night on the plateau."

"Without shelter and proper clothing? If so, I can quite understand that your mild methods are as effective as are stern ones. But what about the less usual cases that don't return?"

"You have yourself answered the question," replied Chang. "They do *not* return." But he made haste to add: "I can assure you, however, that there are few indeed who have been so unfortunate, and I trust your friend will not be rash enough to increase the number."

Conway did not find these responses entirely reassuring, and Mallinson's future remained a preoccupation. He wished it were possible for the youth to return by consent, and this would not be unprecedented, for there was the recent case of Talu, the airman. Chang admitted that the authorities were fully empowered to do anything that they considered wise. "But *should* we be wise, my dear sir, in trusting ourselves and our future entirely to your friend's feelings of gratitude?"

Conway felt that the question was pertinent, for Mallinson's attitude left little doubt as to what he would do as soon as he reached India. It was his favourite theme, and he had often enlarged upon it.

But all that, of course, was in the mundane world that was gradually being pushed out of his mind by the rich, pervasive world of Shangri-La. Except when he thought about Mallinson he was extraordinarily content; the slowly revealed fabric of this new environment continued to astonish him by its intricate suitability to his own needs and tastes.

Once he said to Chang: "By the way, how do you people here fit love into your scheme of things? I suppose it does sometimes happen that those who come here develop attachments?"

"Quite often," replied Chang with a broad smile. "The lamas, of course, are immune, and so are most of us when we reach the riper years, but until then we are as other men, except that I think we can claim to behave more reasonably. And this gives me the opportunity, Mr. Conway, of assuring you that the hospitality of Shangri-La is of a comprehensive kind. Your friend Mr. Barnard has already availed himself of it."

Conway returned the smile. "Thanks," he answered dryly. "I've no doubt he has, but my own inclinations are not—at the moment—so assertive.

205

It was the emotional more than the physical aspect that I was curious about."

"You find it easy to separate the two? Is it possible that you are falling in love with Lo-Tsen?"

Conway was somewhat taken aback, though he hoped he did not show it. "What makes you ask that?"

"Because, my dear sir, it would be quite suitable if you were to do so—always, of course, in moderation. Lo-Tsen would not respond with any degree of passion—that is more than you could expect—but the experience would be very delightful, I assure you. And I speak with some authority, for I was in love with her myself when I was much younger."

"Were you indeed? And did she respond then?"

"Only by the most charming appreciation of the compliment I paid her, and by a friendship which has grown more precious with the years."

"In other words, she didn't respond?"

"If you prefer it so." Chang added, a little sententiously: "It has always been her way to spare her lovers the moment of satiety that goes with all absolute attainment."

Conway laughed. "That's all very well in your case, and perhaps in mine too, but what about the attitude of a hot-blooded young fellow like Mallinson?"

"My dear sir, it would be the best possible thing that could happen! Not for the first time, I assure you, would Lo-Tsen comfort the sorrowful exile when he learns that there is to be no return."

"*Comfort?*"

"Yes, though you must not misunderstand my use of the term. Lo-Tsen gives no caresses, except such as touch the stricken heart from her very presence. What does your Shakespeare say of Cleopatra?—'She makes hungry where she most satisfies.' A popular type, doubtless, among the passion-driven races, but such a woman, I assure you, would be altogether out of place at Shangri-La. Lo-Tsen, if I might emend the quotation, *removes* hunger where she *least* satisfies. It is a more delicate and lasting accomplishment."

"And one, I assume, which she has much skill in performing?"

"Oh, decidedly—we have had many examples of it. It is her way to calm the throb of desire to a murmur that is no less pleasant when left unanswered."

"In that sense, then, you could regard her as a part of the training equipment of the establishment?"

"You could regard her as that, if you wished," replied Chang with deprecating blandness. "But it would be more grateful, and just as true, to liken her to the rainbow reflected in a glass bowl, or to the dewdrops on the blossom of the fruit tree."

"I entirely agree with you, Chang. That would be *much* more graceful." Conway enjoyed the measured yet agile repartees which his good-humoured ragging of the Chinese very often elicited.

But the next time he was alone with the little Manchu he felt that Chang's remarks had had a great deal of shrewdness in them. There was a fragrance about her that communicated itself to his own emotions, kindling the embers to a glow that did not burn, but merely warmed. And suddenly then he realised that Shangri-La and Lo-Tsen were quite perfect, and that he did not wish for more than to stir a faint and eventual response in all that stillness. For years his passions had been like a nerve that the world jarred on; now at last the aching was soothed, and he could yield himself to love that was neither a torment nor a bore. As he passed by the lotus-pool at night he sometimes pictured her in his arms, but the sense of time washed over the vision, calming him to an infinite and tender reluctance.

He did not think he had ever been so happy, even in the years of his life before the great barrier of the War. He liked the serene world that Shangri-La offered him, pacified rather than dominated by its single tremendous idea. He liked the prevalent mood in which feelings were sheathed in thoughts, and thoughts softened into felicity by their transference into language. Conway, whom experience had taught that rudeness is by no means a guarantee of good faith, was even less inclined to regard a well-turned phrase as a proof of insincerity. He liked the mannered, leisurely atmosphere in which talk was an accomplishment, not a mere habit. And he liked to realise that the idlest things could now

208

be freed from the curse of time-wasting, and the frailest dreams receive the welcome of the mind. Shangri-La was always tranquil, yet always a hive of unpursuing occupations; the lamas lived as if indeed they had time on their hands, but time that was scarcely a featherweight. Conway met no more of them, but he came gradually to realise the extent and variety of their employment; besides their knowledge of languages, some, it appeared, took to the full seas of learning in a manner that would have yielded big surprises to the Western world. Many were engaged in writing manuscript books of various kinds; one (Chang said) had made valuable researches into pure mathematics; another was co-ordinating Gibbon and Spengler into a vast thesis on the history of European civilisation. But this kind of thing was not for them all, nor for any of them always; there were many tideless channels in which they dived in mere waywardness, retrieving, like Briac, fragments of old tunes, or like the English ex-curate, a new theory about *Wuthering Heights*. And there were even fainter impracticalities than these. Once, when Conway made some remark in this connection, the High Lama replied with a story of a Chinese artist in the third century B.C. who, having spent many years in carving dragons, birds, and horses upon a cherry-stone, offered his finished work to a royal prince. The prince could see nothing in it at first except a mere stone, but the artist bade him "have a wall built, and make a window in it, and observe the stone

209

through the window in the glory of the dawn." The prince did so, and then perceived that the stone was indeed very beautiful. "Is not that a charming story, my dear Conway, and do you not think it teaches a very valuable lesson?"

Conway agreed; he found it pleasant to realise that the serene purpose of Shangri-La could embrace an infinitude of odd and apparently trivial employments, for he had always had a taste for such things himself. In fact, when he regarded his past, he saw it strewn with images of tasks too vagrant or too taxing ever to have been accomplished; but now they were all possible, even in a mood of idleness. It was delightful to contemplate, and he was not disposed to sneer when Barnard confided in him that he, too, envisaged an interesting future at Shangri-La.

It seemed that Barnard's excursions to the valley, which had been growing more frequent of late, were not entirely devoted to drink and women. "You see, Conway, I'm telling you this because you're different from Mallinson—he's got his knife into me, as probably you've gathered. But I feel you'll be better at understanding the position. It's a funny thing—you British officials are darned stiff and starchy at first, but you're the sort a fellow can put his trust in, when all's said and done."

"I wouldn't be too sure," replied Conway, smiling. "And anyhow, Mallinson's just as much a British official as I am."

"Yes, but he's a mere boy. He don't look at things

reasonably. You and me are men of the world—we take things as we find them. This joint here, for instance—we still can't understand all the ins and outs of it, and why we've been landed here, but then, isn't that the usual way of things? Do we know why we're in the world at all, for that matter?"

"Perhaps some of us don't, but what's all this leading up to?"

Barnard dropped his voice to a rather husky whisper. "Gold, my lad," he answered with a certain ecstasy. "Just that, and nothing less. There's tons of it—literally—in the valley. I was a mining engineer in my young days and I haven't forgotten what a reef looks like. Believe me, it's as rich as the Rand, and ten times easier to dig up. I guess you thought I was on the loose whenever I went down there in my little armchair. Not a bit of it. I knew what I was doing. I'd figgered it out all along, you know, that these guys here couldn't get all their stuff sent in from outside without paying mighty high for it, and what else could they pay with except gold or silver or diamonds or something? Only logic, after all. And when I began to scout round, it didn't take me long to discover the whole bag of tricks."

"You found it out on your own?" asked Conway.

"Well, I won't say that, but I made my guess, and then I put the matter to Chang—straight, mind you, as man to man. And believe me, Conway, that

Chink's not as bad a fellow as we might have thought."

"Personally, I never thought him a bad fellow at all."

"Of course, I know you always took to him, so you won't be surprised at the way we got on together. We certainly did hit it famously. He showed me all over the workings, and it may interest you to know that I've got the full permission of the authorities to prospect in the valley as much as I like and make a comprehensive report. What d'you think of that, my lad? They seemed quite glad to have the services of an expert, especially when I said I could probably give 'em tips how to increase output."

"I can see you're going to be altogether at home here," said Conway.

"Well, I must say I've found a job, and that's something. And you never know how a thing'll turn out in the end. Maybe the folks at home won't be so keen to jail me when they know I can show 'em the way to a new goldfield. The only difficulty is—would they take my word about it?"

"They might. It's extraordinary what people *will* believe."

Barnard nodded with enthusiasm. "Glad you get the point, Conway. And that's where you and I can make a deal. We'll go fifty-fifty in everything, of course. All you've gotter do is to put your name to my report—British Consul, you know, and all that. It'll carry weight."

212

Conway laughed. "We'll have to see about it. Make your reports first."

It amused him to contemplate a possibility so unlikely to happen, and at the same time he was glad that Barnard had found something that yielded such immediate comfort.

So also was the High Lama, whom Conway began to see more and more frequently. He often visited him in the late evening and stayed for many hours, long after the servants had taken away the last bowls of tea and had been dismissed for the night. The High Lama never failed to ask him about the progress and welfare of his three companions, and once he enquired particularly as to the kind of careers that their arrival at Shangri-La had so inevitably interrupted.

Conway answered reflectively: "Mallinson might have done quite well in his own line—he's energetic and has ambitions. The two others—" He shrugged his shoulders. "As a matter of fact, it happens to suit them both to stay here—for a while, at any rate."

He noticed a flicker of light at the curtained window; there had been mutterings of thunder as he crossed the courtyards on his way to the now familiar room. No sound could be heard, and the heavy tapestries subdued the lightning into mere sparks of pallor.

"Yes," came the reply, "we have done our best to make both of them feel at home. Miss Brinklow

213

wishes to convert us, and Mr. Barnard would also like to convert us—into a limited liability company. Harmless projects—they will pass the time quite pleasantly for them. But your young friend, to whom neither gold nor religion can offer solace, how about *him*?"

"Yes, he's going to be the problem."

"I am afraid he is going to be *your* problem."

"Why mine?"

There was no immediate answer, for the tea-bowls were introduced at that moment, and with their appearance the High Lama rallied a faint and desiccated hospitality. "Karakal sends us storms at this time of the year," he remarked, feathering the conversation according to ritual. "The people of Blue Moon believe they are caused by demons raging in the great space beyond the pass. The 'outside,' they call it—perhaps you are aware that in their patois the word is used for the entire rest of the world. Of course they know nothing of such countries as France or England or even India—they imagine the dread altiplano stretching, as it almost does, illimitably. To them, so snug at their warm and windless levels, it appears unthinkable that anyone inside the valley should ever wish to leave it; indeed, they picture all unfortunate 'outsiders' as passionately desiring to enter. It is just a question of view-point, is it not?"

Conway was reminded of Barnard's somewhat similar remarks, and quoted them. "How very sensible!" was the High Lama's comment. "And he

214

is our first American, too—we are truly fortunate."

Conway found it piquant to reflect that the lamasery's fortune was to have acquired a man for whom the police of a dozen countries were actively searching; and he would have liked to share the piquancy but for feeling that Barnard had better be left to tell his own story in due course. He said: "Doubtless he's quite right, and there are many people in the world nowadays who would be glad enough to be here."

"*Too* many, my dear Conway. We are a single lifeboat riding the seas in a gale; we can take a few chance survivors, but if all the shipwrecked were to reach us and clamber aboard we should go down ourselves. . . . But let us not think of it just now. I hear that you have been associating with our excellent Briac. A delightful fellow-countryman of mine, though I do not share his opinion that Chopin is the greatest of all composers. For myself, as you know, I prefer Mozart. . . ."

Not till the tea-bowls were removed and the servant had been finally dismissed, did Conway venture to recall the unanswered question. "We were discussing Mallinson, and you said he was going to be *my* problem. Why mine, particularly?"

Then the High Lama replied very simply: "Because, my son, I am going to die."

It seemed an extraordinary statement, and for a time Conway was speechless after it. Eventually the High Lama continued: "You are surprised? But surely, my friend, we are all mortal—even at

Shangri-La. And it is possible that I may still have a few moments left to me—or even, for that matter, a few years. All I announce is the simple truth that already I see the end. It is charming of you to appear so concerned, and I will not pretend that there is not a touch of wistfulness, even at my age, in contemplating death. Fortunately little is left of me that can die physically, and as for the rest, all our religions display a pleasant unanimity of optimism. I am quite content, but I must accustom myself to a strange sensation during the hours that remain—I must realise that I have time for only one thing more. Can you imagine what that is?"

Conway was silent.

"It concerns you, my son."

"You do me a great honour."

"I have in mind to do much more than that."

Conway bowed slightly, but did not speak, and the High Lama, after waiting awhile, resumed: "You know, perhaps, that the frequency of these talks has been unusual here. But it is our tradition, if I may permit myself the paradox, that we are never slaves to tradition. We have no rigidities, no inexorable rules. We do as we think fit, guided a little by the example of the past, but still more by our present wisdom, and by our clairvoyance of the future. And thus it is that I am encouraged to do this final thing."

Conway was still silent.

"I place in your hands, my son, the heritage and destiny of Shangri-La."

At last the tension broke, and Conway felt beyond it the power of a bland and benign persuasion; the echoes swam into silence, till all that was left was his own heartbeat, pounding like a gong. And then, intercepting the rhythm, came the words:

"I have waited for you, my son, for quite a long time. I have sat in this room and seen the faces of new-comers, I have looked into their eyes and heard their voices, and always in hope that some day I might find you. My colleagues have grown old and wise, but you who are still young in years are as wise already. My friend, it is not an arduous task that I bequeath, for our order knows only silken bonds. To be gentle and patient, to care for the riches of the mind, to preside in wisdom and secrecy while the storm rages without—it will all be very pleasantly simple for you, and you will doubtless find great happiness."

Again Conway sought to reply, but could not, till at length a vivid lightning-flash paled the shadows and stirred him to exclaim: "The storm . . . this storm you talk of. . . ."

"It will be such a one, my son, as the world has not seen before. There will be no safety by arms, no help from authority, no answer in science. It will rage till every flower of culture is trampled, and all human things are levelled in a vast chaos. Such was my vision when Napoleon was still a name un-known; and I see it now, more clearly with each hour. Do you say I am mistaken?"

Conway answered: "No, I think you may be

right. A similar crash came once before, and then there were the Dark Ages lasting five hundred years."

"The parallel is not quite exact. For those Dark Ages were not really so very dark—they were full of flickering lanterns, and even if the light had gone out of Europe altogether, there were other rays, literally from China to Peru, at which it could have been rekindled. But the Dark Ages that are to come will cover the whole world in a single pall; there will be neither escape nor sanctuary, save such as are too secret to be found or too humble to be noticed. And Shangri-La may hope to be both of these. The airman bearing loads of death to the great cities will not pass our way, and if by chance he should, he may not consider us worth a bomb."

"And you think all this will come in my time?"

"I believe that you will live through the storm. And after, through the long age of desolation, you may still live, growing older and wiser and more patient. You will conserve the fragrance of our history and add to it the touch of your own mind. You will welcome the stranger, and teach him the rule of age and wisdom; and one of these strangers, it may be, will succeed you when you are yourself very old. Beyond that, my vision weakens, but I see, at a great distance, a new world stirring in the ruins, stirring clumsily but in hopefulness, seeking its lost and legendary treasures. And they will all be here, my son, hidden behind the mountains in the valley of Blue Moon, preserved as by miracle for a new Renaissance. . . ."

The speaking finished, and Conway saw the face before him full of a remote and drenching beauty; then the glow faded and there was nothing left but a mask, dark-shadowed, and crumbling like old wood. It was quite motionless, and the eyes were closed. He watched for a while, and presently, as part of a dream, it came to him that the High Lama was dead.

It seemed necessary to rivet the situation to some kind of actuality, lest it become too strange to be believed in; and with instinctive mechanism of hand and eye Conway glanced at his wrist-watch. It was a quarter past midnight. Suddenly, when he crossed the room to the door, it occurred to him that he did not in the least know how or whence to summon help. The Tibetans, he knew, had all been sent away for the night, and he had no idea where to find Chang or anyone else. He stood uncertainly on the threshold of the dark corridor; through a window he could see that the sky was clear, though the mountains still blazed in lightning like a silver fresco. And then, in the midst of the still encompassing dream, he felt himself master of Shangri-La. These were his beloved things, all around him, the things of that inner mind in which he lived increasingly, away from the fret of the world. His eyes strayed into the shadows and were caught by golden pin-points sparkling in rich, undulating lacquers; and the scent of tuberose, so faint that it expired on the very brink of sensation, lured him from room to room. At last he stumbled into the courtyards and by the fringe of the pool; a full moon sailed behind Karakal. It was twenty minutes to two.

Later, he was aware that Mallinson was near him, holding his arm and leading him away in a great hurry. He did not gather what it was all about, but he could hear that the boy was chattering excitedly.

11

THEY reached the balconied room where they had meals, Mallinson still clutching his arm and half-dragging him along. "Come on, Conway, we've till dawn to pack what we can and get away. Great news, man—I wonder what old Barnard and Miss Brinklow will think in the morning when they find us gone . . . still, it's their own choice to stay, and we'll probably get on far better without them. . . . The porters are about five miles beyond the pass—they came yesterday with loads of books and things . . . tomorrow they begin the journey back. . . . It just shows how these fellows here intended to let us down—they never told us—we should have been stranded here for God knows how much longer. . . . I say, what's the matter? Are you ill?"

Conway had sunk into his chair, and was leaning forward with elbows on the table. He passed his hand across his eyes. "Ill? No, I don't think so. Just—rather—tired."

"Probably the storm. Where were you all the while? I'd been waiting for you for hours."

"I—I was visiting the High Lama."

"Oh, *him*! Well, *that's* for the last time, anyhow, thank God."

"Yes, Mallinson, for the last time."

Something in Conway's voice, and still more in his succeeding silence, roused the youth to irascibility. "Well, I wish you wouldn't sound so deuced leisurely about it—we've got to get a considerable move on, you know."

Conway stiffened for the effort of emerging into keener consciousness. "I'm sorry," he said. Partly to test his nerve and the reality of his sensations he lit a cigarette. He found that both hands and lips were unsteady. "I'm afraid I don't quite follow . . . you say the porters . . ."

"Yes, the porters, man—do pull yourself together."

"You're thinking of going out to them?"

"*Thinking* of it? I'm damn well certain—they're only just over the ridge. And we've got to start immediately."

"*Immediately?*"

"Yes, yes—why not?"

Conway made a second attempt to transfer himself from the one world into the other. He said at length, having partly succeeded: "I suppose you realise that it mayn't be quite as simple as it sounds?"

Mallinson was lacing a pair of knee-high Tibetan mountain-boots as he answered jerkily: "I realise everything, but it's something we've got to do, and we shall do it, with luck, if we don't delay."

"I don't see how——"

"Oh Lord, Conway, must you fight shy of

everything? Haven't you any guts left in you at all?"

The appeal, half passionate and half derisive, helped Conway to collect himself. "Whether I have or haven't isn't the point, but if you want me to explain myself, I will. It's a question of a few rather important details. Suppose you *do* get beyond the pass and find the porters there, how do you know they'll take you with them? What inducement can you offer? Hasn't it struck you that they mayn't be quite so willing as you'd like them to be? You can't just present yourself and demand to be escorted. It all needs arrangement, negotiations beforehand——"

"Or anything else to cause a delay," exclaimed Mallinson bitterly. "God, what a fellow you are! Fortunately I haven't you to rely on for arranging things. Because they *have* been arranged—the porters have been paid in advance, and they've agreed to take us. And there are clothes and equipment for the journey, all ready. So your last excuse disappears. Come on, let's *do* something."

"But—I don't understand . . ."

"I don't suppose you do, but it doesn't matter."

"Who's been making all these plans?"

Mallinson answered brusquely: "Lo-Tsen, if you're really keen to know. She's with the porters now. She's waiting."

"*Waiting?*"

"Yes. She's coming with us. I assume you've no objection?"

223

At the mention of Lo-Tsen the two worlds touched and fused suddenly in Conway's mind. He cried sharply, almost contemptuously: "That's nonsense. It's impossible."

Mallinson was equally on edge. "Why is it impossible?"

"Because . . . well, it is. There are all sorts of reasons. Take my word for it; it won't do. It's incredible enough that she should be out there now—I'm astonished at what you say has happened—but the idea of her going any farther is just preposterous."

"I don't see that it's preposterous at all. It's as natural for her to want to leave here as for me."

"But she doesn't want to leave. That's where you make the mistake."

Mallinson smiled tensely. "You think you know a good deal more about her than I do, I dare say," he remarked. "But perhaps you don't, for all that."

"What do you mean?"

"There are other ways of getting to understand people without learning heaps of languages."

"For Heaven's sake, what *are* you driving at?" Then Conway added more quietly: "This is absurd. We mustn't wrangle. Tell me, Mallinson, what's it all about? I still don't understand."

"Then why are you making such an almighty fuss."

"Tell me the truth, *please* tell me the truth."

"Well, it's simple enough. A kid of her age, shut up here with a lot of queer old men—naturally she'll

224

get away if she's given a chance. She hasn't had one up to now."

"Don't you think you may be imagining her position in the light of your own? As I've always told you, she's perfectly happy."

"Then why did she say she'd come?"

"She said that? How could she? She doesn't speak English."

"I asked her—in Tibetan—Miss Brinklow worked out the words. It wasn't a very fluent conversation, but it was quite enough to—to lead to an understanding." Mallinson flushed a little. "Damn it, Conway, don't stare at me like that—anyone would think I'd been poaching on *your* preserves."

Conway answered: "No one would think so at all, I hope, but the remark tells me more than you were perhaps intending me to know. I can only say that I'm very sorry."

"And why the devil should you be?"

Conway let the cigarette fall from his fingers. He felt tired, bothered, and full of deep conflicting tendernesses that he would rather not have had aroused. He said gently: "I wish we weren't always at such cross-purposes. Lo-Tsen is very charming, I know, but why should we quarrel about it?"

"*Charming?*" Mallinson echoed the word with scorn. "She's a good bit more than that. You mustn't think everybody's as cold-blooded about these things as you are yourself. Admiring her as if she were an exhibit in a museum may be your idea of what she deserves, but mine's more practical, and

225

when I see someone I like in a rotten position I try and *do* something."

"But surely there's such a thing as being too impetuous? Where do you think she'll go to if she does leave?"

"I suppose she must have friends in China or somewhere. Anyhow, she'll be better off than here."

"How can you possibly be so sure of that?"

"Well, I'll see that she's looked after myself, if nobody else will. After all, if you're rescuing people from something quite hellish, you don't usually stop to enquire if they've anywhere else to go."

"And you think Shangri-La is hellish?"

"Definitely, I do. There's something dark and evil about it. The whole business has been like that, from the beginning—the way we were brought here, without reason at all, by some madman—and the way we've been detained since, on one excuse or another. But the most frightful thing of all—to me—is the effect it's had on you."

"On *me*?"

"Yes, on you. You've just mooned about as if nothing mattered and you were content to stay here for ever. Why, you even admitted you liked the place. . . . Conway, what *has* happened to you? Can't you manage to be your real self again? We got on so well together at Baskul—you were absolutely different in those days."

"My *dear* boy!"

Conway reached his hand towards Mallinson's,

and the answering grip was hot and eagerly affectionate. Mallinson went on: "I don't suppose you realise it, but I've been terribly alone these last few weeks. Nobody seemed to be caring a damn about the only thing that was really important—Barnard and Miss Brinklow had reasons of a kind, but it was pretty awful when I found *you* against me."

"I'm sorry."

"You keep on saying that, but it doesn't help."

Conway replied, on a sudden impulse: "Then let me help, if I can, by telling you something. When you've heard it, you'll understand, I hope, a great deal of what now seems very curious and difficult. At any rate, you'll realise why Lo-Tsen can't possibly go back with you."

"I don't think anything would make me see that. And do cut it as short as you can, because we really haven't time to spare."

Conway then gave, as briefly as he could, the whole story of Shangri-La as told him by the High Lama, and as amplified by conversation both with the latter and with Chang. It was the last thing he had ever intended to do, but he felt that in the circumstances it was justified and even necessary; it was true enough that Mallinson *was* his problem, to solve as he thought fit. He narrated rapidly and easily, and in doing so came again under the spell of that strange, timeless world; its beauty overwhelmed him as he spoke of it, and more than once he felt himself reading from a page of memory, so

227

clearly had ideas and phrases impressed themselves. Only one thing he withheld, and that to spare himself an emotion he could not yet grapple with—the fact of the High Lama's death that night, and of his own succession.

When he approached the end he felt comforted; he was glad to have got it over, and it was the only solution after all. He looked up calmly when he had finished, confident that he had done well.

But Mallinson merely tapped his fingers on the table-top and said, after a long wait: "I really don't know what to say, Conway . . . except that you must be completely mad. . . ."

There followed a long silence, during which the two men stared at each other in far differing moods—Conway withdrawn and disappointed, Mallinson in hot, fidgeting discomfort. "So you think I'm mad?" said Conway at length.

Mallinson broke into a nervous laugh. "Well, I should damn well say so, after a tale like that. I mean . . . well, really . . . such utter nonsense . . . it seems to me rather beyond arguing about."

Conway looked and sounded immensely astonished. "You think it's nonsense?"

"Well . . . how else can I look at it? I'm sorry, Conway—it's a pretty strong statement—but I don't see how any sane person could be in any doubt about it."

"So you still hold that we were brought here by blind accident—by some lunatic who made careful plans to run off with an aeroplane and fly it a thousand miles just for the fun of the thing?"

Conway offered a cigarette, and the other took it. The pause was one for which they both seemed grateful. Mallinson answered eventually: "Look here, it's no good arguing the thing point by point. As a matter of fact, your theory that the people here sent someone vaguely into the world to decoy strangers, and that this fellow deliberately learned flying and bided his time until it happened that a suitable machine was due to leave Baskul with four passengers . . . well, I won't say that it's literally impossible, though it does seem to me ridiculously far-fetched. If it stood by itself, it might just be worth considering, but when you tack it on to all sorts of other things that are *absolutely* impossible—all this about the lamas being hundreds of years old, and having discovered a sort of elixir of youth, or whatever you'd call it . . . well, it just makes me wonder what kind of microbe has bitten you, that's all."

Conway smiled. "Yes, I dare say you find it hard to believe. Perhaps I did myself at first—I scarcely remember. Of course it *is* an extraordinary story, but I should think your own eyes have had enough evidence that this is an extraordinary place. Think of all that we've actually seen, both of us—a lost valley in the midst of unexplored mountains, a monastery with a library of European books——"

"Oh yes, and a central heating plant, and modern plumbing, and afternoon tea, and everything else—it's all very marvellous, I know."

229

"Well, then, what do you make of it?"

"Damn little, I admit. It's a complete mystery. But that's no reason for accepting tales that are physically impossible. Believing in hot baths because you've had them is different from believing in people hundreds of years old just because they've told you they are." He laughed again, still uneasily. "Look here, Conway, it's got on your nerves, this place, and I really don't wonder at it. Pack up your things and let's quit. We'll finish this argument a month or two hence after a jolly little dinner at Maiden's."

Conway answered quietly: "I've no desire to go back to that life at all."

"What life?"

"The life you're thinking of . . . dinners . . . dances . . . polo . . . all that. . . ."

"But I never said anything about dances and polo! Anyhow, what's wrong with them? D'you mean that you're not coming with me? You're going to stay here like the other two? Then at least you shan't stop *me* from clearing out of it!" Mallinson threw down his cigarette and sprang towards the door with eyes blazing. "You're off your head!" he cried wildly. "You're mad, Conway, that's what's the matter with you! I know you're always calm, and I'm always excited, but I'm sane, at any rate, and you're not! They warned me about it before I joined you at Baskul, and I thought they were wrong, but now I can see they weren't——"

"What did they warn you of?"

230

"They said you'd been blown up in the War, and you'd been queer at times ever since. I'm not reproaching you—I know it was nothing you could help—and Heaven knows I hate talking like this. . . . Oh, I'll go. It's all frightful and sickening, but I must go. I gave my word."

"To Lo-Tsen?"

"Yes, if you want to know."

Conway got up and held out his hand. "Good-bye, Mallinson."

"For the last time, you're not coming?"

"I can't."

"Good-bye, then."

They shook hands, and Mallinson left.

Conway sat alone in the lantern-light. It seemed to him, in a phrase engraved on memory, that all the loveliest things were transient and perishable, that the two worlds were finally beyond reconciliation, and that one of them hung, as always, by a thread. After he had pondered for some time he looked at his watch; it was ten minutes to three.

He was still at the table, smoking the last of his cigarettes, when Mallinson returned. The youth entered with some commotion, and on seeing him, stood back in the shadows as if to gather his wits. He was silent, and Conway began, after waiting a moment: "Hullo, what's happened? Why are you back?"

The complete naturalness of the question fetched Mallinson forward; he pulled off his heavy sheepskins and sat down. His face was ashen and his whole body trembled. "I hadn't the nerve," he cried, half sobbing. "That place where we were all roped—you remember? I got as far as that. . . . I couldn't manage it. I've no head for heights, and in moonlight it looked fearful. Silly, isn't it?" He broke down completely and was hysterical until Conway pacified him. Then he added: "They needn't worry, these fellows here—nobody will ever threaten them by land. But, my God, I'd give a good deal to fly over with a load of bombs!"

"Why would you like to do that, Mallinson?"

"Because the place wants smashing up, whatever it is. It's unhealthy and unclean—and for that matter, if your impossible yarn were true, it would be more hateful still! A lot of wizened old men crouching here like spiders for anyone who comes near . . . it's filthy . . . who'd want to live to an age like that, anyhow? And as for your precious High Lama, if he's half as old as you say he is, it's time someone put him out of his misery . . . Oh, why *won't* you come away with me, Conway? I hate imploring you for my own sake, but damn it all, I'm young and we've been pretty good friends together—does my whole life mean nothing to you compared with the lies of these awful creatures? And Lo-Tsen, too—*she's* young—doesn't *she* count at all?"

"Lo-Tsen is not young," said Conway.

Mallinson looked up and began to titter hysterically. "Oh, no, not young—not young at all, of

232

course. She looks about seventeen, but I suppose you'll tell me she's really a well-preserved ninety."

"Mallinson, she came here in 1884."

"You're raving, man!"

"Her beauty, Mallinson, like all other beauty in the world, lies at the mercy of those who do not know how to value it. It is a fragile thing that can only live where fragile things are loved. Take it away from this valley and you will see it fade like an echo."

Mallinson laughed harshly, as if his own thoughts gave him confidence. "I'm not afraid of that. It's here that she's only an echo, if she's one anywhere at all." He added after a pause: "Not that this sort of talk gets us anywhere. We'd better cut out all the poetic stuff and come down to realities. Conway, I want to help you—it's all the sheerest nonsense, I know, but I'll argue it out if it'll do you any good. I'll pretend it's something possible that you've told me, and that it really does need examining. Now tell me, seriously, what evidence have you for this story of yours?"

Conway was silent.

"Merely that someone spun you a fantastic rigmarole. Even from a thoroughly reliable person whom you'd known all your life you wouldn't accept that sort of thing without proof. And what proofs have you in this case? None at all, so far as I can see. Has Lo-Tsen ever told you her history?"

"No, but——"

"Then why believe it from someone else? And all

233

this longevity business—can you point to a single outside fact in support of it?"

Conway thought a moment and then mentioned the unknown Chopin works that Briac had played.

"Well, that's a matter that means nothing to me—I'm not a musician. But even if they're genuine, isn't it possible that he could have got hold of them in some way without his story being true?"

"Quite possible, no doubt."

"And then this method that you say exists—of preserving youth, and so on. What is it? You say it's a sort of drug—well, I want to know *what* drug? Have you ever seen it or tried it? Did anyone ever give you any positive facts about the thing at all?"

"Not in detail, I admit."

"And you never asked for details? It didn't strike you that such a story needed any confirmation at all? You just swallowed it whole?" Pressing his advantage, he continued: "How much do you actually know of this place, apart from what you've been told? You've seen a few old men—that's all it amounts to. Apart from that, we can only say that the place is well fitted up, and seems to be run on rather highbrow lines. How and why it came into existence we've no idea, and why they want to keep us here, if they do, is equally a mystery, but surely all that's hardly an excuse for believing any old legend that comes along! After all, man, you're a critical sort of person—you'd hesitate to believe all you were told even in an English monastery—I

234

really can't see why you should jump at everything just because you're in Tibet!"

Conway nodded. Even in the midst of far keener perceptions he could not restrain approval of a point well made. "That's an acute remark, Mallinson. I suppose the truth is that when it comes to believing things without actual evidence, we all incline to what we find most attractive."

"Well, I'm dashed if I can see anything attractive about living till you're half dead. Give me a short life and a gay one, for choice. And this stuff about a future war—it all sounds pretty thin to me. How does anyone know when the next war's going to be, or what it'll be like? Weren't all the prophets wrong about the last war?" He added, when Conway did not reply: "Anyhow I don't believe in saying things are inevitable. And even if they were, there's no need to get into a funk about them. Heaven knows I'd most likely be scared stiff if I had to fight in a war, but I'd rather face up to it than bury myself here."

Conway smiled. "Mallinson, you have a superb knack of misunderstanding me. When we were at Baskul you thought I was a hero—now you take me for a coward. In point of fact, I'm neither—though of course it doesn't matter. When you get back to India you can tell people, if you like, that I decided to stay in a Tibetan monastery because I was afraid there'd be another war. It isn't my reason at all, but I've no doubt it'll be believed by the people who already think me mad."

Mallinson answered rather sadly: "It's silly, you know, to talk like that. Whatever happens, I'd never say a word against you. You can count on that. I don't understand you—I admit that—but—but—I wish I did. Oh, I wish I did. Conway, can't I possibly help you? Isn't there anything I can say or do?"

There was a long silence after that, which Conway broke at last by saying: "There's just a question I'd like to ask—if you'll forgive me for being terribly personal."

"Yes?"

"Are you in love with Lo-Tsen?"

The youth's pallor changed quickly to a flush. "I dare say I am. I know you'll say it's absurd and unthinkable, and probably it is, but I can't help my feelings."

"I don't think it's absurd at all."

The argument seemed to have sailed into a harbour after many buffetings, and Conway added: "I can't help *my* feelings either. You and that girl happen to be the two people in the world I care most about . . . though you may think it odd of me." Abruptly he got up and paced the room. "We've said all we *can* say, haven't we?"

"Yes, I suppose we have." But Mallinson went on, in a sudden rush of eagerness: "Oh, what stupid nonsense it all is—about her not being young! And foul and horrible nonsense too. Conway, you *can't* believe it! It's just too ridiculous. How can it really mean anything?"

236

"How can you really know that she's young?"

Mallinson half turned away, his face lit with a grave shyness. "Because I *do* know. . . . Perhaps you'll think less of me for it . . . but I *do* know. I'm afraid you never properly understood her, Conway. She was cold on the surface, but that was the result of living here—it had frozen all the warmth. But the warmth was there."

"To be unfrozen?"

"Yes . . . that would be one way of putting it."

"And she's *young*, Mallinson—you are so *sure* of that?"

Mallinson answered softly: "God, yes—she's just a girl. I was terribly sorry for her, and we were both attracted, I suppose. I don't see that it's anything to be ashamed of. In fact in a place like this I should think it's about the decentest thing that's ever happened. . . ."

Conway went to the balcony and gazed at the dazzling plume of Karakal; the moon was riding high in a waveless ocean. It came to him that a dream had dissolved, like all too lovely things, at the first touch of reality; that the whole world's future, weighed in the balance against youth and love, would be light as air. And he knew, too, that his mind dwelt in a world of its own, Shangri-La in microcosm, and that this world also was in peril. For even as he nerved himself, he saw the corridors of his imagination twist and strain under impact; the pavilions were toppling; all was about to be in ruins. He was only partly unhappy, but he was infinitely and rather sadly perplexed. He did not know whether he had been mad and was now sane, or had been sane for a time and was now mad again.

When he turned, there was a difference in him; his voice was keener, almost brusque, and his face twitched a little; he looked much more the Conway who had been a hero at Baskul. Clenched for action, he faced Mallinson with a suddenly new alertness. "Do you think you could manage that tricky bit with a rope if I were with you?" he asked.

Mallinson sprang forward. "*Conway!*" he cried chokingly. "You mean you'll *come*? You've made up your mind at last?"

They left as soon as Conway had prepared himself for the journey. It was surprisingly simple to leave—a departure rather than an escape; there were no incidents as they crossed the bars of moonlight and shadow in the courtyards. One might have thought there was no one there at all, Conway reflected; and immediately the idea of such emptiness became an emptiness in himself; while all the time, though he hardly heard him, Mallinson was chattering about the journey. How strange that their long argument should have ended thus in action, that this secret sanctuary should be forsaken by one who had found in it such happiness! For indeed, less than an hour later, they halted breathlessly at a curve of the track and saw the last of Shangri-La. Deep below them the valley of Blue Moon was like a cloud, and to Conway the scattered roofs had a

238

look of floating after him through the haze. Now, at that moment, it was farewell. Mallinson, whom the steep ascent had kept silent for a time, gasped out: "Good man, we're doing fine—carry on."

Conway smiled, but did not reply; he was already preparing the rope for the knife-edge traverse. It was true, as the youth had said, that he had made up his mind; but it was only what was left of his mind. That small and active fragment now dominated; the rest comprised an absence hardly to be endured. He was a wanderer between two worlds and must ever wander; but for the present, in a deepening inward void, all he felt was that he liked Mallinson and must help him; he was doomed, like millions, to flee from wisdom and be a hero.

Mallinson was nervous at the precipice, but Conway got him over in traditional mountaineering fashion, and when the trial was past, they leaned together over Mallinson's cigarettes. "Conway, I must say it's damned good of you. . . . Perhaps you guess how I feel. . . . I can't tell you how glad I am. . . ."

"I wouldn't try, then, if I were you."

After a long pause, and before they resumed the journey, Mallinson added: "But I *am* glad—not only for my own sake, but for yours as well. . . . It's fine that you can realize now that all that stuff was sheer nonsense . . . it's just wonderful to see you your real self again. . . ."

"Not at all," responded Conway with a wryness that was for his own private comforting.

Towards dawn they crossed the divide, unchallenged by sentinels, even if there were any; though it occurred to Conway that the route, in the true spirit, might only be moderately well watched. Presently they reached the plateau, picked clean as a bone by roaring winds, and after a gradual descent the encampment of porters came in sight. Then all was as Mallinson had foretold; they found the men ready for them, sturdy fellows in furs and sheepskins, crouching under the gale and eager to begin the journey to Tatsien-Fu—eleven hundred miles eastward, on the China border.

"He's coming with us!" Mallinson cried excitedly when they met Lo-Tsen. He forgot that she knew no English; but Conway translated.

It seemed to him that the little Manchu had never looked so radiant. She gave him a most charming smile, but her eyes were all for the boy.

Epilogue

IT was in Delhi that I met Rutherford again. We had been guests at a Viceregal dinner-party, but distance and ceremonial kept us apart until the turbaned flunkeys handed us our hats afterwards. "Come back to my hotel and have a drink," he invited.

We shared a cab along the arid miles between the Lutyens still-life and the warm, palpitating cinematograph of Old Delhi. I knew from the newspapers that he had just returned from Kashgar. His was one of those well-groomed reputations that get the most out of everything; any unusual holiday acquires the character of an exploration, and though the explorer takes care to do nothing really original, the public does not know this, and he capitalises the full value of a hasty impression. It had not seemed to me, for instance, that Rutherford's journey, as reported in the Press, had been particularly epoch-making; the buried cities of Khotan were old stuff, if anyone remembered Stein and Sven Hedin. I knew Rutherford well enough to chaff him about this, and he laughed. "Yes, the truth would have made a better story," he admitted cryptically.

We went to his hotel room and drank whisky. "So

241

you *did* search for Conway?" I suggested when the moment seemed propitious.

"Search is much too strong a word," he answered. "You can't search a country half as big as Europe for one man. All I can say is that I visited places where I was prepared to come across him, or to get news of him. His last message, you remember, was that he had left Bangkok for the north-west. There were traces of him up-country for a little way, and my own opinion is that he probably made for the tribal districts of the Chinese border. I don't think he'd have cared to enter Burma, where he might have run up against British officials. Anyhow, the definite trail, you may say, peters out somewhere in Upper Siam, but of course I never expected to follow it far that end."

"You thought it might be easier to look for the valley of Blue Moon?"

"Well, it did seem as if it might be a more fixed proposition. I suppose you glanced at that manuscript of mine?"

"Much more than glanced at it. I should have returned it, by the way, but you left no address."

Rutherford nodded. "I wonder what you made of it?"

"I thought it very remarkable—assuming, of course, that it's all quite genuinely based on what Conway told you."

"I give you my solemn word for that. I invented nothing at all—indeed, there's even less of my own language in it than you might think. I've a good

242

memory and Conway always had a way of describing things. Don't forget that we had about twenty-four hours of practically continuous talk."

"Well, as I said, it's all very remarkable."

He leaned back and smiled. "If that's all you're going to say, I can see I shall have to speak for myself. I suppose you consider me a rather credulous person. I don't really think I am. People make mistakes in life through believing too much, but they have a damned dull time if they believe too little. I was certainly taken with Conway's story—in more ways than one—and that was why I felt interested enough to put as many tabs on it as I could—apart from the chance of running up against the man himself."

He went on, after lighting a cigar: "It meant a good deal of odd journeying, but I like that sort of thing, and my publishers can't object to a travel-book once in a way. Altogether I must have done some thousands of miles—Baskul, Bangkok, Chung-Kiang, Kashgar—I visited them all, and somewhere inside the area between them the mystery lies. But it's a pretty big area, you know, and all my investigations didn't touch more than the fringe of it—or of the mystery either, for that matter. Indeed, if you want the actual downright facts about Conway's adventures, so far as I've been able to verify them, all I can tell you is that he left Baskul on the 20th of May and arrived in Chung-Kiang on the 5th of October. And the last we know of him is that he left Bangkok again on the 3rd of

February. All the rest is probability, possibility, guesswork, myth, legend, whatever you like to call it."

"So you didn't find anything in Tibet?"

"My dear fellow, I never got into Tibet at all. The people up at Government House wouldn't hear of it; it's as much as they'll do to sanction an Everest expedition, and when I said I thought of wandering about the Kuen-Luns on my own, they looked at me rather as if I'd suggested writing a life of Gandhi. As a matter of fact, they knew more than I did. Strolling about Tibet isn't a one-man job; it needs an expedition properly fitted out, and run by someone who knows at least a word or two of the language. I remember when Conway was telling me his story I kept wondering why there was all that fuss about waiting for porters—why didn't they all simply walk off? I wasn't very long in discovering. The Government people were quite right—all the passports in the world couldn't have got me over the Kuen-Luns. I actually went as far as seeing them in the distance, on a very clear day—perhaps fifty miles off. Not many Europeans can claim even that."

"Are they so very forbidding?"

"They looked just like a white frieze on the horizon, that was all. At Yarkand and Kashgar I questioned everyone I met about them, but it was extraordinary how little I could discover. I should think they must be the least explored range in the world. I had the luck to meet an American traveller

244

who had once tried to cross them, but he'd been unable to find a pass. There *are* passes, he said, but they're terrifically high and unmapped. I asked him if he thought it possible for a valley to exist of the kind Conway described, and he said he wouldn't call it impossible, but he thought it not very likely—on geological grounds, at any rate. Then I asked if he had ever heard of a cone-shaped mountain almost as high as the highest of the Himalaya, and his answer to that was rather intriguing. There was a legend, he said, about such a mountain, but he thought himself there could be no foundation for it. There were even rumours, he added, about mountains actually higher than Everest, but he didn't himself give credit to them. 'I doubt if any peak in the Kuen-Luns is more than twenty-five thousand feet, if that,' he said. But he admitted that they had never been properly surveyed.

"Then I asked him what he knew about Tibetan lamaseries—he'd been in the country several times—and he gave me just the usual accounts that one can read in all the books. They weren't beautiful places, he assured me, and the monks in them were generally corrupt and dirty. 'Do they live long?' I asked, and he said, yes, they often did, if they didn't die of some filthy disease. Then I went boldly to the point and asked if he'd ever heard legends of extreme longevity among the lamas. 'Heaps of them,' he answered; 'it's one of the stock yarns you hear everywhere, but you can't verify

245

them. You're told that some foul-looking creature has been walled up in a cell for a hundred years, and he certainly looks as if he might have been, but of course you can't demand his birth certificate.' I asked him if he thought they had any occult or medicinal way of prolonging life or preserving youth, and he said they were supposed to have a great deal of very curious knowledge about such things, but he suspected that if you came to look into it, it was rather like the Indian rope trick—always something that somebody else had seen. He did say, however, that the lamas appeared to have odd powers of bodily control. 'I've watched them,' he said, 'sitting by the edge of a frozen lake, stark naked, with a temperature below zero and in a tearing wind, while their servants break the ice and wrap sheets round them that have been dipped in the water. They do this a dozen times or more, and the lamas dry the sheets on their own bodies. Keeping warm by will-power, so one imagines, though that's a poor sort of explanation.'" Rutherford helped himself to more drink. "But of course, as my American friend admitted, all that had nothing much to do with longevity. It merely showed that the lamas had sombre tastes in self-discipline. . . . So there we were, and probably you'll agree with me that all the evidence, so far, was less than you'd hang a dog on."

I said it was certainly inconclusive, and asked if the names "Karakal" and "Shangri-La" had meant anything to the American.

"Not a thing—I tried him with them. After I'd gone on questioning him for a time, he said: 'Frankly, I'm not keen on monasteries—indeed, I once told a fellow I met in Tibet that if I went out of my way at all, it would be to avoid them, not pay them a visit.' That chance remark of his gave me a curious idea, and I asked him when this meeting in Tibet had taken place. 'Oh, a long time ago,' he answered, 'before the War—in nineteen eleven, I think it was.' I badgered him for further details, and he gave them, as well as he could remember. It seemed that he'd been travelling then for some American geographical society, with several colleagues, porters, and so on—in fact, a pukka expedition. Somewhere near the Kuen-Luns he met this other man, a Chinese who was being carried in a chair by native bearers. The fellow turned out to speak English quite well, and strongly recommended them to visit a certain lamasery in the neighbourhood—he even offered to be the guide there. The American said they hadn't time and weren't interested, and that was that." Rutherford went on, after an interval: "I don't suggest that it means a great deal. When a man tries to remember a casual incident that happened twenty years ago, you can't build *too* much on it. But it offers an attractive speculation."

"Yes, though if a well-equipped expedition had accepted the invitation, I don't see how they could have been detained at the lamasery against their will."

247

"Oh, quite. And perhaps it wasn't Shangri-La at all."

We thought it over, but it seemed too hazy for argument, and I went on to ask if there had been any discoveries at Baskul.

"Baskul was hopeless, and Peshawur was worse. Nobody could tell me anything, except that the kidnapping of the aeroplane did undoubtedly take place. They weren't keen even to admit that—it's an episode they're not proud of."

"And nothing was heard of the plane afterwards?"

"Not a word or a rumour, or of its four passengers either. I verified, however, that it was capable of climbing high enough to pass the ranges. I also tried to trace that fellow Barnard, but I found his past history so mysterious that I wouldn't be at all surprised if he really were Chalmers Bryant, as Conway said. After all, Bryant's complete disappearance in the midst of the big hue and cry was rather amazing."

"Did you try to find anything about the actual kidnapper?"

"I did, but again it was hopeless. The Air Force man whom the fellow had knocked out and impersonated had since been killed, so one promising line of enquiry was closed. I even wrote to a friend of mine in America who runs an aviation school, asking if he had had any Tibetan pupils lately, but his reply was prompt and disappointing. He said he couldn't differentiate Tibetans from

248

Chinese, and he had about fifty of the latter—all training to fight the Japs. Not much chance there, you see. But I did make one rather quaint discovery—and one which I could have made just as easily without leaving London. There was a German professor at Jena about the middle of the last century who took to globe-trotting and visited Tibet in 1887. He never came back, and there was some story about him having been drowned in fording a river. His name was Friedrich Meister."

"Good heavens—one of the names Conway mentioned!"

"Yes—though it may only have been coincidence. It doesn't prove the whole story, by any means, because the Jena fellow was born in 1845. Nothing very exciting about that."

"But it's odd," I said.

"Oh yes, it's odd enough."

"Did you succeed in tracing any of the others?"

"No. It's a pity I hadn't a longer list to work on. I couldn't find any record of a pupil of Chopin's called Briac, though of course that doesn't prove that there wasn't one. Conway was pretty sparing with his names, when you come to think about it—out of fifty odd lamas supposed to be on the premises he only gave us one or two. Perrault and Henschell, by the way, proved equally impossible to trace."

"How about Mallinson?" I asked. "Did you try to find out what had happened to him? And that girl—the Chinese girl?"

"My dear fellow, of course I did. The awkward part was, as you perhaps gathered from the manuscript, that Conway's story ended at the moment of leaving the valley with the porters. After than he either couldn't or wouldn't tell me what happened—perhaps he might have done, mind you, if there'd been more time. I feel that we can guess at some sort of tragedy. The hardships of the journey would be perfectly appalling, apart from the risk of brigandage or even treachery among their own escorting party. Probably we shall never know exactly what did occur, but it seems tolerably certain that Mallinson never reached China. I made all sorts of enquiries, you know. First of all I tried to trace details of books, et cetera, sent in large consignments across the Tibetan frontier, but at all the likely places, such as Shanghai and Pekin, I drew complete blanks. That, of course, doesn't count for much, since the lamas would doubtless see that their methods of importation were kept secret. Then I tried at Tatsien-Fu. It's a weird place, a sort of world's-end market town, deuced difficult to get at, where the Chinese coolies from Yunnan transfer their loads of tea to the Tibetans. You can read about it in my new book when it comes out. Europeans don't often get as far. I found the people quite civil and courteous, but there was absolutely no record of Conway's party arriving at all."

"So how Conway himself reached Chung-Kiang is still unexplained?"

"The only conclusion is that he wandered there, just as he might have wandered anywhere else. Anyhow, we're back in the realm of hard facts when we get to Chung-Kiang, that's something. The nuns at the mission hospital were genuine enough, and so, for that matter, was Sieveking's excitement on the ship when Conway played that pseudo-Chopin." Rutherford paused and then added reflectively: "It's really an exercise in the balancing of probabilities, and I must say the scales don't bump very emphatically either way. Of course, if you don't accept Conway's story, it means that you doubt either his veracity or his sanity—one may as well be frank."

He paused again, as if inviting a comment, and I said: "As you know, I never saw him after the War, but I understand he was a good deal changed by it."

Rutherford answered: "Yes, he certainly was, there's no denying the fact. You can't subject a mere boy to three years of intense physical and emotional stress without tearing something to tatters. People would say, I suppose, that he came through without a scratch. But the scratches were there—on the inside."

We talked for a little time about the War and its effects on various people, and at length he went on: "But there's just one more point that I must mention—and perhaps in some ways the oddest of all. It came out during my enquiries at the mission. They all did their best for me there, as you can guess, but they couldn't recollect much, especially as they'd been so busy with a fever epidemic at the time. One of the questions I put was about the manner Conway had reached the hospital first of all—whether he had presented himself alone, or had been found ill and been taken there by someone else. They couldn't exactly remember—after all, it was a long while back—but suddenly, when I was on the point of giving up the cross-examination, one of the nuns remarked quite casually—'I think the doctor said he was brought here by a woman.' That was all she could tell me, and as the doctor himself had left the mission, there was no confirmation to be had on the spot.

"But having got so far, I wasn't in any mood to give up. It appeared that the doctor had gone to a bigger hospital in Shanghai, so I took the trouble to get his address and call on him there. It was just after the Jap air-raiding, and things were pretty grim. I'd met the man before during my first visit to Chung-Kiang, and he was very polite, though terribly overworked—yes, *terribly*'s the word, for, believe me, the air-raids on London by the Germans were just nothing to what the Japs did to the native parts of Shanghai. Oh yes, he said instantly, he remembered the case of the Englishman who had lost his memory. Was it true he had been brought to the mission hospital by a woman? I asked. Oh yes, certainly, by a woman, a Chinese woman. Did he remember anything about her? Nothing, he answered, except that she had been ill of the fever herself, and had died almost immediately. . . . Just

252

then there was an interruption—a batch of wounded were carried in and packed on stretchers in the corridors—the wards were all full—and I didn't care to go on taking up the man's time, especially as the thudding of the guns at Woosung was a reminder that he would still have plenty to do. When he came back to me, looking quite cheerful even amidst such ghastliness, I just asked him one final question, and I dare say you can guess what it was. 'About the Chinese woman,' I said. 'Was she young?'"

Rutherford flicked his cigar as if the narration had excited him quite as much as he hoped it had me. Continuing, he said: "The little fellow looked at me solemnly for a moment, and then answered in that funny clipped English that the educated Chinese have—'Oh, no, she was most old—most old of anyone I have ever seen.'"

We sat for a long time in silence, and then talked again of Conway as I remembered him, boyish and gifted and full of charm, and of the War that had altered him, and of so many mysteries of time and age and of the mind, and of the little Manchu who had been "most old," and of the strange ultimate dream of Blue Moon. "Do you think he will ever find it?" I asked.

WOODFORD GREEN
April 1933

Other titles in the
Charnwood Library Series:

SWEETHEARTS AND WIVES
by C. L. Skelton

This sequel to *The Maclarens* tells the story of a new generation of the famous Highland clan—its regiment, its wars, its loves, its honour. *Sweethearts and Wives* follows the Maclarens through the Egyptian Campaign to the Boer War. A credible tale of battle and bravery, and of what men call cowardice: a tale of officers and men, and of the women they love. For Donald Bruce it begins when he is unable to give the order to kill one of his own men. For Ian Maclaren, eldest son of the Laird, it begins with his passionate love for Naomi— a half-caste, a bastard and forbidden. This is their story and that of their fathers—proud men with their strong memories of the past.

MAN ON FIRE
by A. J. Quinnell

Creasy and Guido had served together in the French Foreign Legion. They knew all about discipline, guns and grenades, and were first-class soldiers. Now Creasy had no purpose in life and was fast becoming an alcoholic, until Guido finds him a job as a bodyguard to the daughter of a rich Italian family. A close and happy relationship develops and Creasy enjoys life once more. But then something terrible happens, and Creasy sets out to exact a fearful revenge.

I KNOW MY LOVE
by Catherine Gaskin

Ballarat, Australia, 1854 . . . a bleak encampment of tents in a valley. Here 30,000 men
scramble for the gold under their feet by
day—and every night drink it, gamble it away,
or spend it on their women. Strange circumstances at Ballarat bring two of these women
together. Rose Maguire, ravishing and flamboyant, who meets life with open arms and
a calculating brain . . . Emma Brown, lonely,
shy and gentle—who has killed two men.
Their lives are inextricably tangled when they
fall in love with the same man.

BREAD UPON THE WATERS
by Irwin Shaw

Allen Strand and his family were ready for
dinner, except for his teenage daughter who
had not returned from a tennis match. When
she finally did, it was in the company of a very
bloody stranger whom she had rescued from
muggers in Central Park. The stranger, an
eminent lawyer—and a lonely man—was
strongly attracted by the harmony of the
Strand family. As his involvement with the
family increased, so did his desire to use his
influence and wealth on their behalf. For
Allen Strand it becomes a struggle for the survival of his family against the overwhelming
efforts of their would-be benefactor.

TESS OF THE D'URBERVILLES
by Thomas Hardy

This age-old tale of the maid who goes to the greenwood and returns a maiden no more becomes in Hardy's hands an indictment of all the crimes and hypocrisies of 19th century England. Of all of the author's heroines, the milkmaid Tess is, by common consent, the most touching, and of all his novels this is the one with the most universal scope.

THE KEY TO REBECCA
by Ken Follett

"Our spy in Cairo is the greatest hero of them all", said Rommel in 1942. The man referred to was Alex Wolff, who presented as great a danger to British hopes of containing the German army as Rommel himself. This story of the Second World War is woven around Wolff, who arrived out of the desert, armed with a radio set, a copy of Daphne du Maurier's *Rebecca*, and his own conviction that he would triumph. Only Major William Vandam could stop Wolff's infiltration of British troop movements and strategic plans. A dramatic novel of a subtle, intricate relationship between spy and spy-catcher, between pursuer and his prey. The stakes are the survival of the British in North Africa . . . or the collapse of the resistance to the Axis powers.

XPD
by Len Deighton

On the morning of June 11th, 1940, Winston Churchill, Prime Minister of Great Britain, met in secret with the would-be conqueror of Europe: Adolph Hitler. Forty years later, the truth about that meeting remains Britain's most closely guarded secret—a secret still so dangerous that anyone who might reveal it is marked down for "expedient demise": XPD . . . Set in the summer of 1979 this novel of intrigue and suspense moves from the mansions of Hollywood, to the back streets of London, from Lake Geneva to the Baltic Sea, until it reaches a climax on a film set of the Fuhrer's study under the shadow of a Nazi eagle.

LOVING
by Danielle Steel

Bettina Daniels had everything: youth, beauty, a glamorous life that circled the globe—everything her father's love, fame and money could buy. Then, without warning, Justin Daniels was gone. Bettina stood alone before a mountain of debts and a world full of strangers—men who promised her many things, who tempted her with their words of love. Bettina had to live her own life, take her own chance, but could she pay the bittersweet price of . . . loving.

SEASON OF PASSION
by Danielle Steel

Kate and Tom were the original star-crossed lovers. Kate, a beautiful model, Tom, a successful American football star at the peak of his career. It almost seemed they were made to share their lives together. Then one day the bubble bursts. A gunshot ends Tom's career and puts him in a sanitorium—forever. Kate is left alone in a world with nothing to live for. And the fear that she will never love again.

NO LOVE LOST
by Helen Van Slyke

Pauline and Howard Tresher live in a twelve room apartment on Fifth Avenue. They have two children, a son called James and a daughter Lindsay. A quarrel between her parents—sparked off by Howard's many infidelities—is overheard by Lindsay who, at ten years old, is not quite sure what it is about but realises that something is radically wrong. Much was wrong at that time because it was 1930, the time of the Depression, and Adele, one of Lindsay's friends, was left fatherless by suicide. The story of Lindsay and Adele, James, Geoff the man Lindsay marries, their loves and fortunes through World War II and the strange twists that emotions and fate take, makes this an unusual and absorbingly readable narrative.

BLOODLINE
by Sidney Sheldon

Elizabeth Roffe was the only daughter of one of the world's richest and most powerful men. When, without warning, he died mysteriously while mountain climbing in the French Alps, she had to take command of the family-owned drug company, a giant international pharmaceutical manufacturer. As Roffe and Sons' new president, she discovers that someone unknown in the highest echelon of the firm is not only out to destroy the company, but is determined to kill her.

WOMEN IN LOVE
by D. H. Lawrence

This novel, which Lawrence himself considered his best, is the story of the lives and emotional conflicts of two sisters. Gudrun and Ursula Brangwen, who also appeared in *The Rainbow*, live in a Midlands colliery town. Ursula falls in love with Birkin (a self-portrait of Lawrence) and Gudrun has a tragic affair with Gerald, the son of the local colliery owner. These four, and such well-drawn characters as Hermione, the sensuous and intellectual hostess and Loerke the sculptor, clash in thought, passion and belief. The tale reaches its tragic conclusion in the Alps as the reader is gripped by the deeply held convictions about love and modern society.

THE MACLARENS
by C. L. Skelton

The first volume of the author's projected "Regiment Quartet", a saga which will take one family through nearly a hundred years of history, is a story of love, war and honour, spanning three continents. The Maclarens are a famous Highland clan. Andrew Maclaren, young, sensitive, is serving with his regiment, the 148th Foot, in India when the Mutiny of 1857 breaks out. After the shocking carnage, he discovers Maud, raped and homeless, who becomes inextricably involved in his life. But the good of the Regiment would be damaged by his marrying a sullied woman.

THE OSTERMAN WEEKEND
by Robert Ludlum

John Tanner, network news director, is looking forward to a weekend party with his closest friends—the Ostermans, the Tremaynes, and the Cardones. But then the CIA tells him that they are all suspected Soviet agents: fanatical, traitorous killers working for Omega, a massive Communist conspiracy. From this moment Tanner and his family are caught up in a nightmare whirlpool of terror, helpless isolation, violence and slaughter. Until the shattering climax, Tanner cannot know who are his friends, who are his implacable, deadly enemies . . .

ROUGH DIAMOND
by James Broom Lynne

Born two hundred million years ago, the 8-carat diamond was to mark the beginning of a long journey into fear and intrigue. Its discovery was destined to play the catalyst in the lives of many people. The reader is taken along the unique corridors of the diamond monopolies and into Central Africa; to Sierra Leone and across the Atlantic to Brazil and the murderous Quaqueros of Colombia, and to the urbane, but no less dangerous cities of London, New York and Geneva. A strong cast of characters tells the story of diamonds, from the mines to the glittering showcases of Tiffany's. But, between discovery and final polishing lies double-dealing, theft and murder.

THE FOXES OF HARROW
by Frank Yerby

Set in New Orleans and Louisiana State in the troubled days between 1825 and the Civil War, *The Foxes of Harrow* has a broad sweep and is charged with colour and action, with white-hot animosities, with strife and warfare and the clash of races. Dominating this fast-moving story is the figure of Stephen Fox, who is loved by three women, who has the face of an angel and a mind which can conjure visions of both beauty and evil.

CRUSADER'S TOMB
by A. J. Cronin

In relating the story of Stephen Desmonde—an artist so dedicated to his art, and of such integrity, that he is willing to sacrifice everything, fame, fortune, the responsibilities of a son and the loyalty of a citizen, in order to devote himself singlemindedly to his vocation—the author spans the first quarter of the twentieth century in a rich variety of settings in England, France and Spain with a colourful cast of characters.

NEVER LOVE A STRANGER
by Harold Robbins

The odds seemed stacked against him from the start, but Francis Kane was determined to come out on top. Born of an unmarried mother, raised by an orphanage in the New York slums, he never knew love, security or family life, and he despised them all. A natural leader with no scruples, he worked out his ruthless campaign against the society that had forced him into nothingness. Throughout the Depression and the hard times that followed, he never lost sight of his goals. But years later, when his cherished dreams came true, he realised his mistake—the pinnacle of power can be a very lonely place when men hold you in contempt instead of awe, and women only want you because you can pay them well.

THE MANCHURIAN CANDIDATE
by Richard Condon

Sergeant Raymond Shaw, secretly brain-washed and then freed with the rest of his patrol after being captured in Korea, comes home as a hero and winner of the Congressional Medal of Honour to be idolised by the whole of America. Only the Communists who indoctrinated him know when and where he will explode, and they alone control his actions as the fateful hour approaches. His mother, power-hungry behind the Washington scene, and his stepfather, an unscrupulous demagogue, are quick to exploit Shaw's sudden fame for their own purposes, while, implacably, the mechanism buried in his subconsciousness ticks away.

THE KING'S GENERAL
by Daphne du Maurier

There are only two main families who count for anything in Cornwall: the Arundells and the Grenviles. Honor Harris is a very unusual heroine: she is crippled in a riding accident shortly before her wedding to Richard Grenvile—the "red fox", and the King's General. This intriguing novel tells of her life during the Civil War years, her involvement with the Grenvile family and her love abiding for Richard.

79 PARK AVENUE
by Harold Robbins

Behind this story of the turning point in the lives of two lovers, one risen from the gutter and the other unashamedly drifting towards it, lies the ugly background of the seamy side of New York life. The story of the trial of Maryann Flood, a "model" at 79 Park Avenue, who has been arrested on charges of procurement, bribery and blackmail; and of the dilemma of Mike Keyes, who is conducting the prosecution. For fate seems to have played against Mike in offering him the chance of advancement in his career, through the trial of the woman he loves.

WATERSHIP DOWN
by Richard Adams

One dim, moonlit night a small band of rabbits leave the comfort and safety of their warren and set out on a long and dangerous journey. Not one of them knows where they are heading, only that they wish to find a new warren where they can live in peace. And once they have gained the longed-for place, then begins an adventure which makes all their previous adventures seem like child's play . . . This is a story of rabbits—*real* rabbits who act throughout in accordance with real rabbit behaviour and instincts, living their terrors and their triumphs with them.